"IS BARUCH ABOARD?"

Tahn squinted, trying to focus on Dannon. "What the hell are you doing here? Get off my bridge!"

"I want to know if he—"

The alert sirens went deadly quiet and the blood drained from Dannon's head, making him feel faint.

With sudden dread, Tahn gazed around the bridge. "No . . . he can't have—"

Yes, he can. The truth made Neil sick unto death. Jeremiel had this ship!

"Captain," a bridge officer yelled, "I've got decompression readings from all over the ship. We—"

"Gas Engineering!"

"Can't, Captain. He's rerouted control."

"Bypass!"

". . . Can't."

"Oh, God!" Neil screamed. Jeremiel was evening the numbers! With all the locks open, he could completely decompress the ship in less than five minutes. . . .

KATHLEEN M. O'NEAL
TREASURE OF LIGHT

DAW BOOKS, INC.
DONALD A. WOLLHEIM, PUBLISHER

375 Hudson Street, New York, NY 10014

DEDICATION

To Julie and Lloyd Schott of Lakewood, Colorado.

For your infinite patience and your unending

warmth and kindness.

ACKNOWLEDGMENTS

I owe deep debts of gratitude to the superb work of several scholars: Gershom G. Scholem for his numerous works on Jewish mysticism; James H. Charlesworth for *The Old Testament Pseudepigrapha;* Jean Doresse, *The Secret Books of the Egyptian Gnostics;* Kurt Rudolph, *Gnosis: The Nature and History of Gnosticism;* Mircea Eliade, *Patterns in Comparative Religions;* James M. Robinson, *The Nag Hammadi Library.* Without their exacting research on the ancient magical papyrii and secret books of the Merkabah, Kabbalah and Gnosticism, I would not have been able to complete *Treasure of Light.* The prophecies, theological framework, and idea of the *Mea Shearim* as a stone which opens a gateway to God are not my creation—they're revealed in the most ancient texts of the Near East. The original creators, the prophets Ezra, Enoch, Sibylline, Asenath, Baruch and others believed they were writing history—not fiction.

I'd also like to thank Michael Gazzaniga, Fred Allan Wolf, Nora Levin, Richard Rubenstein, Malgorzata Niezabitowksa, Barbara Myerhoff and Elie Wiesel. Their nonfiction scholarship gives this book its heart—and perhaps its soul, as well.

Karen Sue Jones is and always has been the silent overseer of Mikael and Sybil. Katherine Cook spent endless hours reading and rereading the manuscript. My editor, Sheila Gilbert—the best editor in the business—provided invaluable comments on plot and character development.

W. Michael Gear, my best friend, shared the long walks through the mountains, and the intense discussions about chaos theory and null singularities, God and human frailty—many of which occurred over a few bottles of stout at the Ramshorn Inn. I can never thank Mike enough for the joy of our life together.

Lastly, to the reader who finds that events, names, numbers, and often dialogue in this trilogy ring with a frightening echo of recent history, I admit my belief that in remembrance lies redemption.

THE BOOK OF THE CAVE OF TREASURES
First Century, A.D.
Old Earth Standard.
Fragment found on
Orillas VII, 4411

These mysteries and this narrative were handed down even to our fathers, who welcomed them with joy and who passed them on to us. And these books of the hidden mysteries were placed in the Mountain of Victories to the east of our country of Seir, in a grotto: The Cave of Treasures of the Life of the Silence.

Listen that I may reveal to you the prodigious mystery concerning the great king who must come into the world.

The land and the heavens will wear mourning for his violent death and, from the depth, he will mount up on High. Then he will be seen coming with the army of the Light, for he is the Child of the Word that engenders all things.

So then my people, you who are the Seed of Life issuing from the Treasury of Light and of the Spirit, who have been sown in the soil of fire and of water, you must be on your guard and watch.

For you will know beforehand of the coming of the great king for whom the captives are waiting to be freed.

PROLOGUE

One hour before the end of **An Abyss of Light.**

The white com box buzzed.

Magistrate Slothen grimaced at it, looking up impatiently from the mass of reports scattered over his desk. His office spread in a fifty foot square around him. The room had a high arching ceiling and lavender walls. Holographs of a variety of galactic solar systems hung at his eye level, seven feet off the floor. His round white desk sat before the broad expanse of windows that gazed out over Naas, the capital city of Palaia Station—the center of galactic government.

He shuffled the sheets on his cluttered desk. Over fifteen thousand complaints of increasing pirate activity and floundering trade had already poured in, each planet raging about inadequate protection by the government. Gamants were to blame. A primitive human cultural group, they formed an infinitesimal part of his jurisdiction, yet caused fully fifty percent of the problems. Their rebellions sparked across the galaxy. He had no choice but to deploy his forces to suppress the increasing violence—but that left peaceful planets open to attacks from raiders. At this moment, starvation ravaged quadrant seven.

Slothen ignored the com and heaved a perturbed sigh. He'd given his secretary strict orders not to disturb him. No doubt Topew would have realized his error by now and be sheepishly preparing for the verbal lashing he knew awaited him when Slothen had the time.

11

"Gamants," he muttered tonelessly.

Slothen had often wondered if it wouldn't have been better to have wiped out the group millennia ago. He'd done that with the Viveka when he'd first become ruling Magistrate and had never regretted it. A wild and brutal species of crimson-skinned, four-armed ruffians, they'd threatened war against his government. He'd had no choice. Or perhaps he should have enslaved Gamants? That had worked remarkably well with the amorphous gelatinlike Octopii of Huron II. But, no. Instead, he'd underestimated the ingenuity of Gamants and waited too long, until they'd formed themselves into a formidable fighting force, stolen ships and weapons and fought their way out of his neatly bordered system to land on remote, hostile planets at the edges of the galaxy. The worst of the lot had coalesced into a strong Underground movement that waged a constant guerrilla war against his forces.

"I've been lenient for too long," he huffed, slapping his open palm on his desk.

As for the rest of humanity, he'd implemented a stringent process of information control or blackout, keeping them from discovering his efforts. Most of the human planets remained peacefully oblivious to the plight of Gamant civilization. Those few who knew of his efforts agreed with them. After centuries of careful manipulation, many human worlds possessed a rabid hatred for their brethren Gamants, blaming them for everything from Galactic financial instability to mysterious disease outbreaks. Humans were such irrational creatures—their emotions careened like ancient roller coasters. But with the right devices, they could be controlled.

His only major worry came from his own military. One entire branch of his forces was composed of superb human-commanded ships. He couldn't keep the information from his own officers—so he'd instituted a clandestine "scare" program designed to make them too frightened to commit treason. He'd isolated them from other galactic species—leaving only humans on those ships—and he immediately and publicly corrected the brains of any deviants who developed traitorous ideas.

The com buzzed again.

Slothen contemplatively followed the machinations of

his tri-brains, halting the flood of violent irritation that ravaged his mind. Eons ago, Giclasians had developed a third hemisphere from the proto-basis of what humans called the corpus callosum. That third brain served him now as a separate identity, a highly sophisticated interpreter which could trace every neural pathway in his left and right hemispheres to locate and study the origins of each fragment of mental stimulation. He'd actually initiated neurophysiological investigations to see if the human corpus callosum was capable of growing into a third brain, hoping he could stop Gamant aggressiveness by civilizing the beasts—but so far the results had been inconclusive.

He pressed the response button. "Topew, I told you I didn't want to be disturbed."

"I apologize, Magistrate, but this is urgent. Colonel Garold Silbersay, the former military governor of the Gamant planet Kayan is here, sir. He demands to speak with you."

Slothen bared his needle-sharp teeth in irritation. "Didn't I order Brent Bogomil to get him to a neurophysiology correction center?"

"Yes, sir, you did. But he's here, in my outer office, slamming his fists into the walls like a madman."

Slothen caressed his blue chin. Madman? The last message he'd received had reported Silbersay on the verge of violent schizophrenia. Bogomil said it had taken five guards to drag the colonel to a secure cell and lock him in. Had he gone over the edge in isolation? Possible. Should he risk seeing Silbersay? The man *had* been on the front lines of the skirmishes on Kayan. He might possess critical information about Gamant politics.

Slothen bit his lower lip and gazed out the window. The mirrored buildings of Naas sprouted like spears from the grassy plains of Palaia Station. The original terraqueous architects had done a superb job recreating the painstakingly ordered environment of Giclas IV, his home world. Thypen trees marked each street intersection, their bare crimson limbs like streaks of blood against the green background of parks and fountains. Today, the yellow skies gleamed like transparent amber.

"Sir!" Topew's imploring voice came over com again. "Colonel Silbersay is shouting obscenities at my staff. He claims he has confidential information critical to galactic security. Shall I send him in or call security to have him removed?"

Slothen twined the twelve fingers of his upper left hand and squeezed tightly—a sign of nervousness in one of his race. "Have two armed security officers escort him down the hall and wait outside my office door. I want no incidents."

"Yes, sir."

In the interim, Slothen pulled out his drawer and checked his image in the 3-D mirror. His physical appearance frequently upset humans. They weren't accustomed to the brilliant colors of Giclasian life. Behind his back he knew they called him the "Squid." *Idiots.* He'd seen pictures of Earth squids and it took a vivid stretch of imagination to compare them to Giclasians. He lifted his chin at the mirror. His balloon-shaped head gleamed like polished azure in the sunlight streaming through the window, accenting his wormlike hair and round ruby-red mouth. He tucked four of his limbs beneath the desk, leaving only two visible.

In a few moments, the door snicked back and Silbersay stormed in, fists clenched tightly at his sides. "Magistrate," he said stiffly, "I come to you on a matter of urgent diplomatic business." He looked older, his hair totally gray now. Against the lavender background, it shone like a wealth of silver threads. Tall for a human, he had a pug nose and black bushy brows that formed a solid line across his forehead. His purple uniform looked dreadful, as if he'd slept in it.

"I'm so glad to see you again, Colonel," Slothen said and smiled. Humans thought that Giclasian speech had a stiff, mechanical quality. He deliberately tried to counter that by imitating human tones.

Silbersay's eyes slitted. "*Don't patronize me.* You ordered my mind corrected specifically so you'd never have to worry about me again! Well, you've got something else—"

"That's not true, Garold." He mimicked an expression he knew humans took for injured dignity. "Captain Bogomil reported that you were suffering intense emotional pain over the Kayan episode. I merely wanted to ease your torment."

"Ease it? By destroying critical personality centers in my brain? I thought that sort of treatment was only for

14

dissidents who disrupted galactic harmony. *But me,* Magistrate?" Silbersay put his hands on his hips and paced across the purple carpet, stopping and starting erratically like a windup toy with a faulty spring. "What's happened to us? Are dirty dealing and murder so fundamental now that your administration can't function without them?"

"I don't know what you're talking about, Garold," Slothen responded quietly.

"Stop it! I've been on the front lines, I *know* the sort of insane politics you've been playing. First you assassinate Zadok Calas, then—"

"We did *not* assassinate Calas." The elderly Gamant leader had been a curious sort, stubborn beyond reason, flamboyant in his own brusque way. "Intelligence reported a disgruntled Gamant fanatic ended Zadok's life. We had nothing to do with it."

Suspicion still lit the depths of Silbersay's dark eyes. He kept forebodingly silent.

"I don't order murders, Garold," Slothen lied. "I thought you knew that. Tell me what other falsehoods are circulating about me among my top staff members. I know the past year has been difficult. What else is bothering you?"

"What else?" Silbersay mumbled in a low savage voice. His gaze darted over the floor as though searching for something he'd lost. The collar of his purple uniform had darkened with perspiration. *"What else?"* He squeezed his eyes closed a moment and Slothen could see his jaw tremble. "A *damned* fool question if ever I heard one."

Slothen sucked in a breath. Gently motioning to a chair, he repeated, "Sit, Garold. Tell me what's been going on out there."

He cataloged Silbersay as the man tiredly dropped into the formfitting chair. Dark rings of fatigue shone beneath the colonel's eyes; they made his alabaster face seem even paler. Slothen thought about that. Silbersay must have escaped Bogomil's grasp, which meant he'd undoubtedly hired illegal transportation and that implied criminal associations. Had he also hired assassins? Covertly, Slothen's gaze slid to the huge windows behind him. No ships marred the lemon skies of Palaia, but unease crept up his spine. The penalty for military personnel associating with enemies of the Union of Solar Systems was death. And Silbersay knew it better than anyone. Slothen casually reached beneath his desk to press a button which would signal the guards in the corridor to be on top alert.

"Are you all right, Garold? You don't look well."

"I'm not well, Magistrate."

"Are you upset about my relieving you of your command on Kayan? It was nothing personal, I assure you."

Silbersay tugged nervously at the fingers in his lap, not looking up. "You killed thousands . . . needlessly."

The scorch attack. Yes, Slothen vaguely remembered the details. "They were destroying government military installations. You lost—how many men? Over a thousand, wasn't it? Gamants broke the treaty first. We took what action seemed necessary to defuse a potentially explosive situation."

"Well, you've done it now," Silbersay hissed, and when he lifted his head, his eyes flared insanely, nostrils quivering. Slothen tensed. "You didn't listen to me and now you're in for it. You've unleashed the dragon. You're on the verge of another full-scale Gamant revolt."

"I don't think so, Garold. We've thoroughly contained every outburst so far."

"You really believe that, don't you?"

"Yes," Slothen said and extended two of his arms to cover the reports on his desk which confirmed the opposite. "Besides, Garold, their new leader is a seven-year-old. I hardly think he'll be a threat, at least not for a few years. In the interim, I'm sure we can effectively manipulate him."

Still, one could never tell. Slothen wrung two of his hands nervously. The last Gamant Revolt, led by the old war-horse, Zadok Calas, had shredded the Union. Perhaps the boy had the same suicidal instincts.

Silbersay shifted suddenly, glaring like a man on the verge of violence.

Slothen extended a blue hand and made a desist motion with it. "Garold, please, calm down. I wasn't disputing your word. If I receive information supporting your theory, I guarantee I'll deal with the situation immediately."

"Deal with it? *Deal with it!*" The colonel waved both arms wildly. "You mean you'll—you'll send the battle cruisers in to turn their planets into molten slag. That's what you call *dealing* with it?"

"It stops the problems on individual planets and sets examples by which other Gamant worlds can judge how far to push us."

A twitch jerked Silbersay's left cheek. "You don't understand. None of you do. You're not human. You've no idea what fires the souls of primitive peoples. They're afraid all the time. They live on the edge of survival. All you have to do to turn the tide of violence is make some concessions. Give back some territory, send them some food or medical supplies. In no time they'll return to herding their goats and tending their miserable crops. *You mustn't push them!*" He shoved suddenly out of his chair. *"They go* crazy *when you push!"*

"You needn't shout, Garold. I—I'm listening. Truly, I am," Slothen assured gently, finger poised over the button that would bring the guards rushing through the door. He vacillated. He could simply have Silbersay dragged down to the neuro center and find out most of this information—but perhaps not the most significant details. High level human officers had developed skilled methods of blocking data extraction in recent years. His biologists had yet to discover how.

"Please, Garold, sit down and tell me precisely where you see the problems in our handling of Gamant affairs. We certainly don't want another full-scale revolt on our hands. I respect your opinion. You know that. You've been one of my most valued advisers for thirty years."

Silbersay tilted his head and tears filled his eyes. Pathetically, he protested, "But you relieved me of my duties. You killed my planet."

"Yes, I'm sorry I had to do that, Garold. I—"

"It was that damned Mashiah on Horeb."

The subject shifted so suddenly, it took Slothen's third brain a moment to reorient his thoughts. The Mashiah? Oh, yes. Adom Kemar Tartarus, the presumed savior of Gamant civilization. "What about Tartarus, Garold?"

"He caused it all. He sent emissaries to convert the Gamants on Kayan. After hearing about his new God, they went wild. They threw themselves at my men in wave after wave, using primitive weapons against our pulse cannons. And there were so many." He stared forlornly at the floor for a time, trembling hands clasped

17

together, as though in prayer. The silence stretched so long that Slothen fidgeted.

"Garold? . . . Garold?"

Silbersay whispered in a strained voice, "How could *anyone* believe some lunatic notion of a crystalline god sent to deliver them from *our* bondage and destroy us? We outnumber them a million to one!"

"It's simpleminded. All religious belief systems are—especially the Gamant notion of Epagael. I know, Garold, but they can do a great deal of damage if they decide to. We've heard rumors that he sent emissaries everywhere. Are Gamants still fired up about his religion even now that he's dead?"

"He—he's dead?"

"Yes. Apparently his lover murdered him."

"And Baruch's forces? They haven't intervened?"

"No. His cruisers are picking up survivors off Abulafia and Ahiqar. We had to take punitive action in that system several weeks ago. I've considered dispatching a convoy to see if we can't corner them there before they get away again, but—"

Silbersay pounded a fist into his palm. "Ridiculous. The Underground never splits its forces. So long as they're there in strength, you'll lose as many vessels as they will."

"Yes, my opinion exactly. At any rate, we've also just initiated a new suppressive action on Tikkun. We've set up a series of neurophysiological experiments to explore Gamant brain structure. We're taking the inhabitants of small isolated villages first and slowly working on the mind-sets in the major cities—to forestall any foolish attempts by Gamants to join forces and escape us."

"I—I can't believe Baruch hasn't descended in a ball of fire! He never leaves his people at our mercy for long."

"I've been meaning to tell you, Garold. This will make you feel better. Baruch should already be under lock and key aboard the *Hoyer*. We—"

"*We captured Jeremiel Baruch?* Impossible!"

Slothen allowed a wry smile. His blue hair writhed, pleasantly caressing his skull. "But we've done it. We've been working with a man named Ornias, a powerful politician on Horeb. He lured Baruch in by telling him he needed assistance in halting the civil war there. The thought of Gamants killing Gamants brought Baruch running like a mother hen."

"War?" Silbersay's face slackened, eyes widening in horror. Sweat beaded across his forehead and nose, gluing his white hair to his temples. "*War!* What actions have you taken? Dear God, you haven't ordered another scorch attack, have you? No. *Oh, no.* You can't kill more innocent people!"

Slothen threw out two of his hands. "It's all right, Garold. Don't worry about it. Cole Tahn is in charge. It's not your concern."

"What have you DONE? Tell me?" Silbersay cried and took three quick strides forward, face twisted with madness. Slothen hit the button beneath his desk, then lurched out of his seat and raced toward the window, his six legs swirling in a blur. Two security guards burst through the doors, rifles aimed at Silbersay's back.

The colonel spun, staring insanely into the cold hard eyes of the human guards. "Oh," he whispered forlornly, on the verge of tears. "Poor Cole. Poor, poor Cole."

"Garold," Slothen said quietly. "You're not stable. Let me get you some help. The psych professionals on Palaia are the best in the galaxy. We'll—"

"No!" he screamed. "I won't let you destroy my mind with your probes! I got away from Bogomil and I'll escape you, too!" He lunged at the guards, forcing his way past. The surprised officers glanced to Slothen for further guidance.

"Stop him," he ordered. "Minor Force."

The dark-haired guard scrambled into the hall and a shot rang out. He heard a body thud dully against the walls, then slam to the floor.

"He's down, Magistrate. What now?"

"Take him to Doctor Zirkin. Tell him the colonel is a top level military official and needs special retraining. I want all of his memories purged from the first instant he contemplated joining government service."

The guard's expression darkened, fear in his eyes. Slothen bared his needle teeth again and feigned a malignant smile. The guard hurried into the hall. "Yes, sir," he responded and hit the button to close the door.

Alone again, Slothen twined his fingers so tightly they hurt. "Now I've lost my best Gamant specialist. Where am I going to find someone else? Maybe I ought to look within Gamant civilization itself? Subvert someone, give him a little power, and use him for all he's worth?" It was a problem he'd have to think more about. If Silbersay proved right about the coming revolt, he'd have to find someone soon. Worse, he might have to contact the other Magistrates and that could prove catastrophic. Isolated and sleeping in classified Peace Vaults in the Giclas system, he hadn't had to disturb their rest in centuries.

Taking a deep breath, he dropped heavily into his chair and opened a line to the front office. "Topew?"

"Yes, Magistrate."

"Send a dattran to Captain Brent Bogomil. Tell him I'm *not* happy with him. I want him to report to me immediately."

A pause, then Topew replied. "Your last order told him to swing by Horeb and see if Tahn needed assistance in the scorch attack there. Shall I cancel that?"

"Yes. Tahn's done enough of these things. I'm sure he can handle it in his sleep."

CHAPTER 1

Captain Cole Tahn strode down the long corridor of the battle cruiser, *Hoyer*, absently returning the salutes of the occasional crew members he passed. Turned low to simulate nighttime, the overhead panels threw light like tarnished silver over the white walls. He grimaced at the odor that filled the hall. Level seven housed the technoscience division and they must have been performing some peculiar experiment for the air smelled acrid, like putrifying corpses beneath a searing desert sun.

In a bitter voice, he accused, "Or maybe it's just your own goddamned guilt you smell."

Though he'd just showered and changed clothes, his purple uniform clung in clammy folds to his sides and back, already drenched in sweat in anticipation of the next hour. A tall man with broad shoulders, he had brown hair and piercing blue-violet eyes that, on this somber evening, took in everything: the wall clocks flashing the hour in blue at every intersection; the depressing gray carpet beneath his boots; the dull annoying thudding of his heart.

He rounded a corner and his steps faltered. Ahead, the numbers 955 shone in silver on the cabin door of Mikael Calas, the new leader of Gamant civilization—an innocent child caught in the midst of a government hurricane that looked certain to destroy everything in the universe in its wake.

Tahn inhaled deeply, fighting the tide of futility and despair that rose. He'd retrieved Mikael from Brent Bogomil's protective grasp just after Cole had finished obliterating every known population center on Kayan. Before that, the boy's mother and grandfather had been brutally murdered. Mikael still bore deep emotional scars. Tahn had tried to befriend him to ease those hurts. Immediately after on-loading Mikael, Tahn had taken the boy to his cabin and stretched out on the floor beside him, showing Mikael his galactic stamp collection, talking, trying to get him to open up and eat something. Reports said that the boy hadn't so much as touched a crumb of bread since the death of his mother.

Resolutely, Tahn forced his feet forward. He lifted his hand to the black com patch outside the boy's door. "Mikael? It's Captain Tahn. Can I speak to you?"

A brief pause ensued, then a frail voice responded, "Yes, sir."

The door slipped open. Standing stiffly in the middle of the room, Mikael was dressed in the long brown robes characteristic of Kayan Gamants. Small for a seven-year-old, he had jet black hair and dark brown eyes. Just now, those eyes glinted with fear—as wide and terrified as those of a rabbit caught in a trap. Tahn quietly took a step inside and winced when Mikael ran backward, lips pressed tightly together to stifle tears.

The door slipped closed with a soft snick, leaving them in near darkness. He struggled to project a friendly smile as he looked around the cabin. It spread ten by fifteen feet and had a table and two chairs on the right side and a bed on the left. In the back, a desk with a computer unit filled a small niche. Only one light panel glowed, its glare sneaking around the edges of the almost closed door to the latrine.

. "Are you all right, Mikael?"

"Yes, sir."

"You're keeping it pretty dark in here."

Mikael wet his lips and didn't say anything for several seconds. Then he pointed to the overhead panels and whispered, "Those bright lights scare me, sir."

Tahn nodded, silently chastising himself for not thinking of that. On Kayan, Gamants had lived in primitive caves. Oil lamps and candles provided their only source of illumination. "Would you like me to have a lamp brought up? We could secure it to the table and you wouldn't have to use the lustreglobes at all if you didn't want to."

"Yes, sir. Thank you, sir."

The words had been uttered so softly, Tahn had barely heard them. He shifted uncomfortably, putting the weight of his two-hundred pound frame on his left foot. Mikael flinched at the movement and it dawned on him how daunting his physical presence must be to this boy. He knelt down. "I brought you something," he said, trying to sound cheery.

"What?"

Tucking a hand inside his shirt pocket, Tahn pulled out three stamps sealed in clear petrolon and handed them to Mikael. They'd been the boy's favorites, ancient stamps portraying the first starships. Mikael peered across at the gifts and his shoulders hunched defensively; he turned away.

The posture affected Tahn like a truncheon slammed into his gut. He bowed his head, fighting with himself, silently shouting obscenities. Then, gently, he said, "It's all right, Mikael. I just thought you might like to have these. I want us to be friends."

Silence—but the boy's dark eyes hurled bitter recriminations: *You killed my world. You killed my family!*

Tahn lifted a hand to massage his taut forehead. He had no excuse to offer, other than his own self-hatred, and he doubted the child would appreciate such an irrelevant excuse.

He took the stamps and carefully spread them out across the gray carpet, facing Mikael; but in the darkness, he couldn't be certain the boy actually saw them. He tapped one, asking, "You remember this one?"

The boy shivered and hugged himself.

Tahn frowned, seeing the goose bumps on the boy's arms. "Are you cold, Mikael?"

"Just a little."

"I'm sorry. The ship shuts down the cabin temperatures at night, and I forgot to show you where the thermostat is." *Damn it. Kayan was a tropical forest most of the year. Of course, he's cold.* Getting to his feet, Tahn went to the control panel over the boy's rumpled bed. He increased the temperature to seventy degrees.

"Just turn this dial to the right, Mikael. That will make it as warm as you need it to be."

Mikael didn't answer. He had his lower lip clamped between his teeth, staring fearfully at the stamps as though they were some hostile form of life that might rear up and attack him.

Tahn came back across the floor and knelt again in front of the stamps, pointing to the stamp on the far right. "This one is the first star freighter humans ever built. Do you remember? It came from Old Earth."

Mikael looked up and whispered, "I remember."

"Do you recall how old that stamp is?"

"No, sir. I don't care."

Tahn exhaled slowly. "But I thought that was the one you liked most. I wanted to give it to you." He picked up the stamp and handed it to the boy.

Mikael took a step backward. He cocked his head and the dim light frosted his long lashes in pewter. "I don't want it. *I don't want anything from you!* You're a bad man!" His chest puffed spasmodically. The glare he leveled at Tahn was pure hatred.

Tahn lowered the stamp to the carpet again. *In the name of God, can none of us ever escape the terrible memories of murder and destruction?* Mikael watched him intently and began to cry very quietly. In the same way Tahn would demonstrate to an enemy that he was unarmed, he opened and lifted his hands, then cautiously slipped an arm around the boy's shoulder, squeezing comfortingly.

Mikael's face went livid with terror. He let out a high-pitched shriek and started flailing against Tahn with his fists, striking him in the face and shoulders, struggling to get away.

"Mikael, don't." Tahn gathered the boy in his arms and hugged him, feeling the desperate sobs that wracked

23

Mikael's body. Tears soaked the collar of Tahn's purple uniform. He held Mikael tighter, stroking his dark curls. Every muscle in the boy's body had gone rigid. "I'm sorry, Mikael. I just wanted you to know that I'm here to help you. If you—"

"No, you're not! You're a liar!" Mikael screamed and writhed in Tahn's arms. "You hate me! You hate all Gamants."

Like a stiletto between Tahn's ribs . . . "I don't hate you, Mikael. It's just that I have to do things to protect all of galactic civilization and sometimes Gamants make that hard."

"We don't!"

Tahn held Mikael at arm's length and gazed seriously into those dark eyes. "Listen to me. I'm going to tell you the truth. You know how the Underground goes around fighting all the time?"

"Yes," Mikael sobbed. "Jeremiel Baruch, the leader of the Underground, is a very great hero. When I grow up, I'm going to be just like him." A shining light gleamed in Mikael's eyes when he spoke of the most hated criminal in Magisterial space—and Tahn's most vehement enemy.

"I understand that you feel that way, but sometimes Baruch hurts Magisterial citizens."

"Like how?" Mikael charged disbelievingly.

"At this very moment the Underground is stirring rebellions on lots of Gamant planets and, as a result, half of quadrant seven—that's over on the Orion arm of the galaxy—is starving."

"Why?"

"Because the Magistrates only have a limited number of battle cruisers, so they can only protect so many people at once. When they're off fighting against the Underground, that leaves other planets open to attack from raiders. They—"

"Are raiders like pirates?"

"Yes, just like that." He softly patted Mikael's arm. The boy tilted his head so that the light iced his black hair with a veil of silver. "Raiders come in and cut off supply routes to blackmail planets into giving them their goods and resources for free."

"You mean raiders steal things?"

"Pretty much. They make demands that no planet can really meet and then . . ."

24

When the door com buzzed, Mikael jerked and glowered at Tahn as though he'd been betrayed. From outside, a deep voice called, "Captain Tahn? It's Doctor Iona."

"Just a minute," he called back. All the strangling tensions that enveloped him increased.

Mikael seemed to sense it. He gazed up in utter terror. Tahn hugged him one last time. In Mikael's ear, he whispered, "Sorry. I was going to tell you before he got here. There's something we need—"

Mikael wrenched free from his grip and stood panting. "That doctor's going to hurt me, isn't he?"

"No, no. I won't let him hurt you."

"Then why's he here?"

"I want you to sleep for a while. You know you haven't been sleeping very well. You wake up a lot at night, don't you?" The hospital monitors they'd installed had recorded dozens of wakings during the night, most accompanied by screams and flailing arms. He'd watched the holos with mounting alarm. He'd felt that way himself once upon a time, unable to sleep for even a few minutes for fear some terror would slither out of the darkness to twine around his body and squeeze the life from him. But there were more reasons he wanted the boy to sleep—reasons of his own.

Mikael closed his eyes and tears traced glistening lines down his cheeks. "Sometimes I have nightmares. I can't help it."

"I know that. But you—"

"I'll be good. I'll go to sleep. Don't let him hurt me!"

"Mikael, you're the best boy I know. It's not your fault you can't sleep." He lifted a finger and tapped it against Mikael's temple. "It's just that there are some . . . oh, sad things in your head that keep you awake. But you need to sleep. Doctor Iona is going to give you a shot. It won't hurt. I promise. You'll sleep for a few hours and when you wake up you'll feel better. Here, let me help you lie down."

Tahn stood and led Mikael to his bed where the boy sat on the edge, refusing to look at him. Cole's stomach roiled. Mikael took a deep breath and dragged a sleeve over his eyes, trying to be brave. Cole patted Mikael's hair and went to the door, turning on the light panel over the table before hitting the entry patch. The door slipped open and Iona stood in the hall. He was a medium-sized man with close-cropped salt-and-pepper hair and a bulbous nose; the gold braid on his shoulder epaulets glistened in the dim white light.

"Come in, Doctor. Mikael's calm and ready for you."

Iona entered, glancing surreptitiously at Mikael before putting his bag on the table and rifling through it. "I'm glad to hear it, sir, given the insanity running rampant across the rest of the ship."

Tahn grimaced in understanding. He had a few final arrangements to make with the High Councilman on Horeb who was "selling" Baruch to the Magistrates, but it looked like they'd finally ended the Underground leader's reign of terror. The crew was going wild with joy. In the off-duty lounges champagne flowed like a river. Only a year ago, Tahn would have been in one of those lounges, celebrating with his crew, exulting in that triumphant flush of victory.

But he no longer knew what he was fighting for. He glanced back at Mikael. The child sat hunched on his bed, his brown eyes as wide and hate-filled as an innocent prisoner facing his executioner.

Once again, all the old doubts consumed Tahn, gnawing at his insides. He started pacing. When he passed the mirror over the table, he caught his reflection and stopped. He looked as frantic as a man caught in a cross fire, not knowing which way to turn. Disturbed, he dropped his gaze to the floor. In the circle of light thrown by the table lustreglobe, he saw, for the first time, the tiny piles of lint scattered across the carpet, beside the table legs, beneath the chairs, humped like anthills against the walls. He frowned, wondering what they were. They had no toys aboard. Had Mikael created his own game?

He turned halfway around, pointing to the lint. "What're these, Mikael?"

The boy blinked owlishly. "They're mountains."

"What happens in those mountains?"

Mikael licked his lips anxiously, like he didn't want to tell him. Then, in a suddenly violent voice, he blurted, "People kill each other!"

Tahn clamped his jaw tightly. Undoubtedly the boy's game centered around killing Magisterial soldiers, taking revenge for the destruction of his world. In a kind voice, he asked, "Did you win?"

26

"My side always wins."

"Good. Sometime, if you want someone to play with, I'll fight on your side."

Iona turned around and Tahn saw Mikael blanch. The boy pushed jet black curls out of his eyes and twisted his fingers in his lap, watching the doctor fill a syringe with sedative. The breathless look on Mikael's face made Tahn queasy.

"For God's sake, Iona. He's only seven. Do you need so much?"

The doctor straightened indignantly. "I thought you said you wanted him out for the next twelve hours, Captain? Was I mistaken?"

"Does it take that much?"

"This dosage is adequate to keep him out for twenty. I think he needs the rest and that should give us enough time to complete our Horeb mission and be far away before—"

"That's enough, Doctor." The words cut as sharply as glass, and Tahn knew it, but anger and futility taunted too powerfully just now for him to be civil. The last thing in the world he wanted was Mikael to know that he was going to kill another Gamant planet.

"Forgive me, sir. I didn't realize—"

"Forget it."

Guilt swelled in Tahn's breast. He'd been treating his crew like strangers for the past week. So much so that they seemed to tiptoe around him. He couldn't help it. He felt trapped, on the verge of reckless actions. His mind had gone round and round the circle of possible alternatives and the only way he could see of resolving his inner conflicts was to resign his commission.

At the thought, a cold wave of fear splashed him. The Galactic Magistrates would erase all the memories he'd gained while in government service, claiming it was a matter of galactic security. Then he'd be confined to an institution for the rest of his life. They had little sympathy for captains incapable of carrying out their orders, no matter how onerous.

And they'd gotten goddamned onerous in the past year. How many planets had he killed? Four? Or should he count the half measure on Nuja? And at this very instant he stood on the precipice of another attack on Horeb.

The ache in Tahn's stomach intensified as he watched Iona lift the syringe again. "This just looks big, Mikael. It won't cause any pain. Sometimes, though, it makes you hear or see funny things. You just ignore them, all right?"

"Like what?"

"Oh, strange voices or flashes of light. But they aren't real. Don't let them scare you."

The boy looked up at him accusingly from beneath dark lashes. "Are we orbiting Horeb, sir?"

Tahn held his breath. "Yes."

"I have a cousin on Horeb. Can I go see her? I think she lives in a city named Seir."

"We're not going to stay for very long. We're just here to pick up a prisoner."

"But the doctor said we'll be here for hours. Maybe if you didn't give me that shot I could go down for just a few minutes."

"No. I—I'm sorry."

Mikael fumbled with the sleeve of his brown robe. "I guess it doesn't matter. My cousin probably thinks I'm dead anyway. Just like everybody else does."

Tahn shoved his hands in his pockets, straining at his own impotence. He had no choice. His orders from Slothen obliged him to target the capital first. In an hour, this boy's cousin would be swallowed by a massive wave of molten rock and debris.

He fought to keep his voice steady, "Why don't you lie down, Mikael. This won't take very long."

"Yes, sir." Bravely, Mikael stretched out on his back. He dug tiny fingers into the gray blanket and watched intently as Iona came across the cabin to lean over him. The syringe gleamed silver.

Gently, Iona said, "I'm going to push up your sleeve, all right, Mikael?"

"You'd better hurry. I might throw up."

"Oh, don't do that. This isn't nearly as bad as it looks."

Iona moved the brown cloth from Mikael's left arm and then placed the barrel of the syringe against it. A whoosh of air sounded and the cold barrel went away. Mikael opened his eyes and looked curiously at the cold spot on his arm.

"See? That didn't hurt, did it?" Iona asked.

"No, sir."

"When the sedative starts to be absorbed, it will ache a tiny bit, but by then you should be asleep. So you won't feel it except for just a minute." Iona backed away.

Tahn heaved a sigh and walked to Mikael's bedside. Kneeling, he forced a confident smile. "Are you okay?"

Mikael just glared.

Tahn pulled the blanket up and tucked the edges around Mikael's legs, making sure he'd be warm enough. "There's nothing to worry about, you understand? You'll just sleep for a few hours and when you wake up—"

"You'll take me to Magistrate Slothen? So I can talk to him? I need to talk to him. An angel told me I had to."

"An angel?" A tingle touched Tahn's spine. Imaginary friends? Defense mechanisms came in many forms. He had a number of his own that were no less exotic—like having to position chairs to form a barricade around his bed every night after a major battle to keep the ghosts at bay. Thank God his crew knew nothing about such things or they'd wonder about his sanity.

"Yes, sir. The angel's name is Metatron. He comes as a big dark shadow, then turns into a bright and shining man. He's the one who took me down the mountain to Colonel Silbersay's office before . . ."

At the pained look, Tahn's heart slammed against his ribs. "I'll take you to Slothen. Under the Treaty of Lysomia, it's your right. I'll make sure nobody stops you. Don't worry, now. You just get a good sleep."

Mikael's mouth pursed and his eyes glistened with bitterness. Tahn felt sick to his stomach. Gently, he ruffled Mikael's hair before standing up.

"I'll see you in a few hours. I have some arrangements to conclude with a Councilman on Horeb, then I'll come back and we'll—"

"About the prisoner?" Mikael demanded.

"I'm afraid so."

Mikael's face contorted. "You're going to hurt Horeb, aren't you?"

Tahn opened his mouth to give some quick lie, but no words would come.

"Aren't you?" Mikael demanded, bracing himself up on his elbows.

Tahn blindly studied the boy's tiny shoes placed so carefully at his bedside. "Sometimes, Mikael, I have to do things I don't like. It's just that—"

"Because the Magistrates tell you to?"

"Yes. I'm an officer in their fleet. I have to obey orders."

Mikael wiped a hand beneath his runny nose. On the verge of angry tears, he said, "You're a bad, bad man."

"Mikael, I—"

"Go away! I don't want you here anymore!" He curled on his side and closed his eyes, evading everything Magisterial that filled the world around him. Tucking a finger in the corner of his mouth, he sucked softly.

Tahn backed away, then turned and strode out the door into the corridor. A handful of technicians walked briskly by, saluting. He returned the gesture hollowly.

Finally, Iona exited to stand beside him and Mikael's door slipped closed.

Tahn pointed a finger sternly. "Baruch isn't going to come aboard easily. I want a member of your staff on the security team. Have him prepare a dose large enough to handle a raging Orillian lion."

Iona nodded contemplatively, fastening his bag. "You're sure Horeb will turn him over?"

"I'm damned sure. The Magistrates haven't given them any choice. And find Dannon. I want somebody to give a positive ID of Baruch. Nobody else has ever seen him in the flesh."

Iona threw out his chin indignantly. "You want *me* to find Neil Dannon? Begging your pardon, sir, but I have more important things to do than turn every female crew member's cabin upside down."

Neil Dannon had once been Baruch's closest friend and second in command of the Underground fleet until he'd betrayed Baruch during the Silmar battle a few months ago. Tahn's crew had despised Dannon from the day he'd stepped aboard.

Angry with indecision, feeling impotent, Tahn snapped, "Then start with the bars, Doctor! I'll expect a report from you in half an hour."

He spun on his heel and headed for the bridge, practically running down the white corridors to the closest transport tube.

When he walked out onto the bridge an ominous silence descended. Composed of two levels, the room opened around him in an oval. On the lower level, officers sat in twos stationed side by side in four niches.

His chair, with its massive array of buttons and computer access links, occupied the upper level, giving him a complete view of every action on the bridge. His second in command, First Lieutenant Carey Halloway, swiveled around to pin him with cool green eyes. A tall athletic woman, her auburn hair hung straight over her brows and fell to her shoulders to brush the epaulets on her formfitting purple uniform.

Tahn ignored her and turned to his redheaded communications officer. "Macey? Get me that High Councilman on Horeb. Let's get this over with."

"Aye, sir," Macey responded. The com aura burst to life, glowing like a golden halo around Macey's head.

Halloway's eyes narrowed and Tahn's jaw muscles jumped at the look she gave him. They'd been arguing for a week, debating the rights and wrongs of the curious orders they'd been getting lately. And just now, he could see that same mutinous gleam in her emerald eyes—as though she were clandestinely saying: *Don't do this, Cole.* Only days ago, after they'd scorched the planet of Kayan, she'd stamped into his cabin and demanded a stiff scotch. He could still hear her strained voice . . .

"What the hell are we doing, Cole?"

"I'm obeying orders. I'm not sure what you're doing anymore."

"Goddamn it! We've just been ordered to kill another planet! How can you sit there so calmly?"

"It's only a level two attack, Carey. We'll destroy all the known habitation centers. The planet's resources will be intact. Some of the people might even survive. But the nuisance factor will be completely eliminated."

"And you can live with that?"

At the time, he'd wanted to tell her, "No." But he couldn't. They'd had orders to carry out. And now, as she lifted a brow and studied him pensively, he wanted to tell her again. Instead, he strode forward and dropped into his command chair.

"Captain," Macey informed him, "I have the Councilman."

"On screen, Lieutenant."

Councilman Ornias' tanned face formed. His braided beard, sandy hair, and smug smile looked store-window perfect despite the civil war that currently raged across the surface of his planet. Dressed regally in a gold silk

31

robe, he seemed to be standing in some underground rock chamber. Red stone walls glimmered darkly in candlelight. "Greetings, Captain. I understand the Magistrates have considered my offer?"

Tahn glowered. The bridge crew had gone rigid, eyes glued to the screen. At her console, Halloway cursed. Ornias had outrageously demanded that the Magistrates give him the planet Grinlow in exchange for Baruch.

"Let's get this on the table quickly, Councilman. The Magistrates say no to your request for Grinlow. However, they will up the reward for Baruch to five billion notes. Do you accept or reject?"

The Councilman's face tensed, his lime green eyes hardening. "Five billion is hardly enough to—"

"Yes, or no."

"You don't mind if I think about it for a short time, do you, Captain?"

"I'll give you five minutes. In the meantime, *put Baruch on. I want to see him.*"

Ornias inclined his head cooperatively and Tahn's stomach muscles tightened as two guards in gray uniforms shoved a tall muscular blond in front of the screen. Standing with his hands bound behind his back, the blond lifted his bearded chin defiantly. He had the most piercing blue eyes Tahn had ever seen. A sheen of sweat matted the man's hair to his forehead and temples.

"Baruch," he said tautly.

"Tahn."

They stared hard at each other and a hollowness boomed in Tahn's chest. The brain death that awaited this brilliant military commander was less than he deserved—but Tahn couldn't do a damned thing about it. Feeling trapped and indecisive, he lightly pounded a fist against his chair arm.

"You'll be well-treated, Baruch. I give you my word."

"Until you get me to the nearest neurophysiology center."

"Nonetheless—"

"Did you give your word to the innocent victims on Kayan? Or Pitbon?"

Tahn shifted uncomfortably. Both worlds had been devastated by beam cannon fire—almost nothing had survived. "I wasn't at Pitbon."

"No," Baruch challenged, struggling against the hard

32

hands of the guards who held him. "How about Jumes or Wexlen? I *know* you were there."

Tahn looked up slowly. Baruch had pulled magnificent maneuvers in those battles, slipping through his fingers before Tahn knew what had happened. *But not this time, Baruch. Not this time . . .*

"Councilman?" Tahn called, indicating the discussion with Baruch was over. He sat up straighter when Ornias stepped back in front of the monitor.

CHAPTER 2

On Horeb, the third moon rose over jagged maroon peaks, washing the sandy plains with a brooding silver light. Jeremiel Baruch shook the cuffs that cinched his hands behind his back and gazed steadily at the dusk sky. *Hoyer*'s shuttle dove out of the heavens like a deadly lance. How long did he have? Two minutes? Three?

Rage burned inside him. Ornias had slipped away in the fight that erupted just after Jeremiel's conversation with Tahn. The Councilman's henchmen had died to the last man to provide covering fire while Ornias escaped through the honeycomb of secret passageways that laced the rock beneath the palace. *My fault. I should have shot him the instant I got my hands on a pistol.*

Baruch braced his feet, watching the shuttle. Around him, charred and broken buildings loomed blackly. People raced through the smoky war-torn streets, clubs or rifles clutched to their bosoms. Somewhere, a baby wailed. In the distance, flashes of fire from the continuing war splashed the desert.

He took a deep breath as he studied the way the ship banked, circling the spaceport. "Blessed Epagael," he prayed softly. "Just one more time. Let this work and I swear I'll become a Believer again." Operation Abba was an untried plan—an insane plan meant only for times as desperate as he now faced.

Around his shoulders, he felt ghostly ancestors crowd. People who'd fought arrogant conquerors all their lives. People who'd been crushed beneath the wheels of fate and refused to stay down. Their confident voices whispered encouragements to him, eerily real in the still winds of dusk.

"Harper?" he called to the tall black guard standing behind him. Harper stepped forward, leveling his rifle at Jeremiel's stomach. Baruch looked at it and threw him a weary smile. "Sure you don't want to change your mind?"

Harper shook his head faintly, glancing up at the shuttle. "Too late for that. Janowitz? Uriah?" he called to the other guards. "Get ready."

The shuttle landed in a burst of dirt and hot wind. Jeremiel ducked his head. Three Magisterial guards in purple and gray uniforms flooded down the shuttle's gangplank and ran toward him. Another man, redheaded and short, stayed by the shuttle entry, his rifle clutched tightly as he studied the mayhem that filled the streets of Horeb. People still ran screaming, trying to get into ships before the Magisterial attack.

"That's him," the tall dark-haired lieutenant said as he pointed at Jeremiel. "Put him in the shuttle. And hurry. We've only got a few minutes before this entire planet goes up in flames."

The blond corporal grinned maliciously. "Come on, Baruch. We've got a nice cold lab chair waiting for you."

"Yeah," the lieutenant chuckled. "And the probe helmet's included for free."

All three soldiers laughed uproariously. The two corporals grabbed Jeremiel by the arms and brutally searched him, then forced him toward the ship. Harper, Uriah, and Janowitz brought up the rear.

Jeremiel stepped into the narrow crew compartment lined with padded blue benches. He could see the entire length of the white fuselage. Four round portals dotted the hull. He went to the far side and waited pensively. When Harper and his team tried to follow, one of the Magisterial soldiers threw out an arm to block their entry.

"Where the hell do you think you're going?" the sergeant asked Harper.

"With you, mister!" Harper declared defensively. "My orders are not to release Baruch to anyone but Captain Tahn!"

"You don't trust us with a five billion note prize, eh?"

"No."

Jeremiel glanced from one man to the next. The tall dark-haired lieutenant exhaled hard and scrutinized Harper. "I'm Lieutenant Simons. Who the hell are you? My orders are to take Baruch *alone*."

Harper's mahogany face went stony. "I'm Councilman Ornias' agent, Lieutenant. My name's Harper. The Councilman ordered us to go along to insure his investment." Harper subtly regripped his rifle. "If we don't go, Lieutenant, neither does Baruch."

"Oh, for God's sake! Just a minute," Simons huffed, throwing up his hands. "Let me tran the *Hoyer* and get Tahn's okay. We don't have time to argue."

Jeremiel gritted his teeth, watching Simons and his red-haired copilot head for the command cabin. The other two members of the Magisterial security team shuffled aimlessly, cursing under their breath about "goddamned Gamants." Through the open door, shouts and cries rose in a deafening crescendo. Gunfire shredded the city streets. A brilliant flash of purple lit the interior of the shuttle and both soldiers spun to peer out the side portals.

Jeremiel screamed, *"Now, Harper!"* and lunged forward, leveling a kick at the closest soldier's throat. The man fell backward, dead before he hit the floor. Jeremiel whirled as Simons raced back, his pistol aimed.

The shuttle blazed with rifle fire.

* * *

Jamie Ryngold sprinted down the long white hall. Of medium height with broad shoulders and blue eyes, he had short brown hair that brushed the tops of his ears as he ran. Five other members of the security team weaved around him. They hurried toward the landing bay to meet Captain Tahn and the shuttle transporting their prisoner up from Horeb. A smile of excitement touched Jamie's lips. The great Jeremiel Baruch, leader of the Gamant Underground and murderer of dozens of his friends—*at last, they had him.* He silently raised a fist to the ceiling in exultation.

"You look happy," Kell Gilluy, his lover, said wryly.

He smiled at her. Tall, with a mass of blonde curls and blue eyes, her purple uniform hugged her body, accenting every toned muscle. "Happy? That's an understatement." He affectionately patted the med pack on his belt. "Maybe I should have overfilled this syringe and taken care of Baruch without any further fuss."

"Not a good idea, love. The Magistrates prefer to have him alive so they can drain him dry of every shred of information first."

"Yeah, I know. With Baruch's wealth of knowledge, we ought to be able to permanently kill his damnable Underground Movement." The faces of a dozen dead friends flashed before his eyes. His jaw hardened.

"Let's hope Iona finally found that scum, Dannon, so we'll have a positive ID on Baruch. I won't believe it's actually him until we verify it."

They passed a few engineering technicians dressed in brown jumpsuits. The glare of the dim overhead panels spread like a veil of dove-colored silk over the walls, glinting in the metallic facets of bulkheads. The wall chronometers flashed the time.

"Damn," Kell said, "Tahn's going to kick our asses for being late."

"You think Baruch's already on board? I doubt it. Simons left less than an hour ago to pick him up off Horeb."

They slowed to a brisk walk as they rounded another corner and from the edge of his vision, he saw Kell whirl. He turned in time to see her flinch as though at the flick of a whip. Her knees went weak and she grabbed for the wall, bracing her hands against it to steady herself.

"Kell?" He lunged for her arm, supporting her. Her beautiful face twisted hauntingly. "What's wrong?"

Obliviously, the rest of the team raced down the hall toward the transport tube.

"What's . . . what's happening?" she whispered.

"What do you mean? Are you okay?

She stared wide-eyed at the blank wall, almost as though she sensed the faint outline of some bright alien form. He traced the path of her gaze, feeling a little eerie himself, like something invisible stood just beyond his shoulder, watching.

"I can't seem to . . . I thought I saw a shadow as we turned the corner. "I—I don't feel very well."

"I can tell. You act like you just looked into the abyss and it looked back."

She put a hand over her stomach. Kell, the tough rock-steady woman every security team hoped to have in its ranks, trembled like a leaf in a gale. His brows drew together. He gently enfolded her in his arms. Trying to make light of it, he teased, "I thought you looked pale when we first left the mess hall. Must have been that soup—I told you it smelled like something we scraped off the bulkheads after the last party."

"Don't . . . . Something's wrong somewhere, Jamie. *Terribly wrong.*"

He swallowed hard. "I hate it when you say things like that. The last time Janice Cogle didn't come back from that routine mission on Ikez III."

He let himself drown in the familiar feel of her body against his. "Hey, Kell, why don't you go to the infirmary and I'll report you sick. We can pick up another member for the security team when we pass Defense."

"But it'll make you even later. You know how jittery the captain's been. He'll roast you."

"Don't worry. I know how to handle Tahn. You just have to look pathetic and he commutes your sentence from a year of hard labor to a week."

He kissed her gently, then put his hands against her hips and shoved her in the opposite direction. "Love you. See you in a couple of hours." He charged off, trying to catch up with his companions.

As soon as he rounded the corner, anxiety pressed hard fingers into his throat. Goddamn, she wasn't the flighty type. Her dependability and ability to sense danger were legendary among a half-dozen starship crews. Like a sixth sense, she'd often *felt* ambushes or traps, saving her teams before they ever got in trouble. Was that what this was all about? A warning?

He ran harder, dodging around the corner for the transport tube. Lieutenant Sam Morcon held the door open, scowling. Short, with sandy hair, his mouth had a hard set to it.

"We were wondering if you'd gone to hell or something, Ryngold. What was the delay? Where's Gilluy?"

Jamie slipped into the tube and hit the patch for level nineteen. He damn sure couldn't tell Morcon what Kell had said. The entire team would get the jitters so bad they'd be incapable of functioning at top level. "Kell's sick. I sent her to the infirmary. We need to pick up somebody else for the team."

"Sick? She looked fine. When did—"

"I don't know," he answered tersely, waving it off. "I told her it must have been that cheese soup she had for lunch. Did you *smell* that stuff? Sheesh, like slime that's been breeding for a month."

Morcon looked slightly relieved. "Yeah. I did. That's why I sat on the opposite side of the table. Well, okay, let me near the com." He pushed between Jamie and Norman Linape, going to the black patch on the wall. He input the numerical sequence for level nineteen security standbys.

"Security," a laconic voice boomed through the tube.

"Banders? This is Morcon. We've had an illness in our team. Have somebody meet us at tube nineteen-three immediately."

"Aye, Lieutenant."

Morcon stepped back and lazily leaned a shoulder against the wall. Jamie quietly exhaled and turned his gaze to the numbers that flashed in blue on the wall as they descended.

CHAPTER 3

Neil Dannon grinned as he entered the *Hoyer*'s fifth-floor lounge. He'd been diligently avoiding responding to any of the urgent calls coming over the ship's com system. He didn't want to talk to any of these despicable purple-suited martinets. If they wanted him, they could damn well hunt him down.

His gaze drifted around the large room. It reminded him of some of the nicer taverns on Farben. Lit with jasmine-scented oil lamps, it had thirty small wooden booths and a series of magnificent holographs lining the walls. The holos pictured mountain scenes so breathtaking a man could almost feel the chill of the snow that frosted their peaks. The raucous music came from Giclas V. Its painfully sharp notes affected him like darts shot out of an old-style cannon.

Forty off-duty officers crowded the lounge tonight, most sitting, but several stood in the center of the room, just beyond the rim of the empty marbleoid dance floor. The white oval shimmered pearlescent in the soft light. Neil took another sip of his Ngoro whiskey and eyed Farin Wyncol admiringly. A petite shapely brunette with enormous green eyes, she noticed his attention and smiled seductively. He returned the gesture.

The officers standing nearby gave her disdainful, almost malignant looks. Dannon took a good long swallow of his whiskey. It was his sixth drink in two hours, and much of his pain had receded into a blessed haze. For the past four days he'd tried to stay as drunk as he possibly could. He started drinking before breakfast mess and went from one lounge to the next throughout the day, until he fell into bed at night ill, but too numb to feel, too stupefied to have any of the nightmares that tormented him like demons with fiery pitchforks.

That way he didn't have to seriously think about Kayan being scorched or do the horrifying silent calculations of how many Gamant lives had been lost. The ache in his gut started to rise again. No. *No!* He took another long drink and forced it down.

Farin smiled coquettishly. He strolled boldly toward her, melting into her circle. The other officers glared with repugnance, some gritting their teeth so hard they set their jaws at awkward angles. He knew why they despised him. Military fanatics had an unwritten law: Any soldier who betrays his own people is beneath contempt. Even though his act of treason against the Underground could have greatly benefited the Magisterial government—if they hadn't screwed up the operation—they still hated him for it.

But Farin didn't care. She knew only that he was exceedingly handsome, a superb lover, and Gamant. To a Magisterially born and bred woman, all things Gamant rang with the exciting timbre of the forbidden. Gamant civilization had alternately warred with the government and fled its tyranny, hiding in the most inaccessible, hostile regions of the galaxy.

In the soft golden light, Farin's dark mass of curls glinted. He let his gaze caress the smooth lines of her oval face, lingering on her full lips. Her turquoise off-duty clothing drew his attention even more fully. The sheer, formfitting gown belled at the sleeves and below the hips, clinging like the finest of shimmering spiderwebs. His gaze lingered on her protruding nipples. Large, dark nipples, he recalled.

She surreptitiously watched the movements of his gaze and when he again looked into those magnificent eyes, he saw the dilated pupils, the silken flush of her skin.

"Farin, dear, your beauty soothes even the most persistent of concerns."

Her lips parted provocatively. "Are you concerned about something tonight, Neil? I'm sure we can figure a way of—"

"For God's sake, Wyncol," Lieutenant Jason Delio turned sharply. A short man with bright orange hair, he had a crooked nose and thick brows. He jabbed a thumb in Neil's direction. "What do you hang around with scum like him for?"

"Mind your own business, Delio," she snapped. "I'll keep company with whoever I damn well please!"

Anger stirred in Neil's breast, but he gave no evidence of it. He'd endured this sort of treatment for months now. He ought to be accustomed to it—but he wasn't. He sipped his whiskey and draped an arm possessively around Farin's shoulders.

Delio grimaced as though ready to spit. "You like turncoats, do you, Wyncol? Prefer 'em over the rest of us?"

Neil unconsciously glanced down at his purple uniform. Old friends and familiar places flashed in his mind and his heart began to pound. He squelched the feeling, forcing happy memories away before they slashed through the alcoholic haze he'd nurtured so carefully.

Farin propped a hand on her hip. "What I do or don't—"

"You've got no more pride than a Giclasian sewer rat," Delio accused. "At least have the decency to go hide somewhere if you're going to sidle up to trash like—"

"Shut your goddamned mouth!" Neil shouted.

A hush descended over the room. The shrill strains of

the metallic music seemed louder, more poignantly violent. Delio's freckled face glowed beet red and he clenched his fists, spreading his feet as though ready for a fight.

"You're filth, Dannon!" he spat. "Drunken, cowardly filth!"

Coward . . . coward. . . . The word stung like salt in a gaping wound. Dannon pushed Farin an arm's length away. A good fistfight might be just what he needed. Maybe it would ease the ache caused by the bitter indictments hurled from the darkness of his soul.

"Jealous, Delio?" he asked, smiling. "Because she has better taste than to cast her pearls at the feet of a swine like you?"

The little man's jaw shook with rage. He clutched his glass so hard his fingernails went white. "*Me* a swine? Do you know what this ship is doing right this very instant, Dannon? Or have you been too drunk since Kayan to know anything?"

"What are you talking about?"

"Tahn just headed for Transportation to pick up your friend Baruch. Once we've got him, we're scorching Horeb. It's a level *one* attack. The entire middle section of the planet's going to get wasted. This is definitely Baruch's last stand. You tried to betray him on Silmar and got a hell of a lot of his people killed, even though he escaped. How does that make you feel? Another Gamant named Ornias finally finished your work for you. We're going to deliver your friend to the nearest neurophysiology center and have his brain probed until he's nothing but a vegetable."

Neil paled. *Jeremiel . . . on board?* How had he missed such talk? Surely the crew had been discussing it everywhere. But then, no one would have seen fit to whisper it to him so he could prepare himself.

Farin shouted, "What do you care, Delio? Baruch's been your enemy since the day you stepped out of Academy! You sound like you want to hold a wake in his honor!"

Some of the anger faded from Delio's face. He frowned down into his drink. "Anybody who's fought against Baruch respects him—that doesn't mean I like him. I hate his filthy Gamant guts."

From the corner of his eye, Neil saw Doctor Iona stride

into the lounge with two security guards. The white in his hair glimmered in the lamplight. His gaze darted anxiously around the room, then, spotting Neil, he trotted forward.

"Dannon, move. Tahn wants you in Transportation, now."

He eyed the security staff, one red-haired, one black-haired. Both with hard faces. "What for?"

"Baruch will be here any minute. Tahn wants you to give the positive ID."

"What?"

Iona waved him toward the door. "Come on. You haven't got much time. Baruch should just about be here."

In a staggering moment of lucidity, memories burst wide in Neil's mind. His thoughts riveted on strategy sessions held over a few cool amber ales, just he, Jeremiel, and Rudy Kopal.

"Oh . . . God."

Terror welled. No, it couldn't be. *Operation Abba?* Seven years ago, they'd been stretched out on the lush dry grasses of Lysomia VI, drinking ale, watching the towering clouds, bantering strategy. *Insane strategy—things to be tried only when they were already dead men, trapped, and no other path lay open to them.* An autumn-scented wind blew up the canyon, dry and brittle, rustling in the maple forests. A few crimson leaves spiraled from the limbs to cartwheel across the meadow.

Jeremiel had contemplatively brushed his fingers over the dry grass, his blond hair shimmering a reddish gold in the slanting rays of afternoon light. His deep voice rang like thunder in Neil's ears. *"No, six would be too many. If you're going to take a cruiser, it'll have to be a small strike force. Maybe three or four. They'll have no more than forty-five seconds total to . . ."*

Neil threw his glass to the floor and ran for the exit. Behind him, he heard Iona shout, "Guards! Stop him! I don't care if you have to physically drag him, get him to transportation!"

Neil almost made it to the door before two men tackled him and knocked him to the floor. He rolled, punching, kicking, struggling to get away. One of the security men slammed a hard fist into his solar plexus and Neil gasped, unable to catch his breath.

"You . . . fools!" he croaked. *"You stupid . . . stupid fools! Baruch is going to . . . to take this ship! I have to get to Tahn. For God's sake! Let me go!"*

* * *

When the tube stopped, Jamie Ryngold and the security team flooded out. Sergeant Yocup met them, still hastily fiddling with the charge in his rifle. Together, they trotted in single file into Transportation. Jamie saluted, glancing quickly at Tahn, expecting a reprimand for being late. He frowned when it didn't come. Tahn looked like hell, nervous as a tiger on a hunt, sweat matting his brown hair to his forehead. His blue-violet eyes gleamed with such desperation and uncertainty Jamie tensed involuntarily.

"Ryngold," Morcon ordered. "Hang back. Run the final check."

"Aye, Sam." He faded back to stand by the security com on the wall.

Tahn hit the button to open the doors to the landing bay foyer. Lieutenant Halloway and the security team followed. Jamie tried to ease his anxiety by letting his gaze drift admiringly over Halloway. A tall woman with shoulder-length auburn hair, she had pale translucent skin and blazing green eyes. No man aboard had ever been able to approach her. Cool and tough, she kept to herself for the most part, shunning parties and rarely appearing in any of the lavish lounges on the ship. But everybody admired her from afar.

Jamie brought his attention back, accessing the bay monitor and keying in a level one alert on deck nineteen. The alarm panel above him flashed blue in silent rhythmic pulses, changing the stark white walls to pale azure. He could see the empty landing pad, Mike Fritz manning the control console.

"Sergeant?" Tahn inquired tersely of Fritz. "What's the status of the shuttle?"

"Simons reports he has Baruch in custody. No problems. ETA is two minutes, sir."

Tahn's face paled visibly as though he waged a violent battle with himself. He looked like he'd clenched his fists to keep them from shaking under the tension. Finally, Tahn pulled in a deep breath and ordered, "Notify the bridge to commence Prime Mover One."

"Aye, sir."

Jamie closed his eyes a moment, bracing himself. The ship lurched slightly as violet beams lanced out, blasting the surface of Horeb. He glanced at the close-range planetary monitor. Three hundred miles below, he could see a huge crimson wave rise from the melted sandstone ridges, rolling toward the capital city of Seir—a sea of blood to drown Gamant inequities. Damn them all, anyway. The *Hoyer* had been forced to initiate a level two scorch attack against Kayan less than a week ago. Gamants were all insane. They'd wantonly broken the Treaty of Lysomia, attacking Magisterial military installations, killing hundreds of soldiers. Horeb had compounded the sins by flaring into civil war and hiding a Magisterial criminal. They had to be heroes, protecting one of their own. Baruch ranked number one on the government's hit list, and they knew it. Even though a Gamant Councilman had betrayed and turned Baruch over in the end, the Magistrates didn't tolerate disobedience very well.

"Oh." He heard Halloway whisper emptily to herself as she turned away from the planetary monitor.

Jamie felt the soft reverberations through the ship like widening rings across an enormous pool of black. He could almost hear the screams of the thousands. It made him ache a little, but he quickly dismissed it. Horebians had brought it on themselves. Obeying orders, that's what the *Hoyer* was doing, just keeping peace in the galaxy.

"Shuttle docked, sir," Fritz acknowledged. "Simons reports all clear."

Tahn swallowed convulsively. "Open the doors."

The foyer emptied as people flooded into the broad white-tiled bay. The ceiling stretched seventy feet high.

In an abrupt movement that made Jamie stiffen, Tahn whirled, eyes scanning the bay as he dropped into a combat crouch.

"What the hell . . ." Jamie whispered nervously to himself. His monitor showed nothing! Simultaneously, the communications light on his console flared. He cursed at it and struck the key, demanding the origin point. "Level five lounge? Damn it! Can't you guys wait another ten minutes to know for sure that we've got Baruch?" Jamie put the com request on hold.

44

Halloway's hand dropped to the butt of her holstered pistol as she carefully scanned the bay. To Tahn she whispered, "What is it?"

He shook his head. "Nothing . . . I—I thought I saw a shadow. Something black . . . moving over the walls. I'm just skittish, I guess."

Blood drained from Jamie's face until he felt light-headed. *A shadow?*

"Materialized guilt," Halloway murmured.

Tahn heaved a disgusted breath. "Remind me to prosecute you for insubordination."

"Aye, sir," she responded curtly, but her eyes still searched the wall.

Jamie forced his gaze to the newly arrived shuttle. *Forget it! You don't have time to worry about your imagination or anybody else's.* The com light flashed urgently now, changing from blue to red, demanding attention. The shuttle sat like an ebony spear point on the floor. After a short time, the side doors parted and a man fitting Baruch's description stepped out. Tall and muscular, his hands were bound behind his back. Blond hair clung to his chiseled face in damp curls, but his blue eyes gleamed like fiery sapphires. He looked haggard, desperate. Did he know what the Magistrates had in mind for him? That he'd be a living vegetable in less than two weeks? Four more men stepped out behind Baruch, dressed in the purple and gray of security personnel. Simons prodded Baruch in the back with his rifle to make him walk.

Jamie ran a check of the shuttle. No more life-forms. He exhaled in relief and briefly propped his forehead against the cool petrolon hull. *No Trojan Horse Move, thank God.* He struck the button on the security com. "All is well. Stand down from level one alert. Go to three."

The blue alert panel stopped flashing and the walls returned to their whiter than white hue. Jamie pulled the syringe and checked the fluid level again. He tucked it in one of the outer fabric shells of his waist pack, within easy reach. Unslinging his rifle, he trotted out into the bay to stand behind Morcon. Tahn paced beside him, clenching and unclenching his fists.

Baruch started walking and the tension in the room

felt as concrete as a brick wall. He came to a halt no more than three feet in front of the captain. Stiffly, he greeted, "Tahn."

"I keep my promises, Baruch. You'll be well-treated."

"You're a butcher. Have you initiated the scorch attack yet? How many babies do you think you've already killed?"

For the briefest of moments, Jamie felt time stop, as though they all hung suspended over a chasm of dark swirling nothingness. Then . . . the ship lunged sideways, g-force making them all stagger.

"Cole! *Look out!*" Halloway screamed.

Jamie had just gotten his feet under him when he saw Baruch's hands flash from behind his back and he slammed Tahn in the temple with the butt of a pistol.

Shrill whines erupted, rifle fire bursting from everywhere. Men all around Jamie slumped to the floor in bloody heaps. He dove, rolling to come up with his rifle aimed at Baruch's broad back when a blinding flare of violet slashed his legs. He toppled forward, screaming, writhing, trying to reach for his rifle which had clattered away across the floor. A spread of crimson widened around his body; he looked down to find his legs severed just below the hips. Shock and terror overwhelmed him.

"Harper, GO!" Baruch shouted and threw himself on Tahn, kicking and repeatedly bashing the captain's head with his gun.

The three shuttle officers dressed in *Hoyer* uniforms sprinted into a transport tube and disappeared. Impostors. His fault! Jamie tried to drag himself to his rifle, but he felt so weak, so very weak. What the hell had the lurch been? It felt like the very fabric of space heaved. Phase-change? Stunned, his eyes riveted on Halloway, she lifted her pistol, trying desperately to get a clear shot at Baruch, but he and Tahn were twined so tightly, she had no chance. Finally, she aimed at the floor and fired. The diversion shot flashed around the bay, whining like a shrieking banshee.

Baruch lunged to his feet, dodging into the tube before Halloway could get off another shot.

"Someone'll stop them," Jamie murmured to himself. But . . . but if they headed directly for Engineering, they'd have the element of complete surprise on their side. *Impossible!* Four men couldn't take a battle cruiser!

No! Oh, dear God, no! Why had he given the order to stand down! But there'd been no negative indications. How could he have known Baruch would try something so insane?

Jamie saw Tahn crawl weakly to his knees. Nausea overwhelmed the captain and he vomited repeatedly onto the white tiles. Halloway gripped Tahn by the arm and pulled him to his feet.

"Lean on me. Cole? *Cole!* We've got to get out of here!"

Tahn seemed disoriented, unable to focus his eyes. Concussion? He reeled in her arms as Halloway supported him across the bay and through a side entry that led to Defense.

Jamie lay still, staring blindly at the mangled corpses surrounding him on all sides. Morcon had been cut in half by the beams. Jamie blinked. A gray haze fluttered around the edges of his vision. He worked his leaden fingers in the copper-scented pool of blood that shot in jets from his femoral arteries. With the slow deliberateness of an assassin, blackness closed in, and he felt cold, so cold. . . .

His consciousness waned just as the First Alert sirens wailed through the bay.

CHAPTER 4

Harper braced himself in the tube, breathing hard, adrenaline searing his veins. Jeremiel had said they'd have no more than thirty seconds maximum. Dear God, he prayed Baruch was still alive. He had a baseline competency in the systems, but he'd never be able to handle this massive twenty-level cruiser without Jeremiel. He stared at Uriah, a skinny youth with black hair, then at Janowitz, short and stocky and platinum blond.

"You know the plan," Harper said. "Full-scale attack. No prisoners."

Janowitz's eyes glowed. "We're ready."

The tube door snicked open and they lurched into the corridor, panning it with their rifles. Shrill whines erupted as purple beams lanced out. Four Magisterial crew members fell dead before they knew what had happened.

Harper led the charge, racing down the hall toward the double doors that led into Engineering. Jeremiel had explained that all C-J class cruisers had the same design. Engineering was a tri-level round chamber manned at any given time by about twenty people. Duty stations perched like wire birds' nests on each level—making it damned easy shooting if you surprised the crew from below.

He burst through the doors, lifted his rifle, and took the top level. Janowitz and Uriah braced themselves behind him, taking the floor and second levels. Men and women screamed and struggled to get up to run. A few grabbed for guns as purple arcs sliced off arms and legs.

"Throw down your weapons!" Harper demanded, and kept firing.

A cascade of pistols and rifles clattered on the floor. The dead hung from their wire duty cages, mouths agape, eyes wide with shock. Starbursts of crimson splashed the white walls, running in streaks and bars to pool on the floor. Several members of the crew had escaped. Only one man, a red-haired lieutenant, still remained. He'd been trapped in the square niche of blocky white consoles that controlled the entire ship.

"Janowitz, Uriah, go check the adjacent corridors. Clear them. Use whatever force is necessary."

"Aye, Harper."

Both men raced to the exit that most of the crew had escaped through. Harper watched them disappear, then whirled when he caught a glimpse of his remaining prisoner reaching for the nearest console. He leveled his rifle.

"Get away from those controls, mister."

"Who—who are you?" the lieutenant shouted shakily. "You can't just walk in here and—" He lunged for the console, fingers groping.

Harper's shot took him squarely in the chest, bursting it wide. Blood and bits of bone shredded the air as the enemy soldier slumped face-first over the console. Sporadic gunfire continued in the corridors outside. Harper prayed Janowitz and Uriah were doing the firing.

He spun when he heard the pounding of feet. Jeremiel raced into Engineering, his black battlesuit spattered with blood. Baruch took in the room and immediately headed for the console beside Harper. His fingers flew, inputting data.

Harper watched words come up on the screen: *CANNOT DISCONNECT EMERGENCY BAFFLES WITHOUT PROPER AUTHORIZATION CODE. PLEASE INPUT.*

The emergency baffles, Harper knew, kicked in the instant any section experienced decompression, sealing off the rest of the ship and protecting the crew. To Harper's amazement, Jeremiel keyed in a lengthy sequence and waited pensively.

UNACCEPTABLE CODE.

Jeremiel input a new sequence. He tried six before the com responded: *CODE ACCEPTED. BAFFLES DISCONNECTED.*

The Underground must have had spies in all the right places. Baruch struck a different series of patches, wetting his lips nervously.

The doors to Engineering snapped closed and the alert sirens ceased. Harper asked, "What are you doing?"

"Rerouting control of the ship. Sealing off this section, level seven, and the bridge and decompressing every other level."

In a sudden wash of understanding, Harper sucked in a breath. The emergency baffles? When Jeremiel opened the locks, every unsealed portion of the ship would be swept clean as the oxygen rushed out into the vacuum of space. Anyone standing in those corridors . . . . "You're . . . you're going to kill thousands of people?"

"You want them in here with us?"

The desperate tone struck Harper like a fist in the stomach. He sank down into a chair. "No."

* * *

Dannon lunged for the nearest transport tube, wondering how long he had? The sirens shredded his composure. Obviously, Jeremiel had made some move. Neil's guards in the lounge had released him the instant the klaxons wailed. *It's too late now to go anywhere but the bridge.* If Baruch had initiated Operation Abba, he'd first

49

create a diversion so his team could get out of the bay and into a transport tube. They'd be at level twenty in exactly fifteen seconds if they'd worked it right. And Engineering would be lost. The very structure of the section left it open to such a devastating attack. The crew couldn't move fast enough to get out of the way. They'd be sitting ducks for soldiers with rifles. Already he could picture the slaughter, people hanging from their cages, blood spattering the white walls.

When the tube stopped, Neil ran out onto the bridge into the midst of a half-dozen panicked officers all talking at once. Overhead, a three hundred and sixty degree monitor flashed data from every part of the ship.

Rich Macey, the red-haired communications officer, bent over his terminal, shouting, "Simons? Fritz? *Somebody* answer me! Transportation? What the hell's going on down there?"

"Where's Tahn?" Neil shouted into the melee, but no one paid him the slightest attention. "Goddamn it! Find your captain first. Nobody else matters now! Baruch's responsible and we've got to . . ."

The door to the bridge snapped open and Halloway, panting from exertion, hauled Tahn into the room—he looked ill, staggering in her arms. His purple uniform clung to his muscular body in wrinkled bloody folds.

"Tahn!" Neil shouted. "What's happening?"

Halloway eased her captain into his command chair before rushing for her nav console. Tahn struggled to keep himself sitting upright. "Ship's status, Lieutenant?" he called to Macey.

"We—we don't know, sir. We can't—"

Neil stepped forward. "Is it true?" he demanded, bracing his hands on Tahn's chair arms to stare wild-eyed into Cole's tortured face. His gut tightened as he noted the vastly different sizes of the captain's pupils. *"Is Baruch aboard?"*

Tahn squinted, trying to focus on him. "What the hell are you doing here? Get off my bridge!"

"I want to know if he—"

The alert sirens went deadly quiet and the blood drained from Dannon's head, making him feel faint.

With sudden dread, Tahn gazed around the bridge. "No . . . he can't have—"

Yes, he can. The truth made Neil sick unto death. He

released the chair arms and straightened. Jeremiel had this ship. Dannon tingled from shock. So the crew in Engineering was dead. Jeremiel's next move would be to tap into the Master Engineer's damage control override circuitry, rerouting all major functions of the ship to his own console. The override programming stood as the fundamentally weak link of all C-J class cruisers. Through that system, one man could kill the rest of the ship.

But, no, no. Don't think it! Tahn would find a way of incapacitating Engineering. It would be four against over three thousand trained Magisterial soldiers. Jeremiel may have captured the vessel, but he couldn't hold it. All they had to do was bide their time until they could smoke him out. A giddy feeling of relief wound through him. Yes, they'd pry him out in the end. Baruch couldn't hold a ship this large with a strike force so small.

"Captain!" Macey yelled shrilly. "I've—I've got decompression readings from all over the ship. We—"

"Gas Engineering!"

Halloway's fingers fluttered over her console. Her voice came out strained, quiet. "Can't. He's rerouted control."

"Bypass!"

". . . Can't."

"Oh, God!" Neil screamed hysterically. Decompression wasn't a part of Operation Abba! Jeremiel was evening the numbers! With all the locks open, he could completely decompress the ship in less than five minutes. He lunged for Tahn, shouting, *"He's taken your ship. You fool! You let him take your ship!* You should have known he'd—"

Tahn pushed up to sway erratically on his feet. He slammed a powerful right cross into Neil's mouth. Stunned and in pain, Dannon staggered backward, sobbing as he hit the floor. Jeremiel would kill him! From the corner of his eye, he saw Halloway's hands flying over her console. She'd pulled up the cryptography library and frantically sought to delete file after file. The idiot! Couldn't she see the pattern? She was already too late! He saw her screen flare, *Access Denied.* She tried something else. *Unauthorized entry.* Her fingers tapped another possible sequence. *Can't retrieve clandestine files from this access route.* She made a deep guttural sound of frustration and slammed a fist repeatedly into her console. Then, in a violent move, she reached beneath her console and ripped a panel down, then fumbled with another card. The long-range communications link? Clever, it might take Jeremiel a few hours to figure it out—maybe longer if he got overwhelmed with problems. But would anybody out there be trying to reach them?

Someone screamed and Neil's gaze riveted on the forward screen. Bodies tumbled from the *Hoyer*, scattering in the blackness of space like bloody ghouls just escaped from Aktariel's legendary pit of darkness. They tumbled end over end, contorted faces seeming to stare directly in at those on board, pleading even in death for help.

Desperately, Dannon crawled for the nearest suit locker and jerked one out. He swiftly slipped into it.

"Halloway . . ." Tahn whispered, face ashen. "Carey . . . estimate casualties?"

"Approximately two thousand, seven hundred and fifty."

"Which level did he seal. Seven?"

"Aye, sir."

Of course, he'd sealed seven! Dannon slammed a fist into the floor at their stupidity. Cruisers possessed between thirty-three and thirty-four hundred crew members. Jeremiel might need those science specialists—but the others represented excess, armed baggage. Tahn slumped in his chair, body going slack; his head lolled back as he mumbled incoherently. Delusions?

"Captain?" Macey said, on the verge of tears. "What's happening?"

On the screen, dozens of planetary ships surged toward the *Hoyer* and Neil abruptly understood Jeremiel's plan. He'd adapted Operation Abba to make room for the refugees fleeing the destruction of Horeb. The scorch attack would have initiated a series of horrifying chain reactions. Soon, the planet would be writhing beneath major climatic upheavals. *That would give Jeremiel a ship full of loyal Gamants to do his bidding and they'd methodically search every inch of the* Hoyer *until they found him!*

"Macey," Tahn ordered. "Get me Engineering."

Neil pushed back against the wall, shielding himself behind a console. The forward screen flared to life. Jeremiel's hard blue eyes stared out at Tahn. He looked just as he had six months ago, blond hair and beard neatly trimmed. Dannon shivered involuntarily. His best friend for fifteen years. . . .

"Baruch," Tahn said. "Let's talk."

"I'm listening."

At the sound of Jeremiel's deep voice, Neil shrank in upon himself, soul withering. Happy, hurtful memories whirled out of the blackness of his liquor-laced mind. He felt like he'd been gutted.

Tahn shifted in his command chair, voice unsteady. "I should think . . . telling you we surrender is a little redundant, but if you need to hear it—"

"I don't."

Neil got on his stomach and slithered across the floor, taking a path he knew lay below the visual range. He saw Halloway's cold green eyes leveled on him, brimming with disgust. He headed for the door to the bridge conference room. From there, he could duck into one of the air shafts and when Jeremiel repressurized the ship, he could head for the tangled guts of the *Hoyer*. No one could easily find him there.

He heard Tahn ask, "What can I do to . . . save the lives of the rest of my crew?"

Jeremiel responded tiredly, "I want your cooperation. The people I'm bringing aboard are able, but not trained. Tell your science division to school my people and I guarantee I'll put you off alive and well on the nearest Gamant planet."

"I'm not sure that'll be doing us a favor . . . but we'll manage."

Neil reached up and palmed the entry to the conference room, then scrambled inside and pounded the patch to close the door.

"Calm down!" He smoothed his black hair away from his eyes with shaking hands. "Jeremiel can't hold the ship. Even after killing eighty percent of the crew, he's going to have a hell of a time battling Tahn for control."

He fought to force his breathing to return to normal. "All you have to do is hide long enough for Tahn to take his ship back."

53

Locking his helmet down, he got to his feet and ran around the long table. Jerking off the air duct panel, he scrambled inside.

* * *

Harper put down the gold circlet of his com headset and watched Jeremiel cut the connection with the bridge. Baruch looked dead tired, drained of every ounce of energy that had kept them alive over the past few days. His blue eyes had gone dull, lifeless. He propped a trembling fist on the white console.

"Avel," he said tensely. "I have to go meet the incoming *samaels*. There are two things I need you to do. First, I've set the ship's scanners on maximum. All you have to do is use this board to search the polar ice cap for life. If you get confused, ask the ship, she'll help guide you. *I want to know if Rachel's still alive.*"

"I understand," Harper responded. "If she is, I'll dispatch a *samael* immediately to get her."

Just before Horeb's civil war had flared, Baruch had sent Rachel Eloel in, undercover, to kill Horeb's leader, the Mashiah Adom Kemar Tartarus. The Mashiah had taken Rachel to the polar ice cap just as the first battles began. She'd completed her mission the same day, killing Tartarus while he was in the middle of a broadcast to bolster his flagging troops in Seir—Harper and Jeremiel had seen the holo film of Rachel stabbing Tartarus in the chest. But no one had any idea what had happened to her afterward.

"Good," Jeremiel continued. "Second, use a narrow beam transmission. Aim for somewhere around Pitbon. See if you can contact my fleet. If so, tell Rudy Kopal we've got another battle cruiser for him. Ask him to meet us at Tikkun."

"I will."

Harper watched Baruch go to the closest vacuum-suit locker and suit up. Though he'd begun repressurizing the decks, it would take another two hours to completely restore the life systems. Harper saw Jeremiel disappear into the dark hallway beyond and turned back to his console. He input a series of basic "search" commands and waited. A grid of the polar cap appeared on his screen, showing clearly the distinct topography of ice ridges and windswept plains. A barren foreboding place, the temperatures dropped to as much as a hundred below

54

zero at this time of year.

"Oh, Rachel," he murmured. "Be all right."

While the ship searched for her, Harper accessed the communications panel again. He'd already assigned his most experienced people—refugees from the civil war and damned fine fighters—to land first and secure the bays. Two ships, *samaels*, were easing in now. They settled like feathers on the white tiles.

"Klausen? This is Harper. Be careful when you step out of that ship. Baruch suspects that another hundred soldiers managed to suit up before the decompression. They're probably waiting for you."

A pause. Then, "Affirmative, Harper. We'll be ready for them."

Harper looked back to the vast wasteland of ice and blue shadows at the pole. Bitter glacial winds swirled over the surface, kicking snow up to the dark star-strewn skies.

"Be alive, Rachel. We need you. We . . ."

He leaned forward suddenly. A red dot flared on the screen and began to flash. Harper let out a whoop of exultation.

"Got her!"

CHAPTER 5

Fitful, frightening dreams tormented Rachel Eloel. Wind shrieked around the ice cave where she lay, filtering through the narrow entrance to crust her white weather-suit and long black hair with snow. Half-conscious, she felt the fatal fingers of wind stroke her face in ghostly patterns. Her arms and legs had grown too numb to move.

She whimpered obliviously. Adom's image came again, smiling innocently down at her, filled with love. Shining blond hair streamed over his broad shoulders. That vision soon melted into another—terrifying in its clarity. They stood in the depths of the polar chambers, watching battle scenes from the civil war rage across the wide screen. Adom turned and when he saw the knife lifted over her head, he backed away, stumbling into the screen.

"No," he said softly, "Rachel, no. . . ."

She plunged the knife deeply into his chest. Blood spattered his ivory robe in an irregular starburst. He sank to the floor, gazing up with all the tenderness, the boyish innocence that had always ravaged her heart.

"Rachel. . . ." A red froth bubbled at his lips. "Hold me?"

She'd dropped to her knees and gathered him in her arms. "Adom, forgive me." *Forgive me . . . forgive me. . . .*

Even in sleep, tears drained from her eyes to crust on her lashes. She rolled her head to the side, sending icy locks of waist-length hair slithering over the gritty floor like frosted serpents. Adom had never shown her anything but kindness and love—and she'd betrayed both. Ornias, Adom's High Councilman, had promised revenge and she'd fled into the vast glacial wilderness of the pole, following the lee of the icy cliffs until she found the cave and took shelter. And she'd had strange, strange dreams of talking to God—Epagael—and of being visited by the wicked angel, Aktariel.

Dreams. Just the fantasies of a dying mind.

Somewhere, through the mists of sleep, she heard a soft footfall and felt herself float upward into a golden shimmering haze. The sounds of the chilling polar cap vanished as though they'd never existed and light played across her closed eyelids, fluttering, misty, moving, bathing her in heat. Her frozen limbs ached miserably for a time, then felt as though a million needles pricked them. After an eternity of pain and cold, warmth began to seep inside her and she fell deeper asleep, floating, just floating in the immeasurable ocean of light.

A soft soothing voice swirled out of the gold. "What did God say, Rachel, when you asked him why the universe suffers so?"

"Who . . . who are you?"

"What did He say?"

"He told me I wasn't worthy to ask. He asked me where I was when he laid the foundations of the universe."

A tired sigh fluttered around her on saffron wings. "And if you could bind the sweet influences of the Pleiades or loose the bands of Orion, I'll wager."

"Yes. How did you know?"

"Oh, it's his standard rebuttal. A weak appeal to authority."

"He told me the spinning patterns of chaos give him great pleasure."

"And what did you say?"

"I . . . I told him Aktariel was right. I told him it would be better if we were never born than to live in misery all our lives."

"There are things we can do to end the misery." A hand of flame descended, stroking her hair with comforting fingers. "Rachel, Rachel, last of the sefira. Will you help me stop the suffering? Together, we can."

"But . . . What is that? A sefira? I read about it in Middoth's journal in the polar chambers."

"It's a vessel. A vessel of pure Light."

Terror tightened at the base of her throat. Why did that kind, soothing voice suddenly sound so familiar? *"Who are you?"*

"Someone who loves you. I've loved you and waited for you for uncounted millennia."

"I don't understand."

A roar of thunder vibrated through the golden womb. Cannon fire? The civil war? Rachel shuddered.

"I'm sorry, Rachel. You have to wake up now. Jeremiel needs you desperately. We have to hurry."

Jeremiel? For a single blessed moment her heart soared like an eagle on the wind. *"Jeremiel? He's all right?"*

"For the moment. But he won't be if you don't wake up soon."

"Why?"

"He's in a lot of trouble."

The void moved, swirling like topaz fire. Her leaden eyelids fluttered open, lashes covered with ice. Prismatic reflections sparkled, faces broken into crystal facets, like seeing through a kaleidoscope. A thousand amber eyes stared down, singularly gentle. She let herself drown in the warmth she found there.

The ground shook.

"We must hurry, Rachel. I'm sorry."

The golden void dissolved like clouds in hot winds. She jerked awake, panting, shouting, *"The War! Ornias!"*

She tried to sit up and found herself staring into the glimmering amber eyes of Aktariel. She froze. *Not a dream. . . .* He had her cradled to his bosom. The hood of his blue cloak ruffled softly in the wind penetrating the ice cave. Within the hood, his face shone a brilliant gold, handsome features seemingly chiseled from light.

"Leave me alone!" She shoved out of his grasp, scrambling madly on hands and knees to get away. Dear God, this bright alien was terrifyingly real. How could that be? *Am I losing my mind?*

"Rachel, we must talk."

She pressed back against the far wall. Her white weather-suit screeched with every movement, ice cracking off to tinkle against the cave floor. The temperature had to be eighty below zero, though her body still felt warm where he'd held her.

"No! I read Middoth's journals, I know you misled and killed him! And you killed Adom!"

In a fluid graceful motion, he braced a hand on the floor and got to his feet. She couldn't catch her breath. In the gleam cast by his body, the walls glittered as though crusted with diamonds. "I made a mistake with Middoth."

"You made mistakes with everyone! *They're all dead!* Everyone you've ever used—"

"Yes, I've made mistakes. The major one being that I should have given Middoth a *Mea*, so he could challenge God himself. That's why I gave you one. Don't you see? I've tried very hard not to make any mistakes with you."

She reached up to touch the dull gray ball that hung from the golden chain around her neck. When Adom had first given her the *Mea*, it had glowed with such glaring blue light, it had been hard to look at directly. "But . . . Adom gave it to me."

Aktariel shook his head. "No. I just didn't want him to tell you where it came from. I was afraid it might hinder your use of the device. And I wanted you to know the truth firsthand."

Anger and confusion swelled to suffocate her. "How many dupes in the past believed that only to discover on their deathbeds that you'd toyed with them as cruelly as a cat does with a mouse before the kill?" Gauging the distance to the exit, she vacillated. Outside, starlight plated the ice cliffs in silver. Wind howled, throwing snow like sparkling lances at the dark heavens. "Middoth wrote that you'd stolen all the *Meas*. That you'd—"

"True. I did."

She inhaled sharply. He sounded so calm, so chillingly matter-of-fact, as though confessing to a cold-blooded murder that he only vaguely remembered committing. "If you're so anxious to have people face God themselves, why not spread them around?"

"Because . . ." He clenched his fists tightly, as if to control an emotional outburst. "Rachel, most people in the past who've used the *Mea* have been weak, simple fools, easily influenced. When they went to talk to God, He had no trouble bending them to His will. Believers when they left, they were fanatics when they returned." He shoved his hands deep in the pockets of his blue cloak and eyed her askance. "I had to counteract His propaganda. And . . . I had other reasons."

"Then why did you give me one?"

"I bet everything on the hope that when you faced Him you'd be angry and desperate enough to ask the right questions. And you did. That's why He locked the gate to you. The *Mea* you're wearing is dead. That's why it doesn't glow anymore."

In a gentle loverlike gesture, he opened his glowing arms, reaching out to her. Against the shimmering background of ice, he seemed a magnificent angelic sculpture of gleaming gold. She backed farther away, edging for the cave entrance.

"Rachel, listen to me. There are some things I cannot do. You think of me as being like God, but I'm not. Chaos has clear, distinct patterns. I can't—"

"They why can't you predict and change them?"

"Because I wasn't standing there when Epagael established the initial conditions of this universe—though Lord knows I *should* have been. Unless one knows those conditions, one can never truly predict chaotic turbulence. Patterns that were set in motion eons ago are too strong for me to alter—except in minor ways. Occasionally, I can add an element of nonlinearity and reshape certain parameters. And I can set new ones in motion. But Adom's path had been determined long ago." Forlornly, he murmured, "Just as Moshe's had and

Yeshwah's and Sinlayzan's. Though I tried to help them, too. But they'd been forsaken by God before I descended into the void."

Angrily, she accused, "So all the Old Stories are wrong? You're really a saint?"

He shook both fists futilely. "No, not a saint. A prisoner! A tool, just as you are! We are all pawns in Epagael's cruel game. *But if you'll help me, if you'll only—*"

He took three quick steps toward her and she screamed, "No! I just want to go home and live with my daughter in peace. Leave me alone!"

Aktariel's blue cloak waffled in the wind penetrating the cave entrance. "Rachel, please, we must discuss Tikkun and Jeremiel. What happens on Tikkun will determine the fate of this universe. If we don't plan—"

"NO!"

She shoved past him, ducking out of the cave to run madly along the base of the towering white cliff. Starlight turned the wind-sculpted world into a pewter and black painting, throwing her shadow like an amorphous giant over the bluff.

"Rachel?" He called from somewhere behind, voice carried away by the wind. "Rachel, you'll freeze to death out here! It's a hundred below zero. *And Jeremiel needs you!* He'll be looking for you. You have to stay near the cave!"

An amber glow fluttered like a thing alive over the rough-hewn parapet. She stifled a cry of fear and turned in the opposite direction, climbing a rocky slope to escape him. Cold blue shadows clung to the hollows. The words about Jeremiel were certainly false. He knew nothing of her location. How could he? She'd left Seir with Adom only hours ago. No one knew where she'd gone—except Ornias. A prickle of terror touched her spine.

For an eternal time, she just climbed and ran, until at last, she dragged herself to the top of an icy plateau. Wind hurled itself out of the silvered blackness, shoving her back and forth, draining the warmth from her body. Starlight fell like strewn pearls across the gravel-pocked ice at her feet, shadowing every undulation.

She forced her leaden legs forward, breaking over the

crest—and stopped dead in her tracks. A fiery violet halo grew on the horizon. Like a massive bank of roiling clouds, it swelled with each second. The war? No, it couldn't be. They had no weapons on Horeb that could wreak such terrible devastation.

"What is that?" she whispered to herself.

From behind, a soft and startlingly beautiful voice answered. "A scorch attack."

She spun. He stood regally, arms crossed over his breast as though against some pain. His golden face flared like a beacon of salvation.

A scorch attack? But that would mean that the Magistrates had come to Horeb. When had that happened? Adom hadn't even mentioned the possibility.

Aktariel looked up at her curiously, as though judging what she'd do next. "At this very moment, Jeremiel is fighting for his life and the lives of every living thing on your world."

Her gaze went to the starry sky, seeking the source of the violet fire. "He's not on Horeb?"

"No." The gale buffeted Aktariel's blue cloak, whipping it into snapping folds around his legs. Against the pewter maze of rock and ice, he seemed a lonely embodiment of light and color. "The civil war here ended an hour ago, but Captain Tahn of the Magisterial battle cruiser, the *Hoyer*, was ordered to scorch Horeb anyway for breaking the Treaty of Lysomia. Jeremiel thought he might be able to stop the attack if he willingly went along with Ornias' plan. Ornias sold Baruch to the Magistrates for five billion notes."

"He used himself as a bargaining lever?"

"Of course. You know him. There was nothing else he could do. But the Magistrates just took him and continued with the attack—punishing Gamants for disobeying in the first place."

"Then what's happening now?"

"Ah," Aktariel breathed, cautiously walking forward to stand a few feet from her. He lifted an arm and pointed to the starry horizon just above the lavender halo. "Jeremiel and Harper took over the shuttle transporting him to the *Hoyer* and are now trying to take the cruiser."

Rachel's fear of Aktariel ebbed, replaced by a deeper terror—the loss of her entire world. She clenched her fists, lifting her chin to stare him defiantly in the eyes. "Will he win?"

"For a time."

"What does that mean?"

The crystalline glory of starlight gilded his upturned face with a frosty shimmer. "It means unless you get aboard that ship with him—he'll die."

The word cracked like thunder. She wanted to run, but couldn't force her feet to move. "Why? Why does he need me?"

"Because, Rachel, you are a bridge *to me.*"

As though in response, the lavender fires on the horizon died, leaving them in a shadowy world. The glacial wilderness seemed to close in around her. Towering snowscapes leaned inward like huge hunching beasts. "You mean you can save him—but won't—unless I cooperate with you?"

"I mean *we* can save him. And everyone else in the universe for that matter. Including your beautiful daughter."

There it was. The deal laid out clearly. Jeremiel and Sybil in exchange for her. Her voice trembled when she spoke: "And if I refuse?"

"It's your choice. It always has been."

"What happens if I say no?"

"Truly . . . everything you love will die."

She squeezed her eyes closed in futility. "I hate you! I can't bear the thought of being your pawn."

"You'd rather allow billions upon billions to suffer terribly until Epagael gets bored?"

"But you're the Deceiver! All the Old Books—"

"Yes, yes," he said shortly. "We've already discussed Epagael's propaganda and I'll be happy to discuss it further in the future, but right now, my dear Rachel, you must make a small decision. You've met God. Who's more the monster? Him, or me?"

"I don't know!"

"Well," he sighed and put his hands on his hips, pacing with such charismatic grace she couldn't take her eyes from him. "Perhaps we can compromise?"

"How?" *All this is gamesmanship. I've no choice. To save Sybil and Jeremiel, I'll do anything. And he knows it.*

He gazed at her from wounded eyes, as though he'd

62

heard that thought. "For all the eons I've waited, I can wait a little longer for an answer from you. But you *must* get on that ship."

He extended a hand and his face seemed to glow more brightly, splashing the plateau with a wavering pool of gold. His cloak billowed around him like the great blue wings of a monstrous bird.

"Rachel," he said with soft urgency, extending his hand a little further. "It's now or never. Jeremiel just stopped the scorch attack and has dispatched a *samael* for you, but you're in a much different place than the captain expects. If he has to waste a lot of time looking for you, Jeremiel's enemies on board will change their plans and target him. You're going to lose a friend you love and your world will be next. You must return to the ice cave. Let me help you."

"Don't touch me!" She backed away. "I just want you to leave me alone."

"I can't do that, Rachel."

He gazed at her through stony amber eyes and held up his crystalline hand. A whirling blackness appeared in the glacial air, like a gaping hole in time and space. Rachel's heart thundered. She'd seen that maw before. The last time it had burned all her faith, all her dreams, to blackened empty husks. The warm winds of eternity brushed her, blowing her long hair like a midnight breeze of summer.

She turned to run, but the ebony vortex swirled out, hovering over her like a huge black beast. She slipped and cried out as she fell down the slope. The vortex descended, swallowing her up. Rachel screamed, falling, falling. . . .

An instant later, she landed before the ice cave again. She panted and clawed her way toward the cave entry to get out of the fatal wind.

"One last thing," Aktariel called from out of the disappearing maw. "Make sure you're armed when you step off that *samael* into the landing bay of the *Hoyer*."

Then the void spun closed, leaving her alone in the windswept silver wasteland. Rachel got on her knees and lifted her fists to the heavens. *"What's happening to me?"* she shouted. *"What game is this?"*

Only a roaring rush of wind answered.

CHAPTER 6

Avel Harper ran a hand through his six-inch halo of hair. He stood beside Jeremiel in the tiny ward room outside of Engineering. On a series of overhead screens, they studied the distribution and numbers of vessels bringing up Horebian refugees. It had been only four hours since they'd taken over the ship and already massive numbers of people had fled the planet, seeking refuge from the fire storms that ravaged Horeb. Many of the ships appeared barely able to fly. Hastily applied patches marred the hulls and blast marks scarred the wings and sides.

"For God's sake, how can we take care of them all?" Harper whispered. "We've only secured four levels and most of those refugees are starving or hurt. How can—"

"We just have to get organized. Quickly."

Reaching over to the white control console on his right, Jeremiel input a series of commands. The images on the screens changed, showing a dozen landing bays. People disgorged from ships to flood down the gangplanks. Children filled many arms. Others supported wounded. Some carried the dead, faces still contorted in long-forgotten agonies.

"Avel," Baruch said wearily. "None of the refugees are to get into the *Hoyer* until we've secured decks ten through twenty. Keep them locked in the bays."

"Understood. I'll organize security details immediately."

"We also need to set up a hospital and establish a command hierarchy. Rank goes as follows: Me first, you second, Rachel third and . . ." He squeezed the bridge of his nose. "Who else? Who can we depend on?"

"Now that we know Mikael Calas is alive, shouldn't he be included in the—"

"No. He's just a boy. I'll consult with him, yes, but . . . make Yosef Calas fourth in line, got it? He can act as Mikael's guardian."

"What about cabin assignments?"

"Four people per room. Try to accommodate families where possible. There's no telling how long these refugees will be aboard. We want to make them as comfortable as we can."

"I'll input personal data into the computer as soon as we obtain it. That should make assignments considerably faster and easier."

"Thank you." Baruch turned around and leaned heavily against the console, folding his arms over his breast. His blond hair had taken on a dull sheen of sweat and dirt. "Let me just rest a moment and then we need to go down and take an inventory of the wounded. Many are going to need immediate attention."

Harper gazed back up at the monitors, watching hundreds more people flooding out of the ships. Blood drenched nearly every tattered garment. "Yes."

Baruch turned sideways and struck an adjacent monitor. When it flared to life, Harper frowned. Soldiers in purple uniforms battled *against each other!* One man went down beneath a barrage of fire, his upper torso slamming the wall before tumbling across the floor to stare wide-eyed into the monitor. His four assailants ran back down the long white corridor.

Harper straightened up. "Where is that happening?"

Baruch's mouth tightened. "Level six."

"Why? What's—"

"Every battle cruiser has spies aboard. Undoubtedly the resident Clandestine Services officers are trying to take control of the ship from the 'incompetent' officers who lost it."

"By killing their own people?"

"Oh, yes." He smiled tiredly. "It's standard procedure."

"Will the turmoil help or hurt us?"

"Unknown."

Baruch started to straighten up but seemed to lose his balance. He stumbled sideways and grabbed the console to steady himself. Harper reached for his arm, supporting him.

"You all right?"

Jeremiel rubbed hands over his face. "I will be—once I get some rest."

Harper tried not to notice the way his commander's

legs trembled from fatigue. He wanted to tell Jeremiel to go to bed now, that he could handle things—but that would have been a lie. They all needed Baruch awake. Jeremiel hadn't slept for two days and the past several months had already taken their toll on his strength. Baruch had come to Horeb directly from hot fighting in the Akiba system.

Harper released his arm and stood by, waiting for instructions. As of three hours ago, he understood why Gamants all over the galaxy worshiped Baruch as a savior. On some of the more backward worlds, stories had even begun to circulate that he was the promised Mashiah, foretold eons ago in the Old Books—the savior who would free the people from the cruel hands of their tormentors and establish the millennial kingdom in this galaxy. He half believed it himself. He'd seen Jeremiel hurt, worried, desperate, he couldn't ever recall seeing him afraid. No, some inner strength flowed in the man's veins. Why not think of it as the power of God? He'd always been a deep believer and the religious overtones provided a curious sort of comfort.

Fondly, Harper reached out and gripped Jeremiel's shoulder, squeezing it hard. "Well, things may look bad, but, thanks to you, Horebians have an ark to carry them away from this catastrophe."

Jeremiel's shoulder muscles bunched beneath the fabric of his black jumpsuit. He bowed his head a long moment, as though struggling with himself. Then he turned to Harper and the expression on his face made Avel loosen his grip.

"What's wrong?"

"You think this is an ark?" Baruch's deadly quiet voice lashed out. His eyes had taken on a haunted gleam. *"Wrong.* Epagael has just lifted his fist over our heads, my friend. This is the belly of the whale and we'd damn well better find a method of cutting our way out—fast. *Or we're all going to die in here."*

Harper's mouth dropped open. He felt strangely as though the words had kicked the foundations of the universe apart and all the stones of hope had come tumbling down around his ears.

Jeremiel lifted a hand uncertainly. "Sorry, Avel. I shouldn't have said that."

"No, it's all right. I see what you mean."

"Do you? Then I'm doubly sorry. It's not to our benefit to have both of us scared to death.'"

"You? Frightened? I don't believe it. God's armor shields you from fear."

Jeremiel laughed softly, bitterly. "God's armor? Where are your eyes, Avel? *Can't you see?*" He stabbed a finger at the bright light panels overhead.

Harper glanced up. "See what?"

"God sitting up there. Right there! You see Him watching us? Every time we cry out to Him for help, every time we beg for mercy, He demands more of our blood! For millennia we've given it to Him willingly, blaming ourselves because we broke His commandments or misunderstood His *goddamned* teachings! Gamant blood has washed clean every soul in the universe, and still God raises his fist and slashes open our hearts for more." He took a breath. "When Tahn wakes up, you'll see what I mean."

Jeremiel's bearded jaw quivered with emotion. He shoved away from the console. "I wouldn't take God's armor if He gave it to me." He strode for the exit and pounded a hard fist into the patch. The door pulled back, revealing a blood-sprinkled hallway. Baruch stopped, shaking his head. His voice came out lower, softer. "Avel . . . I'm tired."

"I know you are."

Jeremiel nodded gratefully. "Check in with Janowitz. I need to know the numbers of people we'll be dealing with. Then please meet me in landing bay nineteen-four."

"Aye, Jeremiel."

* * *

Cole Tahn tossed and turned, writhing across his sweat-drenched blankets, reaching pleadingly for people who weren't there. The hallucinations hurled themselves at him from the dark void of unconsciousness. He had vague memories of Carey hauling him to his cabin and shooting him up with steroids, but since that moment, time had ceased.

"You're on . . . *Hoyer!*" he screamed at himself. The echoes of his voice rang through his mind, clanging like the bells of Notre Dame.

Distorted, monstrous images flared and died. He fought them, but still they came. . . .

He ran through the narrow streets of Paris, rifle gripped in clammy palms. Millennia before, the entire city had been declared a planetary historic site and preserved in its twenty-first century splendor. Magnificent buildings with arches and delicate scrollwork lined the streets. Marble sculptures still filled the flower gardens. But today the scents of the roses had vanished—replaced by the bittersweet odor of death. To his left, the Seine glinted a rich green in the morning sunlight. In front of him the ruined towers of the cathedral of Notre Dame stood, broken and battered against a tarnished mustard-colored sky. Overhead, a Pegasan battle cruiser hung like a black oblate coin. The roar of cannon fire split the air as violet arcs streaked from the cruiser to lash the earth, kicking dust and debris a hundred feet high.

"Maggie?" he screamed to the blonde woman running headlong in front of him. "No, no! Not that way! Turn left. *Left!*"

She vacillated, confused. Terror had held them both by the throats over the past half hour as the battle intensified. "No, Cole, this way! We have to . . ." Her voice faded as she turned right, leaping a pile of bloody corpses and racing down a dark alley.

He glanced at the cruiser, seeing the arcs sweeping their way. *"Maggie!"*

He ran after her, jumping the bodies and bounding into the alley just in time to see the cruiser's fire slice through the medieval buildings lining the alley. As though in slow motion the ancient walls tumbled inward, cascading down around them like a gray mountain.

"No!" he shouted in agony and—for a brief moment—felt the sleek fabric of his own bed . . . *sheets* . . . but where? He couldn't quite find it in his memory.

Then it was gone.

He woke in the streets of Paris, blinking at yellow skies hazy with airborne dust. The bars of his light cage gleamed. Agonizingly, he rolled to his side. Maggie lay in the next cage, wavy hair spreading like a blanket of sunlit cornsilk over her bloody uniform.

But she must be alive or they wouldn't have caged her!
"Maggie?"

"Cole . . . oh, Cole, forgive me . . . forgive me. . . ." The sound of her muffled sobs made every muscle in his body go tight.

"Maggie, don't. We're alive. They have obligations under the Treaty of Carina. Prisoners of war have to be treated humanely."

He pulled his battered body forward and extended a hand through the bars, snaking it across the dry weeds toward Maggie's cage. "Take my hand. Can you reach me?"

Weakly, she rolled to her stomach and wiggled her arm through the bars. They could just barely touch fingertips. But the warmth of her hand eased his fears.

"It wasn't your fault we got captured, Maggie. Don't blame yourself. Isle St. Louis was cut off. They'd have gotten us sooner or later anyway."

He struggled to get closer to her, pressing his wounded shoulder hard against the bars of the cage. Pain lanced him, but he could just curl his fingertips around hers.

The dream shifted.

Hallucinatory images swirled, spiraling down on him, random, terrifying. Wave after wave of pain tormented him. He screamed . . . and could hear Maggie's screams, high, breathless. Darkness, so much darkness and pain, constant pain. Agony seared his back and legs, as though a thousand tiny saw blades spun through the hot wounded flesh.

Someone asked him a question, but he felt too drained of strength to answer. The attempt brought on nausea. A short time later, lights flashed through his skull. Probes! He recognized the feel, like hot tendrils of wire snaking through his thoughts. His throat had gone too raw to scream. Only a soft groan escaped his lips. Why torture if they had probes? Why? He caught a glimpse of a hideous face: *a gruesomely twisted ruby-eyed demon.* It hovered over him, smiling, teeth bared. Then the pain returned, stunning in its intensity. Someone asked another question. He vomited and vomited. . . .

After days, he learned a trick to evade them. He reached inside himself, found his soul, and put it in the rocky fortress of the walls of Notre Dame, a place so cold and hard the probes couldn't reach him there. *Abandon yourself. Leave your body in the cage and just go. . . .*

And he did. He stayed gone for what seemed an eternity. Finally—it seemed years later—he awoke to stare up at the cathedral. Sunrise. Light streamed through the shattered fragments of the rose window that clung to the stone wall, falling in dappled shades of red and pink over his cage. How long had he been captive? A month? Two? Ten? Somewhere in the interim he'd ceased to be a man. All the social conventions that told him how to be human had blown away like dust in the wind. He was an animal—even less than that—a bloody piece of meat to be carved upon at his torturer's whim.

"Maggie?" he called hoarsely. "Maggie. . . . Are you all right?"

He battled his bruised body to move his head three inches to look at her cage.

. . . And in that single moment, all his dreams, all his hopes died. Her emaciated body had gone rigid. Blonde hair cascaded over her face. She'd stretched her arm out of her cage, trying to reach him with her last strength.

And he hadn't been there.

He gazed blindly at her contorted hand. Rolling over onto his back, he stared at the sky for hours. Days? The sun burned his face and eyes until he barely felt their pain. It seemed as though he lay there in utter stillness endlessly, timelessly.

He heard soft footsteps in the grass—and turned.

The demon had returned.

It crouched outside his cage, smiling in. Tahn pulled himself up, sliding back, away from it. "What are you?" he questioned disbelievingly. "Are you some Pegasan creature?"

The demon's ruby eyes flared like fiery pits in its grotesque face. "Pegasan? No." It laughed a laugh that made Tahn's blood run cold. "I'm Nabrat. Naar sent me to prepare you for Moriah."

"Who's Naar? What's Moriah?"

The demon smiled; it crawled inside the cage and lunged at him. He fought, but the beast wouldn't let him go. They wrestled, trying to tear each other to pieces, screaming, crying. Waves of pain accompanied each battle. But in the background of their cries, he heard the crackle of dry weeds rustling in the cold winds of winter. Rustling and rustling, growing coated with frost, then covered with snow—and still the demon refused to leave.

Sometimes . . . sometimes they just sat on opposite sides of the cage and stared at each other for hours. The

70

hideous creature's ruby-colored eyes glistened more wildly at those moments and it smiled. Then without warning, the demon would lunge at him again and they'd grapple with each other for days and weeks without end. Pain . . . so much pain. . . .

Images swirled again, coming close and speeding away. Colors spun a rainbow of shapes . . . he heard Maggie's voice . . . and he tried to reach for her. . . .

Unaware, his arms flailed and he knocked over the pitcher of water sitting on his bedside table. The splash across his face brought him half-awake. He shook himself out of the nightmare. His head ached so violently, it incapacitated him.

"You're . . . on . . . *Hoyer.*"

Through blurry, half-lidded eyes, he struggled to make out any feature of his cabin. Only one item caught and held his wavering vision. The dim glow of the light panels glimmered from the transparent case mounted on the wall at the foot of his bed. He saw woolly patches of medals and ribbons—decorations for valor.

Bile rose into his throat as memories of the landing bay and Baruch swelled. Weakly, Cole Tahn lifted an arm and draped it over his eyes—blocking the vision of those colorful bits of metal and cloth. By now his crew would be going mad, wondering if he'd ever be all right, blaming him for losing the ship. Anxiety twisted in his stomach. *I have to do something. They need me.* He tried to push up on his elbows, but he fell back to the sheets, images whirling again, Maggie's tormented screams echoing in his ears. . . .

CHAPTER 7

The 4th of Tishri, 5414. Capital city of Tikkun, Derow.

The soft pearlescent gleam of dawn played over the streets of rough-cut stone, glimmering like frost from the marble window sills of apartment buildings. A chill barley-scented wind wound through the city.

Jasper Jacoby stopped at an intersection, watching four children race across the road in front of autos to catch a purple bus for school. They shoved one another playfully, crowding onto the steps. As the bus eased back into traffic, it belched a dark, foul-smelling puff of smoke into the air around Jasper.

"Damned buses. I hate them." He waved his hand in front of his face, coughing expressively. A few people looked up from their newspapers to stare. The streets bustled this Thursday morning, business people striding quickly to and fro on the sidewalks. Jasper straightened the knotted ends of the blue babushka he wore beneath his gray derby and looked both ways before dodging into the crosswalk. It was an old woman's trick, the babushka, to cut the wind, but he'd turned three hundred last month and felt no compunction to prove his masculinity when he might catch a dreadful cold as a result. Besides, the silver star dangling from the pocket of his red shirt proved his manliness to anyone with a shred of sense. He'd fought in the last Gamant Revolt, right alongside the legendary Zadok Calas.

Jasper crossed the street and turned down an alley, plodding steadily. He passed in and out of the shadows of buildings. He had to get to the square outside the Fine Arts building before all the best seats were gone. Every Thursday, the senior centers emptied out, people flooding into the square to resolve the galaxy's greatest problems. Jasper had no intention of missing today's discussions, not after the frightening events of yesterday.

As he rounded the final turn, he shielded his eyes from the glare of the slanting morning sunlight and surveyed the benches. Over a dozen people had already seated themselves. On the far side, he spied Chaim Losacko and nodded to himself. That's the bench he wanted today. Chaim had an illegal dattran receiver in his basement. He'd know what was going on.

When Losacko saw Jasper striding purposefully toward him, he lifted a hand in greeting. Chaim looked more frail than the last time Jasper had seen him a month ago. A withered stalk of a man, wisps of gray hair clung to his bald head, fluttering in the cool breeze. Short and stooped, Losacko had eyes the color of dead grass. A large fleshy nose hooked over his brown lips. He'd dressed stylishly today, wearing a lavender leisure suit and purple ascot.

"Chaim, how the hell are you?" Jasper asked as he gingerly lowered himself to the bench. Mist from the fountain in front of the Arts building chilled his face as the wind changed.

"I'm doing great. I took the long way around to avoid Mildred's sharp tongue."

Jasper looked over his shoulder surreptitiously. "Is she here? I saw her downtown earlier and she tried to fasten onto me, but I took fifteen back ways and lost her."

"Sure, she's here." Chaim pointed to the other side of the square where a nest of women chattered. "First thing she did was ask me if I'd seen you. I guess she's pretty taken by your charms."

"What a curse."

Chaim snorted a laugh and for a time they just watched the parade of people rushing by on the street. In the distance, they could see fields of ripe golden grain rippling beneath the caressing fingers of wind. Jasper's grandson, Pavel, worked as a botanist in the government labs, developing better plant strains. He wondered idly if Pavel had anything to do with this year's wonderful barley crop. Not that it mattered, that's what he'd tell his friends anyway.

Chaim shifted, groaning softly, to drape an arm over the back of the bench. "How's your son, Toca?"

"He's worried about me. He wants me to come live with him."

"You're not going to, are you? He's going to get himself in trouble someday soon. Mildred told me he's been holding illegal religious rituals in his basement."

"Of course!" Jasper growled. "He's been a Rev on Tikkun for sixty years. What do you think, eh? That he's going to stop now just because the damned Magistrates closed all the temples and made our rituals against the law? Bah! He'll never get caught. He's too smart."

Jasper eyed Chaim hostilely.

"Don't look at me that way," Losacko warned. "I know what I'm talking about. You should come over tonight and listen to my dattran machine."

"Yeah? What's it saying?"

Nervously, Chaim looked over his shoulders and wet his withered lips, leaning closer to whisper, "The Magistrates scorched Kayan."

"What?"

"Sure, I got that news straight from a battle cruiser called the *Jataka*. It was only a level two attack, but—"

"Level two? They wiped all the known population centers? What for?"

Chaim shrugged and cautiously looked around again. "I caught a bunch of different snatches on the seventh dimension band. It looks like *our people* revolted because they thought the Magistrates killed old Zadok."

Jasper frowned. Most citizens whispered when they said "our people," or "True Gamant." Though Tikkun acknowledged itself as a Gamant world, so many government military and educational offices existed that the numbers of native population had slipped below that of the Magisterial personnel. They had to be careful what they said in public. Already acts of rebellion stirred across the planet, Baruch's secret Underground forces attacking military targets.

"Our people," Jasper enunciated proudly. He threw out his bony chest as Chaim cringed, "were probably just trying to protect themselves. Goddamned Magistrates!"

Losacko blinked nervously, then leaned back and pulled open the jacket of his leisure suit to scratch his stomach. As the sun rose higher, the day warmed pleasantly and the scent of ripe barley grew stronger. Jasper untied his babushka and took it off, tucking it into his pocket before putting his derby back on.

"You better watch out, Jasper. Nobody's safe anymore. Just look what happened to Wexler's store—and Cavage's factory."

"I'm too old to worry about being 'corrected.' I haven't got any brain left anyway." But unease crept up around his heart. The square had filled; people shouted and waved arms as they talked. Laughter filtered through the crowd. Life went on as usual, though two Gamant businesses had been burned to the ground yesterday. Eyewitnesses claimed Magisterial officers stood by and watched the blazes until the flames consumed every shred of the properties. And strange holograms had begun to appear throughout the city, caricatures of elderly Gamants, showing long noses and slit eyes.

"I think maybe the Magistrates are punishing us for what the Gamants on Kayan did. They . . ."

Losacko stopped abruptly as a young dark-haired man strode casually over to stand nearby. Dressed in a formfitting synthetic suit, he opened a book and pretended to read.

"Assimilant," Chaim whispered.

Jasper nodded. Assimilants were those who'd willingly abandoned their Gamant heritage for rewards from the government. They were dangerous.

"Serpents we've nursed at our bosoms," Jasper hissed.

"Where's your heart? You should feel sorry for them."

"What for?"

"Don't you see? They aren't worthy of their heritage. Truth is like a great stone. These poor-spirited creatures are too small and frail to bear up under the burden of it. They can't carry the Covenant. You and I have to do it for them."

"Bah!" Jasper spat quietly. "Anybody who can't bear the Covenant by himself doesn't deserve its blessings!"

"I'm glad our forefathers didn't think like you. If they'd abandoned the people every time they strayed, none of us would be here now. Where's your kindness?"

"Don't preach at me, you old fanatic." Jasper shook a fist.

"Calm down, Jacoby. Didn't your doctor tell you not to get excited? How's your heart? Does it hurt? Maybe you should take one of those baby-shit green pills he dishes out to you."

Jasper opened his mouth to say something viperous, but stopped. The young Assimilant scowled openly at them. In response, Jasper reached down to stroke the cool silver medal on his chest. He scowled back.

Losacko heaved a disgruntled sigh and looked sideways at both of them, then he grunted and got to his feet. "Well, Jacoby, it's been nice seeing you again. Come around next week. We'll talk some more."

He gave Jasper a worried look as he hobbled away toward the busy street below. A traffic jam crowded the intersection. People honked horns in irritation. Jasper watched Chaim go, then studied the two commuter buses stuck in the crosswalk. On the side of one of them a green and red hologram glared. An elderly Gamant woman with straggly hair and beady eyes held up the sacred triangle of the faith, sucking it like a baby's bottle.

Jasper glowered at the ugly Assimilant.

* * *

Mikael woke panting from a terrible dream. In it, people ran, screaming, trying to get away from something—but he didn't know what. He'd hidden between two big spikes of rock that people in the dream had called the Horns of the Calf. He'd been a lot older in the dream, maybe twenty or so and a pretty woman had been with him. She'd had long curly brown hair and brown eyes. Ships swooped through the yellow skies around them, firing down to kill people.

Mikael lifted a heavy hand to brush black hair out of his eyes. Tiny blue and white lights winked throughout the room. He blinked lazily at them. It was funny. He could almost hear them talking to him, but their voices were too high and soft to make out the words.

"What?" he asked sleepily. "What did you say? I can't hear you. Is it about the dream?"

The flashes grew brighter, bursting like fireworks—then they died. The room dimmed again. It reminded him of the silver sheet they put over dead people before they buried them. He looked at the shadows for a while, seeing how they pooled in the corners.

He felt so tired. Maybe that nasty drug they'd given him wasn't working? He groggily rolled over to his side and the *Mea Shearim* that the angel Metatron had given him fell out of his brown robe to lie like a blue marble on the pillow. His people called it a sacred gate to God. His grandfather had worn this one for hundreds and hundreds of years. In his mind, Mikael could see his grandfather's wrinkled face smiling at him. His heart ached with longing. He had vague memories of hearing his grandfather talk to him just after Captain Tahn and that mean doctor had left. What had his grandfather said? Something about a man named Jeremiel Baruch coming aboard. He was supposed to tell Mister Baruch something . . . but he couldn't remember exactly what.

He snaked a finger up to touch first the golden chain of his *Mea*, then the ball itself. In a brilliant flash of light, a blue gleam like fire spread over his walls.

"Mikael," his grandfather said in a soothing voice. *"You go to sleep now. Don't worry about the dreams."*

"Can you make them go away, Grandpa?"

"Yes, for a while—then we have to talk more about Mister Baruch and the coming of the Antimashiah. But for now, close your eyes, grandson. That's it. Good. Sleep . . . sleep . . ."

Mikael heaved a deep sigh and rolled over onto his back again. He felt floaty, like he wasn't really in his cabin. He started dreaming again, and found himself lying on the floor of his bedchamber on Kayan, wrestling with his grandfather, laughing. In the golden light of the oil lamps, he could see his mother's round face where she sat on his bed. She gazed at him with love in her eyes and Mikael thought his heart would burst from the happiness. . . .

"Grandpa?" he asked so softly he could barely hear himself. "Can I stay home for a long time? I'm pretty lonely here on this big ship."

"As long as you need to, Mikael. I'll stand guard to keep the other dreams away."

"Thanks . . . Grandpa."

He fell into a deep, deep sleep.

CHAPTER 8

Rachel stood anxiously at the portal and watched the *Hoyer* loom closer. She'd showered and dressed in a tan jumpsuit she'd found on board. Damp black hair draped in waves to her waist, accenting the unnatural paleness of her olive skin. She could see dozens of ships, shimmering like white and black beetles against the background of sunlight that washed space. Most waited in line behind her ship, but some edged in from the side trying to squeeze ahead.

It amazed and frightened her. She'd lived her entire life on a backward planet at the edge of the galaxy. As a result, she had only a bare understanding of technology. What she could see, she could understand almost immediately. Rifles came second nature to her, regardless of fancy gadgetry or sophistication, but invisible things still baffled her: shields, EM restraints, "Uncertainty Principle" wizardry such as the engines that powered these ships.

She edged closer to the portal, studying the planet whirling below. Only the polar caps still lay untouched by the runaway fires and devastation. A roiling band of maroon clouds coiled around the central regions like a great deadly serpent.

"So that's what a scorch attack does," she whispered. She'd heard about such attacks on other Gamant planets, but had never grasped the awesome magnitude. The drought on Horeb had been so bad that the dry vegetation covering the deserts must have ignited instantly.

She forced herself to look away, turning to the dimly lit room. Her heart ached for a home that no longer existed, and for her daughter. It was such a painful longing, she felt if she stayed another moment on this starkly lit *samael* her soul would waste away to nothingness. She needed the warmth of candlelight and the calming salve of her daughter Sybil's love to ease her inner anguish.

For hours, her tired mind had gone round and round the same deeply graven circle of confusing thoughts. Aktariel . . .

"No," she whispered harshly to herself. "Not now. Wait until you can stand it."

She couldn't allow herself to think about Aktariel or Adom just now or she'd fall into a million . . .

A soft creak sounded behind her and she whirled breathlessly, expecting Aktariel to materialize out of nothing. Only a silent white room met her searching gaze. So often, now, she imagined hearing the soft rustle of a long velvet cloak. Her heart hammered at such moments. She found herself always waiting for him, as though she stood in an enormous palace with thousands of rooms and he toiled just on the other side of the wall. At every small noise she strained to hear the sound of his too-silent footfalls coming for her.

She gripped the fabric at her throat, trying to calm her breathing.

"Miss Eloel?"

The tall copilot, Emil Bakon, peered around the open door. He had a swarthy face and eyes as black as coal. Dressed in the gray uniform of one of Adom's palace guards, he cut a debonair figure that sent a violent ache through her. Was he still loyal to the Mashiah? Did he know she'd murdered Adom?

"Yes?"

"We're going in soon. Jeremiel sent word that he'll meet you in the landing bay. Could you strap in, please? Just hit the blue patch on the arm of the chair."

"Yes, of course."

He nodded and disappeared into the command cabin. Rachel went to a seat. Hitting the button, she felt the restraints pull tight around her like a curious tingling net.

She closed her eyes against the foreign feelings it stirred.

* * *

The cramped admin room outside of Engineering smelled of sweat and stale coffee. Yosef Calas smoothed a hand over his bald head and gazed at the guard who lounged over a long white console reading a technical manual, then he looked around the half-moon shaped cabin. Computer screens covered the walls of the small, efficiently organized room. They displayed information in a variety of colors. Through the rectangular portal, Yosef could see dozens of ships lining up to debark into the *Hoyer*. The bays were already packed. Where in God's name would they put them? In the background, stars glistened like melancholy diamonds in an onyx sea.

Yosef pursed his withered lips worriedly. Short, bald, and over three hundred years of age, he felt worn and hollow. He pushed back a short distance from the table and gazed at the tired little girl in front of him.

"It's your move, Sybil."

The eight-year-old heaved a breath and frowned at the tri-level checkerboard. A beautiful olive-skinned child, she had a perfect oval face with a button nose and huge brown eyes. Mahogany curls clung to her forehead and dropped to her shoulders. She fidgeted nervously. Yosef knew why. She missed her mother so terribly she could barely stand it. That's why he'd asked her to play with him, to take her mind off Rachel's continued absence.

"I don't know where to move, Yosef." She wiped sweaty palms on her blue robe.

"You're just tired, Sybil. Would you rather take a nap?"

"No. I—I have bad dreams when I close my eyes."

"Do you want to talk about them?"

She shrugged. He'd tried to get her to discuss her dreams for hours, hoping he could defuse their insidious terror, but she refused. Yosef cocked his head sympathetically, studying the way her young mouth quivered. Were her dreams about the death of her father? Sybil had told him in great detail about that horrifying day in the temple when the Mashiah's guards burst through the doors and opened fire, strafing the temple with beams of violet, killing men, women, and children indiscriminately. She and her mother had escaped only to be captured by Ornias and confined with a thousand other people in a tiny square where they stood for three days without food or water. On the third day, the guards opened fire, burying Rachel and Sybil beneath a mountain of bloody dead. Undoubtedly, the gruesome ordeal had saved their lives—but damned them to horrifying memories. *The stuff of terrifying nightmares.*

Sybil moved to three different squares before she ambivalently settled on a new one. "There, Yosef. I guess I'm done."

He reached across the table and patted her arm gently. "We don't have to play. Would you like to do something else?"

"No, I just . . ."

Ari Funk lunged awkwardly into the room waving a pulse pistol. A tall willowy old man in a soiled gray robe, he had a shriveled triangular face tucked inside a gray mop of hair. A broad smile creased his lips.

"Watch this!" he called, shoving the gun in his holster and doing a remarkable fast draw. Yosef jumped backward. The guard, noticing the barrel pointed at his left eye, let out a shrill gasp and dove for the floor. His elbows and knees banged against the wall.

"What'd you think of that?" Ari asked conversationally and grinned like a demented imp.

Yosef scowled and thrust a hand toward the far wall. "You idiot. Put that thing away. Look what you made the guard do!"

Ari blinked at the young man sprawled like a dead spider in the corner. "You were worried, eh?" Pride lit his old face. "Wait till you see what else I learned in that holo library of yours. I've been battling those 3-D ghosts for hours."

With all the dignity he could manage, the guard pulled himself to his feet and straightened his black uniform before throwing Ari a hard look and going back to his technical manual. Under his breath, he murmured, "Crazy old bozon."

"He's not crazy," Yosef defended indignantly. "He's senile. There's a *big* difference."

"Don't help me, Yosef," Ari urged.

Heedlessly, Yosef waved a hand at the guard. "Just wait until you're three hundred and seventeen. You'll find things don't work the way they used to either."

Ari's gray eyes jerked wide. "Good God!" He slapped his pistol on the table with a painful clang. "You're not going to bring up Agnes again, are you?"

Yosef blinked owlishly. "Don't be stupid. I wouldn't mention your problems in front of strangers."

"My problems! Don't forget I know about the time you took Agnes out on that date to watch the chickadees mate and got het up over all the fluttering."

"*Will you sit down?* I meant that what's between your *ears* doesn't work right!"

Ari's eyes narrowed suspiciously, but he took the chair beside Sybil. "You get on my nerves, Yosef, did you know that?"

"You've only got one nerve left. A person can't help but get on it."

Laughter bubbled up from Sybil's stomach. "You two are pretty funny." She had a soft luminous look in her dark eyes, betraying the desperately tired little girl beneath.

"It's good to see somebody around here has a sense of humor." Ari leaned across the table to kiss her forehead affectionately. From the very instant they'd met, they'd grown to be fast friends—though why Yosef couldn't imagine. Ari was the last person he'd suspect of paternal inclinations.

"How come you aren't sleeping?" Ari pointed a crooked finger reprovingly. "When I left, you said you were going to take a nap."

Sybil's smile faded and she stared down at her restlessly twisting hands. "I can't sleep, Ari. The Mashiah's face keeps coming."

"He can't hurt you anymore, Sybil. He's dead."

She gazed up ominously from beneath jet black lashes.

"Only in real life."

"But that's the only place that counts, sweetheart." He opened his skinny arms. "Come here. Tell me about these dreams you're having of another man."

Sybil slid down from her chair, running to climb into Ari's lap. She nestled against him, rubbing her cheek over the soft gray silk of his robe. "They're bad ones. Not *funny* ones, but bad ones."

Yosef frowned, wondering how "funny" dreams differed from other kinds. Ari spoke softly in her ear, confidentially, and Yosef heard Sybil sniffle and whisper in response. Gradually, their two low voices intertwined, barely audible, and he could tell the little girl's fears had ebbed. Her tone grew calmer, brighter. Yosef shook his head, amazed that gruff, sharp-edged Ari could speak so kindly to anyone.

"Uh-huh," Ari whispered. "So he came and floated over your bed?"

Sybil nodded, twining fingers tightly in the fabric over Ari's chest. "Yes."

"Did he look dead?"

"Only a little. He was kind of pale."

"He was always pale," Ari responded incredulously, squinting down at her.

"Then he didn't look dead at all, okay?"

"Did he say anything?"

"I don't remember. I think he just looked at me."

He stroked her hair warmly. "I get the picture. What if I hold you while you sleep? You won't be scared then, will you?"

"I might." She pleated the robe over his shoulder between nervous fingers.

"I'll keep watch. And I know how to handle girl-getting ghosts." He pulled his pistol and held it up impressively.

Sybil nuzzled her forehead against his bony shoulder. "Okay, Ari. I'll try." But she lifted her head again. "Ari? Have you heard anything about my mom? Is she okay?"

"I talked to Jeremiel an hour ago. He said your mom would be coming aboard any time now."

Sybil looked up through wide, wounded eyes. Her mouth puckered, tears glistening on her lashes. She patted Ari's withered throat. "You're sure? You're not lying to me?"

"I wouldn't lie to you about something like that. Other

82

things, maybe, but not your mother. She's fine. Now try to get some rest, sweetheart. Once Rachel arrives, you'll probably be up for a long time."

"You'll wake me as soon as she gets here?"

"Sure, I will."

She closed her eyes and sank deeper against his chest. He gently pressed his lips to her cheek, and rocked her slowly. It seemed only minutes until slumber loosened her grip and her arms slid back to rest at her sides. When Ari looked up, a gentle expression lit his ancient face.

Yosef whispered, "You two get along too well to have been strangers only hours ago. Are you sure you haven't been holding out on me?"

"I've always had a way with women. You're just jealous."

"For once in your scurrilous life, you're right." Taking the chair closest to Ari, he braced an elbow on the table and leaned his temple against his fist. Weariness made his arm tremble. Ari noticed and frowned.

"Why don't you try to sleep, too, Yosef. We don't have anything else to do. Do we? Have you gotten any news from Jeremiel since I last talked to him?"

"A little. He said they'd managed to secure most of the ship. He's trying to empty shuttles as quickly as he can so they can go pick up more people from Horeb."

"I can understand that. Have you looked at the planet lately?"

Yosef heaved a bitter sigh and nodded. Anxiety burned in his chest. Roiling oceans of smoke billowed into the atmosphere from the fires that raced over Horeb. Across the night half of the planet, flames spread in irregular patchwork patterns, like splatters of brilliant orange paint cast against an indigo canvas.

"Yes," Yosef said softly. "If we don't get the shuttles emptied more quickly, we'll lose a lot more people down there."

Sybil groaned softly and Ari pulled her closer, rocking her again as he murmured soft words in her ear.

Yosef lowered his gaze to the checkerboard and shook his head, whispering, "God almighty, what's happening, Ari? We're in the midst of the worst mess we've ever been in in our lives."

"There's not much we can do about it. Quit worrying. At our age it's suicidal."

"Suicide might be healthier than waiting for the Magistrates to catch us." He massaged his brow. Was it really only last night that they were stuck in the middle of a civil war? Memories of lavender lightning arcing across midnight clouds burst to life on his mental screen. Ragged screams of dying soldiers and fleeing people tormented his ears. "I'm so tired."

"Of course you're tired. A few months ago you were sitting around your yard sipping beer and enjoying the sun on your face. Now you're in a death duel."

"How soon do you think they'll find out Jeremiel captured the *Hoyer*?"

"Too soon."

Yosef felt like he'd been poleaxed. "I hope to God Jeremiel can contact his fleet before the Magistrates get here to crisp us."

"Go take a nap, Yosef. Worrying yourself sick won't change what's going to happen. It's in Jeremiel's hands. He'll figure something out."

Ari's eyes shone bright with concern. Yosef got to his feet and unsteadily went to place a warm hand on his best friend's shoulder. "All right. Wake me in an hour if I'm not already up, hmm?"

"Sure. You sleep. I'll keep an eye on this guard to make sure he doesn't let us get overrun by any purple-coated balloon brains."

The young man gave Ari a disgruntled look but said nothing. Yosef forced his tired body toward the long padded bench lining the far wall. He curled up on his side and rested his head on his arm. Sick to death of the idleness of waiting, he felt anxious beyond exhaustion. The last thing he saw before he closed his eyes was Ari propping a knee against the table to help support Sybil's weight, and then staring contemplatively at the white ceiling.

CHAPTER 9

Jeremiel walked through landing bay nineteen-four with slow deliberation. In eight hours, he'd barely managed to set up a fundamental crew structure. He'd assigned people with basic technical skills to critical consoles in Engineering, Security, Navigation, and Communication. Cleanup crews worked tirelessly as well, going into corridors and cabins after the security teams had thoroughly searched each area. Harper followed on Baruch's heels to keep track of any and all people with medical skills.

Both Jeremiel's black jumpsuit and Harper's purple uniform hung in tatters, revealing bruised and battered arms and legs. The huge room throbbed with a sourceless pounding of sobs and angry shouts. Refugees moved about like mindless ghosts, wearing fragments of clothing, yelling to each other to make themselves heard over the raucous jostling of the crowd. Abandoned children sat crying and reaching pleadingly for anyone who passed, calling the names of family members who would never answer again. Hard crackers and empty bottles lay strewn around the youngest infants like the first shovel of gravel into a grave. Scents of urine and blood rose suffocatingly.

"My God," Harper murmured darkly. "Almost two thousand have already come aboard. How are we going to feed them all?"

"How many more do we suspect are coming?"

"Maybe three thousand. Tahn struck Seir first and fanned out into the desert, killing most of the surrounding nomadic villages before you stopped the attack. A few isolated villages and army units fighting in distant regions are alive—so far."

A sinking feeling invaded Jeremiel's stomach. He felt as though he balanced on a knife edge, waiting for someone to tell him which way to fall—which side led to heaven and which to hell. "Fire storms move fast. Keep emptying the shuttles as quickly as you can, then return them for more survivors."

"I will."

"Any word from Rudy Kopal yet?" Kopal ranked second in the command of the Underground forces. He needed Rudy. A tight loneliness tormented him. His friend's last disgruntled warning about Horeb rang in his ears: "Jeremiel, for God's sake, this is suicide and you know it." *Might still be, old friend, if I can't keep the takeover of the* Hoyer *secret from the Magistrates long enough to collect all Horebian survivors and space for God only knows where.*

"No," Harper responded. "I've been trying to contact your fleet for the past several hours, but they must not be around Pitbon like you thought. Do you want me to switch to wide beam?"

"Negative. We can't take the chance that the Magistrates might pick up the tran. Keep focusing on Gamant planets in Sector Seven. If that doesn't work, switch to Sector Four. Maybe they're tangled in some battle in the Lysomian system. Any word from the Underground bases on Tikkun?"

"Negative."

He ran a hand through his damp blond hair. What the hell was going on? Why wasn't Tikkun answering? Had everybody on his side vanished into the pit? Or was it just that Harper and the green Gamant crew he'd assigned to communications didn't grasp the complexities of the system yet? A few of the soldiers from Horeb had a fundamental understanding of the cruiser's systems and could handle basic functions—like security, mess halls, crude navigation and communications—but none of them had a true grasp of the intricacies of Magisterial technology. He'd have to tend to the communications problem himself, as soon as he could. *When will that be? When the* hell *will that be?*

Those with the worst injuries had been placed around the walls of the bay. Moans penetrated the melee. Harper followed a winding path which led by them and Jeremiel looked on the wounds with a horrified feeling of despair. Many had limbs missing, others had heads or chests bandaged with filthy, blood-soaked rags. Most of these people were dying, dying swiftly, their strength too drained by the civil war and flight from the scorch attack to battle infection and loss of blood.

They broke from the press and Jeremiel caught sight of a scarecrow child. Blood clotted in greasy mounds over the boy's chest. Five or six at most, the gaunt victim stared up at him with eyes that held a resolute courage. The boy watched him intently, recognition on his sunken face.

Jeremiel forced a confident smile. Stepping around two sleeping people, he went to the boy's side, and knelt down. The frail child beamed. Jeremiel gently stroked his bruised cheek and felt the searing heat rolling off the boy's flesh. High fever. "Hello. What's your name?"

"Andy," the child said weakly and fell into a coughing fit. Jeremiel watched and something in his soul cried out. Blood spilled from the boy's mouth to form a glistening crimson pool on the floor. Wounded lung. They had only two doctors on board and both were engaged in surgery in a temporary hospital outside of Engineering.

"You hang on, Andy. A doctor will be here in no time. He'll make you feel better."

"You're . . . Jeremiel Baruch . . . aren't you?"

"Yes, but you shouldn't talk. It's not good—"

"I know stories about you. My . . . my mom . . . tells me them at night." The boy smiled. His breathing grew more labored. The rattling sound seemed to vibrate in Jeremiel's own lungs. He gripped the boy's sticklike arm and squeezed tightly.

"You need to stay still and quiet, Andy. All right? Let me—"

"'Member? 'Member . . . that fight where you had fifteen bad ships . . . shooting at you . . . and you only had two . . . but you blew up ten of theirs before you . . . got away. Where did that happen? Salonica? I—I'm too tired to remember."

Andy beamed his admiration and love. Those soft misty eyes made Jeremiel's heart pound. He smiled back, patting the boy's hand tenderly.

"You remember just fine. It was Salonica."

"You know what? Sometimes? I used to play with my cousin Tarin . . . in my backyard and . . . and I'd pretend I was you." Andy feebly reached out to touch Jeremiel's torn black sleeve. He caressed it reverently between dirty, blood-caked fingers.

"Well, I hope you also pretended that the Underground stole a lot more ships and weapons from the Magistrates. We need them."

"I did. Then I beat up Tarin with them."

Jeremiel smiled. "I hope Tarin got to play Cole Tahn occasionally so he could beat you up, too."

Andy blinked wearily, not seeming to hear.

Jeremiel brushed the boy's hair from his burning forehead. "The doctor won't be long, Andy. I promise."

"It's okay," Andy whispered. "I'm brave . . . just like you." To prove it, he clamped his jaw hard and lifted his chin defiantly, daring death to take him.

"I can see that," Jeremiel praised softly. "Some day, when you grow up, I'm going to make you a captain in my fleet."

Andy's eyes glowed like brilliant suns as he smiled.

From the corner of his vision, Jeremiel caught sight of a young woman with long brown hair rushing across the room, a precious cup of water in her hands. He watched her hurriedly step over people to get to Andy, her shredded blue robe fluttering behind her. She sat on the floor beside Jeremiel, giving him a curious look as she lifted Andy's head and tipped the cup to his lips. Water spilled down the sides of his emaciated face. "You have to drink something, son. It's been hours since you've had water."

And he's lost so much blood. "You're his mother?"

"Yes. Mara Kunio. Who are you?"

"Jeremiel Baruch."

She blinked in surprise. "Oh, of course. Forgive me. We've all been told what you look like, but few of us know for certain." She gazed at him through worshipful eyes and he felt half-ill. Did she have any idea how slim their chances of survival were if he couldn't contact his fleet soon? Behind him, he heard Harper's belt com beep, then a low interchange of words.

Mara said, "I'm one of Horeb's Old Believers, Commander. For all of us, I thank you. Because of you, we can start a new life on a different world without worrying that Ornias' marines will come into our homes in the middle of the night and kill everyone in their sleep." She turned back to her son and caressed his fevered cheek. "Try to drink a little more, Andy. It will make you feel better."

The boy sipped, smiling up at Jeremiel, dreaming. Then suddenly, Andy shivered. The tremors came feebly at first, increasing until his body convulsed in terrible waves.

"Oh, God, what's happening?" Mara screamed.

Jeremiel grabbed for a wooden toy soldier on the floor, trying frantically to slip it into Andy's mouth, between his teeth. But the boy's body went limp. His sweat-drenched head lolled back, eyes wide.

"Andy?" Mara shook her son gently. "Andy!" She shook him harder, sobs rising to choke her. *"Andy!"* Oh, my God. No!"

Jeremiel carefully examined the boy's slack face and wide dead eyes and lamely murmured, "I'm sorry." He heard Harper suck in a difficult breath.

"Oh, not my son," Mara sobbed. "Not my only baby!"

Jeremiel got blindly to his feet and strode for the far exit, hurrying, hurrying, because he couldn't bear it any longer. Behind him, he heard Avel whisper pleadingly, "Where is God, Jeremiel? How can he allow such terrible suffering? Where is God? *Where is He?"*

Jeremiel wanted to stop, to shout, to slam his fists into the closest wall. Instead, he took a breath of the death-tainted air and answered, "You just saw Him, Avel—in the eyes of that little boy. *Dead."*

Harper's heavy steps pounded a dull cadence against the dirty white tiles. After a minute of winding through the crowd, he came up beside Jeremiel. "That was Janowitz on my belt com. This is going to get worse. They found a new pocket of survivors in the Kemah Desert. They'd been caught in the midst of the fire storms. Most of them are hanging on by a thread, suffering third-degree burns."

A weary fury seared Jeremiel's veins. The time would come—*too soon*—when he'd have to order his search parties to abandon the severely wounded because they'd die just as quickly here as on the flaming surface of Horeb. "Notify Doctor Severns. Keep the shuttles moving."

As they neared the exit, a different group of people stood knotted by the door. They'd deliberately separated themselves from the other refugees. Dressed in fine, bright silks of lilac and saffron, many of the women still wore jeweled hair nets. They glimmered obscenely in the landing bay's white light. They must have been remnants of the Mashiah's elite worshipers. The ones who'd funded Ornias' death squads against the Old Believers? They'd probably bought their way into the first shuttles to escape the devastation. Jeremiel noticed that one woman even wore a pair of white lace gloves—*clean.*

The flagrant foulness of the spectacle made him sick to his stomach. He forcefully shouldered through the crowd.

"You!" a tall man wearing a long green satin cape called. He waved a hand as though addressing one of his servants. "You're Baruch, aren't you? When are we getting out of here? We've been here for four hours!"

"We have to secure the ship first. We'll let you inside as soon as we—"

"We're dying out here!" the plump woman with the gloves responded. Her red hair blazed beneath her ruby-strewn net. "Let us in now! Surely part of the ship must have been . . ."

Jeremiel gave her a look so hard the words died in her mouth. She glanced fearfully to her companions for support. He stood a moment, unable to take his eyes from her golden gown and priceless Orillian diamond necklace; it sparkled like a strand of dew in the lavender rays of dawn. *I could buy a hundred new rifles with it.*

"Avel," he said, "belay that order about cabin assignments. I want all the Old Believers separated from the New. Put all of Tartarus' followers on their own floor. After cabins have been assigned, I want each sealed so they can't get out under any circumstances. Arrange mess crews to deliver food."

"Trying to avert problems before they happen?"

"I'm taking no chances these people have brought the civil war on board with them. We've got enough to worry about without fighting our own people."

Like the Hoyer's *crew is doing.* The battles on the upper levels had grown worse. He'd been keeping tabs, watching the intensification with growing alarm. The only positive effect was that with the Magisterial people at each other's throats, they'd ignored him and his refugees.

"Harper, when am I scheduled to meet Rachel's shuttle? I've lost track of time. When is she coming aboard?"

"I thought she'd already be here, but several ships with wounded pushed in ahead of hers. We have dozens more lined up awaiting entry. Shall I order them to stand to and usher her in first?"

He exhaled hard. "No. Get the rush of injured aboard. Just let me know when I should go meet her."

He forced his legs to take him around the brooding group and out into the stark white halls of the *Hoyer*.

* * *

"Go, Joe! Move!" Carey Halloway ordered, firing wildly as she raced down the second level corridor. Sergeant Joe Mie pounded after her.

A shot flashed off the wall and Carey dove, rolling to come up at the intersection of corridors. She scrambled around the corner, lungs burning, legs aching.

More gunfire split the corridor and Carey heard a jagged cry. She held her breath, fingering the sweaty trigger of her pistol. The lights of the corridor seemed unusually bright and harsh. She squinted against their brilliance.

Hatred ravaged her. How many spies had the Magistrates worked into the command heirarchy of the *Hoyer*? Fifty? A hundred? At least fifteen had survived and gathered together a formidable fighting force from the crew members who'd managed to suit up and find shelter before the decompression could catch them.

"They've split the crew in half," she muttered.

Baruch was meticulously searching the duct system and sealing each secured level—which forced more scum her way. The Clandestine Services forces had taken refuge on this level. She'd come down to try and talk to them, to tell them they had to band together to fight Baruch or they were all lost. But they'd killed her messengers and assaulted her temporary base of operations. They'd just assumed that every surviving officer loyal to Cole Tahn was either traitorous or incompetent. *It's probably part of their goddamned instructional code.* They wanted control of the ship. Nothing less.

"Well, by God," she whispered to herself. "They'll take it over my dead body."

Her gun felt clammy in her palm. She caressed the cool petrolon. She'd gone in to see Cole only an hour ago, but he still writhed in the grips of his concussion—shouting garbled sentences, tossing and turning on his sweat-drenched sheets. She prayed that the amount of jeno-steroids she'd given him would at least reduce the swelling of his brain and ease his pain. She couldn't do anything else.

When the hell would someone finally get around to trying to tran them? Why hadn't Slothen already tried? Surely Palaia realized they hadn't checked in to confirm their receipt of Baruch? If somebody, *anybody*, would just try to tran them they'd find out *Hoyer* didn't respond—maybe help would come.

Carey froze as a din of babbling broke out down the hall. Someone shouted a command and the corridor went quiet. Carey strained to hear any sound, any word that would tell her it was safe to get up and try to make it back to the bridge.

Joe, where are you?

But deep inside, she knew. She waited several more minutes, wiping perspiration from her brow. Finally, she eased forward and peered around the corner.

The "enemy" had gone.

Only Joe's bloody body was sprawled against the wall. One of his arms had been severed at the shoulder, but the heat of the low-intensity shot had cauterized the wound. A blackened stump stuck out from his purple uniform. His blasted chest had pumped blood in an irregularly braided river across the gray carpet.

Carey fought down the welling tide of emotion. Dead? *Probably.* Anger smothered her . . . then she saw Joe's right hand twitch. She lunged to her feet and ran, sliding to a halt beside him. He gazed up at her through eyes drowsy with death.

"Joe, hold on."

Slumping to the floor, she pulled his mangled body into her lap, heedless for the moment of the possibility that the spies might return. Splintered ribs protruded from his back, spiking into her legs. Carey stroked his dark matted hair. "It's all right, Joe. Just hold on. You're going to be all right."

He shook his head slightly and gave her an understanding smile. He knew as well as she did that Baruch had captured the level six hospital and none of the *Hoyer*'s physicians had survived the decompression. Futility swept Carey so violently she wanted to slam her fists into something.

"Goddamn it," she whispered hoarsely. "How can we fight Baruch when we're waging war against our own people?"

Joe gazed at her hollowly, then his body went slack. His remaining arm fell to the floor.

"Joe. . . ?"

Carey pressed her cheek against his. Her gaze landed on the place where she'd last seen the spies and cold rancor overwhelmed her.

CHAPTER 10

Jeremiel squinted at the amber letters on the com screen. He struggled to keep his mind from wandering. The letters had begun to blur every time he took a deep breath. The faint odor of cleaning fluids still clung to the walls, stinging his bloodshot eyes.

"You're losing it," he chastised himself.

But he had so little time. So *goddamned* little time. The twelve hours since the takeover of the ship had swept by like minutes while he fought to organize enough people to handle basic necessities.

He propped a fist on his desk and struck the key to abandon the rich personnel file. Pushing up to stand, he weaved so badly on his feet he had to thrust a hand against the wall to steady himself. He calculated how long it had been since he'd last slept. Fifty-six hours? And there was no end in sight. He'd been giving himself injections of stimulants, but the human body could only take so much before it just plain collapsed. He needed help. He'd delegated as much authority as he safely could, but Harper, Janowitz, and their rough-hewn crew had their hands full securing the ship and implementing the rescue program for Horebians.

"Just hang on. Rachel's on her way."

He forced a series of deep breaths as he looked around his cabin. The door to the latrine stood open. Stark white light shimmered from the shower fixtures. He stared at them longingly.

"Yes. Take the time. It might revive you a little."

He couldn't afford to sleep—not when the ship swelled with injured refugees and enemy soldiers scared to the point of madness. Horebians crowded like ghostly sentinels around every portal and monitor. They stared blindly down at their beloved world, watching it spin in the horrifying contortions of a wounded planet. He could feel the emotions growing to monstrous levels. Rage, hatred, and desperation seethed, ready to burst the seams of the *Hoyer*.

He put his hands on his hips and stretched his taut back muscles. Crossing to the pack sitting beside his bed, he unfastened the closures and pulled out a dark blue jumpsuit and laid it across his gray blanket. Reaching inside again, he patted around for socks, but his hand touched something else—cold, tiny.

It set off an earthquake in his weary soul. He steeled himself, and gently pulled out the silver locket.

"Syene."

He gripped it tightly in his hand and closed his eyes. Her face filled his memories. Beautiful long brown hair spilled around her shoulders. She gave him a confident smile and laughed, that sweet little girl laugh that always made him smile in return, no matter how desperate the circumstances. *"Well,"* her voice echoed softly. *"God help Tahn if he ever catches you. Your unrefined habits will make him wish to hell he hadn't."*

They'd been standing in his cabin, dressing in battlesuits for the Silmar fight. Crystal sheets lay scattered over the desk and table, stacked a foot high in various spots on the floor. They'd studied and restudied every facet of the plans, every possible thing that might go wrong, and hedged their bets accordingly. Still, his nerves hummed so tightly he thought they'd tear him apart.

He watched her pull on her boots, and clenched his fists. "Syene, I don't like this. Let me go. I can't bear the—"

"We've been all through this," she said, giving him one of those wry smiles meant to ease his tension. "You're too valuable to send down on a routine subversion mission. I'm going."

"*Listen to me.* There's a trap here somewhere. I—I don't know where, but I can feel it. Something's just . . . *wrong.*"

She cocked her head and hair cascaded over her shoulders, glinting like polished brass in the light. Her dark graceful brows drew together. "Shall we discuss Neil again?"

He stiffened. They'd argued about it before, shouting at each other until he felt physically ill. "Not now, Syene."

She nodded amiably. "All right. Getting back to our former discussion, then, there's always a trap somewhere. The trick is to stay out of it. I'm fairly good at that, don't you think?"

"Of course, you're a brilliant—"

"Glad you agree." She straightened up. "Now, I'd better get going. Lichtner isn't going to wait all day for me."

She strode past him and he grabbed her arm and embraced her frantically. Her muscular body felt suddenly frail in his arms, too slender for fighting endless wars. They stood silently and he fought to memorize the feel of her, the way her shoulders rested against his chest, the silken touch of her hair tangling in his beard, her thighs pressing warmly against his. Deep inside him, a terrible ache grew.

"Be careful," he said, kissing her fragrant hair. "I love you."

She tightened her grip around his waist, pulling him closer, stroking his back tenderly. "Don't be foolish. I'm coming back to you, Jeremiel."

Coming back . . . back. . . .

He stared at the locket. Raped and left for dead, he'd held her in his arms as she died. Silmar had been the last battle before Horeb, hadn't it? Or were there others in between? His tired mind rambled over the question. Yes, yes, of course, the last battle . . . before Horeb. Syene had paid the ultimate price for his unquestioning loyalty to Dannon. He wondered now how he could have been so blind. She'd tried to warn him.

"How many strategy sessions has he missed, Jeremiel? *Where is he when he isn't* here *with us?*"

"He has a personal life, too. Leave it be. I trust him." But it had been Syene who'd deserved his utmost

95

confidence. Why hadn't he given it to her? Why hadn't he checked on Dannon's whereabouts during those terrible last days? Syene had pretended not to be hurt, but he knew. Still, she stood by him, loving him, fighting for him with passionate loyalty, shielding him from any and all criticisms.

Dying for him.

He turned the locket over and over, drifting with the delicate triangular shape, remembering the hundreds of times she'd worn it. Had it only been four months ago that he'd burst into that blood-spattered apartment on Silmar? His love for her still hurt deep inside.

Gently, as though it were made of glass, he put the locket back in his pack. It made a silken scratching sound against the petrolon. Tipping up his chin, he mentally searched the ship. His voice came out surprisingly calm. "You can't hide, Neil."

He'd found the records in his search of the *Hoyer's* files. Tahn had picked Dannon up off Silmar, but he'd never set him down. Somewhere in the depths of the vessel, Neil would be scrambling for cover. A hot feeling of rushing adrenaline bolstered Jeremiel for a few seconds. Furiously, he stripped off his soiled black battlesuit and threw it on the floor. Setting the heat dials in the shower for eight out of ten, he stepped beneath the spray, flinching when the water washed the cuts and abrasions like a river of fire. He stood there for an eternal ten minutes.

"Forget about Dannon! Later. Think about him later. You have to be sane to meet with Halloway." Tahn's second in command had demanded a meeting and he'd put her off for as long as he could, hoping to get things figured out better before he had to face her.

When he stepped out of the shower, he felt better, not quite so painfully exhausted. He dressed in his blue jumpsuit and went to stand before the mirror. The reflection caught him off-guard. He barely recognized the man who gazed back. His shaggy brows drew together over his straight nose. Inflamed blue eyes studied him from dark circles. His mouth had a cynical twist to it, boding ill for all concerned.

"Well, you certainly look the part of an evil conqueror."

He picked up his brush and took a few swipes at his hair and beard, then shoved his pistol in his belt holster and headed back for the com unit and the precious personnel files. The buzzing of his door com made his steps falter. He swung around, stumbling sideways before he gripped a chair back and regained his balance.

"Jeremiel? It's Harper."

He took a deep breath. "Come in, Avel."

The door slipped open. Harper stood tall in a clean gray jumpsuit, a sleeping boy in his arms. Behind him, Chris Janowitz and two unknown men stood, rifles cradled in their arms. "Jeremiel, meet Wen Howard and Rumon Kaufa." He gestured to the two skinny bald-headed men. "They'll be working with Janowitz."

Jeremiel nodded to each one, then his gaze shifted to Mikael. "How's the boy?"

"Fine, we think. We found him just where you said, cabin 955 on level seven. They've been keeping him heavily sedated."

Mikael Calas' seven-year-old face looked serene. His black curly hair twined across his olive cheeks. Jeremiel heaved a sigh. "But is he all right? Has Doctor Severns checked him over yet?"

Harper shook his head. "No, I was on my way there. I just wanted to bring Mikael by here first, so you could rest easier."

"I appreciate that, Avel. How is security faring? How many decks have we searched?"

Janowitz answered, "Levels eight through twenty. We haven't had a chance to get to the bridge yet. The infighting on the upper levels has been so intense we didn't want to try it until we'd organized more security teams."

Jeremiel nodded. He'd instituted a rigorous investigative search before any refugee was allowed to serve as part of the ship's Gamant takeover forces. He couldn't risk allowing a Magisterial sympathizer or a former marine loyal to Ornias into a critical position. But it meant that the assignment process took a great deal of time.

Janowitz continued, "We found a bunch of Magisterial soldiers skulking around in the air ducts. I'm sure there's a lot more. We disarmed those we captured, jerked them out of their vacuum suits, and herded them to level seven."

"Good, Chris. As the cleaning crews complete their

97

work on each secured level, start assigning refugees to rooms. I'm sure they're going mad waiting in the bays. Avel, have you had time to arrange mess crews to deliver meals?"

"Not yet. Sorry."

"No apology necessary. The dispensers in the rooms will give the refugees soup and drinks. Just tell them we're working on full meals, Chris."

Janowitz nodded. "I will."

Harper cleared his throat and hesitated. Jeremiel turned abruptly, sensing something unpleasant. "What?"

"The search teams you assigned to look for Dannon have found nothing. I provided all of them with pictures, but—"

"Keep them looking." He silently promised himself that when he had the majority of the critical problems out of the way, he'd go looking *himself.*

Harper licked his lips and nodded. "We also picked up a tran from Ornias. It was sent right after he left Horeb. He got away safely. He's on his way to Palaia Station to pick up his reward."

Silently, Jeremiel stared into Harper's black eyes, sharing a conspiratorial look of anger and a promise of revenge.

"Well, blessed be Milcom," Howard said, "at least the High Councilman got away."

Rage tensed Harper's face. He turned like a bear about to attack. "I'll let that pass, Howard, since you don't know Ornias is the cause of all this."

The skinny man blinked. "What? The blessed Mashiah's right-hand man—"

"The High Councilman laid a trap for Jeremiel, seducing him away from his forces by sending a false message that the very survival of Gamant civilization depended on his coming to Horeb. The entire civil war was nothing more than a ruse to capture Baruch. Jeremiel came, all right, and Ornias turned him over to Tahn for five billion notes."

Howard frowned incredulously. At his side, Kaufa blinked and shifted uneasily; in the stark light of the hallway, his cheeks reddened to crimson. Jeremiel scrutinized him. Did he agree with Howard, or was that just nerves?

Howard threw out his chest indignantly. "The High Councilman sold out Gamant civilization? Why, I can't believe it! He had the purest of souls. He did everything in the world to help us on Horeb. He fed the people after the drought and—"

"He killed thousands of Old Believers!"

"Well . . . yes," Howard acknowledged as though it had little import. "They revolted against Milcom's Mashiah, tried to kill him by blowing up his temple with him in it!"

Jeremiel leaned against the wall. Not a marine, but certainly an Ornias devotee. He'd have to revise his questionnaire. How many others had they missed? "Harper, when's Rachel coming aboard?"

"About two hours."

"Contact Calas and Funk and have them bring Sybil—"

Howard sucked in a sudden breath. "Rachel Eloel? The Mashiah's *murderer?*"

Jeremiel lifted his chin at the indignant look Howard gave him. Every ache, every pain in his deathly tired body cried out.

"Chris," he ordered. "I'm supposed to meet First Lieutenant Halloway in one hour. Why don't you and Kaufa go up and spend some time checking the security arrangement on level eight. When Halloway steps out of the tube, inform her I want to alter our meeting place. Tell her I'll meet her here, in my cabin at 07:30. If she can't make it—cancel the meeting. I'll reschedule later."

"Aye, Jeremiel." Janowitz and Kaufa stalked away down the hall, Kaufa throwing harsh questioning looks over his shoulder.

"Howard," Jeremiel ordered sternly. "Please go and check in with the deck twenty security chief. I want to know how many more people have come aboard in the past four hours."

"Aye, sir," Howard saluted lazily and stalked down the hall.

Jeremiel's hand unconsciously gripped the butt of his pistol. "Avel—"

"I didn't know, Jeremiel. We've been trying to weed them out, but things are so confused sometimes—"

"We're all rushed. Pull Howard off security duty. I don't want you to use him at all. Not even for a cleaning

99

team. As quickly as possible, assign Howard and any of his obvious friends to the same level where you're putting all the Tartarus fanatics. I want them sealed in their cabins—just like the others."

"Understood." Harper shifted nervously from one foot to the other. "Get some rest, Jeremiel."

"When I can."

Harper nodded and walked quietly down the hall, steps easy so as not to jar the sleeping boy in his arms.

Jeremiel closed his door. Sourness roiled in his stomach. He felt like a soldier lost in the midst of a firefight, running in a nightmare country, his path lit only by flashes from enemy rifles that might bring him down for good.

"You're just tired. Goddamn it. That's all it is. Let it go."

But he couldn't. He had an overwhelming urge to grab a shuttle and space for nowhere—anywhere away from Gamant civilization. Insanity. He'd spent his entire adult life trying to protect Gamant culture and religion from being destroyed by the Magistrates. Why did doubts consume him now, after they'd just achieved a major victory by capturing the *Hoyer*? That look on Howard's face had stirred it. He'd have to put Rachel somewhere relatively safe or the refugees still loyal to Tartarus and Ornias would tear her to pieces.

"Why are Gamants always trying to cut each other's throats? Especially now, when each other is all we have left in the galaxy?"

How many had died in the past ten years? Maybe two million? So damned much death. Magisterial cruisers, even now, probably hovered over a Gamant planet, blasting it to scattered bits of nothingness. And his Underground, *God willing,* circled dozens of Magisterial military installations, blasting them to dust. Horeb had been the worst—with Gamants gleefully killing Gamants. Damned fools. *All of them!* Because of the endless petty juggling of political priorities, less than a million Gamants now inhabited the galaxy. In the past year, the Magistrates had scorched four planets: Wexlen, Jumes, Pitbon, and Kayan, and completed half-measures at Horeb and Nuja. And it was escalating, he could *sense* it in the fact that he couldn't find his fleet or contact his bases on Tikkun.

Am I ready for another series of insane battles?

He stood stiffly until he could suppress the desperation. "Torture yourself later. There's too much to be done."

He went back to slouch into the chair before his com terminal. "Computer?"

"Running."

"Access personnel file of Lieutenant Carey Halloway again. This time, I want the personal data. Family, friends, hobbies, likes, and dislikes. Full psych profile." With Tahn still down from the concussion he'd given him, she'd be the force to reckon with. What scrap of data could he find to use against her? The Clandestine forces? She'd skillfully managed to isolate them on level two. How long could she keep them there? *Should he let her?*

"Searching."

A full-length picture of her appeared on the screen. A beautiful woman, the picture showed her with shorter hair than he remembered from the landing bay. Her soft translucent skin stood in stark contrast to the hard eyes that looked out at him. Age: 35. Born: Columbia VIII, the 9th of Sivan, 5381. Parents: Lorne and Miza Halloway. Fruit orchard laborers. Siblings: One. Brother: Timothy Sean Halloway. Family killed during Centauri Revolt, 5398.

The record continued to scroll up, forty-two screens worth. He didn't have time for it. He had to get everything he could on the key players and quickly, before the enemy resolved their own inner conflicts and combined forces again to take their ship back.

And they would—the instant Tahn could sit up.

"Computer? Stop. Give me a split screen. Correlate files of Captain Cole Tahn and Lieutenant Halloway. Highlight comparisons and contrasts in psych profiles, particularly stress test results."

The screen filled with data.

He leaned back in his chair and caressed his beard, trying to concentrate past the deepening fear. Halloway would be just as bad as Tahn. Maybe she'd been one of the driving forces behind him all along. Looked like it. It paid to give that some thought. How would Tahn do without her? But, no. He couldn't afford to do that—the stakes were too high. He *knew* how they worked together.

101

They'd be unpredictable if separated.

He wearily massaged his forehead before reaching for another syringe full of stimulants. The drug tingled through him, giving him a momentary flush of vitality—but it didn't last very long anymore. Closing his eyes for a moment, he sighed, then turned back to the split screen, hoping he could get their probable strategies worked out before they did.

He'd damn well better.

* * *

Brent Bogomil tugged at the tight collar of his purple uniform. His hand came back coated with sweat. *Slothen had demanded he* immediately *reroute to Palaia?* Lord, it wasn't his fault Silbersay had managed to slip through his fingers when they'd made that routine maintenance stop at Ourano II. But who'd believe that?

He shifted uncomfortably in his command chair and looked around the bridge of the *Jataka.* In an oval room composed of two levels, nine people worked the monitors and consoles. His chair with its massive net of computer links sat on the upper level overlooking the lower where eight officers sat in twos, stationed side by side at four niches around the oval.

How in hell could they look so bored, when he felt like the world might be coming to an end at any moment? Actually, not any *moment,* it would take them days to reach Palaia.

He ran a hand through his moist red hair. Blast, he needed to talk to someone about what Slothen might do. Who could he call on such a confidential matter? He had to think of someone who despised Slothen as much as he did. His thoughts drifted.

After a few minutes, he leaned forward, looking at his dark-haired communications officer. "Winnow? Put in a tran to the *Hoyer.* I want to talk to Cole Tahn."

"Aye, sir." The com aura glowed like a golden halo around her head as her nimble fingers flew.

He waited, leaning back in his chair. Slothen wouldn't order him to be corrected, would he? Sweat popped out over his face, running in rivulets down his neck. He lost himself for a moment in practicing how he'd explain his blunder to the Magistrate, but after several seconds he came back, grimacing.

"What's taking so long, Winnow? The *Hoyer*'s just on the other side of—"

"Yes, sir. I know their whereabouts, but I can't seem to get a response to my trans. I've tried three times now. Let me try again."

He frowned at the forward screen. At their speed, the stars looked like blue-violet tubes streaking an ebony sea.

"Negative, Captain. No response from *Hoyer*." She swiveled around in her chair, curious eyes meeting his. "Could be a routine malfunction of the long-range link, sir."

"Could be." He rubbed his chin reflectively. On the other hand, Tahn had just gone to retrieve the famed Jeremiel Baruch. He ground his teeth softly. Could the Underground fleet have intervened? No. He'd have been notified of their proximity. And Baruch damned sure couldn't take the *Hoyer* out from under Tahn by himself. It probably was the long-range link.

Then again, it never paid to underestimate Baruch.

"Dharon?" he called to his navigation officer. "Calculate how late we'll be if we backtrack and swing by the *Hoyer*? Just to make sure everything's all right there."

"Aye, sir, but let's not forget that Slothen's orders said *immediately*."

"Yes, yes, I know, but if Tahn's in trouble, it'll be worth a tongue-lashing from Slothen to help him. He's pulled us out of enough fires."

His gaze darted nervously over the bridge. Maybe he ought to tran Palaia and find out if Cole had checked in after retrieving Baruch? But if he did that, Slothen would suspect a delaying tactic on his part and that wouldn't help his case any. Plus, the blue beast would probably be difficult and deny permission for the course change.

"We'll be approximately thirty hours overdue to Palaia if we reroute, sir," Dharon reported.

"Thirty?" Too long. Slothen would hit the roof if he didn't request authorization first. "All right. Winnow, send a dattran to Slothen's secretary, what's his name? Topew? Tell him we suspect a problem aboard the *Hoyer* and want to offer assistance as originally planned. Request permission to delay our arrival at Palaia for another two days."

"Aye, sir."

He rubbed his chin pensively, gazing out at the dark, star-streaked skies. "Dharon, while Winnow's checking with Palaia, see if you can contact the *Scipio*. The last I heard, Gen Abruzzi was delivering med supplies in Sector Two. If we can't help Cole, maybe he can."

CHAPTER 11

Carey Halloway absently watched the level numbers flash as the transport tube descended. Her knees trembled.

"Goddamn it."

Pressing her hot cheek against the cool white tiles, she fought the overwhelming urge to vomit. "Pull yourself together. You can't let Baruch see you like this."

Arranging this meeting with the Underground leader had been nearly impossible. For the past thirteen hours, he'd allowed no visits from the *Hoyer*'s officers, not even a visual communication.

Gamant refugee ships had been unloading, Baruch orchestrating each movement personally, like a man terrified to even take a deep breath lest he miss something. And all the while, his soldiers tramped tirelessly through the tatters of her world, securing different levels, searching everyone, confiscating belongings, tearing the ship apart looking for hidden people or caches of weapons. The only levels left to her now were one through five. And they were a blazing mass of gunfire.

Nothing of her old ordered life remained. All sanctuaries had been looted. Her crew—what remained of it—had gone nearly mad with grief and terror. They'd started questioning Cole's abilities, threatening to lynch him for the loss of their families and friends. And there was nothing she could do. Bodies still twisted lifelessly in the star-strewn silence, silhouetted blackly against the flaming surface of a devastated planet hundreds of miles below.

Tahn continued to reel in the grips of his concussion, half here, half somewhere else. The last time she'd gone to see him, he'd just moaned, reliving some terrible nightmare from his past. If she didn't get him a doctor soon, she'd no idea what would happen to him.

The tube stopped. She kept her palm pressed securely against the "close" patch, preventing the door from opening. "Come on," she commanded her trembling knees. "*Come on!* You don't have any choice. Your crew is killing itself from the inside."

For a moment longer, she delayed, gathering her strength. Finally, she brushed auburn hair from her brow and hit the "open" button.

The door snicked back. Her stomach cramped at the sight of the hallway. Crimson splashes stained the walls, marking the places where bodies had slammed before being sucked out the hatches. A fine brownish mist sprayed the ceiling—body fluids released during repressurization. Four hard-eyed Gamant guards aimed rifles at her chest.

"I'm Lieutenant Halloway. I'm meeting Commander Baruch in conference room 8015."

The short stocky blond nodded. Dressed in the purple and gray of *Hoyer* security, he seemed a vile abomination. "I'm Christopher Janowitz, ma'am. There's been a change of plans."

She rubbed sweaty palms on her pants, then took a deep steadying breath. "Don't tell me he's canceling this meeting. I've got to see him, damn it!"

"He understands that. He just wants to meet you in his quarters on level twenty within the next ten minutes."

Anger flared. Was that the only place he felt safe? "He's afraid to meet me in a conference room?"

"His cabin or nowhere, ma'am. Make up your mind."

"My crew can't wait, mister. Let's go."

She stepped out into the blood-splashed hallway. The odors of human wastes tainted the air. A Gamant cleanup crew labored a short distance away, using mechanical shovels to pick up and deposit the dead bodies of Magisterial crew into the wall compactors. Carey tried not to watch, not to study each face in anticipation of recognition, but one woman, a sergeant, held her gaze riveted. She'd been caught in a door. Her arms extended pleadingly across the floor as she stared from hauntingly bare eye sockets. *Lorene Saunlon?* Carey swallowed hard, looking away.

Janowitz motioned with his rifle. "Please put your hands against the wall, ma'am. I need to search you."

She braced her fists against the petrolon and spread her legs. He expertly patted her down and ran a supplementary check with his hand-corder, looking for hidden substances.

Satisfied, Janowitz stood and pointed. "This way, please."

"I'm well aware of the route to level twenty, soldier." She started forward, but the hard hand on her forearm stopped her.

"I don't doubt it. But please follow me anyway. Jeremiel would be a mite upset if I let you lead."

"Really? Does he think I can take the ship back by myself?"

"I think he's more concerned about your safety, ma'am." Janowitz said the words with such reverence, she gritted her teeth. Did these fanatics consider Baruch a damned god? *Yes, undoubtedly. And why not? My own crew's starting to believe it.*

Janowitz stepped out in front of her while the other man, thin and bald, fell in behind. Her spine prickled ominously, knowing a rifle centered on her back. They marched down the hall to the far transport tube and caught it, descending rapidly. She kept her eyes focused on the lighting panels on the ceiling, contemplating what she'd say to him, how she'd stand up under a grilling if he decided to torture her. Gamants were well-known for refusing to use mind probes. Instead, they utilized primitive, brutal methods of information gathering.

When the tube stopped, Janowitz got out first, checked the corridor and motioned for her to exit. She walked into a hall crowded with Horebian refugees. Groans and sobs filled the air. Many people wore bandages, black bloody tatters of cloth wrapping heads and legs. One old man, with a face like a weather-beaten mountain, gazed at her through hate-filled eyes, watching her every movement. She took a step forward, maneuvering around the line of people lying prostrate against the wall. The other guard followed her, prodding her in the back with his rifle barrel. Pain lanced her kidney. She winced, stumbling forward.

"It's cabin 2017, Lieutenant. March."

She marched, evading the hostile glares that came from the wounded. An old woman with a leg missing spat at her, crying, "Magistrate filth! You killed my family. You killed my whole family!"

Carey's heart thundered. At the end of the corridor she saw a tiny girl of maybe two struggle up from a tangle of sleeping children. She had red curls and a gaunt face; she started crying pathetically. Just as Carey neared her, the girl weakly toppled across the floor and tried to crawl away, but she was too weak to move more than a few inches. Carey stared down into those bright wet eyes and her soul withered. The little girl feebly lifted her arms to Carey, begging to be held, sobbing suffocatingly.

Carey vacillated—Baruch might cancel the meeting if she were too late. But . . . dear God. . . . She knelt and picked up the little girl, hugging her. "It's all right," she whispered softly into the child's ear. "Everything's going to be okay."

The girl gripped handfuls of Halloway's auburn hair and tugged, pulling Carey closer so she could wrap tiny arms around her throat in a death grip. For several seconds, Carey just rocked the little girl and whispered confidently to her. *How many more like this are aboard? Hundreds?* The thought struck her like a blow in the face. She stroked the girl's back to soothe her tears. "Shh, don't cry. Don't cry."

Memories of Jumes rose. After they'd scorched the planet, they'd gone down to inspect what remained and she remembered too clearly the multitudes of orphaned children wandering the far reaches of the planet, crying, searching for family they'd never find again. Cole's eyes had possessed a haunted gleam for days after that reconnaissance. She'd wandered the ship at his side, silent, aching.

Janowitz came over and nudged her shoulder. "Come on, Lieutenant. We'll take care of the baby."

Carey hugged the child tightly one last time, then got to her feet and handed the girl to Janowitz. The girl shrieked wildly, fingers reaching for Carey—her whole body went numb. Janowitz delivered the child into different arms and pointed down the hall. "Go on, Halloway. Commander Baruch's waiting."

Carey hurried around the corner, lungs heaving. This

hall had no refugees, but the stench of their soiled clothing and tainted wounds still clung to the air.

Janowitz hit Baruch's com. "Jeremiel, Lieutenant Halloway's here to see you."

A lengthy pause ensued. Finally, the door slipped open and Carey gazed up into the face of the one man she'd feared for most of her adult life. Tall, he had broad shoulders and strong handsome features. Blond hair clung to his forehead and cheeks in wisps. His reddish-blond beard was neatly trimmed close to his face and his blue eyes flashed piercingly, though it was obvious he could barely stand from weariness.

"Lieutenant, please come in." Baruch stepped aside and made a tired sweeping gesture with his arm.

"Thank you," she said as she walked into his cabin. The door slipped closed behind her and her stomach muscles tensed. The lights gleamed softly, casting a dim silver glow over the bare walls. Identical to hers, the cabin stretched ten by fifteen feet and smelled astringent from cleaning fluids. A table and two chairs nestled against the wall on her right, next to the door to the latrine. His bed sat in the back. One small bag dotted the floor beside it. It seemed to be the only item of personal gear he possessed.

Walking past her, Baruch went to stand in the middle of the room, hands propped on his hips. "Please sit down. May I get you a cup of taza or—"

"A stiff scotch would be much better."

"All right." He went to the cabinet over his desk, pulling out a bottle and two glasses. Bringing them back to the table, he wearily commented, "My people found this in Engineering. I've no idea about the—"

"*Found* it?" Hatred and rage formed a fine hot brew in her breast. "You mean *stole* it."

"Since we currently own this ship, I mean *found* it."

"Arrogant bastard. You don't own all of it. Not yet."

He nodded nonchalantly and filled two glasses, handing her one. She accepted it with a jerk. Cool liquid washed her hand. Their gazes held: hers icy with desperation, his hard and unyielding.

She took a solid drink of the liquor, relishing the fiery path it burned down her throat. A few more of these and she'd be able to face the world, no matter how bleak it looked.

She glanced at the heavy pistol on his belt and her anger increased. "Did you wear your gun to threaten me? I assure you, Commander, I'm in no position to be dangerous."

"I don't meet any Magisterial officer unarmed. Especially not one who's won the Orillian silver star and the Columban cross. You're dangerous—regardless of your 'position.' I advise you not to make any sudden moves."

"Been researching personnel files all night?"

"Mostly."

She sipped her scotch, watching him intently over the rim of her glass. Her stomach cramped threateningly. She tipped her glass and drained it dry. Baruch studied the action detachedly. He seemed to be bracing himself up by locking his knees. Dead tired. Through the V-shaped opening in his neckline, she could see a thick mat of blond hair streaked with deep cuts. Hurt and tired. Could she find a way to use that? Wring information from him he wouldn't ordinarily reveal? *Maybe.*

She went to the table and dropped into a chair. A brief expression of relief crossed his face. He took the opposite seat and stretched long legs out across the gray carpet, crossing them at the ankles.

"Baruch," she began, "I'd be grateful if we could just talk like human beings for a few minutes before we get down to my reasons for requesting this meeting. Humanity is something the past few hours have been sorely lacking."

He nodded agreeably. "I understand that need, Lieutenant. Well, then, how's Tahn?"

"Still delirious. He keeps reliving the Pegasus Invasion of Old Earth."

Baruch frowned at his drink, swirling the amber liquid. "He was captured there, wasn't he?"

"Yes. Captured and jammed into a six-foot-square cage where they tortured him for five months. When Magisterial forces defeated the invaders, he crawled out of his cage, a little mad, they said. He spent several months in a rehabilitation center."

"He's an interesting sort, isn't he? Did he authorize the wide-beam emergency message requesting all ships within range to pick up Horebian survivors?"

"He did."

"Thoughtful of him, considering the message could

109

have brought my own fleet down on the *Hoyer*."

"He knew that."

"Then why did he take the chance?"

"To save a few *goddamned* Gamant lives."

Baruch ran a hand through his damp sunny hair. "That's rather difficult to believe, considering the hundreds of thousands he's taken in the past fifteen years. But I'm sure he had his reasons. I've promised myself that after I've had a thick steak and ten hours of sleep, I'm going to think about it. Or maybe I'll just ask him. I look forward to meeting him."

She lifted a brow. "He looked forward to exchanging a few fists with you."

"I can't think of anything that would make me happier. Except maybe the chance to kill every Magistrate alive."

She clamped her jaw, watching the way the dim light shadowed his gold-fur red forearm above his wrist. His hand shook slightly from exhaustion. "You're not very subtle."

"But I'm a good host. Your glass is empty. Can I refill it?"

"Damn better."

He poured it full again. *Keep him talking, think of something.* If he'd let her push him, maybe she could surreptitiously get him to answer critical questions.

"You're also a lunatic, Baruch. That was a crazy stunt you pulled in the Jayhawk system."

He looked at her curiously, noting with interest the change of subject matter. "You had my people in detention. What did you expect me to do?"

"Something saner. You rushed a heavily armed prison planet with six cruisers to rescue *two . . . two* people?"

"I liked them."

"You must have. Your maneuver around Antares Minor, however, was brilliant." She gave him a small smile, watching him closely.

He smiled back—hard and calculating—as though he saw right through her congenial act. "I didn't know you were a fan of mine, Lieutenant."

She lifted a shoulder and studied the way the light refracted through her glass to cast coppery designs across the black surface of the table.

In Antares Minor, they'd had his fleet boxed tight in an

asteroid belt, outnumbered five to one. Rather than surrendering like any sane commander who knows he's lost, Baruch stationed four of his ships in strategic locations, secretly evacuated his crews, set his matter/antimatter engines on time-delay for merge and ran the rest of his fleet like bats out of hell for the light vault. They'd shot three of the bats out of the sky before they realized the stationary ships were decoys. The entire asteroid belt, including fifteen Magisterial vessels, vanished in the explosions. He'd wasted six quality ships and two crews to get the remaining six out. The Underground fleet barely had fifteen vessels left.

"You killed fifty thousand government soldiers in that maneuver," Carey informed.

"Really? I'm disappointed. I thought it was more."

"Hopefully Epagael will cast you into Aktariel's pit of darkness for such feelings."

"I doubt it. I deserve at least a week in the seventh heaven as a reward."

"You think the archangel Michael will let you in? His reputation for justice must be greatly exaggerated."

He massaged his forehead. "Your file didn't say you were an expert on our religion. Perhaps we should discuss the pros and cons of Sinlayzan's rationalistic philosophy?"

She ground her teeth. She'd always had what Cole called "an unhealthy interest" in Gamant theology. Maybe some of those long hours of studying ancient texts would finally come in handy. "If you like. Don't you think his views on teleological ethics are myopic?"

Baruch laughed softly. "You're a surprise, Lieutenant."

"Answer my question."

"Myopic? A little, yes."

"More than a little. Implementation of his philosophy on Secus IX in 5102 resulted in nearly total genocide for the native life-form. The end, Commander, doesn't always justify the means."

"Basically, I agree, but I'm surprised to hear a Magisterial officer express such a sane opinion. I can't see any of you caring about methods given your—"

"*Your vision's pretty limited, isn't it?* You and Sinlayzan. Is that a Gamant trait?"

He set his glass down and looked her over in detail, as

111

though distastefully examining a slab of maggot-ridden meat in an open bazaar. She took another long drink, letting the amber saint warm her stomach and bolster her courage.

He cocked his head. "Let me clarify my former statement. Under certain conditions, Lieutenant, I think the end *can* justify the means. For example, I'd lie, cheat, steal—do anything, say anything—to overthrow the Galactic Magistrates and their brutal alien government."

"And I suppose you think that's ethical? A lot of innocent—"

"I've watched millions of my people die under your cannons, Lieutenant. Do you know what it's like to witness old men, women, and helpless children running in terror before they're slaughtered by anonymous villains from the skies? Do you have any idea—"

Desperate rage smothered her. Unthinkingly, she slammed a first against the table, coming halfway out of her chair. *"You just murdered twenty-seven hundred of my crewmates, Baruch! Don't be so damned righteous!"*

He leaned forward tiredly, blue jumpsuit rustling loudly in the sudden quiet. "And you've killed four of my planets in the past year. Half a million people, Lieutenant. My Underground kills *soldiers*, not babies. Didn't you ever feel a twinge of conscience murdering innocent people?"

Unsteadily, she lowered herself back into her chair. "No soldier likes to kill civilians, Commander."

He tipped his chair back on two legs, resting his head against the white wall as he scrutinized her. "Well, maybe the Magistrates have human beings in their service after all."

She gripped her glass hard, taking another long drink. "Baruch, what are you going to do with all the refugees aboard?"

"Put 'em groundside somewhere."

"And then?"

"Explain."

"I'm no fool. I suspect your fleet is on their way here right now." *Are they?* "When they arrive, are you going to use me and my crew as sacrificial offerings in the stead of the Magistrates?"

"Gamants aren't fiends, Lieutenant, no matter what

112

you've heard. Our hoofs and horns vanished centuries ago. Evolution, you know."

"Does that mean your men won't rape me and pillage my ship?"

"First, it's not your ship. Second, they'd certainly want to, but I assure you I'll forbid it."

"Gallant of you." She shook her head. Her stomach had started to ache again.

"Let's get down to business, Halloway. You called this meeting. What do you want?"

"I . . ." She squared her shoulders and took a deep breath. "I need your help."

His face was bland, but his blue eyes glittered questioningly as though wondering how she had the guts to ask. "Indeed? What for?"

Carey reached out and retrieved the whiskey bottle, refilling her glass again. "I want you to open the locks on level two." When she looked up, she found him watching her like a cat at a mousehole.

He thumped his thumb against his glass. "And what will I get in return?"

Carey swallowed hard. "I . . . I'll order my crew to lay down their arms. And I'll cooperate as best I can with your orders. That's what Cole intended when he talked to you last."

"And will your crew obey you?" A suave brutality tinged his voice.

Carey lifted her head and glared. *"Yes."*

He smiled as though intrigued by the entire conversation. "Let me get this straight. I'll kill your enemies for you and you'll willingly become my prisoner. Is that it?"

"Yes, Commander, that's it. I'm trying to save as much of my crew as I can. You said you'd put us down on the nearest Gamant planet alive and well. I assume you intend to keep that promise."

"I do."

"Do we have a bargain?" Carey held her breath.

"You'll also order your scientific staff to train my people, correct?"

"Correct—just as Tahn agreed."

He eyed her closely, then finished his drink and set the glass on the table. "I'll open the locks."

She exhaled in relief and slumped back in her chair.

"One other thing, Commander. I have several wounded people stashed in a wardroom on level three. And Captain Tahn is very ill. He might be dying for all I know. I need medical personnel. When you decompressed the ship, you killed all—"

"We have two physicians in our group. I'll send you one for exactly one hour."

"I won't have to worry about him murdering Tahn in his sleep, will I?"

"I'll leave orders that that task is my *sole* prerogative. What else do you need?"

"Permission for my bridge crew to go back to their own cabins. They—"

"Negative. Once they've officially surrendered, however, we will prepare cabins for them on level seven and have their nonmilitary possessions brought up. You and Tahn will continue to stay on level four."

"You want to keep us separated from our crew?" She laughed shortly. "Your people outnumber ours four to one and you're still bringing up more refugees. What do you think—"

"Even if the odds were a million to one, Lieutenant, I'd take the same precautions." He braced a hand on the table and pushed up, reeling slightly before he caught himself. Even in exhaustion, his physical presence was daunting. He moved with a leashed power that struck her unsettlingly. "Please keep me informed about the status of your crew. If I can do anything else to ease—"

"I'll let you know, Commander. Thank you for talking with me."

She hurried by him, hitting the exit patch and striding out into the rifle barrels of a half-dozen guards.

* * *

Gen Abruzzi rubbed his square jaw as he studied the now blank forward screen. A middle-aged man, he had a long narrow face the color of varnished walnut. Deep black eyes sat in darkened hollows beneath his drooping lids. Gray hair formed a woolly, close-cropped mat around his head. He shifted uncomfortably in his command chair, contemplating the things Bogomil had said. Oh, Brent had tried to sound nonchalant, merely asking the *Scipio* to keep an eye on the *Hoyer*'s location, to report if the vessel undertook any unusual maneuvers.

But there was more to it. Cole would have never allowed a routine malfunction to go on for so long. A few hours, yes, but ten hours, no. And who knew how long the link had been out before Bogomil tried to tran him?

Something had gone wrong aboard the *Hoyer*.

Abruzzi leaned forward slightly, gazing at his second in command. Tenon Lamont, a tiny Oriental woman with short black hair, looked back pensively. They all felt it—that anxious foreboding in their bellies. If somebody had dropped a net around Cole, they'd be on their way. But it had to be done delicately—especially if the "somebody" turned out to be Baruch. The lunatic Underground genius might do something desperate. "Lieutenant," he said, "what's the location of the *Klewe*?"

She ran a check through her com, then swung back around to face him. "They should be just finishing up a delivery mission in Sector Three. Do you want me to contact Captain Erinyes?"

"What course has he logged for the next week?"

Tenon hit a few more keys on her console. "He's cutting across Sector Two, heading for Four to provide strategic support for Governor Puyo on Komati. They apparently have a civil war brewing in the Mysore system."

Abruzzi pursed his lips disdainfully. *Strategic support, my ass.* Erinyes was probably maneuvering for political leverage, trying to make himself look good. Rumor had it he planned on running in the next election for a seat to the Magistrates' military advisory council. A pompous two-bit politician, Erinyes' uncle—Nafred—already served on that board. As a result, the *Klewe* hadn't seen battle in twenty years. Worse, Erinyes was rarely where his flight plan said he would be. The *Klewe* could be sitting in dock at Palaia right now. If anybody else neglected to update their flight plan the central command would kick the hell out of them—but not Erinyes.

He hesitated. "Oh, hell . . . No, no, let's wait. With his reported course, he shouldn't be more than a few hours away at any given point in the next few days if we need his assistance to pull Tahn out of some fire."

"Aye, sir.

"In the meantime, keep monitoring the *Hoyer*. I want to know the instant they send another long-range dattran. We're too far away for them to pick us up on their scanners, but as we get closer I want you to keep us hidden behind Horeb's sun." He slid back in his chair, rubbing his chin again as he eyed each of his bridge crewpeople in turn. They fastened him with worried gazes. "If there's an applecart tilted out there, we don't want to push it over. Not yet."

CHAPTER 12

Carey sat immobile in the command chair on the bridge. Baruch had taken over the *Hoyer* exactly twenty-four hours ago—but it seemed like centuries. Her purple uniform hung in a mass of blood-spattered wrinkles, accenting her pale complexion and the reddish sheen in her auburn hair. A dull glitter lit her eyes as she watched her crew. Only an hour ago, Baruch had opened the second level lock. After he'd shut it, she'd taken a security team and gone down herself to scout the area. No sign remained of the Clandestine Services officers— but she couldn't be sure that some hadn't escaped in the final moments. Baruch had released the shipwide communications link to her so she could comply with her side of the bargain. She hadn't used it yet.

She didn't need her bridge officers' concurrence before ordering the crew to lay down their weapons, but it would help to have their backing. Until Tahn regained consciousness she needed every ounce of support she could get.

Scarlet blazed on Rich Macey's freckled cheeks as he paced before the blank forward screen. The other seven officers hunched over their consoles, lips pursed, nostrils flaring in fear and indecision. Hera tapped a pen irritatingly.

"It's our only choice," Carey pointed out.

"To give up?" Macey blurted. Skinny and red-haired, his blue eyes had a wild look. He threw up his arms.

116

"What the hell is going on? First Tahn lets us get slaughtered, then you make a deal with Baruch—"

"Tahn did not let us get slaughtered, Lieutenant," Carey said coldly. "I've served with the man twice as long as you have and I can tell you for a fact that he's risked his life repeatedly to save his crew. Losing the *Hoyer* was nobody's fault. Baruch just outmaneuvered us, that's all."

"Outmaneuvered," Macey grumbled hostilely. "Sure. My friends are dead, Halloway! I can't . . ."

He stopped when he saw Hera drop her pen and bury her face in her hands. A series of muffled cries rose. Her husband Kevin was still missing, and almost certainly dead.

Carey tightened her grip around her chair arms. "I'm not suggesting we give up, Macey. I'm suggesting we pretend to cooperate—which is what Tahn wanted us to do. Once we assure Baruch that we're peacefully resigned to our condition, we can start organizing. And once Tahn is back on his feet—"

"What?" Macey blustered incredulously. "After what's happened, how could we ever trust him again? I won't trust him with my life!"

Carey's gaze slid to the faces of every other officer on the bridge. Some looked away, trying to keep her from seeing that they agreed with Rich. Others met her gaze squarely, supportively, loyal to her and Tahn to the end. But how many? If she took a vote, would she have enough to win? *Doesn't matter, sweetheart. You're going to order your crew to lay down their weapons anyway. You've no choice. If you break your bargain with Baruch, he's liable to cut off the oxygen to the bridge. But, blessed God, if you lose the vote and go ahead with it, every man and woman who voted against you is going to be waiting to slip a knife into your back . . . and Tahn's.*

Without moving a muscle, Carey quietly promised, "I want to start organizing to take this ship back. But I need unity. If we split into factions and spend all our time trying to slit each other's throats, we're lost. How many of you are with me?"

Hera's hand went up immediately. Others slowly followed. Six in all. Only Macey and Jim Reno dissented. Carey inhaled a silent breath of relief, meeting Macey's hostile glare with one just as glacial.

"I'll inform the crew," she said and reached for the com patch on her arm console.

* * *

Neil Dannon hid in the utter blackness beneath a series of clanging pipes. The past day had been sheer agony. The soft hiss of steam venting encircled him. He'd been crawling desperately from one level to another for hours, flinching at every sound. At least a dozen men dogged his trail. He'd counted them, noting the different sounds their boots made, cataloging the occasional voice. The Magisterial infighting had obviously stopped, for Gamant soldiers flooded every corridor from the bridge down. He had to keep moving.

Cold leaked from everywhere. He shivered and curled into a fetal ball on his side, trying to sleep. The chill of the deep niche assaulted his torn uniform like grasping fingers, twining inside to stroke his warm flesh.

Unconsciously, he reached up to clutch the sacred triangle he always wore. He patted his throat, searching, then heaved a tremulous sigh. He must have lost it somewhere in his mad flight. Maybe it was a sign? Jeremiel had given it to him. *Jeremiel . . .*

Neil rolled to his other side, pressing his back against one of the pipes. A slight warmth crept into him. Slowly, he drifted off to sleep. Images flashed, distant, scattered, spinning through time.

And the voice that haunted his nightmares called to him again, as it had a thousand times in the past few months . . .

"Neil? Neil, for God's sake, get up! Get up!"

Suriel. Rabbah system. Fifteen years ago. Round habitation domes lined the street, people visible inside, crying, wringing their hands as they watched the snow fall on bloody corpses and racing children. Black ships hung like deadly goblins in the air. Lights flashed rhythmically as they used instruments to search the windswept ground.

"I'm hit, Jeremiel. I'm hit!"

His leg dangled lifelessly, the thigh blasted wide. Blood ran hot and sticky to pool on the icy sidewalk. He pulled himself forward on his elbows until his strength ebbed, draining out with his blood like water from a bucket with the spigot left open.

"Neil?"

Baruch ran back to him, firing down the street to cover them. Neil squeezed his eyes closed against the blinding purple glare and felt a strong arm slip beneath his shoulders, trying to lift him. Another shot rang out.

"Neil, help me. Grab onto me. Try to stand!"

"I can't! Jeremiel, get out of here! Go!" He violently shoved his best friend away.

Then he saw the Magisterial soldiers surging down the street toward them and terror laced his gut. God damn, there were so many. The Underground had raided a Right School to free the children held captive—but something had gone wrong—some element of the plan had failed.

"Jeremiel, for God's sake, go!"

"I'm not leaving you. Damn it, get up or you'll get us both killed!" He leveled his pistol, firing into the purple-suited tidal wave. "Hold onto me, Neil. Come on! Damn you, help me!"

Feebly, he draped an arm around Jeremiel's shoulder and felt Baruch grip the sleeve of his black battlesuit, dragging him to his feet, supporting his hundred and ninety pounds as they stumbled around the corner and down a dark alleyway.

Winding through the streets like amorphous fog, Jeremiel finally hauled him into a ramshackle building on the edge of town. Panting so hard his lungs heaved, he'd gently lowered Neil to the hard floor. Quickly, Jeremiel undressed, removing the white shirt beneath his battlesuit and tearing it into strips.

"Feeling any pain yet?"

"Pain?" Neil gasped incredulously, sweat drenching his face. "My whole body feels like it's on fire."

Jeremiel gave him a broad flashing smile and casually remarked, "Good. You probably won't even feel this, then."

Neil suppressed screams for the next five minutes while Jeremiel bandaged his leg.

Insanely, he laughed, lifting his head to stare into the utter blackness. A warm feeling rose in his chest. He shook himself, but the deep emotions wouldn't leave him be. Pain and hatred swelled, remnants of old love taunting around the edges of his heart—relics of the damned that he'd kept bottled up for months.

He forced himself to imagine what must be going on in the lower levels. Jeremiel had brought up a few thousand refugees he'd heard one of his pursuers remark.

"How are you doing, Jeremiel? Losing it, yet? You can't hold on, old friend."

Can you?

Neil clenched his fists futilely. He had to know. He had to get down to those lower levels and find out for himself or he'd go stark raving mad. If he could just steal some refugee's clothes, he might be able to fade into the Gamant structure and discover what the hell Baruch was up to—and where his weaknesses were.

Gathering his courage, he slithered foward.

* * *

Rachel watched the brightly lit landing bay fill the portal. The seconds seemed to drag by until finally she felt a slight lurch and heard a dull scraping sound as the ship came to rest.

She switched off the restraints and got to her feet, rushing toward the exit. The pilot and copilot met her at the door.

"Please stand aside, Miss Eloel. We'll need to check the bay before you exit. Baruch's orders."

"I understand." Reluctantly, she slid back against the stark wall and watched as they hit the appropriate buttons. The gangplank descended and the door snicked open. Sanders, the pilot, cautiously stepped out. Bakon stayed, guarding the ship and her.

Strange scents wafted in, stale fear-sweat and dirt, mechanical lubricants, and astringent cleaning fluids. Her thoughts drifted back in time to Aktariel's warning and she fidgeted uncomfortably, then blurted, "Where's the weapons compartment. I need a pistol."

Bakon looked her up and down. The incredulous expression on his swarthy face said he thought her a little made. "I'll protect you. You don't need—"

"*Nobody* protects me but *me,* mister. Where're the weapons?"

He pointed to a compartment on the far wall. "Help yourself."

She strode across the cabin, palming the control panel. Her gaze went over each weapon. Finally, she selected a pulse pistol and strapped it around her waist. Expertly, she pulled the gun and checked the charge, then tested the balance.

Bakon peered out the entry and nodded, then turned to Rachel. "All clear, Miss Eloel."

From outside, a sweet voice, high with desperation called, *"Mommy?"*

In one swift turn, Rachel raced down the gangplank. The landing bay stood almost empty, except for a series of crates piled three high, and a knot of people standing in the center. Sybil ran toward her breathlessly, brown curls bouncing, eyes enormously wide. Dressed in a long orange robe, she seemed a tiny dagger of flame.

"Sybil?"

"Mommy! Mommy!"

"Oh, baby." She opened her arms and ran, scooping her daughter up, smothering Sybil's face and hair with wet kisses. "I missed you so much."

"I thought you were dead, Mom," Sybil whimpered. She squeezed Rachel's neck like a choking vine. "I tried and tried to get people to take me to you, and nobody would. I was so scared."

"I know, sweetheart. So was I. But it's all right now." She stroked her daughter's hair softly, drowning in the feel of Sybil's warm breath against her throat. "It's all right. I love you. How long have you been here? On the ship?"

"A few hours. Ari and Yosef have been taking care of me."

Sanders, Bakon, Funk, and Calas crowded around them. The soldiers cautiously scanned the landing bay, rifles aimed at nothing in particular.

"It's good to have you home, Rachel," Yosef Calas said gently as he patted her shoulder. He seemed balder and shorter than the last time she'd seen him. His spectacles rode low on his blunt nose, accenting his moist brown eyes. Correspondingly, Funk seemed to have grown six inches, his tall lanky frame adorned by a fuller mop of gray hair. Both were dressed in gray jumpsuits that made them look even older, if that were possible.

Rachel exhaled a tired breath. "I thought Jeremiel was meeting me here." She frowned questioningly at Calas.

He shrugged, lifting his hands. "I thought he was, too. Perhaps he got detained somewhere."

"Perhaps. Well, I'm sure he'll be in contact. Has

anyone arranged a cabin for Sybil and me yet?"

"A security man did," her daughter answered. "It's number 1901. There's a dispenser in the room that shoots cups of tea and soup out at you." Sybil demonstrated with her hands and laughed. The tinkly silver bell sound penetrated clear to Rachel's wounded soul.

She hugged her daughter tightly again, then wiped tears from her cheeks before standing up. "Mister Funk, Mister Calas, thank you for taking such good care of Sybil. If I can ever—"

"Oh, never mind that now," Yosef said, pushing up the spectacles. "Let's get inside where it's warmer."

Rachel's eyes probed the old man's. Worry shadowed his withered face. As they walked, she asked, "Is the situation so bad here?"

"I think so, though Jeremiel doesn't discuss such things in public."

"I remember. Has he contacted his fleet yet?"

"That's another story, I'm afraid. The spaceways seem to have gone very quiet when it comes to the Underground. He can't even reach his units on Tikkun." Yosef gripped her elbow paternally, leading her toward the exit.

Rachel gratefully allowed him to guide her through a small foyer, into a transportation tube for a few seconds, then down a long white hall. People in a variety of uniforms and tattered multicolored clothing raced around, anxious looks on their faces. Sanders and Bakon brought up the rear, rifles still cradled menacingly in their arms. Sybil clung to her leg in a death grip.

They rounded a corner and Sybil released her mother and charged ahead, short legs pumping as she led the way to cabin 1901. Standing on tiptoe, she hit the patch to open the door. It snicked back and Rachel could see a section of the dim cabin interior.

"Here it is, Mom. Come on! I'll show you how to work the dispenser." Sybil disappeared inside.

Yosef released her arm when they reached the door and looked up at her through adoring elderly eyes. "Go and get reacquainted with your daughter, Rachel. Ari and I are in cabin 1909. Call if you need anything."

"I will, Yosef. I—"

From the edge of her vision, she saw six men round the corner, pistols aimed. Instinctively, she screamed, "Get down!"

Funk threw himself at Calas, knocking the old man to the floor with a dull thud. The shrill whine of rifle fire thundered, casting a deadly luminescent web through the corridor. Sanders collapsed in front of her, head lopped off, throat gushing blood like a hose turned on full.

"Get in your cabin!" Bakon shouted at her.

She tried to back away, but couldn't without turning. One of Sanders' arms blocked her path. She fired insanely at their attackers. Calas and Funk slithered into the cabin. A young man with thinning brown hair charged forward, leaping corpses, shouting, "You killed the Mashiah! In the name of Adom Kemar Tartarus!" His gun lanced the air with an arc of purple.

Bakon pitched backward into her, shoving her against the wall so violently he almost knocked the gun from her hand. Before she lost the cover of his body, Rachel panned the hall, slicing her wild-eyed assassin in half, watching blindly as his upper torso pounded the wall and thudded down the corridor. The remaining men fled, silently, expertly. From within the cabin, she heard Sybil crying, "Mommy? Ari! Let's go help my mom!"

"Sybil, don't move!" Funk ordered sternly.

Hardly breathing, Rachel stared at the fragments of bodies lining the corridor. Blood flowed like a livid river. Stunned by the assassin's words, terrified at what might come next, she stood rigidly, feet braced, pistol trembling in her hands. But no one else stepped into the gruesome corridor. Agonizingly, she waited.

"Rachel?" Yosef called. "Hurry, come inside. Rachel?"

A frail old hand twined in her tan sleeve, pulling her backward. "No, no, wait!" She jerked loose and ran forward, collecting every weapon in the hall, piling them in her left arm.

Then she backed up into the cabin. Dim silver light cascaded over her as she pounded the patch to close the door. Sybil ran forward and hugged her leg.

Yosef gazed at her worriedly. "Sit down, Rachel. I've locked your door. Let me call Jeremiel and find out what's happening."

"Yes. C-call him," she whispered, but couldn't convince herself to sit. Instead, she moved into the center of the room, gaze welded to the door, expecting another madman to burst through it at any moment.

123

He'd told her to be armed. *He'd* warned her . . .

As the full truth dawned, reaction set in and she trembled uncontrollably.

"Rachel," Ari said in a strong voice. "Give me those rifles. You sit down. I'll guard the door."

"No . . . I—I—"

"It's all right. I'm good with guns." He gripped the weapons, prying them from her rigid arm, then helped her to a chair where she sat down. Reluctantly, she put her pistol on the table beside her.

Sybil climbed into her lap and hugged her around the neck. "Mommy, who was shooting at you?"

"I don't know." *Someone who loved Adom.* She clutched Sybil tightly to her breast, kissing her brown curls.

Sybil buried her face in Rachel's long black hair. "I love you, Mom."

Over the table, Yosef keyed in a sequence of numbers and called, "Jeremiel? It's Yosef Calas. Are you in?"

Another voice came from the box, a voice Rachel vaguely recognized. "Yosef? This is Avel Harper. I'm afraid Jeremiel is out on urgent business. We've just had a series of murders on level six. Apparently the old Horebian civil war has been carried to the *Hoyer.* Did you get Rachel safely aboard?"

Yosef looked at her and a deep frown etched his face. "She's safe, but I'm afraid we had similar problems. We were attacked by six men—I don't know who they were. The hall outside her cabin is littered with dead. Please send a security team to guard this corridor."

A brief pause ensued and Rachel heard Harper sigh tensely. "Immediately. Tell Rachel not to set foot outside her door until Jeremiel personally gives her authorization. Understand?"

Yosef looked at her and she nodded once. "We understand. Is there anything else we can do?"

"No. I suspect Jeremiel will be detained for a while. Why don't you tell Rachel to get some sleep. I'm going to try to force Jeremiel to do the same thing before they meet. He's weaving on his feet."

"I think that's a good idea. As soon as the security team arrives, Ari and I will meet you at his cabin. Perhaps together we can convince him."

"I'll welcome the help. Give my best to Rachel and

124

Sybil. I'll see you soon. Harper out."

Yosef palmed the controls and Rachel gazed up at him numbly. Her body, so lit with the fires of adrenaline a few moments ago, had gone stiff and unfeeling as though it belonged to someone else.

"Sybil," Yosef said gently, tugging at her brown curls. "Why don't you fix her some soup?"

Sybil nodded, fear still widening her eyes. "Sure. All right." She slid down from Rachel's lap and ran to the dispenser on the wall, but her gaze stayed glued to her mother.

Silence settled like a leaden blanket over Rachel's shoulders. Ari and Yosef grouped against the far wall, talking in low dread-filled tones. Her gaze drifted aimlessly. A small compact room, the bunk beds took up one entire wall at the back. Beside them, a desk with a computer terminal sat, cursor blinking rhythmically. She vaguely knew how to use computers. She'd run a few on Horeb. The table and two chairs dotted the floor near the entry.

Sybil pulled two cups from the dispenser on the wall and set them on the table, then went back and hit two more buttons.

"Wait till you try this, Mommy. Ari made me eat some about an hour ago. It's good. It'll make you feel better."

A rich odor wafted from the cups on the table. Her hunger had vanished, but she lifted the cup anyway. "It's delicious. What is it?"

"Ari said the Magistrates call it Orion mushroom soup." Sybil looked at Funk and smiled lovingly before looking back. "Mushrooms are little plants that grow in the dark. I guess they grind them up and throw them in water to make the soup."

Carefully, Sybil retrieved two more cups and carried them back to the table, spilling only a little before setting one in front of Rachel. She reached out and caressed her daughter's olive cheek, seeing a scar beneath her left eyebrow. She shook her head. When had Sybil gotten that scar? Odd that she couldn't remember. She knew Sybil's body better than her own. She fought the welling anxiety by turning her attention to the new cup. "What's this?"

"It's just tea, but it tastes kind of like the greasy grass tea we used to make. Except this tastes more like dirt."

125

Rachel tasted the concoction. It had a crystalline flavor as delicate and sweet as spun sugar. "Oh, it's wonderful."

Sybil pulled her chair so close to Rachel that when she sat down, her knees touched her mother's. The stark light of the lustreglobes frosted her orange robe with silver, so that every time she moved, waves undulated visibly over her arms and chest.

". . . too many refugees aboard," she heard Funk whisper.

Calas responded, "Jeremiel can't leave those people on a barren planet. The fire storms are consuming everything."

Rachel tried to imagine what the capital city of Seir must look like. The crimson sandstone ridges must have melted into a smooth glassy sea of blood. Suddenly she felt hot and the scent of death stung her nostrils. Sounds from the holocaust in the square fluttered in her memory, people gasping, crying, an old man screaming madly, "Gamants, listen to me! I see a sea of blood rolling down over us! A sea of burning blood! Don't you see it?" He'd lanced out a hand toward the mountains glimmering maroon with the flames of sunset. "Oh, dear God, dear God, we can't escape!"

She bowed her head. *Prophecies did come true.*

A buzz came from the black box near her door. "Mister Calas? This is Chris Janowitz. Are you in there?"

Yosef briskly walked across the room, palming the entry patch. The door snicked open and a short, stocky blond stood outside, face stern with apprehension. He looked inside at her and then back to Calas. "Any injuries?"

Yosef shook his head and gripped Janowitz's sleeve, hauling him inside. "Just the men in the hall. Come in and meet Rachel Eloel and her daughter Sybil."

Too tired to stand, she simply formed her hands into the sacred triangle of greeting. "Thank you for coming so quickly, Mister Janowitz."

He nodded and returned the symbol of greeting. "I'm sorry we didn't meet you in the bay, ma'am. We had no idea—"

"It's all right. I understand things have been hectic here. Will you be guarding my door all night?"

"My team will. You rest easy, ma'am. They'll be just

outside." He smiled reassuringly and exited into the hall.

Funk and Calas followed him. Before he closed the door, Yosef called, "Rachel, there are twenty guards in this corridor. Don't worry. We'll see you again soon."

Funk winked confidently at Sybil and she winked in return.

"Good night, Yosef."

He smiled paternally. "Good night."

Her door slipped shut and she and Sybil studied each other. "I love you, baby."

"I love you, Mom."

As they finished eating, they stared at each other, basking in one another's gaze, occasionally touching beneath the table to reassure themselves. Finally, when they'd finished, Rachel leaned her head back against the wall and smiled at Sybil. "You're prettier than I remember."

Sybil glowed beneath the praise. "Mom? I haven't seen Jeremiel, but Ari talked to him on the ship's com machine, and he said you're a hero. He wants to give you a medal because you saved thousands of lives on Horeb when you killed the Mashiah."

Rachel's smile faded. Tears filled her eyes. She fought to blink them away before Sybil could see. "Does he?"

"Yes. I'm very proud of you, Mom. Me and everybody else."

Fluttering images of Adom's handsome face tormented her. Their last day together, he'd held her gently in the huge bed in the polar chambers, murmuring tenderly how much he loved her. His frail smile and wide blue eyes had created a space all their own in her soul. *A medal? For murdering an innocent man?*

All the weariness Rachel had been suppressing swelled to an incapacitating burden. "Sweetheart? I think I'm going to take a shower and go to bed. Would you sleep with me if I take the bottom bunk? I want to be able to hold you in my arms, like I used to, before the war."

Sybil finished the last of her tea and jumped to the floor, running to turn down the gray blanket and white sheet beneath. She pulled her orange robe over her head and draped it over the foot of the bed, standing in her T-shirt and panties. "I've been dreaming about holding you, Mom. Maybe I'll finally be able to sleep through the night. For the past few months, I haven't slept very good." She sat on the side of the bed, waiting eagerly.

Rachel pushed up from her chair and smiled, then began undressing, draping her jumpsuit across a chair, and removing the *Mea* from around her throat. She stared at it for a moment, noting its dull, lackluster appearance. Dead, *He'd* said.

Gently, she laid it on the table and walked into the bathroom.

Sybil watched her mother go and heard the water come on, sounding like the patter of rain, then she got up from the bunk and cautiously went to stand beside the necklace. It looked different, but she felt nearly sure it was the same necklace she'd had the *funny* dream about when she'd slept in the caves of the Desert Fathers on Horeb. She remembered talking to Avel Harper about it.

"Have you ever seen a necklace that looks like a lustreglobe, Avel?"

He'd given her a curious smile, mahogany face shining in the light of the fireplace. "No, but it sounds like the infamous *Mea*. Where did you hear about it?"

She hadn't told him, because grown-ups always teased her about her "funny" dreams and made her feel stupid. She cocked her head, staring at the ball. She'd been a lot older in the dream. Her hair had grown long enough to hang to the waist of her ivory robe. The sounds of cannons and squealing rifles filled her ears and she could see the young man with curly black hair putting the *Mea* against his forehead. She'd pressed her forehead to the opposite side and they'd kissed. His lips had felt warm and soft, making her tingle deep inside. A golden man had floated up above them, whispering to Sybil. She remembered because his voice had made her head hurt real bad. And the necklace had glowed so brilliantly between them she'd had to close her eyes.

But this one didn't glow.

Timidly, she extended a finger, tracing a wide circle on the table around the ball. After a few seconds, she got up enough courage to prod it gently. Still, nothing happened. Finally, she picked it up and—as in the dream—pressed it against her forehead while she thought about the young man.

A blue light flashed briefly. She jerked it away, startled. *But in the dream, the light had been good.* When she put the ball back against her forehead, the light flared in a constant flood, splashing the walls with such brilliance they changed from white to a pale glittering blue. And a soft, kind voice called her name.

"Oh!"

Frightened, Sybil dropped the ball back onto the table and ran to crawl beneath the covers of the bed, heart pounding. She stared wide-eyed at it, watching the light die again. In her dream, no one had spoken to her from the ball. And that voice had sounded a little like her dead father.

When her mother finally came out of the bathroom, drying her long black hair with a towel, a lump of fear had formed in Sybil's throat.

"Mom? What's that necklace?"

"Hmm?" She looked to where Sybil pointed. "Oh, it's a . . . just a glass necklace, baby. I wish I didn't own it. It reminds me of the Mashiah." Her voice quivered with that last.

"It's pretty."

"I suppose it is."

Sybil slid to the back of the bed and let her mother curl around her. She pulled the blanket up around her throat and clutched it tightly as she thought. Someday, she'd have her own *Mea* and, on a battlefield far away, she'd use it to stop a war. The dream had told her.

Sybil nervously crushed the blanket beneath her fingers. The warmth of her mother's body felt good against hers, but she couldn't sleep now. The scary voice had called her by her full name, *Sybilline*. Nobody had ever called her that in real life, except her father. And he only called her that when she'd done something bad.

She frowned, thoughts drifting from her father to the young man with black curly hair and back again.

*   *   *

CHAPTER 13

Cole Tahn weakly pushed the gray blanket off his chest and rolled onto his side, blinking at the hazy ceiling. His flesh burned hot with fever. Thirst plagued him. Dim green light from his com terminal lit the overhead panels so that they looked like fuzzy patches of grass. His thoughts drifted to Old Earth, the grass around the Cathedral of Notre Dame. Bodies piled ten feet high around the magnificent structure, blood spattering the ancient stones . . .

"Stop," he commanded himself with as much strength as he could muster. With effort, the wrenching vision dissolved.

He heaved a small sigh of relief. How long had he been out, he wondered? Hours? Days? He recalled a series of vivid hallucinations, dreams which threw him back to the hellholes of Paris, Orillas VII, and Kayan. He took a deep breath and the room swirled around him. He braced a hand against his bedside desk to still it.

"What a . . . headache."

His skull throbbed agonizingly, as if his brain might burst through the sutures at any moment. Gently, he tried to push up on one elbow to reach for his blurry water glass, but the effort sent his mind tumbling, thought after thought, memory after memory. From the corner of his eye, he saw his door slip open. A long rectangle of bright light slid into the room. He blinked and fell back to his sweat-soaked sheets. Closing his eyes, he struggled to control the cascading images.

"Are you finally awake?" Halloway called irreverently.

"You don't . . . sound happy about it."

He pried an eye open; even that hurt hellaciously. A nebulous purple splotch wavered near his door.

"Oh, but I am. Now I can stop wasting energy cursing you."

130

"Glad to . . . to finally be of some use. How long . . . how long has it been?"

"Since the takeover? Forty hours and twenty-two minutes."

Carey methodically went around the room, dragging a chair with her, checking every monitor, undoubtedly disconnecting each. He closed his eyes and listened to her quiet movements.

"Don't you think . . . Baruch . . . will catch on?"

"Certainly. But for now we're safe." She moved closer, the purple splotch hovering over his bed. He squinted and thought he could make out the shape of her face. Her eyes looked more red than green.

"You look like hell," he commented conversationally.

"Probably because I've been slaving to kill a dozen spies and their cohorts, keep a hysterical crew under control, maneuver around a herd of insane Gamants, and deal with the worry I've harbored about you."

He smiled. "Hand me my water glass?"

She sat on the edge of his bed, sliding an arm beneath his shoulders to gently lift him. Then he felt the glass touch his lips and he drank greedily. Liquid spilled from the corners of his mouth to run coolly over his bare chest. He finished it and let his head fall back against her arm.

"Better?"

He nodded, but as she pulled her arm from beneath his shoulders, his mind tumbled again. Confused memories telescoping, coming close and fading away. Where was he? Suddenly, he couldn't remember. He shook his head, struggling to recall. In the background he heard the shrill whine of cannon fire.

"Cole, are you all right?"

"Daryl?" Paris. 5407. Daryl Williston, his voice had sounded a little like that before a cobalt mortar landed on top of him.

"No, Captain. It's Carey."

Images of yellow skies filled with airborne dust pulsed behind his closed eyes. He could smell the vile metallic odors of ionized air and blood. Williston gave him a look of utter terror. "Daryl, get the *hell* out of here! I gave you a direct order. What do you—"

Explosion. Dirt cascading. Someone screaming . . .

"Captain. Do you remember that Jeremiel Baruch captured the *Hoyer?"*

"Baruch?" His mind struggled to sort images of war in the Akiba system from those on Old Earth. "He . . . he what?"

"He took our ship."

Not Daryl. A female voice, it rang with such foreboding, it brought him back. He shuddered, twining fingers in his damp blanket. The landing bay . . . Baruch smashing him again and again with his pistol . . . trap, *ambush* . . . first alert sirens ringing . . . Carey's hard voice demanding, "Cole? *Cole!* We've got to get out of here!"

"I remember—Carey."

"Good. Lie still. We've got a doctor coming in about ten minutes to take a look at you."

"Doctor? But I thought . . . When Baruch decompressed—"

"Yes, they're all dead," she said matter-of-factly. "He's sending us a doctor from his own staff. Somebody named Severns."

He threw her a cockeyed look. "Search him . . . before he touches me, all right?"

"Don't worry, Cole. Baruch assured me he wanted to kill you himself."

Bizarrely, he felt like laughing. But he figured it would kill him, so he didn't. "How's the crew?"

She shrugged, puffing a taut breath. "Not well. I had to order the screens on the bridge turned off. Every time we cross the path of the decompression, Hera keeps searching the bodies outside for Kevin."

Hera's husband had worked in Security on level eighteen, surrounded by a dozen major hatches. He'd almost certainly been sucked out.

"Carey? What's the crew . . . thinking about me?" Even in his haze and pain, he'd been worried to death about that. Surely the ones who'd lost family would be blaming him, praying he'd die. When he was able to take control again, would they obey his commands?

"They're worried, Cole. Some of them aren't sure they can trust your judgment. But most of them are with you. *I'm with you.* You know that."

"I . . . I know that."

With hushed violence Carey demanded, "Goddamn it, Cole, what are we going to do? To kill the Clandestine moles I made a deal with Baruch that our people would willingly comply with his orders. Our—"

132

"Good. You . . . should have."

"But it scares me to death. Our techno-science division is training his people. He's got two thousand civilians crawling all over our ship and he's bringing up more. *What are our options?*"

Pain ran rampant through his mind, images of flashing rifles and dying crew bursting wide. He sucked in a deep breath. "What actions . . . have you . . ."

She stood up and started pacing. "I sabotaged the long-range com link, but I suspect he'll find the problem soon."

"Maybe not. If somebody . . . trans and can't—"

"I'm praying that happens. But we can't count on the cavalry coming over the hill."

"Can you get . . . to level seven?"

"He's forbidden it so far."

"What about Dannon? Did he . . . did he survive?"

She stopped pacing to stare down at him. "Did you want him to?"

"Not really. I just . . . thought he might come in handy." Everybody on board despised Neil Dannon, but Tahn had special reasons for hating his guts.

Carey started to laugh, a strange, near desperate sound. Since he felt the same way, he chuckled with her—and instantly regretted it. His head felt as though it would shatter like a glass vase dropped from a five-story building. "Carey . . . when possible . . . get to seven . . . to Millhyser. Get . . . get organized."

"I will. We've already arranged a roundabout course of message delivering. I'll have Macey slip data through to Phil Cohen or someone."

"Good."

He thought he saw Carey run a hand through her hair, but it was a splotch on splotch movement so he couldn't be sure. Her voice came out soft, strained. "I've missed you, Cole."

He smiled warmly. "Glad to be back." He tried to reach up and pour himself another glass of water, but his hand shook too badly.

"Let me do that for you." She walked over and he heard the splash of water. Gently, she lifted his head again, tipping the glass to his lips. He drank and drank until he emptied it.

"I should probably let you get back to sleep." She eased his head back against his pillow and stood. "I'll go to the bridge. The doctor will be here any minute."

"Carey? You . . . scared?"

"Terrified."

"Don't be. Baruch . . . may have taken . . . *Hoyer*, but he can't . . . can't hold her."

"I think you're right. If he keeps bringing up more Gamants, it won't be long until he overloads the *Hoyer*'s systems. When his people are going hungry and can't get enough water, tensions will rise. He'll have his hands full just managing his own refugees' quarrels. And it won't be long until Palaia realizes we haven't called in to report the completion of our Horeb assignment. We might be dead before they get here, but—"

"No . . . we won't."

She took a deep breath and spread her feet, looking like she'd just braced herself for hand-to-hand combat. "You have more faith in the Magistrates than I do."

A treasonous tone flamed in her voice. Damn, why did she do that to him so often lately? It set him on edge and she knew it, ringing like an ominous warning bell inside him. He lay still, thinking, until he felt the silence so desperately, he knew he had to get up, to get the crew organized himself. He pushed up on his elbows and a sharp pain nearly fragmented his skull. He fell back weakly, thoughts rolling, jumbling, pieces of images swirling, slips of different voices shouting. . . .

Carey watched him writhing and her heart pounded. She shouldn't have come. But she'd needed to talk to him, to bolster her own flagging spirits.

"Maggie?" Tahn called frantically. "Don't . . . don't leave me." He feebly lifted a hand, reaching out.

Carey felt like she intruded on some private memory. But she couldn't force herself to leave him in this condition. She'd wait with him until the doctor came. Resolutely, she walked to his liquor cabinet. Removing a bottle of scotch and a glass, she poured herself a stiff drink and looked down at him. His pale face contorted against the pain. "This is a hell of a mess we're in, Cole."

She paced anxiously, distracting herself by wondering who Maggie was? Some lost lover? She knew Tahn's open personnel record nearly as well as her own, but they didn't put things like that in open files. Thank God. If they did, somebody might know about the corporal who'd dumped her in Academy and how she'd damn near fallen to pieces over it. Curious, she thought sarcastically, that Tahn's memories would trigger her own of Buchard Mead. Bucky. Sonofabitch.

She took a strong belt of scotch. It burned a pathway down her throat, warming her mangled stomach. From the hallway, a loud thud rang. She whirled, heart in her throat. Probably cleanup crews washing the corridor, but in Tahn's mind they came from some distant memory.

"No!" he screamed. "No! Don't! *Oh, God,* Annum. *Not . . . our fault! Com malfunction. We . . . Let me . . . let me talk to Slothen himself, damn it!*" He raised his hands to his head, squeezing hard as he tossed from side to side.

"Cole! Stop it! You're on the *Hoyer*. You're safe!" What a lie that was.

"*Hoyer?*"

"Yes, your ship. We're still circling the godforsaken planet of Horeb."

He shook his head, as though clearing the feverish mental fog. "No. No. . . . Oh, God. Even if we . . . Pegasus . . ."

He turned toward her and the soft pained look in his usually hard eyes made her feel like he'd ripped her guts out. Vague memories of the name, *Annum*, tried to stir, but she couldn't place it. However, she knew quite well what he meant by the Pegasus Invasion. He'd spent six months in a rehab center after he'd crawled out of his torture cage, unable to sleep a full night without waking screaming. The Magistrates had given him a commendation letter accompanying his promotion to captain: "For uncommon courage and indomitable will," it had said. She'd often wondered specifically what had happened to him, but the psych files had been closed by Slothen's personal order. Had this concussion tapped into those forbidden neural pathways? It might be dangerous for all of them if it had.

"Cole," she assured him, "you're not on Earth. The year is 5414. Calm down."

"No, I . . . I'm so frightened, Maggie. Glatzer has filed charges. I—I don't. . . . *Hold me?*"

He weakly lifted his arms out to her. She put her glass down and sat on his bedside again, hugging his shoulders. "You're safe, Cole. Get some sleep."

135

He tightened his arms around her back and feebly pulled her against his bare chest, tenderly rubbing his chin in her hair. "Never safe . . . no . . . never. *Annum* . . . *Annum*."

Drained from his outburst, he blinked wearily, drifting off. His arms slowly slid back to his sides. Carey got up and reached for her scotch, downing the entire glassful. Then she poured herself another and resumed her pacing. What the hell was the *Annum*? And why did it disturb him so? Would he be stable enough to command after the doctor treated him? How would he perform under pressure?

Halloway shook her head. After several minutes and another healthy belt of scotch, the com rang. She strode to answer it and grimaced when the door snicked back.

Baruch loomed tall and hard-eyed in the entryway. A shorter man stood behind him, a bag beneath his arm. "Lieutenant," Baruch greeted. "How's the captain?"

"Pretty damned bad, Commander."

"Severns," he ordered, "see what you can do."

The Underground leader walked inside and stood out of the way as the doctor went to Tahn's beside. Carey met and held Baruch's stern gaze. He looked rested, as though he'd had at least a few hours of sleep. Behind her, she heard Tahn whimper and her heart ached.

"Maggie?" Cole lifted a hand feebly. "No . . . no, reach . . . farther. I can almost touch. . . . Don't! I—I need you. I—"

"It's all right," the doctor soothed. "Calm down. You're going to be all right."

"No! *Let me go!* Don't . . . not the probes. Dear God, *please.* No more! I can't . . . *Maggie!*"

Carey shifted uncomfortably. Baruch had no right, *no right,* to see Tahn like this. She gazed up at him through fiery eyes, but he looked over her shoulder to Tahn's bed. The hard set of his jaw slackened and she saw a swallow bob in his throat. He lowered his gaze suddenly, glaring uneasily at the floor. Softly, he said, "I'll come back later."

He turned and left in a dark smear of black battlesuit.

She lifted her chin, blindly contemplating the closed door. What had he felt? she wondered. His expression had betrayed deep grudging emotion.

"Lieutenant?" the doctor called.

"Yes?"

"Could you stay with the captain for a half hour or so? I've given him a rather large dose of uro-steroids. I'd like someone to monitor him to assure he doesn't have an adverse reaction."

"I'll stay."

"Good. I'll be on level three with your other injured soldiers if you need me."

"Thank you, Doctor."

Severns nodded and packed up his bag. He strode past her, disappearing into the hallway.

Carey studied Cole. He'd quieted down, though his breathing still came erratically. "You all right, Cole?" she whispered.

No answer. Idly, she wandered around his cabin, picking up one object, then another. Tahn's cabin brimmed with unique items from a variety of worlds, many Gamant in origin. She retrieved a small tapestry, beautifully woven in shades of blue and white and held it up to the light.

"From Jumes. When did you get this, Cole?" she asked almost inaudibly. "Before or after we destroyed the planet?"

The face of the little girl in the hallway rose in Carey's mind. She heard again those pathetic suffocating cries and her stomach knotted. Hastily, she put the tapestry down.

CHAPTER 14

Ari leaned over the table, grimacing down at the plate of food the stewards had just delivered. Their cabin glowed warmly with candles they'd found in the supplies index. He glanced up hopefully at Yosef. "Do you know what it is?"

"Taste it. You're brave."

"Not me. I don't eat anything gray."

Yosef lifted a utensil and cautiously poked at the "meat." Slicing off a miniscule piece, he put it in his mouth and forced it down his throat, unchewed. "It tastes like . . . no, never mind. That wouldn't help matters." A trickle of red seeped out from the wounded steak, draining with unnatural viscosity across his plate.

Ari watched the trickle critically. "Well," he huffed. "At least it looks like it was alive once."

"A philosophical conclusion, I'm sure."

Yosef sighed and got to his feet. Grabbing Ari's plate and his own, he carried them across the bright cabin and unceremoniously dumped the contents into the wall compactor.

Ari lifted his knife and gestured rudely with it. "You should have saved a specimen. That way we could have gone and demanded what it was and who was responsible for it."

"Don't be stupid. Somebody might answer."

Dejectedly, Yosef waddled back to the table and flopped into his chair again. His gaze darted around their cabin, landing on the pile of empty beer bottles collecting beneath Ari's bed. "Well, you know what it means, don't you?"

"The kitchen crews have been pared down to nothing. Jeremiel can't help it. A place like the kitchen has to be staffed by trustworthy people."

"Arsenic-laced food might taste better than tonight's dinner."

"Not for long enough to make it count."

Yosef looked at him over the rim of his spectacles, then frowned disconsolately. "How much longer do you think we'll be here? I hate ships. They're all white and smell antiseptic." He longed for the familiar fragrances of ripe barley and wet leaves.

"Jeremiel said we should be finished rescuing refugees in a couple of days." He reached across the table to pat Yosef's forearm comfortingly. "We'll be home soon."

"Home?" He winced at the sound of his own voice: like a five-year-old who rips open a beautiful gift at Chunuk and finds the box empty. "I'm not sure where that is anymore, Ari."

"You don't want to go back to Tikkun?"

"I don't know." He shook his head forlornly. Images of his little house on Mandean Street flickered through

138

his mind, the trees shading crimson and gold with autumn's strength. Homesickness overcame him. He threw up his hands miserably. "I have to find some place safe to take Mikael."

"Is he still out from that drug they gave him?"

"Yes, I checked in on him just before dinner. He was having another nightmare. Jeremiel was there. We talked for a few minutes. He said it was the second time he'd tried—you know, as a formality, Baruch feels he should be one of the first people to greet the new leader of Gamant civilization. Jeremiel said he couldn't understand why Mikael hadn't awakened yet. It worried him—and me."

Ari waved a hand. "Don't let it. After what that boy went through on Kayan, he probably needs a week of sleep."

"What planet can I take him to, Ari? Where can we live without worrying the Magistrates will fly over the horizon and kill us all?"

Ari sighed expressively and stretched his long legs across the carpet. "Tikkun may be all right. We don't know—"

"Then why haven't Jeremiel's bases there contacted him yet?"

"Who knows. It could be anything."

"It could be that they're all dead."

Ari gazed at him levelly and into those faded gray eyes rose a flame of battle. In the flutters of candlelight he looked like a fierce gray mop. His withered face underwent a slow metamorphosis, as though Yosef had lifted a fist and shouted, "Thou shalt see me at Phillipi!"

"Well, if that's so, then you won't have to worry about a safe planet for Mikael—because the only safe place will be in a cruiser surrounded by a dozen others. There'll be a full-scale Revolt, Yosef. It might take the people of Tikkun months to get the courage, but they'll kill every Magisterial soldier alive—or die trying."

A sharp ache invaded Yosef's heart. He looked around the white cabin, going over the gray carpet and gray blankets, the white and black furniture. He felt he'd suffocate. "Pray God spares us that."

* * *

The 6th of Tishri, 5414

Jasper opened the gate and plodded up the narrow dirt

walkway toward his grandson's home. Noon sunlight streamed down through the latticework of the wrought iron canopy over the porch, landing in searing patches of molten gold on the brown tiles beneath.

Jasper wiped his tennis shoes and rang the bell, inhaling the dry sweet smells of autumn. Salome trees in full color lined the winding street like a twisting amber and ruby necklace. Leaves showered the ground with every strong gust of wind, cartwheeling over dying lawns and into the streets.

"Coming!" he heard Pavel yell and in a few short moments his grandson appeared at the door, bearded face flushed, black hair awry. Dressed in blue pants and a black shirt, he looked hot. "Grandpa! Come in. Why didn't you call to tell me you'd be early? I'd have gotten some beer or—"

"You haven't got any beer? I'm going home."

He started to turn and walk away, but Pavel gripped his white sleeve and dragged him back, smiling reproachfully.

"I have two cans. After that, you're on your own."

Jasper shrugged. "Okay."

He stepped through the front door into the parlor. It was a broad sunny room spreading twenty by twenty-five feet. A tan leather couch and two matching chairs squatted against the wall to his left. On his right, a long table with eight chairs sat. An oval rug sporting geometric designs in blue and gold covered the center of the wood floor.

Jasper strolled to the couch and dropped down in a brilliant patch of sunlight; it set the silver threads in his white shirt glimmering. "Where's Yael?"

"She's in the backyard. She brought young Jonas Wallace home to play this afternoon, to help her celebrate her great report card."

Jasper nodded. Yael, twelve, was retarded, but the Magisterial doctors on Tikkun made no attempt to correct the problem—though every non-Gamant child suffering the same problem had long ago been fixed. The government took Gamant children like Yael and put them in classes learning useless things like coloring and ceramics. Jasper roughly brushed off his pant leg. "Where's your father? I thought he was coming early to get that fancy dessert of his started?"

Pavel spread his arms a little forlornly. A veil of sunlit dust swam with his movements. "You know how he is when he gets caught up with weddings or funerals. Everything else fades from his mind."

Jasper pursed his lips, drumming his bony fingers on the warm back of the couch. Blast Toca! In his entire life, he'd never known his son to be on time for any family gathering. Outsiders, his "flock," always came first. He glanced at Pavel and saw the small lines of hurt etching a web around his dark eyes.

"Was it a joining or a burying."

"Burying. And, too," Pavel hurriedly explained, "he had some business to take care of in the city. Major Lichtner called him in to talk."

"Lichtner? That military pimple brain? About what?"

"I don't know. We'll have to ask . . ."

Pavel stopped. From outside came the sound of the gate slamming. "I didn't forget!" Toca's voice penetrated the room. "I'm coming." He burst through the front door, breast heaving. Tall, his hair had grown sparse and gray, but the fire in his black eyes still blazed. Herringbone wrinkles deeply lined his face. Dressed all in black, the silver triangle around his neck shone brightly. "You've been bad-mouthing me anyway, I suppose."

"You deserved it!" Jasper tormented. "You think a corpse is more important than a breathing granddaughter?"

Toca's mouth tightened in guilt—a practiced look Jasper had seen a thousand times, designed to make his accusers recant and plead for mercy.

"Well," Toca said apologetically. "I didn't mean—"

"Don't bore us. Pavel and I have heard this same story too many times to buy it. Who died?"

A twinge of real shame reddened Toca's cheeks which made Jasper feel better. Pavel gave him a look of suppressed amusement.

"Old Benjamin Powe. And he couldn't have had a better send-off. Lots of tears and wailing. The line of autos following the hearse to the graveyard stretched for miles."

"Of course it did. He owed everybody money," Jasper noted irreverently, contemplatively studying the dirt under his fingernails. "His debtors were probably hoping

141

to corner the family before they could get away with dignity."

Toca gave him a disgruntled look, then walked to the couch and dropped down on the other side. From the backyard, sweet high giggles rose.

Pavel smiled. "Jonas came to play with Yael."

"Ah . . ." Toca nodded in understanding. "Well, let me see this spectacular report card? Where is it?"

"In my room. I framed it and hung it on the wall. I'll get it." Pavel ran out of the room and down the long hall, steps echoing.

Jasper eyed his son seriously and Toca frowned. "So you went to talk to Lichtner? What did that idiot want?"

"Oh, nothing very important, Papa. The Magistrates are initiating a registration program. Starting tomorrow, they're setting up temporary offices all over the city. We each have to report."

"Report what?"

Pavel trotted back in the room and handed Toca the framed card. Standing with his hands on his hips, he waited for his father's response. Toca glanced admiringly down, then gave Pavel a broad smile. "She's the smartest girl in school. I've always known it. What did her teacher—"

"Report what?" Jasper pressed. Fear had risen to thump a little out of time with his heart.

"What's going on?" Pavel inquired, taking the frame back and setting it on the table.

"Oh." Toca waved a hand in irritation. "Papa's upset because the Magistrates are starting a registration program. We each have to go in and report our names and addresses. We also have to provide a list of our whereabouts, twenty-four hours a day, for the next two weeks straight."

Pavel shook his head. "That's crazy. What if we don't know? I haven't the vaguest idea what I'll be doing tomorrow night."

"You'd better. Any errors or omissions will be punishable by imprisonment. They're serious."

"Registration?" Jasper whispered to himself. Long-forgotten memories rose to choke him. The Magistrates had done the same thing before the last Revolt. He remembered. All Gamants had been required to update

their whereabouts daily. A chill climbed his spine. He looked fearfully at Toca. "What for?"

Toca blinked, a little taken aback by his vehemence. "They say they're afraid Baruch's forces might be going to attack Tikkun and they want to be able to evacuate the populace efficiently if the time comes."

Pavel groused, "Jeremiel would never attack civilians! Instead, they should be evacuating their military installations."

"What does it matter?" Toca asked. "So we go somewhere and put our names down in a book? What's so terrible about that?"

Jasper's face contorted in anger. He exchanged a deeply disturbing look with Pavel and stabbed a finger into Toca's chest. "I'll tell you what's so terrible. They can find us any time they want, day or night, that's what."

"So?"

"For the sake of God!" Jasper shouted, leaning forward to stare nose to nose with Toca. "Are you brain-dead? The Magistrates just killed another Gamant planet. They're burning our businesses to ashes and now they're demanding we register and you can't see the danger?"

Toca leaned back in defense. "What are you talking about? Another Gamant planet?"

"Losacko told me days ago that Kayan got scorched."

"I don't believe it. He misunderstood the message."

"The hell he did! The Magistrates are out to kill all of us and it will damn sure make it easier if they know where we are every moment of the day and night. I won't register!"

In the silence, Jasper glared out the window. People leisurely strolled by on the street, some laughing, others holding the hands of children and talking. The crimson leaves of the trees suddenly seemed forebodingly red. He felt acutely the warm wind that brushed the back of his neck like a warning hand.

Toca's thick gray brows lowered. "You have to register. If you don't, they won't let you—"

"*I won't!*"

143

CHAPTER 15

Carey Halloway brushed auburn hair behind her ears and braced her elbows on her desk. The utter darkness of her cabin wrapped around her like a silken burial gown.

"I've got to do something."

All the moments in her life when she'd ever been ill with fear came back to her, their horror magnified a thousand times. Her com screen flared in blue, the flashing cursor sending a spurt of color over her five times a second. The title page of the file read, *"Pegasus Invasion:* Annum *Incident Inquiry."* Her eyes rested on Cole's name and the charges against him. For a timeless moment, she just sat still, feeling the wintry chill of her cabin against her bare arms. Every tiny sound seemed louder, the shhh of air from the cooling vent, the hammering of her heart, the barely audible male voices in the hall outside.

Finally, when she could bear it no longer, she shoved her chair back and got to her feet, circumnavigating her cabin like a dazed sleepwalker.

It had happened twenty years ago. Cole had been a rookie lieutenant, just out of Academy, graduating number two in a class of over four thousand. His specialty: singularity engineering. His first assignment had been aboard the starcruiser, *Annum.* Less than a year after shipping out, the *Annum* had been frantically redirected to Old Earth to protect the planet from Pegasan invaders who sought to enslave the native population to operate the lethal and highly profitable neuro-gas wells on the planet of Lad.

The fighting had been insane, cruisers dying by the dozens. During the seventh month, the *Annum* had been hit hard—the ship virtually cut in half. Communications between halves had ceased. Cole had been stationed in Engineering, fighting to contain the reaction in the old style singularity tapper engines. His report claimed the heat gauges showing the status of the primordial black holes had climbed to level five: "extreme danger," singularities on the verge of complete evaporation. He'd signaled Top Alert and ordered his crew into the nearest pod. He tried for another hour, alone, to contain the mass deterioration. Then he'd climbed into that pod with his crew and jettisoned, hurling through space to land in the midst of hot fighting in France. He'd been immediately recruited to command a ground unit and performed "with superior valor." A year later, he was captured.

Moments after he'd jettisoned, however, a Pegasan special forces team had boarded the *Annum,* killing the captain and taking the ship. The engines, apparently, were not as threatened as Cole had thought. The war had lasted for another two years, until Magisterial forces crushed the invasion and the surviving remnants of the *Annum*'s crew were returned. The Magistrates immediately set up a board of inquiry to determine whose negligence had resulted in the loss of the *Annum.* First Lieutenant Glatzer, second in command, had charged that Tahn's assessment of the engines was in error and his abandonment of the ship had left it defenseless, unable to access the weaponry, directly resulting in the takeover. Cole had defended himself vehemently, reciting the sequence of events in excruciating detail, claiming there must have been a computer malfunction. His crew had supported him to the last man. Though Slothen's report termed him a "brilliant young hothead," he'd declined to prosecute, citing Cole's valiant performance in France as evidence of the youth's competence and value to the service.

A week later, the rest of the Annum*'s crew had been marched to the nearest neurophysiology center and spent weeks undergoing intense mind probing to find out what really happened, who made errors and why.* No definitive conclusions were ever arrived at, but the crew came out of it irreparably damaged, critical centers of their brains destroyed. The government had housed them in institutions until they mercifully died.

Carey stood rooted, bare feet tingling from cold, staring blindly at the magnificent holo of the Teton Mountains on Old Earth that covered half the wall by her door. The towering snow-capped peaks shimmered coral in the first rays of dawn. Above them, a battle cruiser gleamed like a polished silver triangle. The holo had a presence, a power—just like the *Hoyer* and her captain.

The *Annum* had been the last ship in the Magisterial fleet to succumb to enemy takeover—the last before the *Hoyer*. No telling what Slothen would do to them when he discovered their predicament. Would he reconsider his verdict of Cole's innocence in the *Annum* Incident? He might, and that fact had to be tormenting Cole at this very moment. Slothen would demand to know where they'd blundered, what went wrong, who they'd underestimated, and why. What if the ship's log didn't give it to them? *The* Annum*'s log hadn't.*

"Don't jump to conclusions!" she raged at herself. "Things are different now. The *Annum* didn't have our sophisticated computer recording system. Our logs *will* tell the Magistrates most of what they need to know. They won't have to do any deep probing."

And if they do it anyway—as punishment?

She tucked her freezing fingers beneath her arms as she paced, frowning hard at the gray carpet. She wished she could access the com security system to see for herself what Slothen would find, but Baruch had cut it off. Thank God he hadn't seen any threat in the supplementary personnel files or she'd have never been able to access the data on the *Annum*.

"Damn it. *Damn it!*"

The only way to make sure the crew, including herself, stayed healthy was to win back their ship. Otherwise, the instant Baruch put them groundside, the Magistrates would pick them up, order an inquiry . . . and haul them kicking and screaming to the nearest neuro center. At least, she'd go kicking.

If they could regain the ship before the Magistrates got wise to their current predicament, Baruch would make a superb prize to appease any dismay they might experience after they discovered what had happened.

But how the hell could they defeat Baruch? Tahn's mental state still reeled precariously, though he seemed better, able to hold longer conversations. She couldn't rely on him yet. Which meant she'd have to handle the major burden of planning the assault herself. It left her nauseous.

"Where are your weaknesses, Baruch? Do you have

any? Goddamn it, do you?"

She wandered her cabin for another two hours, laying out one line of attack, then another, then backtracking and redefining the first. None of it worked—Baruch would guess her strategy before she'd completed the first maneuvers.

Glaring at the dark ceiling panels, she clenched her fists. What in the name of God could she do to incapacitate . . . A hot flush of adrenaline rushed through her as her thoughts shifted. "Oh. . . . Maybe. Just maybe."

She ran back across the room, dropping heavily into her desk chair. The cursor pounded in time with her heartbeat. "Computer, correlate all known data on Syene Pleroma. Highlight personal habits and emotional traits. I want to know *everything:* what her laugh sounded like, her perfume, the way she walked."

A picture of a beautiful, athletic woman filled her screen. Long brown hair was pulled back behind her ears, draping in luxurious waves down the front of her black battlesuit. Carey's eyes riveted on the woman's expression; it was as frail and fine as a porcelain doll, eyes wide with vulnerability.

* * *

Gen Abruzzi glared at the forward screen. They'd slipped out from behind the sun and had gotten a faint picture of the *Hoyer*. It gleamed like a winged silver bird as it circled Horeb. Even from their distant location, Abruzzi could tell Tahn hadn't completed his scorch attack.

He ran a hand beneath the woolly gray hair at the base of his skull, massaging the taut muscles. "Tenon, you're sure those ships coming up from the surface of the planet aren't ours?"

"From the mass readings, some of them are. But most are too small to be of Magisterial construction."

"Planetary ships? *Doing what?*"

Tenon got out of her chair and walked slowly up to stand beside him. Her flaxen skin and short black hair shone silken in the bright light. Together they studied the faraway images. Horeb blazed with a marmalade sheen beneath the fires of the midday sun. "The only thing I can imagine that would take so many trips is if they're shuttling refugees."

He swallowed down a parched throat. His dark palms

had gone clammy. "Blast. We might need help. See if you can contact Erinyes, but let me do the talking. We'll play this one close to the chest."

"And Palaia? I don't think Slothen will take kindly to our going maverick and intervening without orders."

He breathed a long exhale, nodding reluctantly. "Tran Palaia. Request guidance on our next course of action."

"Aye, sir." She nodded to Jylo Weri, the communications officer.

Abruzzi bounced anxiously on his toes while he waited for the reply.

CHAPTER 16

Rachel moaned softly in her sleep, trying to rise, to run, but she seemed to be wrapped in a straitjacket of nightmare. Adom's handsome face hung above the rest, watching, forgiving, as dozens of other scenes flashed. All the people she'd fought against on Horeb, the men who'd murdered her husband and tried to murder her and Sybil, now walked the corridors of the *Hoyer*. And they still wanted to kill her. But now, in space, she had no vast empty desert to run to for shelter. She tried to turn over but couldn't move. What could she do? Where could she go to escape? Her stomach knotted so agonizingly she could think of nothing but the pain.

In a swirling wash of warmth, a hazy void enveloped her, glittering like gold dust, curling around her dreams in a lover's strong embrace. Tears of relief traced down her cheeks. For an indefinable time, she simply floated on the undulating waves of warmth, letting them soothe her inner aches and the persistent fear that tore her apart. Then Ornias' tanned face appeared and her body went rigid. A cruel smile lit his . . .

A gentle voice penetrated her terror, bright and soft as eiderdown shining in the sun. "You're safe, Rachel. Sleep. Just sleep. We'll talk in an hour or so."

148

She fought to wake. Her soaked blanket pressed coarsely against her chest. She struggled, fighting to find a way out of the peace and warmth. Her arms and legs went numb. Terror began to beat a thrumming chorus in her heart. It lasted until she felt dizzy.

"Just go away."

"I can't. I have something important to tell you. But it doesn't have to be now. I can wait until—"

"I don't want to hear anything you have to say!"

"Not even if it means saving a quarter of a million Gamant lives?"

Indecision twisted like a knife in her stomach. She strained against the warmth of the glittering void, wanting it, hating it. All the while, the rhythmic movements caressed her tormented soul like a huge tender hand.

"What do you want?" she demanded.

"Tikkun is in trouble. In a matter of days, the Magistrates will be dispatching five cruisers to aid in suppression efforts there. Jeremiel needs to know so he can think about it. Mention the long-range link to him. He'll need to monitor—"

"What is that?"

"Just tell him. He'll understand."

"Why does it matter? He has enough problems trying to figure out what to do with Horebian refugees. He can't do anything for Tikkun."

"Give him the chance."

The haze danced around her. A warm womb outside of time, she let herself bask in the tingling sensations of bliss and oneness. She felt safe, beyond anyone's harmful reach.

His patient voice echoed. "Never believe that, Rachel. We're always in Epagael's reach. So long as this universe exists."

She flinched, almost waking. *"I'm not ready to give you an answer yet."*

"I know. I didn't press, did I?"

"No, but—"

"Then don't worry about it. Soon, when you're more receptive, I'll take you away from here, to a place where we can talk unfettered, and I'll answer all the questions you want to ask me. But for now, can I teach you some things? They're pleasant. They won't disturb your rest and you won't understand the equations anyway."

149

"Equations? About what?"

"Redemption. They're called the Treasures of Light. Regardless of your answer to me, someday soon you'll need them."

She hesitated, not certain she wanted to know, but after the attack in the corridor, fear prompted her. *"What are they?"*

He paused a long moment, letting her drift on the soothing waves of nothingness. The golden haze seemed to penetrate every pore, filtering inside her to fill her so completely she could almost lose herself, almost escape the imprisonment of her own flesh and soar like the formless wind.

"Sleep, Rachel. Go deep, deeper than you've ever gone. Find that one place inside that always listens. Deeper, deeper. Yes. There. Good. Listen, now. *Listen very carefully, Rachel-Sophia, for this is what you have done and must do. It is what you are and are not yet. I want you to repeat these words. . . ."*

His voice lilted and she heard the words, but didn't understand them. Still, she floated through the melody, whispering the strange musical sentences as he'd instructed: *"I am the riches of the Light. I walked in the depth of the Darkness, and I persevered until I attained to the middle of the prison, to the foundations of Chaos where I stood next to the white pillar of light: Jachin. On my left, stood the shadowy pillar of darkness: Boaz. Upon each sat a celestial ball of divine energy. I took one of the sapphires, a sacred stone formed of heavenly dew from the Treasury of Light, and threw it into the abyss. . . ."*

* * *

Sybil woke, frightened. She curled into a tight ball on her top bunk, pulling the covers over her head like a suit of armor as she listened to the strange words her mother spoke. What did they mean? She'd been in the middle of a *funny* dream before her mother's voice startled her. Scenes still drifted in her mind. Huge ships swooped through yellow skies, flying over a city filled with tall pointed buildings. She'd been standing next to a little boy in a big lavender room with beautiful pictures on the walls. The boy's voice had mixed with her mother's, forming a strange scary sound in her mind.

"Aktariel . . . let me go," her mother whispered.

Sybil squeezed her eyes closed so hard the lids hurt. A

horrifying thought dawned. Was her mother having *funny* dreams, too? Did the wicked Aktariel have something to do with her and the little boy and the lavender room with pretty pictures? She'd always thought God sent people funny dreams. Was Epagael trying to tell her something? Her mother called to Aktariel again and Sybil felt sick.

She slid deeper under her blankets until her feet thudded against the metal rail at the bottom. Twining fists in the sheet, Sybil pulled it down over her mouth and cried softly.

* * *

Mikael woke and blinked lazily at the ceiling above him. The dim silver light gave the overhead panels an opalescent sheen like frosted glass under water. He'd been dreaming about yellow skies and those funny rocks, called the Horns of the Calf. In his dream, Metatron had come to him and they'd talked about how to win the war that raged on the plains below. It had been a funny talk, because all through it, Mikael's head had hurt, as though Metatron's voice did funny things to his brain. He reached up to run fingers through his black hair.

How long had the shot made him sleep? He remembered that his grandfather had come to him and told him he had to sleep longer than Captain Tahn had wanted—that it was important or a lot of people would die. So he'd played with his grandfather for hours on the floor of his chamber on Kayan, listening to story after story about Jekutiel and the *Mea* and ships coming out of whirlwinds to destroy bad people. He'd crawled through the rain-drenched forests, smelling the earth and pine, making forts behind fallen logs. Being home again had made him happy . . .

. . . and now he was back on the *Hoyer*.

Tears hurt his throat. He lifted the corner of his sheet to wipe his eyes. Then, violently, he threw the gray blanket off, kicking it to the foot of his bed.

Rolling to his side, he froze.

A man in a gray uniform sat sleeping in a chair by the table. Mikael's eyes went suddenly over the cabin. Groggily, he sat up. The bed was in a different place and his bathroom door opened on the opposite side. When had they moved him?

151

Yawning, he threw his legs over the side of the bed and looked at the sleeping guard. He had a square face with a long black beard and mustache.

"Excuse me?" he whispered softly. "Sir?"

The man stirred, shifting to a different position in the chair.

A bit louder Mikael called, "Mister? I'm awake now. Are we at Palaia Station yet?"

The guard opened his eyes and heaved a sleep-worn sigh. "I certainly hope not."

"But I need to get to Palaia Station to talk to Magistrate Slothen. Captain Tahn promised he'd take me." A small shiver of fear prickled at the back of his neck. Something was wrong.

The guard got to his feet. "I'm Nikos Kilom, son—a doctor, of sorts—if you count a day's worth of training. How are you feeling. A little hazy, I'll bet."

"Yes, sir. A little. My head hurts."

"It should. That was some dose of sedative they gave you to keep you out for two days straight."

Mikael blinked and dug his fingers into his sheet. He licked his lips anxiously. Mister Kilom said that like it was bad. "The captain wanted me to sleep. I have nightmares sometimes."

"Well, a lot has happened since you closed your eyes, Mikael Calas. A lot, indeed."

The doctor stood and stretched his arms over his head, then went to a black metal pack on the table and opened it, taking out several instruments that looked cold. Mikael braced himself for their touch.

"What are those?"

"Hmm? Oh, I need to check your heart and lungs and some other things."

"You don't want my blood, do you? I gave Doctor Iona a river full."

"I won't take near that much."

Mikael's heart sank. He squirmed while he waited. Why did doctors always sound so glad to be hurting kids? Kilom smiled as he brought the pack and opened it on Mikael's bed, then sat down beside him. First, he took a gray box with lights and dials and pressed it against Mikael's chest for a moment. The boy bit his lip to keep from flinching when the icy metal touched him.

Kilom took the box away and squinted at the dials,

writing something in a book he'd laid open on Mikael's blanket. "Well, that looks pretty good."

"What did it say?" He tried to read the book but couldn't get a good enough view. He struggled, peeking around every way he could.

"Oh, it said your heart's still a little slow, but your lungs sound clear."

"Is that okay?"

"I think so. For now." Kilom reached into his pack again and drew out a needle and Mikael winced, groaning. The doctor patted his cheek hard. "I'll get it over fast. Why don't you roll up your sleeve."

"Yes, sir."

He pushed up the wrinkled brown fabric and gritted his teeth as the doctor laid the needle against his flesh. A soft swish sounded and the needle went away filled with his blood. It only hurt a little. He rubbed his arm vigorously to get blood back into the empty spot.

"What happened while I was asleep, sir? How far are we from Palaia Station?"

Kilom studied the readings on the analyzer where he'd dumped Mikael's blood. "Oh, it's a long story. Let me just tell you you're among friends now. A Gamant crew is running this ship and we have most of the Magisterial officers locked up on level seven."

"I thought I was on seven?"

"Not anymore. Now you're on level nineteen. Jeremiel insisted we put you in the safest place possible."

Mikael stopped breathing, eyes widening as excitement flooded through him. "Jeremiel . . . *Baruch?*"

"The same."

Mikael let out a small cry and lurched off the bed, running barefoot across the cool carpet for the door. *"Where is he? Where is he? I have to see him! I have to tell him something very important! The Antimashiah is here right now! We have to . . ."* he stopped suddenly, remembering that he wasn't supposed to tell anybody but Mister Baruch.

Kilom got to his feet and threw out a calming hand. "I don't know where he is right now, Mikael. Come and sit back down and let me call him for you. He's been by twice to see you while you were asleep. I'm sure, if he's not busy, he'll come again."

Mikael punched his door patch again and again, tears

of frustration stinging his eyes. "No! I have to see him now. *Right NOW!* My grandfather told me something to tell him. Why won't my door open?"

"It's locked, son. Here, come and sit down with me. Let's talk. It's locked to keep you safe. As the new leader of Gamant civilization, your life is very precious to all of us."

Mikael wiped his running nose on his sleeve. "But . . . but I have to see Mister Baruch *now!*"

Kilom came slowly across the room. In the dim light, his black hair and beard looked like a dark tangle of brush. He put a gentle hand on Mikael's shoulder and guided him to one of the chairs by the table. He went, but not willingly. He shuffled his feet as much as he could.

"Why can't I see Mister Baruch? My grandfather told me something that I have to tell him. *Please!*"

He looked up into those dark, disbelieving eyes and suppressed the tears that shook his chest. He crawled into the chair and fiddled with his fingers.

Kilom went to the dispenser and came back with a steaming cup, setting it on the table beside Mikael.

"What's that?"

"It's hot cocoa, son. You need to drink something before we start giving you solid food. It'll make you feel better."

He frowned, looking curiously at the cup. Wreaths of steam rose like smoke, twisting toward the ceiling.

Kilom leaned across the table to pat his shoulder. His gray jumpsuit rustled loudly. The sound reminded Mikael of the autumn forests on Kayan and his heart ached. He felt all the more desperate to see Mister Baruch.

"Mikael, you drink this first and then I'll call Jeremiel for you, all right? Once you have something in your stomach, then you can talk to him."

He didn't really feel like drinking hot cocoa. He felt like running down the halls screaming until he found Jeremiel Baruch, but this doctor didn't look like he'd let him. Reluctantly, Mikael picked up his cup and sipped it. It tasted good, making a warm spot in his stomach.

Kilom smiled. "There, see? Isn't that better? Now, what's so important that you have to tell Jeremiel immediately? He's very busy."

He frowned into his cup, watching the bubbles on top

of the brown liquid stretch and die. "I can't tell you. My grandfather said I could only tell Mister Baruch."

"I see," the doctor smiled indulgently, like he thought Mikael was only four instead of almost eight. "Well, you finish your cocoa and I'll contact Avel Harper. He's running interference for Jeremiel."

"Yes, sir, if I have to."

Kilom smiled, cocking his head slightly. "There's also someone else who's been waiting for a long time to see you. He kept coming in while you were asleep just to look at you and make sure you were still all right."

"Who?"

"Yosef Calas. Your uncle."

Mikael's mouth dropped open. He licked the mustache of cocoa from his upper lip and set his glass down. "I thought he was dead."

"He looked pretty alive to me."

Mikael lifted his brows in amazement. After his grandfather's murder on Kayan, his mother had searched and searched for his uncle but hadn't ever been able to find him. Idly, Mikael wondered where he'd been. He'd have to ask him.

"Where is he?"

Doctor Kilom smiled and his mustache wiggled. "Want me to call him?"

"Maybe we could call Mister Baruch first? Then Uncle Yosef?"

"Business before family? You'll make an excellent leader for our People, Mikael. All right, Baruch first, but don't be disappointed if he can't see you for awhile. The last I heard, he was in an important meeting."

Mikael nodded and sipped the hot cocoa as fast as he could without burning himself.

CHAPTER 17

Yosef rushed around the cabin, dressing in a brown jumpsuit he'd gotten from the uniform dispenser in Engineering before all the other refugees ran the system completely out. Joy leapt like flames in his soul.

He gazed in the mirror that lined the wall beside the door to the latrine. His faded brown eyes gleamed with moist happiness. He adjusted the glasses on his fleshy old nose, and smoothed the few strands of gray hair that still dotted his bald head. In the jumpsuit, his paunch didn't seem quite so noticeable. He sucked it in and studied his reflection. In the mirror, he could also see under Ari's bed. The collection of beer bottles had grown so vast, they'd started to ooze from underneath.

"Ari, hurry up. Aren't you going with me? The escort will be here any minute."

"Huh? What?" Ari asked absently. He stood before the com unit on the desk, a hand caressing his withered chin as he sniggered. Images of some ancient black and white movie fluttered across the screen, the slapstick crude at best.

"Quit watching that thing!" Yosef ordered. "Change clothes so we can go see Mikael."

"Sure, sure, I'll go with you for a little while. But don't forget I have to take Sybil to the 3-D library in half an hour," Ari said, chuckling again as he tried to back away without losing sight of the screen. Dressed in an orange jumpsuit, he looked like a scrawny gray-topped carrot. "Good God, this is the funniest movie I've ever seen. Did you see that girly bite that fellow's—"

"You can't even understand the words. How do you know it's funny?"

"You don't have to know words in movies like this. Sheesh, those twentieth century Earthlings had great senses of humor."

Yosef glanced at the screen and scowled at the writhing

bodies. "They were sick."

"You've never had any savvy for wit."

"It takes a half-wit to enjoy that. Now, will you hurry! We haven't got all day. Kilom said Jeremiel was in a meeting and that's the only reason we get to see Mikael first."

Reluctantly, Ari turned off the screen and sighed, going to the mirror to scrutinize himself. He spit in his palms and briskly rubbed them together, slicking down the wild silver twigs that shot from his head.

In the meantime, Yosef wrung his hands nervously. He'd felt so empty thinking Mikael had been killed on Kayan. Oh, he'd had a good, long life, but there were so many things he'd wanted to do. He'd dreamed fondly about telling Mikael the Old Stories, the stories that kept the People together despite the vast distances between Gamant planets. And the family things that a young boy ought to know. Like the fact that his grandmother had been as ugly as a weabit and played the violin so sweetly it made a man's heart ache. He'd wanted to tell Mikael about how his grandfather, Zadok, had led the Gamant Revolt and won when the odds were a million to one.

"And another thing," Ari said, rudely interrupting Yosef's reverie. "You should talk to Mikael about leading another Gamant Revolt. If we somehow survive this, I mean if the Magistrates don't knock us out of the sky anytime soon—"

"What's the matter with you?" Yosef huffed in irritation. "Here I am feeling great and you talk about more war! Instead of thinking about that, you should be taking account of your soul. Aren't you sorry you might just be hovering over death?"

"Me? Bah! Do you know how many good fights and great women I've had in my life? Enough to exhaust the talents of five men."

Yosef cocked an eyebrow. "Except you never had any talent. You just exhausted people."

"How many times after *your* dates with Agnes did she call in sick because she was too tired to—"

"You mauled her."

Ari puffed out his bony chest proudly. "I know."

"Egotist. You *irritated* her, that's all. Just like you do everybody else."

Ari chuckled at first, then as Yosef's scowl deepened,

he threw back his head and guffawed. His mop of gray hair fell away from his face, lying like a mat of frosty grass against his skull.

"Stop that, you old fool," Yosef reproached. "What are you laughing at?"

"I hope God doesn't send you to the pit. I'd miss you."

Yosef waved a hand irritably. "I'd be down there with all my friends—including you."

The door com buzzed. "Mister Calas? This is Chris Janowitz. I've come to escort you to see your nephew."

"Oh! Ari, are you ready?"

"Sure, I'm ready. Let's go. I don't know why we need guards though. Who cares about us?"

Together they walked to the door and opened it. Six guards dressed in purple and gray uniforms filled the hall. Chris Janowitz bowed slightly at the waist.

"Good to see you again, Mister Calas. Please follow me. We'll try to circumvent the worst halls."

"Is it getting worse?"

Janowitz nodded, wiping away the sweat that dripped from his long nose before looking up through worried green eyes. "I'm afraid, sir, that level eighteen looks damn near like a battle zone. Most of the people coming up now are in bad shape. They had to stay down there through the worst of the fires and fighting."

"Why are they in the halls, then? Why aren't they—"

"The hospital and all the auxiliary rooms are full, Mister Calas. They're waiting to get in."

They started down the hall, three guards in front and three behind and Yosef threw Ari an anxious look. His old friend just pursed his withered lips in response.

"Is there still fighting on the planet?"

Janowitz barely turned, casting over his shoulder. "Not much anymore, but it took the people trapped in the desert regions a while before they realized the civil war was over and by then it was too late to escape the effects of the scorch attack. They got pretty well cooked. Fortunately, we're almost done picking up survivors. And none too soon. The fire storms have ravaged the entire central portion of the planet."

They walked to the nearest tube and descended. When they stopped, everyone exited and headed down a long corridor that stood empty—except for a series of heavily armed guards dressed in the multicolored fabrics of rough homespun wool. It came as a strangely comforting sight. Yosef breathed a little easier.

Ari glanced at the door numbers, and lifted a brow. "Is all this muscle and hardware for Mikael?"

"Of course," Yosef whispered. "He's the new leader of Gamant civilization. And he's aboard a government ship. He needs all the protection he can get."

Janowitz called to a tall dark-haired man standing next to the door of cabin 1911. "Slome, tell Kilom we're here."

The guard's hard facade softened. He gazed at Ari and Yosef with kindly camaraderie. "The boy'll be mighty glad to see another friendly face. Hold on just a moment."

He struck the door com. "Doctor Kilom? Calas and Funk are here."

Ari folded his arms over his bony chest and spread his legs. Yosef glanced up nervously at his tall friend. Ari nodded confidently, but Yosef still felt awkward and anxious.

His thoughts kept revolving around all those people who had lost their world, their family, everything. His own grandnephew had endured such a fate—except he still had Yosef.

Finally, the door to cabin 1911 snicked back and Kilom stepped into the hall, his black beard canted at a funny angle, as though he'd slept on it. He smiled, nodding. "Please come in. Mikael's waiting."

Even before the guard waved them forward, Yosef started running, his ancient legs pumping unsteadily. From the open door, the sweet treble laughter of a little boy lilted and iron hands clenched tight around Yosef's heart. What if Ari was right? What if, even now, the Magistrates plotted to silence that bright sound? He felt sick with fear.

He hurried, breathing hard as he stepped into the dimly lit room. On the floor before him sat a tiny black-haired boy with wide brown eyes. A checkerboard adorned the floor between his spread feet.

Yosef took another cautious step and water welled in his ancient eyes. His tongue seemed so thick he couldn't speak.

Mikael smiled shyly. "Hello, Uncle Yosef."

Yosef rushed forward, surprising the boy by hugging

him desperately and passionately kissing his cheek. "Mikael, I didn't think you'd remember me. The last time I saw you you were only four."

"I remember you pretty good. Grandfather used to let me sleep in his lap when he talked to you late at night. 'Member?"

"Yes, I do."

"I love you, Uncle Yosef. I missed you. Me and Mama, we wondered where you were."

Those few words, so simple, brought Yosef more joy than any others in his long life. He tenderly stroked his grandnephew's dark curls. "I love you, too, Mikael."

* * *

Dannon held his breath, listening to the hurried footsteps coming up his back trail. He stood hidden behind an uneven line of crates stacked eight high on level twelve. A shrapnel explosion of machinery parts was scattered across the narrow white-tiled floor. Jeremiel's security teams had been gradually, efficiently cutting off Dannon's territory. All levels below twelve and above eight had been secured and sealed. Soon, he'd have nowhere left to run.

"I saw him, I tell you!" a big rawboned man with a bald head insisted. Dressed in a dirty black robe which hung in tatters around his ankles, he seemed the looming image of Death.

"Shut up, Harmon," his thin friend with thick spectacles growled. "You've let that million note prize that Baruch's offering go to your head. Look at this picture. Are you sure this is the man you saw?"

Harmon fidgeted, gazing at the holo. "Well, no. The fellow I saw didn't have a beard and mustache, but he had black hair and was about Dannon's height."

Neil sucked in a breath. They must be using the picture of him taken when he'd first come aboard the *Hoyer*. He'd always worn a beard in the Underground. Now, he thanked God he'd shaved it. It had been an impulsive act, designed to change his appearance even to himself so he could forget the face of the man who'd spent his entire adult life fighting at Jeremiel's side.

"You're wishing!" the bespectacled man accused. "I didn't see anyone."

"I'm telling you—"

"Come on, Harmon, we're wasting our time. I'm going

160

back to the air duct central outlet where we smoked out those cowardly Magisterial soldiers. I'd lay you five to one odds that's the sort of place Dannon would be hiding."

A thudding of boots sounded. Neil waited. Five minutes. Ten. Finally, he peered around the stacked crates. Harmon still stood in the semidarkness, a pistol clutched in his hands. He had his back turned to Neil, examining the far wall.

With the skill of a professional assassin, Dannon edged along behind the crates, getting as close as he could without exposing himself. Harmon grumbled something harsh and started for the door.

Neil leapt from behind the crates, knocking the man to the floor. He slammed a fist into Harmon's throat before he could scream for help, then calmly, efficiently, broke his neck.

Quietly scanning the room, Dannon made certain no one had seen. Hurriedly, he undressed Harmon and threw off his own purple uniform. Slipping the tattered black robe over his head, Neil grabbed the rifle and slung it over his shoulder, then picked up Harmon's feet and dragged him over to an air duct. He grunted as he stuffed the tall corpse into the narrow chamber. Racing back, he retrieved his purple uniform and tossed it in on top.

After he fastened the duct seal again, Neil searched the pockets of his new robe, finding a meager amount of cash and a small round badge. He lifted it to the light to read it.

"*A security clearance badge?*" He chuckled in relief. "This is going to be easier than I thought."

He clipped it to a fragment of black cloth on his shoulder and unslung his rifle before heading for the door. He cautiously opened it a slit.

The stench struck him first, overwhelmingly vile— scents he knew from his days of warfare, festered wounds and urine-soaked clothing. The sound of childish whimpers and groans from the injured assailed him.

He stepped out and closed the door behind him. The hall was bursting with people, most hunched against the now-grimy walls, their faces gaunt and eyes hollow. One mother with a blood-streaked face held a dead baby to her breast. She sang a soft sweet lullabye as she rocked it in her arms.

Neil's shoulders tightened. *The effects of Tahn's scorch attack? God Almighty . . . how many died?* His gaze swiftly calculated the numbers of injured. At least a hundred crowded this short corridor. How many more were aboard? A thousand? Five thousand?

I told you, Jeremiel. I told you!

He walked swiftly through the moaning crowd, side-stepping the dead that sprawled like limp bags of bones down the line. Feelings of violation and despair overwhelmed him. Would the Magistrates' vengeance never end?

CHAPTER 18

Rachel glared ominously into the mirror over her table. Her heart-shaped face had shrunken to cadaverous thinness, high cheekbones protruding so that her black eyes seemed huge eclipsed moons. The hair which cascaded in glistening waves to her waist shimmered darker than midnight silk, forebodingly black against her long jade gown. She'd ordered the garment from her room clothing dispenser and thought it immensely strange that a ship like a battle cruiser would stock such feminine accoutrements. She pushed her wavy hair away from her face and glimpsed the brand in her forehead: AKT. Adom's initials. The tiny letters had been burned into her forehead just at her hairline by the Desert Fathers of Horeb. They'd suspected she might need a sign of anointing to convince Adom of her kinship with him. But he'd never seen them, not that she knew of anyway. In fact, no one had, except Jeremiel and the elderly gray-headed Father who'd put them there so expertly. They remained hidden unless she deliberately pushed her hair back from her forehead.

She anxiously milled around the cabin, waiting for Jeremiel. He'd arranged to have dinner with her, but was already forty minutes late. Stewards had brought their food almost an hour ago. It sat in a pile of covered dishes on the table, the sweet scents of curried lamb and Halosian wild rice strong in her nostrils—special treats now that the food system labored under the number of refugees.

Rachel slowly walked her cabin, concentrating on how she'd tell him the things she needed to. Would he think she'd gone crazy? Probably. Why shouldn't he? She wasn't convinced of her sanity herself.

Thank God, Ari had come by a half hour ago and taken Sybil to the 3-D library to teach her how to do quick-draws. He seemed genuinely fond of her daughter. And Sybil needed friends, especially now when the entire world might crumble at any moment and she herself was little use as a comforter.

A buzzing sounded and Jeremiel's deep voice penetrated the room. "Rachel? It's Jeremiel. Sorry I'm late."

She ran to the door, pounding the entry patch. When the door snicked back, she saw him standing tall and broad-shouldered in a gray shirt and white pants. He looked so tired he could crumple at her feet at any moment. Four guards surrounded him. His perfectly chiseled face and blond hair seemed relics from another life.

She smiled. "Jeremiel, it's so good to see you. Come in."

He stepped into her cabin, giving curt instructions for his guards to wait. In the soft light, his smile seemed an ethereal beacon. "You're still beautiful. How are you?"

He opened his arms wide and she hurried into them, twining her fingers in the soft folds of his shirt. The steady rhythm of his heartbeat acted as a salve to her fears. His strong hand stroked her hair tenderly.

"Are you all right?" he murmured.

"Yes, better now. How are you?"

"As well as can be expected. Come, let's sit down and eat before the food gets stone cold. I'm afraid I haven't much time."

"Avel prepared me for that. He said you'd spent all day trying and condemning the men who attacked me."

"Attacked you and several others. The murder rate has been mounting for the past two days. The leader of the assassins was Rumon Kaufa. I ordered him and all his cronies jettisoned from the ship." As though they'd been discussing the poor weather, he lifted a hand toward the food. "Shall we?"

They went to the table and dropped into chairs. Jeremiel began uncovering the dishes, piling the lids, one inside the other, at the rear of the table. Obviously in a rush, he lifted the serving ladle for the curry.

"May I fill your plate?"

"Yes, I'm starving. I figured if you didn't get here soon I'd eat without you."

"I wouldn't have blamed you. Besides, you're going to need your strength."

"Really? Good. What do you have in mind?"

He filled both their plates and poured the alizarin wine into crystal goblets. Lifting his fork, he smiled wryly. "Let's get the eating over, all right? That way my tortured stomach will be eased and I'll be able to concentrate."

"Sounds good to me." She reached for her fork. Barely warm, the curry tasted a little pasty, but spicy and good.

Jeremiel ate heartily, smiling at her whenever she looked up. She'd forgotten how good it was to be close to him. He always radiated an inner strength that infected everyone around him. And never more so than now when she desperately needed someone strong to talk to.

When she'd finished, she laid down her fork and picked up her wine, watching him scrape his plate to get the last spoonful of rice.

He looked up, noticing she'd finished. "You're a fast eater."

"I'm just not as thorough as you. You eat like this might be your last meal."

"You've always been too observant." He threw her a bare-soul look of worry, then quickly scooped up the last grain of rice. Getting up from the table, he dragged his chair closer to hers and sat down again.

She studied him, seeing the leaden smudges of exhaustion below his eyes. From this range, she could see lots of things she hadn't before. Tiny lines around his mouth pinched tightly. Already a pale stain of sweat darkened the collar of his gray shirt. Had he been caught in a strategy session on his way here? Is that why he'd been late and why he had so little time to spend with her?

"Forgive me for noticing," she said, "but you look a little ragged around the edges. I know some of what's going on, why don't you fill me in on the rest?"

He crossed his legs and took a long drink of his wine. "I'm in trouble."

"You're never in trouble."

"I knew you'd say that. That's why I've been so anxious to see you, for moral support."

She cocked her head. "I'll bet. What's going on?"

His face went deadly serious. The rich scent of curry still lingered sweetly in the air, like a fragrant shawl of golden spices cast about their heads.

"To begin with," he said through a long exhale, "we've stolen a C-J class battle cruiser and as soon as the Magistrates discover that fact, I suspect they'll be a bit dismayed."

"So we've got to find some place to run, right?"

"Right. After we finish loading the refugees, which shouldn't take more than another day or two."

"Why do we have to collect everyone from the planet? Can't some people stay where they are?"

"That would make things a great deal easier, but we can't. A scorch attack sets off a series of chain reactions, even as brief a one as Horeb experienced. A fire storm flashes over the surface engulfing nearly every thread of vegetation, then the clouds set in and the rains come, drowning everyone and everything, washing away top-soil. But, more importantly, we can't leave anyone because the Magistrates will be back to finish the job someday soon. I cut their little show of force off in mid-swing. They won't be happy about that."

"I suppose we're hoping the Magistrates don't catch on before we collect our people and get away safely. Do you have any information which suggests they might be on their way here?"

He heaved a tense breath. "No, but it doesn't pay to underestimate the devil. I haven't had time to fully research it, but I think the Magistrates have initiated some sort of silence program regarding the Lysomian system, particularly Tikkun. It terrifies me."

Rachel's throat constricted suddenly, blood rushing in her ears. Aktariel's words whispered in her memory. She fumbled unsteadily with her wine glass, spilling some on the black tabletop. She retrieved a napkin with a shaking hand and sopped it up.

Jeremiel watched her intently. "Want to tell me about it?"

"Let's finish discussing our predicament here first. Tell me more about the refugee problems? I tried to walk the—"

"*Don't . . .*" he almost shouted, eyes gleaming suddenly. Catching himself, he lowered his voice. "Rachel, please, don't do that. Call Janowitz or me if you want out. We'll assign you an escort."

"I'm armed. I can take care of myself."

"In a fair fight, yes. But these boys don't play by our honorable rules."

"I thought you'd captured them all?"

"We may have, but I'm not sure. Until I am, I don't want you taking any unnecessary chances."

She looked away, despair and futility taunting her. Adom's death weighed more heavily with each living breath she took. "I have more enemies than just Kaufa?"

He pressed his lips tightly together for a moment. "You're a hero in my eyes, Rachel, but not everyone from Horeb is as broadminded as I am. As well, not everyone knows the facts like I do. We've necessarily thrown together both sides of the civil war and tensions are extreme. There were two more murders this morning."

"*More?*"

"Yes. Inside the hospital. Somebody made an error. They unknowingly placed an Old Believer's bed next to a New Believer's."

She closed her eyes, fighting the horrifying images that rocked her soul. Memories of the square flashed . . . night birds tugging relentlessly at mangled corpses . . . the whimpers of suffocating children buried beneath a massive mountain of dead. "Jeremiel, I'll do almost anything you need, but if you came here to ask me to mediate—"

"No, I didn't. Though I'll admit that I thought about having you coordinate the Old Believers just as you'd done on Horeb, but too many people saw the city-wide broadcast of you killing Tartarus. I'm afraid your presence among the refugees would only polarize the people, fanning the flames—one side hating you, the other considering you a savior. Besides, I have a more critical problem I need you for."

"I'm relieved," she said, letting out a slow breath. "But where can you put me where I won't be amongst Horebians?"

He thoughtfully swirled his wine, watching the silver light flash through the liquid. "I need someone I can trust to join the security team on level four."

"What's on level four?"

"Two enraged Magisterial soldiers who can't wait to get their fingers around the throats of the first Gamant who walks by. I've confined Captain Cole Tahn and his second in command, First Lieutenant Carey Halloway, on four. The rest of the crew is on level seven."

"I'm getting nervous."

"You won't be alone for even a second until we've thoroughly secured the upper levels. I have ten—"

"I know nothing about security, particularly not technical systems like the sort this magical ship possesses."

He had a hard glint in his eye. "What you do know, Rachel, is the *cost* of poor security. You've seen firsthand what happens when somebody, anybody, gets lazy or overconfident. I can assign Harper to teach you the basics of security in a day, then set you up for accessing the tech manuals in the ship's library. Your fellow security officers have already been trained—by the best, I might add."

"Meaning you, I hope."

He smiled and caressed his reddish-blond beard. "Somebody better."

"There is nobody better."

"The soldiers in the last Gamant Revolt might argue with you. They'd think Zadok Calas a far superior—"

"Zadok?"

"Quite. Every security officer on level four is a former member of Harper's clandestine group on Horeb, all men originally handpicked by Zadok himself. They're loyal to a fault, and most are Old Believers who've followed your path for years, watching while you organized Seir's populace against Ornias, cheering you on, praying for you to win. They know you're a hero. Having you in their ranks will unquestionably bolster their spirits."

A tingle of dread went through her, but she suppressed it. "Well, I have to do something fast or I'll go mad. When do I start?"

"Immediately." In a fluid movement, he got to his feet and stood over her, smiling down regretfully. "And now, I'm sorry, but I have to go."

She stood up beside him. "Give me another two minutes. I want to talk to you on a more personal level."

He nodded apologetically. "Go on. I'm sorry. It's just that I have a strategy session in Engineering in five. But I can be a little late."

"I won't keep you longer than that. I know things are frantic here." She gave him a grateful smile and walked to the other side of the room, thinking how to start. She'd planned for hours how to approach him with the subject. Obviously, she wasn't going to have the time to break it gently.

"Jeremiel, when I was on Horeb, at the pole, I—I had some very strange nightmares."

"For example?"

"Well . . . I dreamed that Aktariel came to me."

He paused, then said, "Really? I hope you told him we could use some of his power to kill every Magisterial soldier alive."

"Don't joke. I'm still terrified."

"I wasn't joking. That's some nightmare. What did he have to say?"

"He told me Epagael enjoys our suffering. That . . . that God withdrew a part of Himself in order to spawn the Void of creation and that now He's flexing his muscles around the perimeter to throw galaxies into one another, to increase the chaos he loves and, thereby, our torment."

Jeremiel crossed his arms as though in defense. "Misery is on the increase, you mean? I'll admit it certainly feels that way."

"Aktariel told me he's trying to save us."

"Hmm. . . . Well, if I recall the old lessons, he's been telling people that for centuries, hasn't he? That's why our legends call him the Deceiver."

"Yes, but—"

"Rachel? Let's be straightforward. You were frightened and enduring great emotional stress down there, weren't you? I remember the horrified look on your face when you got into the *samael* with Adom to head for the pole."

"Yes, Jeremiel. *But I thought* . . . I thought I really *saw* Aktariel. That he appeared before me, touched me, talked to me."

He cocked his head, appraising her curiously. "And?"

She threw up her hands. "What do you mean *and?* Isn't that enough?"

"You sound worried about it."

"Of course, I'm worried! Wouldn't you be?"

He lifted both brows and thought for a second, then shook his head. "No. I'd use any help I could get right now. I'd only worry about Aktariel if he told me to sell out all of Gamant civilization. Did he tell you to do that?"

She wet her lips nervously. "No."

He embraced her affectionately. "I have to go. If Aktariel comes to talk to you again, defer to me. I'll gladly bargain my soul for a dozen more battle cruisers. I'll call you soon."

She shuddered slightly. "If you have time. Things sound pretty desperate."

Keeping his arm around her shoulders, he guided her with him to the door. "One last thing. I've been thinking about arranging a ceremony to publicly acknowledge your bravery on Horeb. When do you—"

"*Don't*. It would only complicate the situation with the refugees. And something like that would make my guilt over murdering Adom increase."

He nodded understandingly. "Whatever you want."

They reached the door and he hit the com. "Janowitz? You out there?"

"Aye, Jeremiel. Me and Uriah are standing right here."

He waited for the door to slide open. When it did, his guards unslung their rifles, getting into position to escort him down the hall.

In a strained voice, Rachel said, "Jeremiel? One last thing?"

"What?"

She blurted, "I—I dreamed that the Magistrates are going to dispatch five cruisers to Tikkun and that your Underground bases are frantically trying to contact you, but can't because the link is down. I don't know what that is, but—"

"The link?"

"Yes, I guess it has something to do with communications, but I don't—"

"*The long-range link? Oh, my God.*" His gaze went rapidly over her. "Rudy could have been trying for days and I'd have never . . . I've got to get to Engineering."

169

He pulled his pistol from his holster, letting it melt into his hand before he started down the hall, one guard in front, one in back. "We'll talk more about these *dreams* later, Rachel."

"Yes," she whispered.

She watched him until he ran around the far corner, then closed her door and gazed around her cabin. As the desolate silence returned, she sprinted to the control console, turning all the lights on full. The stark brilliance drove out some of her fears.

Jeremiel *had* known what that meant. Though she didn't, still. She wandered insecurely around her cabin, feeling afraid and lonely.

* * *

CHAPTER 19

The 8th of Tishri, 5414.

"People are missing," Jasper said ominously, glaring at Pavel. "Old Ruth hasn't been coming to the benches on Thursdays. Sumino has vanished. Something's happening."

"They're all from the village hinterlands," Pavel pointed out. "Maybe the skirmishes with the Underground have cut them off and they can't get to the city."

"Sure, or maybe the Magistrates have hauled them off into the pit of darkness."

"The government doesn't kidnap people."

Jasper leaned back against the couch into the splash of sunlight pouring through Pavel's windows. He had a cold beer clutched in one hand and gestured roughly with it to make his points. "You're a blockhead, you know that?"

A warm breeze blew around the room, fluttering the curtains, carrying the sweet scent of flowers and baking bread.

Pavel crossed his arms over his short-sleeved blue

170

shirt. "Don't be difficult, Jasper. I think if we all just do as they say, we'll be all right. They're not monsters. They're human beings, just like us."

"Bah!" Jasper waved a harsh hand, his wrinkled face falling into deeper lines. "They may be human beings, but they're ruled by a bunch of blue bastards."

Pavel pointed out the window to the yellow house across the street. "Just yesterday, that lieutenant the government moved in with the Richmond family brought Marjorie a sack of groceries. What do you think of that? He—"

"He's the neighborhood spy! He's covering his butt. He's alone in the middle of hostile territory right now. Just wait until he finds something bad to report to his superiors. The groceries will vanish and the guns will come out. Then you'll be sorry you didn't kill him right off the bat."

Pavel threw up his arms in exasperation. "Grandpa, troops have been marching through the streets of Derow day and night and nothing bad has happened. They're keeping the peace, for God's sake! Why is it you think the only solution to problems is to wipe out innocent people?"

Jasper leaned forward and squinted an eye malevolently. "For one thing, it's a damn sight easier to kill people when they're still innocent than after they've killed your entire family and grabbed a bunch of hoodlums to guard their guilty asses!"

"Diplomacy *works!* I've seen it."

Jasper examined his fingernails as though something mighty interesting had sneaked beneath them. "You know what?"

"What?"

"I think maybe you were born without a brain. Hmm? Should we have a doctor check that out? They do great things with transplants these days."

Pavel laughed, but his mirth came mostly from indignation. He shook a fist at Jasper. "Why would you say something like that when we were having a good discussion?"

His grandfather eyed Pavel hawkishly and lazily draped an arm across the back of the couch. Sunlight reflected like strewn glitter through the gray hair on his forearm. "Because you act like a brainless yog some-

171

times. The only time diplomacy has ever helped Gamants was when old Zadok rammed it down the Magistrates' throat with an army of a million at his back."

"You're ignorant! You see only what you want to. And if you don't get down to the registration center and put your name on that piece of paper, you're going to go to prison, because I'm going to stop lying for you!"

"Don't be a stooge."

"Stooge nothing. I'm breaking the law just to keep you from obeying it. Did it ever occur to you that I'm a criminal now because of you? Just this morning I lied to another soldier who asked where you lived. I told him you were homeless!"

"I am," Jasper agreed. He'd been afraid to go home, so he'd been snatching naps at friends' homes or spending a few hours each day at the hundreds of derelicts' camps that covered the outskirts of Derow. He had to keep moving—he knew that—just like the smart people had done during the last Revolt. Even coming to Pavel's had been a risk—but Jasper had scouted the area thoroughly before chancing it and slipping in the back way. "Besides, if you'd had any smarts, Pavel, you'd have become a criminal long ago. If it weren't for your hoity-toity job working in the government labs, we could all be far away now, living safe on some island."

"Oh, Jasper," Pavel huffed, scratching his black beard expressively. "You make me so mad sometimes I want to hang you."

"Well, if you're going into the kitchen to get a rope, bring me another beer while you're at it." He crumpled his petrolon can in his fist and smiled impudently.

"Sure. Anything to get away from you for a few seconds."

Pavel virtually threw open the kitchen door and strode toward the frigerator. He jerked so violently on the handle that the appliance rocked as though animate. As he searched the contents, he thought he vaguely heard the front gate slam and Yael's steps come hurriedly up the walk. A small glow touched him, cooling his ire. He pulled a can of Imperial Stout from the bottom rack and turned, just in time to hear Jasper yell:

"*Pavel!* Get out here, now!"

Then Yael's soft whimpering made its way to him and

he dropped the can and ran, leaving the frigerator door wide open. He heard it crash against the counter, bottles jingling, as he burst back into the living room and stopped dead in his tracks.

Jasper knelt on the floor, holding Yael and patting her back. When she looked up at Pavel, her beautiful face ran with tears. A series of red welts and the faint blue underpinnings of bruises swelled around her eyes.

"Oh, Yael, what happened?"

"Daddy?" She cried, holding out her arms to him. Her shoulders shook with renewed tears.

"Baby." He ran and gathered her into his arms, lifting her off the ground and hugging her tightly against him. "Did you get into a fight?"

She nodded against his shoulder, trying to suppress her tears.

"You didn't hit first, did you?"

"No! Daddy, no."

"All right, it's okay. Hush, now." He stroked her back tenderly, kissing her moist forehead. "Did you say something you didn't mean and somebody—"

"No, I don't know why Maren hit me, Dad! The teachers put us in different rooms today and I—"

"Us, who?" Jasper inquired.

"Us Gamants. I was just walking to coloring class with Jonas, and Maren jumped out from behind a bush and shouted at me. He shouted, 'You dirty Gamant,' then he hit me and hit me! Then Jonas picked up a rock and smashed Maren in the ear and he let me go."

"Good for Jonas," Grandpa muttered furiously. His ancient face had taken on the alert dangerous look of a wolf on the hunt.

Pavel glared at him. He'd been teaching Yael all her life that physical violence did no good, it only got a person into deeper trouble. "Yael," he whispered lovingly, tipping up her chin to gaze into her glistening eyes. "Next time Maren does that, you just cover your head with your hands and tell him you're sorry—even if you didn't do anything. He'll stop hitting you then."

"Okay, Dad," she moaned and sniffed, burying her face in his blue shirt.

From the corner of his eye, he caught Jasper's nearly ferocious glowering, but ignored it.

"I love you, baby. Are you better now?"

173

She sucked in a deep halting breath and looked up, giving him a frail little-girl smile. "A little."

"Good. Why don't you go and wash your face in cold water. And grab a cookie off the counter in the kitchen when you come back."

"Aunt Sekan's cookies?"

"Yes, she brought them this morning."

"What kind are they?"

He winked at her excited expression and set her on the floor. "Go see for yourself."

She smiled broadly and ran, casting over her shoulder, "I bet they're nutbutter! She knows they're my favorite!"

"I bet you're right," he said, laughing.

Once Yael had vanished and they could hear her steps retreating toward the bathroom, Jasper violently shoved Pavel's shoulder, swinging him around to face him. The old man's cheeks blazed as red as the roses in the front yard.

"You stupid imbecile!" Grandpa accused. "You want to get her killed?"

"No, I want to keep her safe! Fighting does no good, it only exacerbates—"

"You're teaching her to be a *mouse,* for God's sake! You think she should get used to being a victim, huh? That she should come to like it, maybe?"

Pavel's heart beat as rapidly as a bird's. He met Grandpa's hot stare with one of his own. "Maybe being a victim isn't as bad as being *dead,* huh?"

The anger drained from Jasper's face and he straightened to his full rail-thin height—getting ready to bully Pavel. He clenched his jaw in preparation. They stared at each other in silence for what seemed an eternity.

"This Maren kid, he's a Magisterial yog, right?"

Pavel grimaced at the word. Yog: non-Gamant. "What difference does it make?"

They heard Yael's steps in the kitchen and the scritching of the cookie platter as she pulled it across the counter, with a gay giggle of delight.

Jasper moved closer to Pavel, breathing, "Teach her to fight, and you'll teach her how to live. People who want to kill her aren't going to stop just because she lies down and covers her head."

"You've never tried to understand me or my ways! They're different from yours!"

"You listen to me, boy!" Jasper poked a crooked finger hard into Pavel's chest and he felt his anger swell even more. "All the 'I'm sorrys' in the world won't make murderers put down their rifles. *Why do you think they separated Gamant children from Magisterial brats?* You'd damned well better think about it!"

Jasper turned and stamped across the room, flinging the door wide and slamming it closed with a loud bang. Wind caught in his white sleeves, flapping them into snapping folds as he hurried down the walk.

Pavel couldn't help himself; he ran to the screen, shouting, "The Magistrates aren't murderers! They're not!"

"Bah!" Jasper shouted over his shoulder as he turned down the street.

Bright sunlight streamed down through his latticework porch, falling like irregularly placed golden stepping-stones over Pavel's porch. Across the street, Lieutenant Warick emerged from the Richmonds' house, his purple uniform looking crisp and freshly ironed.

Pavel lifted a hand in greeting—and paled a little when the man gave him a malignant stare in return.

* * *

Jeremiel strode purposefully toward the transport tube, ten guards following. "Bridge," he ordered tersely.

How many dattrans had the *Hoyer* received in the past four days and failed to respond to? Were a dozen cruisers even now on their way here to verify Tahn's status?

Silently, he cursed himself. He'd been too caught up in the whirlwind to think of the minor things that could be done to sabotage his hastily laid plans. And the green Gamant crew he'd assigned to communications knew only rudimentary facts about com units. Of course, they hadn't noticed the anomaly. Only he would have. It had been expertly done, shutting off the link and circumventing the com alert. Whoever had initiated it had been betting on his preoccupation with Horeb and the refugees—and she'd been right. *How had Rachel known?* Her words about the dream haunted him. As soon as he had time, he'd arrange a long, long talk with her.

The tube halted and Janowitz got out first. He went to the four Gamant guards routinely stationed on the bridge and coordinated tactics, then took his elite team of ten to check and recheck every member of the *Hoyer*'s crew, getting only a few curses from women who balked at his thoroughness. They glared hotly from the lower level, uniforms stained darkly with sweat around collars and beneath arms, jaws clamped. Jeremiel had ordered the bridge crew rotated, only allowing five at a time to sit at the inoperable consoles—just in case Palaia tranned and he needed familiar faces in the picture.

Jeremiel walked out, pinning Halloway with a murderous gaze. She slouched tiredly in the command chair, auburn hair tucked behind her ears. Her cheeks seemed more sunken, delicate facial bones sharp.

"What do you want, Baruch?"

He watched Janowitz going through his security routine, then shifted his eyes to the forward screen. Blank, it stood out like a huge locked door of the deepest gray. Had she turned it off to keep her crew from hysteria every time the ship recrossed the path of the decompression? Probably.

"They're all clean, Jeremiel," Janowitz confirmed. Then, waving, he instructed his security team to fan out around the bridge. They stood with rifles cradled in their arms, sharp eyes constantly moving.

With infinite patience, Jeremiel walked over to Halloway and gazed down at her. Conversationally, he commented, "I wanted to let you know I reconnected the long-range link. And I've tended to all the minor reroutes necessary to completely disable the bridge."

Her shoulder muscles tensed, but subtly. "I thought you'd find it sooner. Slipping in your old age, Baruch?"

He gave her a pleasant smile. "Let's go into the bridge conference room and have a chat, shall we?"

She stood up, and swayed, groping for her chair back. Instinctively, he reached out to take her arm, helping to steady her. She glanced at his hand, but made no move to throw it off. Slowly looking up, she met his gaze. A curiously vulnerable light gleamed in her eyes, as though her soul lay open for his appraisal. It affected him strangely, making him feel more hollow than he already did. He released her arm and gestured to the conference room. She stepped forward, leading the way.

A round chamber, it spread thirty feet in diameter. An oval table sat in the center surrounded by fifteen chairs. Holos of exotic landscapes dotted the walls. Most showed majestic mountain scenery, but some displayed eerie wind-sculpted rock formations.

He pulled out a chair for her. "Have a seat."

Without looking at him, she accepted and leaned her head tiredly against the high back.

He crossed his arms over his gray shirt and strolled around the room. She clasped her hands in her lap defensively, but it was a frail, almost childlike gesture.

"Tired?" he asked.

"What would give you that idea?"

"You're not your usual hateful self."

"My, you're charming tonight."

He came back around and sat down next to her, propping his elbows on the table. She looked at him wearily. Her purple uniform possessed wrinkles where no uniform should. Had she slept in it while sitting in the command chair? He knew what that was like.

"Stop plotting against me. You'd have a lot more time to rest."

Her dark graceful brows lifted. "Why don't you ask me to turn into a toad?"

"What do you think I ought to do with you? I certainly can't let such sabotage go unpunished. It would set a bad example for your crew. They might think I'm soft on treachery."

"What do you usually do?"

"I usually kill the offender."

"Well . . . that would give me some rest."

She'd said it so nonplussed that it made him lean back in his chair. "Why don't we discuss now what other 'problems' I might find in the ship's operation. That way we can both rest easier."

She gave him a feeble smile. "Go to hell."

"Perhaps we're not communicating. I'd really rather not lose you."

She fumbled insecurely with her hands. Beautiful, tired, this display of unguarded emotion struck him disturbingly.

"Halloway, let's be straightforward. I can't—"

"*Neither can I!* We're playing a high stakes game, Baruch. You're fighting for your people. I'm fighting for mine. And it's all or nothing. You know that."

He shook his head in confusion. "No, I don't. We made a deal. You said you'd follow my orders. I told you I'd put you and your people off safely on the nearest

177

Gamant planet. And I intend to. You're making this a lot harder for yourself than it has to be. Just hang on for a week and you'll be down somewhere, can tran the Magistrates to reroute the nearest cruiser to pick you up, and you'll be fine. Alive!"

"Tahn's right. I do give you more credit for brilliance than you deserve."

He shook his head. "What does that mean?"

"It means you don't know Magisterial history very well. Now, either kill me or let me go back to my bridge."

He frowned. The only history that interested him was Magisterial technological development. He'd been searching for years to find a way of blowing the hell out of Palaia Station. It occurred to him to tell her that, but he stopped himself. He studied her, burning to know what frightened her so. Magisterial history? His mind flashed over the elements he knew, major events. All the while his gaze held hers. She must have realized he was running events through his mind, for her face changed. A worried swallow went down her throat, as though she feared she'd revealed too much. Too much about what? He'd told her she'd be fine and she'd fundamentally responded that he was stupid . . .

The *Annum* Incident?

"Oh, Lord," he murmured tautly, massaging his brow. Her labored breathing seemed suddenly loud in the quiet. "You think you have to get your ship back to stay healthy."

A gleam came into her eyes, as though a scarcely endurable fear gnawed at her vitals. But she said nothing.

"You mean the *Annum* Incident, don't you?" he asked.

"How do you know about it?"

"I've made Tahn a hobby of mine. It helps to know a man's personal history. It gives you clues as to how he thinks. So it is all or nothing. Well, at least we know where we stand."

He steepled his fingers over his lips as he thought. A rabid indignation beat in his chest, but he kept it out of his voice, speaking softly. "I'm sorry. I know the fear you're feeling. For decades the Magistrates have been sending Gamant children to Right Schools to strip their minds in the same way they did the crew of the *Annum*. Oh, our children aren't totally incapacitated like they were, but we've lost entire generations of fine minds.

178

They function only at median levels in society. Where Gamants are concerned, the Magistrates call it 'eliminating the nuisance factor.' What do you think they'll call it in your case? 'Galactic security'?"

A tense silence settled over the room. He nervously fiddled with the cuff of his gray sleeve, not looking at her. Something akin to self-ridicule tingled inside him. How damned dare he feel pity for her, this woman who had been instrumental in the murders of so many innocent Gamants! But he did feel pity—pity and a startling sense of shared desperation. She must be going through a living hell, worrying what the future held. And so was he. That made them even in his heart, though his head rebelled, shouting at him to just kill every Magisterial soldier on board. That way he wouldn't have to lie awake nights writhing in worry about what they might think up next to murder him or his people. But he damn sure couldn't train refugees by himself and worry about keeping them alive at the same time. And they needed training, badly. He'd never be able to handle this ship in a battle unless he had a crew with a baseline competency in the systems.

She leaned forward, her face no more than two feet from his. He studied the beauty of her auburn hair and delicate features, the bare sprinkle of freckles across her nose. All the while, he was acutely aware that her gaze searched his face, probing deeply for something he didn't understand.

"So," she said at last, "the great Jeremiel Baruch is indeed human. I've often wondered."

"What makes you think that?"

"You look like a damned soul hanging by a thread over the pit of darkness. It makes me feel better."

"Don't let it comfort you too much. I haven't fallen in yet."

"It's just a matter of time, Baruch." Tiredly, she braced a hand against the table and got to her feet. Tiny upright lines formed between her brows. "May I go back to my duties now?"

He ground his teeth as he held her gaze. Should he let her? She'd been doing an invaluable job keeping her crew sane in an impossible situation. But her knowledge of the ship put her at the top of his list of dangerous enemies.

"No, I think not."

She looked surprised. "Why? If you've really taken

179

care of the minor reroutes, there's nothing more I can do to hurt you from the bridge."

"True, but there are things you can do to *help* me in Engineering. And I can keep a closer eye on you. Especially now that we know all deals are off. I'll let you come back to the bridge often enough to keep up pretenses."

He walked forward and lightly gripped her arm, guiding her toward the door.

* * *

Rudy Kopal paced the bridge of the *Zilpah*, black battlesuit rustling with his strained movements. Perspiration drenched his brown hair, stinging in his gray eyes. His gaze darted around the bridge. Ten people worked the control consoles in evenly spaced niches at the edges of the round chamber. Above him, twenty-two screens displayed different-colored information. He'd shouted so often at his crew in the past ten hours that now they all refused to meet his eyes, pretending to study the cursors on their com screens.

Damn it, Jeremiel. I told you. I told you not to go to Horeb.

He'd had his jaw clamped so hard for so long his facial muscles ached. Tightly, he said, "Merle?" letting the unspoken question dangle like a threat.

She swung around in her chair. A petite woman with a round face and pointed nose, long raven hair fell over her shoulders. Her dark eyes echoed his own deepest fears.

"Nothing more so far, Rudy. The message from the *Hoyer* to Palaia simply said they'd made arrangements with some Councilman named Ornias for a price of five billion notes. That was dispatched four days ago."

He glared anxiously at the forward screen. "What's the *Hoyer*'s current location? Do we know?"

"We assume they're still circling Horeb. But that information is unconfirmed."

He stepped toward the screen, eyeing the distant star-strewn skies. They'd been holding their position for hours, waiting for more data before they moved. To his eyes, the stars glistened darkly, like a sequined burial shroud thrown over the heavens. "At maximum vault, how long to get there?"

Merle's mouth went tight. She dropped her gaze. "Rudy, even if—"

"How long!"

The bridge hovered in deathly quiet. No one moved a muscle, but his officers seemed to cringe without moving.

Merle got up from her nav console, striding to stand beside him. The top of her dark head barely came to his shoulder. Under her breath, she said, "Let's go somewhere and talk."

Reluctantly, he spun and strode full tilt for the transport tube. She followed, gently pounding the patch for level twelve. They descended in grave silence, neither daring to speak to the other for fear of a blowup. When the tube stopped, Merle stepped out first, leading the way down the hall to the observation dome.

Rudy followed. They both stepped into the room and waited until the door snicked closed. A circular transparency lined with padded blue-plaid window seats, it had a diameter of about twenty feet. The lighting, always turned low, gleamed with the strength of a full moon. It cast their shadows like dark giants across the back wall. Through the dome, the Wind River Cloud Galaxies flared brilliantly, seeming so close he could reach out and grab a handful of stars.

And somewhere out there, somewhere, Jeremiel had fallen into a black abyss of trouble.

After several minutes of just standing and gazing at the stars, Merle sighed and went to sit on one of the long benches.

She ran a hand through her ebony hair, commenting, "You're wound pretty tight, Rudy."

Roughly, he folded his arms and fixed his gaze on the Crowheart Z-1, a neutron star of majestic splendor. Just now it seemed the center of everything bright in a desperately dark galaxy. "What the hell are we going to do, Merle? Leave him there? *You know what they'll do to him?*"

"Of course, I know."

"I won't leave him to that! If it was one of us, he'd run the whole goddamned fleet ragged to get us out."

"I know, but—"

"You've raided enough of those neuro labs. Do you want to see Jeremiel like that? I won't be able to look at myself in the mirror unless I know I did everything I could to get him out of Tahn's hands."

At the thought of Tahn, he couldn't help it, he whirled around and slammed a fist into the transparency. A muffled thud rang out. Clenching his fists, he struggled to gain control again.

Merle's soft voice penetrated his emotional haze. "I love him, too, Rudy. But let's take a good *professional* look at the data. First, Jeremiel probably *is* in Tahn's hands. And if he is, he has two options, to fight or to commit suicide. You know as well as I do that the chances of him allowing himself to be probed are minimal. He'd reveal too much critical information about Underground operations. Second, we're on the verge of doing something that may well endanger the entire Underground movement. If we leave half our fleet here to complete rescue operations around Abulafia and Ahiqar, we'll deplete our firepower dangerously. And we may need every erg we've got in the next month. *Because* . . ." She let the word hang dreadfully. "From the bits of information we've pieced together the Magistrates have already initiated a genocide program on Tikkun. What do you—"

"We don't *know* that!" he snapped hostilely. "All we have is some fragments of trans that have used words like 'sterilization' and 'relocation.' We can't be certain—"

"Don't be an *idiot!*" she shouted, lurching unsteadily to her feet. Her dark eyes blazed. "Do you want to take the chance? *Do you?* Tikkun is the most heavily populated Gamant planet left in the galaxy. There are a quarter million of our people there!"

"Merle, we can't split the fleet! It's too risky, damn it! And we can't just abandon—"

"What happens, Kopal, if the Magistrates initiate a massive sterilization program on Tikkun? *What happens to Gamant civilization* if twenty-five percent of its people are incapable of fertilization?" In a violent gesture, she clenched both her fists. "If they succeed, Rudy, Tikkun will only be the beginning."

"Don't be a doomsayer."

"Prophet maybe, doomsayer, never. I just believe the Magistrates. When they vowed to end *all* Gamant problems, I think they meant it."

"You've got faith in Slothen? The next thing I know you'll be revering him as a zaddik just like the rest of the galaxy."

She jerked his sleeve hard, forcing him to turn and look down at her. "When has he ever broken a promise,

182

Rudy? When he said he'd put an end to Gamant raiding, we lost the planet Jumes. When he said Gamant agitators would be stopped, Pitbon and Kayan died. *He keeps his promises.*"

Rudy dropped his arms to hang slackly at his sides and walked to the edge of the dome, staring out into the cold blackness of space. The dusty glow of hundreds of galaxies tarnished the sable background. In the distance, he made out the bare smudge of pewter marking the Orion arm of the Milky Way. His people had run a long, long way to escape persecution, but it seemed to follow them wherever they went. From the corner of his eye, he thought he saw movement—like a darkness slipping along the far wall. He turned to stare quizzically at it.

"And maybe," Merle pressed, "just maybe, Jeremiel owns the *Hoyer* by now."

He shook his head, looking back at her taut face. "Operation Abba was insane. I never thought it would work."

"You always said you did."

"I lied."

She eyed him consideringly. "But it might have."

"It might, if he'd had *you* and *me* to help him."

"Maybe he found somebody just as good."

The shadow seemed to have frozen in place. He frowned at it, wondering what object in the room cast that curious animallike shape. "It's possible. But if that's the case, why hasn't he tranned us? And even if through some miracle, he's in control of the *Hoyer* and he's got a com malfunction, he's going to have one hell of time keeping the cruiser. Tahn is nobody's fool. He'll know every thread to pull to make the whole damn thing fall apart around Jeremiel's ears."

"We don't have a choice, Rudy. Jeremiel's life is a second priority." Her voice quavered. "Retrieving survivors here and protecting Tikkun have got to be our primary concerns."

Their gazes locked and they shared their silent desperation. In the far reaches of Rudy's mind, he thought he heard a bare whisper—soothing, pointing him in a certain direction. "No. We can't split the fleet."

"Name of God, Kopal!" Merle threw up her hands. "What do I have to say to get it through your thick skull that we've got no . . ."

She kept talking, but Rudy's mind closed in upon itself. The voice in his head grew stronger, prompting in wordless ways. It became so strong that he shook his head to try and rid himself of it. "Merle. Merle . . . stop. I've changed my mind. You're right. Lord, I can barely stand the thought, but contact Martin Qaf."

"Does that mean I can set course for Tikkun?"

He shifted uneasily, vying with himself, not quite able to utter the word that might well condemn Jeremiel to a fate worse than death. At last, he forced himself to nod.

Merle exhaled a relieved breath and slipped an arm around his waist, pulling him close in a friendly hug. "I know it's hard. But if Jeremiel were here, that's what he'd order us to do."

Rudy tightened his grip around her, gazing at the dark shadow that clung unmoving in the corner. It gave him an eerie feeling—as though it watched him. "When you reach Martin, tell him he's in charge of the Abulafia operation. Inform him we're on our way to Tikkun, which means he'll have only seven cruisers at his back here."

"I will."

"He's going to have to make the evacuation of refugees damned fast—if he wants to get out of here alive."

Merle nodded solemnly. "I'll remind him—though I doubt he needs it."

* * *

Abruzzi ran a hand through his woolly gray hair and pounded a mahogany fist into the back of Tenon Lamont's chair. She looked up at him through dark eyes. Her pretty Oriental face had gone hard, unpleasant. Around them, the bridge hummed with quiet dismay, officers shaking their heads.

"This is ridiculous, Captain," Tenon whispered angrily. "Tahn obviously needs help!"

"I'm well aware of that." Abruzzi glared at the Clandestine One message that filled the forward screen:

Greetings, Captain Abruzzi.

Take no action to intercept or interfere with the Hoyer. *Continue monitoring and keep us informed. We have recently initiated an action against the Underground fleet and can afford no complications at this time.*

Please await further instructions.

Tenon swiveled around and leveled a fiery look at Abruzzi. "We can't just sit here when we know the *Hoyer* is in trouble."

Abruzzi propped his fists on his hips. "Those are our orders. I'm afraid we haven't any choice."

"Blast it, Gen! We told Slothen about the half-finished scorch attack and the shuttles filled with Gamant refugees. What possible complications could we cause if we rescue Tahn!"

"Slothen knows more about the galactic situation than we do, Lieutenant. Maybe he's afraid Baruch will get off a message before our attack and the Underground will rush to his aid and . . ." he lifted a hand uncertainly, "and he'll slip out of the trap Slothen has set."

Abruzzi walked back and dropped into his command chair on the top level. Out of habit, he checked the three-sixty monitors encircling the bridge. Everything aboard the *Scipio* looked normal—except his officers. They had anxious looks on their faces. Each stared at him, waiting. He felt it, too—as though every moment they hesitated in rescuing the *Hoyer* was a knife in Tahn's back.

Abruzzi expelled a breath. "Please keep monitoring the *Hoyer*'s actions, Lieutenant. We need to be prepared to advance on a moment's notice."

CHAPTER 20

Ornias gazed at his reflection in the wall of mirrors adorning Slothen's outer office. He was a tall man with light brown hair and a neatly braided beard, which accented his cold, lime green eyes and tanned face. He smoothed the wrinkles in his scarlet robe, watching the way the bright light flashed in the gold embroidery

185

adorning his broad chest. Yes, he looked the perfect picture of a soon to be wealthy gentleman.

"How much longer?" he sharply asked the beast sitting behind the desk. Its blue Giclasian skin and blood-red mouth set him on edge, bringing back too many unpleasant memories. Slothen had already kept him waiting for two days with no explanation.

"That is unknown, sir. Magistrate Slothen will call when he's ready for you. Please sit down." It extended three of its arms toward a chair. Its utterly toneless voice set him even more on edge.

"No. Thank you."

Didn't this pusillanimous animal know he'd been the one to trap the great Baruch? Irritation burned in his breast. Why hadn't he been met at the spaceport by a marching band and a dozen beautiful women? Not that it really mattered. Once he had his five billion notes, he'd go buy enough communications coverage to assure himself of a place in history.

Looking around the outer office, he grimaced. Ten by ten feet square, the place had putrid lavender walls and stark white furniture—none of the rich wood or stonework of Horeb or other Gamant planets. It disturbed him that he'd come to care about such things. He'd been born on Palaia Station, after all, he ought to value some of the things of his scurrilous youth. Idly, he wondered if any of the lice-infested friends of his childhood still lived. Abandoned by his parents when he'd turned twelve, Ornias had made his own way in the world.

He shuddered just thinking about it. He'd started selling bonds for nonexistent power plants when he turned fourteen. After that, stocks in supposedly rich uro-platinum mines on uninhabited worlds had gone well. Only one man had tried to kill him over the scam after he'd hired a fast transport and found his mine to be nothing more than a meteor crater. But Ornias had gotten rid of him quickly. He'd run into real trouble, however, when he decided to hoodwink war widows into buying land on the parade grounds of prison colonies. Weeping women could affect the most charcoal of hearts. The Magistrates had ordered him arrested. He'd been forced to steal a ship, change his identity, and flee to the hinterlands of Gamant obscurity where he'd flourished like a Giclasian sewer rat. And snaring Baruch had been his greatest achievement.

Annoyed by the delay, he moved to the broad window which looked out over Naas. Spiked buildings spread like a sea of bayonets, their mirrored surfaces gleaming beneath the lemon-colored skies.

"Topew?" a gruff baritone came over the com on the beast's desk. "Send in Councilman Ornias."

"Yes, Magistrate. He's on his way." Pinning him with catlike amethyst eyes, the beast pointed down a hallway. "It's the last door on the left, Councilman."

Ornias' mouth pursed disgustedly, then he strode past Topew and down the short corridor. Two human guards dressed in purple and gray uniforms stood outside, rifles cradled in their arms. They eyed him speculatively as he approached.

"I'm here to see Magistrate Slothen," he announced.

"He's expecting you, sir." The tall black-haired guard pressed a button on the wall. The door snicked back, revealing a large room, at least fifty feet square, with a high arching ceiling and more putrid lavender paint. Holograms of astronomical features hung high on the walls. Ornias stepped inside, inhaling deeply of the rich spicy fragrance. Exotic, it had an almost sexually intoxicating effect. His gaze lingered on one particular hologram: Palaia Zohar—the black hole companion of the star around which Palaia Station's enormous bulk orbited. Once every fifty-six years the station complex came perilously close to the singularity, requiring some fancy navigational maneuvers to escape the overwhelming gravitational pull. How old had he been the last time? Well, no matter, the next conjunction had to be at least ten or twelve years away.

"Councilman," the blue beast behind the broad white desk greeted. "I'm Magistrate Slothen." He tilted his balloon head toward the corner. "And this is Captain Brent Bogomil of the Magisterial cruiser *Jataka*, and Captain Joel Erinyes of the *Klewe*."

Ornias lifted his chin, wondering why Slothen had invited military officers to their meeting. A veiled threat? He scowled at the captains. Bogomil stood maybe five feet ten inches tall, had close-cropped red hair, emerald eyes, and a bluntly squared jaw. Sweat beaded across his pale forehead, running down his plump cheeks. He looked terrified. Erinyes, on the other hand, seemed uncommonly placid—almost gloatingly so. Tall with a thin face and hooked nose, he had coppery hair.

Ornias' stiffened instinctively and looked back to Slothen. "Why do we have an audience, Magistrate?"

"Do have a seat, Councilman." Slothen's wormy hair writhed and Ornias flinched. "Let me offer my congratulations on behalf of the Union of Solar Systems for the valiant services you've rendered. Baruch has killed millions of Magisterial citizens in his wild rampages across the galaxy. We are all deeply in your debt for ending his reign of terror."

"Uh-huh," Ornias muttered, eyes narrowing. He could feel something coming. The very air itself seemed to crackle with tension. He braced himself for the worst. "If you don't mind, Magistrate, I'm simply here to collect my five billion notes, then I'll be on my way. I've no desire to take any more of your precious time than is absolutely necessary to conclude our—"

"Let's not be rash, Councilman. I'd like to get to know you better."

Bogomil exhaled, his chair squealing as he suddenly shifted positions. Ornias' gaze slid furtively sideways. The captain's breathing had gone shallow, quickening like an ancient steam locomotive picking up speed to climb a steep hill.

Ornias swallowed hard. The Giclasian tried to smile, but the expression came off as more of a malevolent scowl, like a dog baring its teeth before gleefully pouncing on an unsuspecting rat.

"To *know* me better? Pray tell, Magistrate, what does that mean?"

Slothen shuffled through the mass of papers on his desk, picking up a stack six inches thick and riffling the shimmery crystal sheets. "There is some business pertaining to your presence on Palaia Station that I'd like to discuss with you. *Do sit down*, Councilman."

Panic tingled up Ornias' arms. Gracefully, he dropped to a formfitting chair and perfunctorily straightened his scarlet collar. Beneath the desk, he could see four of Slothen's arms writhing like mating serpents. His stomach roiled. "What business?"

"You were born on Palaia, is that right?"

He didn't answer, stalling until he figured out the angle.

Slothen continued. "And your real name is Ephippas Ornias Lix Tetrax?"

Good God, they weren't going to try and prosecute him for crimes committed over twenty years ago, were they? "Do your questions, Magistrate, relate to the valiant service I recently rendered to the Union?"

Slothen shoved the stack a short distance away and laced his slender fingers before his red mouth. In the yellow light streaming through the window, the blue skin of his shoulders glittered greenish. In a mechanically flat tone, he answered, "I'd no idea when we originally spoke through Captain Tahn that you were so . . . shall we say, 'well known' around Palaia?"

Blessed Gods! They were going to try it!

Ornias sighed expressively. "Are we still bargaining, Magistrate? I do hope not. It was my understanding that all that was over when I delivered Baruch."

Slothen's red mouth puckered into a shriveled circle. "Surely you can see that it would be most inadvisable for me to pay out five billion notes to a man who's wanted for everything from petty theft to murder. My constituents would hang me." He blinked, trying to look sympathetic.

"You're *reneging* on our deal!"

"Not exactly."

"Well, *what* exactly?"

Bogomil exhaled a nervous breath and leaned forward pensively. "May I explain, Magistrate?"

Slothen nodded. "Of course, Captain. Please go ahead."

Ornias watched Bogomil suspiciously as the man crushed and recrushed the purple hat in his hands. Erinyes sat by calmly, scrutinizing Ornias. "Councilman, we find ourselves in an unenviable position. We suspect we are currently standing on the brink of another Gamant Revolt, which—I'm sure you can understand—we'd like to avoid at all costs."

"Uh-huh." He surreptitiously glanced back at Slothen. The Magistrate watched him through demonic, half-lidded eyes. No matter how hard Ornias tried, he couldn't get over the feeling that Giclasians were all just sophisticated robots. They even moved with a mechanical stiffness.

"Of course, we've taken some measures to contain it. For example, the Underground just split its forces and we have several cruisers on their way to see if we can trap them around Abulafia and Ahiqar. Penzer Gorgon, one of our finest commanders, is in charge, but even if he crushes them, it won't be enough. And, well, our former Gamant specialist, Colonel Silbersay, has recently been institutionalized and we have no one to replace him. Are you following me?"

"Too well, I'm afraid."

"Well, we were thinking . . . that is, with Baruch in Tahn's custody . . . Yes, in custody, we . . . well . . ."

The uncertain tone in the captain's voice set Ornias to squirming. "You sound like you're not sure Baruch is in Tahn's custody, Captain. Don't tell me the government fouled up again?"

"No, no," Bogomil hastily assured, brows pulling together. "Please let me continue. With Baruch in our hands we thought it would benefit galactic peace if we spent several months taking Baruch around to Gamant planets. You know, making an example of him to those who might seek to follow in his footsteps?"

"I see."

"But we, well . . ."

"What the captain is trying to say," Slothen finished, smiling that dog smile again that made Ornias queasy, "is that we need someone who understands Gamant psychology to make the most of this venture."

This looked bad. Ornias contemplatively fiddled with the golden embroidery around his scarlet sleeve cuffs. Of course, it had possibilities. Though it would require him to put off retirement and expensive behavior for a short time, if he played it right, he could double his fortune and escape prosecution to boot. "You mean you want someone who can play up the Baruch capture for all it's worth."

"Precisely."

"It's an intriguing idea. But a Baruch sideshow could backfire in your faces and fuel the Revolt."

"*That,* Councilman, is why we need an experienced hand at the helm."

He stroked his beard thoughtfully, and returned

Slothen's smile. "And my compensation for this service?"

"We would, of course, be willing to pay you the standard salary of every Magisterial ambassador. Say—"

Ornias threw back his head and laughed condescendingly. "Surely, you're joking. You're asking me to defuse the entire Gamant Underground movement and you want to pay me a pittance? Be *realistic*."

Slothen's purple cat's eyes narrowed. For a long moment, he simply stared, then he said in a frighteningly deep voice, "I could simply lock you up, Tetrax. Given your background, I seriously doubt the judiciary committee would even request a hearing."

"Come, come, Slothen. You'd waste the talents of the one man in the galaxy who could lure Jeremiel Baruch away from his fleet and into a foolproof trap? I'm the perfect man for the job of undermining the impending war. And obviously you realize it or we wouldn't be having this discussion."

Bogomil waved his wrinkled hat, huffing, "Why are we listening to this drivel? We can find a hundred other—"

"What's your price, Councilman?"

Ornias smiled and considered for a moment. "I'll promise you six months of my time and take another five billion notes in payment."

From the corner of his eye he saw Bogomil jerk as if someone had slammed him in the stomach with a hard fist. Erinyes, however, grinned appreciatively. *"Magistrate,"* Bogomil blurted, "what he asks is simply outrageous! We can't—"

"Shut up," Slothen ordered and swiveled around in his chair as though following a well-rehearsed automated routine. His blue jaw vibrated as he gazed out over Naas. In the distance a huge fountain sprayed mist a hundred feet into the air, spawning a glistening rainbow over the center of the city.

Ornias smiled deprecatingly at Bogomil, who scowled in return. This was going better than he'd anticipated. A few months of scheming and he'd be able to afford his own planet. Maybe he'd select one of the jewels in the Mysore system. What a comforting idea. In his mind, he pictured the six-mile-high mountain peaks and marvelously muscular women in their scanty local costumes.

Already he could feel the grip of an athletic female's legs around his back as she milked him dry. Tingling in anticipation, he crossed his legs.

Slothen swiveled back and studied him harshly. "I'll give you one billion for two years' service."

Bogomil's sharp intake of breath made him smile. "Make it three for one year."

"I'll make it two for one year and that's my final offer."

A surge of adrenaline pricked his veins. "Just two other things then, Magistrate."

Slothen hesitated, eyeing him suspiciously. "They are?"

"I want that quaint stack of reports in front of you destroyed and my record erased from every com file in the galaxy. Despite my past, I expect, when this is all over, that you'll formally acknowledge me as the hero I am."

"I'll erase the com files."

Ornias shrugged, only mildly perturbed at losing hero status. "All right. I expect to have a battle cruiser at my command. I want no mistakes which might jeopardize my ability to survive and enjoy my rewards—if you know what I mean." He glanced at Bogomil, looking him up and down disparagingly.

Slothen tapped his twelve fingers on his desk. A curiously hollow thudding resulted, like the irregular staccato of distant rifle fire. It was a little unsettling.

"Not at your command, *Ambassador,* but I will agree to grant you First Lieutenant status aboard the *Klewe.*"

Chuckling softly, Ornias stood. "It's a pleasure doing business with you, Magistrate. When may I expect an armed escort to accompany me to the *Klewe*?"

"Armed? Afraid some of your old comrades might see you in the streets, Ambassador?"

"Comrades I wouldn't worry about. *When?*"

"Day after tomorrow. Say eight o'clock in the morning?"

"I'll be ready. Out of curiosity, where will our first stop on the Baruch sideshow be?"

Slothen heaved an irritated sigh. "Tikkun. I'll send a dattran to Tahn and have him meet you there. We've had so many violent attacks on Magisterial personnel recently, we've been forced to take punitive actions. Major Lichtner is in charge of the planet. I recently ordered him to intensify his efforts. But from what little intelligence we can gather, the Underground is growing in strength. Rebellions are flaring everywhere. Perhaps seeing their hero in a cage will dampen some of their ardor for battle."

Ornias smiled and bowed deeply. "I'll make certain it does, Magistrate."

"You'd better."

A small tendril of unease wound through him, but he smiled pleasantly and strode out the door, irreverently saluting the guards and starting down the hall. Before he reached the end, Erinyes had trotted to catch up, amiably walking at his side.

"Ambassador," Erinyes said smoothly. "Let's go somewhere and talk. I believe we can help each other."

CHAPTER 21

Long after midnight, Cole Tahn still wandered around his cabin, picking up things and slamming them down, clenching and unclenching his fists—fit to explode. His goddamned Gamant guards had just come in to reconnect his monitors again and it irked him no end. He'd been a prisoner on his own ship for five days! He could barely stand it. He hadn't been a prisoner since . . .

"Don't think about it," he whispered to himself, massaging the back of his stiff neck.

The pain in his head had nearly gone. But the concussion had left more perilous scars, as though the blows to his skull had shattered the inner gates in his mind that he'd worked for years to lock and bolt. He had to walk a tightrope around his own thoughts, physically keeping them from straying to Maggie and the Pegasus Invasion. Still, lightning flashes of scenes tormented him at unpredictable moments and for those few seconds, he found himself lost in a whirling storm of fragmented rose windows and actinic bursts of violet.

"If Palaia knew, they'd undoubtedly order me confined to a psych center for treatment." An involuntary shiver went through him. "Well . . . that may happen anyway. What the hell am I doing to stop it?"

He shook a fist futilely. Halloway had been acting as messenger between him and his crew. Suspicions about his capabilities among the crew still ran high, she'd said, but most had ceased to blame him for the debacle. He and Carey had set up a tentative organizational structure already, but he needed more time, more data, so he could discover precisely where Baruch had left himself vulnerable. Tahn had ferreted out possibilities, like the access Baruch had given the techno-science division to teaching programs, but killing the *Hoyer* through those narrow channels would be difficult, if not impossible. The thought of turning his ship into a mini-supernova left him trembling.

"Cool down. You're not that desperate yet. There has to be a method that will leave somebody alive."

He let his gaze drift over his cabin. He'd shuffled his books for the fifth time, rearranging them in descending order of size from left to right. In the bare pewter glow cast by the overhead panels, the gold gilded bindings gleamed as though sewn with the finest threads of saffron.

He needed more information! In a gruff movement, he spun in first one direction then another, feeling as though he wallowed in a vacuum. "Damn it!"

Unthinkingly, he pounded the com over his table. He'd tried every other cabin aboard and gotten nothing, but maybe . . . He keyed in cabin 2017. "Baruch? It's Tahn."

A long pause, then the Underground commander's deep voice responded. "I'm busy, Tahn."

"I don't give a good goddamn! When the hell are you going to meet with me? Are you afraid—"

"How's your head?"

Tahn propped a fist against the wall and ground his teeth. Baruch sounded vaguely concerned; it annoyed him like grains of sand in his eyes. Stiffly, he responded, "I'm fine. I want to talk to you."

"Severns says you're still suffering occasional hallucinations. I'll wait until—"

"Get your ass up here. I'm telling you, I'm fine!"

194

"Well, you do sound better. But I can't, Tahn. Not for a while. Get some sleep. I'll arrange a meeting as soon as I can."

He leaned a shoulder against the wall, squinting curiously at the com box. He had the overwhelming urge to ask Baruch why the duct in his cabin was still open. But that would be insane. Baruch had probably overlooked it in the melee of refugees and intership war—*and if so, Cole would be able to use that duct once and only once.* He had to pray Baruch never noticed and he could save it for just the right moment to get to his crew.

"Affirmative, Baruch. Tahn out."

Haggardly, he pushed away from the wall and walked to the center of his cabin. Raising fists over his head, he glared helplessly at the dim light panels. Carey had told him Baruch had reconnected the long-range link.

"Name of God, Slothen! Why haven't you tranned us demanding an explanation for our failure to report on the Horeb mission?"

It made no sense. No sense at all. His mind danced around the issue. It had been five days, for God's sake! Did nobody . . .

He stopped, slowly lowering his fists. But Palaia would have tried to tran. Unless they suspected something had gone wrong.

A tingling flush taunted him. He forced his fuzzy mind to think. How many cruisers had been in the approximate vicinity a week ago? He remembered checking the flight plans. *Jataka. Scipio.* Had there been others?

Hope welled so powerfully, his knees shook. He walked to his table to ease down into a chair. Maybe, just maybe, the cavalry stood on the hill overlooking the *Hoyer* at this very instant.

Excitedly, he shouted, *"Yes! Brent . . ."*

The room seemed to tip sideways, walls warping as though seen through a series of distored mirrors. *"Cole?"* Maggie's voice cried pleadingly.

"No. No!" He lurched unsteadily to his feet, grabbing his head between his hands as though to press the memories back inside. But the images rolled over him like a powerful wave: Slothen's misshapen face at the *Annum* Inquiry. The haunted eyes of the crew, his friends, as they were marched from the huge room. His own voice demanding, "Slothen! It wasn't their fault.

Magistrate, if you have any shred of decency you must see . . ."

His feet went out from under him. Minutes, or maybe hours, later he found himself lying on his floor, knees pulled up, head tucked.

The sick dread that filled him left him unable to get up. He rolled to his stomach and buried his face in his sleeve.

* * *

Sybil sat on the floor in the corner of their cabin, pretending to play with the checkerboard Ari had given her. She moved a red piece here and a black there, all the while keeping an eye on her mother. Something had happened to her, something bad, Sybil could tell. Though her mother had just showered and dressed in a beautiful cream-colored robe, sweat glistened across her nose. Sybil sighed and regarded her secretly. Deep inside, she felt afraid, though why, she couldn't say. But her mother felt it, too—her eyes gleamed darkly and she paced their cabin as though expecting the Magistrates to swoop down and kill them all at any second.

Sybil fiddled with another checker, shoving it aimlessly across the board with one finger. The room had been so very still and quiet, she ached to hear any word. The moments seemed to drag by as though she waited for something terrible. She'd tried talking to her mom about what the polar chambers had been like, or what had happened with the Mashiah in the palace, but her mother answered shortly as though Sybil were disturbing her, so she'd mostly stopped talking. It hurt deep inside, this strange scary silence and the haunted look on her mother's face. Loneliness tormented Sybil. She felt more lonely now, with her mother in the same room, that she had when she'd know her mother stood thousands of miles away in the polar chambers with the Mashiah.

Bravely, Sybil ventured, "Mom?"

"Hmm?"

"Are you scared? You look scared about something."

Her mother frowned.

"Are you scared, Mom?"

"No, baby. I'm just tired."

Sybil figured that was true, because her mom had terrible nightmares every time she closed her eyes. Sybil hadn't gotten very much sleep either because of them. "But you keep twisting your hands and walking around like you're afraid to sit down for even a little bit. Like you think something might get you if you do. You've been studying those security files all the time. Are they making you feel bad?"

Her mother folded her arms tightly over her chest. "I'm just worried, Sybil, that's all."

"You mean about learning enough to be good at security, or about the Magistrates coming to take the *Hoyer* back?"

Her mother swung around, mouth open. "Where did you hear that? Did Ari and Yosef—"

"No." Sybil nervously fiddled with another checker piece, lowering her gaze so she wouldn't have to see her mother's eyes. "No. I—I had a *funny* dream about it."

"Dream?"

She grabbed her mother's hand, bringing it down to kiss it lovingly, before pressing it to her cheek. "I know you always told me dreams weren't real, but I dreamed the Magistrates were coming in big ships to hurt us."

Her mother's eyes went glassy as though she were seeing something faraway. "When did you dream that?"

"Yesterday."

"How many ships were there in your dream?"

Sybil cocked her head, trying to count the ones she'd seen. "I don't know, Mom, maybe fifteen or twenty."

"Oh," her mother laughed as though in relief and patted Sybil's cheek. "Well, don't worry about your dreams, sweetheart. Jeremiel will keep us safe."

Sybil formed the blue fabric of her pant leg into a peak and smoothed it away, thinking all the while. She wanted to tell her mom that sometimes people couldn't, no matter how hard they tried, but she figured her mom didn't want to talk about it anymore. Her mom had that faraway look in her eyes again. When they'd lived on Horeb and Sybil had had a *funny* dream, she'd run into her parents' room and crawled into bed between them. They'd both put their arms around her and patted her until she went back to sleep. The closeness had chased her fears away. She had the urge to ask her mother to hold her now, but somehow, she didn't think it would work anymore. Her mom seemed too nervous and frightened herself to comfort her. "If it's not the Magistrates that are worrying you, what is it?"

"Oh, I—I just . . . I'll get over it. Don't worry, baby."

Sybil thought about that for a while, wondering why her mother wouldn't tell her. They used to talk all the time, telling each other their most horrible secrets. But that was back before her daddy got killed. She swallowed the hurt that rose like a suffocating bubble in her throat. Things had changed. Sybil tried to think of something to say to make her mom feel better, but before she could, a deep voice rang out from the com box.

"Rachel? It's Avel Harper. I have a message from Jeremiel for you."

"Avel!" Sybil yelled in excitement. He'd kept her safe when her mother had gone away to kill the Mashiah. He'd played with her and treated her like his own little girl. Her anxiety briefly changed to joy.

Her mother went to the door and palmed the patch. Stark white light from the hall streamed into their dim cabin, making a huge rectangle on the floor that stretched to touch Sybil's checkerboard. Avel stood tall and thin in the entryway, black hair shimmering in a halo around his head. His tan robe looked startling pale against his mahogany skin. One of the guards who constantly stood in the hallway peered over his shoulder.

Sybil got to her feet and ran to Harper, happiness overwhelming her. She swerved around her mother to grab his legs. "Avel! I've missed you. Where have you been?"

He knelt and gathered her into his arms to kiss her hair. "I've missed you, too, Sybil. I'm sorry I haven't been by to see you before now, but Jeremiel has kept me running."

She smiled up into his face, then patted his dark cheek affectionately. "It's okay. I'm glad you came today."

He kissed her forehead again and looked at her mother. The lines around his eyes crinkled. "How are you, Rachel?"

"All right, Harper. Is something wrong?"

"No, don't worry. It's just that Jeremiel wants to meet you briefly tonight. You're scheduled to report for security duty on level four tomorrow morning. Is that all right with you?"

Her mother's pretty face hardened. "Yes, of course. When does he want to meet me?"

"In his cabin at 1900 hours."

"Tell him I'll be there."

Sybil felt ill watching her mother drop her gaze and walk unsteadily back to stand in the center of the room. She folded her arms and hugged herself tightly. Avel's brows drew together, but he squeezed Sybil's shoulder warmly.

"One other thing, Rachel?"

"Hmm? What?" Her mother turned halfway around, grimacing as though she hadn't really heard the question.

"There's someone I'd like Sybil to meet. Would you mind if I take her down the hall? We'll be in cabin 1911."

Sybil bit her lower lip, wondering what was going on. "Who, Avel?"

He winked at her. "Someone I think you'll like. He's a little younger than you, but not by much."

"Another kid? Oh, Avel, that's wonderful! I *need* somebody to play with. Can I go, Mom? Can I?" She bounced hopefully. "Please, Mom?"

"Yes, sweetheart, but call me if you're going to be gone for more an than hour."

"I will."

Sybil charged into the hall, grabbing Avel by the hand and dragging him down the white corridor. Guards stood at each intersection of corridors, rifles held across their chests. Once outside that forebodingly silent cabin, her dread lifted like mist in the morning sun. "Who is he, Avel? Did he live on Horeb? Maybe I went to school with him. What's his name?"

Avel dutifully allowed himself to be led along, smiling. "I don't think you know him. He lived on Kayan. His name's Mikael Calas."

"Calas like Yosef?"

"Yes, he's Yosef's nephew."

"And he's seven? When's his birthday?"

"I don't know for sure, but you can ask him."

Sybil wanted to race down the hall to Mikael Calas' cabin and find him by herself. But she didn't, knowing that would probably hurt Avel's feelings. He'd want to introduce them, she figured. Grown-ups were like that. Once they'd planned something, they hated to have a kid mess it up. She forced her steps to slow to match Avel's.

"Thanks for coming to get me, Avel. I haven't felt very good."

"Why not? Are you sick?" He lowered a hand to feel her forehead, checking for fever.

"I'm not sick. I mean I haven't felt very good inside my heart."

"Ah," he said, nodding thoughtfully. He looked down at her in a kind way and for awhile they just walked, looking at the white walls. "Are you worried about your mom?"

Sybil wiped a hand under her nose and studied her feet. "She's not like she was before she went away to kill the Mashiah, Avel. She's different."

"How do you mean?"

"I don't know, she's . . . quieter. She hasn't talked to me very much."

He pulled her closer and stroked her face gently. "Well, you have to give her some time. She's trying to learn a whole new job and probably still thinking about what happened on Horeb. It wasn't easy for her, you know? Killing—"

"But she hated the Mashiah!"

"Hatred doesn't make killing easy, Sybil."

She thought about that. Avel squeezed her hand. "How long do you think it'll take her to get back to normal?"

"Oh, that's hard to say. But I'll bet she'll be pretty much her old self in a month or so. Can you wait that long?"

She nodded. They passed another guard who smiled down at Sybil. She smiled back and looked up at Avel. "I'll be extra nice to her. Maybe that'll help her to get over it sooner."

"I suspect that will help a lot. You're the most important thing in her life, you know?"

"I know. She's my best friend, too." Sybil exhaled a relieved breath. She'd forgotten that because her mother acted so much like a stranger, but now she remembered again and felt better. Sometimes friends had to be quiet with each other so the other could think hard.

As they neared cabin 1911, two guards appeared, each carrying a rifle. Sybil brushed brown curls out of her eyes, wetting her lips as Avel guided her through the crowd and rang the door com.

"Mikael? It's Avel Harper. I brought Sybil, just like I promised."

"Just a minute," someone said excitedly from within. *That voice!* Sybil's knees went suddenly weak. Where had she heard it before? Deep inside, she felt she'd always known his voice.

In a few moments, the door slipped open and a little boy with black curly hair and wide brown eyes stared at her. He was dressed in a lime green robe, and had a shy smile on his oval face. Sybil's insides shriveled. *She knew him.* He'd been in hundreds of her *funny* dreams.

"Mikael," Avel said happily, "this is Sybil Eloel. She's eight and lives down the hall in cabin 1901. Sybil, this is Mikael."

"Hello," Mikael said, forming his hands into the sacred triangle of greeting.

Sybil stared uneasily, seeing him as he would be in a few years, noting how his jaw would get squarer, his brown eyes harsher and she wondered what would happen to set his mouth into hard lines. "Hi." It came out smaller than she'd intended. She returned the sacred triangle.

"Come in! I've got games and candy in here."

He trotted across the room to pick up a bowl of brightly wrapped candies that had been on the floor by his bed, then raced back to set them on the table. Sybil stepped over the threshold into his room. Avel followed and the door zipped shut. Her heart pounded as she gazed around. The room looked the same size as hers, except there was only one bed and it sat in the back. It had the same ugly gray carpet. He had the overhead lights turned off. Only one panel lit the room; it glared dimly behind his bed.

"Come and sit down, Sybil," Mikael invited, crawling into a chair himself and patting the table. He smiled shyly again.

"Sure." She slid into the chair beside him.

"Here, try one of these candies. The blue ones taste like licorice." He shoved the brown bowl at her.

"I never heard of licorice, but thanks." She picked out one of the blue ones and unwrapped it, putting it in her mouth. The burst of wonderful flavor made her laugh. "This is good."

He laughed with her, eyes never leaving her face. Maybe he'd had dreams about her, too? The thought made her relax a little. She sucked in a deep breath and smiled.

"Sybil?" Avel said, touching her shoulder. "I have business to take care of for Jeremiel. Will you be all right here?"

"Sure. Me and Mikael will be fine. Go do what you need to, Avel."

"All right. I'll see you later." He started for the door. "Don't forget to call your mother if you're going to be longer than an hour."

"I won't."

"Bye, Avel, " Mikael called. "Thanks for bringing me Sybil."

Avel nodded, smiling as he left. "You two have fun together."

When the door closed, Sybil cocked her head, studying Mikael with interest. His hair hung in thick black curls over his ears, framing his turned up nose and big eyes. He dug into the bowl and pulled out a red candy.

He held it up for her to see. "These taste like hot cinnamon. You should have one next."

She nodded. "When's your birthday, Mikael? Avel said we were almost the same age."

"September-Uru," he said. "The fifteenth."

"So you're about four months younger than me. My birthday's Jano twentieth."

"My mom's birthday was in Jano. She . . ." He stopped, dropping his gaze to the table. Sybil blinked seeing his tears well.

"You okay?"

He nodded quickly, wiping a sleeve over his eyes. "It's just that my mom . . . The Magistrates killed her. They came in big ships and fired into the cliffs where we lived. Rocks rolled down on top of her."

"I'm sorry," Sybil forced herself to say, "My dad's dead, too."

Mikael lifted his eyes and looked seriously at her. "Is your mother all right?"

"She's down the hall in our cabin. Where's your dad?"

"He died before I was born. I don't know very much about him. Just that he was a cantor in temple. People used to talk about what a beautiful voice he had."

Sybil's heart ached for him. She remembered the terrible fear of wondering what life would be like with both her parents dead. It had ripped at her insides like the claws of a huge cat. He must feel the same way. She

202

reached across the table and squeezed Mikael's hand tightly. "It's okay, Mikael. Someday the Magistrates will all be dead and they won't ever be able to hurt our people again."

His smile faded and he gazed at her gravely—*through the same worried and fierce eyes that filled her dreams.* She couldn't help but stare into them.

"You know why they'll be dead, Sybil? Because I'm going to lead a new Gamant Revolt and kill them. Just like my grandfather did. You can come if you want to."

She nodded, knowing she would. She'd seen the battlefields since the day she'd turned three and started having *funny* dreams. "I do."

"Do you? Really?" he asked anxiously.

"Yes. I need to be there with you. So we can kill them right."

"Do you know how?"

She shrugged. "Not yet. But I will someday."

He formed his hands into the sacred triangle and nudged her to do the same. When she did, he wove his fingers with hers, locking the triangles together. "Let's make a pact that we'll both learn, on our parents' graves."

She looked at his fingers linked with hers. It sounded reasonable. "Okay, what do I have to do?"

"Just say you promise on your dad's grave that you'll help me lead the revolt."

"I promise—on my dad's grave."

A lump rose in her throat. She didn't even know where her father's grave was. That hurt. She swallowed hard and saw Mikael gazing steadily at her, as though she were his only friend in the universe.

"Thanks, Sybil. And I promise on my mother's grave." Then he cocked his head and hastily warned, "You can't back out now."

"I won't back out. You need me."

Slowly, he released her hands and they stared at each other for a long moment. Sybil smiled first, then he followed.

An hour later, she got on her knees on the chair next to the com, punching in her room number. "Mom? It's me."

After a short wait, her mother responded, "Are you all right, Sybil?" There was something brittle about her voice, like she might break into a million pieces if she talked too long. Sybil heaved a tense sigh.

"Fine. Me and Mikael have been wrestling. I won."

"Don't hurt him, sweetheart."

"I won't."

Sybil smiled down at Mikael. He was stretched out on his side on the floor. He grabbed his ribs like they were broken, then shook a fist at her. They both laughed. A warm feeling flooded her chest. "Mom? Could I stay here for another hour or so? We want to play checkers."

"Yes, Sybil. Just call me every so often to let me know you're all right."

"I will, Mom. Bye."

Sybil switched off the com and climbed down from the chair. Mikael looked up at her through shining eyes.

"Your mom sounded worried."

"Yeah." She shook brown hair out of her eyes and sat down cross-legged beside him. "She's been like that since she got back from Horeb. She had to kill a bad man and I think she's still feeling funny about it."

Mikael pursed his lips and rubbed his fingers thoughtfully over the carpet. The glare of the single light panel reflected silvery through his hair, casting the gray shadows of wispy curls over his cheeks. "It must be hard to kill somebody."

"I guess so."

"I don't really want to, but we'll have to, you know."

She nodded, stretching out on her side next to him. "Yeah, I know."

"I'll try to make it easier for you. Once I learn how to do it, I'll show you."

"Okay."

Sybil let out a long breath and picked at her fingernails for a little while, thinking. "Mikael? Have you ever had dreams about me?"

He frowned in confusion. "I don't know. Maybe."

She crushed her pant leg in one hand, feeling her palm getting wetter as her heart thumped against her ribs. "I think I've dreamed about you."

"Really? What was the dream?"

She hesitated. Maybe she'd better only tell him about one to start with—he might feel weird if she told him she dreamed about him all the time. "Well . . . it . . . it was funny. We were standing on a green hillside and there

204

were horrible sounds. Screams and things. People were dying all around us. Purple fire burned in the clouds for as far as we could see." She closed her eyes, shuddering, remembering the brilliant lavender reflection flashing across the evening sky. It was huge, not like the small purple fires that had lit up Horeb during the civil war. Her nostrils ached with the coppery scents of blood and battle.

He shifted suddenly and she pulled her eyes open, meeting his tense gaze. "I've seen that kind of fire before. When the Magistrates killed my mom."

"So, it's real?"

"It's real. It comes out of the big ships the Magistrates own. Like this one."

"Oh." Her gaze darted nervously over the table and chairs, his bed and desk.

"What else happens in your dream?"

Should she tell him? What would he do? Would it make him afraid of her? Maybe she could tell him part. "Mikael, do you have a *Mea*?"

He jerked as though she'd hit him, sitting bolt upright. His breathing quickened. "How do you know about it? My grandfather told me not to tell anybody but Jeremiel Baruch. And he's so busy, I haven't seen him at all."

Sybil's throat had gotten scratchy, making it hard to swallow. "In my dream, we hold it between our foreheads and—and do something."

Slowly, as though he feared doing it, he tugged on the golden chain around his neck, pulling a *Mea* out of his robe. The brilliant blue ball threw light like a glowing shawl over the walls.

Sybil's heart thumped louder. "Where did you get it?"

He lifted his chin a little, staring at her in a doubtful way, like he thought she might not believe him if he told her. "An angel brought it to me."

"An angel?"

He nodded. "He's bright and shining. His name's Metatron. He—"

"Hey! I think I've dreamed about him, too! He came and brought you a *Mea*? Why? So you can talk to God?"

Mikael's shoulders sagged. Abruptly, he got to his feet to pace, hands clasped behind his back. "I don't think I can tell you, Sybil. I'm sorry. I'll have to ask my grandfather first."

"It's okay," she said, playing with her shoelaces—only a little hurt. "Is he on board?"

Mikael's breathing stopped, face puckering as though he were trying to decide if he could tell her. "Sort of."

At the strained look on his face, fear tightened in her chest. She didn't like feeling afraid with Mikael. She wanted them to be friends. "You know what? I think we ought to play checkers for a while. *Meas* are funny things. They scare me."

She jumped up and ran across the room, pulling the checkerboard off the desk by his bed and carefully carrying it back to the table.

He smiled gratefully and tucked the *Mea* back in his green robe before climbing up on the chair opposite her. They set out the playing pieces, glancing sideways at each other.

"Sybil?"

"What?"

"In your dreams? When you talk to Metatron, does your head hurt?"

Sybil swallowed hard. "Yeah. Real bad. Like maybe he's putting poison in my brain or something. Does yours hurt?"

Mikael nodded heartily. "I don't really know why. But I talked to my grandpa about it and he said that sometimes angels do funny things to people. But he didn't know why Metatron was talking to me either."

"What else did he tell you?"

"Well . . . I'm not supposed to say. I'll tell you someday, okay?"

"Sure. You don't even have to if you don't want to. You'll still be my friend."

He sneaked a hand across the table and patted her arm. His fingers felt warm. She looked up. He watched her from under his lashes, a sad smile on his face.

"You can move first, Sybil. I don't want to."

* * *

CHAPTER 22

Jasper Jacoby rounded a corner, heading down another aisle in the grocery store. His basket had a wobbly wheel, making it difficult to control. He had to aim it to the left and lean into it to get it going straight. People who noticed him coming at them fled liked scared chickens. It was a little exciting, since the place brimmed with people today, especially women buying fresh fruits and bread for the Shabbat. Their freshly-ironed dresses gleamed brightly down each aisle. He liked the startled looks on their faces when they observed his tenacity with the basket.

"But you're still a damnable beast," he cursed, giving the malevolent wheel a swift kick.

For the past two days he'd been staying at one of the largest vagrant camps north of Derow. Those bums knew how to live. They never told anybody their real names and they never asked him his. Soldiers had come through a few times, but all the derelicts had clammed up tight. Still . . . Jasper had a feeling of impending doom—like time was running out.

He pushed his cart toward the checkout. A young fat woman with two ugly children stood in line in front of him. The younger boy clung to his mother's skirts like a leech, whining for a toy he'd seen.

"I *want* that bear, Mama! You promised you'd get me a toy. You lied. You lied!"

"Shh!" his mother hissed, slapping at his hands, which made the child worse. His whines rose to shrieks and he started to jump up and down. "You're embarrassing me! Stop it!" She cast a sideways glance at Jasper. "See that man staring at you, Tomasz? He thinks you're a bad boy."

Jasper's mouth puckered wickedly as the boy frowned up at him. "Boy, hell. He's a little wild animal. Why didn't you raise a human being?"

The fat woman's mouth dropped open. "How dare—"

"Don't dare me. You'd regret it."

"You old lout! Get out of my way!" She jerked her basket backward, forcing Jasper to move, then hurried toward another checkout. Her son stuck his tongue out at Jasper in a final coup.

He sniggered. The woman in front of him was just finishing paying for her food. He pushed his basket forward as she grabbed her bag and left.

"Good morning, Mr. Jacoby," the dark-haired boy behind the counter greeted. Eighteen, with a heavy brow and hooked nose, Smuel looked like a primitive caveman.

"Hi, Smuel. How's your father's gout?"

"Oh, he's much better, thanks. That new doctor gave him some pink pills and he's on his feet again."

"Glad to hear it. He needs to be to keep running from Mildred Slone. *I know.*"

Smuel suppressed a smile and pulled Jasper's basket into his checkout niche. Looking up pleasantly, he held out a hand. "May I see your ration card, Mr. Jacoby?"

"My *what?*"

"Your ration card. That's the yellow card they gave you when you registered."

"I didn't register!"

Smuel's face paled. He glanced uneasily at the people in line behind Jasper, lowering his voice. "I'm sorry, sir, but I can only sell food to people with ration cards."

"What? You mean my money's no good in your store?"

"Money's not the issue. Nobody in Derow can sell you food without seeing your ration card. The Magistrates have declared a death penalty for all food vendors who disobey."

Jasper grabbed the counter hard to steady himself. *So that's the way they're working it. If you don't register, you don't eat.* Rage flared. "What are you going to do, eh?" he shouted at Smuel. "Let your relatives starve because they won't knuckle under to the Magistrates?"

A crowd had gathered, whispering behind Jasper's back, pointing rudely. He spun on his heel, waving his arms. "Quit that! Get away from me! You over there? Did you register?"

The little old man in the worn brown derby timidly raised a yellow card.

"You imbecile! When they come to get you, I hope you remember some of us resisted! And you could have and didn't!"

Gruffly, Jasper shoved his basket into Smuel's stomach and strode from the store.

Rain fell outside, a drenching shower that turned the gray day into a nightmare of tears. He could have walked beneath the canopies of the shops lining the busy street, but he walked in the open, letting the rain soak him through—hoping the cold would ease some of the qualm of terror that blazed in his chest.

* * *

Penzer Gorgon glanced at the three hundred and sixty degree monitors that encircled the bridge. Everything looked ready.

"Take one final deep breath everybody," he said softly. "After we exit light vault, we're not going to have another one for hours."

He dropped back into his command chair and gripped the armrests. Around the broad oval bridge of the *Hecate*, officers sat deathly still in their niches, as though walking a knife's edge over a fiery apocalypse. The entire spectrum splashed his forward screen, waves of purple and yellow eddying around the edges. He was a short man with pale blue eyes and sparse gray hair; the gold braid on Gorgon's shoulders gleamed like strands of spun sunlight beneath the harsh lusterglobes.

"Meursault," he called to his skinny brown-haired navigation officer. "What's our status?"

The boy answered without turning. "So far as we know, sir, we're still in formation with the other twelve ships in the fleet. We should all exit vault at exactly the same time and take the Underground cruisers by complete surprise."

Gorgon nodded, pursing his lips tightly. "Delaney? Ready?"

"Aye, sir." Blonde with green eyes, she leaned forward over her console. "Weapons powered up, sir."

"Good. Since we're the lead ship, target the first enemy vessel you see. We'll initiate the attack in approximately thirty seconds. Meursault . . ."

His voice died as the lights dimmed. Gorgon lurched from his chair. "Goddamn it, is that a power fluctuation? Get me Engineer Horner before I—"

Delaney screamed, arm stretched out toward the back wall. A huge dark shadow undulated across the bridge. The faces of his crew twisted in terror, people lunging out of their seats.

Gorgon stumbled backward. "What the hell is that? *What is that?*" he shouted.

"Exiting vault, sir!" Meursault yelled. "Enemy vessels on screen!"

* * *

Aktariel quietly observed.

Martin Qak barely had time to whirl to see the brilliant streaks of cruisers dropping out of the blackness of space. The twelve men and women on his bridge went white. His dark eyes widened in shock. "Oh, my God . . . Nunes! Get us the hell out of here! Weslan, shields on full. Get us—"

Aktariel winced, closing his eyes as Gorgon's first shot lanced out of the blackness. The bridge of the *Khezr* vaporized, hull breaching. Atmosphere and bodies boiled into the blackness of space around Abulafia.

Aktariel clutched the blue velvet over his heart and closed his eyes against it. Quietly, he drifted to level sixteen, walking the long white halls in silence. His cloak billowed out behind him. People in black battlesuits rushed by, panting, some whimpering.

"Oh God, oh God," a woman with blonde hair prayed. She knelt in the hallway beside him and jerked a cover from the wall, then frantically began inputting a series of commands into a computer unit. "Please, Epagael. Just one more time, let us get out of this and I'll do anything you say. Oh, Jeremiel, Jeremiel, I wish you were here. You'd get us out of this. I know . . ."

A shrill sucking sound deafened Aktariel. He put his hands over his ears.

"No!" the woman screamed. "No, no, God! *Please!*"

She clawed at a doorway as the oxygen vanished. Her lungs burst, eyes popping from her skull, then her body slithered down the corridor toward an open hatch.

Aktariel bowed his head.

He descended to level fourteen, into a crew cabin where the forces of decompression worked more slowly. A young man writhed on the floor. No more than twenty, he groped frantically for the vacuum suit lying just out of his reach. The boy rolled over and his eyes widened.

"Help . . ."

Aktariel blinked in surprise. This one had blood from the House of Ephraim. A curious find. Only a handful remained in the universe. He'd made certain of that. "I can't."

The boy stretched out a hand. *"Please?"*

"I'm sorry. This must be—for all of us." He knelt, tenderly stroking the corporal's brow. "Forgive me. If I could save you, I would."

When the last of the air vanished, blood trickled from the boy's nose and his eyes went vacant.

Aktariel stood, listening to the pounding of his heart, studying the corpse. The boy's face had contorted. His horror and disbelief reflected starkly in the glaring white lusterglobes.

The ship went black, power gone.

Aktariel looked up, seeing beyond the thin veil of metal to the dark star-strewn skies. All around him, ships flared and died. The screams of thousands burst forth, borne silently on the solar winds, spreading out eternally. One Underground cruiser veered off from the rest, hurtling wildly through space, picking up speed for the vault. It vanished.

Aktariel absently watched six Magisterial cruisers disappear in pursuit. He extended his senses, searching beyond the battle, searching for some residue of understanding or pity that might have penetrated the fabric between the Treasury of Light and the Abyss. But he found nothing.

He bowed his head and faintly, ever so faintly, he heard a tiny childish voice call to him—a boy's voice filled with tears.

It called. And called again.

Wearily, he pulled his *Mea* from his cloak and lifted a hand to the darkness that engulfed the dead starship.

CHAPTER 23

Jeremiel leaned a shoulder against the wall of his cabin, sipping his taza. Dressed casually in a charcoal gray shirt and black pants, he looked at Rachel with an intensity that made her spine stiffen. She hunched over the table, impatiently playing with her own cup. Perspiration glued her brown jumpsuit to her sides.

"So these dreams come over you without warning?"

"Yes," she responded, evading his eyes. "I don't understand it."

Steam whirled around his handsome face as he lifted his cup again, taking a long drink of the rich earthy brew. "Prophetic dreams are pretty common among Gamants. Have you had them all your life?"

"No. Just recently."

"How do you feel otherwise?" His eyes glittered.

"Fine. Why?"

"No symptoms of sleeplessness, tendencies toward violent behavior, unjustified nervousness?"

She examined him severely. "Oh, I get it. You're psychoanalyzing me. All right. In the current context, define 'unjustified' nervousness?"

The corners of his mouth curved in a reluctant smile. "You're feeling perfectly normal, I take it, other than for the dreams?"

"Perfectly normal."

"You haven't seen Aktariel physically again since you left Horeb?"

"No."

He nodded. "Good." Relief eased the hard set of his face. "Then let's discuss the ship and your duties. We've thoroughly searched the duct systems and sealed levels seven through the bridge and levels twelve through twenty. You should be safe alone on any of those—but *don't* set foot on the others. I'm fairly certain we've weeded out the old Ornias devotees, but not positive. If they're still alive, that's where they'll be, in among the wounded waiting for treatment." He took a drink of his taza. "There are also a few special things I want you to do with the level four security, even though they'll sound . . . unusual."

"For example?"

"Tahn continually disconnects the monitors in his cabin. I want you to check them periodically, and reconnect them, *but let Tahn finish talking to Halloway each time before you do so.*"

She studied him curiously. "I don't understand. Why?"

"Let's just say I want him to feel comfortable. You will also notice that the air duct in Tahn's cabin is open. Leave it that way. It currently leads nowhere."

"Currently?"

"Yes. Don't worry about it."

She lifted dark graceful brows. "I didn't realize you liked Tahn so much."

"Don't." His lips smiled, but his eyes remained stony. "And I want you to give Halloway free access to him—any time she wants."

Rachel shook her head as though she hadn't heard right. Long black waves fell over her shoulders. "I'd think you'd want exactly the opposite, to separate them to keep them from plotting behind your back."

He pushed away from the wall and strolled lazily to stand by the table, gazing down at her seriously. "They'll be plotting anyway. There's absolutely no way I can prevent it unless I kill them."

Rachel held his gaze. What possible reason could he have for giving them the chance to get their crew organized? "Why *don't* you kill them? It would seem to me—"

"Bear with me, Rachel. Let's say I'm playing a hunch. As soon as I know more about how the Magisterial forces are operating, I'll explain my bizarre orders."

"I'll bear with you. You're usually right." She finished her taza and stood up. "Incidentally, I've had some other interesting nightmares."

His brow wrinkled. "Indeed?"

"Yes. My worst fears made manifest. Try not to make them come true. I don't know how we'd survive without you, Jeremiel."

He tightened his arms over his chest and gave her a fleeting smile. "Don't worry. I don't have time to die."

* * *

Sybil dashed across her cabin past the table and chairs near the entry, giggling wildly. In her long silver robe she looked like a tiny splinter of moonlight. Ari crept across the floor, eyes squinted. "Now I've got you!"

"No, Ari! No!" Sybil yelled, laughing shrilly. She scrambled to hide behind the bunk beds. They'd been playing war for over an hour. She'd kicked and bitten him just about every place she could. "It's not fair. That's not in the rules!"

"Lesson number twelve," Ari said wickedly. "When it comes down to you against them, forget the rules."

"Ah!" Sybil shrieked as Ari dove at her, picking her up and swinging her over his head. She laughed, arms flailing. Grabbing handfuls of his gray hair, she jerked.

"Hey!" Ari growled. "Wait a minute!"

Sybil gritted her teeth so hard her head shook. She jerked harder, throwing all of her strength into it. "Yeow!" Ari swung her over his shoulders like a sack of potatoes and dumped her on the floor. He glared down at her.

"You little wildcat!"

Sybil lay prostrate, grinning. "'Member that one, Ari? Lesson number four: Honorable people play by rules. If they don't, you can kick them wherever you want."

He scratched his head briskly. "I've been teaching you too much about strategy. Before I know it, you'll be as sneaky as the Magistrates."

Sybil's smile faded. She blinked and pulled her eyes away to stare at her hair and the way it shimmered against the gray carpet. Biting her lip, she kept quiet for a little while, thinking.

Ari frowned at her. "What's the matter, sweetheart?"

"Ari? Have you ever heard of a man named Captain Erinyes?"

Ari put his hands on his hips and shook his head. "Can't say that I have. Who is he?"

Sybil frowned and heaved a sigh. Ari cocked his head curiously. He didn't understand it, but she seemed so much older now than when they'd met—as though some eerie power had invaded her body and stimulated her

214

mental growth. But the same could be said of Mikael. In the six days they'd been aboard the *Hoyer*, he'd seen Mikael four times and each time, the boy seemed more mature. Stress, probably. Even protected children felt it. But . . . it struck him as odd. Both Sybil and Mikael acted more like ten- or eleven-year-olds now.

He gazed back at Sybil. She looked vaguely frightened —like she thought he might laugh at her, but she said, "I don't know who Captain Erinyes is. But he's a bad man, Ari."

"What does he look like?"

She stretched her arms over her head. "He's tall and has a mean face with a hooked nose like a stone eagle."

"Hmm." Grunting, Ari slowly lowered himself to sit on the floor beside her. He folded his wrinkled hands in his lap. "Where'd you hear about him?"

"Well, I don't know if I should tell you."

"What? Who can you tell if not me? Huh? I thought we were friends." He formed his mouth into a fine pout.

"Yeah. We are." She smiled and extended a hand, grabbing his sleeve and tugging it affectionately. Then her gaze fell. "But people make fun of me sometimes, Ari. I don't like that."

"I'm not going to do that. Tell me."

She heaved an uncertain breath and looked at him suspiciously, as though weighing his trustworthiness. "Well—I have *funny* dreams."

Ari's bushy gray brows drew together over his nose. "You mean like dreams that scare you or—"

"No," she said in a small voice, embarrassed. "Do you promise not to tell anybody, Ari? It would make me mad if you did."

"I won't tell. What?"

"I have dreams that . . . that come true." She looked up apprehensively.

"Oh, I see." He nodded in grave understanding. "And you had one of these dreams about this Captain Erinyes?"

She nodded, curls bouncing against the carpet. Breathlessly, she waited for him to say something.

Ari picked lint from his green robe and dropped it on the floor. "So—what happened in your dream? With this Erinyes?"

Sybil opened her mouth, then closed it—obviously holding back.

"Look," said Ari. He stretched out full-length beside her, so their faces would be on the same level. He gazed seriously into her eyes. "I'm going to tell you something, but you can't tell either, okay?"

"Sure. What?"

He reached out and gently pulled one of her curls, straightening it out. She watched his face intently. "I know somebody else who has 'feelings' that come true. When something's wrong, he just knows it." Ari tapped his chest. "He feels it in his heart. If your dreams are like his 'feelings,' you should tell somebody. That way we can prepare for whatever's going to happen."

She bit her lip again. "Yeah. I guess. Who's this other person, Ari?"

"Yosef."

Her eyes widened, as though that fact lent more credence to her own dreams. "He does?"

"He does. The legends of our people say that everybody with blood from the House of Ephraim has the sight of a prophet. So, tell me about this Erinyes? Who is he?"

"The House of Ephraim?"

"The House the final Mashiah is going to come from."

"Sure. That's right. I remember from school. Okay, Ari, here goes. Erinyes is the captain of a big ship. It has a purple sign on it."

"The shield insignia of the Magistrates. Go on. Is his ship shaped like this one? A battle cruiser?"

"Yeah. Just like this one." In a violent burst, she threw out her arms, whistling shrilly. "And other ships come. Bad purple light shoots out from them and hits this one. And . . . and . . . me and Mikael?"

"What? What about you and Mikael?" A tiny flicker of horror built in Ari's breast. His old heart pounded painfully.

"Well, I don't really get it, but me and Mikael go with Captain Erinyes. And we're both real scared and Mikael cries a little."

The flicker grew into a devouring flame. Ari swallowed hard and pushed up on one elbow. "When does this happen?"

"I don't know. But I . . . ." She tilted her head as though

seeing the dream images again. Her soft brown eyes took on a faraway look. "I think it's soon."

Ari reached out and dragged her across the carpet, pulling her against his bony chest. "What happens after that? Did your dream say?"

She shook her head. "Nope. But sometimes they come back and are longer. Maybe next time I'll see."

Ari couldn't keep the dire quality from his voice. "If it does, I want you to come tell me. I don't care what time it is. *You come tell me.*"

Sybil nodded. "Okay. Ari? Thanks for not making fun of me. It hurts when people do that."

"I won't ever make fun of you, Sybil. You're my best girl."

"Thanks, Ari."

In a swift, expert motion, she lunged for his stomach, digging her fingers in and tickling ruthlessly.

"Good God!" Ari blurted, trying to grab her lightning fast hands. "Quit that! What do you think you're—"

"Lesson one: Get them before they get you!"

He squirmed away and Sybil leaped to her feet, braced for combat. An eerie glitter lit her eyes. She circled him like a hawk spying a juicy grasshopper. He distracted her by looking suddenly over by her bed. When she whirled to look, too, he dove for her legs. Her bright giggles filled the room.

CHAPTER 24

Jeremiel stood behind Halloway in Engineering, watching her teach Janowitz the principles of navigation. They'd been working sixteen hours straight and all felt a little numb. Work crews had thoroughly cleaned the tri-level round chamber, dragging out the bodies and scrubbing blood from the walls. The wire duty cages now contained a handful of Gamant specialists manning the critical consoles. In front of Halloway and Janowitz, seven computer screens displayed calculations in red, gold, and green. She pointed at the middle screen, eyes glowing darkly as she talked to Chris. He frowned in determination, blond hair hanging in damp strands over his ears. Most of it he didn't understand, but he was trying very hard.

"Not quite," she said patiently, "the Belk solution to this empty space field equation is asymptotically flat. I mean by that the value of the Reimann-Christoffel tensor goes to zero as the coordinate r approaches infinity and also the physical . . ."

"Lieutenant." Janowitz licked his lips anxiously. "I don't understand a word you're saying. I'm sorry. Could you tell me why this is important?"

She blinked, obviously unnerved by the question.

Jeremiel leaned forward, bracing his hands on their chair backs, gently interjecting. "He's been raised and taught on a backward planet at the edge of the galaxy, Halloway. Singularities aren't common topics of discussion in the schools."

She turned to look incredulously up at him. "Why not?"

"Because they don't directly relate to the procurement of food and shelter—those are the primary concerns on places like Horeb."

She heaved a tired sigh. "Well, let's take it from the top, Janowitz." She swiveled her chair back around and squinted at the screen as though trying to focus, then leaned back in her chair and closed her eyes a moment.

"Things starting to get blurry?" Jeremiel asked sympathetically. He'd been pushing her hard, deliberately.

"Afraid so."

"Chris, why don't you take a break and come back in an hour or so."

Janowitz vented a disgruntled breath and nodded. "Aye, Jeremiel, I could use a sandwich—and some time to clear my head." Getting up from his chair, he eagerly left.

Jeremiel smiled at Halloway. She looked dead tired, dark circles forming beneath her eyes. "Can I buy you a cup of taza? Coffee?"

She ran a hand through her damp hair and exhaled

wearily. "Are there any computer screens where we're going? If so, I'll decline."

"There aren't. My people just finished cleaning the level twenty lounge."

"Then I accept."

He led the way out of Engineering and down the long white hall in silence. They passed several Gamant guards and a few technicians. When they came to room 2012, he input the entry sequence and ushered her inside, then sealed the room. He didn't want to have to worry about security tonight.

He almost breathed an audible sigh of relief. This was his favorite cruiser lounge, soft, sensuous. Real, inefficient candles lit the hardwood tables; it had fifteen small wooden booths lining the walls and a series of magnificent holograms of exotic architecture on the walls. The soft music came from the Arctur Colonies, but its mournful lilting notes took him back to early twentieth century Earth and the jazz era. His one off-duty passion consisted of collecting every scrap of music ever recorded by Billie Holiday. Not an easy task these days.

A circular marbleloid dance floor adorned the center of the room, shining like a mother-of-pearl pool in the candlelight.

Halloway nodded admiringly. "Good job. Your people did more than clean. This place sparkles."

"An architect from Horeb, originally born on Jumes, took charge of the effort."

Neither looked at the other. He knew the woman had fled from Jumes just before Tahn's scorch attack. Halloway would suspect as much.

He put a hand lightly against her back and guided her to a far booth. They took opposite sides of the table and Jeremiel turned to the dispenser built into the wall.

"What can I get you?"

She gave him a tired smile. "How about a glass of sweet Silanian sherry?"

He keyed in for two. The honey-flavored liquor came out in fine crystal goblets. He handed her one, watching the way the light refracted through the glass to cast beautiful geometric designs across the tabletop.

"Thanks."

"You're welcome."

She leaned back against the booth and exhaled slowly. The rich wood made her auburn hair seem redder, her alabaster complexion more like smooth cream.

He sipped his drink and braced his elbows on the table. "Thanks for being so patient. You've done a superb job teaching today."

She shook her head. "I didn't realize it would be so difficult. Janowitz is very bright, but his last question made me cringe. Anyone who could ask why understanding singularities is important to navigation knows absolutely nothing about gravitation."

He turned his glass between his hands. "I know. It's one of the constant battles in the Underground. Training takes a very long time. People have to work their way up through the ranks a step at a time."

"But it's insane. Why aren't basic physics courses taught in the schools?"

"Because, my dear Lieutenant, they're not important."

"Really? When Janowitz flies you edge-on into a singularity, you'll think differently."

"Space is your environment, not theirs. What I mean is that on wilderness worlds where most Gamant communities have taken refuge, it's far more critical to teach children about native plant and animal species—which are dangerous, which are safe. It's more important that they learn how to use stone to construct stable dwellings, how to till the soil to plant crops. Basic survival is all they have time for. Sophisticated sciences are the supreme luxury."

She shifted positions, pushing back against the wall and bringing her feet up onto the seat. She propped her glass on her drawn up knees. From this side view she seemed all the more slender, almost frail. It touched something inside him, some illogical masculine need—as if this highly decorated officer in the Magisterial fleet needed anybody's protection. Nonetheless, it softened his guarded responses to her.

"Baruch, tell me something?"

He lifted his brows, expecting something unpleasant. "Are we going to talk business?"

"Only in an offhand way."

"All right. Go ahead."

"Why is it Gamants fight like panthers to keep living in medieval squalor? The government could significantly

220

improve the lives of people on isolated planets like Horeb."

"Cost, Lieutenant. It's the price that bothers my people." He took another sip of his sherry and listened to the lilting strains of the violin that tenderly caressed his ears. If he let himself, he could almost feel as though he'd stepped backward in time a few thousand years to a more civilized galaxy. A galaxy where officers were simply humans who could understand each other.

"Cost?"

"Yes, the government demands a price for helping struggling worlds. First, they'd want to establish a Right School—to insure our children thought correctly—and we've already discussed the problems with that. Next, they'd order the planet to allow the establishment of military installations. And then, if the planet ever objected to *any* policy implemented by the government, in the schools or otherwise, the Magistrates would have the military muscle on site to enforce their will. Which they do constantly." He took a deep breath. "We can't afford the government's help."

"Some planets have accepted, though."

"Yes, like Tikkun. I remember when the first Right School was established. My father hid me in the basement to keep me from having to attend, thank God."

In a graceful, ballerinalike motion, she made a sweeping gesture at the ship. "So, you owe all this to your father? And you're grateful?"

He lightly stroked the fine grain of the wooden table. "I'm grateful. He taught me that a whole healthy mind is the most precious possession of any human being. He taught me self-reliance, self-respect, and the importance of never knuckling under to anyone who isn't *right*." He fixed her with a harsh look and her beautiful face clouded.

"Sorry," she said. "I didn't mean to offend you. Those are all important lessons every soldier must learn, and the earlier, the better. Your father clearly did a superb job. You're a brilliant commander."

The words soothed some of his inner sting. In the candles' glow, the usually coppery glints in her hair shaded golden, as though a glistening web of real summer sunlight netted her head. He fumbled with his glass, suppressing the ache for familiarity, for the scents of wet

221

dirt and wildflowers, the rustling of wind through pines. Something about her made him want to let himself be vulnerable.

"Sorry, Halloway. I didn't mean to sound so defensive."

"You should be defensive. The Magistrates have pushed your people around for a long time."

He looked at her curiously. She took a healthy drink of her sherry, evading his eyes. He wanted to call her on what she meant. How, if she knew that, she could fight so hard to kill so many of his people—but he refrained—adopting a different tack. "That almost sounded friendly."

"Did it? I must be more tired than I thought. But I'm not blind, Baruch. My general angle of vision is just different from yours. I've seen the government do a lot of good, too."

"It's hard for me to put that in perspective, given Gamant realities."

She contemplatively pleated the purple fabric over her knee. "You know why they target Gamants for abuse, don't you?"

"Pretty much. But I'd appreciate hearing your thoughts on the matter."

She looked up briefly, as though unsure how he'd receive what she wanted to say. "Your people are untamed. Nobody ever broke you to harness. That makes you damned difficult to fit into any social system."

"Uh-huh. Are you familiar with the old adage that the first sheep to get an original idea is the first to go into the pot?"

"What's a sheep?"

"A domestic animal from Old Earth. There aren't any smart ones left. All the intelligence was deliberately bred out of them—so they'd be easier to handle in the pens, you see. No fence-jumpers were allowed." She squinted and he smiled. "What I mean is that we don't want to fit into your society; it requires us to give up too much that we consider precious."

"You mean you're all fence-jumpers?"

"Exactly. And we like it that way. In fact, we encourage nonconformity, believing it strengthens, rather than weakens, our culture."

"That makes you stumbling blocks to every move the

222

Magistrates try for galactic unification."

"For example?"

"Take programs for communal redistribution. The philosophy is that the entire galaxy is a community—we pool our resources at Palaia and the government redistributes those goods where they're needed most. Everyone has enough to eat, everyone's warm. We all benefit from each other and take care of each other. Except Gamants, who refuse the goods offered and insist on charging for their own, or—"

"Lieutenant, I know a little about Magisterial history, do you know anything about Gamant history?"

"I'm an expert in your religion, remember?"

He smiled. "I meant profane history."

"I know some details."

Thoughtfully, he shoved his almost empty goblet across the table to his opposite hand, then shoved it back again, playing it between his palms. "Do you know about the diasporas?"

"I know about the Exile and Edom Middoth, where your people were hauled off to slave camps. There were others?"

"Many, many others. Every time my people got settled into a nice comfortable society and became productive members of the system, something went wrong. They ended up running for their lives. Our philosophy of isolationism comes from the fact that those marvelous communal economic systems can shut off goods any time they damn well please. Government officials are rarely saints. And food is the greatest of all tools for manipulation."

"True." She finished her sherry and set the goblet on the table where it glittered wildly. She put a hand to her mouth, covering a yawn.

"Am I boring you?" he asked.

"No, it's not you. I just don't think I've been this tired in my entire life."

"Shall we cut this short? I'll cancel Janowitz's next lesson. That way you can go back to your cabin and get some rest."

He started to get up from the table, but she reached a hand across to touch his sleeve. He could feel the chill of her delicate white fingers through his shirt.

"I'd rather talk with you, if you don't mind," she said.

223

He lowered himself back to the seat. "I don't . . . so long as we abandon the business of culture conflict. I can't bear much more right now."

"All right. Let's let the trumpets sing truce for an hour."

"Gladly."

"Can I get personal?"

He lifted a shoulder noncommittally. "Probably. What do you want to know?"

"Only things that don't matter. Tell me . . ." She inhaled a deep breath and shrugged. "Tell me your favorite food?"

He smiled and saw the lines around her eyes crinkle softly in return. "A dish so spicy almost no one but me can eat it. It's called Luzin Jamboli, from the Kaj Colonies on Bedford. What's yours?"

She returned his smile, a true gesture, not one of those carefully contrived to ease tension. It made him feel better. "A crazy dish made with green sea monsters that have ten legs."

"Sounds wretched. Where's it from?"

"Harvest Moon."

He leaned forward over the table, hands laced. "I'll have to try it the next time I'm there."

"Do. I think you'll like it."

They fell silent, gazing across the table at the other, smiling genuinely for a time. A small connection of warmth grew between them, like a strengthening current of electricity. When he started to feel it so clearly that a tingle began in all the wrong places, he dropped his gaze to the wood grain on the table.

A long silence stretched.

"Halloway . . ." He pressed his lips tightly together. "I'm sorry that all this—"

"You did what you had to, Baruch, and with disarming efficiency, I might add. Just as I'm trying to do now."

He watched the brassy splashes of light cast over the table by their glasses. They fell irregularly, like diamond-shaped puzzle pieces of the finest gold.

"As Cole says, we just have to do our jobs." A gentleness foreign to her usually gruff manner suffused her voice. It made Jeremiel feel desperate. Oh, how he'd love to be able to drop his defenses and speak to her honestly, just one human being to another.

He roughly shoved his glass around the table. "You sound like you'd rather not do your job."

"Sometimes. But I don't see any viable alternatives out there."

"You're not looking very hard." He contemplatively caressed his beard, then gave her a sudden brash grin. "There *are* other sides to fight for."

She lifted a brow and laughed softly. "Don't be ridiculous. You're doomed."

"Another hope dashed. We could use you."

"Thanks anyway, I'm not that frantic yet. But I'm intrigued by your faith in the future."

"You mean that we'll both be around to make such decisions? You're right, that is presumptuous. The offer, however, still stands."

She laughed again and shook her head as though she doubted his sincerity. "I'll keep it in mind."

"Good. I'm serious."

Something about the softness of her expression touched him deeply, building a warmth in his heart. It worried him. He wanted to stay, to drink another sherry and talk more with her, but he couldn't let himself. This was much too pleasant.

He slid out from behind the table and shoved his fists deep into the pockets of his white pants. "I'll walk you to the end of the hall and have a security team escort you back to your cabin."

As she started to slide out, he instinctively offered her a hand. She leaned forward and put her fingers into his. He clutched them tightly as he helped her to her feet. When she stood and looked up at him, time seemed to stop. Conflicting emotions danced across her beautiful face: a magnetic attraction to him, fear, desperation. They stood side by side, the physical contact lasting for fifteen seconds, then thirty. The longer he touched her, the more loudly blood rushed in his ears.

Finally, Carey gently pulled her hand back.

"Let me walk you to the security station," he said.

"Thank you."

* * *

Dannon stood in the midst of four guards outside of Engineering on level twenty. Dressed in multicolored

225

ragged robes, each held a rifle and wore a pistol on his belt. The bright corridor stretched endlessly white in front of Neil. He'd managed to work his way into the lower echelons, acting as gopher for the main security personnel. In the process, he'd learned a great deal about Jeremiel's operations—including the deep problems. Horeb's civil war still raged on a sporadic basis, factions slitting each other's throats in the hallways or hospital. After the wounded received adequate treatment, they were immediately locked in a cabin and not allowed out. As a result, the lower levels had gradually begun to clear. Jeremiel's greatest difficulty, it seemed, was that he possessed only a handful of officers capable of manning the basic control consoles aboard the *Hoyer*. Everybody else with brains had been stuck into the teaching programs being run by Magisterial staff on level seven.

Good move, Jeremiel, but I doubt Tahn's going to give you enough time to get them fully trained. You're in a hell of a mess, old friend.

Lucius, the short, blocky redhead beside Dannon whispered, "Yeah, well I heard Tahn was half-crazy from the concussion Baruch gave him. Even if he is back on his feet, I doubt he'll be a threat."

Dannon leaned a shoulder against the wall and calmly inquired, "Where did Baruch put Tahn?"

Lucius jabbed a thumb at the ceiling. "Level four. Tahn's old cabin, I hear."

Damn it. Jeremiel would certainly have sealed it, which meant Neil had no hope of gaining entry. But he *could* make it to level seven and contact some of the Magisterial officers before anybody in the Gamant regime caught wind of his identity.

"So," Neil said casually. "How many people have we got in Engineering now?"

Lucius scratched his scraggly red hair and squinted in thought. "Six, I think. Though a couple more may have come up from the teaching programs."

Six! Barely enough to keep the ship in orbit and maintain a watch on the primordial black holes in the engines. *Incredible.*

Dannon started to ask another question, but Lucius went suddenly stiff. He and the rest of the group came to attention and saluted crudely. Neil quickly snapped up his hand only to have his knees go weak when he saw Jeremiel and Halloway walking down the hall toward them.

Carey shot Dannon a knowing glance, but kept her face blank as she passed. Jeremiel's steps seemed to falter for a split second. He looked Neil straight in the face and Dannon stopped breathing. In those piercing blue eyes Neil saw *recognition—painful remnants of old friendship—hate—silent questions of "why?"*

Then Jeremiel quietly walked by, catching up with Halloway.

When Baruch rounded the corner and disappeared, Neil sank back against the wall, forcing himself to take deep breaths while he pretended to listen to Lucius' inane monologue.

If Jeremiel knew, why hadn't he . . .

I've got to get out of here, now!

Dannon amiably excused himself and moved briskly down the hall. For days he'd been avoiding the upper levels—but now he headed straight for seven, flashing his security badge at every intersection.

CHAPTER 25

Mikael sat alone on his floor, playing with the stamps Captain Tahn had given him. Avel Harper had picked them up when he found him in room 955. Mikael liked the one with the old style starship best. It had lots of purple and green in it. He looked around his white cabin and groaned softly. He missed colors. On Kayan they'd had so many, every color you could think of played over the tall mountains—but here only white and gray seemed to exist.

He rolled over on his back and stared at the ceiling, trying to think what Kayan would look like at this time of year if it weren't a dead planet. It would be fall, and the Kayan oaks would be turning yellow, little green veins

227

still striping the leaves. He used to sit for hours in the forest, smelling the rain-wet wood while he piled leaves into huge mounds. His mother used to play with him, throwing him into the leaf beds and laughing at him when he crawled out, spitting them from his mouth.

He missed her.

He closed his eyes for a while, trying not to think about it. But he only felt worse. He reached over and picked up the purple stamp again, studying the triangular shape of the ship. He laid it down and kicked his feet for a while, listening to them thud on the gray carpet.

His throat started to tighten, to ache. He swallowed to make it go away, but it didn't help much. Tears blurred his eyes. He looked at the ceiling again.

"God? Are you up there?" He reached out with his hand, holding it open to the heavens. "I'm scared . . . a little."

After a minute, when no answer came, he lowered his hand and turned over on his stomach to pick aimlessly at the lint on the carpet. He rolled the gray fibers into balls and made a growing pile in front of him.

He remembered his mother's round face and her long black hair. His nose ran. He wiped it on his sleeve and bit his lower lip. He pulled his *Mea* from inside his robe and held the blue ball up to swing before his eyes.

"God?" he called. "Grandfather? Maybe I could talk to you for just a little bit? I feel pretty lonely. Everybody's busy here, and nobody seems to want to talk to me. Except Sybil, but she only gets to come every so often and . . . and . . . I feel scared."

"Metatron? Are you in there? Could you come talk to me?"

Mikael had been calling for hours, but no one had answered. He couldn't help it, his mouth trembled. He covered his eyes with his hand and cried, feeling the tears warm against his fingers. A spot of gold flared and he jerked his hands down.

"Oh!"

"Are you all right, Mikael?"

Metatron stood before him. Tall and beautiful, the angel's body shimmered like polished glass in the light. His amber eyes glittered. Dressed in a hooded blue cloak, he smiled warmly and Mikael felt it like sunshine on a cold winter's day. The angel walked forward and gazed down at him.

"Thank you for coming, sir. I'm just lonely, I guess."

Metatron nodded understandingly. "You're never really alone, Mikael. I'll always be close if you call."

"But sometimes I feel awfully bad." He lowered his gaze and fumbled with his bare foot.

"I know you do. I should have come sooner. You sounded pretty gloomy when you called me." The angel sat cross-legged on the floor and threw back his hood. The brilliant light from his body splashed the walls like an ocean of gold. He smiled brightly and opened his arms wide. "Come, let's talk."

Mikael got on his knees and crawled into Metatron's lap. The angel held him tenderly, stroking his back. He gazed at Metatron's beautiful yellow hair. Shyly, he reached up to touch it.

The angel smiled. "Feels just like yours, doesn't it?"

"Yes, sir, except it's softer and warmer." Some of his fear went away. He heaved a sigh of relief. "Metatron?"

"Yes, Mikael?"

"The people here—they're all running around scared, like things aren't going very good. Are we in trouble?"

His feet were getting cold, so he tucked them into the hem of the angel's warm cloak. Metatron reached out and grabbed his icy toes and held them. Mikael shuddered at the sudden warmth that coursed pleasantly through him.

The angel nodded, heaving a tired breath. "Yes. I'm afraid we're in pretty bad trouble.

"Because the Magistrates want to come get their ship back?"

"Oh, that and other things. You see, there are a lot of bad people who are trying to hurt us."

"My grandfather told me! He told me the Antimashiah is here, *right now!* And she—"

"Yes, I know he did." Metatron's amber eyes seemed to glow brighter.

"I guess God told Grandfather about her."

"I guess."

"I'm supposed to tell Mister Baruch, but he's always so busy. I haven't even seen him at all."

Metatron pulled him closer, hugging him tightly for a moment. It felt good, like being swallowed by a pool of molten gold. Mikael wished he'd never stop, but he did.

Metatron relaxed his hold and looked down through kind eyes. "Don't worry about delivering that message. Jeremiel doesn't need to know for a time yet. Just now he's very, very busy trying to keep everybody on this ship safe."

"I know, but I *want* to tell him. Maybe you could make him come and talk to me?"

Metatron gently pushed Mikael's curls away from his face, and cradled the boy's chin in his golden palm. "I'll try, but you shouldn't be disappointed if he doesn't come immediately. Soon, he's going to have to take this ship far, far away to try to save Gamant civilization. And it's going to be very hard. The Magistrates are setting up an ambush for him."

Mikael's chest felt hollow. He nuzzled his cheek against the angel's hand. "But I could help him. If he'd only—"

"I know. But maybe you should wait for just a little while, until things get straightened out better here. You need to play with Sybil and be happy for a time before . . ." He smiled sadly, kissing Mikael's rosy cheek. "Before the strands of destiny pull tight around you."

"You mean like the war? Is that going to happen soon?"

"Too soon, I'm afraid."

"I don't mind. Me and Sybil, we're ready."

Metatron nodded proudly. "I knew you would be. But it's not for a while yet. God and I, we want you to play a while longer. Just be happy before you have to come back to the Cave of Treasures."

Mikael cocked his head inquisitively. "Where is that?"

"Well," the angel sighed, looking serious. "It's a place Sybil's mother knows about. God and I, we call it the Cave of Treasures, but Rachel calls it the polar chambers."

"Where she killed the Mashiah? Sybil told me about that."

"Yes, that's where. There are a lot of old books there. They'll help you win the war."

"Sybil's mom is going to fight with us, too?"

"Yes, she'll be an important asset for you."

"Where are the books? I know how to read. Can we go get them?"

Metatron smiled, but shook his head. "It's not time yet. We have to make things work just right or they won't work at all."

"Okay." Mikael patted the soft velvet of the angel's cloak, leaning his head against Metatron's warm chest. "Metatron?"

"Hmm?"

"Can't you kill the Antimashiah or something? You could kill her and all the bad people who want to hurt us. And then things would get better."

"I'm sorry, Mikael. There are some things the universe just doesn't allow me to do."

Mikael looked up at him, blinking thoughtfully. "But God could. Maybe if you talked to Epagael—"

"He's . . . he's pretty busy right now, too. There are a lot of other universes he has to keep an eye on."

"More than just ours?" Mikael asked, startled. No one had ever told him that before.

"Oh, yes. A lot more. More than you could ever imagine."

"But ours is his favorite, isn't it?" He remembered the old stories about how God had chosen the Gamant people to make His Covenant with. "Isn't it?" He cocked his head to see the angel's face. A look of grief etched lines around Metatron's mouth.

"Yes . . . it's His favorite." He exhaled heavily and then smiled down again. "Tell me what else is bothering you?"

"I'm just lonely mostly."

"Well, that's all right. Everybody is, deep down. Don't you like Sybil?"

"Oh, yes, sir. She's pretty awesome."

Metatron laughed and the sound seemed to echo, swirling around his cabin like warm spring winds. "I'm glad. She's very important to us."

"Is she? Her mom doesn't let her come very much. She has chores she has to do in their cabin. I don't know what, but they must take a lot of time."

"Do you want her to come more often?"

"Oh, yes. That would be great."

"I'll talk to Rachel about it."

"Sybil's mom talks to you?"

"Not as often as I'd like, but occasionally. You probably shouldn't tell Sybil that, though. It might scare her."

"She's pretty brave. I bet it wouldn't. But if you don't want me to, I won't."

"Thank you. You're a good boy."

Mikael smiled broadly and reached a hand up to tenderly pat the angel's beautiful golden cheek. It looked like glass, but felt like silk. "Sybil's had funny dreams about me. Did you know?"

"Yes. I've known for a long time. I'm going to tell you something you won't really understand for a few years, but it'll give you some time to think about it."

"What? I might understand."

"Yes, you might. You're a very smart boy. Well, Sybil is one of those rare people in this universe who only has a limited number of parallel futures. And they're all close and powerful. They send . . . um . . . *waves* to her all the time and she feels them very strongly. That's why she has those *funny* dreams. You listen when she tells you about them."

Metatron's crystal hand patted his leg gently and for a minute Mikael just watched the movements of those glittery fingers. "Waves like the ocean?"

"Something like that."

"I used to have funny dreams, too. When I was little, I used to dream that Aktariel came and tried to get me." Mikael laughed brightly.

The angel inhaled a deep breath and leaned forward to wrap his arms snugly around Mikael. "He won't hurt you, Mikael."

"But he might. He's a very wicked angel who fell from heaven. God says so. In the old books."

"Well, Epagael has his own perspectives."

"I guess so. Did you ever know Aktariel, Metatron?"

"Oh, yes. Very well, as a matter of fact. He was the leader of the angels, you know? I worked very closely with him in the beginning."

"You mean like the beginning when God created the universe?"

"Exactly like that. Do you remember the teachings about how God destroyed the first two universes?"

"Yes. My grandfather told me. All the angels told God those universes were bad. Isn't that right? Isn't that what happened?"

For a time Metatron rocked Mikael back and forth in his lap, his golden arms tender and warm—so warm that

232

Mikael started to feel sleepy. He yawned.

"Yes, Mikael. We advised God to destroy the first two. Some angels told him the same thing about the third. But Epagael wouldn't listen. And that's why we're here. What do you think about being here? It's pretty sad, isn't it?"

Mikael's thoughts turned back to his mother and he bit his lower lip, keeping the tears inside. "Sometimes it's real sad."

"I know." Metatron rubbed his back comfortingly. "We'll make it better soon."

Mikael's eyes felt so heavy he let them fall closed. Relaxing, he melted against Metatron, softly kneading the angel's cloak between his fingers. When he was a baby, he used to have a pillowcase made from one of his mother's old nightgowns. He kept it with him all the time. He couldn't sleep if he didn't have it against his face. This soft cloak made him feel the same way.

In a little while, Mikael felt himself being lifted and quietly carried across the room. His eyes fluttered open a time or two and he saw the door to his bathroom and his desk pass by, then Metatron gently laid him down and covered him up with his gray blanket, tucking the edges around his legs. His mother used to do that. It felt good.

Mostly asleep, Mikael murmured. "Could you sit by me? Just for a little while?"

"I'll stay as long as you need me."

Mikael sighed in contentment. Metatron's warm hand tenderly stroked his hair as he fell deeper asleep.

Almost like an echo in his mind, he heard Metatron whisper, "Maybe we can even talk while you're asleep. If you want to."

"Can we do that?"

"Sure, it's easy. And I sense that even though you're tired, you're worried about other things. Are you?"

"Yes, sir." Mikael's thoughts swirled aimlessly for a while, like fluttering flames in the wind. Slowly, a golden fog grew up around him, soft, warm. He floated in it. *"Maybe you could tell me why my grandfather doesn't talk to me very much. I need to talk to him. I don't feel so lonely when I can hear him."*

"Oh, it's mostly because your grandfather is in a place where time works differently. To you it's been days since you heard his voice, but to him it feels like only seconds ago."

"Where is Grandfather?"

"He's in a place called Authades. It's a dark dark void just on the other side of here."

"Why can't he come out?"

"That's kind of hard to explain. You remember when you went to his funeral?"

Mikael's chest hurt and he felt tears press against his closed eyelids. *"Yes, sir. It rained that day. It rained and rained."*

"I remember. The forests of Kayan glistened like a veil of rainbows. But, because your grandfather died, he no longer has a receptacle to return to in this universe. If he came through the void the light that composes him, you call it a soul, would just disperse. That means he wouldn't be Zadok anymore."

"Who would he be?"

"He wouldn't be anybody. He just wouldn't be at all."

"You mean he'd sort of disappear?"

"Yes, sort of. He wouldn't be able to talk to you anymore. And God and I need him to talk to you."

"Sir, could you maybe get him to talk to me more?"

A hesitation, and Mikael felt a curious sense of sorrow and reluctance swirl around him. It made him afraid. But then the feeling vanished and the warm light came back. The fog thickened, shimmering like gold dust in the sun.

"I'll see what I can do. There are some other angels I know who might be able to help."

"Thank you, sir. I'm glad you came today. I feel a lot better."

"Whenever you need me, just call. I'll come as soon as I can. Sometimes, if I'm far away, it might take a while. But you just keep calling and eventually I'll come. You sleep now. You're very tired. Sleep . . . sleep. . . ."

Mikael let himself go, feeling safe for the first time in what seemed forever. Against his skin, the glittering fog felt as soothing as a velvet blanket left beside the fire. Faintly, he felt the angel kiss his forehead and heard him say, "Yes, we'll make it better. God wouldn't listen back then. He'd already seen the spinning patterns of chaos and been drawn into their magnificent beauty. No matter what the angels told him about suffering in this universe, he didn't care. But He'll have to pay attention again soon. We'll *make* him.

"Soon, Mikael."

Just before Mikael fell asleep, his head started to hurt again, *badly*. He whimpered. Sybil had said it felt like brain poison, but to him it felt like little bugs eating tunnels in his head.

Then it stopped and the golden haze returned, warm and soothing. Mikael slept.

CHAPTER 26

It began as a dream.

Rachel heard the heavy blows of a hammer on an anvil. The sound rang with such rich clarity, she thought at first it was a silver bell. She listened and it grew louder, like the temple chimes of her youth, calling her to worship. Curious, she walked toward it.

She found herself plodding along a narrow dirt path, dressed in a long, coarsely-woven white robe. A great ocean spread to her left, surreally blue and vast. Birds soared through the halo of sunshine. A warm breeze caressed the land, flapping the hem of her robe. Her long hair danced in the gusts. In the distance, she could see a mountain rising, its top rounded as though scoured by the salt-laden sea winds for millennia. Dark green blankets of trees covered the long slopes.

The clanging of the hammer grew so loud she could almost feel its pounding against the air. She crested a hill and plunged down the other side into the narrow streets of a village. An old crone of a woman sat combing wool in front of a mud house. A black and white goat chewed straw at her elbow. The crone cackled and lifted a hand, waving at Rachel as she passed. Down the street, a man yelled ferociously at a great hump-backed beast loaded down with merchant's goods. The curious animal brayed and tugged against his lead rope, finally resorting to spitting on his master. Rachel laughed long and hard at the look of surprised rage on the man's hawk-face.

Turning down a shadowed alleyway, she lifted her arms and spun around. A feeling of sheer freedom possessed her. None of the terrible burdens on her soul existed any longer. Whether or not the Magistrates would find and kill her and everyone she loved was an irrelevant question. The Magistrates didn't exist here. She felt as though she'd stepped out of her own universe and into a sanctuary nestled in the calm heart of space and time. Two-story buildings rose on either side of her. On bars extended out windows, clothes hung drying, waffling in the warm breezes that swept the village.

The savory odors of burning logs and roasting meat met her nostrils. She inhaled deeply and hugged herself. *But this is only a dream, Rachel. Soon you'll wake up.* She fought the truth by picking up her feet and running like the wind, winding down the hill. Breaking out of the alley, she burst into the bustling environment of a picnic.

A broad plaza spread before her, filled with racing children and barking dogs. Men and women laughed around a long table filled with baskets of fruit and bread. Nearby, the roasting pit glowed. Flames leapt four feet high to taunt the sizzling flesh of three animals on spits. On the far side, in a shaded grove of trees, a tall man lifted a hammer and slammed it down on a red-hot piece of metal. Each clang sent her heart soaring. He'd called her here. Why?

Rachel watched him as she slowly meandered through the crowd. She listened to fragments of conversations she didn't understand, but the rich guttural quality of the language reminded her vaguely of Gamant. It made her smile. She felt an almost euphoric sense of contentment. *She'd escaped . . . escaped. . . .*

She walked to stand behind the circle of men watching the blacksmith and maneuvered so she could see between two men to watch his crafting. He smiled at her when he noticed her attention. Nudging a man standing next to him, he indicated Rachel with a tilt of his head. The man turned. Tall, with a tanned face and a mass of blond curls, his gaze made Rachel's heart stand still. In the bright afternoon sun, his deeply set brown eyes shone magnetically warm—eyes that swept her away like the powerful waves of a flood. A gust of wind flattened his tan robe across his broad muscular chest.

She dropped her gaze and started to back away, but the

blacksmith's robust, teasing voice stopped her. She shook her head, "I don't know your language," she answered. "I'm sorry."

The half dozen men in the circle turned to smile at her, talking animatedly among themselves and gesturing toward the tall blond. He made some comment and smiled as though in embarrassment. Backing out of the circle, he gracefully walked over to Rachel. He smelled faintly of crushed spices and desert-scented winds.

He bowed at the waist. "Forgive me, lady. My name is Hasmonaean. My friends here correctly assume that my language is very similar to yours. Though you give your Aramaic a slightly different accent. Where are you from?"

Rachel opened her mouth to answer, then laughed. "I don't think you'd believe me if I told you." *This is a dream, Rachel. You can tell him anything you want.* She laughed again. Oh, it felt so good to laugh.

He smiled. His gaze caressed her face with an almost breathless anticipation. "Perhaps, if you'll allow me, I could escort you around our celebration? I'd like to hear your stories."

"Whether you believe them or not?"

"Oh, belief is all a matter of perspective, isn't it? You see, I'm not from the Dor vicinity either. I travel a great deal and like hearing stories from different places."

"Mine might shock you, I'm afraid."

"Then I look forward to hearing them all the more."

He offered his arm and she hesitantly accepted it, feeling his hard muscles beneath the tan fabric of his robe. They strolled leisurely across the plaza. A gaggle of children crossed back and forth across their path, weaving in some game. Giggles and shrieks laced the air. He guided her out of the press of people and up a hill into a grove of sweetly scented trees overlooking the plaza. He led her beneath the overhanging boughs of a tree filled with ripe red fruit. Stopping before a wooden barrel propped on a table, he reached for a clay goblet and placed it beneath the spigot, filling his cup with dark maroon liquid.

"The wines here are strong, but they have a wonderful spicy flavor. May I get you some?"

"Yes, thank you."

He handed her the cup he'd been filling, then filled one

237

for himself. "What is your name?"

"Rachel Eloel."

"A beautiful name. *Eloel Souel.*"

She frowned inquiringly. "What does that mean?"

He shrugged as though wishing he hadn't said it. "I don't think anyone really knows anymore. It's a very old phrase."

He flashed her one of those charismatic smiles that made her heartbeat quicken, then took her arm again and guided her through the grove. Finally, at the peak of the hill, he sat gracefully on a mat of thick green grass and extended a hand to her. "Come, sit with me."

Rachel pulled up the hem of her white robe and dropped down beside him, gazing out over the blue ocean that sparkled in the distance. Behind her, sandy hills dotted with trees undulated endlessly. She sipped her wine and tipped her head back to the scented breeze, letting it flood her face.

"You look happy," he said.

"You can't imagine. Being here is like paradise." *No, better.* After all the horrors of her life the past three years, all the weary burdens she'd borne, this simple land of villagers wearing homespun robes and laughing seemed far superior to any of the promised seven heavens. Her thoughts shifted briefly to Epagael and a tired bitterness gripped her heart. She sipped her wine, forcing the thoughts away. When she looked up, she found Hasmonaean studying her taut face anxiously.

"Oh, I think I can imagine. Being in Dor affects me that way, too. Take care though, paradise is rarely what it seems." He smiled and she had the feeling he'd done it deliberately to cheer her up.

"What do you mean?"

"For example," he said and extended a hand toward the cackling group of people below them. "The water system here is contaminated. The women have to walk three miles a day to carry each bucket. And the local political official was assassinated last week for er . . . 'indiscretions' with his brother's wife."

She grinned and leaned back on her elbows. The wind blew long strands of her wavy hair over her eyes. She brushed them away, drinking her wine, relishing the aniselike flavor. "What charming problems."

He gave her a wry smile. "Charming? You do have a

238

different way of looking at things. Where did you say you were from?"

"I don't know where it is in relation to here. You see, I think I'm dreaming. It was nighttime when I left. The ship's halls were mostly empty."

"Dreaming?" He lifted bushy blond brows and chuckled. "Well, the important thing is that you're happy. I say you enjoy it, Rachel."

"Yes, I plan on it." Her smile faded. "Because the world I come from is terrible."

A potent gust of wind swept them with stinging grains of sand. They both threw up their arms to protect their faces. The tree branches overhead creaked like rusty hinges.

When he lowered his arm, he asked, "Terrible how?"

"Filled with sadness and discord."

A woman's loud husky laughter rang from around the roasting pit. Hasmonaean stretched out on his side, propping his head on his hand. His blond curls ruffled in the wind. "Yes, discord is always the enemy, Satan in the truest form. The region of Truth has no shadow in its heart, for the immeasurable light fills it entirely. But the limbs of Truth are dark, boundless chaos. Do you know the writings of Basilides?"

He shifted to look at her and his eyes gleamed softly with power. Strange, she thought, that dreams always conjured people easy to love. This handsome man's gaze buffeted her like a gale-force wind. Perhaps that was why she was having this dream. To help her work out the ache that lingered in her soul for Shadrach. Regardless, she planned on letting herself drown in the pleasant feelings.

"I don't know the work of Basilides, but his idea of the shadow seems similar to something else I'm familiar with. The *reshimu*. Have you heard of it? I don't know very much about it."

"You mean the notion that the forces of evil come from God Himself?"

"Yes," she responded eagerly. "Could you explain it to me? I'm not sure I grasp it."

He inhaled the scents of spiced meat that drifted to them on the breeze. "I'll try. Stop me when I bore you."

"I doubt that this discussion could ever bore me. It's too important."

"Why do you think so?"

"Because I believe suffering is the heart of everything."

He nodded contemplatively and studied the dark red contents of his goblet. "Yes, I think you're right. Well, then, the story goes something like this. In the beginning, Light was all there was—God, if you will. Light withdrew a part of itself from itself, leaving a void: an empty space within which creation could take place. But Light could never again enter that space." He waved a hand airily. "Or else the Light would be One again, if you follow me?"

"The dichotomy of God and not-God would vanish, melt into Oneness again. I understand. Go on."

"Within the void, a residue of light remained, like the perfume that scents a bottle long after the contents have been emptied. That residue, the *reshimu*, is the source of evil because it's a partial reality."

Rachel took another sip of her wine. Her head had started to feel light, the alcohol making her vision seem clearer. The turquoise sky contrasted sharply now with the azure of the ocean. She rolled over on her side, closer to him, their faces only two feet apart. He looked at her speculatively, that same warm glint in his eyes.

"I don't understand. How is it the source of evil?"

He smoothed his fingers over the green grass. "Oh, Basilides' followers would talk about the fall of the light of the *Pleroma* down to the lowest depths of the abyss. Other mystics would put it differently. In the beginning, the *reshimu* simply existed as pure light, but soon this light, 'atomized,' or soured, forming clots in the body of the void. When God infused the pure vessels of light into the midst of the clots, they picked up the taint and soured, too, bursting. Their wealth spilled forth across the universe. From those fundamental bits of light, all this—" he gestured to the sky, sea, and earth. "—came into being. And, as most intelligent people know, *all this* is fundamentally chaotic."

"Most people in my faith view the universe as fundamentally ordered," Rachel challenged.

"That's because they view only the surface of reality."

Rachel toyed with her cup. "So chaos is equated with the *reshimu*?"

"Not exactly. Chaos is an effect of the *reshimu's* isolation in the void. When God put the stopper on the perfume bottle, he condemned the aroma to a tragic fate.

In perfect equilibrium, a top can spin eternally. But perfection exists only in God. The *reshimu's* isolation shattered that perfection. The 'top's' motions became chaotic, turbulent; it's begun to wind down. The very nature of the creation is to struggle against itself, seeking an equilibrium it can never find. We experience the struggle as suffering."

She inhaled a deep breath and let it out slowly. The words wafted like a silk scarf through her mind, soft, familiar, as though she'd heard them before. In the deepest recesses of her mind, a forbidden voice spoke in gentle tones about God and Milcom and the "naked singularity." Adom. Her heart ached.

"Some thinkers have actually proposed," Hasmonaean continued, "that the *reshimu* soured because it went insane, because it was always seeking the glorious memory of the fullness that lingered in its essence and could never find it."

Images of her visit to the throne of God tormented her. Rachel could feel the heat of the River of Fire on her face, hear Epagael's arrogant voice. She swallowed hard. "How could there be a God so cruel He would sacrifice a remnant of Himself to appease His own curiosity? It's like cutting off your hand just to watch it bleed."

"But once the hand has been severed, the body ceases to feel its pain. The hand can cry out in agony forever and the body will never know."

"Are you saying God doesn't know we suffer?"

"No, no. He knows."

"How could He if He can't enter this universe to see for Himself?"

"In the beginning, He created messengers, angelic beings who could traverse the interuniversal void between the Treasury and the Abyss. They told Him—a thousand thousand times."

"And He didn't care?"

"He loves the spinning patterns of chaotic turbulence. They're quite beautiful, you see." Hesitantly, he reached over and gently caressed her hand. The warmth of his skin, the tenderness of his touch made her turn her palm up so they could twine fingers. He gripped her hand tightly and heaved what sounded like a sigh of relief. He closed his eyes a moment as though drowning in the feel of her flesh against his.

When he opened his eyes, he said, "God had no curiosity before He spawned the void. Since then, it's become His greatest passion." He sounded bitter, as though he were voicing an achingly human and heart-rending protest against suffering. One she understood.

"Then the seeds of curiosity must have been in the Pure Light to begin with. Couldn't the original taint have come from God rather than isolation in the void?"

He smiled admiringly. "A good question. Many brilliant women and men have proposed exactly that—but I don't think so. I don't believe that in the beginning the Light was either good or evil. Rather, I think the original separation tainted it as well as the void. Before spawning the Abyss, the Light felt no hatred or envy, no love or greed. You see, if there's only One reality, no element of dualism can exist. Only after God had 'seen the light' was He drawn into the magnificence of chaos. *That* is the point when he developed a personality."

Rachel thoughtfully swirled her wine, watching the dark waves wash the cup. "Too bad we can't go back to a time before that point. But, if God loves the web of chaos so much, aren't we all doomed to endless suffering to provide Him with entertainment?"

He nodded. "Yes. Unless we do something to force Him to feel what this universe feels." He gave her a solemn glance. "We have to 'reconnect' the hand so he can feel its anguish."

"And how can we do that?"

He looked down at the people in the plaza. They'd started dancing, whooping, and singing, arms locked as they kicked their legs joyously. "We must penetrate the Treasury of Light and slap Him in the face with chaos."

Rachel's breathing went shallow. He no longer sounded like he was discussing philosophy. No, he sounded like he *knew* what he was talking about. She looked down at the large tanned hand that twined so comfortably with hers and she felt slightly faint. She jerked her gaze up to his, cataloging every element of his classically handsome face: the high cheekbones and patrician nose, the large, magnetically wistful eyes. The similarity jolted her like an electric shock.

"Oh." Her gasp came out small and pained. She tried to jerk her hand away from him, but he held it tightly.

"Rachel . . . don't. Just talk to me. I'm not as bad as you thought, am I?"

She frantically fought to get away from him.

He pressed his lips tightly together and released her hand. "I'm sorry. I wanted to be with you in a world where the myths about me don't exist."

An iron cage tightened around her chest. Rachel slid a few feet away. "Why do you play the name-games? Aktariel. Hasmonaean. You're a trickster. What is your name really?"

"I've had thousands over the millennia. Too many to remember. At this point, one seems as good as another. But forgive me, Rachel. I couldn't see any other way of showing you I'm not the monster you believe."

She concentrated on the warm wind that ruffled her long hair, fighting the revulsion, trying to take her mind off the powerful natural attraction she felt toward him. "You tried to *deceive* me! I—I don't . . ."

He waited, giving her time, but when she refused to finish, he said, "Talk to me, Rachel. *Let's just talk.* I'm not asking anything of you—except your companionship at this moment."

"*Is* that all you want?"

"Yes. I swear it."

She absently creased the hem of her robe. "Is this a dream we're in? Something you manufactured? Or is it real?"

"It's real. I've wanted to bring you here again for a long long time. I just—"

"*Again?*" Her lungs went stone cold still. "What do you mean *again?*"

His smooth jaw moved with grinding teeth, as though he were silently berating himself. He lifted his goblet and finished it to the last drop. "I don't think you're ready for that discussion yet. Let's talk about—"

"I'm ready for the truth, damn it! Do you ever tell that?"

A buried hint of desperation glistened in his eyes. "I've never lied to you."

Rachel gazed miserably into that handsome face framed in blond curls. She had the passionate urge to strike him, or slip into his arms and let him soothe the terror and confusion that twisted her soul. But she did

243

neither. She braced her forehead against her drawn up knees and stifled the emotions that threatened to consume her.

After a few moments, she felt a gentle hand stroke the long hair that draped down her back. "Do you want to go back? I'll take you."

"Stop touching me!" He took his hand away. In the depths of her heart, she wanted to stay here—far away from the realities of Magisterial tyranny and murder. "You frighten me, Aktariel."

"Why?"

"You're the Deceiver, for God's sake! How can I believe anything you tell me?"

"Rachel, please, try to see beyond the propaganda Epagael has spun around me. Do I seem frightening—as a man?"

". . . No."

"Let me prove myself to you. Give me the chance—"

"But you're not a man. Are you?" She lifted a hand and gestured to his perfect body. She could see his stomach muscles tense at her words, bulging through his silk robe. "How do you do that? Lose your glow, I mean?"

He broke off a blade of grass and pondered its softness, brushing the tip over his fingers. "It's a simple matter of refocusing the vortex around myself. And, yes, I know you think I'm talking gibberish again. I'm not. Let me teach you, Rachel. Let me show you . . ."

She got to her feet and backed away. "Aktariel, if you care about me, *leave me alone!* Prove you truly care by . . . by giving me this dream—without you. Let me walk these streets alone for a few hours." Lord, how she needed that. Just a little time to feel the solidity of a planet, the comforting simplicity of a less complicated time.

He nodded and stared at his empty goblet. "Of course. I want you to be happy."

She quickly trotted down the hill, out across the plaza. In the distance, the ocean beckoned, crystal blue and immense. She just wanted to walk barefoot in the sand and listen to the crashing of waves while she thought.

When she neared the white beach, she turned, gazing back at the hill where they'd sat. He was gone. Only an empty grove of swaying trees stood tall and quiet. "Why do you torment me, Aktariel? What have I done that I deserve such attention from you?"

Rachel took off her sandals and ran out onto the shimmering sands. The afternoon sunlight brushed her cheeks with warmth. She took her time, picking up each shell she passed, turning it over and over in her palm, feeling its texture, smelling the salty scents of fish and kelp that clung to it. She struggled to keep her mind off anything important. All she wanted was to play for a few blessed hours.

Her running steps left pockmarks across glimmering white grains.

On a distant hill, Aktariel braced his arm against a fig tree, watching Rachel on the shore below. She raced childlike down the beach, running for a short distance, then stopping and lifting her arms to whirl like a dervish in the glorious sea breezes. Even from here, he could feel the joy in her heart, as though a long aching wound had at last been salved.

He pressed a fist to his mouth and shook his head at himself. He *wanted* her to feel that. For too long, he'd been forced to watch her suffer, to feel her despair from afar—all the while knowing her essence had been created for greater things. He could endure the sight of starving millions, the bloodied corpses of innocent children, but to see Rachel miserable broke his heart. He'd rather have endured the holocaust in the square himself than to have witnessed her horror.

Yet . . . she had to experience that herself.

He folded his arms tightly over his breast and leaned a shoulder against the cool trunk of the tree. He had urgent business to take care of, but he couldn't leave. He hadn't wanted to tell Rachel she couldn't get back to her own universe without him. That would have frightened her even more. He'd wait, watching from afar until she seemed to have satiated her need for earth and wind and sun. Then he'd take her home.

He ran a hand through his blond hair. An ache had grown in his chest, pressing painfully against his heart. "You're a fool," he whispered harshly. "A damned fool."

* * *

CHAPTER 27

Dannon lay prone in a narrow power tunnel, trying to catch an hour of sleep. His shredded black robe had grown grimy in the past twenty-four hours while he struggled to get close enough to contact a Magisterial officer on level seven.

In the darkness behind his closed eyes, memories flooded out. The massive numbers of injured and dying Gamants mixed with the silent questions and pain he'd seen in Jeremiel's eyes. A hornet's nest of emotions hummed inside him. Neil's thoughts kept returning to the candlelit saloon on Vensyl. He and Jeremiel had slouched in one of the outside booths, gazing up at the magnificently jagged mountain peaks which pierced the full moon. Light penetrated the soughing trees, carelessly throwing moonglow like silver coins over the veranda where they sat. He remembered so clearly, so very clearly, the pine-sharp winds that ruffled their sleeves, the strong handclasps they'd shared.

When had it all gone wrong? He searched his memories. He couldn't quite pinpoint the exact moment, but sometime, somewhere, the Underground had stopped being a rescue organization for Gamants in distress and had become a full-scale war machine. Blind. Desperate. Hitting hard and running fast.

He'd pleaded with Jeremiel to stop and take a good look at what they'd become. But he never did—couldn't, he said. Even now, he could hear Jeremiel's deep voice: "The whirlwind has caught us up and twisted us around so much, Neil, the only way out I can see is to fly into the storm."

"But Jeremiel . . ."

The hands over Dannon's face trembled. He dug his fingers into his flesh to still the nervous attack. How many innocent people had died while they spouted Gamant righteousness? *An eye for an eye.*

For a while it had escalated to five eyes for one—making up for past Magisterial murders, they'd justified. Then ten for one . . . twenty for one.

And Neil couldn't bear it anymore. When they'd been planning the Silmar attack, he'd shriveled in upon himself, so staggered by the anticipated casualty figures, he could no longer turn his head.

When he'd gotten up from the strategy table, he'd been sick, sick to death with the horror, the screams that filled his dreams, the terrified faces of little children running, running through streets devastated by cannon fire.

"Jeremiel," he'd begged, "let's go have a beer. I need to talk to you. *Let me talk to you?*"

Baruch had frowned contemplatively, eyes distant—already lost in the battle, mind weaving the strategy he devised so well. He'd warmly grabbed Dannon's shoulder and murmured, "I promised to meet with Rudy. He's coordinating ballistics. Later, huh? Maybe tomorrow after we've . . ."

But there'd been no tomorrow. Neil had made his decision that instant. Then the Magistrates had started hitting back and entire Gamant planets had died in a flood of vengeance.

He groaned softly to himself. "Why wouldn't you listen, Jeremiel? *I begged you.*"

He brought up his knees and curled into a ball. Tendrils of the love he'd tried so desperately to kill rose, twining up from his unconscious to wrap themselves around his heart. He hurt as though he'd been bludgeoned. The faces of the dying children in the hallways haunted him. . . .

"Why wouldn't you talk to me, Jeremiel?"

* * *

Cole Tahn lay sleeping soundly, dreaming of the pleasant lazy days of his youth in Academy. The sweet pungent scent of Giclasian apple blossoms wafted through the scene. He and Maggie Zander lay side by side beneath a huge tree, her beautiful face dappled with soft shadows, golden hair streaming around her shoulders. She gave him a reproachful look.

"I mean," she said, "you're so brilliant at physics, how could you fail that simple Intergalactic lingua test?"

He laughed. "I'm only good at useless accomplishments. Singularity drives and—"

"Be serious. You'll never get out of Academy if you don't study harder about things you find uninteresting."

He smiled and took her hand, pressing it tenderly to his lips. "My dear Maggie, don't worry about me. If I have to, I'll stay up all night before finals and get it straight in my head."

"Yes, unfortunately, you probably will. Most people have to study all semester long. I think it's bad to be so brilliant. Things come too easily. You'll regret that some day."

"Will I? Why?"

"Because eventually it's going to make you over confident, which means you'll make mistakes at exactly the wrong moment. That is, if your classmates don't kill you in jealousy first. Except me, of course. I'm fool enough to love you."

She laughed teasingly. It reminded him of warm winds through autumn-brittle aspen leaves. He cherished it, engraving it in his memory to hear again and again when he thought he could bear no more of the horrors of war or the futility of command. In the farthest regions of his memory, scenes of her death struggled to rise, flitting like butterfly wings through the dream. Forcefully, he pushed them down.

"Maggie," he said with an urgent gentleness. "I love you, too. I wish we could . . ."

Faintly, he heard faraway sounds. The door to his cabin snicked open. He fought against it, not wanting to wake up. A dozen booted feet rushed in.

"Get up, Tahn!"

In a swift trained motion, he rolled off his bed and to his feet, crouching ready for combat, panting from the shock. In the dim green light cast by his com unit, he made out five men. One he recognized.

"What the hell do you want, Baruch?"

"You."

The tall blond's jaw was clamped so hard, his entire face seemed skewed. It sent a frigid wave through Tahn. He girded himself for war, straightening slowly. "What for?"

"Magistrate Slothen is on com. He requests visual contact with you."

Tahn breathed a small sigh of relief, straightening up. "Let me get dressed."

Baruch used the barrel of his pistol to motion to the uniform draped carelessly over the desk chair. "Hurry. We haven't much time."

"I'm hurrying. Don't get nervous." He slipped on his pants and tucked in his shirt, then sat on the edge of his bed to pull on his black boots. All the while, Baruch stood rigidly, eyes glued to his every movement. In the rectangle of light streaming in from the corridor, Baruch's blond hair shimmered platinum. A beautiful woman Cole had never seen before stood behind Baruch, a rifle held expertly in her arms. Tall, she had long, wavy black hair and intense midnight eyes.

"What com should I take?"

"I want you on the bridge where everything will look perfectly normal."

"All right." Tahn started walking, exiting into the long white hall. Ten other Gamant guards greeted him, rifles aimed unambiguously at every conceivable part of his anatomy.

Baruch came up to walk beside him, eyeing him gravely. "Let's discuss your conduct."

"I think I know how to act before Slothen."

"My people have just sealed off level seven. One wrong word, one suspicious move—if you blink too quickly, Tahn, I'll gas the entire deck. Do we understand each other?"

Rage flared, but he controlled it. "We do." He stepped into the tube, accompanied by six Gamants, and looked at Baruch. Their gazes locked, each taking the other's measure. A silent tug-of-war ensued. The tube smoothly ascended, level numbers flashing in blue on the wall panel as they passed.

"I want you to ask Slothen one question for me."

Tahn squinted suspiciously. "What is it?"

"Ask him where my fleet is."

"You mean you don't know?" He laughed. "And to think I've been worrying about—"

Baruch's muscular arm slammed him painfully against the tube wall. He stared Cole hard in the face. *"Just ask him."*

"Affirmative," Cole responded mildly. A seed of hope lodged in his breast, quickening his breathing. If Baruch didn't know, they could be a month away. He studied the Underground leader. Baruch fidgeted like his nerves

249

were strung tight as an ancient cat-gut fiddle.

The tube halted and four of the guards stepped out first, securing the bridge. His crew responded with practiced ease, as though for the thousandth time. Baruch gripped him by the arm and shoved him out in front, a pistol stabbed uncomfortably into his kidney. He winced as Baruch forced him to walk to his command chair where he shoved him into the seat and glared down through fiery eyes.

"Don't forget, there are five hundred people depending on you."

"I'm aware of that, Baruch."

The Gamants moved back, out of visual range, to cling like shadows against the walls. Tahn studied his bridge crew. They looked at him breathlessly, awaiting instructions. Some were obviously worried sick that he couldn't handle the situation. It made his gut ache. Halloway's hard eyes assessed the Gamants and flicked to him. She gave him a fleeting smile. Damn, he ought to be reassuring her, not the reverse. But he appreciated it.

"Relax people," Tahn said in the calmest tone he could muster. "We'll proceed just as though this were a casual conversation with Palaia. No heroics. Our friend Baruch has level seven sealed with the intent of murdering the entire techno-science division if we so much as breathe wrong."

A sharp gasp followed by a soft whimper drew his attention to Shelly Ronan. Her husband, Juno, served as a chemist. She pressed a hand to her trembling mouth as tears filled her eyes.

"Shelly," he said softly, forcing a confident smile. "Why don't you wait in the tube. We don't need you here for this."

"Yes, sir." She got to her feet and quickly ran off the bridge. A Gamant guard followed. The door snicked closed behind them.

"Good work, Tahn," Baruch praised, caressing the trigger of his pistol as he looked around. "Anybody else here who might get his friends killed by breaking at the wrong moment?"

Cole eyed each of his crew in turn. Those he might have suspected bucked up beneath his gaze. Pride warmed him. "No. Everybody else will hold up fine."

"All right." Taking one last deep breath, Baruch

250

turned toward Halloway. "Lieutenant, reroute control of communications to your console. I want you handling the dattran. And remember, this pistol is pointed at your head."

"That would be hard to forget, Baruch." She hit the necessary keys, acutely conscious that Baruch's eyes monitored her every movement. "Rerouted."

"You ready, Tahn?" Baruch asked in a strained voice.

"As ready as I ever am when I have to talk to Slothen."

A small round of nervous laughter went through his officers, just as he'd intended. They all knew how much he hated conversations with Palaia. Giclasians gave him the fidgets.

"All right, Halloway," Baruch ordered. "Narrow visual, focused solely on Tahn. Go."

The forward screen flared to life. The familiar lavender room with the gorgeous background of Palaia Station appeared. Fluffy clouds drifted through the magnificent lemon skies. Slothen bowed his blue head in greeting. "Greetings, Captain Tahn."

"Greetings, Magistrate. What can we do for you this fine day?"

"We were growing concerned. Why haven't you reported confirming receipt of the Horebian cargo and requesting further instructions?"

Cole straightened indignantly, setting his jaw. "With all due respect, Magistrate, our last dattran notified you we had concluded arrangements regarding Baruch and requested two weeks off-duty time on Lopsen. We've been *patiently* awaiting *your* reply."

Slothen blinked as though taken off-guard. "Did you?" In his most juddering mechanical voice, he continued, "Oh, forgive me, Captain. Now that I think about it, I do recall that message. Things have been rather hectic here, as I'm sure you can imagine. I'll certainly have to reprimand my staff for not reminding me."

"May I take that as authorization for a vacation, sir?"

Slothen's blue hair writhed and Tahn grimaced, just as he always did. "No, I'm sorry. We have a new mission for you that is of urgent strategic importance."

"I see." He ground his teeth a moment, concentrating on looking disgruntled. In irritation, he lightly pounded a fist into his chair arm.

"I do apologize, Captain. Please assure your crew that

251

we will make amends as soon as possible by giving them a full month off on a planet of your choice."

"How soon, Magistrate? My crew has been riding herd on these lunatic Gamants for nearly a year straight. We're—if you'll excuse me—goddamn tired. You cannot expect mentally and physically exhausted soldiers to perform at peak capacities."

"I realize that. Please ask them to be patient. I'll take the matter up with the military advisory council."

"We'd appreciate that. Thank you for allowing me to express my dismay. What is our next mission?"

Slothen turned slightly and acted as though he were speaking with someone else in the room, but no sound of voices penetrated the bridge. He must have doused the audio. A moment later, Brent Bogomil's face filled the monitor.

"Cole?" Bogomil called affably. "How are you? How did the scorch attack on Horeb go? *I hope you reached a hundred and one percent efficiency.*"

Tahn's heart stopped. Bogomil knew! The 101 code was brand new and only used to clandestinely inform another commander of desperate problems. "Yes, Brent. A hundred and one percent."

"Good. You had me worried. We've tried to tran you twice since we arrived at Palaia and couldn't get through."

Tahn responded calmly, "We had some downtime on the link, Brent. Nothing major. So tell me, how the hell did you get a vacation at Palaia when we're still stuck orbiting Horeb?"

Sweat seemed to pop out over Brent's pale face. He wiped at it nonchalantly. "Unfortunately, this isn't a vacation, Cole. *Jataka* has simply been rerouted. We're to rendezvous with the *Hoyer* around Tikkun."

"Oh, in the name of God, Brent! Another Gamant mission?"

His crew responded to his outrage by shifting disgustedly. Moans and subvocal curses laced the air. He wanted to kiss them.

"Sorry, old friend. It looks like we'll be doing a dog-and-pony show for the next few months. Slothen promises me, however, that our crews will have ample planetside time to enjoy themselves in lieu of full vacations."

He leaned back in his chair, briskly rubbing the knots out of the back of his neck. "It's not the same and you know it. But I guess we don't have a say in the decision. What's the show?"

Bogomil hesitated a moment, then lifted a shoulder apologetically. "The Gamant Underground is wreaking havoc across Sector Four. We have rebellions cropping up everywhere. The Magistrates think that if we make a spectacle of Baruch—you know, haul him around and point the condemning finger at him—his people will lose some of their fervor for war. What do you think?"

From the corner of his eye, he caught the wolfish looks exchanged by the Gamant guards. Baruch himself, however, glared unblinkingly at the screen.

Tahn responded, "I think it'll be a witless debacle, Brent. What idiot thought it up?"

Bogomil glanced sideways at Slothen. "We'll be accompanied by a new Gamant ambassador. Hopefully, he can make the thing work."

"Uh-huh. Who's this new ambassador? Some soft diplomat we'll have to cart around?"

"I believe you know him, Cole. He's the former High Councilman of Horeb. His name's Ornias."

He lifted his chin, eyes narrowing. "I know him. He's about as slimy as they come."

Baruch took a deep breath and quietly leaned a shoulder against the wall. He scanned the bridge, eyes gleaming with deadly intent.

"Can you work with him, Cole?"

"I can work with anybody. Well, I guess we'll meet you at Tikkun, Brent. What's our timetable?"

Bogomil's face vanished to be replaced by Slothen's. The Magistrate pursed his mouth into a stern circle. "We have some arrangements to conclude—in the capital city of Derow, Captain. Why don't you take it slow? Say you meet the *Jataka* in two weeks standard time?"

"Aye, sir. One last thing."

"Yes, Captain."

"We've been expecting some sort of appearance by Baruch's forces. A rescue mission, if you will. Have you received any intelligence on the whereabouts of his fleet?"

"Yes, I have very good news to report on that score. We've destroyed half his fleet. We—"

Tahn sat forward abruptly. "Begging your pardon, sir? *Half?*"

Baruch straightened, eyes narrowing as though he'd just heard his own last rites read.

"Yes, Captain. Eight Underground cruisers were picking up survivors in the Abulafia system. We cornered and destroyed all but one. The other half have vanished, however. We suspect they're headed for Sector Four—and probably the Lysomian system."

Anxiety tingled in Tahn's chest. If the government had severely wounded the Underground fleet, the rest of the cruisers would be regrouping, preparing a counterattack. That "other half" could be right on top of him this very moment and he'd never know it. But if Baruch hadn't been able to contact them. . . .

"Well, we'll keep our eyes open. Please let us know if you receive further intelligence."

"We will, Captain. Slothen out."

The screen went blank and the entire bridge seemed to heave a sigh of relief.

Baruch stepped forward, expression strained. His voice came out unsettlingly soft. "What happened around Abulafia?"

Cole blurted, "How the hell would I know? I haven't been in any condition to tap clandestine trans." Then his voice went hard. "So, how many people you think you lost? Twenty thousand? More?"

Baruch glared, fingering his pistol before leveling the barrel on Carey. She blinked and lowered her eyes in a gesture so fragile it made Tahn want to get up and offer some kind of aid, anything to make her feel better. He grimaced uncomfortably. When the hell had she developed that look?

"Halloway," Baruch ordered, "*find out* what happened in the Abulafian system."

"Certainly, Commander. Please have your people in Engineering release dattran control to me."

"I have a better idea." He motioned for her to come to him. She stood and walked toward him. When she got near, he grabbed her roughly by the arm and she let out a small cry of surprise.

Instinctively, thoughtlessly, Tahn lunged for Baruch, trying to protect Carey.

"No, Cole! Don't!"

He saw only a glimpse of her frightened green eyes, before five Gamant guards had him laid out like a slab of meat on the bridge floor. Their smothering bodies and hard hands convinced him to stay there.

In the kindest voice he'd ever heard, Baruch murmured, "Sorry, Halloway. I didn't mean to scare you. I want you to use the com in my cabin. That way I can watch your every move."

"Try asking next time. I'm not deaf."

Baruch gently shoved her into the tube. Two Gamants gripped Tahn's arms and jerked him to his feet, then forced him in after her. Carey glanced over her shoulder, face lit with concern, to make sure he was all right.

They exchanged a brief look of shared understanding and Cole smiled faintly. They might be outnumbered ten to one, but they both knew what they had to do now. Until Bogomil or the Underground fleet showed up, Baruch had a few thousand civilian amateurs to work with. But he and Carey had five hundred trained Magisterial soldiers.

CHAPTER 28

Jeremiel squinted against the harshness of the lustreglobes in the transport tube. Though he'd spent most of his life in this stark light, after living on Horeb for a few months, he missed the soft silken glow of candles and braziers which reminded him so much of the halcyon days of his youth on Tikkun. Slothen's hideous face had ripped the sack of his memories wide and they tumbled in a flood into his waking consciousness. While he'd listened to that stiff monotone speaking intergalactic lingua, he'd seen the dead faces of a hundred friends, the smoking devastated surfaces of a dozen planets—and he'd longed to retreat from the harsh lights and hear someone speak to him in Gamant again. He glanced at Rachel. She stood tall and stoic on the other side of the tube, dark eyes taking it all in. Dressed in a gray Magisterial uniform, perspiration shone in a shiny patch across her forehead. He wished he could get close enough to talk to her, to ask if she'd had any interesting *dreams* lately, but the tube was too crowded.

He bowed his head to avoid the glare of the overhead panel, and found himself gazing into Halloway's eyes. Pressed close as they were now, he could smell the subtle fragrance that clung to her, something earthy, like wildflowers after a rain. Where had he smelled that scent before? She had a strained alert look on her face that made him avert his gaze, feeling raw inside. Was she afraid he might hurt her again?

He lowered his voice for her ears alone, "On the bridge . . . I was on edge. I didn't mean—"

"Didn't you?"

"No, I'm sorry. I just . . ." He stopped when Tahn turned to pin him with a wary, calculating gaze.

"What are you going to do if you can't find your fleet before we get to Tikkun, Baruch?"

"We're not going to Tikkun."

Tahn braced an arm against the tube wall and gave him an amused look. "No? Come on. You know if you don't at least head the *Hoyer* in that direction, the Magistrates will be all over this ship and you and your friends will be dead. And second—"

"But in that case, Captain, so will you and yours."

"Second, something's up. And I know the way you think. If the government has destroyed half your fleet and initiated some sort of suppression action on your home world, you won't be able to keep your fingers out of it."

Jeremiel's gaze drifted back to Rachel. She looked at him fearfully. *Five cruisers, she'd said. Dear God.* His gut had been crawling since she'd first mentioned it. But he couldn't base future strategies on someone's "dreams." He needed concrete data. And yet . . .

The transport tube stopped on level four and Jeremiel pulled Halloway back against the wall. "Rachel, take Janowitz and Uriah, make certain Captain Tahn gets back to his cabin safely. Post a guard to make sure he stays there."

"Wait a minute, Baruch." Tahn struggled against the hard hands that gripped his arms. His purple uniform

256

clung to his back in sweat-damp folds.

"What do you want?"

"Let's discuss ship psychology. You know what happens when a commander is absent. The crew gets crazy."

"Your point?"

"Let me go to the bridge. So long as you have the controls routed to Engineering, I can't do anything, but my presence there will damn sure help my crew to stay calm. And the closer we get to Tikkun the more anxious they'll be."

Jeremiel ground his teeth and probed the depths of Tahn's blue-violet eyes, seeing the pleading, but something else lay deeply buried there, too. What? He scrutinized his enemy a while longer. Naturally Tahn wanted to be with his crew, any commander in his position would, if for no other reason than the comfort of camaraderie. But beneath the emotion openly expressed in Tahn's gaze, a logistical undercurrent flowed.

Jeremiel shook his head. "Negative. Maybe after we've—"

"You're cutting your own throat, Baruch! My people won't get any funny ideas if I'm there to ride herd. But if I'm not, there's no telling what sort of trouble they'll dream up. For God's sake, if you want this to work, *let me go to my bridge!* Let me . . . let me be with my crew."

The struggle in his imploring voice made Jeremiel's brows draw together. "I want *four* guards on his door, Rachel, including you."

"Understood."

"Damn it, Baruch!" Tahn shouted, fighting the hands that dragged him out of the tube.

Jeremiel hit the patch to close the door and then punched level twenty, glaring threateningly at Halloway. "He's persistent."

"What did you expect?"

"I expect—"

"The hell you do. You're just being cruel. Are you tormenting him for his past? All he ever did was follow the orders of the Magistrates. Would you have done differently in his place?"

Her eyes gleamed like frozen emeralds. An ache rose to thump with Jeremiel's heartbeat. He didn't answer.

"He's lost his ship, Baruch. His crew is all he has left. Can't you ease up a little?"

257

"He lost his ship. I may have lost twenty-five thousand friends. Tahn still has his life, Lieutenant. And if he wants to keep it, he won't push me."

"Kill Tahn, Commander, and his loyal crew will sacrifice everything to destroy you." Her eyes narrowed threateningly.

The tube halted and the door snicked back. The remaining guards flooded into the hall and nodded their approval, but Jeremiel pulled his pistol and gripped her purple sleeve anyway, pushing her out in front of him, checking the hall himself. Finding it clear, he cautiously released Halloway.

"Walk, Lieutenant. You know the way. I'll be right here behind you."

"I'm walking."

She strode forward and Jeremiel followed, pistol aimed at her back. He doubted she'd try anything foolish, but after seeing Slothen's malignant face on the monitor, his nerves wouldn't let him stand anywhere in the open without his pistol in his fist. Had the blue beast been telling the truth about destroying half the Underground fleet? Or was all that a clever lie? In either case, he was in even worse trouble than he'd thought, for if Slothen had lied, he more than suspected problems aboard the *Hoyer*.

Jeremiel's gaze darted defensively over the corridor, noting every soldier they passed, logging each in his memory. He felt like he walked a flaming tightrope over a sea of sharks. Fear knotted his guts, doubts throwing taunts from his subconscious: *You don't own this ship; this is all a precarious charade of time; one minute it's yours, the next Tahn's. And thousands of people are depending on you.*

When Halloway reached his cabin door, she asked, "Shall I just walk in, or would you prefer me to wait for you?"

"You can't get in, Lieutenant." He moved up beside her and blocked her view, then keyed in his code. He'd programmed the unit himself, allowing no one entry without the appropriate authorization sequence. The door opened.

He bowed slightly and made a sweeping gesture with his hand. "After you."

"Don't squander gallantry on me. I'm not one of your

258

soft Gamant women." She strode past him, going to stand in the center of the room.

Jeremiel straightened; haunting visions of Syene's magnificent muscular body swam out of his memories. A week before she'd died, she'd stood naked before the full-length mirror in his cabin and given herself a critical appraisal. "I guess I'm not in bad shape for being thirty-two." He remembered shaking his head in disbelief as he braced a hand against the wall over her head. Her deep olive skin had glistened wetly from her shower, accentuating every perfect female curve. "You're the most beautiful woman I've ever known. And vain, too." Her laugh rang sweetly in his memories, making him long for her. His mind still felt the softness of her touch, the warmth of her body against his.

And half his fleet might be dead? People they'd both known and loved? Unbeknownst to him, his eyes had gone hollow, face twisting miserably. When he looked up, he found Halloway staring probingly at him.

"Seeing ghosts?" she asked.

He strode in, closing the door behind him. "You know where the com terminal is. Get to work. And in case you forget the correct access codes, I've printed out the entire cryptography library. It's there on the corner of the desk." He pointed to a thick stack of crystal sheets as he strode across the room. Going to the drink dispenser, he ordered a glass of Numonian taza, took it to the table and slumped into a chair. He quietly watched the light refract through the amber liquid to cast geometric designs across the tabletop. Pain and fear stabbed him with dagger-sharp intensity.

Halloway eased into the desk chair and said, "Avel Harper wants you to call him."

"Thanks. Anything else?"

"No."

"Erase the message and get to work."

Halloway input several commands and waited, staring at the screen. He ignored her, his mind locked on the empty task of calculating how many days it had been since he'd heard Syene call his name. *"Love you,"* she'd whispered, barely audible, her bloodstained chest rising and falling erratically. *"Knew . . . knew you'd come. . . . Jere . . . Jeremiel. Dannon . . . Tahn. Betrayed . . . us. He was . . . was here. Half-hour ago."*

"I'll kill him, Syene. I swear."

"Baruch?" Halloway interrupted.

He didn't look up. Agony slashed his heart. *Stop it. She's been dead for months.* "Yes, Lieutenant?"

"What I said earlier—about Gamant women. Sorry. I just felt vulnerable and hostile after what you did to Tahn."

"What you do or don't think about Gamants is irrelevant to me, Halloway. I brought you here to do research that my own staff would find extraordinarily difficult and time-consuming. *So, do it.*"

But that wasn't quite true, was it, old boy? Silently, he chastised himself. He could have done the research just as effectively himself, probably more so. In fact, he'd check and recheck every shred of data she gave him. He'd just *wanted* her here.

In a quick motion, he slammed a fist into the com over his table, then programmed it for cabin 1912, calling, "Avel? This is Jeremiel. Are you in?" He swirled his taza, watching the amber liquid shimmer like ocean waves beneath a bright noonday sun.

A pause, then, "Yes, Jeremiel, thanks for getting back to me so quickly."

"I hope it's nothing critical, Harper. After staring into Slothen's eyes, my nerves are humming."

"No, don't worry. It's just that Mikael Calas has been pleading to speak with you. He claims it's urgent, about something his grandfather told him to tell you."

Jeremiel frowned curiously. "When? I was the last person to speak with Zadok. Why wouldn't he have told me—"

"Mikael claims his grandfather spoke to him a few days ago."

"Zadok's been dead for months, Avel. You know that."

"Mikael has gone through a great deal of trauma. You have to understand—"

"Yes, I do understand." They'd all been through hell, but Mikael's entire family and world had been brutally torn from him within a few short weeks of each other. "Tell him I'll arrange a meeting as soon as I can. The stakes have just been upped enormously, Avel. I've got to spend all my time on strategy for a few days. Please send him my sincere apologies."

"I will."

He kept his voice neutral. "Avel? Any word on Dannon yet?"

"None."

"Did you tell the searchers the Underground's standing reward is a million notes?"

"I did. But they've found absolutely nothing, Jeremiel."

"Cancel the search parties, then. I've concluded he must be dead."

Jeremiel caught Carey's fleeting look of interest. He lowered his gaze to the table and smoothed his fingers over the black tabletop.

"But why?" Harper asked. "I don't understand? What if he's—"

"See to it immediately, Avel. Baruch out." He switched off the com.

Halloway turned halfway around in her chair and examined him uncertainly. The light accented the smooth curves of her alabaster face. Why did her eyes affect him so? It was as though she'd decided to let him see through her carefully maintained professional mask and the fragility revealed drew him powerfully.

Be careful. You're still hurting over Syene. And she's a Magisterial officer who'd love to use that vulnerability against you.

Impatiently, he demanded, "Finding out anything, Lieutenant?"

"Yes, but I'm not sure you want to hear it."

"I suspect you're right. What is it?"

She hesitated a long moment, until he felt the quiet like a smothering layer of earth over his face. He looked up, meeting her gaze.

Quietly, she explained, "Apparently units of your Underground organized a series of small-scale rebellions on Abulafia. They attacked Magisterial military installations, killing several thousand soldiers. The Magistrates responded in kind. They—"

"Oh . . . no." He propped a trembling fist on the table.

Softly, she continued. "Casualty estimates range as high as twenty thousand. It was a level one attack. The central regions of the planet were destroyed. Survivors ran to the poles. Your fleet, or part of it, tangled briefly with the cruiser *Shamash*, drove it off, then initiated a rescue operation."

"And the battle Slothen reported?"

"No information in the files. It could be a very recent operation."

"Or maybe it never happened."

"Maybe."

For a brief instant, he felt relief. Maybe Slothen *had* been lying, but if so. . . . God, oh God.

Memories of the rich farmlands of Abulafia rose strongly. His mind overlaid past images with what those fields must look like now—an ocean of dark brown glass. They'd been communal farms, overrun with laughing children and plodding animals. The last time he'd visited the largest cooperative, a tiny dark-haired boy of five had clung to his pants' leg as they walked through orchards redolent with blossoms, smiling his love for the great Underground leader who protected them all from the horrors of the Magistrates. Jeremiel squeezed his eyes closed, gut hurting.

"Baruch?"

"*Don't* . . . Don't talk to me just now." Hatred smothered him like a black leaden blanket, the weight of it so great he felt he'd be crushed if he didn't do something.

Getting blindly to his feet, he slammed a fist into the wall. Throwing all of his weight behind his hands, he did it again and again, imagining each bolt of sound to be a rifle burst, seeing purple-uniformed soldiers die. When he'd killed enough, when the glassy ground ran thick with the enemy's blood, he dreamed of watching a little dark-haired boy spring back to life, crawling out of a glistening sea of melted rock to run toward him, arms open, laughing.

Finally, the pain in his hands overrode his inner anguish. He dropped aching fists to his sides and stood deathly still, struggling to separate reason from emotion. He forced a deep breath and tipped his chin toward the ceiling.

Carey sat riveted, barely breathing. Baruch looked like a tortured savior, handsome face drenched in sweat. The heavy muscles of his shoulders bulged from contraction, swelling against the fabric of his black jumpsuit.

She glanced back at the com screen, studying the statistics on Abulafia. An agricultural planet, they primarily grew grain crops. A few hardy fruit orchards thrived. Her own parents had labored in fruit orchards. Memories from her childhood swept her up, the sweet scent of Orion peach blossoms in spring wafting through her mind, her mother's crooked smile. Population of Abulafia: 23,000. Half were children. A paltry number of people for such a large, fertile planet. She scanned the data on production. They must have worked their hearts out. They yielded five times what a similar number of Magisterial workers grossed. And they possessed none of the sophisticated technological advantages.

Baruch made a deep-throated tremulous sound and she scrutinized his clenched fists and ravaged face. For a moment, his eyes came back to her, wide and unsettlingly blue. Hatred seethed in the depths, striking her like a brutal slap. She experienced a flicker of his pain. *Goddamn it.* She hadn't realized that adopting Pleroma's vulnerable facade would call forth a response from him that found an echo in her. She laced her fingers, squeezing tightly.

"Don't blame yourself," she said. "There's nothing you could have done. If you'd been there, the outcome would have been the same."

He bowed his head to stare at his glass. Violently, he shoved it across the table; it toppled over the edge, smashing into the chair before rolling onto the floor. The look of desolation on his handsome face brushed her like a frigid wind. When he spoke, his voice held such struggle, she had to clamp her own jaw to defend against the tide it stirred in her breast.

". . . A bunch of farmers. They were no threat to the government."

"Slothen sees all rebellions as threats. Giclasians have a narrow view of what constitutes constructive dissent. Gamant dissent rarely falls into the correct parameters."

He walked slowly across his cabin to stand over her. "And the Underground has split its forces and may be heading for the Lysomian system. What the *hell's* going on out there?"

"I don't know. Honestly. Do you want me to search for something else?"

He ground his teeth, nodding. "Yes, run a scan for every scrap of data that's traversed space concerning Tikkun."

She swung back around to the console, inputting the

correct request sequence—and wondered just why she'd done that. *He would have known if you hadn't. Sure. Right, that's why you did it. It has nothing to do with the fact that a part of you masochistically wants to help him.* The screen gleamed with a wave of amber fluctuations.

The com flared: *Access denied.*

"What?" she blurted.

Persistently, she tried other routes to access the data. Behind her, she felt Baruch's fiery eyes on her. Her spine prickled.

Inadmissible authorization code.

"Indeed? Well, this is interesting."

"What is?" he demanded pensively.

"I can't get through."

"Why not? How can that happen?"

"Sometimes Slothen seals files by sending orders through the main com on Palaia. But hold on. Let me do some fancy rerouting. Perhaps if I try to slip into the files through the back door."

She input a new series of requests under her security clearance code, not based on Tikkun but on clandestine operations. As information appeared, she frowned. Fragmented, words out of order, the data had obviously undergone a thorough and deliberate incoherency cover-up.

She cocked her head. "Well, we're into something deep, I can tell you that. Come look at this."

Quickly, he came across the room, bracing a hand against the back of her chair to read over her shoulder. "They've scrambled the data?"

"Apparently."

He reached over to touch the keyboard, and she felt the warmth of his muscular arm as it softly brushed hers. In a hushed voice, he read: ". . . sterilization . . . have demonstrated domination . . . organize entire populace for . . . bureaucratic progress . . . own annihilation . . ."

His tension had risen to such a violent crescendo, she could feel his anxious trembling through her chair. He hit a new series of keys, scrolling up slowly. ". . . relocation centers in deserts . . . rationalized terror . . . simplifies problem . . ."

As the horror of the possibilities struck him, his breathing went shallow. "No."

Carey swiveled her chair to look up. "Baruch, it can't

264

happen in this day and age. These are just a bunch of fragmented scraps. Don't jump to conclusions."

He looked at her steadily, and all the enmity between them slipped away. Just one human being to another, his eyes seemed to plead, *can't you see?* And she felt almost as if she, too, had heard the faint whisper of a lover's last good-bye, the sudden silencing of a child's ringing laughter, the quiet, quiet murder of an entire civilization.

She went numb as her mind spun images of her parents' death: Battleships diving through the dark skies . . . arcs of purple weaving an eerie luminescent web over their home . . . the sweet smell of orange blossoms mixing with that of ionized air . . . her mother screaming *"Run, Carey! For God's sake, go hide in the trees!"* . . . Timmy's squalls, running behind her, running before the web slashed through him.

The emotions caught her off-guard. She shoved her chair back, forcing Baruch to sidestep, then lunged to her feet. A sob welled in her throat. "I—I have to go."

She tried to push by him, but he grasped her wrist, gently stopping her. She looked up through tear-blurred eyes and saw his handsome face contort in shared pain.

"Your family?" he questioned. She nodded and before she realized what had happened, he'd wrapped his arms around her shoulders, pulling her close. A warm rush of feeling flooded her, frightening in its intensity. His beard softly brushed her face and he murmured something soothing, inaudible. For a blessed timeless moment she allowed herself to drown in the comfort he offered. How long had it been since she'd let a man hold her? Years— so many years. What a safe feeling it was to be held again. The touch of his muscular thighs against hers stirred sensations she thought her body had forgotten.

And with them cold sanity slapped her hard. "Baruch," she said, "the Magistrates call this fraternizing with the enemy. They frown on it."

"I can see why."

Slowly, he released her and took a step backward. They stood silently, facing each other.

"Don't . . . don't worry about the incoherency cover-up," she murmured lamely, embarrassed by how rapidly she was breathing. "It's probably nothing."

"It's something."

"Is there anything else you need from me?"

265

He shook his head and studied her piercingly. "No. Thank you."

* * *

Brent Bogomil walked the floor of Slothen's office, glancing at the beautiful holos of nebulas and distant solar systems that lined the lavender walls. Beyond the broad window, a triangular formation of station security ships flew, making a calculated arc over the city. "I told you Abruzzi was right. The *Hoyer* isn't ours anymore."

Slothen twined his fingers nervously. "It would be foolish to assume so. What do you want me to do?"

Bogomil heaved a sigh and studied the magnificent fountains beyond the window. They threw moisture so high a series of interconnecting streams laced over the spiky buildings. "I noticed the *Aratus* and *Leimon* in docks Seven-C and Eight-A when we arrived. Can you spare them?"

"You mean to accompany you and the *Klewe* to Tikkun?"

"Yes, just in case."

"Are you sure you need them? Gorgon's fleet is headed to the Lysomian system. Can't you rendezvous—"

"We don't know when he might drop out of vault. Worse, we can't be sure when or where the other half of the Underground fleet might appear. I could need immediate support."

Slothen's red mouth puckered. "All right. Let me know what's going on out there as soon as you can. But *try* to leave Baruch alone long enough that he feels it's safe to off-load his refugees on Tikkun; it will give us more research subjects to work with. Our studies there are critical." He feathered through a new stack of crystal sheets on his desk and shook his head angrily. "These Gamant problems have got to stop. Maybe I'll even reroute the *Scipio* as a show of force. Abruzzi nearly begged for that."

Bogomil nodded, eyes narrowing as he thought about the firefight that loomed only a few days distant. Already, he'd started plotting tactics and strategy. They'd need something powerful, foolproof.

Absently, he responded, "Thank you, Magistrate."

CHAPTER 29

. . . the Luminous came down to the innocent Adam and awoke him from a sleep of death that he might be saved. Even as when a just man finds a man possessed of a formidable demon and pacifies it by his art, so was it with Adam when this friend found him plunged in a deep sleep, awoke him, set him astir. . . .

"Let him who hears wake up from heavy slumber!"

Then Adam wept and shed heavy tears and then he dried them, saying, "Who called my name? And from whence comes this hope, while I am in the chains of the prison?"

"I am the pronoia of the Pure Light; I am the thought of the virginal Spirit who reestablishes thee in the realms of glory. Stand up, and remember that it is thyself thou hast heard, and return to thy root. For I am the Merciful! Take refuge from the angels of Destruction, from the demons of the Chaos.

Then the Luminous sealed him with the light and the water with five seals, so that death henceforth should have no power over him.

> **Secret Book of John**
> (Nos. 6 and 36 and No. 1 of the Berlin Codex).
> One of the Forty-Four Secret Books.
> Found on Jumes, 5013.

Rachel stood on the first step of the ladder climbing through the level four security mainframe tunnel. An armored passageway six feet across, its lights glowed dimly. She reached up and removed the silver panel covering the central network of monitors.

Fourteen screens greeted her efforts. She wiped her sweaty forehead on the sleeve of her formfitting brown jumpsuit and shoved her long black hair over her shoulders, studying the rows of computer readouts. Each screen possessed its own unique color. Supposedly the color-coded display helped the reader keep different kinds of data straight.

"So why can't you?" she gritted in angry exasperation.

Taking a notebook out of her pocket, she flipped through the crystal sheets, reviewing the schematic again. As she reached out to input a check sequence, a brilliant flash lit the tunnel. She shielded her face with her hands. Through the weave of her fingers, she saw the sleeve of his carmine cloak. He stood tall, awesomely beautiful. His amber body shimmered like liquid fire in the dim light, blazing against the walls so that they seemed sheathed in gold. The shadows of the ladder and com units wavered in monstrous images up and down the tunnel.

"No," she whispered, stepping off the ladder to the floor. "Aktariel, why can't you leave me alone!" Her knees shook so badly, she had to brace a hand against the wall to keep standing. "I have nothing to say to you. What do you want?"

"Rachel, you'll be on your way to Tikkun soon and I—"

"Jeremiel said we're not going to Tikkun! He said we're going to—"

"Yes, I know he told you that." He gazed at her with an anxious patience. "He's being very cautious. In the end, almost half a million lives will depend upon his sixth sense for battle strategy."

Tightly gripping the rung of the ladder that rested beside her, she stifled the fright and frustration swelling in her chest. As he watched her movements, a peculiar sadness invaded his eyes.

"Rachel, listen carefully. The ships Slothen has dispatched for Tikkun are coming from different directions. Two already have a fix on the *Hoyer*. Jeremiel is walking into a trap."

"What kind of trap?"

"A clever move called the 'Laced Star.' Jeremiel is familiar with it."

"Can he counter it?"

"I don't know."

"What do you mean you don't know? You do know!"

He shifted uncomfortably to lean a shoulder against the wall. "You overestimate my abilities. Epagael is manipulating the void so that I can count on very little. Chaotic parameters of the future are fluctuating wildly. There are too many factors which might change. Ornias is predictable, but Lichtner is another question. He and Tahn have old business to resolve."

"Who's Lichtner?"

"The current military governor of Tikkun."

"Why is he important?"

The haunted look on his face made her hold her breath. "Ask Jeremiel."

"You can't tell me?"

"It would be better if he did. It's his private business." He stood a little straighter, as though a new thought had occurred to him. "*No, ask Tahn.* He'll tell you."

"I can't just walk into Tahn's cabin and—"

"Yes, you can. In fact, he'd welcome the intrusion. He's going a little mad from claustrophobia."

Uncertainty and confusion vied in her stomach. "Why is it I always want to believe you? Even though I know, *I know,* you're lying."

He lowered his voice to a soothing murmur. "I'm not lying. And as to why you want to believe, my dear Rachel, you and I have an ancient connection. You sense my own deepest fears. Our paths have been joined for millennia."

"*Not* if I don't choose to align myself with you."

". . . That's mostly true."

Terror throbbed like a living creature in her chest. What did he mean by that? He gave her a pained shake of his head and looked away. His tension seemed to affect the very air, making it thicker, heavier.

"I don't understand," she quavered.

"Do you want me to explain?"

"Yes. *Now.*"

He cautiously took a step toward her, amber eyes gleaming with a strange light. He opened his palm and extended it. "Take my hand."

"Why?" She backed away.

"Because I can't explain such important things to you here. I need to feel wind in my face and dirt beneath my feet. Come with me. You'll like this place. It's warm and beautiful."

"Dor? Or somewhere else? Where are we going?"

He squeezed his eyes closed a minute, then, in a taut

voice answered, "The name wouldn't mean anything to you if I told you. Please, trust me. Share my company for just an hour. An hour, Rachel, that's all I'm asking and I'll answer any question you put to me."

"Any question?"

"Any. I give you my word."

"Including the nature of our *connection?*"

"Yes, yes, anything."

A well of cold expanded inside her, but she felt desperate to know. She hesitantly extended her hand and put it in his.

He lifted his other hand. A whirlwind of darkness spun out from the wall. Rachel's hair danced in the warm wind.

She took a deep breath before they stepped through the darkness.

CHAPTER 30

Cole Tahn ran a hand through his brown hair, grimacing at everything in his cabin, the oil lamp on his table, the subdued colors of the holos on the walls, his unmade bed. His blankets tumbled onto the floor in a heap. "Goddamn, you have nothing to do and you can't even pull up your godforsaken sheets?"

His spine went stiff when a deep voice boomed through his door com: "Tahn. It's Baruch."

"It's about time! Come in."

The door slipped open and Baruch stepped inside. They stood silently, holding each other's gaze in an undeclared dominance war. Baruch yielded first, shifting his attention to one of the bright holos of sunrise over Giclas VII. Yellow peaks glimmered like golden needles.

Tahn slowly backed toward his table, eyes never leaving the Underground leader. He bumped a chair and it scudded across the carpet. Baruch whirled, dropping into a combat crouch.

Cole lifted his hands over his head. "No challenge intended. Can I get you something to drink?"

Baruch vigilantly straightened up. "Whiskey?"

Tahn nodded and slowly walked toward the cabinet over his desk. He opened the latch and pulled out a finely faceted crystal bottle and two shot glasses. Quietly, he brought them back to the table. Watching Baruch out of the corner of his eye, he poured the glasses full. The man had squared his shoulders, standing as rigidly as a statue.

Cole eased into his chair. "You're welcome to the other seat."

Baruch nodded curtly, but continued standing. Finally, he walked across the room and picked up his whiskey, glaring at it suspiciously.

"Oh, I see," Tahn said irritably. He bolted the contents of his own glass and poured himself another. "Feel better?"

"I will in about fifteen seconds. I'm sure you'd only use the best."

"You're astute."

Carrying his drink, Baruch meandered around the cabin, glancing frequently back to make sure Tahn still sat immobile at the table.

Tahn asked, "Are we headed for Tikkun yet?"

"No. And I don't expect to be."

Cole laughed condescendingly. "Going to wait until they force you? That's silly, Baruch. They might cut you a deal if you surrender and plead for mercy."

Baruch smiled, a hard bitter gesture. "Thanks. But I'm well acquainted with Magisterial generosity. I'm not interested." He wandered to the display case mounted on Tahn's far wall and went deathly silent. Retrieving the fine palm-sized tapestry from Jumes, Baruch lifted it to the light, studying the weave.

"What's this, Tahn? Some peculiar form of necromancy?"

"You mind?"

"It's a little blasphemous, don't you think?"

"You consider artistic taste to be ungodly?"

Baruch lifted a brow. "Just when did you develop this taste? Before or after you killed every living thing on Jumes?"

A chilling tingle filled Tahn's breast, like a thousand icy ants crawling around inside him. "Let's discuss the

271

Hoyer, Baruch. Recriminations between us are useless at this point. How's my crew?"

"They're holding up better than I'd have thought. You trained them well."

Cole tilted his chair back on two legs and propped his whiskey glass on his knee, eyeing Baruch speculatively. The compliment sounded honest, a gesture from one commander to another. But it made him even more uneasy. "Glad to hear that Halloway's keeping the lid on."

"She's a fine officer."

Tahn nodded reflectively. A curious light gleamed in Baruch's blue eyes at the mention of Carey's name. Cole contemplatively tapped his thumb against his cool glass, remembering the softness in Baruch's voice when he'd hurt her on the bridge. *Interesting.* Worth investigating.

"Come and sit down, Baruch. You make me nervous pacing around."

He continued standing. "How are you feeling?"

"That's the second time you've asked. Why do you care? Concerned about your hand-to-hand proficiency?"

Baruch's mouth turned up in a sardonic smile. "Not even slightly."

"Then for the last time, *I'm fine.* Severns is a good doctor. How are your refugees?"

Baruch studied Cole for several painfully quiet seconds. "Most of them are dying. Some with agonizing slowness. Others too swiftly for their families to mourn. Why do *you* care? Trying to determine the efficiency of your cannons?"

Memories rolled across Tahn's mind—devastated planets whirling in pale violet hazes, hysterical voices pleading with him over com. His gut tried to tie itself in knots. "I've never liked attacking Gamant civilians, Baruch."

"No? You certainly did it with disturbing frequency. When did you decide you didn't like it? Somewhere between half a million and a million? What was the magic number?"

"Is it time for the mudslinging contest?" He made an airy gesture with his hand. "Just let me know so I can prepare myself. I've got a few charges I could level against you, too."

Baruch drew a deep breath and nodded while he exhaled. "I'm sure you do." He walked back and forth in front of the table, brow furrowed in thought. "You never enjoyed murdering my people, I'm glad to hear that. Perhaps you wouldn't object, then, to telling me what other orders you've received lately regarding Gamant planets?"

Cole laughed incredulously. "You're brassy as hell, aren't you? Why don't you use the mind probes? You could wring lots of things from me that you'd find very interesting."

He'd thrown out the comment facetiously because everybody knew Gamants refused to employ the probes on their prisoners, but now he wished he hadn't mentioned it. The odd gleam in Baruch's eyes gave him the eerie feeling the Underground leader might make an exception in his case.

With unsettling silence, Baruch walked across the room and took the chair opposite him. He braced his elbows on the table and sipped his whiskey, staring hard into Tahn's eyes. "Let's discuss the *Annum*."

Cole barely moved. "Why?"

"I assume it's bothering you."

". . . And?"

"I'd rather it didn't."

Cole chuckled his disbelief. "Well, you're a kind-hearted soul. And just how do you expect to alleviate my worries?"

Baruch reached for the whiskey bottle and started to pour himself another, then stopped. "May I?"

"Please, do. As I recall, I promised you a glass of my best hundred-year-old rye."

"I remembered, but I thought I'd be polite and not mention it."

"Good idea."

Baruch gave him a greatly amused smile. "Out of curiosity, do you know what the Magistrates were doing on Jumes before you were ordered to scorch it?"

"What does that have to do with the *Annum*?"

"Oh, a very great deal."

"I don't see—"

"No, I don't suppose you do. Pity. Don't Magisterial captains ever bother to research why planets that have

273

been peaceful for centuries suddenly flare into revolt?"

Cole massaged his forehead in annoyance. "Your point?"

"On Jumes the Magistrates called it Operation Scythe—a tasteless play on Old Earth images of Death. They rounded up every politician, every religious leader, every serious scientist and ordered them probed until their minds were little more than mush."

Indignantly, Tahn responded, "Come, come, Baruch. I know something of the history of Jumes. The social system was founded on ridiculous and dangerous principles. The politicians promised their constituents that as soon as every vestige of Magisterial government had been wiped off their planet, the true Mashiah would come." He leaned forward angrily, gripping his glass tightly. "And those 'scientists' you're so protective of taught the youths how to make bombs! They preached mass murder in illegal classes, for God's sake! Of course the Magistrates took defensive action!"

Baruch's penetrating gaze never wavered. "They did more than that, Tahn. After they'd probed them, they ordered them all killed."

He sat back, slowly. Deep inside him, a thrumming refrain beat: *Lucky, lucky, lucky.* "So?"

"So tell me, how can I prevent that from happening to you and your crew?"

Tahn shook his head as though he hadn't heard right. This had to be some ploy to gain leverage, but he couldn't quite figure the angle. "What's this? Don't tell me you've started to believe the rumors circulating on backward planets that you're the promised redeemer? And anyway, I didn't know that option existed for Magisterial soldiers."

"If I put you down on an accessible planet, the Magistrates will certainly haul you all off to the nearest neuro—"

"*Not. . . !* Not certainly." He fought the urge to tremble. Blood had started to surge deafeningly in his ears. "Why the hell are we discussing this?"

Baruch's face fell into stiff lines. "I can tell you for a fact, Tahn, the *Hoyer*'s records won't clear you."

Cole jerked involuntarily. "How do you know that?"

"I've reviewed them damned carefully. Oh, mind you, it's evident the point at which the error occurred—just after I stepped out of the shuttle. But it's not clear who was to blame. And the Magistrates will want someone to blame. You know that. *Just like they did with the* Annum."

Hot, agonizing flashes of the probes in the courtyard before the cathedral of Notre Dame taunted Cole. He pulled his hands off the tabletop and tucked them in his lap, hiding their trembling. "Why are you telling me this?"

"Because I knew it would be bothering you and I thought I'd remove that one uncertainty from your mind. To help you make decisions more clearly."

"What *specific* decisions did you have in mind?"

Baruch looked up without moving a muscle. "Decisions regarding this ship."

"Oh, I see." They stared unforgivingly at each other for a time, each silently trying to guess the other's strategy. "Well, if you really want to help me with those sorts of problems, let me look at those files myself."

"I'll release the data to your com immediately."

Tahn's mouth fell open. "Let's talk honestly, Baruch. Is this some bizarre sort of blackmail? If the situation were reversed, I'd never release such files to you."

Baruch heaved a tired breath and smiled. "Perhaps I respect you more than you do me. I sincerely believe that given all the relevant data—you'll make the right choice."

"Which means?"

Baruch lifted his glass and smoothly emptied the amber contents. "Once you're finished reviewing the files, give me a call. We'll discuss it."

In cynical amusement, Cole asked, "Planning on making me an offer I can't refuse?"

Astoundingly, Baruch turned his back on Cole and walked quietly to the door. Over his shoulder, he cast, "Yes. I am." Then he exited into the brightly lit hallway.

* * *

CHAPTER 31

Rachel stood on the crest of a ridge, black hair waving in the warm breezes. Around her, red hills filled with orchards and fields rose and fell with the land. She looked down across a brilliantly blue lake. On the sandy shores a small village sprouted; people in multicolored robes walked the narrow dirt streets.

Aktariel spread his arms wide and turned his glowing face up to the brilliant sunshine, as though absorbing every sight and every scent into his very being. Happiness lit his amber face. "Do you smell that?"

"What?"

"That sweet tang in the air? I didn't know how very much I'd missed the scents of olive trees and thyme."

"Where are we?" Rachel asked.

He put his hands on his hips and tilted his head. "Quite honestly? We're in a universe where I never existed."

"A universe. . . . Where is that?"

He laughed softly. "Here. The village down below us is known as Tverya."

Walking a short distance away, Aktariel removed his blue cloak and draped it over a spiny bush. The long white robe he wore beneath shimmered with a metallic brilliance in the sunlight. A purple sash knotted around his waist, the ends flapping gently in the breeze. He sat down upon a flat stone and took off his sandals. Slapping them against the rock to knock out the dust, he smiled. "There's a wonderful tavern I know in Tverya. Would you go there with me?" He hesitated, frowning. "At least, I think it's there."

"But I thought you'd never been here?"

"I haven't, but . . ." He waved a hand. "I have."

She lifted a brow in angry, frightened annoyance. "You don't plan on answering all my questions in riddles, I hope?"

"No. I promise."

Below, children ran through the streets of the village, a dog chasing them, barking. Giggles rose sweetly on the wind. "Then let's go find this tavern you may know. I have a lot of questions."

"Good. I've wanted to talk to you for a long, long time, Rachel." He stood up and grabbed his cloak, handing it to her. "I'm afraid you'll look a little conspicuous in that jumpsuit. Why don't you put this on?"

"Me? What about you?"

"They'll see me as an ordinary man."

"You're going to transform yourself again?" Her heart thundered suddenly. When he shimmered like a golden god she could successfully fight the deep attraction she felt, but if he again became the striking man of Dor she feared her own responses.

"Yes," he answered. In a tender, intimate gesture, he opened his cloak and wrapped it around her shoulders, then stepped closer and fastened the top clasp. "There," he said, "they'll think we're filthy rich, but we can stand that."

He stepped back away from her and lifted a hand in front of his face. As he lowered it, his inner glow died. Rachel watched the transformation with trepidation. His oval face took on the deep tan, high cheekbones and charismatic brown eyes of Hasmonaean. Blond curls hung down around his ears, fluttering in the wind. Rachel uncomfortably held that powerful gaze. When he smiled she felt as though the sun had come out from behind a dark bank of clouds. She steeled herself against him. "Let's go."

He walked forward, sandals swishing in the red soil. "Yes. Let's. This is a wonderful village. They're known far and wide for their wines."

He offered her a hand. She refused it, gesturing for him to lead. He nodded obligingly, but his expression appeared hurt. Rachel fell in line behind him, following him through the shadow-dappled rows of an orchard and out onto a winding dirt path. Flat-roofed houses lined the street, mud and stone exteriors gleaming like tan and ocher patchwork quilts.

As they turned down a new street, a gaggle of children came racing toward them, playing some sort of tag game. Rachel smiled at their happy faces. Memories of Horeb flitted through her mind. How could these children have such bright shining eyes when those in her own universe gazed out through haunted fear-hardened orbs.

The gaggle raced by, all except for one little boy with a dirty face. He stopped abruptly as he passed and looked up curiously at Aktariel. He asked a question in a language Rachel didn't understand.

Aktariel threw back his head and laughed, then knelt down beside the boy and stroked his grimy cheek. Reaching into the pocket of his white robe, Aktariel pulled out an irregularly shaped coin. He tossed it into the air where it spun, reflecting the sunlight that streamed down between the buildings. Then he handed it to the boy, speaking in soft tones. The child nodded and clutched the coin tightly before running away down the streets to catch up with his companions.

Rachel watched the child disappear. "What was that all about?"

"They think we're Romans, God. forbid. The boy speaks Greek remarkably well."

"Romans? What are those?"

He stood up and lifted both brows. "Something bad in this day and age. They'll view us in much the same way your own people view Magisterial citizens. Well, at least we're not wearing any jewelry."

"Would that make it worse?"

"Considerably. They'd think we were one of Antipas' own. That would be *very* bad. It's a little like being one of Slothen's cronies."

He placed a hand lightly on her shoulder, urging her to walk beside him. "Just play the role and we'll do fine." He turned and examined her carefully. "But you'll have to look more arrogant, dear Rachel. Here, lift your chin. Good, that's better."

She smiled reluctantly, allowing him to guide her down a hill and through the cool shadows of a two-story building that overlooked the lake. Stepping into the doorway, Aktariel jarred it open and peered inside uncertainly. The smell of baking bread wafted out to Rachel, and a number of scents she didn't recognize. A husky female voice bellowed at them. Aktariel called back gaily, then turned to Rachel. "We're in luck, it does exist in this universe."

He opened the door wider. She walked past him into

the flaxen lamplight of the tavern. A tiny place, it stretched no more than twenty feet square with eight rough-hewn tables lining the walls. A plump elderly woman with silver-shot black hair and a deeply wrinkled face waved at them.

Aktariel waved back. "Stay here. I'll get us two chalices of wine and we can go sit at the outdoor tables."

"All right."

She stood alone in the back of the room while he strode forward, chatting happily with the barmaid, who cackled loudly at something he'd said and shoved his shoulder hard. They talked for a while, as if old friends. Then the woman tipped two ceramic chalices and a pitcher beneath a barrel and filled them full. Aktariel tossed a coin on the counter and retrieved all three. Striding across the floor, his grace struck her disturbingly. He seemed to float more than walk.

He handed her a chalice and led her out the door again, around the side of the building. Five tables sat beneath a wooden arbor covered all over with vines. Beyond, the windswept lake glimmered as though frosted with silver.

"What luck that Tzipora has no other customers this afternoon. We may get to be alone all day."

Rachel stiffened. "You said an hour."

He pulled out a chair for her and nodded. "No matter how long we stay here, Rachel, I'll return you at the exact moment you left—or before, if you like. Please, don't worry about time while we're here. I just want you to be happy. Sit. Enjoy yourself."

Uneasily, she took the chair and watched him drop into the opposite one. He smoothed the hair away from his handsome face and tipped his chin to the fragrant breeze, inhaling deeply. Rachel lifted her chalice and sipped the wine. It had a rich robust flavor.

"Tzipora's an interesting character," he said. He lifted his own glass and drank deeply. "I think her feet stay purple all year from tramping the grapes."

"She didn't seem to mind that you were a Roman."

"Oh, she's broad-minded. She serves all kinds, as long as they have money."

Rachel gave him a stare as cold and piercing as a dagger's blade. Why did her heart long to laugh, to be free with him? *Don't. If you ever yield—you're lost.* To counter the welling emotions, she filled her mind with

279

hate, forcing herself to concentrate on all the old legends, the terrible stories of his brutality and cunning.

He seemed to sense the direction of her thoughts, for he smiled indulgently and leaned forward, patiently plucking at the splinters in the table. "How are you, Rachel?"

"Terrified. Feeling trapped."

"By the Magistrates, or me?"

"Both."

He nodded and expelled a breath. "I'm sorry I tried to rush you. It was wrong of me."

"Wrong? You tried to *deceive* me. But then that's what you're renowned for, isn't it?"

"Rachel, please—"

"You said this was a universe where you never existed. Does that mean all the people you deceived in mine are absent in this one?"

He evaded her eyes by gazing up at the birds soaring over the lake. "I didn't deceive them, Rachel. But, to answer your question, no. All those people will be here. They'll just be different. Their lives will have taken an alternate course."

"But now that you're here, doesn't your presence affect them?"

"Not as long as I don't meddle. And I guarantee you, I won't. I like this universe exactly as it is—painfully, mundanely boring."

Rachel frowned into her cup studying the way the shadows played over the dark red wine. "Aktariel . . ."

He looked up and his handsome face pinched. "I'm ready. Go ahead."

"Let's start with your reputation as the Deceiver."

He nodded. The wind tousled his white sleeves, setting them to billowing. "Well, it's a long story, but I've never been very subtle. Have you noticed that?"

She just glared.

He pursed his lips. "Unfortunately, you'll probably notice it again, no matter how hard I try to correct my behavior. It's just part of my nature. Well, anyway, *Deceiver* should be equated with *Tempter*. My fault lies in the fact that I've always tempted people to see the truth about God. And none too gently, I'm afraid. Epagael always made a point of seeking those people out, sending emissaries to drag them to the Throne and contradicting my story by showing them how loving he could be. Of course, they thought I'd lied to them." He opened a hand. "Hence: Deceiver."

"That sounds very neat and clean. Let's discuss the legends about Sinlayzan."

He stopped moving, seemed not even to breathe. Then he hesitantly leaned back in his chair. "All right."

"The stories say that you deceived him into believing you were a messenger from Epagael and you led him into the desert where you brutally tormented him for forty days and forty nights, accusing him of every sin in the old books. He fought you, proclaiming his innocence, but you never relented. You tortured him until he fell to the ground, confessing every minor violation of the Law he'd ever committed. Sinlayzan, the stories say, wept and tore his hair, begging your forgiveness." She gazed hard at Aktariel. His face had gone ashen, lines etching tightly around his eyes. In the cerulean sky behind him, clouds drifted.

"Yes," he said, balefully quiet. "He did—beg my forgiveness."

Rachel glowered into his miserable face. "And then? You dragged Sinlayzan back into the city of Gulgalto and brought formal criminal charges against him, citing every crime against God he'd ever committed." Rachel gulped her wine, feeling the same hatred she had when she'd heard the story as a child. She'd asked her father so often why God didn't just kill Aktariel so he couldn't hurt people, but her father had never found an answer to give her. "After they convicted Sinlayzan, they blinded him and tied him to a pole, then slowly lowered and raised him above a roaring fire. Witnesses claimed they could hear his screams for two days before he died."

Aktariel bowed his head and clenched his hands in his lap. His twisted face reminded Rachel of a long-dead zaddik whose heart had been gnawed out by the worms of doubt.

"Did you do that to Sinlayzan?"

He closed his eyes against the question. "Not . . . not exactly in that way. But—yes."

"You *deceived* him. How could you? He was a good man, a great man! A prophet!"

"Yes. He was."

Ruthlessly, she pressed, "I want to hear your defense."

He looked up at her through empty eyes and she had the feeling he looked through her to some distant and horrifying past. "*Elahi, Elahi, metul mah shebaktani.* . . . That's why, Rachel. Because God had forsaken him."

"What does that mean? What bearing—"

"Don't you see? Sinlayzan lived in a sedate society which prided itself on pure rationalism. They were never hungry, never cold. His people never had to face the terrors that plagued the rest of the universe. God had given him that peace for a reason."

"To defeat you, you mean?"

"Yes. I had to force Sinlayzan and his people to see a different reality."

"The one *you* consider true?"

He reached over and lifted his cup to his lips, drinking slowly. A gust of wind blew across the lake, pushing up white caps, sending them undulating toward the shores. "Rachel, tell me, what lesson did you learn from Sinlayzan's plight?"

"I learned that you were an abomination to be feared."

His nostrils flared. "Sinlayzan's people learned something different. They paraded by his dead body for seven days, until the horror became too much for them to bear—then they began asking terrible questions that they'd never thought of before. *They asked how there could be a God so monstrous He would allow His own greatest prophet to die because he'd violated a few of* His *petty Laws.* They asked where God was on the day Sinlayzan died. Was He watching? Why didn't He save him? Why wouldn't a just God grant a truly holy man forgiveness for such minor sins?"

Rachel's breathing had gone shallow. A fire of righteousness flamed in Aktariel's voice. The paper folded in her breast pocket seemed to cry out to her. She'd written down all the equations he'd told her she wouldn't remember—written them down to try and figure out what they meant. Did they hold the key to a plot like the one he'd used on Sinlayzan?

She lifted her cup and drank her wine as she gazed out across the lake. Birds circled the water, wings flashing in the sun. "When I went through the *Mea*, Epagael told me that you'd deceived me into believing all of existence was suffering. He asked me if I'd never seen a sunset or counted the wildflowers in the deserts in the spring."

Aktariel's jaw hardened. "Did you tell him the beauty of a wildflower pales when your heart is broken, when your baby's crying from hunger, when you're watching your people die by the thousands and there's nothing you can do to stop it? Did you tell him despair clouds every sunset?"

"No, I—I just asked Him if it was going to get worse."

"Good question. And He said?"

"He said that Chaos becomes more intricate as time passes—which I took as a yes."

"You should have. Except that isn't the whole truth. Chaos will grow more intricate for a few billion years more, then it will gradually start to decline as the universe winds down."

Rachel sat quietly, sipping her wine, watching the waves that washed the shore of the lake. "Adom told me something about that. I asked him if entropy wouldn't resolve the problem of evil and he said no. He said that God would simply start it all over again."

"He learned well."

"He loved you."

Aktariel gazed forlornly at the table, caressing the rough wood. "I know."

"God told me something else that I found strange. He asked me if you'd paid me my thirty pieces of silver yet. Then he said you'd deceived Adom and me into—"

"Did he?" Angrily, he lifted his chalice and drained it dry. "Did you, perchance, mention to Him that you hadn't met me yet?"

"No, I didn't have the time. He threw me back to Horeb rather abruptly."

She fumbled awkwardly with her chalice, thoughts jumping with angry confusion. His handsome face darkened as he watched. Slowly, he reached across the table and grasped a strand of her hair that had been twisting in the breeze. He drew it back and pressed it against his cheek. The gentle gesture left her feeling strangely hollow.

"On the ship," she murmured, "you said we had an ancient connection. What did you mean?"

He caressed her hair a moment longer before letting it fly into the wind again. "What I meant is difficult to explain. Perhaps it would be better left for another time

283

when we know each other—"

"*Now*, Aktariel. I'm no simpleminded fool you can control through dallying and misdirection! Tell me!"

He gazed at her steadily, longing in his eyes. "All right. You have a right to know. I just thought it would be easier once you . . . . Never mind. I meant that our paths have twined and missed for millennia."

"I'm thirty-four years old. I don't know what you mean."

"Yes, thirty-four, in this current form. What you are now isn't what you've always been." He tenderly patted the *Mea* that made a bump beneath his white robe. "It relates to the vortex, the field of woven energy that stretches infinitely through the void. It's the heart of everything. Oh, the strands of the tapestry often shake loose and drift away or change color, but they never cease to exist. They simply get rewoven into the fabric of the whole again. Are you following me?"

"No."

"I mean that you and I, and all this . . ." he lifted his arms toward the vine-covered arbor and the sky, sweeping down to include the lake and hilly land, "are intimately interconnected. The strands that form my soul, have often also formed yours. We're a part of each other." He tilted his head, giving her a sad smile. "And neither of us will be whole until we're together again."

Her spine tingled. "I don't—"

"I know you don't. Believe me when I tell you, it will all be clear later. Don't let it frighten you. None of it has to be if you don't want it to. It's just that our paths are so close now, so very close. But, if you decide you don't want to help me, we'll meet again. Maybe next time I'll be more convincing." He nervously fingered the hem of his sleeve. "But know this, Rachel. I'll never be able to end the suffering in this universe without you. And I hate to think of all the misery that will ensue before our next conjunction."

She stared breathlessly at him. "I'm the key to stopping the suffering?"

"Oh, yes. You always have been. I can't do it alone. Though I've tried. But I was younger then—foolish and impatient." He waved a hand negligently. "Epagael's comment about the thirty pieces of silver relates to that foolishness."

She sat quietly, hair fluttering in front of her eyes, partly obscuring Aktariel's serious face. She didn't know how to respond. Could any of this be true? It didn't make sense. Why her? The sounds of the village crept up around her, men talking somewhere down the street, a woman's husky laughter, birds chirping. Rachel finished her cup and reached for the pitcher.

"Oh, let me do that," he said, taking it from her hands and pouring her chalice full again. His expression was pained, as though he felt her terrible confusion, and wished he could end it. "You're very beautiful, Rachel, did you know that?"

She winced slightly. "Why did you tell me that?"

"Because it's true."

"I—I don't know what to think about you, Aktariel," she responded. In the depths of her soul, his strange words of strands and conjunction rang with a foreboding timbre of truth.

"Think whatever feels right, Rachel." He cautiously reached across the table and tenderly touched her cheek. Instinct told her to pull back, but she didn't. The warmth of his hand soothed something inside her.

He studied every change in her face. "What are you feeling?"

"Things I wish I weren't."

"I feel it, too, Rachel—that completeness when we're together. Though I experience it more powerfully than you because my consciousness retains its continuity over millennia. I remember all our pasts."

An involuntary shudder took possession of her. She pulled away from the gentle warmth of his hand. "Don't . . . don't say things like that. I need time to put all this together. Let's go back to the *Hoyer*."

She pushed her chair back and started to stand, but he grasped her shoulder lightly, stopping her. "First, let's discuss Tikkun."

"What about it?"

His eyes took on a gleam. "Rachel, time is short. Jeremiel is planning on taking Carey Halloway down to the planet with him. You mustn't let him. *He has to take Cole Tahn.* If he doesn't . . ."

His voice trailed away as five men swaggered out of Tzipora's and took a table a short distance from them. Their laughter rang through the vines, carrying on the

285

wind. Ranging in age from around fifteen to perhaps fifty, they wore coarse brown homespun robes. They smelled of fish and salt. One of them, a tall man with dark brown hair falling around his shoulders and a long beard, smiled at her. Rachel smiled back, but her heart pounded. He had haunting eyes, filled with a pained emptiness.

Aktariel stood suddenly and gripped her hand, pulling her to her feet. "We must be going," he said quietly. "Hurry."

She stumbled around the table, trying to obey, but the hem of her cloak—his cloak—caught on a splinter protruding from the table leg.

"Wait. Wait!" she blurted, bending down to untangle it, but the tall stranger leapt up from his table before her fingers even touched the hem.

"Let me help you," he said. With deft fingers, he unwound the tangled fabric and released it, then stood, facing her.

Rachel studied him curiously. Why did she understand his language? He had a heavy accent, but the words were clear. Aktariel's grip on her hand tightened and she turned to look at him, but his gaze was leveled over her shoulder, fear in his eyes.

"Pardon me," the stranger said politely to Aktariel. "Don't I know you?"

"No," Aktariel responded coldly.

The unknown man took a step forward, eyes bright, apparently drawn to Aktariel like a moth to flame—even more powerfully, it seemed, than Rachel herself. The stranger shook his head slightly, as though to clear his thoughts. "But I seem to know you." He lifted a hand to grasp the brown fabric over his chest. "In here. In my heart, friend. Are you sure we haven't—"

"I don't know you!" Aktariel said sharply. Then, as though in pain, he squeezed his eyes closed. His grip on her hand grew viselike, so strong that it hurt.

Rachel turned to the stranger. "I'm sorry," she said, "we're in a hurry. Forgive us for being rude."

He nodded once, smiling his forgiveness, and she found her gaze riveted to his. Everything about him affected her like a strong belt of whiskey on an empty stomach. His muscular body, the simple dignity of his face, the haunting light in his dark eyes.

Behind them, one of his friends, a gray-haired man with a square jaw, pounded the table with his fist, "Ben Yosef, for heaven's sake, we were in the middle of a discussion. Get back here! I haven't finished taking you apart yet. Your notions about the nature of sin—"

"Are correct," Ben Yosef said, turning halfway around to smile challengingly. "In everyone, there's something of his fellow man. Therefore, whoever sins injures not only himself but also that part of himself which belongs to another."

"Yes, of course . . ." Aktariel murmured in soft agony.

Ben Yosef smiled curiously, nodding. "You know it, too?"

"Ridiculous!" his friend at the table shouted. "Come back here and explain. Let these Romans go!"

Ben Yosef lifted his chin to examine Aktariel again, vague recognition in his eyes, as though he could almost place where they'd met, but not quite. "Won't you come and sit down with us? Let me buy you a pitcher of wine? I'd like to talk to you. Perhaps if we talk I'll remember where we've—"

"No, no, we can't," Aktariel said, voice shaking. With stern deliberateness he pulled Rachel from behind the table. "Thank you, anyway."

Ben Yosef bowed slightly. "Perhaps another time."

"Yes, perhaps."

Almost running, Aktariel dragged Rachel down the winding dirt path past Tzipora's door. His dread hung like a pall around them. When they finally turned the corner leading out into the orchards, Rachel tugged against his strong grip to make him stop.

Panting, she said, "Wait. Let me catch my breath."

"Forgive me," he said shortly. He began pacing the red soil and she noticed how badly he shook.

"Are you all right?"

"I just need a moment."

Rachel turned partway around, gazing back over her shoulder toward the tavern and the lake. "Who was that? He had the strangest eyes I've ever seen."

"Yes, even in this universe. I was surprised by that. His name is Yeshwah ben Yosef. I didn't expect to see him here. I'm sorry. I . . ." He inhaled a deep breath and struggled to calm himself. "He's a fisherman, Rachel. That's all. Nothing more."

"You say that like he could have been. Why wasn't he? Because you were never here?"

He gave her a moist-eyed look, then came forward and gently linked his arm through hers, leading her out into the fragrant orchard. Shadows mottled his face and blond curls. The scents of lake and thyme surrounded them as they walked.

"He was never tempted," Aktariel answered softly. "He was never beaten by the hammers of unbearable fate, or burned by hatred to forge him into something stronger."

"There was such loneliness in his eyes. I almost—"

"He chose his own path. He's had a quiet uneventful life, living most of his thirty-seven years in his parents' home. The only real excitement he's had was when the woman he loved was stoned to death while he watched."

Rachel looked at him severely. "How terrible. Didn't he try to stop it?"

"No. In this universe, he didn't have the strength to stand up against tradition—even though he knew that tradition was wrong."

"What tradition? Tell me more, I want to understand—"

"I . . . I'd rather not discuss it, Rachel. Grant me that privacy, will you? Back there, I caught myself on the verge of taking up Matthya's challenge about sin and that could have been disastrous. I'd rather forget the entire affair, if you don't mind." He lifted her hand and tenderly kissed her fingers.

Strong feelings welled inside her, revulsion, the urge to pull away from him, a tingle of excitement and longing to be closer. "You can forget it. I won't. Tell me why I understood his language?"

"Actually, I've told you once before. Aramaic is very similar to Gamant. If we'd stayed longer, though, you'd have noticed substantial differences. Gamant has changed quite a lot."

Facts began falling into place, bits coming from here and there. "Aramaic is a forerunner to Gamant?" Her heart did a triple-step. "Does that mean that these people are distant relatives?"

"Very distant. But let me get you back to the *Hoyer*. If you'll share your company with me again, I'll find a new tavern. One less likely to stir old and deep emotions in me. I apologize if I startled you back there."

They climbed up through the orchard and back into the rolling brush-covered hills overlooking the village. His arm felt warm against hers, comforting. When they reached the crest of a hill, she stopped and turned back to look over the lake and fields verdant with golden grain waving beneath the caress of the wind.

"I almost hate to leave here," she whispered. "It's so peaceful, so beautiful."

"Yes, I've missed it terribly. More than I'd realized."

Beneath his robe, she saw the *Mea* flaring blue.

"Rachel," he said quietly. In the flood of sunlight, his hair shimmered like rain-soaked topaz. A gust of wind swept by them, whirling red dust up to tumble through a cloudless sky. "I know you can't trust me yet, but give me more time to show you I'm worthy of that."

"I'll never trust you, Aktariel. You frighten me too deeply."

"I understand—though it's difficult for me. Let's get back, Rachel. We'll have more time to talk later."

In a strange movement, he slowly took her hand and placed it over the *Mea* beneath his robe. A vibration shivered through her. She tried to pull back.

"Don't be afraid. You must learn to wield the vortex. Not even Zadok understood it fully. But you *must*."

She glanced fearfully at his hand that held hers over the *Mea*. "Why?"

"Because you'll find after you've used it enough, that it's part of you, that you can feel its fabric in your soul. And when you reach that stage, I can show you how to walk from here . . ." He opened a hand to the undulating hills and azure sky. ". . . to the Treasury of Light."

"What is that?"

"Your rightful home. Lift your other hand, Rachel."

Hesitantly, she did, raising it as she'd seen him do, palm to the warm fragrant winds.

"Yes. Good. Now, find that one place inside that listens. You've done this before in your sleep, see if you can while awake."

She closed her eyes and followed a winding, treacherous path, taking wrong turns occasionally. When she did, he gently prompted her in different directions. At last, after what seemed an hour, she found the place and let her mind blend with her soul. A euphoric feeling of harmony enveloped her.

"Very good," he murmured. "In time it will come easier. Now grab hold of that essence and think about the *Hoyer,* picture that security tunnel as clearly as you can."

She nodded slowly, the image forming with remarkable clarity. Curious. Did he give her the ability to imagine with such exactitude, or did—"

"No, Rachel. That's your own ability. Open your eyes."

She did. Before her the dark maw spun, gouging an ominous ebony hole in the magnificent countryside. Aktariel gazed down at her, a warm pride on his face.

"You're a natural at this," he said. He reached out and took her hand again. "Three final things. Don't forget what I said about Tikkun. Talk to Tahn. You'll find he's a just man—decent to a fault. And tell Jeremiel the information on Lichtner came from a file listed under the heading of Neurophysiological Experiments. File number nineteen-one-one-eight. He'll only be able to get fragments, but he'll need them."

Rachel steeled herself. Was this part of some plot he was weaving? How many men had believed him in the past only to discover he'd lied to them? How many women had felt the same inexplicable attraction she did? She needed to go back to her cabin and spend long hours contemplating the implications of today.

"Are you ready, Rachel?" he asked.

"Yes. I'm ready."

The void felt oddly cold as she stepped into it, as glacial as a tomb.

CHAPTER 32

The 12th of Tishri, 5414.

Pavel Jacoby reached for his spoon and tasted the Yaguth ox soup. Black hair fell over his brown eyes. He nodded approval at the soup; it tasted rich and earthy, the basil giving it a flowery flavor.

He dipped his spoon again and gazed around the long table. Five members of his family talked and laughed, gesturing with their arms when they wanted to make a point. Grandpa Jasper kept shouting, "I shouldn't even be here! Look at the risk I'm taking to be with family."

They sat in a large room with a high ceiling. The oil lamps on the mantle cast a soft golden light over the wall-to-wall bookcases. The white table linen, crystal wine goblets, and ornate silverware shimmered. People dressed in their best suits this Shabbat erev, even Grandpa. His threadbare white shirt had been starched so stiffly he clawed at the collar constantly, making little choking sounds to emphasize his discomfort. But Aunt Sekan had demanded everybody come dressed as though it were a high holiday . . . for it might be their last meal together. The marines continually tightened the ropes around their necks.

"Pavel?" his father said, gesturing sternly with his spoon. His sparse gray hair glimmered like tarnished silver in the candlelight. "What do you think about these marines telling us we can't go into our own cafes anymore, eh? We can't go to cafes or the spaceport or even be on the streets after eight o'clock. You think they believe such measures will keep us under their thumbs?"

He frowned. He'd prayed they wouldn't discuss the frightening new orders this night. The implications of the restrictions made him deathly ill. "I think they're convinced it scares us. It's a potent step."

His father's ebony eyes narrowed. "Step?"

"Yes, I think—"

"The boy's trying to tell you we've got much worse coming," Grandpa bellowed so loudly the entire table went silent, staring. "I heard downtown this morning that they're planning on walling the whole city in."

Pavel lowered his gaze to his half-full soup bowl. He'd heard it, too, but had hoped no one else had. Now all the fears they'd been suppressing behind kind smiles would surface. He glanced at Aunt Sekan. A tiny overweight woman with curly red hair and huge blue eyes, just now she looked like a terrified owl.

"Grandpa," Pavel said softly and instantly regretted the attempt to use a soothing tone.

"*What?* Speak up, boy!"

He scowled reprovingly but leaned across the table, raising his voice to a shout, "I think those are just rumors the Magistrates started to scare us into obeying their curfew. I wouldn't worry about it."

"You wouldn't, would you? Well, you've never been very bright. Remember when you failed that basic astronomy class in the third grade? Couldn't identify your own planet on a solar system map. I knew then your beam was a little dim."

Pavel sighed and leaned back in his chair. Every time Grandpa wanted to gain leverage, he reminded him of that test score. He'd never live it down.

Jasper continued, "Chaim Losacko told me two days ago that he'd tapped an illegal transmission talking about Horeb getting scorched. *Eh, what do you think of that?* First Kayan, then Horeb. You think these stupid marines aren't serious, you've got another think coming."

Sekan nervously fiddled with her spoon. It clinked repeatedly against her wine glass. She stared at each man in turn, mouth tightening to a thin white line.

"If they put up a light shield around the city," Toca said through a strained exhalation, "then we'll form our own government inside and go back to living like we did before they declared martial law. That might even be a good thing. We wouldn't have to see their hateful faces every day."

Grandpa briskly rubbed his face as though trying to wake from a bad dream. "I can't be hearing right. You think they'll just leave us alone once they wall us in? I'd rather be imprisoned in the pit of darkness with Aktariel himself, than be at the complete mercy of the Magistrates!"

Pavel glanced at his father, who studied his bowl uncomfortably. No one could correct Grandpa once he got on his high horse. Worse, everybody knew he was right, but no one wanted to spoil a joyous family meal by talking about it. Who could eat when they feared their world might die tomorrow?

"Daddy?"

Pavel turned to pat Yael's dark curly hair. Her mother had died giving her life, and the difficult birth had left its scars on Yael. Her snubbed nose, prominent cheekbones and almond-shaped eyes announced her retardation. But she wasn't bad, he told himself. She at least had the mental development of a six-year-old, though she was twice that age. Some brain damaged babies he'd seen were much worse off. And he loved her.

He bent down, whispering in her ear, "How's your soup?"

She beamed up at him. "Good, Daddy. It tastes like the grass."

"It does a little, doesn't it?" He had to watch her constantly when he let her out in the yard or she would spend the entire day grazing and the entire night throwing up. He'd told her over and over that it wasn't good for her, but to no avail. She liked the taste.

"Can I have some bread?" Yael asked.

"Yes, sweetheart. Aunt Sekan, please pass the bread."

"Oh, dear me, I'm sorry," Sekan apologized, reaching for the basket and handing it around the table. "Jasper got me so flustered, I forgot Yael likes to dip it in her soup."

"What'd you say?" Grandpa inquired gruffly, just catching his name.

"I said you got me flustered!"

"Well, you ought to be flustered. We'll be next on the Magistrates' hit list. Losacko also told me he'd heard clandestine trans that Baruch had been captured on Horeb and that's why the Magistrates scorched it, for hiding him."

Toca looked up, spoon held in mid-path to his mouth. "Captured? I don't believe it. Jeremiel wouldn't let himself get captured."

"Who said he 'let' himself? Losacko told me some Gamant on Horeb betrayed him. Sold him to the Magistrates for big money."

"Dear God, let's hope Losacko is wrong."

"He's not. We're next on the scorch list. I tell you—"

"Grandpa may be right," Karyn said softly and everyone turned to her. At twenty-two, her pale skin glowed as satiny as a newborn's. Her blonde hair hung in loose curls over her forehead and ears. "We've been trying to reach Baruch for days and haven't been able to get through. The Magistrates seem to have thrown up some

293

communications block that we can't penetrate."

"See!" Jasper exploded. "I told you. We're going to get scorched!"

"Grandpa!" Pavel shouted as gently as he could. "We don't know that. Major Lichtner said Slothen is going to send us an ambassador to talk things out. They just want peace."

"Peace? Don't be a pimple brain. They want us all dead! The best way to kill us is to make us knuckle under first, then they'll have us right where they want us. First they force us to register, then they put up a light shield. We'll be sitting ducks!"

Pavel gruffly crushed the napkin in his lap. His soup had gone stone cold. Nevertheless, he picked up his spoon and ate heartily, avoiding Grandpa's stern gaze. "This is excellent soup, Aunt Sekan."

She smiled, reaching around the table to squeeze his daughter's plump arm. "I knew it was Yael's favorite."

"I love you, Auntie," Yael said and giggled, putting a hand over her mouth like Pavel had told her to. He winked at her.

"I love you, too, baby." Sekan checked everyone's soup bowl, then pushed back her chair. "Well, I think I'll bring out the main course if everybody's ready."

"Sure," Toca said happily. "It's the perfect time."

Pavel lifted his bowl and finished his soup, eyeing his cousin over the rim. Karyn sat with her eyes downcast, glancing uneasily at him. Pavel sipped his Alizarin wine and looked at her in a kindly way. More his sister than his cousin, she'd been a mother for Yael for all the years since his beloved Absa had died.

"Karyn," he said warmly, "how's school going? Papa said you've been taking mostly physics and chemistry courses."

She gave him a sly smile, as if acknowledging his attempts to find a more pleasant topic of conversation. "Mostly, yes." She lowered her voice to a conspiratorial whisper. "Plus the Underground has been teaching us Magisterial technology. It's very interesting."

The government hadn't installed listening devices yet. At least, he didn't think so. They checked every day. Karyn's actions were just instinctive. Years ago, the Magistrates had burned out the old University and decreed that anyone found attending secret Underground classes would be shot on sight.

"So, if Baruch's alive, you can be the captain for the next battle cruiser he steals, is that right?" he joked.

A small round of laughter passed through the group. Only Grandpa scowled, but everyone knew why. He didn't approve of women learning science. Only in the past fifty years had it been allowed on Tikkun, and then reluctantly. The planet still clung to the old ways in every other respect. But the University meant life for the Gamant people. Nearly everyone realized that now. Once a year, Jeremiel sent scouts to Tikkun, looking for the best the University had to offer to fill his crews. And Karyn had studied very hard in the hope she'd be chosen.

She pushed blonde locks out of her eyes, glancing at Grandpa. "They upgraded my rating last week. I'm now a level one weapons specialist."

"Ah," Pavel said, smiling proudly. "That's even better. When the time comes, you can protect cowards like me."

"You? A coward? Don't be modest," she teased. "I remember when I was seven and you beat up that bully at school who tried to kiss me. You—"

"Weapons," Grandpa muttered under his breath, but everybody heard—just as he'd intended. Once he discovered he had their attention, he blustered, "Women don't have the temperament for things like that. What would you do, eh?" he asked as Aunt Sekan whirled out of the kitchen with a plate heaped high with broiled strips of lamb. "Could you look a Magisterial marine straight in the eyes and shoot his guts out?"

Sekan stopped, a horrified look on her face as she set the trembling platter on the table. "*What* are we discussing?"

Karyn heaved a tense sigh. "War, Mother. If I had to, Grandpa. I don't want to kill anyone, but if they come to hurt me or my family, I will."

"Bah!" Grandpa spat. "You'll fall apart, start crying or something, and they'll kill you before you can see straight again."

Toca, who'd sat quietly through the exchange, intervened. "I've talked to her teacher, Jasper. He says she's the best in her class." He smiled at Karyn. "Freia said she could shoot the eye out of a dove on the wing at a thousand yards."

"With these new weapons, who couldn't?"

"*I* couldn't," Toca said mildly.

"And I doubt you could, you old blowhard!" Aunt Sekan challenged. Pounding a fork on the table, she instructed, "*Let's eat.* I don't want to talk about any more foolishness tonight!"

Grandpa gave her the evil eye, but smiled when he got a whiff of the steaming lamb. "Okay. You'd probably make me go hungry if I tried, so I surrender." He held out his hands for the platter. Sekan handed it across the table.

Pavel waited his turn, hugging Yael, then took the plate of meat his father handed him and forked out three pieces for himself and one for Yael. She prodded it suspiciously with her knife before picking it up in her fingers and munching it like a long strand of spaghetti. A small transgression, he didn't try to stop her. No one cared and it gave Yael great pleasure. He passed the plate back to Aunt Sekan and reached for the salad bowl, shoveling his plate full. The vinaigrette dressing smelled spicy and sour compared to the sweetness of the lamb.

"You remember Moche Oyar, Pavel?" Toca asked.

"Loren's son. Yes, a gangly boy. Isn't he thirteen or fourteen now? He used to play with Yael when she was little."

"Fourteen. I've been teaching him the Merkabah." Toca cut a piece of lamb and chewed thoughtfully. "He's a very good student."

"Is he? He'd make you a better son than me, then. I could never keep all the secret names of God straight, let alone memorize all the guardian angels I was supposed to recite them to. The seven heavens were too complicated for my mind."

"You were more interested in climbing trees."

He laughed. "Guilty as charged. I liked to study the leaves. That's where my first motivation to study botany came—"

"Let's get back to business," Jasper said gruffly, now that his plate was heaped with food. "If Baruch is in the government's hands—we haven't got a leg to stand on to piss!"

Sekan gasped, but Toca just heaved a disgruntled sigh. "Jasper, this is Shabbat. Please."

Grandpa waved his willowy arms wildly. "You think God never heard the word *piss?*"

"Grandpa?" Yael whispered, sitting up straighter in her chair. Her dark eyes gleamed. "What does that mean, 'piss?' I like that word."

Jasper's stern face softened and an indulgent smile creased his withered lips. He reached across the narrow table to pinch her cheek. "Never mind, pretty girl. It's a grown-up word."

"Will you tell me when I get older?"

"Sure."

"Papa," Pavel said. "Grandpa's right about Baruch. If he's—"

A loud siren blared outside. They all whirled, hearts in their throats. Lights flashed through the candlelit house.

"What's happening now?" Jasper demanded.

"Gamants," a voice called in intergalactic lingua. "Prepare to be searched. All artifacts made of precious metals are to be confiscated. Anyone who attempts to hide such belongings will be immediately taken to the prison colony on Tertullian."

Pavel got up quickly and went to the window, pulling back the drapes a slit. A huge ovoid ship hovered over the street, blotting out the stars. Below it, a hundred armed soldiers stood, apparently awaiting instructions.

"They've brought muscle to force us," he said.

He heard Aunt Sekan grabbing silverware, it clanged in the foreboding silence. "They're not getting my great-great-grandmother's silver," she said in a shaky voice. "It came from Old Earth. I won't let them take it!"

Karyn's hushed voice cut the night. "They're afraid we're manufacturing weapons in the city. Our instructors told us last week this might happen."

Pavel let the curtain drop closed and turned to stare hollowly at his family. "Papa, what should we do?"

Boots pounded the pavement outside, the click-clop thundering through the dining room. Toca drummed trembling fingers on the table. "Cooperate. It's all we can do."

"No!" Sekan cried, hugging the silver to her ample bosom. "I won't! They can't have—"

"Sekan!" Toca reprimanded in the hardest voice Pavel had ever heard him use. Sweat beaded on his father's broad nose. Did he know more than he'd been saying? Had he been expecting this? Had Lichtner told him? "They'll be here any second. You don't want to take the

chance they'll kill one of us, do you? Over a bunch of forks and knives?"

Before she could respond, a fist knocked insistently at the door. "Jacoby? Open up!"

Toca got up from his seat and went to the door, unlocking it with fumbling fingers. A cold gush of wind swept inside, fluttering the drapes and white linen tablecloth.

"Yes, officer. Please, come in. We'll give you no trouble."

The tall brown-haired sergeant in a purple uniform pushed past him, throwing Toca off-balance so that he stumbled into Pavel's arms.

"No trouble?" the sergeant said disbelievingly. "You Gamants are all liars. You're born troublemakers."

He motioned to his men and ten soldiers thrust through the door. One corporal grabbed the tablecloth and jerked it hard, pulling it off and onto the floor. Yael screamed, hands pleading to be taken. Pavel started forward, but in a flash, Karyn was on her feet and had Yael in her arms. They backed up against the far wall. Grandpa sat sternly still, eyeing the soldiers as though they were pond slime. Pavel could see the splashes of wine and gravy on the old man's white shirt.

Liquid seeped through the linen as the corporal started to draw up the corners, securing all the silver that Sekan hadn't yet collected.

Pavel looked pitifully at his aunt. She stood shuddering, tears running down her plump cheeks. Several precious forks and spoons were still clutched to her breast. The corporal spied them. "Give me those!"

She took a step backward, mouth quivering. "Let me keep them. They belonged to my grand—"

"I said give them to me!"

"Sekan," Toca pleaded. "Do as he says."

When she hesitated, the private pulled his pistol from his holster and aimed at her pudgy stomach. "You Gamants think you can disrupt every quadrant of space and the government will do nothing. People in my home sector are starving because of you and your filthy Underground! Well, you've just begun to feel the wrath of the Magistrates. Hand them over!"

Sobbing, Sekan walked forward and gently added the

silver to the dirty pile in the tablecloth. Her wrenching cries filled the room, an underlying current of sound that made Pavel's throat go dust dry. He'd seen that silver set the table for every holiday he could remember.

The marines turned over tables, pulled out drawers, shoved cabinets facedown to see if any metal objects were hidden behind them. It took only a little more than fifteen minutes, yet Pavel felt each ticking of the clock as hours.

Finally, the sergeant lifted his chin, glaring at Toca. "Be here, *all of you,* tomorrow morning at six."

"Of course, officer. Why? What's—"

"We're emptying out this nest of rebellion. Everyone will be transported out of the city, street by street."

Toca cocked his head incredulously. "There are over two hundred thousand people in Derow. Where will you take us? What will we do?"

A cruel smile lit the sergeant's face. "Something productive for a change. You'll have the honor of serving the Magistrates."

"But I—I don't understand. We have jobs here. What—"

"*Don't ask questions, old man!* Just pack your bags and be ready to go."

The sergeant spun on his heel and left; his men followed in single file. When Toca closed the door again and turned to meet each of their gazes, tears shimmered in his eyes.

"Come on," he said softly. "We have a lot to do. Pavel, go downstairs and fetch the eggs. We'll boil five dozen and take them with us. Sekan? Sekan, darling, don't cry. We haven't time now for grief. Can you bake some bread? We'll need as much as you can cook over the night."

"Yes, I—I'll get started." Sobbing, she squared her shoulders and trotted from the dining room into the kitchen.

When Pavel looked over, he found Grandpa futilely wiping at his good shirt with a napkin he'd dipped in water. The wine stains grew, spreading across his bony chest like pale blood. After a moment, Jasper glanced up and met his gaze. His eyes glimmered with hate, but his voice was so quiet he could have been giving a blessing.

"They're going to kill us. You know that, don't you, Pavel? You're smart enough to see that."

The question froze his tongue. He stared a moment, transfixed, then ran for the basement, slowing only long enough to stroke Yael's cheek as he passed.

CHAPTER 33

Rachel walked up and down the dimly lit level four corridors, talking briefly with each security officer she passed. They'd pared the staff on the level down to five, three stood strategically at the intersecting corridors around Tahn and Halloway's cabins. Rachel monitored Tahn's door, a job that left her on her own much of the time, which she appreciated. She needed to think.

The silence seemed to thrum—like her nerves. Dread swelled so violently in her chest, she thought she'd explode. Even though Aktariel had specifically told her to talk to Tahn, she couldn't bring herself to do it. She'd tried to see Jeremiel instead, to ask him about Lichtner, but he'd been in urgent consultations with Harper over the refugees. An epidemic had broken out on level fourteen and the children and elderly afflicted with the virus were dying with stunning swiftness.

Desperate to understand *anything* Aktariel had told her, she pulled the sheet of equations from her pocket and glanced at them as she walked. Inverted triangles, strange foreign letters and parallel lines met her gaze. When she reached Tahn's cabin, she slumped against the wall and vented a brusque exhalation.

"I don't know what any of this means. None of it!"

She crumpled the sheet in her hand. Her entire body burned with the need to understand. She'd go mad if she didn't talk to someone soon.

Reluctantly, she looked at Tahn's door.

"No. No, not yet."

* * *

Tahn paced his cabin like a caged lion, nervous, anxious to be at somebody's throat. Baruch hadn't been lying. The *Hoyer*'s records left open the question of fault. He felt combative and ill. He'd showered twice so far today, just to ease some of his tension. His fresh uniform hung in crisp lines, accentuating his broad shoulders and trim waist. His brown hair still clung damply to his temples and forehead.

"Damn it."

Carey had been in three times in as many hours, but every time they'd spoken she seemed more antagonistic, berating his ideas for no apparent reason.

"Stop it," he chastised himself. "She's just on edge. She's carrying the double burden of maintaining crew morale and dealing with Baruch."

He felt trapped—a pawn in a deadly game. He ran a hand through his hair and stared imploringly at the floor.

"Captain Tahn?" a deep feminine voice called through his door com.

He put his hands on his hips, frowning. "Yes?"

"I'm on Commander Baruch's security staff. May I see you for a moment?"

Probably another frisk session. What did they think he did, manufacture weapons out of the goddamned air? "Enter."

The door slipped open and a tall woman stood silhouetted against the nighttime corridor. Dressed in a brown formfitting jumpsuit, long black hair hung in lustrous waves to her waist. He couldn't recall her name, but he remembered their original "meeting" when Baruch had bodily hauled him to the bridge.

"I'm sorry to disturb you," she said.

"I wasn't exactly busy. Come in."

She entered and the door closed behind her. She fumbled nervously with a crystal sheet, crumpling it in one fist then the other. Just watching her obvious discomfort made him uneasy.

"I suspected you wanted in for a reason," Tahn challenged. "Was I wrong?"

"No. I'm sorry, I'm just very nervous about disturbing you."

"What was your name?"

"Rachel Eloel. I'm in charge of security for your cabin."

"Ah, you're my jailer. I wondered what your specific job was. Well, it's good to finally meet you. What may I do for you?"

She stepped forward boldly, feverishly asking, "Who's Major Lichtner?"

Taken completely aback, he shook his head in confusion, but a hot fire blazed in his soul, igniting old hatreds. "Why do you want to know?"

"He's important."

"Well, if he's that important, you'd better ask Baruch."

She took another step forward to stand no more than two feet from him. She fixed him with a look so hard his shoulder muscles contracted. Her eyes blazed. "Tell me."

He kept silent. Some undercurrent of emotion roiled in the depths of her eyes. He couldn't quite figure out the source. Was she in love with Baruch? Is that why she cared about Lichtner? He scrutinized her posture, her face. No, that didn't seem to be the root. It was something else. What?

She clenched her hands into tight fists. "Why won't you tell me? Is it something so terrible that even you—"

"No." He shook his head. "No, it's just that the thought of Lichtner gives me a stomach ache, that's all. He was instrumental in a battle in the Akiba system a few months ago. A battle Baruch won—except in the ways that count."

"What does that mean?"

Grimly amused with himself, he responded, "I haven't the slightest idea. In the game of war, winning should be everything, shouldn't it?"

"I don't think so."

"Miss Eloel, why do you care about Lichtner?"

"He's the current military governor of Tikkun."

He sucked in a breath as though she'd splashed icy water in his face. If true, why would she tell him such a critical bit of intelligence? "How do you know?"

"I just do." She crumpled the crystal sheet again.

He looked at it, wondering if she had some sensitive data written there and if he ought to tackle her to get it. "If you're worried about Lichtner, don't be. He's an idiot."

"Is he?"

"Yes."

302

"But he's dangerous, isn't he?"

"If some imbecile has given him power, he'll undoubtedly abuse it, but he's not creative if that's what you mean."

She wandered sternly around his cabin, hair shining like strands of the darkest, rarest silks in the galaxy. Softly, as if speaking to herself, she repeated, "He's not creative. . . ."

"Why does it matter?"

She brusquely waved a hand to silence him while she thought and he lifted both brows. The only other woman he knew who made him feel like a subordinate was Halloway.

"Excuse me? Is there something else I can do for you, Miss Eloel?"

"Yes, Captain, would you . . . would you help me with a physics problem?"

He almost laughed, but her serious expression kept him from doing it. "It's not a calculation you're planning on using to blow up me or the Magistrates, is it?"

"No."

"Is that what you have in your hand?"

She gazed down at the crumpled sheet and nodded apologetically. "Yes. I hope you can still read it."

"Let me see." He extended a hand.

Quickly, she strode forward, placing it in his palm. He unfolded it and smoothed away the wrinkles. As he glanced at the equations, his brows lowered. "Miss Eloel—"

"Please, call me Rachel."

"Why don't you sit down, Rachel. This might take a while. These are rather complicated."

Without taking her eyes from his, she reached back and dragged a chair around next to him, waiting breathlessly.

He smiled, intrigued. Did she know that despite the pistol on her hip, he could easily have her pinned to the floor to use as a hostage? Why would she give him such a chance? But if he attacked her, Baruch would gas level seven and the next thing Cole knew he'd have a chain around his throat. Rachel undoubtedly was aware of that. Disgruntled, he turned his attention to the equations. For a full two minutes, he went over them in detail, growing more and more fascinated. Finally, he leaned back in his chair and looked at her admiringly.

"You don't need any help from me. This looks perfect. My only questions are regarding your statistics for mass and charge. Are you sure they're correct?"

She looked confused, wetting her lips nervously. "I think so. Why?"

He braced his elbows on the table. She had a curious effect on him. A handsome woman, those stunning eyes held him riveted. She looked at him as though he knew more than God Himself—and damned well better give her the answers she needed or she'd kill him, just because. He bent over the crystal sheet, motioning to her. "Come here, let me show you what I mean."

She obliged, leaning so close her long hair draped over his arm and he could smell the fragrance of some strange flower or place. A whisper of rich soil and sunshine clung to the strands.

"You see," he said, pointing to the questionable figures, "you're correct here and here regarding the event horizons. Obviously charged black holes have two, one reflecting the mass, the other the charge. But here's where I'm a little confused. If you keep adding to the charge, as this series of five equations shows, the inner event horizon will grow while the outer shrinks. You see what I mean?"

"Not exactly."

"Well, the maximum possible charge occurs when the inner and outer event horizons merge. Correct?"

She nodded, but looked gravely uncertain. "Go ahead."

Her forehead lined in concentration, but he had the feeling she hadn't the vaguest idea what he was talking about. "What I'm trying to say is that if you execute this particular sequence, I'm afraid you'll wind up with a naked singularity."

Her face paled to a pasty clay color. "What is that?"

He tilted his head curiously. "Did you work out these equations, Rachel?"

"Answer my question."

He sat back in his chair. "Let's begin with basics. A singularity, a black hole, is a place where gravity is so powerful a 'hole' has been torn in space-time. Around the chasm is a horizon in the geometry of space. We call it an event horizon. When the horizon, or horizons, in the case of charged or rotating black holes, disappears, you have a naked singularity." He put his hands on the table, palms open. "You didn't work out these equations, did you?"

She gazed at him through glittering black eyes. "A friend did. He said I'd need them someday."

Her voice trailed off as she stared over his shoulder. That prophetic look made Tahn's breathing go shallow.

"Why did your friend say you'd need these?"

"Because when I reach the middle of the prison, the foundations of Chaos, I have to throw one of the sapphires. . . ."

She turned, looking at him with such aching confusion, he had the insane urge to reach out and comfort her. Instead, he shoved his chair back and got to his feet. She eyed him warily.

"It's all right. I'm in no position to hurt you. I'm a prisoner here, you see." He smiled wryly, but it faded when her face darkened.

"We're all prisoners here, Captain. I just want to go home, but I haven't got a home to go to."

They held each other's gaze, sharing an understanding deeper than words. Guilt tortured him. She nervously played with the crystal sheet for a few seconds, shoving it around the table, and he felt her tension building.

"Is there something else you want to ask me, Rachel?"

Her gaze lifted, impaling him with its buried desperation. "Captain, you've been everywhere, places I've only dreamed of. Do you think happiness or suffering is more prevalent in the universe? Does it depend on where you are? In some parts of the galaxy is happiness on the increase?"

Almost mesmerized by her eyes, he responded softly. "I don't think so. Suffering seems to be on the high side everywhere I've been in the past decade."

"Oh. . . ."

"Why did you ask?"

She lurched unsteadily to her feet, tears glistening like diamonds on her lashes. "Thank you for helping me, Captain."

"Any time. Unfortunately, I'm nearly always available." He tried to smile, but his face fell into serious lines. "Come again."

She retrieved her crystal sheet from the table before backing away toward the door. "I will. Thank you."

She palmed the exit patch and left. A trail of fluttering ebony waves was the last glimpse he had of her.

* * *

Yosef sat on the floor in Mikael's room, playing checkers with his grandnephew. Two lamps glowed, one over the table where Ari sat reading computer printouts and another focused on the game board. In the soft light, the red and black playing pieces gleamed brightly.

Yosef glanced at Mikael. He had his tongue sticking outside of his mouth as he concentrated on where to move next. A deep and abiding love filled Yosef. What a handsome boy he was. He resembled Zadok so much when his brother had been that age that it made Yosef's heart ache with longing. But . . . Mikael seemed much older than seven. Twelve, maybe. Certainly, the death of his family and the destruction of his planet had played a role in such early mental development. Zadok had lost his mother when a child, too, though his planet hadn't been devastated like Mikael's, but Zadok had never seemed so old.

Mikael smiled suddenly and jumped two of Yosef's pieces. "Ha! I got you, Uncle Yosef."

"Oh, that was a good move, Mikael."

"Sybil taught me that. She's good at checkers."

Ari glanced up from his book. Dressed in a tan robe, he had one long leg stretched out over another chair. His gray mop of hair hung about his ears like dead weeds. "She's good at lots of things. She nearly choked me to death in a wrestling match yesterday.

"She beats me up all the time, too. It's because she squirms so good when you get her arms pinned."

"And she kicks like a pagan mule."

Mikael laughed brightly, eyes shining. "Yeah, I got her down on her back once and she tried to kick my stomach out."

Ari chuckled, then his gray brows drew together malevolently and he pounded a fist against the printout laying scattered over the table. "Maybe that's the answer. We ought to hire Sybil to go find this Dannon character, eh? He could use having his stomach kicked out."

Yosef leaned back, bracing himself on his elbows. "What's that printout telling you? Anything important? Could he still be alive?"

"I don't know yet. Those search teams looked everywhere. They even checked and rechecked areas to make sure he hadn't crept like silent slime back into already secured areas."

"Well. . . ." Yosef sighed and looked back at the checkerboard. Mikael had one bare toe resting on the corner. "If he were alive, they'd have surely found him."

"Bah!" Ari groused, withered face shriveling with disdain. "You and me might have found him, but those amateur searchers Jeremiel had out? They couldn't find their own arses with both hands."

Yosef sat bolt upright as Ari's face suddenly lit with challenge. "*Get* that thought out of your demented mind. No! You're always getting me into trouble. This time I refuse—"

"Don't be such a coward," Ari said in a silken tone, smiling broadly. He adjusted the holster on his hip so that his pistol gleamed silver in the light. "I'll protect you."

"You?" Yosef cried incredulously. "When are you going to outgrow these delusions of godhood?"

"What's the matter with you? Jeremiel needs us and all you can think about is my delusions? When did you get so selfish?"

Yosef blinked. He cast around for something equally spurious to say, but couldn't think of anything. "I'm not going."

Ari slouched back in his chair. "You know, I bet Jeremiel would even give us extra pistols to carry while we hunt. What do you think, Mikael? Doesn't that sound like a good idea?"

Yosef started to explode with something nasty, but he noticed how seriously Mikael had taken the question. The boy contemplatively blinked at Ari, as though he felt the query like the weight of all Gamant civilization on his tiny stomach. His face pinched.

"I guess so. Sybil told me about how her mom had been helping the search teams on level four, before Mister Baruch canceled them. If Dannon is still alive, we need to find him before he hurts our people again." Anxiously, Mikael got to his knees, eyes glowing darkly. "And, and, maybe when you go to see Mister Baruch, you could take me. I need to tell him about what Grandfather . . ."

He swallowed suddenly, glancing from Yosef to Ari, a

307

look of utter terror on his young face. Yosef reached over to pat Mikael's tiny hand in reassurance.

"It's all right, Mikael. Zadok was my brother. I'm sure he wouldn't mind you telling Ari and me something he told you in confidence."

In a choking voice, Mikael said, "He said to tell you hello, Uncle Yosef. That he loves you."

Yosef sat back. "Who?"

"Grandfather. He's been talking to me a lot lately."

Yosef could hear Ari drop a hand against the scattered printout; it swished softly. He turned to meet his friend's anxious gaze. A small glint of horror sparked in Ari's gray eyes. Doctor Severns had warned them Mikael still experienced constant nightmares and might have minor delusions from the shock he'd experienced on Kayan, but they hadn't seen any until today.

"Mikael," Yosef said lovingly, "your grandfather's dead."

"Oh, yes, sir, I know. But he talks to me anyway. Epagael lets him. The archangel Michael was with him last time. He talked to me for a while, too."

"I see," Yosef whispered forlornly. The boy must have more psychological scars than seemed apparent. The thought pricked his bones like a frigid gale.

"Grandfather said you'd help me lead the revolt if I asked, Uncle Yosef."

"Revolt?" Smiling awkwardly, he assured, "Yes, of course, I will."

"Thanks. Sybil and I might need help when the war starts. Though, I don't know, Metatron said he'd help us, too. And he's pretty powerful. He can walk through walls and things."

"Who's Metatron?"

From behind him Ari chastised, "You witless bozon. Metatron is the Prince of the Divine Presence. He took Ezra to heaven to talk to God millennia ago."

Mikael nodded heartily, smiling. "Yeah. That's him. He's golden and beautiful."

Yosef's bushy gray brows drew together. He clumsily creased the hem of his green robe and gazed at his nephew from the corner of his eye. Mikael calmly studied the checkerboard. "An angel comes to you, too?"

"Only sometimes. When I'm feeling sad or confused, I call him and he comes to talk to me."

Yosef's heart throbbed. "You can call me, too. I'll come talk with you whenever you're lonely."

"Thanks, Uncle Yosef. Sometimes Metatron doesn't answer right away and I get pretty crazy waiting. Maybe next time I'll call you."

"I'd like that."

"Metatron's very busy. He goes to other universes a lot. Do you know what those are? They sort of look like this one, but not really."

"Oh, I know they exist, but I've never thought much about them."

"I think about them all the time now. Metatron says you have to get past ones and future ones to hit just right, or the present isn't like it is. And there's a bunch of different ones that hit you all the time."

"Universes hit us?"

Mikael's young brow creased, as though he struggled to find the right words. "Well . . . I don't know for sure, but it has to do with waves."

"Oh?"

"Yes, he says we have a Seer in our brain who uses waves to make things real or not."

"Uh-huh." Yosef glanced at Ari who blinked expressively. "Well, that's interesting."

As though their willingness to talk about it triggered the boy's excitement, words bubbled out in a flood. "Yeah, it is, because, you know what? Metatron says that people in this universe are all a little crazy and they can't help it."

Ari shifted position, shoving his book across the table. "Metatron's right. You should see Yosef's girlfriend. She's about as crazy—"

"She's *your* girlfriend, not mine. Now, hush, you old fool." Yosef pursed his lips disgustedly. "I'm trying to listen to somebody with an IQ above fifty."

Mikael laughed. "You know why people can't help it?" He looked from Ari to Yosef, eyes wide and glistening.

"No, Mikael, why?"

"Because, *because,* the Seer has been crazy so long he can't see very good anymore. So he picks the wrong futures and pasts and just gets more mixed up. And—"

"Like you trying to pick lint out of your navel with your glasses off," Ari declared.

Mikael clasped his hands together in a prayerful position. "But we can fix it, Uncle Yosef. We just have to throw Indra's Net back into the sky! That way, we can go through the naked singularity again and everything will be all right!" He stopped and beamed, looking at them hopefully, as though he knew they'd understand.

Yosef frowned, pushing up the spectacles on his nose. Naked singularity? He had no idea what that meant, but he knew about Indra's Net. The Old Stories spoke about a web of interconnected *Meas* that sparkled in the sky once-upon-a-time. The zaddiks, holy men, of Old Earth had supposedly been able to fly between them to go any place they wanted in the universe—some *Meas* even reputedly led to Epagael. His own brother, Zadok, had claimed to be able to ascend through the seven heavens to the throne of God. Once, during the last Gamant Revolt, Zadok had been in a catatonic state for so long that his soldiers had prepared his body for burial. They were rudely stunned when Zadok awoke, told them Epagael had revealed the path to salvation, then led them to a crushing victory over Magisterial forces on the plains of Lysomia.

But Indra's Net had vanished mysteriously in the mists of the past. Fanatics claimed that the wicked Aktariel had gathered all the *Meas*—except Zadok's—and given them to the Galactic Magistrates, disentangling the net. The Magistrates, so the story went, had put the *Meas* into a big hole at Palaia Station.

Yosef shrugged and smiled indulgently. "I believe you," he said lamely.

Mikael's face darkened, exuberance dying. He looked at Ari, but seeing no light there either, dropped his gaze morosely to the checkerboard. "Never mind."

"No, no!" Yosef hastened to soothe. "It's just that Ari and I don't understand things like that very well. But maybe if you told us more, we could—"

"That's all right, Uncle Yosef." Mikael aimlessly shoved a checker across the board with the heel of his hand. "Metatron said nobody understood anymore.

". . . Nobody. But he's trying to help."

CHAPTER 34

The 13th of Tishri.

Pavel felt bone-tired, arms shaking as he stuffed bags full of clothes, one for him, one for Yael. Then he filled another with food and all the medicines he could find. Yael caught cold so easily. From the kitchen, metallic clangings rang. Sekan and Toca's voices meshed, planning, soothing each other. Grandpa had gone upstairs to sleep and Karyn had disappeared into the night.

He looked over to where Yael slept, curled into a ball on the long couch beneath the window. She had a finger tucked in the corner of her mouth. A terrible fear rose in him. What would they do to her? To his only child? He got up and went across the room, gathering her in his arms, kissing her sleepy head.

"Daddy?" Yael said in a muzzy voice. "What's wrong?"

"Nothing, baby. Nothing. I just wanted to hold you."

She blinked at the window, seeing the lightening heavens. Already the stars had disappeared. "Is it morning?"

"Yes, Yael. But you can sleep another hour if you want. You don't have to get up. I'm sorry I woke you."

She snaked a hand around and tenderly patted his throat. "I love you, Dad. Maybe just another five minutes."

He smiled, but tears stung his eyes. She told him the same thing every morning when he got home from work and kissed her hello. She'd heard him say it once and it had stuck, ". . . just another five minutes." Gently, he nestled her warm body back against the couch and stood.

An hour later, they sat outside, staring at the rising sun. The clouds turned pink and orange, brightening the heavens like strips of colored lace. He looked out over the reddening autumn leaves to the fields beyond the city.

Ripe barley rippled in golden waves beneath the gentle fingers of morning wind. The dark beauty of Tikkun cedars covered the rolling hills.

Pavel hugged Yael against him and watched people emerge from houses across the street to pile belongings in their yards. Elderly matrons kept coming over, sobbing to his father, and Toca did his best to comfort them.

"Now, Patlica, don't fret so much. They're probably just taking us to one of the Magisterial military installations where they can keep a closer eye on us."

"Do I look like a threat to the Magistrates?" the elderly woman demanded hotly through her tears. "Well? Do I?"

"No, no dear. Of course not, but just be calm. Don't give them any reason to hurt us. I'm sure everything's going to be all right."

He patted her shoulder tenderly and she walked back to her own yard and family. Pavel tried not to notice how sunken his father's cheeks looked, how dull with worry his black eyes had grown.

He stroked and stroked Yael's back, whispering soft words in her ear, keeping her still and quiet. Her heart thumped against his chest like a small frightened bird's. For a brief moment, hurt penetrated his fear.

He buried his face in Yael's hair and closed his eyes.

Minutes later, a hum split the cold morning air. Ships swooped down out of magnificent pastel skies. Thousands of purple-clad soldiers disgorged, rifles aimed at the people who waited so innocently in their yards for God only knew what.

Grandpa Jasper hobbled over to slump down next to Pavel and Yael on the step. He clamped a hand over Pavel's, holding it in silence. Toca turned, his withered face dark and tired. In a low voice, he said, "I hope they don't blame us for Karyn's absence."

Grandpa's face went stony. "I just hope she can shoot as well as Freia said. We need the Underground desperately."

"You!" a marine called, pointing the barrel of his rifle at them. Tall and very broad-shouldered, he had stringy blond hair. "Get up and move to the center of the street."

They gathered their bags and complied, huddling with the others who'd been driven from their yards. All around Pavel, people exchanged warm glances or comforting touches. Many clutched prayer books to their hearts.

"Jacoby?"

Toca turned and called, "Here!"

The dark-haired sergeant who'd visited them last night strode haughtily up, a crystal sheet in his hands. His purple uniform smelled sweet, like flowers, but his eyes gleamed maliciously.

"Is your whole family here?"

"Yes."

Pavel felt himself pale. He glanced sideways at Grandpa. The old man subtly shook his head, warning him to keep quiet. Aunt Sekan started to sniffle uncontrollably.

"Answer when I call your names," the sergeant instructed. "Jasper Jacoby."

"I'm over here."

The sergeant grinned malevolently. "You thought you could skulk around the back alleys and hide from us, did you? Well, now you'll find out what we do to cowards." He laughed shortly and called, "Pavel Jacoby?"

"Here."

"Yael—"

"She's here in my arms."

The sergeant looked up and his gaze went over Yael in detail. He scowled as though her retardation disgusted him. Feeling the hatred, she tightened her grip around Pavel's neck, staring back wide-eyed. Hatred rose in Pavel.

"Karyn Landson."

No answer. Pavel's heart pounded so loudly, he couldn't think straight.

"Karyn Landson?"

Toca shifted, but said nothing.

The sergeant eyed each of them threateningly, then went on. "Sekan Landson."

"Here, sir." Her red hair clung to her head in matted curls, accenting the hugeness of her eyes.

Once more, the sergeant said, "*Karyn* Landson."

"Maybe she's somewhere else in the crowd, officer," Toca said mildly. "She has friends—"

"You filthy liar! You think you can deceive me? She tried to escape to go fight with the Underground. *We caught her last night!*"

A tremor climbed Pavel's spine. Truth? Or a clever lie designed to terrify them and make them talk? From somewhere in the crowd, the sweet lilting strains of a violin rose, caressing the very wind that swept around them. Unconsciously, he searched for the source. Who could be playing it? Who could feel such magnificent joy? Such unspeakable beauty? Surely only a divine hand could play such music.

Toca responded, "I—we . . . didn't know."

"You didn't know," the sergeant mocked. He lifted a hand and slashed down through the air as though his palm were a knife. Two privates ran forward, looking at him for instructions. "Gerome, Niniva. This old man is guilty of lying to a Magisterial officer and of protecting a Magisterial criminal. Take him to the reorientation lab."

"No!" Pavel screamed, thrusting Yael into Jasper's arms. He ran forward and tried to keep his voice calm, controlled. "No, no, Officer, please. My father told you the truth! We didn't know Karyn was involved with the Underground. Let him go. He's done nothing."

The sergeant laughed. "Then we'll discover his innocence under the mind probes." He stabbed a finger into Pavel's shoulder. "And if you're lying, Pavel Jacoby . . . you'll be next."

He shuddered. The two privates grabbed Toca and started leading him away. Pavel's mind reeled with horror. The probes destroyed critical centers of the brain! Like a cat protecting her litter, he threw himself on the guards, shouting, "Leave him alone! Let my father go! *Damn you!*"

He jerked one of the guards backward and wrestled him to the ground. The crowd surged forward, hopeful, terrified faces watching in disbelief. Yael's insane screams of "Daddy! Daddy!" made him fight harder. Who'd be next after Toca? Her? Him? The other guard released his father and turned sharply. Pulling a long petrolon bar from his belt, he slammed it into Pavel's back, beating him unmercifully. Pavel writhed, covering his head with his hands. The bar landed like agonizing fists against his legs, his arms.

"Stop! Stop it!" he heard his father shriek raggedly.

"Don't hurt him. It's my fault, *my fault*, I'm the only one who knew about Karyn being in the Underground! Punish me!"

"No," Pavel murmured sickly. "Papa, no." When the beating ceased, Pavel rolled to his side and vomited. Sharp pains ran up and down his spine. Had they broken his back?

The tall sergeant ambled lazily forward. "Take the old man away. I'll handle this one."

Pavel barely heard Aunt Sekan's sobs as Toca was dragged toward a black ship. He forced himself to breathe, but it hurt terribly. He felt as though his lungs swelled with fire. Then he saw the sergeant kneel beside him. An eerie glow filled the man's eyes.

"I've got a special place to send problem cases like you and your family, Pavel Jacoby. You'll like it there. Just wait."

His sudden laughter left Pavel frozen with terror. The poignant strains of that faraway violin sang louder. Then—as though to silence the majesty—a burst of shrill rifle fire shredded the wind. The violin stopped. Pavel laid his head on his arm and wept.

CHAPTER 35

A single lamp glowed on Cole Tahn's desk. The decorative shade, which had a series of holes arranged in geometric patterns, cast a polka-dotted glow over his cabin, landing like luminescent opal beads across Carey's taut face. She'd awakened him out of a sound sleep, demanding he get up. Though he'd pulled on his wrinkled uniform, his bare feet tingled from cold. He frowned at her. She had her auburn hair fastened over each ear—a new look for her: softer, more feminine. It made him damned well nervous.

"Well?" he demanded. "Did you come to have a discussion with me or am I supposed to carry on a monologue?"

She propped hands on her hips as she paced. "How are you?"

"Tired. What's wrong?"

"The crew's going out of their minds with anxiety and I thought seeing you would give me some ideas of how to deal with them."

"Uh-huh." He eyed her askance. "This picture's a little sketchy. Want to fill it in for me?"

Her gaze darted to each place in his cabin where monitoring devices existed. He leaned back in his desk chair, disgusted. "Of course, I've disconnected the monitors, Carey. And I made certain again only a half hour ago. So, speak your mind."

Her eyes took on that icy calculating look he was so familiar with. He felt better. "I got word through Macey that Millhyser has an interesting gift for you."

"What gift?"

She smiled. "She found Neil Dannon crawling around in the guts of the weapons systems. Knowing you wanted him, she hid him."

"He's alive?"

"Very."

Cole closed his eyes a moment, thanking nameless deities. The former second in command of the Underground fleet, Dannon could prove to be a deciding factor. He knew Baruch like the back of his hand.

"I've got to meet with him." His mind raced and his gaze slid to the duct. *You'll only be able to use it once. Is Dannon worth it?* Through a tense exhalation, he said, "I guess it's time to use our last ace."

"I agree."

Quickly, she strode across his cabin and leaned over him, accessing the com unit on his desk. He swiveled in his chair, watching the herringbone structure of the *Hoyer*'s duct system appear on the screen. She pointed to a series of interconnected passageways.

"This looks like the best route. You see, here and here. It'll take you about half an hour to reach fourteen C, and it'll be a tight squeeze for you, but I think—"

"I think so, too. But. . . ."

"What?"

He straightened, holding his breath. "I don't know.

316

I've got an uneasy feeling about this."

"You mean like it's a setup?" She shook her head vehemently. "Dannon's been crawling through the ship's deepest recesses for days—trying to stay out of Baruch's sight after that near-miss on level twenty. In fact, he's terrified of the possibility that Baruch recognized him. I don't think he did, but Dannon—"

"That's not what I meant. No, it's—it's something else. Something about the monitoring system. The freedom Baruch's given me to plot in my cabin has a reason. And why hasn't he sealed the duct system from me, hmm?"

"Either because he doesn't know it's open—or because he expects you to use it."

"Maybe he hopes I'll lead him to his ex-best friend?"

"Impossible. No one can monitor the ducts or the weapons niches. There's no system—"

"There may not be a system, but if there's a way, he'll have found it. Something simple, something we're not thinking straight enough to pick up on."

She shifted uncomfortably. "Do we have a choice? I can get a message to Millhyser to put Dannon on hold if you think it's too risky."

"No." He squeezed the bridge of his nose. "We haven't much time. I have to talk to him. We'll work fast. Can you keep Baruch busy while I'm meeting with Dannon."

"Of course." She started for the door.

He got to his feet and reached for his boots. "Carey?"

She turned back, fixing him with a piercing, impatient look, as though she was anxious to be off. "What?"

"I don't care what you have to do, but don't take any unnecessary risks. Just keep his guard down and yours up long enough for me to have a healthy talk with Dannon. Remember, Baruch may seem like a nice guy, but he's as dangerous and unpredictable as they come."

"Thanks for the reminder." She threw him an impertinent smile and left.

Striding back to his com unit, he studied the diagrams once more time. He couldn't risk running a printout. If he were apprehended, he didn't want to implicate anyone else in his activities. Memorizing the sequence of interconnecting passageways, he got on his stomach and crawled beneath his bed.

Removing the rectangular duct covering, he set it aside and slithered into the semidarkness of the tunnel.

* * *

Neil Dannon paced the dim cubicle unsteadily, arms folded across his chest as he listened to the machinery that hummed quietly around him. Six Magisterial science officers spoke in low tones about the *Hoyer*'s predicament, but he barely heard.

He passed a shiny bulkhead and caught sight of his reflection. His chalky face ran with sweat, gluing strands of his jet black hair to his temples and cheeks. The stark terror in his eyes took even him by surprise. He looked like a frightened cat, ready to claw anything to shreds to get out of its trap.

"Dannon."

"What?" he demanded irritably.

Millhyser, a pudgy blonde with an ugly bulbous nose pointed to a chair. "Sit down. You're making me nervous. Tahn will be here any minute."

"I don't take any goddamn orders from you! Leave me alone!"

She threw up her hands and turned away, going back to her discussion with Paul Urquel, weapons specialist.

Neil paced for a time longer, then reluctantly dropped into a formfitting chair. His stomach ached so violently he could barely swallow without feeling it might come back up. In defense, he leaned forward, propping his elbows on his knees and burying his face in his hands.

He felt like a cloth that had been wrung out so hard and so often all the threads had severed, leaving a tattered remnant so flimsy it was no good to anybody anymore. He'd been thinking about Baruch and the refugees so much that he felt ill. *I know you recognized me, Jeremiel. Why haven't you taken any action to apprehend me? What strategy are you working on?*

He dropped his hands and folded his arms over his stomach, rocking back and forth to still the writhing pangs.

"Here he comes," someone whispered.

All the Magisterial officers straightened. Neil listened and could hear faint whisperings of movement from the cooling duct behind Millhyser. She knelt and quietly removed the covering, setting it canted against the wall. Murmurs of excitement went through the crew when

Tahn's face and shoulders appeared. Two lieutenants helped pull him out and for a few moments, the cubicle became a bustling center of embraces and hard hand-shakes. As always, the crew's eyes glowed in Tahn's presence, confident smiles lighting faces that had been taut and worried only seconds before. Only one man eyed Tahn with distrust.

"Corsica," Tahn whispered, "you've checked this place thoroughly?"

"Aye, sir. There's no way Baruch could have tapped this section without us knowing."

Tahn straightened his purple uniform, brushing dust from the gold braid on his shoulders. "Good. We have to make this fast, people. Let's get to work."

When that tough blue-violet gaze fell on him, Neil stiffened instinctively. Tahn walked forward, scrutinizing the grime that covered Neil's torn black robe.

"Dannon, how are you?"

He almost laughed. "As well as can be expected given the circumstances, Tahn."

"You still want to help us capture Baruch?"

He clenched his hands into fists in his lap. He'd never really wanted to do that. He'd just wanted to stop the senseless killing by the Underground. "Yes."

Tahn heaved a tense breath and began pacing before him, hands on his hips. "Let me sketch the situation for you. We've got about five thousand Gamant civilians on board, refugees from Horeb. The—"

"I know. Jeremiel's concentrated them on levels thirteen through eighteen."

Tahn glared, but nodded. "Correct. The Magistrates recently scorched Abulafia and they've initiated a planet-wide suppression action on Tikkun which we've been ordered to assist in."

Neil swallowed the bile that rose into his throat. "And you want to know. . . ?"

"What's Baruch liable to do?"

"Where's the Underground fleet?"

"The government cornered and destroyed half of it around Abulafia. As to the other half, we don't know. We suspect they're on their way to Sector Four, probably the Lysomian system."

Neil's eyes widened. *Half the fleet? Oh, God. Which friends? Which ones?* Maybe that's why Slothen had started hitting Gamant planets so hard—to force the Underground to split its fleet, to spread its resources too thin. That would never have happened if Jeremiel had been there. He'd have never let Rudy make such an error. "When did Jeremiel leave for Kayan?"

"Two months after the Silmar battle."

Neil's lungs burned so that it hurt to breathe. "All right, listen. Rudy will have given Jeremiel a couple of months freedom. Anybody who knows him understands the way his gut works. He would have needed a minimum of two months to recover from—from Syene's death."

"So?"

"It means you'd better hurry." He slowly lifted his eyes to meet Tahn's cool gaze. Dirt streaked the captain's neck, highlighting the tendons bulging from strain.

"What do you mean?"

"Rudy will have been looking for Jeremiel for two months now. When he received no answer to his dattrans, he'd have gone crazy with worry. He—"

"He's on his way, you mean." Tahn stopped pacing and ran a hand through his brown hair.

"I suspect Kopal's close enough to Horeb to smell you, Tahn."

"All right, give it to me quick. What's Baruch's strategy likely to be?"

"I—I don't. . . ." He exhaled anxiously, trying to think like Jeremiel. "He'll probably head this ship for Tikkun to keep the Magistrates thinking you're still in control. He'll be betting on Rudy's eleventh hour appearance. But. . . ." He paused, worrying. "He'll want to be rid of the Horebians before he gets into a firefight. So he'll be trying to figure some place to put them ashore."

"There's nothing between here and Tikkun, not if he takes a straight shot, and any veering off established spaceways will alert the Magistrates that something's wrong on the *Hoyer*."

"So, he'll probably be thinking he has to find a place on Tikkun where the civilians will be safe." He briskly massaged the back of his tense neck. "Is there still a place on Tikkun that's untouched by the Magistrates?"

"How the hell would I know? You were born there." Tahn grimaced, grinding his teeth.

Neil glared at him. "Maybe some of the islands off the

320

continent of Yihud. The Sacla Seven islands. They're small, isolated way stations with very few people living on them. Mostly old Gamants who stick unwaveringly to the traditional life. Have you established military installations in that vicinity?

Tahn pointed sternly at Millhyser. "Next time you get access to the computer, check. I want to know immediately."

"Yes, sir. I have a teaching session in five hours. Fifty Gamants will be breathing down my neck, but they're so inexperienced with com units I doubt they'll realize what I'm doing."

"Good. Let me know as soon as you can."

"Aye, sir."

Tahn nodded approvingly at her, then shoved his hands in his pockets and resumed pacing. "We've been ordered to rendezvous with Brent Bogomil and the *Jataka* in two weeks standard—"

"No, no. I—I don't think Jeremiel will wait that long. He'll want to get rid of the civilians as quickly as he can and he'll need to do a recon of the planet before he knows where to set them down safely. He'll want a thorough look at Tikkun to know what he's up against."

"That's assuming the Underground fleet doesn't find us first," Tahn muttered sarcastically.

Neil couldn't help it, he laughed. "If Kopal contacts Jeremiel before we arrive at Tikkun, you've lost, Tahn. And very likely every Magisterial installation on Tikkun will get wasted before you can blink." A grim sense of pride surfaced. Pride in Kopal's abilities, his one-time good friend. Pride for the fleet, filled with people he'd loved. But that sense soon vanished, replaced by a confusing gnashing in his chest like tiny teeth eating him from the inside out.

"Captain?" Millhyser thoughtfully caressed her ugly chin. A gleam of hope sparked in her eyes. "If we get to Tikkun within the week, and Baruch off-loads—"

"Yes, at least we'll have fighting space—though I imagine Baruch will want at least five hundred of his trainees to stay on board—in case Bogomil is uncooperative. Does that sound reasonable, Dannon?"

"Of course. Jeremiel would never give you a numbers advantage."

"All right, our job today is to work out the basics of

321

three different contingencies. First, we'll plan for an intership battle. Second, we'll try to figure a way of notifying Tikkun's military of our problems and requesting assistance. Third, we'll strategize the outcome if Bogomil can give us aid. Baruch will certainly surrender if he knows cannons are centered over his very heart and those of his people. Then—"

Neil laughed again, this time loud and long, the sound bubbling up from his stomach. He let the mirth roll out over the suddenly silent government officers.

Tahn eyed him like a moldering lab specimen. "I gather you're trying to tell me something, Dannon."

"Indeed. Indeed! Though I'm surprised after fighting against him for so long, you could even suggest something so preposterous. If Jeremiel thinks you've cornered him, he—will—simply—shoot his way out."

"But that's suicidal!" Millhyser accused, throwing out her flat chest. "No one would—"

"Well, maybe. But at least that way he'll take a lot of you with him. And the more the better."

"Ridiculous! He wouldn't risk killing all his friends—"

"Better listen up, Tahn. Box him and you'll have a hell of a fight on your hands. He knows the C-J class cruisers as well as your own engineers. After he's wielded the weapons for a few hours, you'll damn well wish you'd never invented them." He tried to suppress the insane chuckle that shook him. Tears welled in his eyes—but not from amusement. "And if that doesn't stop your attack, he'll just adjust the tappers in the engines to drain your primordial black holes at a rate much faster than you'd feel comfortable with." He smiled and threw up his hands, mimicking the giant explosion that would result. "Better nobody has this ship than you."

The crew stared aghast, some with mouths gaping. Neil folded his arms tightly across his chest and squeezed, rocking back and forth again, trying to force the bitter ache from his heart and avoid stepping over the edge into the chasm that widened in his soul.

Tahn turned away from him, giving stern instructions to his officers. "Carlene, use your chemists. They'll know every ordinary substance on the ship to make lethal gases from. I want them on it immediately. Tell your computer specialists to start looking for a way to break through the training programs and tap the main com. If we—"

"Yes," Millhyser said. "If we can do that, we can disrupt every system on board."

Tahn continued, giving quick precise orders. People nodded, eyes lighting as they plotted how to take their ship back—and how to kill Baruch in the cleanest, least costly way.

Dannon jerked up his head. "Wait a minute." Tahn turned to glare. "*We made a deal!* We agreed off Silmar that you wouldn't kill him, you'd just—"

"Baruch's *brillance* has left us no choice."

He lurched to his feet, fists clenched. "*NO!* We made a deal! You promised you'd—"

"Sit down and shut up, Dannon! I'm not taking any chances Baruch might do this to us again!"

"But you—"

"*That was then.* He's pushed us too far this time."

"Tahn, you filthy liar! WE MADE A DEAL!"

Tahn took a threatening step toward him. Neil braced himself for the punch, but it never came. "You'll still get your goddamned money, Dannon! Sit down! *And the Magistrates will probably pin a medal on your chest for helping us!* You'd like that, wouldn't you? To be a galactic hero."

Neil's knees went weak. He dropped back into his chair and concentrated on the dull nauseating thudding of his heart.

CHAPTER 36

The security access tunnel stretched like a dark gray tube over Yosef's head. He planted a foot on the next rung of the ladder which lined the full length and grunted as he pulled himself up. Sweat ran down his face and chest, soaking his collar and the constricted waist of his gray jumpsuit. Below him, he could hear Ari gasping and groaning protestingly. Too tired to move another inch,

Yosef hooked an arm in the ladder and hung limply for a few seconds, catching his breath. Dim gray light suffused the shaft, landing like a heavy slate curtain over the walls.

"What are you doing?" Ari demanded. When he got no answer, he prodded Yosef uncomfortably in the butt with his rifle barrel. "Climb! I'm suffocating down here."

"Put that thing away, before you put somebody's eye out."

"You don't have to worry about that from this angle." Ari grinned malevolently.

Yosef reached around to slap at the barrel until he shifted its aim—no matter how roundabout—from pointing at his head. "When they circumcised you, they cut out part of your brain."

"You're just jealous because I had enough left that nobody called me stubby when I was a kid. Now, move. We haven't got all day."

Yosef gazed back up the length of the ladder. "I don't know why I let you talk me into things like this."

"Would you rather take a transport tube and have every bubble-brain guard on the ship know what we're doing?

"What *are* we doing? Jeremiel canceled all the search teams. He said he'd finally concluded Dannon must be dead."

"Sure he said that. He's waiting until a better time to smoke the rat out. Where're your guts? Do you want him to have to do it all alone?"

Yosef shifted so he could scowl down at Ari. His friend hung like a gangly spider from the ladder, gray mop of hair sticking out at odd angles. "Where'd you learn such twisted logic?"

"Move!"

Yosef kicked at Ari for a few minutes to release his frustrations, then he gripped the next rung of the ladder and climbed.

* * *

Jeremiel leaned back in his chair. He'd dressed casually, comfortably, for this long night, wearing a black shirt and gray pants. He studied the pale green com screen as he sipped a steaming cup of taza. The slightly bitter flavor refreshed his tired mind. Music played softly in the background, one of the famed "Lost Symphonies" of

Nikos Theodorakis. Beautiful in its melancholy, the sweetly lilting strains seemed to reach inside and soothe him.

He input a new series of commands—and waited, drinking more taza. When the screen flared, he scrutinized the weapons niches scattered throughout the ship. *Yes, that's where I'd hide.* Many of the niches, as well as Tahn's crew, clustered on level seven.

"That's where you went, isn't it, Neil?"

A storm vied inside him. Vestiges of old and abiding friendship competed with hatred. Memories were his greatest enemy. He could still see the light of the flames reflected in Neil's eyes that desperate night on Ebed II. The rest of their team had been killed during the first day of fighting. He and Neil had been running through the burned city for three days, trying to reconnect with their unit—but Tahn's forces had cut them off and cornered them in a battered warehouse. When Jeremiel had led the charge inside, he'd barely noticed that the roof was blazing over their heads. They'd scrambled heedlessly behind a tumbled mound of boxes and crates. The fire's roar had nearly deafened. . . .

"How many you think are out there?" Neil had asked conversationally as he checked the meager charge left in his rifle.

"I'd guess twenty."

"Yeah? That's only ten to one odds."

"Don't you think that's enough?"

As the flames swept closer, heat had seared their faces like a blowtorch.

Neil lifted an arm to shield his eyes and grinned devilishly. "Did you see that redhead? Um, um. Nice. If she hadn't been in a purple uniform I'd have—"

"You'd have been dead in less than a second. She didn't like your looks at all."

"She just needed to get to know me."

Jeremiel laughed. Neil had always done that to him—made him laugh in the most dire of circumstances. A crate exploded, sending a shrapnel spray of petrolon at them. They both hit the floor and covered their heads. The spray pattered against the mound of boxes.

"This doesn't look so good, Jeremiel, old buddy." Neil had shouted. "I don't think we can hang around here much longer."

"I think you're right. I say we pick a direction, use our last photon grenade and pray."

Neil had lifted his brows in amusement, rolled over onto his back and pulled the grenade from his pocket. "Jeremiel? You're my best friend. I've never had a friend like you before. If we don't make it out of this I want you to know—"

"Don't get maudlin! Tell me tomorrow."

Neil had given him one of those reproachful looks filled with warmth. "Always the sentimentalist! Well, all right. What direction did you say we were diving?"

Jeremiel forced the memory away, but not before an incapacitating ache straitjacketed his chest. He leaned forward over his console. *What happened to us, Neil? What did I do to hurt you so much that you'd....* Ruthlessly, he tapped his keyboard, requesting carbon dioxide readings for every niche on board.

"I know you're on level seven. But I'd better search every area with weapons niches—"

A voice filtered from his door com into his cabin. "Jeremiel? Are you awake?"

Hitting the patch above his desk, he called, "Yes, Jonas," to his new door guard.

"Lieutenant Halloway is here to see you."

He swiveled his chair around to face his door and softly caressed his beard, wondering why she'd be here at this late hour. "Go ahead and access, Jonas."

"Aye, Jeremiel."

His door slipped open and she strode in, a look of quiet urgency on her beautiful face. Her purple uniform looked fresh.

"Have a seat, Halloway." He gestured to one of the chairs by the table. "What can I do for you?"

"Jeremiel, I'm sorry to disturb you, I—"

He cocked his head incredulously. "Are we on a first name basis, Lieutenant?"

"Sorry. I. ... How would you prefer to be addressed?"

She lifted a shoulder gracefully in apology and he felt a little ashamed of his reaction. "Well, since there are some names I'd rather you not use, I guess Jeremiel's fine. May I call you Carey?"

"Please."

"Can I get you a cup of taza or a strong belt of

whiskey?" She looked like she needed the latter.

"Whiskey, please."

"I thought so. You know, you drink more than many men I know." He got up and went to the cabinet over his bed, pulling out the bottle and a single glass. On the way to the table, he picked up his taza.

"What an ill-bred remark," she commented.

"Oh, you came to discuss breeding? That sounds like a refreshingly different topic."

She smiled disarmingly, green eyes slanting. "Don't get your hopes up. I also *hold* my liquor better than many men you know. Though guzzling is one of my newfound talents—developed since you came aboard."

He smiled back. "Indeed? I'd have thought Tahn would have driven you to it long ago."

"He's not as bad as you think."

"Our perspectives are different, I'm afraid."

She stood very close beside him while he opened the bottle and poured her glass full. Her perfume surrounded him like a meadow of wildflowers. He gave her a sidelong look. In the bright light, her tightly clenched fists shone starkly white. Surreptitiously, he examined her more closely. She was fighting to keep her breathing even, but it wasn't working. His brows lowered. Either the stakes were uncommonly high, or she wasn't particularly practiced at this. Maybe both. Was she covering for someone? Tahn? A moment of panic set his heart to racing. *Had the time come?* He'd opened the route from Tahn's cabin to level seven two days ago.

He quietly inhaled a deep breath and handed her the glass, noting with interest how long she allowed their fingers to touch before taking it. It sent a small tingle through him, just as she'd intended. Interesting. "Do sit down, *Carey.*"

"I think I'll stand."

"Suit yourself." He pulled out his chair and propped a boot on it, eyeing her speculatively as he sipped his taza. "What can I help you with?"

"Several of my people are refusing to train yours and I don't—"

"Really? I've received no complaints from my staff."

"Nevertheless—"

"I take it you'd rather I not threaten to kill each recalcitrant specialist?"

"Good guess. I think that might exacerbate existing tensions."

He nodded amiably. "Well, I certainly can't tolerate dallying or misdirection. What do you suggest we do about it?"

She gave him an uncertain glance, as though wavering about how to act. Were his suspicions that plain on his face? Or was she just uncomfortable with the role of trickster? Lifting her glass, she finished it to the last drop, setting it in front of him for a refill. He poured her another.

"Is this discussion difficult for you?" he asked.

"Not yet."

"Do you expect it to be?"

"I don't know."

"Really? I'm disappointed."

She cocked an eyebrow. "Yeah? Why?"

"You're a professional. You should have had your strategy worked out before you came in."

She fixed him with a penetrating, slightly frightened look. "What do you mean?"

He shook his head deprecatingly and strolled leisurely back to look down at his com unit, stalling, giving her time to get more nervous. The screen fluttered, still processing the carbon dioxide data, but the preliminary figures told him a great deal. Definitely level seven, none of the other niches had any unusual levels. *Yes, go talk to Neil, Tahn.*

Finally, after the silence had stretched so long she started to fidget, he said, "Tell me something? How distracted am I supposed to be? Enough to forget myself completely?" He brazenly looked her up and down. "Or did you count on my highly vaunted Gamant sense of propriety? Let me warn you that it's overrated."

The pale color of her cheeks grew to a rosy hue. She exhaled haltingly and ran a hand through her auburn hair. "Counting on you in any form seems risky."

He scrutinized her unmercifully. She stood quietly, staring into her whiskey glass, as though vaguely embarrassed.

"Do you want to tell me what we're really discussing?"

She shook her head. "Not particularly."

"Well, why don't you let me start then." He took three steps to stand directly in front of her, a hard look on his face. "Let's discuss how Tahn is plotting to take his ship back."

"Damn it, Baruch. What makes you think he's—"

"It's instinctual. No good commander ever gives up. And Tahn's a very good commander. If he didn't try, I'd be far more worried. Though for the life of me I can't figure out why he hasn't called to talk to me again."

She opened her mouth to say something, then thought better of it, and kept quiet. He took the opportunity to go to the drink dispenser and refill his taza. He hit the light on his way back, dimming it to a soft velvet hue. Jerking a chair out from the table, he ordered, *"Sit down, Lieutenant."*

She stood rigidly a moment, then complied, easing into the chair. He sat on the opposite side and leaned back, his gaze impaling her.

She swallowed nervously. "You think I'm here as a strategic ploy?"

"Aren't you?"

"Why don't you throw me out?"

He ground his teeth audibly. "I like you."

"Is that supposed to ease my tension?"

"Not especially." Swirling his taza, he asked, "So Tahn's finally decided to tap Dannon's knowledge, eh?"

She hesitated, as though wanting to ask him about the level twenty incident. Instead, she played along, "Dannon's dead. You said it yourself."

"Neil knows the rules too well to be dead. I've been through hundreds of decompression training sessions with him. And if he knew I was coming aboard, he certainly knew what I had planned."

She let out a breath. "I don't understand you, Baruch. If you think Dannon and Tahn are plotting against you, why are you just sitting here? Dannon can hurt you."

A small thread of warm emotion tinged that last. He looked her over in detail, from the flushed cheeks to the anxious movements of her hands around her whiskey glass. Strategic or genuine? He couldn't tell.

"I know that."

"You're going to let him? *Just like you did on Silmar?*"

His controlled facade crumbled. He fought to keep the anger, the hurt, buried. But it swept him up like an ocean-born cyclone, dragging him into a dark abyss of pain. She'd done that deliberately, taking charge of the conversation, turning it the direction she wanted. "Careful," he murmured. "Be very careful. What are you getting at?"

Her face seemed to change, as though she'd come to a difficult decision. When she lifted her head, her alabaster skin gleamed pearlescent beneath the velvet lights. "In Akiba, you knew he was off plotting behind your back, didn't you? Surely someone tried to tell you your good buddy—"

"Syene tried to tell me. Didn't matter. I trusted him."

"Like now?"

His gaze drifted slowly from his drink to her tightly pursed lips. *Goddamn, does she know what I'm doing?* Had she guessed his strategy? She was a shrewd, intelligent combat veteran. Had he underestimated her? The possibility stuck him like a jagged timber in the stomach. "What are you getting at?"

She rubbed both hands over her beautiful face as though in disbelief at what she was saying. "Forget it. I've lost my mind."

"This is a rather intriguing discussion we're having, don't you think? Are you trying to *help* me, Lieutenant?"

She lounged quietly back in her chair, looking suddenly weary, weary beyond exhaustion. After an interminable period of peering at the floor, she lifted her right hand—her pistol hand—and opened the palm, extending thin white fingers to the bluish gleam of light. Bitterly, she examined the lines, as though seeing them for the first time and finding the patterns distastefully woven. A somber set of wrongness fell over her beautiful face. In slow motion, she closed her hand into a tight fist and shook it at some inner foe. He watched the action with a strained unwillingness, for he understood that gesture better than he had any of her spoken words. A thousand times, in a hundred battles, he'd cursed fate with that same soundless ferocity.

Softly, she said, "You know, I hated you for years. You killed so many of my friends."

A familiar ache swelled in his chest. He stared at the tabletop, letting her finish.

"But as I watched what you did, I came to grudgingly admire you. You were so damned exact, so *perfect* in your calculations—like a machine. Clean, precise, no emotion."

"That's how it looked from the outside?"

"Yes."

"I guess desperation appears eloquent in its execution," he responded

"I guess. And I suggest you brush up on it. You're in a hell of a predicament. What are you going to do? If you head for Tikkun—and you must—you'll have fifteen Magisterial military installations waiting for you. You can't—"

"Maybe I can."

"I doubt it."

"What a pessimist you are."

"And Bogomil will be there in two weeks. No matter how well you coerce our people into training yours, they'll never be good enough to match Academy-drilled soldiers."

He gripped his cup hard. May Epagael damn her to the pit of darkness for reaffirming his deepest fears. "I'm aware of that."

"Do you have a plan?"

He chuckled at the question, softly at first, then louder. "Shall I tell you about it?"

Her gaze lifted to him with a severity that stopped him short. "I'll know soon enough anyway. Your good buddy Dannon—if he's alive—will undoubtedly tell Tahn exactly how he expects you to act. And here you are—"

"Being far too honest with a woman I like too damned much."

Rashly, he slammed a fist into the table, overturning both her glass and his cup; they smashed into each other with a sharp clink, dumping their contents in an irregular braid over the table and onto the rug. Their gazes held and he noticed how hers softened. He shook his head sternly. "Damn it."

"Well," she whispered, lowering her hands to her lap. "This is uncomfortable. I think I've distracted you long enough."

"You made it uncomfortable. I didn't."

"Because I asked about your strategy? Don't condemn me for that. I figured you needed help."

"Did you? As a matter of fact, I do. Tell me how Tahn plans on retaking his ship?"

His heart pounded at the look on her face. She paused almost as if she wanted to. A ploy? It was a hell of a good

331

one. Every emotional fiber in his body geared up to do anything necessary to help her step across that spun-silk bridge of loyalty to his side. "*Carey,* just tell me—"

"It's time for me to leave." Getting up, she practically ran for the door.

He stood and grasped her wrist tightly as she passed, a subdued urgency in his voice. "I *do* need your help. *Help me, Carey.*"

She pulled hard against his grip. He refused to let go. They stood eye to eye a minute, then two. He could feel her pulse increasing the longer he held her wrist, until it raced as rapidly as his own and he felt a desperation that verged on futility. In only a few hours, he'd have to head this ship down the serpent's throat, praying to God he could find a way out again. His gaze caressed the brassy glints of her hair, the smooth lines of her face, the silken feel of her skin against his. In a brusque gesture, he released her wrist and wrapped his arms around her, kissing her.

She struggled halfheartedly, then seemed to melt against him, her body conforming to the hollows of his. She kissed him back, lips soft, enticing, moving slowly, as though they had hours to play. A surge of warmth flooded Jeremiel's veins. He tightened his arms powerfully around her shoulders, pulling her against him, and in the back of his mind a voice whispered: *A game. This is all a game. We'll both use whatever leverage we can. . . . Yet, it feels so good. What harm is there in soothing each other for an hour? What harm . . . !*

He threw up his hands and backed unsteadily to the center of the room. His shirt clung in sweat-drenched folds to his chest and he noticed with irritation that his arms shook.

"Carey," he said in a low voice, "leave. And tell Tahn that Dannon's right about one thing. If he pushes me, *I'll blow this ship to hell.* Got it?"

She ran a hand through her auburn hair, nodding. "I've got it, all right. When are we leaving orbit?"

He walked to stand over his com, absently focusing on the screen. "Immediately."

She hesitated for an excruciating amount of time and he heard her uniform rustle with uneasy movements. "Jeremiel, if I could. . . ."

He closed his eyes, and balled his fists, fighting with himself. "You *can*."

"No. I can't," she said quietly. "I'll give Tahn your—"

"If he's with Dannon, he already knows."

Without a word she exited into the corridor, disappearing from his view. He caught a glimpse of Jonas' curious face before his door slipped closed again.

Jeremiel wandered around his cabin. In a quick violent gesture, he pulled his shirt over his head and threw it at the foot of his bed. For hours, he'd secretly endured the same fear that lined the faces of those closest to him, wondering how they'd get out of this impossible dilemma. But it angered him to be reminded of it every moment by their eyes—eyes reverent with faith in him. They believed he could get them out safely—and of all the things that could be said about him, that was the most difficult to live up to.

He sat heavily on his bed and put his hands on either side of his head, pressing hard, trying to force some sense into his worry-laced brain.

"Come on, Neil. Come on, damn it! Tell Tahn *exactly* what you think I'll do."

And yet, when push came to shove, if they got trapped in the heat of battle—he knew he wouldn't have time to second-guess Neil. A sharp ache invaded his chest. He fought it, filling his mind with so much hate, he felt he'd explode. *Remembering Syene*. After fifteen or twenty minutes, he looked back at the com screen, noting the finished calculations, listed in descending order of highest concentrations.

Section fourteen C, level seven.

He stretched out on his back and stared at the ceiling, trying to thoroughly examine his narrowing options. Too often, too damned often, thoughts of Carey Halloway intruded—as powerful as a polished golden calf in the searing deserts of old.

* * *

Carey got into the transport tube with Jonas Wilkes. Short and built like an inverted pyramid, he stood stiffly, eyes on her. She leaned against the wall, letting the chill of the petrolon filter through her uniform to taunt her flesh. A barren wind swept her soul. Too deep. She'd gotten in too deep. How had that happened? How had she let it happen?

The game had gone awry. . . .

The sensation of Jeremiel's strong arms around her had stirred feelings that terrified her.

CHAPTER 37

Dim bluish light filtered between machinery to land like a crumpled silk scarf across Dannon's face. He rolled uncomfortably to his back and struggled to get to sleep. Cramped into a narrow four by six space between two enormous cooling units, he could barely stretch his legs their full length. Worse, the constant low hum of the ship slashed through his dreams, becoming Jeremiel's voice every time he drifted off.

Would he never escape the nightmares about Silmar?

After an eternity of restless tossing and turning, he finally sat up, pulled his knees against his chest, and leaned back against the cool gray metal. Sweat drenched his face, rolling down his neck to soak the collar of his fresh purple uniform.

He wiped his forehead on his sleeve and stared blankly at the patchwork patterns of light that scattered the carpet. What time was it? Morning yet? No, it couldn't be. Weariness clung like an iron cape around his shoulders. He probably hadn't lain down more than three hours ago.

"Stop it," he whispered, bracing his forehead on his knees and closing his eyes. "Stop torturing yourself. Gamants bring it on themselves. You did the right thing."

Didn't you . . . didn't you? But . . . maybe Jeremiel was right . . . about flying into the storm?

Several minutes later, he felt himself sinking deeper and deeper into sleep. His breathing melted into soothing rhythms. The sounds of the ship faded. Darkness smothered the light. . . .

And the snow fell around him in huge wet flakes.

"Where, Dannon?" Tahn's voice grated, wavering in the icy gusts of Silmar wind that lanced their uniforms.

He gazed down the street at opaque botanical domes and apartment buildings, then pointed. "There. The one in the center. They're on the third floor."

Tahn held his pistol pointed at the sky. "Let's go."

Two sergeants grabbed Neil's arms, protecting him as they half-ran down the sidewalk, stopping frequently to duck into shadowed doorways to wait until fleeing Gamant civilians passed. Already the attack had ripped the city wide and desperate people sought escape. Several women dragging suitcases by long straps swept by, one weeping fearfully when she saw them.

Neil wet his lips, imagining the fire play in the dark heavens where battle cruisers hurled violet lances at each other.

"Hurry!" Tahn blurted, and they ran again.

The Akiba oaks lining the street hunched like old men under the heavy mantle of snow, branches drooping to touch the frosted grass.

Tahn's security team encircled him as they dashed for the peak-roofed building. The lead lieutenant, a burly man with a bald head, slammed a boot into the front door and hit the foyer rolling, coming up with his rifle pointed.

Tahn darted through the entry and charged the stairs, taking the steps two at a time. In a bunched file they ascended, breathing raggedly by the time they reached the third-floor landing. "Dannon?"

"Last door on the right."

Tahn hesitated, then motioned with his pistol barrel. "You go first. In case Baruch's been here before us."

"All right." He swallowed convulsively and walked ahead. Before he got to the door, he heard the raucous laughter and throttled female cries. He grimaced, not understanding.

Sliding against the wall, he extended a fist and banged the door. "Syene?"

"Oh, God! Neil? Neil, get away! Don't—"

He saw Tahn and the security team hugging the walls, waiting for him to give the all clear. Tahn was too cautious for his own good. Just because he'd never met Lichtner didn't mean they weren't on the same side. He shoved open the door and entered.

The living room looked as though a bomb had blasted it. Furniture lay overturned, broken glass shimmering like diamonds across the pale green carpet. Blood splashed the far corner in an irregular oval. She must have fought like a wildcat when she realized the true nature of the situation. They'd set her up to believe she'd be bargaining with Lichtner, buying him off so he'd pull his troops out of the Gamant section of town and leave it safe at the critical moment when the Underground cruisers combined fire to blast all the Magisterial military installations on Silmar. In reality, she'd be bait to lure Jeremiel's forces into a huge net where they couldn't maneuver.

A final resting place for the Underground fleet.

Dannon had personally guaranteed Lichtner that Jeremiel wouldn't leave Syene, no matter how hot the fighting got, until too late—until he couldn't escape anymore.

He sprinted past the kitchen and down a long white hall to the rear bedroom where he knew Lichtner had set up his ambush. Bursting through the door, his legs suddenly went wobbly at the sight that met his eyes.

"Neil!" Syene sobbed. "Neil . . . oh, Neil. . . ."

She lay naked on the bed, her beautiful olive skin drenched in sweat and blood. Four marines held her arms and legs spread-eagled. Another man, a corporal by his uniform, crawled off her when Dannon entered, and proceeded to tuck himself into his pants and fasten his fly. Down the insides of Syene's thighs, whitish fluid trickled. Some spots appeared long dried. Had they all taken turns?

He stared, too stunned to speak.

Trembling all over, Syene's lungs heaved as the men released her. She curled into a ball on her side and looked up at Neil through eyes stark with pain and terror—half insane.

Tahn and his security team raced down the hall, dodging into the room to line the walls like purple pillars. Lichtner's people briefly studied the *Hoyer* insignia on their shoulders and lowered their weapons.

"Neil?" Syene mewled pathetically, as though he were her only reference point for sanity. She held a hand out to him. "Neil . . . help?"

His throat tightened as tears rose to choke him. He turned away in shock and walked toward the bedroom door where he dropped to the floor. Why hadn't he realized Lichtner would do something like this? Guilt tightened like a rope around his throat. Anger and hurt jumbled inside him so wildly, he vomited in the corner.

Through tear-blurred eyes, he saw Tahn's jaw harden. Meticulously and quickly the captain took in the scene. Syene weakly pulled a sheet up to cover her nakedness and Tahn turned away, toward the major who leaned so superciliously against the wall, smiling, a cigarette in his right hand.

"Are you Lichtner?" Tahn asked in an unsettlingly calm voice—like the hush that falls before the hurricane strikes.

Lichtner stepped forward, grinning proudly. "Yes, I deserve full credit for this capture, Captain. I hope your report will reflect—"

"Tell your men to get out."

Lichtner blinked. "What? Why?"

"Do it!"

Lichtner took a step back, ordering, "Terengi, take your men and guard the front entrance."

Glancing at each other, they filed out, striding past Neil and closing the bedroom door behind them. The scent of Syene's perfume clung to them, sweet, cloying.

Tahn's face went livid. Eyes on Syene, he stood so still, so quiet, that Lichtner fidgeted nervously.

"Captain, thank you for heeding our call for assistance so quickly. We'd not anticipated—"

Tahn swung around and slammed a devastating right into Lichtner's stomach, then brought up his knee and struck the man agonizingly in the groin. The major sank to his knees, gasping.

Tahn hissed, "You damned fool! What the hell did you think you were doing? If I didn't need you, you'd be dead. Get up! Tell me what information you've gleaned about Baruch's plans for Silmar?"

Lichtner gripped the back of a chair and staggered to his feet, shaking. "You struck—an officer! I'll have you strung up from the highest—"

Tahn grabbed him by the front of his uniform and

threw him brutally against the wall. *"What information!"*

"N—none," Lichtner stuttered, glaring at Syene.

Her long brown hair spread across the pillow like damp silk. Through huge eyes filled with the certainty of death, she watched, shoulders heaving with silent sobs.

"What do you mean *none?*"

"She's told us nothing! We tried everything, but she—"

"You kept her here as your private toy and learned *nothing?* Goddamn you! If you'd turned her over to us, we'd have long ago gained that information through mind probing!"

"As planetary commander, I outrank you, Captain! You take *my* orders!"

"The hell I do!" Tahn backhanded Lichtner with lightning speed, sending him toppling over a chair to land hard against the wall. Lichtner got to his feet and bellowed like an enraged bull, rushing insanely. Tahn's kick caught him in the chest.

But Dannon's eyes shifted, watching Syene. The fracas seemed to have shaken her so badly that a glimmer of sanity had returned. She edged toward the window, fingers crawling spiderlike until she could grip the sill.

"She's getting away!" Lichtner shouted from where he lay sprawled over the floor.

Syene dove, trying to escape, but Tahn lunged for her bare legs, dragging her halfway back inside just as a shot drowned out everything. The purple flash blinded him for a second.

From below, Lichtner's guards shouted, *"They're here! Run! Baruch's forces. . . ."*

Neil's heart seemed to stop. *Here?* He sprinted for the window, and saw Jeremiel running toward the apartment building, Rudy close behind. But closer movements took all his attention. Tahn gently released Syene and pushed up from the bed. His uniform bore spatters of her blood.

Neil saw Syene's beautiful chest blasted wide. The shot had been a glancing blow but had ripped a lethal gash.

Lichtner still held his pistol high, eyes gleaming. "She was getting away!" he explained, seeing Tahn's clenched fists and enraged face. "I didn't mean to kill her! I just wanted to stop her!"

"Simons, go!" Tahn shouted to his security chief,

frantically waving at his men. "We've got to get the hell out of here. If that's Baruch down there, his forces are surely behind him and this whole damn section of town is about to go up in a ball of fire!"

Dannon got to his feet and stumbled back against the wall, watching men race by. Everyone filed out, leaving him alone. The sudden silence fell over him like a leaden sheet. For the last time, his gaze took in the overturned furniture, the blood.

"Syene," he murmured miserably. "I didn't know he'd do this. I swear."

Faintly, almost inaudibly, he heard a voice plead, *"Neil?"*

He fell back against the wall, breaking into sobs. *She was alive!* He took a fumbling step toward her, then blindly turned and ran. As he neared the end of the hall, he heard Rudy's urgent shouting below, "They're coming fast, Jeremiel. *Hurry!*"

Boots pounded violently on the stairs and Neil lunged for the nearest apartment, ducking inside and locking the door. He pressed his ear against the wall, hearing Jeremiel's agonized shout, *"Syene?"*

Wildly, frantically, Neil ran to the rear of the apartment, trying to enter the circle of Tahn's protection before. . . .

* * *

The sudden loud whir of a cooling unit kicking on brought him bolt upright from where he'd slumped across the floor.

"Oh." His voice quaked. "Just—just a—dream."

Shuddering as though from deadly cold, he folded his arms tightly over his aching stomach. Breath rushed in and out of his lungs in huge desperate gulps.

"Oh . . . God, oh God, ohGod."

He wiped soaked hair from his brow and leaned his head back against the chill metal, staring unblinkingly at the ceiling fifteen feet over his head. Shadows wavered, monstrous against the stark lustreglobe-dyed walls.

People walked. Second shift? Or morning? He hadn't the strength to rise and ask. Soft voices echoed around the rows of machinery and he could see two soldiers in purple uniforms wandering aimlessly through the niche. He clenched his fists. Like severed nerves shocked by a laser's edge, his despair, despair he'd carried for four months and twenty-two days, reawakened and his agony returned.

The abyss in his soul yawned wider.

* * *

The 14th of Tishri.

Autumn's dusty breathless heat choked the streets of Derow, adding a leaden weight to anxious hearts.

After a day and a half of standing, Pavel's injured back ached as though demons with hot pokers prodded it. He straightened painfully, gazing around the ominously quiet crowd that packed the long street. Children stretched out across the pavement, mothers protectively holding their heads in their laps. Several of the elderly had formed a group beneath the shade of a crimson leafed tree. Yet no one moved, no one spoke—he wondered if they even breathed for fear the marines would hear and tear them to pieces.

Dozens of ships waited above them, hovering like still black beetles against the brilliant azure sky. Armed guards patrolled the boundaries of the gathering, rifles held threateningly.

Pavel bowed his head and looked at Yael. She slept at his feet, her young face serene and innocent. A balmy warmth caressed the air, redolent with the scents of ripe fields of barley and freshly harvested alfalfa. Along the road, golden masses of ivy bordered lawns, climbed trellises, and wound over rooftops. He exhaled painfully. On beautiful fall days like this, he and Yael usually spent the afternoon leaning with their arms on the sill of an open window, drinking in Tikkun's beauty, talking about things that interested her: cats and oxen, colors and grass.

"How do you feel?" Grandpa asked. He sat next to Yael, ancient knees drawn up. His withered face had taken on a hard, hateful set.

"Sore, but all right. Where did Aunt Sekan go?"

"Patlica Urbikeit begged her to come and talk. Her heart is broken."

Pavel swallowed hard and nodded. Tears stung his eyes, but he sucked in a deep breath, forestalling the emotional tide. Toca's absence weighed heavily on all of them—a great black blanket that smothered their strength.

340

"How are you, Grandpa? Do you need some water? There's a canteen tied to that bag behind you."

Jasper reached around and unfastened it. The petrolon made a harsh scritching sound as he dragged it across the pavement and handed it up to Pavel.

He gingerly sat down beside Yael. His spine felt worse when he sat than when he stood or lay down. He twisted so he rested on his right hip. Uncorking the canteen, he took a long drink and gave it back to Grandpa.

Jasper sipped a little. "As for how I am, fine so far, but I'm not expecting miracles."

"What do you think they're going to do with us?"

"Work us until they kill us. You've heard the rumors about the camps they set up on Jumes before they scorched it. I suspect we're in for the same thing."

He said the words mildly, but they made Pavel shiver. "What have we done to deserve such punishment, Jasper?"

"We're Gamants. That's enough."

"What has humanity come to that we can do this to each other? We're all *humans,* for God's sake!"

"Humans have always persecuted each other. They enjoy it. Look at Pleros of Antares. History is full of examples where brutality worked wonders to wipe out opposition and whip up the fury of *patriots.*"

Pavel shook his head, wondering how it was possible to convey such contempt in such a virtuous word.

A roar like the wash of the ocean over rocks rose. Pavel looked up and saw the black ships moving, landing here and there. People stood, alarm on their faces. The guards started running.

"Jacoby!" the ugly sergeant cried. "Over here. You're going with this bunch."

Pavel gently woke Yael. Picking her up, he rose, offering Jasper a hand. The old man refused it, grunting as he stood and wiped sweaty palms on his black pants. They'd all dressed in their sturdiest everyday clothing. Yael wore blue pants and a red and black plaid shirt. He wore a red shirt and brown pants.

"Are we going, Daddy?" Yael asked, hugging him tightly around the neck.

He kissed her ear. "I think so, baby."

In the distance, cloud shadows roamed the barley fields, darkening the golden grain with splotches of gray.

"Where to?"

"We don't know yet. But everything will be all right. Don't be scared."

Aunt Sekan came running up as they followed the sergeant. Her green dress bore sweat stains down the front and beneath her arms.

"Jasper?" she asked pathetically, as though on the edge of hysteria. Her eyes looked as stark and wide as Yael's. "What's happening?"

Grandpa patted her shoulder gently. "We're going with this group. That's all we know. Don't worry yet."

She crushed and recrushed the balled handkerchief in her hands as they moved along in the flow of people. About fifteen others were herded with them toward a ship sitting at the far end of the street. Guards with truncheons waited at the doors, striking people indiscriminately, yelling, "Hurry, you filthy Gamants! We don't have all day to wait on your lazy asses."

Yael closed her eyes as they neared the doors, burying her face in Pavel's collar. "Daddy?"

"It's all right," he whispered soothingly. "Only a little longer." Her shallow breathing warmed his cheek.

"Get inside! Damn you! You waste our time dawdling!"

The guard struck Grandpa Jasper on the shoulder. He groaned, lifting his arms to shield his face as he ran up the gangplank. Pavel gripped Sekan's dress sleeve and dragged her behind him, dodging between people to avoid the beating. She let out a small cry, but came.

A huge white room stretched in an oval around them, people packed wall-to-wall. Mustiness filled the air, a queasy odor of fear and dirt. Somewhere, a man recited the Kedis, tears straining his voice. Pavel silently accompanied him, saying the holy words with all the terrible reverence he could muster. *Are you listening, God?*

Buttercup sunlight poured through the round portals, landing in spots of gay color on a hundred faces drawn with terror. Pavel and Yael shuffled back against the far wall. Out the portal behind him, he saw rows of daylilies bordering a family garden. The flowery lanes spread over the earth like lace doilies, accenting the golden stalks of dead corn.

He concentrated on the beauty, the tranquillity.

The doors snapped closed and the ship lifted, shooting

away through the warm skies. Pavel rocked Yael in his arms, singing a soft lullaby, but she wouldn't sleep. She hugged him in a death grip and stared up in grave silence.

He smiled, but his throat ached with the urge to shout at someone. He wanted to strike out, to hurt as he'd been hurt. Where was his father? What would happen to their home? Would the marines separate them, or leave families together. *Dear God, don't let them separate us! Anything but that.* How long would the torture last? Where was Karyn? Dead? Or was the Underground even now planning their rescue?

Yes, yes, of course. A brief welling of hope calmed him. He let himself drown in it. People shifted, shoving each other to find a comfortable standing position in the cramped ship. Yes, he forced himself to believe. Surely the Underground would come soon, before the marines could hurt them. Baruch and his officers wouldn't let them suffer at the hands of the Magistrates. They'd come as soon as they could and set them free.

For an hour, Pavel watched the undulating surface of Tikkun flash by beneath the ship, then they started to descend. A barren stretch of the Yaguthian Desert glowed like polished coral in the light of the setting sun. Rocky ridges cast long indigo shadows over the sands.

A man pushed through the crowd, whispering to people, shaking hands, speaking sharply on occasion. Short and thin, he had the lean pointed face of a hungry weasel. Pavel's stomach muscles went tight as he neared.

His voice rasped like stone against sandpaper. "That's a nice little girl you've got."

"Thank you."

"When you get to the camp—*she's a boy*. You understand?"

"No," Pavel said, shaking his head in confusion. "She's a—"

"*Fool!* Don't argue! She's a boy and she's under twelve!"

"But, that doesn't make any sense. Why should we. . . ."

Pavel stopped when Grandpa's hand tightened on his arm. He turned to stare questioningly. The elder's withered face shone with grief.

"We understand," Jasper said softly. "Thank you for telling us."

The weasel man nodded and glanced sorrowfully at Sekan, shaking his head before hurrying away through the crowd, finding and speaking to others with children.

Pavel frowned, holding Grandpa's stern gaze. What possible difference could age and sex make for . . . *work . . . camps.* . . . As understanding dawned, Pavel began to shake. He clutched Yael more closely. "Oh, no."

"What did he mean?" Sekan asked frantically, turning up her tear-bloated face. Red hair dangled in damp curls around her ears. "Jasper?"

"Hurry," Grandpa said in a gentle voice. He produced a key ring with a tiny pair of scissors on it. "We need to cut Yael's hair. Maybe if she looks more like a boy, they won't check."

"Yes, yes." Pavel set her on the floor and smoothed brown curls away from her eyes.

"Jasper. . . ?"

"Shh, Sekan. We'll discuss it later."

Yael's mouth puckered miserably. She looked up at Pavel as though the end of the world had come. Her dark eyes searched his face imploringly. He cursed himself for being such a fool. She couldn't have missed his terrified voice or trembling. He forced a smile and stroked her side.

"Sweetheart, don't cry. I was just being silly. All right? You know I act stupid sometimes. Forgive me. Don't worry."

"You're going to cut off my hair?" she asked, fingering her curls. Tears leaked from her eyes and her chest puffed spasmodically.

"Yes, but it will grow back in no time and you'll be as beautiful as ever. Can you pretend to be a boy? You'll have to be a lot meaner."

"You yell at me when I'm mean."

"I won't this time. Grandpa, let me have those scissors."

Jasper handed them over and Pavel quickly cut Yael's hair very short, leaving bangs over her forehead. When he'd finished, he ruffled her new hairdo and lifted his chin in judgment.

"You're still beautiful," he assured. "You look more like Karyn now."

Yael's eyes glowed suddenly. She smiled that sweet

little girl smile that always melted his heart. "Thank you, Daddy."

"You're welcome. Can you remember to say you're ten, not twelve?"

"I'm ten."

"And you're a boy. Remember?"

"Ten and a boy. Yes, I remember."

"That's my smart angel." He grabbed her and hugged her playfully. "Smart and beautiful."

She giggled, but tears still clung to her lashes. Pavel's throat constricted. "Don't worry, baby. I won't let them hurt you."

"I love you, Dad." She patted his cheek and reached out a hand to Jasper. "And you, too, Grandpa—Auntie."

Jasper took her fingers and kissed them, squeezing them tightly. "You're my best girl."

Sekan leaned over and kissed Yael's forehead.

The ship juddered a little as it set down. When the doors opened, a man outside shouted, "Hurry it up! Come on!"

People flooded out across the vast desert. Pavel looked around at the livid sky behind them, at the tall dark rocks hemming them in on two sides like a prison wall, at the frightened figures stumbling from fatigue on the hot sands. Had he gone crazy? Surely this couldn't be happening.

The gleam of sunset lay like a sheet of translucent lavender over the hostile faces of a hundred guards. A huge building surrounded by a photon fence sprang from the desert. Ships lined the grounds outside, marines lounging in their cool shadows. Cruel smiles lit their faces.

A scream sounded from behind and Pavel whirled. A guard slammed a rifle butt into a woman's jaw. She fell to the sands in a heap, blood gushing from her mouth. People started pushing, jabbing Pavel in the side and his injured spine to make him move forward. He gripped Yael's hand tightly, shuffling through the open gate and into the compound.

"Lord above," Grandpa whispered at Pavel's elbow. "What is this place?"

"It—it looks like more than a work camp," Sekan whimpered. She kneaded Jasper's sleeve in clammy palms as she looked around.

From inside, the photon shield seemed to rise infinitely into the sky, a wall of gold that sparkled in the fading light. Beautiful. The buildings formed a huge square complex. But strangely, no windows or doors dotted the grayness.

"Attention, Gamants!" Someone shouted from near the front of the mob. "Attention!"

Pavel stood on tip-toe to see over the heads of people. A tall, dignified looking man stood on a platform. He had light brown hair and a drooping mustache. His square face made his dartlike nose seem even sharper. His purple uniform stood out brightly against the background of gray buildings.

"Welcome to Block 10," he shouted, smiling pleasantly. "I'm Major Lichtner. You are all political prisoners, *troublemakers,* labeled as dangerous by the Galactic Magistrates. That's why you're here. Your value to the government rests in your ability to tell us about Gamant thought processes. The Magistrates want to know exactly what it is in your brains that causes such disruptive behavior patterns. As a result . . ."

Pavel's knees shook. He couldn't breathe. He felt Grandpa's hand on his arm, holding him up.

Sekan looked with dread from Pavel to Jasper. "What . . . what does he mean?"

"It means Toca may have been the fortunate one," Jasper whispered.

"Move!" a guard shouted and started jamming his rifle barrel into people's backs. "Go on! Head toward the booths! Run! Run!"

As they charged forward, they passed a series of enormous translucent bins. At first no one recognized the contents, then a rumble of gasps went up. The mob stumbled over each other, slowing. The dead eyes of thousands of children stared out, noses smashed against the petrolon, cheeks white and bloodless.

All were in their teens. Over twelve?

Pavel's knees locked. People flooded around him. He stared, unable to pull his gaze away. Tears burned his cheeks. Inside his chest, a violent horror rose.

* * *

CHAPTER 38

Rachel stood in the nighttime corridor outside Tahn's cabin. She felt confused, desperate, her stomach aching. Her mind had gone over and over her conversation with Aktariel in Tverya until she could barely think at all. One thing she knew—every human who'd ever believed him in the past lay dead in a long-forgotten tomb.

And in the back of her distraught mind, the name Yeshwah rang alarmingly. Was Yeshwah ben Yosef the same Yeshwah as in: Avram, Yeshwah, and Sinlayzan, the holy fathers of the People? The possibility struck her frighteningly. What did that mean in the end? If the Yeshwah ben Yosef in Tverya had never known Aktariel, did that mean he hadn't become one of the sacred patriarchs? *Did it mean the Gamant people had ceased to exist in some misty past?* Had Aktariel manipulated the strings of this universe to keep her people alive? *Why?*

Her gaze drifted over the gray ceiling panels, the gray carpet, the dark gray shadows outlining each doorway down the hall. How could human beings live like this? The colorless, odorless environment grated on her nerves, draining her energy.

She closed her eyes, trying to feel again the warm, olive-scented breezes on her face, trying to taste Tzipora's rich wine on her tongue. Aktariel's words about strands and conjunction haunted her, as did his joyful laughter and gentle touch. Both rang some warning bell. The Deceiver. Despite his words aligning deception with temptation, the old teachings proved hard to dispel. Could he make her trust him through deception? Is that why she *wanted* to believe him? When he'd returned her to the *Hoyer* and vanished, a hollow place of longing had torn open in her soul. Soon, very soon, she'd have to decide whether or not to tell Jeremiel the things Aktariel had told her to. She'd held off too long already. But she hadn't been able to force herself to do it because she

347

knew Aktariel was playing his own game and couldn't be certain it didn't culminate in all their deaths. Yet Aktariel seemed so sincere. Could he make her feel that way against her will? Through his power, could he *shape* personal thoughts?

From behind, a tender voice said, "No, Rachel. I don't have the ability to control your thoughts."

Adrenaline flooded her veins. She turned. He stood tall and handsome at the end of the hall, his glow gone. Blond curls brushed his forehead; they seemed almost flaxen against the hood of his chocolate-colored cloak.

"But you read thoughts."

"It's a simple matter once you understand the mechanics of the vortex. Since it's connected to everything, you can follow it anywhere. But your free will is your own. If I could force people to believe things, I wouldn't have had nearly as much trouble with the Deceiver reputation, would I?" His cloak billowed out behind him as he walked forward.

Rachel's muscles tensed instinctively. "Why are you here?"

"We need to have a serious talk."

"Why?"

"You haven't yet told Jeremiel about the Laced Star maneuver the Magistrates have waiting for him. Why not?"

He stopped an arm's length from her, gazing down through magnetic brown eyes. The scent of roses clung to his robe, sweet, delicate.

When she didn't answer, he asked, "Testing me? Have I been wrong before?"

"You don't read thoughts perfectly, I see."

"Especially not ones that are imperfectly formed. Let me help you make the decision you're wavering on. You're afraid to tell Jeremiel?"

She haltingly took two steps away from him. His gaze followed her every movement. "I don't know how to approach him with it. If I go down and tell him—"

"Instead of relying on the 'dream' theory, why don't you tell him the truth?"

She laughed disdainfully. "Oh, yes, if I tell him you're quite real, that'll make him feel better."

"Well." He braced a shoulder against the wall and frowned. In the pewter light, his tanned face had a faint

348

silver sheen along the cheekbones and forehead. "It's not his feelings we're concerned with, is it? We're trying to help him prepare his half-trained crew for the greatest challenge most of them will ever face."

"*Is* that what we're doing?"

She spread her legs, bracing herself, ready for a battle. If she delivered every message he told her to, what would the outcome be? Was he 'pulling strings' to adjust chaotic patterns more to his liking? Who would die this time? Her? Jeremiel? *Sybil?*

"Ah, you think I'm lying to you. For my own gain?" He lifted a hand to thoughtfully stroke his chin. "I'm not going to argue with you, Rachel. I've told you the truth. We'll all pay a tragic price if you don't believe me."

"What price?"

"A few hundred thousand lives. Most of them are currently suffering terribly in the Yaguthian Desert, praying every moment that the Underground is on its way to free them. Would you rather they weren't freed?"

"You're saying I'll be to blame if they die?"

He gazed at her steadily, a curious longing on his face, almost whispers of fear. "Let's just say your actions are critical to their salvation."

"Why can't *you* tell Jeremiel? Why do you need me to serve as your handmaiden? I don't like it!"

"Oh, Rachel, Rachel. . . ." he whispered forlornly. Tenderly, he reached out to stroke her hair. She flinched and he drew back as though she'd burned him. He gazed contemplatively at his fingers before slowly closing his hand. "Rachel, there are many things we don't like in life, but what bearing do they have on duty?"

"Duty?" she whispered incredulously. "*Duty!* If those people's lives mean so much to you, Aktariel, why don't *you* save them? You have powers I can't even conceive of." Desperately, she blurted, "Why don't you destroy all their enemies or . . . or call down twelve legions of angels to save them?"

For a time, he stared hauntingly into her eyes. "I wish you hadn't used that choice of words, but, to answer you, I don't have any angels at my command." He extended a hand to her. *"All I have is you."*

"It was a poor choice of words," she answered coldly. Fear and indecision knotted in her stomach, making her frantic. "Perhaps I should have said *demons.*"

"Oh, Rachel." He shook his head, as though trying to convince himself she hadn't said that. She could feel the noose his charm had thrown around her throat tightening, strangling her.

A warm night-scented wind swept the hall and Rachel jerked around. The vortex whirled outward, huge, spinning to hover around her like black rippling fingers.

Wearily, Aktariel said, "Rachel. Pick up your *Mea* before you go to see Jeremiel. You're going to need it."

He stepped through, melting into the darkness. The black cyclone consumed him before it vanished.

She stood riveted, staring breathlessly at the white hall. What had he meant by that?

"But it's dead. Why would I need it? Aktariel? *Aktariel, tell me why!*"

* * *

Jeremiel stood in the level twenty conference room, lights off, a huge holographic display of Tikkun hanging like a gold, blue, and green ball over the oval table. The three major continents stained the globe irregularly, two in the northern hemisphere, one in the southern. The vast oceans shone deep azure, dotted with thousands of islands.

Avel Harper pointed to a section of the North Amman continent. His black hair glimmered green in the holo's light, accenting the khaki color of his robe. "What about here? This is fairly isolated."

Jeremiel caressed his beard. "True, but we don't know the locations of Magisterial operations in the deserts. And there are no facilities in those regions—just nomadic way stations at the scattered oases."

Harper shrugged. "I don't think that will matter to most of the Horebian refugees. They've always lived precarious lives."

"I know, but starting over is hard enough as it is. I'd rather set them down somewhere where they'll be in the company of like-minded communities."

"That'll be difficult." Harper tapped a wazer pen on the edge of the table. "With the refugees already having split into two distinct groups: Old Believers and Tartarus' Believers. Maybe we should set each group down in a different place?"

Jeremiel heaved a confused sigh. He was a soldier not an expert on long-range social evolution or its techniques. In the Underground fleet, he had professionals who worked out details such as this. He wished he had them here now. What if he made some critical mistake that doomed these people to miserable existences? Mara Kunio's hopeful face prodded him like the barrel of a rifle. "That'll encourage separate evolutions of ideas. Do we want to do that?"

"Well, I don't know, but if we put them together, I can tell you for a fact that we'll be staging a war. Do we want *that?*"

Jeremiel shook his head and frowned at the holo. The place called to him, taunting his cluttered mind with fragments of memories. He saw long roads and tawny fields of barley waving beneath the wind; cool Shabbat evenings of stories and song, robust laughter and gay smiles; starlight falling in pale silver bars over rough-hewn streets lined with squat houses. He hadn't been home in too many years to count. "No. No more war between Gamants."

Harper sat on the edge of the table, thoughtfully studying the globe. The green glimmers of islands seemed to draw his eyes. He lifted a hand, pointing to a new location. "How about these islands off the coast of Samran?"

"For which group?"

"The Tartarus Believers."

"You want to isolate them, you mean."

Harper shrugged. "Might not be a bad idea for a few years. That'll give them a chance to work out the specifics of their belief system and stabilize their social structure."

Jeremiel pulled out a chair and propped a boot on it as he considered. The Samran Four Islands had a lush, tropical environment with hundreds of native food resources, mostly vegetable, though. Horebians accustomed to a largely meat diet would have to make a substantial shift of emphasis—but they'd have plenty of food, and he could arrange a staff of teachers from Tikkun's Underground University to help them the first few years. A malevolent voice in his mind taunted that he ought to just let them all die, that that was what they deserved after the horrors wrought by their belief system on Horeb and the murders they'd committed on the ship. But they were Gamants—despite their fanatical attachment to curious new philosophies. Zadok had once told him it was that ability to change, to adapt the religion to new times and strange places, that kept Gamant culture alive.

"All right. The Samran Four for Tartarus' Believers. How about the others?"

Harper lifted his brows and folded his arms. "You tell me. We need a safe place where the Old Believers will be among similar religious rigorists."

Jeremiel reached over to the control panel on the table and hit the appropriate button to set the globe spinning. Continents rotated slowly, flashing alternately in amber and green. Much of the rest of the planet consisted of empty ocean, but a few ancient communities thrived on distant islands, holding diligently to the Old Ways. Their daily lives swelled with mystical precepts based on the magical papyrii found in cubbyholes around the galaxy —allegedly they'd originally come from Old Earth, pirated during the Middoth Exile.

"I suppose the most deeply religious communities exist off the continent of Yihud." He stood and went to the holo, indicating a clump of islands known locally as the Sacla Seven. Filled with high volcanic peaks and rich soil, a wealth of bird and fish life provided the major dietary element. Nut trees abounded as well.

"How exclusivistic are they? Will they accept a new horde of sibling believers?"

"I suspect they'll welcome them with open arms. Saclans have a reputation for being charitable to a fault. They adopt strangers—people they consider true seekers —almost immediately, making them part of respected families in an elaborate ceremony of anointing. Old Believers will have no problem fitting in."

Harper nodded. In the flashes of rotating gold and green, his dark skin gleamed like polished mahogany. He tugged absently at the collar of his robe. "It sounds good. Do you have any reservations about either of those locations?"

"No. We'll just have to assure ourselves that no Magisterial programs have been initiated which might harm the refugees' ability to assimilate the new environment."

"Agreed." He stood up and glanced again at the whirling globe. "Well, I'll see to the organization of the shuttles. I think I'll dispatch the Tartarus Believers first, if that sounds all right. There are more of them."

"Yes. Good. That will also leave the trainees in place on board until the last minute."

"True, that way we'll have a reserve of talent in case we need them. Speaking of which, before I left my cabin, I got a message from Halloway. She says her duties trying to keep the crew together preclude her from meeting with you personally on a regular basis anymore. She requests you assign an intermediary to operate between you."

Jeremiel's brows lowered, a sudden hollowness pounding in his chest. It fueled an angry fire that had been building for days. Sharply, he ordered, "Negative. I've no intention of giving her more time to complete her plots with Tahn. Deny the request. No . . . no, I'll talk to her myself."

"Affirmative. Before I go, do you want to discuss Plans A and B more? I think I have contingencies C and D staffed out, but—"

"Janowitz and Rachel are key players. Do they understand their roles?"

Harper nodded with certainty. "Yes. As a matter of fact, Chris has been foaming at the mouth to begin the isolation process."

"And Rachel? Is she ready for her role with Tahn?"

"I think so. She balked when I first told her she'd be his only guard during the battle, but she seems to have accepted. . . ."

He stopped as the door to the conference snicked open. In the brilliant white light that flooded the room from the corridor, Rachel stood tall, black hair cascading in thick waves around her shoulders. Her brown jumpsuit showed dirt around the cuffs.

Jeremiel frowned. Her face glowed an unnatural ashen shade. "Come in, Rachel."

She stepped inside and the door closed, leaving them in the yellow glare of the holo. She glanced at Harper. "Hello, Avel."

"How are you, Rachel?"

"Fine, thanks. Would you mind if I speak to Jeremiel?" Obviously, she meant alone.

"Not at all," Harper responded, bowing obligingly. "I think I'll start working on the passenger lists for each shuttle."

"Thank you, Avel. Let me know your final arrangements."

"I will." He strode for the door, nodding pleasantly to Rachel before he exited. She barely seemed to notice. Her huge eyes were riveted on the globe spinning over the table.

In a clipped voice, she said, "That's Tikkun, isn't it?"

"Yes."

"Where's the Yaguthian Desert?"

He cocked his head curiously, but turned around, drawing a rough circle around the dark basin east of Derow. "About here. Why?"

She seemed to be watching him breathlessly, like a tiger stalking a gazelle, waiting for *the* movement before making her own. It made the hair at the back of his neck prickle.

"Is something wrong, Rachel?"

"Yes. Charles Lichtner is the current military governor of Tikkun and he's confined a number of people to that desert region. I don't know why."

He felt like she'd just kicked out his guts. Syene's voice filled his mind. He leaned heavily back against the table, gripping the edge with hard hands. "*Lichtner. . . ?* How do you know?"

"I was going through some classified security files and found his name listed."

A sharp pain pounded in his head, like flashes of electrical arcs trying to connect up with his throat to form a cry of agony. He rubbed a hand over his flushed face. "Which files? I'll want to review them."

"They're under the heading of Neurophysiological Experiments. Nineteen-one-one-eight."

"*Neuro . . .*" Sterilization . . . relocation. . . . Brain experiments? Stunned, he didn't even think to ask how she'd accessed a file he'd never have thought to. "I'll check it immediately."

She slowly walked around to lean next to him against the table and he felt her unspoken words like a brisk slap. His face stung with a rush of blood.

"Is there something else, Rachel?"

She wet her lips, letting her hand rest on the butt of her holstered pistol. Her fingers clutched the gray petrolon like a child's security blanket. Green from the holo flashed in her black eyes, then gold. She didn't look like she wanted to tell him. He kept quiet, observing numbly the struggle on her beautiful face. "Jeremiel, do you know what a Laced Star maneuver is?"

"Yes." He pinned her dark eyes with his own and fear crept like a deadly virus through him. "Why?"

"Those five ships that Slothen dispatched? They're converging on Tikkun from different directions and they already have us located on their. . . ."

He lurched away from the table, staring at her in terrified disbelief, lungs heaving. Lord in heaven, did she have the remotest idea what she'd just said? The Laced Star was nearly impossible to defeat if a commander fell into the trap. Being caught in the midst of the maneuver was a death sentence!

"How do you know that?"

She gazed up at the holo. Black hair glistened like a curtain of spun silk around her shoulders. Tikkun rotated, its motion now appearing labored, turning in a slow agonizing roll of anticipation. "I beg you to trust me and not ask."

He shook his head violently. "*What?* Tell me!"

"Jeremiel, I—I can't."

"We're not discussing more of your dreams, are we? Because if so, I've got no time for—"

"*I'm telling you the truth! Listen to me!*"

"And how do you know something that neither I nor any of my top communications staff have. . . ."

The air went out of his lungs. For an awful moment, his life floated in a timeless void of distrust. Old aches surfaced, seizing his mind, twisting it into new and horrifying patterns. Like a clock ticking off distinct known sequences and their relationships, his mind correlated, correlated. The hot fire that seared his veins burned all the way to his bones. Calmly, he said, "Janowitz told me you've been spending a lot of time with Tahn—*alone.*"

"That's not true. I've seen him twice."

"Why?"

She shook her head in confusion, searching his stern face. "To talk. He's helped me with some physics problems I've been studying. And other things. I have the right to a personal life, too. Don't I?"

He straightened slowly, memories swirling, seeing Syene's tormented face, hearing his own insistent voice,

"He has a personal life, too. Leave it be. I trust him."
Goddamn it, how could Rachel have said that so blithely, knowing as she did about Dannon and Syene? Had Tahn confided in her? Bought her off? Seduced her? A feeling of bottomless dread swallowed his objectivity.

"No, Rachel. You don't have the right to a personal life. Not when it involves the enemies of Gamant civilization. What the hell are you doing? *Trading information?*" In a flood of angry despair, he shook both fists. "Rachel, I'm sorry. Forgive me. It's just that—I must know. Where did you hear that information?"

"Jeremiel. . . ." her voice faltered. As though immersed in a subjective world of nightmare, her eyes took on a faraway look. Then, insistently, she responded, "You know I would never hurt you or Gamant civilization. Can't you just accept on faith that I—"

"No! The game is too desperate for me to alter my carefully laid plans based upon *faith.* I need *facts.* And if you're right about the Laced Star, I'd damned well better start making new plans or we'll all be dead! Did Tahn tell you about it?"

She shook her head.

Almost tangibly, like the foul breath of a dying beast, he felt a presence swelling in the dark corners of the room. It grew to monstrous proportions in only a few moments. His mind went back in guarded terror to the desperate days on Kayan after Zadok's death, to the shadowy creature that had attacked and stolen the last *Mea* from Sarah Calas' very hands. A vague ripple touched the darkness, moving toward Rachel.

In a velvet smooth movement, Jeremiel drew his pistol. "Rachel, get back!"

"What's wrong?"

"Don't you see it?"

"What?" Her gaze searched the blackness.

"I don't know. Some . . . *shadow.* Like the one we both saw in the caves of the Desert Fathers!" He backed up, fingering the trigger of his gun.

Rachel took a step toward him and a sudden flash of brilliant blue lit the room. Startled, he jerked around. The light pulsed from beneath the brown fabric of her jumpsuit.

"Rachel. . . ?"

"Oh," she murmured in a choking voice. "No!

356

Aktariel? Not Jeremiel. NO!"

Aktariel?

As though in pain, she groaned, "Oh, no. It burns. It *burns!*" A small cry of agony escaped her lips as she gripped the chain around her neck and pulled a *Mea* over her head. She threw it on the table. The gold chain curled around the sacred globe like a living serpent.

For a time, they simply stared at it, both breathing hard. Then Jeremiel cautiously reached out and grasped the chain. The *Mea* flared more brilliantly in his hand, casting a cerulean blaze over the room. "I thought every *Mea* in the universe had vanished. Where did you get this?"

"Adom."

"Why didn't you tell me you had it?" The longer he held the sacred device, the warmer the chain grew against his palm. He could feel the heat rolling off the globe. All his anxieties about Rachel seemed to increase. Had she traveled through the gate to the Veil of God where all the preexisting events of creation were recorded? Was that how she knew so much about the future? He'd never really believed in the sacred journey to the Veil.

"I thought it was useless," she defended. "The glow had died."

"Indeed. It seems to be fine now. Was it dead when Adom gave it to you?"

"No. It died. . . ." Words tumbled end over end in a flood, as though she feared if she didn't spout them all at once, her courage would fail. "Jeremiel, when I was at the pole, I—I dreamed I went to talk to Epagael. We argued about suffering and I called him a monster for allowing it to exist. That's when the light in the *Mea* went out. And Aktariel told me later that it was dead, that Epagael had locked the gate to me."

He stood resolutely silent.

"Jeremiel, *listen to me.* Unless there's no other way, don't use it. Do you hear me? It will turn all your dreams to dust."

A shiver played along his arms. "I believe you." The *Mea* ooomed to hear for it flared even brighter, so bright he had to shield his eyes against the glare.

"Oh," Rachel murmured.

A heartbeat later, he heard her steps heading for the door. A white rectangle of light briefly lit the room, then vanished when the door slipped closed.

He sank back against the table, seating himself on the edge as he slowly lowered his arm. White swirls, like sea foam, eddied across the surface of the *Mea*.

He glanced back at the wall again, seeking the black form that had drifted through the room. He'd seen it twice before. Once on Kayan. Once on Horeb. Each time, it had heralded a massive upheaval in the course of the future.

He lifted his sleeve and wiped his forehead. Taking a deep breath, he held it for several seconds before boldly calling, "Aktariel? Are you here? If you are—talk to me. *I'll do anything you want.* Just help me put these refugees down safely and . . . and tell me how to blow up Palaia Station."

CHAPTER 39

Ornias sauntered around the bridge conference room on the *Klewe,* idly studying the holos of Old Earth that decorated the walls. Dressed in a long sable robe, Gamant style, he looked kingly. The glass of Cassopian sherry in his hand echoed the color of his light brown hair and braided beard. At the other end of the room Erinyes tapped a wazer pen impatiently on the table.

"It's a *ridiculous* idea," Erinyes commented haughtily.

"You're a man of limited perceptions, Captain." Ornias strolled to the next holo on the wall, admiring the red and gray banded canyon that rose out of the sunrise mists. He sipped his sherry. "Only pathetically ordinary men are upset by discussions of assassination or kidnapping. I thought you had more backbone."

Erinyes snorted and leaned back in his chair, folding his arms. "Backbone has little to do with rationality. Your idea makes no military sense."

"Of course, not." Ornias lifted a brow. "I want something that *works.*"

Erinyes furiously tapped his pen. "Gen Abruzzi will never go for such a plan and I seriously doubt that even that half-wit, Bogomil, will." He stabbed out a finger menacingly. "Your plan may get a lot of Magisterial soldiers killed."

"Surely you can arrange to have Bogomil's strategy altered, can't you? All we have to do is drop out of his Laced Star maneuver."

Erinyes shook his head as though in disbelief. "Ambassador, really. You can't expect me to use my influence on your petty, questionable—"

"It's up to you, of course," Ornias said, smiling unpleasantly. "If you don't think you can handle it, tell me. I'll talk to Slothen myself." Military people annoyed him. Few of them had the elasticity of morals necessary to win truly important battles. Oh, they understood brute force, but shrewd diplomacy left them floundering.

Erinyes looked like he'd swallowed something bitter. "I can handle *anything,* Ambassador. You'll do well to watch your tongue in my presence."

"Does that mean you're willing to discuss it with Slothen, then?"

"Certainly not!" Erinyes shouted, rising out of his chair in fury. "I wouldn't . . . wouldn't. . . ." He stopped, slowly lowering himself back into his chair. "Did you see that?"

Ornias blinked incredulously. "What?"

"I don't know. I thought I saw a black patch on the wall behind you."

Ornias whirled breathlessly, but saw nothing. In irritation, he snapped, "Let's get back to our discussion. Why aren't you willing to talk to Slothen? Surely talking can't hurt—"

"What? You weren't listening to me, Ambassador. I said *of course,* I'd tran Palaia."

Ornias frowned, blinking curiously. "You did? Well . . . good." Lifting his glass, he finished the sherry to the last drop and set the goblet on the table. "I take it, then, that you agree with my plan?"

"Yes, yes!" Erinyes blurted, pounding a fist into the table. His cheeks had flushed fuschia. "But, listen, Tetrax, *I'll handle the arrangements.* Most men of our ilk can't tolerate the thought of using a child for political gain."

"Believe me, Captain, that little boy will prove a gem in our hands."

"Yes, I suspect you're quite right." Erinyes shoved his chair back roughly and stood. "I'll contact Slothen."

Erinyes strode headlong from the conference room. When the door snicked shut behind him, Ornias tilted his head and shook it, then went back to examining the holos.

* * *

Sybil sat morosely on the floor of Mikael's cabin, methodically tying and untying her green shoes. Mikael watched her anxiously. She'd come in a half hour ago and slumped in the corner, barely talking to him. Brown curls hid most of her face, but every so often she would glance up at him and he could see the hurt in her eyes.

"Sybil? Want to see something really neat? Huh, do you?"

No answer.

He backed a few steps away, then turned and trotted to his closet. Pulling out the three stamps Captain Tahn had given him, he carefully carried them back and knelt beside her. She didn't look up.

He laid the stamps out on the floor by her shoe, putting the pretty one with an old-fashioned starship painted purple in the middle. "Sybil? Look, I want to show you these. This one, on the left, it's from Jubilee. And this one over here, on the right, it came from Bohairic. These ships are both freighters, they carried things like clothes and food to other planets a long time ago. Like a million years, or something."

"Nobody was alive a million years ago," she corrected meanly.

"Well, okay. Anyway, how long doesn't really matter." He looked up to see if she was still listening. She'd stopped tying her shoe. The laces stretched like thick spaghetti over the floor. But she seemed to be paying attention. "And this one," Mikael continued swiftly, tapping the one in the center. "This one with the purple ship came from Old Earth. It's really old. Captain Tahn told me to take good care of it, that someday it might be worth something."

"Well, what is it?"

"Oh, it's a—"

"It *was*."

"Sure. It *was* the first star freighter. See these weird pointed things hanging off the sides? Those are guns. People were afraid when they first went into space. They thought monsters lived there."

"Monsters *do*. What do you think the Magistrates are? Monsters if I ever saw one."

He felt like the wind had been knocked out of him. He stared at the floor.

Sybil glanced at him and wiped her sleeve under her nose. "And anyway, I don't care."

He slumped to the floor to sit cross-legged beside her. "What's wrong, Sybil? You're pretty mean today."

"I don't know. I have a stomach ache."

"Maybe you should drink a carbono. They always make my stomach feel better."

"What are they? I've never had one."

He jumped to his feet and ran to the drink dispenser, programming it. When the glass came out, he walked slowly, trying to keep it from spilling over the sides, but some did anyway. "Here. Try this."

"Okay." Sybil straightened a little and took the glass from his hand.

"They taste like Kayan coconuts. You'll like them, I bet."

"I don't like very many things."

He licked his lips anxiously as he watched her take the first sip. She frowned and he wilted, then a faint smile came to her face. She had a white mustache of foam on her upper lip when she turned to look at him.

"It's good, Mikael. Thanks."

Relieved, he sat down again and studied her pensively. "How's your stomach now?"

"It doesn't hurt near as bad."

He smiled, watching her take another long drink. In the bright light, her olive skin seemed to have washed to a pale clay color. Against the background of white walls, her green pants and brown shirt stood out more than her face. But he figured his blue pants and shirt made his face seem pretty white, too, so he didn't worry about it anymore.

Trying to cheer her up, he said, "Sybil, I'm sure glad your mom's been letting you come so much this past week. It makes me feel better to have somebody to. . . ."

He stopped, seeing her face pucker. She bowed her

head and her shoulders shook with silent tears. Horror gripped him. Had he said something bad? Something that hurt her?

He scooted closer to her and timidly patted her arm, stuttering, "I—I'm sorry, Sybil. Sometimes, I—I say stupid things and don't know it. I didn't mean to, though."

She put down her glass and drew up her knees. Bracing her forehead on them, she cried softly. Mikael bit his lower lip. He tried to look anywhere except at Sybil, at his bed, the bathroom door, the checkers game set up on the table.

After a minute or two, he noticed Sybil's shoe was still untied and he leaned forward and put a double knot in it for her. He'd tried to teach her to do that so they wouldn't come undone so often, but she hadn't got it right yet. Which was okay. He didn't mind doing it for her.

A tear leaked out to run down her arm and Mikael felt very bad inside himself, like somebody'd punched him in the stomach.

"Sybil? I'm sorry. . . . I didn't mean—"

"It's not you!" she said sharply.

"Well, if it wasn't because I said something stupid, why are you crying?"

"Because . . . because . . . ." She gave him a threatening glare. "You better not ever tell anybody. You understand? *Nobody!*"

He nodded quickly. "I won't!"

"It's a secret. A big bad secret. Okay?"

"Sure. I get it."

She wiped her eyes on her sleeve and sucked in a jerky breath. Her mouth puckered miserably again, trembling. "Something's wrong with my mom."

He shifted positions, crawling to sit in front of her so he could see her downcast face. "Like what?"

"I don't know."

She cried silently for a little bit again and Mikael reached out to pat her foot. "You mean she's acting funny? Parents do that a lot. It doesn't mean anything bad."

"She's acting real funny."

Sybil cocked her head helplessly and he figured she didn't really want to talk about it because it hurt. He

362

remembered how he'd felt when his mom had been trying to talk to the leaders of the revolts on Kayan. She'd yelled at him all the time and he hadn't wanted to talk to anybody. But maybe if he'd had somebody to talk for him, he would have felt better. Maybe he could talk for Sybil?

"Sybil?" he said softly. "Before my mom died, you know what? She was cross with me all the time. I didn't know why and I felt like maybe I'd die or something 'cause it hurt so bad? You understand?"

"Yeah," she croaked.

"Then one night I made her sit on the side of my bed and talk to me. She told me she was being mean because the leaders of the revolts on Kayan thought she was crazy, 'cause she told them how my grandfather used to go through the *Mea* to heaven to talk to God. They didn't believe it—but it was true."

She looked up cautiously. "Yeah?"

"Yeah. Sure."

"But I—I tried to make my mom talk to me and she just shouted like—like I was being bad or something."

Tears welled in her eyes again, and he nodded his understanding. "My mom used to do that, too. 'Cause she was scared."

"Of what?"

"She was afraid the Magistrates would come and scorch us because of how the revolts were tearing up the Magistrates' big military houses."

"Those are called 'installations,' bozon."

He smiled and lowered his eyes. "Okay, military installations. They looked like big houses all hooked together."

Sybil laughed shortly and punched his arm hard. He jerked away, grabbing it and laughing. She still had tears in her eyes, but her smile made it seem okay.

"Mikael?"

"What?"

"Did your mom ever talk in her sleep?" She held her breath and looked up at him from beneath her lashes. Her brown hair had fallen into the tears on her face and stuck to her cheeks.

"I don't know. We had different chambers. She said I was too big to sleep with her anymore."

Sybil's mouth pursed disdainfully. "That's silly.

You're not too big until you get to be twelve or something. My parents let me sleep with them all the time."

He nodded. "I always wanted to, but she wouldn't let me. Does your mom talk in her sleep?"

"Yeah." Her voice trailed off and she frowned at the floor, fiddling with her double-knotted laces. "Sometimes."

"What does she say? Bad things?"

"I don't know what most of them mean. Do you know what null singularities are?"

He shook his head. "But dreams are crazy. Sometimes they're just weird and don't mean anything."

"But sometimes they do."

"Oh, you mean like the dreams you have about you and me fighting battles against the Magistrates?"

She nodded, scrunching up her face. "They mean something important."

"Yeah, but those are *funny*, funny dreams. They're different."

He watched her fingers fumbling with the laces of her other shoe and leaned forward, taking the laces from her hands. "Here, let me tie it. Now, watch how I do this." He double-knotted them real slow, so she could tell what he did. "See that?"

"Yeah," she said, but he could tell she hadn't really watched. "Someday maybe we'll work on it again."

"Okay." He looked at her and held her gaze. Some deep hurt crawled out of her eyes. "So what kinds of things does your mom say?"

"Oh, things about the Mashiah. And you know, Mikael, I think maybe she liked him. I think maybe . . . maybe she even loved him."

She looked up suddenly, as though expecting him to shout bad things at her. Did her mother do that?

He shrugged and stretched out on his side, propping his head on his hand. He smoothed his fingers over the soft fibers in the carpet. "What if she did? What difference would it make?"

"A lot. He killed my dad."

"Yeah, but maybe he didn't mean to and she found that out."

"What makes you think so?"

"I don't know. But I've heard Uncle Yosef talk about

how bad that High Councilman was. What was his name?"

"Ornias. He was a pig."

"So maybe he did it and blamed it on the Mashiah? Who knows? Your mom wouldn't like the Mashiah unless he was really okay, would she?"

Sybil shook her head sternly. Her brown curls bounced. "No, she's too smart."

She squinted hard at his arm for a while.

"So what else does she say in her sleep."

Sybil glanced at him fearfully and his stomach gurgled. He patted it to make it be quiet.

"Mikael, this is even a bigger, badder secret."

"It's okay. I keep secrets good."

Sybil brushed hair out of her eyes and took a deep breath. "Okay, listen, I'm going to tell you everything. But you can't ever tell anybody else. She—she talks a lot about Epagael. Like she was living through a time when she talked to him. And it's bad stuff."

"Some people can go talk to God. My grandfather did it all the time. But I think you have to have a *Mea*."

A swallow bobbed in Sybil's throat. "She does, Mikael."

"She does?" Excitement went through him. He opened his mouth dramatically. "Why didn't you ever tell me? That means God likes her. That's good."

"Maybe. I'm not sure."

"But talking to God's always good."

"But. . . ." She looked horrible, like she wanted to say something but was afraid to.

"I'll believe whatever you say, Sybil. What?"

"Maybe I won't tell you that part yet. It's pretty scary. You might have bad dreams like I do." She squinted at him.

"I don't like bad dreams. But one or two would be okay I guess. I want to know. Tell me?"

She played with her brown sleeve for a little while, then lay down beside him, stretching out with her face real close and serious.

"Mikael?"

"What?"

"Sometimes my mom acts likes she's talking to Aktariel, too."

He blinked, fear rising like a black balloon in his chest, but he tried to hide it. God had thrown that wicked angel out of heaven. He was the Deceiver. He lied to people all the time to trick them into doing bad things that hurt God. "What does she say about him? I have nightmares about him sometimes, too."

"These are different," Sybil said gravely. "She talks to him like he was in the room with us, standing right by her bed."

"Do you see him?"

"No . . . no, I never do. But it's kind of like having a ghost in the cabin at night. I snuggle down under my blanket and cover up my head. And sometimes I cry. Because my mom cries a lot. Like—like he makes her feel bad, guilty, or scared, or something."

He tilted his head, thinking about it. It didn't make any sense. If Sybil's mom had a *Mea* and could go talk to God, that would make Aktariel leave her alone. That bad angel was afraid of God. Just like everybody else.

Sybil's face puckered again and she squeezed her eyes closed, crying softly. She rolled over onto her stomach and buried her face on her arm. He shrugged helplessly.

"Sybil? It's okay." He slid closer to her until he pressed against her side, then he put his arm around her and rested his head on her shoulder, patting her opposite arm.

"It's okay, Sybil. I bet she's just having regular dreams. Not *funny* ones. You probably shouldn't be scared."

But he was. He felt like he had a snake crawling in his guts.

She turned hurt eyes on him. "Mikael? If I call my mom and ask her if I can sleep with you, will you let me?"

"Sure. I haven't had a friend to sleep with in a long time."

"Really?"

"Yeah, I don't care. Do you want to go home and get some stuff, like a nightgown or toothbrush?"

"No!" Sybil's eyes got big. "No, I—I don't want to go back at all. Not tonight. I'm too scared."

"Okay. That's all right with me."

She smiled and sat up, wiping her nose on the tail of her shirt which had pulled out of her pants when she'd lain down. "Thanks, Mikael. I'm real scared tonight. Someday, when my mom's all right again, if you're feeling bad, you can come sleep with me, too."

He sat up, returning her smile. "Okay. Why don't you call your mom and see if it's okay?"

"All right." Sybil shoved to her feet to run to the com on the wall over the table. Mikael watched her, a kind smile on his face and she heaved a sigh. He made her feel better, like maybe things really would be okay.

She crawled into the chair and stood on her knees, then punched in her room number. "Mom? It's me, Sybil. Could I spend the night with Mikael? He said it would be okay."

No answer. Sybil glanced fearfully at him. But he just shrugged.

"Ask again. Maybe she was in the bathroom or asleep or something."

She nodded. "Mom? Are you awake?"

"Sybil?" her mother's tense voice came back. "Are you all right?"

"Yeah, Mom. Are *you* all right?"

"Yes. I—I. . . . Are you coming home now?"

"I wanted to know if I could spend the night with Mikael. He has some neat things to show me, like his stamp collection and—"

"Yes, you can stay overnight. But call me first thing tomorrow morning, all right? I want you here for breakfast."

Sybil smiled happily at Mikael. He smiled back. "Thanks, Mom. I love you."

"I love you, too, sweetheart. Good night."

"Good night, Mom."

Sybil jumped off the chair and let out a war whoop, making it last as long and as loud as she could. When she finished, she put her hands on her hips proudly. "Can you do it that long?"

"I don't think so, but let me try." He took a very deep breath and threw back his head, howling like a stone wolf on the hunt.

Sybil lifted her brows, impressed, prepared to tell Mikael how good that was, but he stopped in mid-yell. A crazy look came over his face.

He tilted his head as if listening. "What?"

Sybil shook her head. "I didn't say anything."

His jaw slackened, face going so pale his hair looked blacker than black. He seemed to be staring at the ceiling. Sybil turned to look up, too, but saw nothing very interesting.

"What, Grandfather?" Mikael asked nervously. "Tell me again, I didn't hear you."

Sybil's eyes jerked back to him and she felt suddenly queasy. He hadn't been talking to her. In a sudden burst of light, the *Mea* around his neck glowed like a blue sun, drowning out the white light of the lustreglobes. It flared so brilliantly, the walls turned as blue as the noon sky. She lifted a hand to shield her eyes.

Breathing hard, Sybil backed away, dropping into one of the chairs by the table.

"Yes, Grandfather, I know. He's come to talk to me before. I'm not scared."

He tilted his head forward so that his chin rested on his chest. "No, sir. He came to see me on Kayan. He got me off the planet before the Magistrates scorched it. He saved my life because he said I was the new leader of Gamant civilization and people needed me. Why didn't the archangel Michael tell you before that God had sent Metatron to help me?"

Sybil struggled to listen and could hear a faint, ever so faint, buzz coming from the *Mea*. Is that where his grandfather lived? *In the* Mea*?* Her eyes widened and she felt her cheeks get hot. The voice she'd heard coming out of her mother's *Mea* had sounded like her dad. Could he live in that *Mea*? Excitement swept her and her hands shook. She stuck them under her arms to keep them warm. She'd have to ask Mikael.

He'd know.

He knew lots of things about *Meas* that she didn't.

"Yes, Grandfather," Mikael said lovingly. "When I talk to Slothen, I'll tell him."

As though becoming suddenly aware of her presence, Mikael looked at Sybil and smiled broadly. Nervously, she smiled back.

"Grandfather? Before you go, can I ask you sumpthin'?"

The buzz sank even lower.

"I have a friend now. Her name's Sybil. Can I tell her about you? She's keeps secrets real good."

His face darkened as he listened. "All right. That part

I'll keep secret until you tell me it's okay." He went quiet again, then a slow smile crept over his face and he nodded heartily. "Thank you, Grandfather. I love you. Tell Epagael I'll try to make everything okay for Him here. Sybil promised to help."

Mikael bowed his head for a long minute and Sybil found herself sitting on the edge of her seat, waiting. Finally, he looked up and laughed.

"I can tell you!"

"You can?"

"Yeah, Grandfather says it's okay." He squinted suddenly. "But you can't tell anybody else."

"I won't. I promise."

Mikael got up and ran to her, resting a hand on her shoulder and looking down radiantly. "Sybil. You're the best friend I've ever had. My cousin Shilby used to be a pretty good friend, but we fought a lot. You're a better friend. You don't hit me."

"I wouldn't hit you. I like you, Mikael. Unless you hit me first, then I'd wallop you good." She playfully shook a fist at him.

He grabbed it and laughed, pulling her out of the chair. She landed on the floor with a loud thud. He fell beside her and hugged her. Sybil felt funny having him hug her, but she hugged him back, guessing it was okay. Someday, they'd lead a war together. She guessed the sooner they got to be real good friends the better.

They wrestled for a while, laughing until their stomachs ached. Then when Mikael finally got on top again, he let her arms go and looked down at her, his smile fading to a serious look.

"Sybil? I won't ever hit you. Not even if you hit me first."

"Why not? That would be okay. If I hit you, you can hit me just as hard. My dad told me once. My friend Moshe used to knock me down in the school yard and try to kiss me. So I smacked him good."

Mikael got up, standing awkwardly and looking down at her. "But maybe I won't anyway. I think I'd feel worse if I hit you than if I didn't. And I don't like feeling bad."

She propped herself up on her elbows and noisily blew hair out of her eyes. "Yeah, I think I'd feel pretty bad, too. Maybe we just won't hit each other."

He smiled, lifting his eyebrows. "That sounds good to

me. Hey, do you want to go to bed now?"

Sybil got up and started unbuttoning her shirt. She noticed curiously that he watched her with a shy nervousness. She threw her shirt over the back of a chair, then took off her pants and did the same. Standing in the middle of the room in her undershirt and panties, she propped her hands on her hips and eyed him inquisitively.

"Aren't you going to get undressed?"

"Oh, sure." He slipped his shirt over his head and got out of his pants, leaving both lying in a pile on the floor. He just had on shorts. He looked skinny.

Sybil gazed at his clothes on the floor and frowned, but figured since he didn't have a mother to yell at him, it would be all right. She walked past him to get into his bed and scooted to the back, propping her head on her hand.

He smiled suddenly and ran to turn the lights down real low, sort of like a nightlight, then climbed in bed. They snuggled warmly beside each other and Sybil felt good. For the first time since her father had gotten killed on Horeb, she wasn't afraid of the dark.

She looked at Mikael's face and noticed that he had a black mole beneath his left ear. "Mikael? Sometimes I don't sleep too good. Maybe if I have bad dreams, you could pat me?"

He nodded, biting his lower lip. "Sure. You bet."

"Okay, this is a night of secrets. What did your grandfather say? Does he live in the *Mea*?"

Mikael reached under the blanket to grab her hand and squeeze it hard. She squeezed back. With his opposite hand, he took the *Mea* out and laid it on top of the sheet covering his chest. It shone over the room. Sybil prodded it with her finger. Then jerked back at the unusual warmth it threw out.

"This is different than the one my mom has."

"It is?"

"Hers is cold and only comes on when I touch it."

He frowned. "That's weird. I thought they glowed all the time."

"Hers doesn't. So, does your grandfather live in the *Mea*?"

He let out a breath. "Yeah. God put him there so he could talk to me."

"Why does he have to?"

In the blue glow cast by the *Mea*, she saw him swallow. "Sybil, you know those *funny* dreams you have?"

"Yeah, what about them? Sometimes they're real scary."

He rolled over on his side to stare hard at her. They looked at each other for a long time without saying anything, and she fidgeted, pulling the blanket up around her neck.

Finally, Mikael whispered, "My grandfather says they're true. That someday I have to lead the war. But first, I have to talk to Magistrate Slothen. Lots of people are going to get killed, but we can't help it. It has to happen."

"Okay, so if we have to, we have to."

"But you know what's the bad part? You kind of made me afraid when you were talking about your mom and Aktariel."

He fiddled with the sheet and Sybil said, "Why?"

"Because the final battle between Epagael and Aktariel. . . . Did you learn about it in school? My grandfather taught me."

"I learned about it." She flopped back on the bed and made an explosion with her mouth while throwing out her hands. "Everything's going to get burned to a crisp and only Epagael Believers will get saved. Right?"

"Yeah. But . . . you and me? The battle we lead helps Epagael."

"Of course. We wouldn't help Aktariel. He's a bad guy."

Mikael timidly reached over and stroked her arm. "Yeah. I knew you'd know that. I'm glad you're going to be there to help me, Sybil. I'd be real afraid if I was by myself."

"I won't let you be afraid, Mikael. Besides, you've got Metatron to help you, too. So is the war starting soon? Is that what your grandfather was telling you?"

"Pretty soon."

"You know what? One time, I put my mom's *Mea* to my head and I heard a voice, too. Do you think my dad could live in my mom's *Mea*? I think it was his voice coming out."

He chewed the insides of his cheeks for a while. "I don't know. I don't think so. I think my grandfather living in one is pretty different. It's the first time I ever heard of it. But maybe." He lifted his shoulders. "God does some weird things sometimes."

"Yeah, I guess."

"You know what else, Sybil?"

"What?"

"I really have to see Mister Baruch." He looked away and his mouth puckered. "I have a secret I need to tell him."

"Hasn't he come to talk to you yet?"

Mikael shook his head like it really bothered him. "He tried to a couple of times when I was asleep, but he's been pretty busy since."

A small thread of anger and surprise went through Sybil's chest. "I bet he forgot, Mikael. But, hey! I know him real good. *I'll* take you to see him."

"Can you?"

"Sure, you bet." Her forehead lined with concentration. "Maybe tomorrow or the next day."

Mikael rolled over on his side and put his arm around her, hugging her tightly. "You're my best friend, Sybil. I think maybe you and me together can do just about anything."

"Yeah. Me, too."

They shared a smile and talked long into the night, until Sybil's eyes felt so heavy she couldn't keep them open. She yawned and let them fall closed. Mikael kept talking for a while, the sound of his voice soothing in her ears. The last thing she felt was him curling around her, "spooning her," her mother called it, because it looked like two spoons fitting together. She nuzzled back against him, feeling how warm his legs were against hers. He put an arm around her and squeezed her shoulders.

"You and me and Metatron, Sybil, we're going to make everything all right for God here."

She nodded sleepily, drifting off . . . drifting into a *funny* dream. It was like she was floating, up high, near a tall ceiling. Down below her, a horrible blue creature leaned back in his chair and twined his fingers together like a braided rope. . . .

* * *

CHAPTER 40

Carey Halloway drew her saffron shawl around her shoulders, letting the long fringe drape down over her bare legs. Just out of the shower, she'd put on a silver gossamer sleep shirt which hung below her hips. She sat on the chilly floor of her cabin, gazing up at the magnificent peaks of the Tetons. Their coral color salved her tormented soul like the soft strokes of a pink silk scarf across her face. A candle burned in the center of her table, casting a tawny glow over the room.

"You're being a goddamned fool," she whispered roughly to herself.

A tight band of self-pity and resentment constricted her chest. Through her emotional haze, she caught the sweet scent of soap drifting from the shower.

"How could you have let this happen?"

But she knew. When she'd decided to adopt Pleroma's facade, she hadn't figured on the consequences. The hallmark of Syene Pleroma's character was her open vulnerability to the eyes of the universe, though beneath the facade, all records showed her to be a shrewd, tough soldier. For Pleroma, the vulnerable characteristics came naturally, but they were nonetheless a facade. Carey's personality operated differently. Her facade was that of a hard-eyed, ruthless soldier—she had no ability to contrive a vulnerable facade in its place. *No, she had to* be *vulnerable to pull off the play.* And Baruch had responded to her bared soul unexpectedly. She'd only wanted him to let down his guard so she could find a way of cutting his throat. She hadn't dreamed he'd lower the shield enough to share his desperation with her, to really show her the galaxy from his perspective. He'd planted doubts in her soul that burned like raging fires.

She propped her chin on her drawn-up knees and gazed at the sooty shadows clinging in the corners. Never in her professional career had she erred so outrageously. How could she mend the damage? How could she unfeel the things she was feeling for her side's greatest enemy? Falling in love with Baruch was suicidal.

She buried her face in the saffron fringe of her shawl that tickled her knees. What should she do? Should she tell Cole her objectivity in the matter had dropped off somewhat? Oh, yes, he'd be intrigued by that. He'd probably shoot her on the spot for insubordination.

Jeremiel had already initiated light vault. They were four days from Tikkun. She didn't have much time for pleasant feelings of self-pity.

She slipped a hand beneath her auburn hair and massaged the back of her neck, easing the tension in the muscles. How could this happen now when everything she'd ever cared about in her life was on the line? *They had to get their ship back.* And they had to turn Baruch over as an appeasement to the Magistrates to keep their crew healthy.

That fact gnawed at her vitals like a demon from the darkest pit.

"Five hundred people are counting on you."

She dropped her hand to the carpet, drawing her fingers back and forth across the soft gray fibers. She prayed to all the Gamant gods in history for them to kill the hollow glow that spread through her when she was near Baruch—the tingling of forbidden want that tortured her dreams.

Her door com buzzed and she jumped, looking up somberly.

"Carey? It's Jeremiel. Can I talk to you?"

"Oh, God. Not now," she whispered to herself, but to the com she called, "Just a minute."

She pushed to her feet and threw off her shawl, draping it over a chair she passed on the way to the closet, searching for a robe. She pulled out the first one she saw and slipped it on.

Jeremiel put his hands on his hips and stood uncomfortably before the door. He'd taken care of the refugee preparations, briefed his shuttle pilots, and reviewed all the available files he could find on Tikkun. He had a blessed hour to try and resolve the problem with Halloway. Behind him, Janowitz and Uriah guarded the hall, casting curious looks his way. Undoubtedly, they wondered why he hadn't just ordered Halloway to level twenty, as he had in the past. But he wanted to meet her on a different battlefield, one where she felt more at ease and they could talk openly.

"Come in, Jeremiel."

Her door opened and he stepped inside, listening to it snick closed behind him. The candlelight cast a flickering glow over the room, revealing the real leather bindings on the books stacked on her table and the magnificent holos of mountains that adorned the walls. As his eyes adjusted to the darkness, he clenched his hands into fists. She stood in the center of the cabin, dressed in a floor-length turquoise robe with tiny bands of lace around the hem and sleeves. Auburn hair tumbled in loose wisps around her shoulders. Through the vee in the collar of her robe he could see a gossamer sleep shirt.

"Forgive me if I disturbed your sleep. I'll come back later."

"I wasn't asleep."

"Can we talk?"

"I don't know. I don't want. . . . About what, Baruch?"

The room smelled subtly of a flower-scented soap. Pleasant. "Harper told me you requested an intermediary between us. I'd like to know why?"

She crushed the fabric of her robe in nervous fingers and walked across the room, getting as far away from him as she could get without going to stand by her bed against the back wall. He noted it with mild interest.

"It's a simple matter. You've made a Cole a prisoner in his cabin. I'm solely responsible for crew psychology and the closer we get to Tikkun the more precarious it becomes. If you want me to keep things under control, you have to give me more time with my people."

He folded his arms and stood silently, thinking. She expertly evaded his gaze, pretending to have found something fascinating on the carpet. His shaggy brows drew together. He moved to stand before the holo of the magnificent mountains. They sparkled like ethereal granite giants in the pink rays of dawn. "They're breathtaking," he said. "Where are they?"

"The Republic of Wyoming. Old Earth. They're called the Grand Tetons."

"Magnificent."

375

"Yes."

He looked at her over his shoulder. "Ever been there?"

"No."

"It looks peaceful. I'd like to go there someday—when we're out of this insane mess."

She laughed bitterly, scoffing at his optimism.

Bowing his head, he absently studied the way his black boots reflected the candlelight. "Carey, let's be honest. We both know the reason you want an intermediary is so that you'll have more time to coordinate tactics with Tahn. I can't—"

"Do we?" she asked sharply.

He lifted his gaze. She looked away quickly, but not before he caught the buried desperation. Shaking her head, as if angry with herself, she turned in a whirl of turquoise and went to stand before her table, playing with the candle flame, warming her fingers in the glow.

He tilted his head. "Don't we?"

"Damn it, Baruch, just set up an intermediary. I'll agree to anyone you assign."

Standing before the dusty radiance of the candle, her hair glinted as though each strand had been hand-polished until it shimmered.

"No."

She looked up, startled. "Why not?"

"I don't want an intermediary. I want to meet with you."

"You don't. . . . I don't care what you want. I *refuse* to continue meeting you on a regular basis. What do you think of that?"

He lifted a brow. "*Vox et praeterea nihil,* I always say."

Her eyes narrowed. "Did you just insult me?"

"I said you're gorgeous when you're angry." Striding across the room, he stood on the opposite side of the table. The candle glow cast his shadow like a huge beast on the far wall. "Carey, talk to me. We don't have time for useless games. Tell me how I've offended you and I'll find some way to—"

She gazed at him from beneath her lashes. "You don't even have the brains Epagael gave a gnat, do you?"

He started to say something, but decided against it. Instead, he caressed his beard, hoping she'd finish that thought and enlighten him. But she clamped her jaws tight, the muscles jumping beneath the creamy veneer of skin.

"Carey, it's too late to change communication lines. We've built up a rapport that I—"

"A rapport?" she asked hostilely. "A *rapport*? Is that what you call it?"

Her eyes leveled a scorching examination that made him blink in confusion. "Ah," he said in a flash. "I understand. That is, if you're referring to what happened in my cabin—"

"Of course, that's what I'm referring to."

He made an airy gesture of self-reproach. "If my conduct offended you, I sincerely apologize." He stopped short. "No I don't. I take it back. I enjoyed your company. For the briefest of moments, you made me forget all about the terrors we're facing, and, *damn it*, I liked it." He'd more than liked it. He'd felt flashes of wholeness for the first time since Syene's death.

Her emerald eyes narrowed incredulously. "What does that have to do with anything?"

"It has everything to do with anything."

"*What?* What does that mean?"

He planted his hands firmly on his hips. "I haven't the faintest idea."

She frowned at his stance. A malevolent glimmer lit her eyes. "You know, in that position, I could kill you with one swift punch to the solar plexus. You'd never know what hit you."

Uneasily, he glanced down at his vulnerable chest. "Uh . . . yes." Slowly, so as not to alarm her, he took a step backward. "I appreciate the warning."

"You should. A week ago I wouldn't have given you one."

"A week ago you wouldn't have needed to."

"Do you know, I wish . . . I wish desperately that you were the inhuman beast I used to believe you were."

"Glad to disappoint you. But I thought that's what this discussion was about. My animal nature."

She gazed at him over her shoulder and a warm, worried expression strained her face. He walked over to her. The candle cast a saffron aura around them. Halloway observed him quietly. Flickers of gold glimmered in her eyes.

377

"No intermediary, Carey. This entire affair will be settled within a week. Surely we can stand each other for that long."

She suppressed a shiver, and instinctively, he lifted an arm, then hesitated to drape it around her shoulders, letting it hover awkwardly behind her back. After two or three agonizing seconds, she took a small step forward and eased into his arms. He pulled her close.

"I didn't really intend this. I only meant—"

"Just hold me."

He let himself drown in the fragrance of her hair and the feel of her breasts against his chest. A hot tide flooded his veins with fiery intensity. "I have to go, Carey. I—"

"No." She looked up at him and he saw desire and something more in her eyes, soft, fearful. "I'd like you to stay."

"I—I can't."

"Why?"

"It would change everything."

She shook her head lightly, as though denying some inner admonition. "Everything's already changed. Jeremiel, I . . . I'm falling in love with you."

Mentally, he closed in upon himself, hiding. Her words echoed around the chasm in his soul, swirling, sounding different. *I love you . . . I'm coming back to you, Jeremiel.* "Don't."

"Then assign an intermediary so I don't have to be near you."

"That's why you asked?"

"Yes. I thought if I could just avoid you for a few days, I could get you out of my mind."

He hesitated, dredging up unpleasant thoughts. It could be part of Tahn's plot—but it didn't feel like it. He silently reprimanded himself. It didn't matter. Tomorrow, or the next day, she might have to kill him. Or he her. "I've felt the same sorts of emotions, Carey, but you know as well as I do that they're not healthy for either of us. Besides," he sucked in a deep breath and gave her a grudging smile, "you're my enemy. Unless you've decided to take me up on my offer?"

"Don't ask me for a decision about that yet. I can't tell you, Jeremiel. I don't know."

He let her go and took a step away, shoving his hands in his pockets. "When you do, let me know."

She shook her fists at him. "Damn it. Can't you just share an hour with me without demanding—"

"No."

"Then go!" She thrust an arm toward the door. "I wasn't even necessarily propositioning you!" she clarified. "More than anything, I just wanted a few minutes to talk with you—to *be* with you. Get out!"

Tears of what looked like fury filled her eyes. She turned her back on him and walked angrily toward her bed. In the wavering light of the candle, her turquoise robe shimmered opalescent, making her seem a slender pillar of dawn sky. He stood awkwardly. She just wanted to talk? He had nothing critical to do for an hour.

He formed the hands in his pockets into tight fists. "What did you want to talk about?"

"You. Gamant civilization. Freedom. I don't know. A thousand things that have nothing to do with whether or not we have to kill each other tomorrow." She folded her arms and hugged herself fiercely. "Leave, please."

He gazed at her solemnly, shifting his weight to his other foot. Deep inside he thought he heard the first muted wails of the shofar, calling to him, warning him. But he found himself saying, "I'd like to stay."

Uncertainly, she turned. "Don't do it on my account. I can live without you."

He tried not to smile. "What do you have to drink around this place—that's nonalcoholic?"

"How about. . . . Maybe a cold glass of Sculptorian cherry cider?"

"Never had it before."

She gracefully crossed to the wall frigerator over her desk, hand hovering over the latch. "I think you'll like it."

Dropping into one of the chairs, he pulled out another with his toe and propped his boot on the seat. "I imagine I will. Thanks."

* * *

An hour later, they lay twined in each other's arms in her narrow bunk. Her forehead pressed against his chin, auburn hair tangling in his beard. He stroked her bare back slowly, letting the silken texture soothe him as he thought.

"You asked about freedom," he murmured. "I think it means being free to fight for a cause you know is right, to fight with all your heart without ever expecting—"

"You mean being free to die for the salvation of your people, don't you?" She lifted her head and he gazed into her eyes. They shone now with a strange warm light, so warm that he felt buffeted by that gaze.

"There is no greater freedom than that."

She lay her head back down, nuzzling her cheek tenderly against his shoulder. "Good Lord, I think I'm beginning to understand Gamants."

She'd said it with such a tone of reluctance, his breathing went shallow. He looked down at her and squeezed her arm. "Sorry you asked me to stay?"

"No. You taught me something important tonight."

"What's that?"

"I'd always thought soldiers fought to win. I always have. I think Cole has. You taught me there's another kind of soldier: One who considers the battle itself redemption and fights without either fear of defeat or hope of victory."

He smiled. "I didn't say anything about fear. And as for hope—"

The door com buzzed and Jeremiel tensed. Janowitz's voice rang out. "Jeremiel. Harper checked in. We've got problems on level twenty."

Carey exhaled in disappointment and lightly pounded a fist against the sheet. Jeremiel gently touched her cheek. "I'm sorry."

"So am I."

Reaching up to the com unit over her bed, he struck it and called, "On my way, Chris."

CHAPTER 41

Yosef hobbled along in the rear, his blasted arthritic knees aching. Down the dim corridor in front of him, Ari darted like a great gangly ostrich. They seemed to be in a maze of interconnecting passageways, as though stand-

380

ing at the hub of a spiderweb. Thick shielding covered the walls, ceiling, and floor, gleaming with a haunting silver reflection.

"Ari?" Yosef called quietly. *"Ari!"*

His oldest friend turned around. "Hurry up. What are you doing way back there?"

Yosef trudged forward, glaring. Stopping five feet from Ari, he accused. "You got us lost! Didn't you? You and your boasting about knowing how ships are laid out. Bah!"

"Me? It's your fault. If you hadn't slunk down that dark corridor trying to find the men's room, we'd have never wound up here."

" 'Slunk?' Is that a word?"

"Sure it is. I just used it, didn't I?"

"The only thing that proves is that you're illiterate."

Ari squinted down the hall suspiciously as though he'd glimpsed a shadow reflected against the wall. "Words are unimportant. When you shout, people understand just fine."

Yosef sighed and waddled forward, turning left down the connecting passageway. A long dark corridor, only the faint light from adjacent halls lit it. He headed for the next intersection, hoping he'd find a place to sit on before he crumpled. A faint scraping sound found his ears, then Ari's hurried footsteps pounded behind him. A skeletal hand clamped over his mouth and jerked him back against the wall.

"What's that sound?" Ari demanded.

"How would I know?"

They both stood still in the near darkness, listening. A muffled thudding sounded, accompanied by more scrapes.

"Sounds like the mummy coming to get us," Ari said.

Yosef turned around and swatted his nose. *"You're not watching any more of those blasted Earthling movies*! They're warping what little mind you have left. Haven't you got anything more—"

"Shh! Be quiet!"

Yosef reluctantly obeyed. The thudding closed in around them. Ari gripped his arm and dragged him hurriedly back around the corner again. Both of them peered around the wall, squinting into the darkness.

A muted squeal of metal against metal touched the

darkness and from near the end of the passageway, a duct covering fell onto the floor. Yosef could hear Ari's heavy breathing over his head. From out of the duct, Lieutenant Halloway and Captain Tahn crawled. They'd studied both officers long and hard on their room coms. Ari and Yosef pulled their heads back, staying out of sight. Yosef's heart pounded. What would happen if the Magisterial crew found them? They'd probably be executed as spies on the spot.

A few minutes after Tahn's hushed whispering died, Ari nudged Yosef. "Come on," he mouthed. "Let's follow them."

Yosef grimaced.

Ari cautiously eased around the corner. Yosef heaved a sigh and reached down to rub his spasming knee muscles before gingerly following.

* * *

Joel Erinyes sat in his command chair squinting unpleasantly at *Ambassador* Ornias—the title had begun to grate like glass in his belly. Any thoughts of using this man to his own best political ends had vanished. The slimy politician had proved impossible to deal with. He'd ordered a new console moved onto the bridge and placed squarely before the forward screen. He lounged back now, boots propped on the top of the com controls, dressed in a purple uniform heavily adorned with gold braid running around the collar and down the sleeves and pant legs. Nauseating.

The com aura snapped on around his com officer's head. A pretty bronze-skinned beauty, Saren Lil nodded obliviously. "Captain? Major Lichtner from Tikkun requests visual with you."

"Put him on."

The forward screen flared to life, Lichtner's face looking out at him. They'd met only once, years before. Erinyes had forgotten how strikingly square the man's face was, how limp his light brown hair.

"Greeting, Captain Erinyes, I hope you're well?"

"Fine, Major. What can we do for you?"

"Magistrate Slothen just tranned saying I should take some special security precautions here. They're rather extraordinary and he wouldn't clarify his reasons. He said *Klewe* is in charge of operations and suggested I discuss the situation with you."

"Oh, I'm sure they relate to—"

"To the very *real* possibility," Ornias rudely interrupted, "that Jeremiel Baruch is in charge of the *Hoyer*, and he's coming right at you, Major." Laughing grimly, Ornias lowered his boots and stood up, to pace before the monitor.

Lichtner's eyes narrowed, but Erinyes couldn't see the rest of his face for the top of Ornias' head. He shifted angrily, waving a hand. "Will you either sit down or get out of the way, Ambassador!"

Ornias lazily strolled to the side. "Introduce me to the Major, Captain."

"Major Johannes Lichtner, this is Ambassador Ornias. He's our new Gamant specialist."

Lichtner sniffed, lifting his chin. "You're not *Gamant* yourself, are you?"

"No."

But Lichtner eyed him suspiciously as if he could tell just by the shape of his face or the color of his eyes. "Well, good." He turned back to Erinyes, jaw going hard. "Captain, is the information about Baruch confirmed?"

"Negative. We only suspect he's compromised the *Hoyer*. We have no clear evidence to support that suspicion."

"I see." Lichtner fingered his chin. "Well, what am I to expect? Slothen said the *Hoyer* had already vaulted. When will you arrive?"

"We have some minor equipment problems to deal with here, but we should be initiating vault within four hours. Expect us day after tomorrow."

Lichtner spread his arms wide, angrily asking, "Well, this is rather ridiculous, don't you think? What am I supposed to do with the *Hoyer* in the meantime? I mean, am I responsible for trying to save Tahn from—"

"Negative. *Negative*," Erinyes ordered harshly, leaning forward in his chair. "You will take no action regarding the *Hoyer*. Comply with whatever Tahn tells you. Do not, I repeat, do *not* attempt to resolve any matters relating to Baruch's status. We'll handle that which we arrive in force."

Lichtner perfunctorily picked a shred of lint from his chest and dropped it on the floor. "Very well. I suppose it would be safer to wait until we have a dozen or more cruisers in our skies to convince Baruch he's outgunned."

Erinyes grimaced. "What do you mean, a dozen? My understanding was that five—"

"Not as of an hour ago, Captain. Slothen said Penzer Gorgon and six cruisers were headed our way. They're apparently pursuing an Underground cruiser toward the Lysomian system."

"Oh, mother of God," Erinyes muttered under his breath. He straightened. Gorgon's six vessels, plus the five he and Bogomil had commandeered made eleven. "This could turn into a circus."

Then to Lichtner, he said, "Please rush those extra security precautions, Major. We've no way of knowing precisely when the *Hoyer* will drop out of vault and into your skies."

"Affirmative, Captain," Lichtner said in a silky voice. "We'll be more than prepared. One last thing. Can you tell me what Baruch looks like? To my knowledge, no spectrum prints exist."

"That is correct." Reluctantly, Erinyes gestured to Ornias. "Ambassador, could you describe Baruch?"

Ornias stroked his elaborately braided beard and strolled in front of the forward screen again. "He's over six feet tall. I should guess around six feet four inches. He has blond hair, a reddish-blond beard, and blue eyes. If you see him, Major, you'll know him. He carries himself with an air of authority." Ornias stopped, smiling up gloatingly into Lichtner's face. "But most of all, Major, you'll know him because he'll probably go straight for your throat when he finds out who *you* are."

Lichtner's nostrils flared indignantly, but Erinyes saw the blood pulse more rapidly at his temples. "I'll be ready for him, Ambassador," Lichtner answered menacingly. "Tikkun out."

The screen went blank abruptly and Erinyes glared at Tetrax. "Did it ever occur to you, *Ambassador*, that I might have had another question for Lichtner?"

"No." Coolly, Ornias wandered across the bridge, smiling seductively at the female crew members before walking into the transport tube.

Erinyes gritted his teeth and gruffly flopped back in his chair.

CHAPTER 42

Neil Dannon sat in the near darkness of the weapons niche. Scents of dirt and oil tainted the air. Tahn and Halloway had been taking turns grilling him hard for over an hour and he felt crazed, on the verge of violence. "I—I don't know, Tahn."

The captain stood like a tall iron column before him, hands on hips, brown hair hanging in sweat-damp strands over his forehead. "What the hell good are you, Dannon? Baruch has redeployed his forces throughout the ship, and you haven't the *slightest* idea what he's up to? Damn it! What's he doing?"

"I don't know, I—I. . . . Leave me alone!" He'd stopped answering their questions because discussing Baruch made his stomach cramp so violently he couldn't stand it. He'd gone over and over that brief moment when he and Jeremiel had stared at each other on level twenty. There'd been something in Jeremiel's eyes that he couldn't shake—some remnant of old and abiding friendship, a regret and pain that it had ended this way. It had conjured too many memories of a shared life that had been mostly good. Neil glared up at Tahn and Halloway. Every word he spoke to them made him feel like he was reliving that terrible night on Silmar when he'd made the deal with Lichtner to betray Jeremiel. His stomach cramped again. He bent forward in agony.

Tahn crossed his arms and looked at Halloway, tilting his head toward Dannon. She walked lithely forward.

"Dannon," she said, "maybe we can arrive at some conclusions from a different angle. Let's lay out what we know. Jere . . . Baruch has shifted his security forces, concentrating them in and around Engineering and the landing bays. He's relieved all Magisterial personnel except the teaching staff and sealed them in their cabins. His own green crew is currently running the ship while we're in the vault. Does that mean that he's preparing

385

them to take over completely when we arrive? Or is he just making preparations to usher the refugees into the shuttles as soon as we get to Tikkun? Or is it all a ruse to distract us from something else? Is it possible he's substantially revised his strategy?"

Neil examined her from head to toe. She'd almost said *Jeremiel* and there'd been a hint of softness in her voice. Had his ex-best friend been using his charms to sway her to the Underground's side? In such desperate times, Baruch would use whatever methods worked and damn the ethical considerations—though he'd never known Jeremiel to resort to seduction before.

He ran a hand through his moist black hair and forced himself to respond. "No. Jeremiel would never revise at this late hour, unless he's received critical information that demands it. He wouldn't chance confusing his key players. I suspect he's probably redelineated his people's duties and, for the moment, they're involved in readying shuttles or preparing supplies." He looked up and smiled gloatingly at Tahn. "You know, of course, that he's going to cannibalize the *Hoyer* to make life easier for the refugees when they get to Tikkun."

Tahn's nostrils flared. "You mean he's sending each down with a goddamned Magisterial dowry? Well, there's nothing we can do about that. Let me ask you this, though, Dannon, is it possible Baruch's planning on keeping his word and putting our people down first?" Tahn's eyes gleamed with an eerie light.

Neil chuckled disparagingly. "Be realistic, Tahn. You didn't *believe* that tripe, did you? He needs what's left of your crew to serve as hostages if things really get bad. If somebody corners him, he'll first try arranging an exchange, your people's freedom for his. Then if that doesn't work . . . well, you won't have to worry about anything ever again."

Tahn rubbed his chin, gaze drifting to Halloway. She wandered slowly around the edges of the niche, grimacing at the walls and floor. Neil's eyes narrowed. He'd watched her go about her duties for months; he knew her style, brisk and militarily sharp. What was this new feminine allure? He shook his head, fighting against the clear similarities between her graceful movements and Syene's. Did they affect Jeremiel in the same way? He felt suddenly numb—the thought like a knife in his back.

Perhaps her newfound allure reflected exactly what she knew Jeremiel liked? Or was it his direct, if subtle, coaching? *Have you been doubled, beauty? Whose side are you on?* He had to know and fast.

"I'm worried," Halloway said. "I think he's pulling a fast one and we're too caught up in the mechanics of our own movements to catch it. I'm almost sure—"

"Really?" Neil laughed, a low laugh that made his own blood run cold. "When did Jeremiel tell you that? In *personal* consultation sessions? He's a gem, isn't he? Gentle, willing to bend over backward to compromise so he doesn't have to hurt you. Yes, I can hear it now, 'Carey, darling, just help me and I'll guarantee the safety of everyone you love. *Help me, Carey!*'" She seemed to stop breathing. He leaned forward, eyes sparkling as black as ebony. "And he's got a reputation for being an expert lover. Oh, I'll bet you like that, don't you? Did he promise you the galaxy on a silver platter, too?"

Tahn glanced at his second in command and Neil could see the lurking doubts surface. So Tahn suspected it, too, eh?

In a low warning voice, Tahn said, "Dannon, if I were you, I wouldn't—"

"You're not me! And this is too amusing. Don't you disapprove of treason, Tahn?" He thrust a hand out at Halloway. "God, I've seen this so many times!" he lied, pushing Halloway, trying to force her to show her hand. He ignored the slight shift of her body, the cold glare she gave him. "This is standard operating procedure for Jeremiel. Seducing Magisterial officers is a game with him. He. . . ."

In a graceful dancer's whirl, she kicked out, her right foot smashing Neil in the shoulder. The force slammed him into a cooling unit, then sent him tumbling across the floor. He lunged to his knees to crawl, but she kicked him down on his stomach and her fingertips pressed painfully into his windpipe. From the corner of his eye, he could see her face tighten. He gasped for breath.

She smiled. *"You're dead, Dannon."*

In a quick, catlike movement, Tahn took three long strides and knelt beside her, placing a restraining hand on her arm.

"Carey," he said sternly. He tried to pull her hand away, but she jerked it back, keeping it against Neil's throat. "*Carey!* Cool off. We're all crazy from the tension. Don't let this—"

"You'll back me, won't you, Cole? Dannon was obviously suffering from a bout of Gamant conscience. He was trying to escape to go warn Baruch about our plans. Right?"

A swallow went down Tahn's throat. He hesitated uneasily, then got to his feet and walked a short distance away, turning his back on them. "Right. Make it quick and clean, I don't want any inquiries."

The cool way Tahn had spoken of his murder left Neil reeling. "Wait a minute! The Magistrates promised me asylum! Tahn, you can't—"

"No, but I can." Halloway smiled again, speaking to Neil in a caressing voice. "Let's have a final chat, Dannon, shall we? If I get the right answers, you might even live. Hmm? What do you say?"

He twisted his neck to gaze up into Halloway's icy eyes. "What—what do you want to know?"

"Details. Just minor details of the Silmar debacle."

She toyed with him, smoothing her deadly fingers down his neck like a lover's hand. Every muscle in his body went rigid. And still Tahn kept his back to the entire affair. Goddamn him! He was an agent of the Magistrates and they'd given him their word! A billion notes and a new identity. *But that wasn't the reason you did it. No. No!*

"For example," Halloway said in a silken voice. "We had the Underground fleet in a foolproof trap. Our ships dropped in directly out of vault and started firing. We killed seven of Baruch's cruisers before he could move, but when he did—he pirouetted like a skilled assassin, driving two flying wedges of cruisers between our forces so we couldn't fire at him without killing each other. And in the midst of all this, in a lull when everyone caught their breath, he grabbed a shuttle and flew hell-bent for Silmar—abandoning his fleet. His shuttle even sustained two hits. Yet, he resolutely dodged our fire to get planetside."

Neil's breathing came in shallow gasps now, sweat stinging in his eyes. His position made him most vulnerable. If he could get on his knees, he might be able to take her. He considered it. No, no, it would be suicide. Even if he managed to take Halloway, Tahn would probably kill him out of some bizarre sense of loyalty to his second in command. "To rescue Syene."

"I don't believe that. He's too much of a professional to throw away his life and endanger the safety of his forces simply out of love. Was he supervising a critical ground action? What else—"

"Oh, Halloway, Halloway!" Neil shook his head, chuckling hysterically. Maybe he *could* talk his way out. "I'd have thought you would have picked this up by now! Jeremiel has some fundamental flaws. He's a cool calculating commander only up to a point. He can recover from any military surprise, but if you shock his emotional foundations, he stumbles for a while. In that moment of agony, he loses it! He'll sacrifice himself any day to—"

"Let's discuss Syene. Try to imagine, Dannon, try to see in your mind what her last discussion with Jeremiel must have been like before he let her go into a situation where he knew she might die."

He shook his head violently. "I—I don't. . . ." Her fingers once again pressed coolly into his windpipe. He swallowed convulsively, belly threatening to empty itself if he spoke another word. "He probably said something about how dangerous it was and she told him he was too valuable to risk."

"Would she have discussed you? She had suspicions you weren't the loyal friend Baruch thought, didn't she?"

"Yes, yes, she might have. Syene and I never got along. She was always so fanatically dedicated to Jeremiel that it sickened me. I couldn't even have a decent argument with him without her sticking her nose—"

Halloway shoved to her feet. She glared down, disgust and hatred plain on her beautiful face. Her full lips pursed as though she wanted to spit on him—then she briskly strode away, with Tahn following her immediately.

Neil rolled over onto his stomach and wiped sweat from his eyes, trying to catch his breath.

* * *

The 16th of Tishri.

The indigo shadows of evening crept over the hollows of the rocky cliffs that surrounded Block 10, dawdling like honey to pool in the crevices. Scattered puffs of clouds blew steadily southward, reddening to flame in the last fading remnants of sunlight.

Pavel watched them as he flowed with the herd of men and boys into the huge transparent amphitheater. Stretching in a three or four hundred foot semicircle, the glass walls and ceiling revealed the vastness of the desert. Dust devils whirled across the darkening sands in the distance. He clutched Yael's hand, dragging her down the long aisle in the rear before they sat. Grandpa dropped to sit next to Yael, putting his arm around her protectively as he watched hundreds of others file in.

They'd been in the camp for two days. Guards had thrown white sacklike robes at them and told them where to sleep and eat. Men above puberty age had been asked for blood, urine, and sperm samples, but little else had happened, and their anxious hearts eased more every hour. Rumors weaved rampantly through the ranks that they'd be going home soon, that the Magistrates had only called them here to keep them out of the way while they sterilized the city or to frighten them into submission by separating them from their families.

No one wanted to believe the maw to the pit of darkness gaped before them, ready to swallow them up forever.

All the people had taken seats now, most down front. And guards began to file in, circumscribing the amphitheater, rifles slung over their shoulders. The guards were of two types: Those who refused to look them in the eyes, or those who glowered cruelly as though in anticipation of what lay ahead. Every time Pavel had to be near any guard, a tightening like the hands of doom closed around his throat and he couldn't breathe for a while.

"You all right, baby?" he whispered to Yael.

"I'm okay, Dad," she answered, eyes wide. He squeezed the tiny hand tucked securely in his own. Thank Epagael, no one had asked young boys for medical samples, though his heart stopped when he wondered why not.

On the stage far below, a panel of Magisterial soldiers sat, lips pursed tightly, some with deep curiosity in their eyes, other filled with disdain. The heavy gold braid on their shoulders marked each and every one as a high level officer. Major Lichtner sat at the far end, a detached look of amusement on his square face.

Jasper leaned sideways. "Why so many big boys in this godforsaken place?"

"I don't know."

"What are the special insignias on their sleeves?"

Pavel shrugged and shook his head. "I can't tell from this distance. Maybe some sort of science department designation. I've seen similar ones in the botanical labs."

A few minutes later, a roly-poly little man with white hair, a pointed beard, and ears that stuck out like shells glued to his head walked to the central podium. His voice boomed around the amphitheater, high and a little shrill.

"Good evening. Please quiet down. Yes, that's better. Thank you. I'm Colonel Jonathan Creighton, in charge of the Neurobiology Division of Sciences at Palaia Station."

He went on to introduce the other eight doctors who sat at the long table. Pavel shivered softly. On the horizon, he could see clouds gathering into blue-black bastions piled hundreds of feet high. Their edges shimmered with the palest of greens.

". . . Doctor Hyde, would you like to explain our program, please?"

Pavel watched a thin man over six feet tall stride to the counter. Brown wavy hair clustered around his rosy cheeks. "Thank you, Doctor Creighton." He smiled sternly at the audience. "In simplistic terms, we are studying why Gamants are so easily agitated—why you're quarrelsome and carry out your frustrations through irrational and often violent means. Humans of your type, we've found, have substantially different levels of metabolites in their cerebrospinal fluid. Noradrenaline, serotonin, dopamine, norepinephrine—"

"What the hell's he talking about?" Grandpa groused indignantly, eyes narrowed.

"Brain chemicals. Shhh, let me listen."

"Chemicals for what?"

"Neurotransmitting."

"And what, in the name of God, is—"

"Shhh!" Pavel made a hushing gesture by snapping his fist closed on air.

". . . In short, we suspect Gamants, through the long process of evolution, have developed different arousal systems than non-Gamants. Our goal here is to determine if that is so, and then how we can alter your biochemical profiles to suppress aggressive sensation seeking."

Pavel's stomach roiled. He desperately wanted to ask a question. Would they allow it?

Timidly, he released Yael's tiny fingers and stood up, raising a hand. The men on the stage seemed disconcerted, glancing awkwardly at each other. Lichtner shrugged at Hyde and he responded by exhaling loudly before condescending to ask, "Do you have a question?"

Voice quaking, Pavel responded. "Yes, Captain. Could you tell me, are you studying aberrant chemical processes brought on by environment, or genetic causes?"

Hyde frowned as though uncertain whether to answer. Knees trembling, Pavel waited as the scientists conferred on exactly how to respond. All over the room, people looked to Pavel for guidance, hope bursting in their eyes. As though, he, of everybody there might be able to tell them what all the scientific hoopla meant.

Finally, Hyde cleared his throat, responding, "Both."

"You're . . ." he swallowed nervously. "You're searching for a genetically determined malfunction in the production of a transmitter like—like dopamine?"

"Partially. We're researching how neurotransmitters trigger the misfiring of nerve circuits, and how the misfiring sets the brain's interpreter up for devising a *wrong* method of coping with what it perceives as reality. Now, who else has a question?" Hyde extended a hand and panned the audience, obviously trying to shut Pavel up.

But fear consumed him. He couldn't leave it be. "Wait!" Pavel blurted suddenly, throwing up both hands. "Are you studying limbic system and temporal lobe abnormalities?"

"Certainly. Now, please—"

"Wait! *Wait!* If you find that these abnormalities are genetically linked, then simple chemical correction won't—"

"Please, sit down! You've had your turn."

"Do you think the genetic complement comes from the X chromosome or—"

"What is your name, Mister. . . ?"

He gripped the chair back in front of him for support. "Jacoby. Pavel Jacoby."

Hyde flicked his hand at a man who wrote it down and Pavel quailed. "Sit down, Jacoby. You and I, we'll discuss this in more depth later, all right."

"All right," he mumbled and dropped unsteadily back to his chair, feeling as though his name had just been recorded in Epagael's Book of Judgment.

A man in the front row shouted, "What are you doing with our women? Why can't we stay with our families?"

Hyde looked uneasily to Creighton who, in turn, leaned forward to stare at Lichtner. The major nodded irritably and folded his arms across his broad chest, then signaled the guards to be on the alert. They unslung their rifles, gripping them tightly, daring anyone to object. A din of frightened voices rose to rumble through the ampitheater.

Creighton waddled back to stand beside Hyde. He waved his arms and after several long moments, the cacophony settled down. "You'll be reunited with your families soon. Just cooperate."

Questions continued to be tossed, most dealing with how long the study would last, what the words "control group" meant, and when everyone could go home again.

But Pavel's head whirled in thought, spiraling with terror for Aunt Sekan and all the other women who'd come from his neighborhood. He squeezed Yael's hand so tightly, she patted his arm, whispering, "Daddy? That hurts a little. Just a little, though."

"I—I'm sorry, baby." He released her fingers abruptly and kissed her forehead, then blindly stared at the red socks showing beneath her long white robe. Oh, Lord, *when* would they find out her sex? It was no longer a question of "if." And what would they do?

"Pavel?" Grandpa muttered as he eyed the guards maliciously. "Later, I want you to explain all this. Eh, you hear me?"

"I hear you."

"In boring detail."

"Yes, all right."

Throughout the rest of the lecture, Pavel struggled to remember his neurobiology classes. He hadn't been particularly interested at the time. He'd wanted to refine strains of food crops to feed more people more nutritiously. Now . . . now he wished he'd listened more carefully.

Kraeplein, Bleuler, Gazzaniga, Slomon, Buckner. He recalled the names clearly, but not so clearly what they'd theorized.

Almost unconsciously he voiced his fears. "Jasper, do you think they did this on Kayan or Jumes?"

"I'd say that's a good guess."

"And they resisted. How could the people have mustered the courage? I feel as weak as a baby in the face of this."

"Sure, they resisted. People on the more backward planets get the milk of bravery from birth. Because everything around them is a threat: the weather, the animals, the very soil itself in places like Jumes."

"Are you saying we on Tikkun are all cowards?"

"Most of us. We've lived in the safe palm of the Magistrates for so long, we've forgotten how to act when we're afraid. We expect that if we *lie down and cover our heads* the government will let us live out of the goodness of its heart," he said brutally, but he patted Pavel's back. "We have to learn to fight again—just like the people on Kayan and Jumes."

"How can we learn, here, in this butcher shop?" he whispered in a strained voice, twisting his hands in his lap.

"We'll learn—or we'll die."

Pavel looked around the room at the haunted faces, starved for any scrap of understanding, any lie to make them feel better.

They listened for another half hour and finally Creighton announced, "That will be all for today. We'll be assigning individuals to specific groups tomorrow. Please have all of your biographical information sheets filled out."

Curious, Pavel thought, that Block 10 had even held such an explanatory meeting. Of course, much of it must have been lies, but why hold it at all? Did they want to calm their victims' fears or. . . . Then he noticed that several of the people who'd dared to ask questions were being herded together. *Isolating possible troublemakers?* "Oh, no."

The guards aimed their rifles at the audience, prodding some people to get up and shouting at others to move. Pavel gripped Yael's hand and they followed Jasper down the aisle and toward the rear doors.

Just as they arrived, a big redheaded guard stepped out and shoved his rifle into Pavel's stomach. "You, Jacoby," he said. "Creighton and Lichtner want to see you. Fall out of line and stand here beside me until the rest are gone."

"Why do they want to see me?" he blurted, heart jamming against his ribs. "I've done nothing wrong!"

"Don't make trouble, Jacoby. You're already in enough as it is. You like living, eh?"

"Daddy?" Yael murmured miserably, gripping him tightly around the legs.

Jasper came forward and quickly pulled Yael away. "I'll take care of your son. Go, Pavel. Do as the guard says."

Trembling, Pavel nodded and went to lean heavily against the wall. People shuffled by, some weeping and wiping their eyes on white sleeves.

Pavel lifted his gaze to the world beyond the glass prison. Night had fallen. The dust devils in the distance whirled across the twilit sands like coils of dove-colored velvet. Though the room around him buzzed with conversation and tramping feet, he could feel the quiet of the desert, could almost smell the dry sage-scented winds.

Another guard strode up the aisle to stand on the other side of him. They'd pinned Pavel between them, these huge giants with gleaming rifles.

"You think you're smart, Jacoby?" the new dark-haired guard inquired malevolently. "Hmm? You stupid fool. You opened your mouth and now you're in for it."

Pavel drove his hands deep into the pockets of his robe and clenched them into tight, shaking fists. He didn't make eye contact with the man, for fear the guard would see his terror and take advantage of it. "What are you talking about? I just asked some questions. That's all. Just some simple questions."

Dark Hair chuckled condescendingly. "You'd have done better to have poisoned yourself in your bed last night than spoken up like a know-it-all at this meeting. You think they really want to *talk* to you? Maybe they'll give you a medal, eh? For being smart enough to have figured out what they're up to."

Redhead laughed cruelly, eyeing Pavel like a pile of manure. "You bet. A medal."

"I don't want any trouble. I'll cooperate any way I can."

Dark Hair raised his brows at Redhead. "He doesn't want any trouble. Poor Jacoby. He's just trying to mind his own business."

"Sure. He's a nice guy."

They both laughed rudely and spent a minute shoving Pavel back and forth with their rifle butts. He stumbled, still not meeting their cruel gazes.

"Hey, Jacoby?" Redhead whispered conspiratorially. "You see that big square building out there, across camp? Hmm? You're a smart boy. You know what it's for?"

"No," he murmured humbly.

"You ignorant bastard. You stupid Gamant filth. These scientists here, they're not just going to do some harmless studies. They're trying to figure out how to kill you all the most efficiently—with the fewest outcries from the rest of the galaxy."

"Yeah," Dark Hair threw in. "They can't do it outright. Because some simpering fools might mind. So they're doing it undercover in a war zone. Sure, funny things happen in wars—people understand that."

"But there's no war on Tikkun." He looked up bravely, gaze going from one haughty face to the other. He noticed Dark Hair had a tooth missing in front. "A few skirmishes, a few minor—"

"There'll be a war—next week. We've got battle cruisers coming in from all over this sector to blow the hell out of this planet. Because your filthy Underground has established terrorist training camps here. Everybody knows that. You've had them for years, right?"

"I don't know what you're talking about." But his legs shook so hard he had to lean against the wall to brace himself up.

"Yeah," Redhead said, kicking Pavel's knee so that he fell, sprawling across the floor. He had to get on all fours before he could stand again. "You don't know anything about the Underground University. I don't believe you."

Dark Hair grinned. "Once the Magistrates tell the galaxy, when this is all said and done, they'll understand we were just protecting them by cleaning out nests of vipers here on Tikkun. And so some people end up missing in all the shooting. Who'll ever ask what happened to a few dirty Gamants?"

Pavel locked his knees, barely breathing. The amphitheater stood empty now, except for Magisterial staff. The officers who'd made up the scientific panel carefully gathered their papers and made small jokes. Pavel could hear them laughing among themselves. Were the jokes about how they would kill all Gamants? About how they'd torture them to death to pay for injustices committed by the Underground? *For God's sake! He wasn't a member of the Underground! Would they punish him anyway?* But inside, a dark hope lurked that even now the Underground fleet was dropping out of vault, surrounding Tikkun to kill every Magisterial soldier alive.

The scientists strolled up the aisle toward him, Lichtner bringing up the rear.

"Jacoby," Redhead whispered, "I forgot to tell you about the square building. That's the hospital, that's where they cut up your brains and feed them to machines for analyzing. *It's also the place your women go to be sterilized.*" He snickered at the look of abject terror on Pavel's face. "Sure, all those they find with the gene are killed out of hand, but the others. . . ."

"You're a liar."

"Think so? Just ask the women. They walk into the booths like sheep, thinking they're just filling out papers. But after the flash hits them, they never give birth to any more *filthy* Gamant babies—if they live."

Pavel paled. *The little girls in the bins?* No. No, the thought staggered his mind. The fools were lying to him, torturing him because they hated his people. *Liars!* The Magistrates would never do something so brutal. They wouldn't murder innocent people for no reason! He briskly rubbed his face, breathing easier. He wanted to laugh at himself, at his foolishness for believing these two huge buffoons. But he dared not laugh, not yet. He'd do it later, after he'd returned safely to his room and could relate the ridiculous story to Jasper.

The scientists passed by without so much as glancing at him. Finally Lichtner came over. He stopped briefly, and his lip curled as he glared into Pavel's eyes. He had a small baton in his hand which he slapped rhythmically against his pants leg.

Then he started forward again, calling sharply, "Take him to Ward Four."

Pavel didn't even try to fight the bruising hands that hauled him up the aisle and out of the amphitheater.

* * *

Jasper marched back and forth across the barracks, his gut writhing. Fifty by seventy feet, the building had high

397

ceilings and morose gray walls. Bunk beds lined the walls, stacked three high. The bare concrete floor felt bitterly cold against his socked feet. Pavel had been missing for four hours, so long that he'd nearly gone mad with worry.

"Grandpa?" Yael whispered when he neared her bunk, blinking back tears. "When's Daddy coming back?"

"He'll be here soon, sweetheart. Try to sleep. We have to save our strength."

She stared at him like a wounded doe, her brown eyes wide with anguish. Curled into a ball on the bed, she watched his every move, every breath. Fifty other men and boys lounged on their bunks, speaking quietly, telling stories, trying to reassure each other. They'd tried pumping Jasper for information when they'd first returned, but he'd shouted at them in panicked torment, telling them he knew nothing. Only his grandson had understood the haunting words. He'd promised them Pavel would explain.

And Pavel would. If he came back.

"Don't worry," he soothed. "They're probably just keeping your dad extra long to find out everything he knows about brains. He'll come back soon."

"Sometimes people don't."

"This isn't one of those times."

She rolled over on her back and gazed worriedly up at him. "Grandpa? Where's Aunt Sekan?"

"She's in the barracks next door. She's fine, too. I'm sure of it."

"But. . . ." Yael's innocent face puckered, her chest rising and falling spasmodically in preparation for tears. She creased the corner of her pillowcase between anxious fingers. "Grandpa, these bad men want to hurt us, don't they?"

Jasper grabbed her bare foot. He'd raised two children and never lied to them once—except maybe about small things that didn't really matter anyway—but now he balked as he looked at Yael. Her sorrowful eyes stared back at him, critical eyes, that seemed to weigh his hesitation and find it alarming.

"Baby, I'm going to tell you the truth. Can you be brave about it?"

She nodded hurriedly. "I'm brave, Grandpa."

"I know you are. Well, let me tell you a story first, all

right? Just a short story."

"I like stories, Grandpa. But, could you hurry?"

"I'm hurrying." He squeezed her toes. "Six thousand years ago on a planet called Earth, our forefathers lived in peace until a great power rolled down on them, thrashing them with swords, casting our people to the winds. But the seeds flew far and wide and planted themselves again. They struggled for a while, trying to eke out livings on hostile soil amid people who hated them. But they survived and grew strong off the hate of others. Then two thousand years ago, the Galactic Magistrates came roaring in, gloating that they could make things better for everyone in the galaxy. They forced a communal economic system down our throats—the Union of Solar Systems—and made our people work like dogs to drain our coffers dry so others, less fortunate supposedly, could be fed. The Magistrates set themselves up as directors of the redistribution program."

"They're blue, aren't they? The Magistrates? And there're four of them. We learned about them in school."

"Sure and I'll bet that school of yours told you they were all hunky-dory. Well, I'm telling you something different. They're the biggest bunch of bastards that ever lived."

A slow smile crept over Yael's face. "Bastards. I like that word."

"It's a good word. Just don't use it all the time."

"Okay."

"Anyway, Gamants watched their planets being destroyed and they got together and groused for a while. They told the Magistrates they could manage their own planetary resources better than the government and wanted to. The Magistrates said to hell with you, and our people became soldiers and beat the hell out of them. But it took a long time."

"First the Exile happened, didn't it?"

He smiled at her, and noticed the entire barracks had gone quiet, listening. From the corner of his eyes, he saw the anxious faces focused on him and Yael. Stories of the past always bolstered people's courage, showing them their ancestors got out of some pretty terrible messes and they could, too, if they had the guts to stand on their own two feet. Jasper glanced around. It would be hard for these people—after so many years of being fed by the

Magistrates. But he figured enough Gamant blood lurked in their veins that they could do it.

"Sure," he answered Yael. "First Edom Middoth came to Earth and herded our ancestors into big ships to carry them away to work in horrible labor camps, didn't he?"

She nodded eagerly. "And Epagael gave Jekutiel ships out of a whirlwind to come and save them."

"That's right. And after Jekutiel wiped out Middoth, our people scattered far and wide again, establishing themselves on new planets far away, out of the Magistrates' reach, they thought. But they found us again. And war after war tormented the galaxy, our people getting the backs of all six of the Magistrates' hands, until Zadok Calas took over as Gamant leader, *We*," he said proudly, throwing out his bony chest, "we all stole rifles and took to the dirt to fight. And *we* won on the plains of Lysomia."

Yael smiled up happily, a gleam in her dark eyes. "And that's where all your medals come from, isn't it, Grandpa? You were a hero in the war."

A buzz of voices stirred the room, people eyeing him with more respect, hope lighting some eyes, worry sparkling in others.

"Oh, some people might call me that. But I just did my soldiering the best I could. I fought right beside Zadok and we whipped the blue bastards, by God, we did." Remembering set his own veins afire with longing. His mind flashed with memories of battles and real heroes, friends he'd never forget if he lived as long as God himself. "Gamants had guts back then."

"The Gamants on Kayan did, too, didn't they? They fought the Magistrates."

"And got scorched for their trouble." He hadn't thought she was listening when he and Pavel discussed Kayan and Horeb. Obviously, they'd underestimated her comprehension. "Yael, it's a good idea not to mention that around people, all right?"

She twisted her hands nervously. "Why? Isn't that what happened?"

"Sure. You got it right," he soothed proudly. "But most people don't know about it and it makes them scared."

"Because the Magistrates want to scorch us, too?"

He started to answer, but a din of gasps and pounding

400

boots rose to a violent crescendo in the barracks, people hissing to each other, climbing up on their bunks for safety. Shouts of "They're here!" "Hush!" and, "Oh, God. What are they doing?" reverberated.

And then Jasper heard the harsh voices outside, the vile choking sound that made his blood run cold. Guards laughed. Someone groaned.

"Yael," he ordered harshly. "Stay here in bed. *Don't get up!* You hear me?"

She nodded and pulled the blanket up around her eyes, staring in quiet horror as he headed for the front door. His footsteps echoed like hammer falls in the deafening quiet. Men and boys watched him pass, eyes as wide and glistening as a pack of frightened rats.

Jasper reached the front of the long barracks and pressed his ear to the door. He heard only a small rattling sound, like wind through dead branches. Gently, he pushed down on the door handle. The entire room jumped when it clicked to unlatch.

Jasper peered outside, into the midnight darkness. The Milky Way banded the heavens, sparkling like a wreath of silver dust. And in the starlight, Jasper caught sight of a heap of white on the ground.

His heart went cold and dead in his chest.

He quickly pushed the door open further, so that a long rectangle of light splashed Pavel. Jasper took two steps and dropped to his knees on the cold ground, gathering his grandson into his arms.

"Grandpa. . . ?" Pavel whispered, barely audibly, his bruised lids fluttering.

"Shh, Pavel. It's me. I'm here."

"Jasper . . . kill Yael. *Kill her!*"

"Hush, Pavel. Don't say that. We're going to get out of this."

"No. Please, *please*," Pavel sobbed brokenly.

People crowded the doorway, gazing out wide-eyed at the massive red welts and bluing bruises covering Pavel's body. His face had swollen so miserably, Jasper barely recognized him.

"You!" Jasper waved a hand at a strong looking young man. "Come here. Help me get him inside."

The boy took a step backward, shaking his head. "No. No, I can't." He turned and fled back into the bright barracks.

"Goddamn cowards," Jasper accused, glaring at all of them as though he wanted to spit. "I'm three hundred! I can't lift him by myself. Somebody help me!"

Finally, a little old man with the deeply wrinkled face of an eroded cliff pushed through the dense crowd and hurried to Jasper's side.

"Come on," he whispered, sliding his hands beneath Pavel's battered shoulders. "I'll help you. I fought with Zadok, too. Company Gimel, Fourth Division. I'm Hari Sandoz."

Jasper gripped his shoulder tightly. "Alef Company. First Division. Jasper Jacoby."

Hari took Pavel's shoulders and Jasper took his legs. They grunted as they got feebly to their feet. As they pushed back through the door, and the bright light fell on them like a sheet of gold, they exchanged a tense, knowing look.

No one else might understand what Pavel's beating meant. But they did. They'd seen it a thousand times on the battlefields of a dozen planets.

"You remember Zadok's wife?" Hari asked.

"I remember."

Nelda. She'd been captured by the Magisterial forces in the last revolt. After days of absence in which Zadok had nearly gone mad with rage and fear, she'd appeared again. He'd found her thrown unceremoniously on his doorstep, her abdomen ripped open to reveal gangrenous intestines. Zadok had rocked her in his arms for hours, singing soft lilting songs, until she'd died.

A sign. It had been a sign to him—to them all.

CHAPTER 43

Cole pulled a chair out from the table and carried it to the opposite side of his cabin. Standing on it, he removed the critical overhead panel and meticulously searched the monitoring area. Nothing. He replaced the panel and climbed down, going to the wall panel near the table com. He took it down, searching, searching. Still nothing. He and his jailers had played a game of "disconnect" and "reconnect" on the monitors for days—but something had changed. He dropped into a chair by the table and drummed his fingers on the top, scrutinizing every nook, every shadowed niche. Eloel had taken him down the hall for a private chat about nothing. What had Janowitz done while he was gone? Or was it just a ruse to keep him off balance?

His door com buzzed, Carey's voice filtering through, "Cole? It's Halloway."

"Come in."

She entered and blinked owlishly to accustom her eyes to the nearly complete darkness. Only the lamp on his desk gleamed, casting a bare pewter glow over the walls. He stood up, propping a hand on one hip. The chevrons on her shoulders sparked like fire in the light, her uniform glowing as darkly as old blood.

He turned and deliberately gave her a galled look. She took a step back.

"What did I do?"

He folded his arms, glaring. "Why hasn't Baruch sealed my cabin yet? Surely he knows by now that I'm wandering the ducts."

She started to answer, but he shook his head and walked to the table, motioning her over. He took a tiny hand com unit, shielding its screen with his body while he keyed in: *Suspect new monitoring devices installed, but can't locate. Make plausible conversation.*

She nodded, heaving a sigh of relief, then spat offensively, "How would I know why your cabin's still open? What do you think I am? Baruch's adviser?"

"You spend enough goddamned time with him."

"Was that jealousy in your voice?"

"Not in your wildest dreams. Why do you think he's letting me wander at will through my ship?"

Millhyser's found a way into the main com through one of the training programs. We'll attack just after we set Gamant civilians down on Tikkun.

"I haven't the vaguest idea. Why don't you ask him?"

"Because I think it might be a little ill-advised to discuss strategy with the enemy right now. We each know where the other stands. But the fool must not realize

403

what effect my mobility has on my crew."

She keyed in: *What's the plan?* "Don't be naive. Baruch knows crew mind-set as well as you or I. Better probably."

"You give him too damned much credit. And you always have." He slammed a fist loudly into the table. "I'm sick and tired of your tirades on his brilliance! I'm beginning to question where your loyalties lie."

Millhyser setting up computer virus. Will effectively short-circuit Baruch's ability to run or defend Hoyer *from external attack.*

She caught her breath, staring at him disbelievingly. "My loyalties are clear and you know it. Let's get back to the subject, Captain. Baruch still believes Dannon's alive. Maybe he's willing to risk your presence will galvanize the crew in the hope that you'll lead him to his ex-best friend."

You plan on leaving us open to attack? Goal?

Shields will be functional to defend against Jataka. *But Baruch won't be able to run or return fire. I hope Bogomil catches on after getting silent treatment from* Hoyer. *He may make a few passes, but I know Brent. He'll cut attack if we're not returning fire.*

"Well, in that case, Baruch is wasting a hell of a lot of time and energy—since Dannon's dead."

Goal?

Gives us time to take ship back from inside. Baruch can't get away. Us against them.

"His 'energy' isn't my concern!" Halloway growled indignantly.

"No? That's not what I've heard. Baruch's own people in my hallway have been whispering that you've spent the past three nights—"

"You sonofabitch! I ought to kill you for that!" *You're locking us in the mental ward with the patients and betting we'll come out on top? Sheer lunacy.*

Got a better idea?

Negative.

"Kill me?" He laughed condescendingly. "Come on, let's see you try. Come on, honey, let me see you fight!" *You've been with Baruch. What's his mood? Nervous?*

She shook her head. *Eerie. Calm. Galaxy by the horns.*

"Shut up, Cole! Just shut up, for God's sake!"

"What's the matter? Afraid to try out your level one

hand-to-hand rating on me?" *Probably has an unpleasant surprise for us up his sleeve. Any word on his fleet yet?*

Negative. Suspect, however, that if he'd made contact, we wouldn't still be headed for Tikkun. He'd set up rendezvous some place safer.

"Cole," she said imploringly, "please, I know you're worried. Calm down. Just relax for a minute. I don't want to fight you."

"Worried? Why would I be worried?" he shouted, then exhaled tensely and paused for several moments. "Carey . . . I'm sorry. I'm just—just crazy right now." *We've laid plans.*

She gave him a dubious look. *I'm not going to like it, am I?*

You might. You've got guts. You're the only member of crew who has access to Baruch. Want you with him when we initiate attack. Kill him if possible.

Affirmative. "Cole," she said poignantly, "you weren't serious when you made that crack about Baruch, were you? You don't really think I'd—"

"No. No, of course not, Carey. Forgive me. I just. . . . I'm sorry if I hurt you. I know you'd never betray me."

"Good," she said in a painfully small voice.

She grinned and he shook his head. They shared a look of conspiratorial warmth that set his soul to aching, then Carey picked up the mini-com again. *Timetable for initial stages?*

I'm ordering Millhyser to organize placements of key players immediately. Virus will not be introduced in system until just before refugees start going down.

"Anyway," Carey said. "Just be glad Baruch's too busy to take your freedom of movement seriously."

Tahn lifted both brows and softly rubbed his chin. "He's too smart not to. He's up to something. He goddamn scares me to death."

"Aye, Captain. Me, too."

He tugged his head around to look at her. Something in her voice made him think that statement had a double meaning. He cocked his head questioningly. Taking the mini-com, he keyed, *You all right?*

She closed her eyes, nodding emphatically. "Well, if there's nothing else you want to discuss, I think I'll go back to my cabin."

"I'll see you tomorrow, Carey."

"I hope so, Cole. Depends on how nervous Baruch gets."

He reached out and squeezed her shoulder, nodding confidently to her. A brief smile flickered over her taut face. She patted his hand in return, then headed for the door.

* * *

Carey strode briskly down the hall, stomach rising threateningly into her throat. She forced it down. Eloel walked at her side, escorting her to the tube. She couldn't let the enemy see her vulnerable. *Blessed God . . . I owe Cole my life a dozen times over. But kill Jeremiel? Oh, no. Stop it! Who physically dragged you out of the shuttle wreckage in that firefight on Horin III, at risk of his own life? Who gave you his bed and blankets and nursed you like a sister when you caught Puxa fever during the fighting on Sythian VII? Cole. . . . Always Cole at your side, helping you, encouraging you, smiling away your darkest fears. A hell of a captain—and friend.* When they rounded the corner and caught sight of the tube, Carey's feet faltered, unable to take another step. She slumped against the wall, a sob lodged silently in her throat. Her stomach ached so terribly, she had to bend double.

Eloel stared down stoically, eyes glittering like the darkest obsidian. "Then don't do it, Lieutenant."

The words affected Carey like a brutal fist in the face. Had Baruch slipped in monitors despite their caution? No. Cole would have checked thoroughly. Eloel was guessing. Anger fired Carey's veins, the burst of adrenaline bolstering her. She swallowed and forced her body to straighten up. Bracing a hand against the wall, she carefully made her way to the tube.

* * *

Jeremiel sat at his desk in the darkness. His breathing came quick and light. His blue jumpsuit rustled in the foreboding quiet. He squinted, trying to decipher the jumbled clues. The glow of his com unit cast amber light over his bare chest and hands, glimmering like a golden ghost across the rumpled white sheets of his bed.

NEUROPHYSIOLOGICAL RESEARCH: FILE NUMBER 19118.
Subject: Tikkun Experiments. Planetary Commander: Johannes Lichtner.

. . . strange levels of metabolites in cerebrospinal fluid. Suspect . . . arousal systems . . . aggressive sensation seeking results in inability to accept peace . . . abnormally high number of receptors in basal ganglia . . . misfiring of circuitry sets brain's interpreter up for devising wrong methods . . . responds to endogenous events by delusional referents like journey through the *Mea* . . . serves to cope with turmoil . . . genetically founded. . . .

"I don't understand," he whispered to himself. "Are you saying that Gamant brain structure is different? Or that we have abnormal levels of neurotransmitters? Why is either important to the Magisterial government? Developing new mind probe techniques?"

He lightly pounded his desk with his open hand. Desperation raised its ugly head. The hours slipped by as though each were a millennia of agony. If he could only find the hourglass and smash it, he could thrust them all into the eye of the cyclone and this endless tarrying would be over. He turned his attention once more to the final sentence fragment at the bottom of the file: Suggest massive sterilization of females over the age of. . . .

His chair squeaked as he pushed slightly away from his desk. "God Above, what have we done to deserve such punishment?"

He needed someone to discuss this with. None of his own people knew the slightest shred about the Magistrates' neurophysiology programs. He longed so to rush to Carey's cabin that he found his muscles tensed on the verge of standing. He forced himself to relax.

"You can't."

He'd seen her too often already. He couldn't risk further jeopardizing her position with her captain. Tahn had to trust her implicitly or Jeremiel's own plans would come tumbling down around his ears. He shook his head, self-ridicule stinging in his chest.

To divert his mind from Carey, he turned to gaze at the *Mea*. It lay innocently on his white pillow, the golden chain snaking down to disappear amidst tumbled sheets. "The Magistrates are worried about you. They think the journey to the throne of God is delusional. Is it? I could resolve that question rather quickly, couldn't I? All I have to do is place you against my forehead."

He lifted a hand toward it, then recoiled, turning instead to abandon the neuro file. When it vanished, he input the secret access codes for the new file he'd been accumulating. He leaned back as data swelled on the screen. It took three hours, but he reread every line, once, then twice. He scrolled up to the beginning. His cursor flashed rhythmically on the first line.

Weight: Four billion tons.

He tugged on his beard, frowning. The *Mea* felt feather-light, almost weightless. Could the mass be in another universe and the magnetic trap merely serve as a spatial referent for the edge of a cross-universe vortex? A protective railing around the precipice to the void? The computer had no answer.

Absently, he murmured, "Outer containment vessel consists of cooled beryllium ions organized into a series of concentric spherical shells which form some sort of magnetic trap."

High-energy gamma rays: 10 MeV. But no radiation penetrated the containment vessel. Why?

He exhaled heavily, shaking his head. "A primordial black hole."

In the past several centuries the Magistrates had tried to pry loose the secret of passage through the ring singularities of black holes to the parallel universes predicted by mathematics. But they never had. Though they utilized the holes in their cruiser engines to warp space and time in this universe, they'd never discovered the key to other universes. In fact, the last ship they'd sent through Palaia Zohar carried a Gamant apostate named Zevi in its crew. His desperately insane voice had been the last words anyone heard from the *Bashi*. Jeremiel remembered sitting rigidly on the bridge of the *Zilpah* listening intently to that final haunting transmission:

"Ship breaking up. Crew dead. But I feel like I'm floating . . . free . . . free. . . ."

Maybe they'd been trying too hard, tackling major black holes when they should have concentrated on the tiny singularities that powered their engines and served as power plants on a thousand developing worlds? Maybe *physical* passage was unnecessary . . . impossible? But the pure energy of thoughts traveled unhindered?

"Curious," he murmured to himself, studying the

cerulean gleam of the sacred gate. Legends said the *Mea* had originally freed Gamants from the Magistrates' tyranny millennia ago—though no one knew anymore what that meant since they still seemed to be captives.

"At the quantum level, primordial black holes are indistinguishable from white holes. They pour out so much matter they . . . glow."

He slowly turned in his chair, scrutinizing it more closely. The stories Rachel told of Aktariel seemed far more frightening now. He reached over and picked up the *Mea* by the chain. A hypnotic pendulum, it swung before his eyes. Its light mixed with that of his com screen to make him feel like he floated in a silent aquamarine sea.

"Are you the key? The one device that makes passage to another universe possible? How about transporting the *Hoyer* to heaven? It would certainly make things easier. Better yet, how about taking all of Gamant civilization?"

He ground his teeth softly, thinking.

"You're closed to Rachel, but open to me? *Why?*"

White foamy swirls eddied across the cerulean surface of the *Mea*. The glow grew until it flared so brilliantly he had to look away. His breathing went shallow, gaze landing fearfully on his walls. They gleamed as though crusted with sapphires.

He almost jumped out of his skin when his com buzzed.

"Jeremiel?" Jonas Wilkes called. "I have two small visitors here to see you."

Heart pounding, he said, "Who?"

"Sybil Eloel and Mikael Calas."

He lifted his brows. He'd been feeling guilty about neglecting the boy. He reached over and threw his sheet over the *Mea*, then slipped a black shirt over his head and pulled it down. "Please, let them in, Jonas."

He stood up as the door snicked open. In the square of light from the hallway, he saw them. Sybil stood nearly a head taller, brown curls fluffing around her face. Mikael looked terrified; he was biting his lower lip.

"Hi, Jeremiel," Sybil said amiably. "Can we talk to you?"

"Sure. Come on in."

Sybil put a hand at Mikael's back and gently pushed

409

him inside in front of her. When the door closed, she looked anxiously from Mikael to Jeremiel and back again, then she laughed suddenly and ran forward, arms outstretched. Jeremiel knelt down to catch her, hugging her tightly. Her arms twined like thin vines around his neck.

In his ear, she whispered, "Be nice to him. He's scared."

He hid a smile and nodded against the top of her head. "I will."

Sybil stepped back and winked conspiratorially. "You've been awfully busy and we know it, but Mikael just wanted to talk to you for a few minutes. His grandfather told him something very important to tell you. You *need* to hear it."

Jeremiel nodded seriously and stood up. Blessed Epagael, how she'd grown up since that day on Horeb when she'd crawled into bed with him and begged to be patted because she'd had a bad dream. Bowing respectfully, he greeted Mikael, "Leader Calas, I apologize for not having met with you before this. I'm at your disposal."

Mikael shifted uncertainly, glancing at Sybil. She trotted back across the room, whispering, "That means you can talk to him for as long as you want."

"Oh," Mikael heaved a relieved breath and smiled shyly.

Jeremiel smiled back. "Your grandfather was one of my heroes, Mikael. What did he tell you?"

The boy frowned anxiously and walked forward. He'd taken only four steps when a massive blue light spurted from beneath his brown robe. Jeremiel spun breathlessly when the *Mea* on his bed responded by blazing to life, as well. The combined radiance flooded his cabin with a magical wash of azure. Sybil gasped and backed up until she hit the wall by the table. She stared openmouthed at Mikael who stood in the center of the room; his eyes had gone blank, as though he stared through the light to another universe.

Baruch haltingly began, "Mikael, what's—"

As though his words had triggered it, a beam shot out from Mikael's *Mea* to strike the one lying beneath Jeremiel's sheet. Across that thin bridge of light, a wall of icy blue fountained up, splashing the ceiling and showering down around them in a glittering luminescent veil. The children's faces took on an ethereal sapphire gleam.

Zadok's voice, old and comfortingly familiar, echoed from the blaze:

"Jeremiel, you must hurry. The Antimashiah has come. You will know her by the initials AKT branded into her forehead. You must destroy her before she joins forces with Aktariel."

Heart hammering, Jeremiel's gaze darted around the shimmering room. He could almost perceive faces in the haze—amorphous, fiery images that swam in ghostly patterns. He felt light-headed. *Rachel? . . . the Mea. . . Aktariel . . . the Laced Star. . . .* He glanced at Sybil. She'd hidden behind a chair. Did she know those letters appeared on her mother's brow?

"Zadok?" Jeremiel called frantically, "Are you sure? I can't believe that she—"

"You must kill her, Jeremiel. You have only days. Kill her . . . kill her . . . kill her. . . ."

Zadok's voice faded into nothingness and the ocean of dancing blue light vanished, returning them to the semidark cabin. Jeremiel's breath shuddered in his lungs. He stared piercingly at Mikael.

After a long silence during which Sybil's labored breathing seemed to fill the room, Mikael shook his head and came to again. He smiled at Jeremiel. "Did Grandpa tell you?"

"Yes. You—you didn't hear him?"

"No, sir. But he told me he loved me before he left." The boy turned luminous eyes on Sybil, who hunched against the wall, hiding behind a chair. "It's okay, Sybil. We can go now."

He held out his tiny hand and Sybil ran across the room to take it. Jeremiel watched them head for the door. Sybil kept throwing agonized looks over her shoulder at him.

Stunned, in shock, Jeremiel could only stare as they exited into the hallway and his door slipped shut again.

* * *

Sybil held Mikael's hand as they ran past the guards and down the hallway toward the transport tube which would take them back to level nineteen. Mikael smiled happily, but blood boomed so loudly in Sybil's ears she could barely think. Hearing Zadok's voice come out of the light had scared her badly. She didn't know what to think about Mikael anymore. He was still her best friend, but. . . .

She watched him out of the corner of her eye.

He looked just the same.

They rounded a corner and Sybil worked up the courage to ask, "Mikael? Who is the Antimashiah? Did your grandfather tell you her name?"

"No. He just told me about the initials on her forehead."

Sybil pushed brown curls out of her eyes and thought hard. She'd been dreaming about Aktariel all the time lately, because her mom did. Maybe God was trying to tell her something? Like maybe the Antimashiah was on board with them? She shivered suddenly, her eyes going wide at the terrible thought. From now on, she'd look at the forehead of every woman she passed.

They stopped in front of the transport tube and the guard, Joan Thomas smiled at them. Tall and slender with red hair, she had a friendly face. "Hello, kids, are you ready to go home?"

"Yes, ma'am," Sybil said as she pulled Mikael into the tube.

Joan hit the patch for level nineteen and Sybil cupped a hand to Mikael's ear. "Mikael? Do you think maybe we're supposed to help Jeremiel kill the Antimashiah?" She lowered her hand and looked at him.

He shrugged, then whispered, "I don't know, Sybil. Maybe. Grandpa hasn't told me yet, but it could be part of the war we're going to lead."

"Okay." Sybil didn't want to kill anybody, but if she had to, she guessed one of the best people she could kill would be the Antimashiah.

She grabbed Mikael's hand and squeezed it hard. Together, they could do it.

CHAPTER 44

Rachel shoved her taza cup across the long black table, barely aware that Janowitz and Harper watched her in mute silence. They'd just dropped out of vault and Tikkun rotated lazily below them. Jeremiel had interrupted their rest period, ordering them to immediately assemble in this conference room. It was very early morning, and each looked a little ragged. Janowitz's blond hair hung in spiky strands over his ears. Harper kept yawning and shifting in his chair.

The door snicked open and an irregular rectangle of light splashed the room. Jeremiel stepped inside. Dressed in the purple and gray of a *Hoyer* security officer, his handsome face showed more than gritty tiredness; he looked exhausted, as though he hadn't lain down for even a moment last night. Instinctively, her gaze went to his chest where a small bump rose over his heart. So he wore the *Mea* now? He hadn't tried to use it, had he? She'd called and called to Aktariel, demanding he talk to her. But he hadn't come and she now wondered if the *Mea* was the only way Aktariel could reach her. Is that why he'd told her to give the sacred gate to Jeremiel? *He'd given up on her and was trying to find a new stooge?* She dropped her gaze and began puttering with her taza cup.

Jeremiel quietly studied the rotating holo of Tikkun that hung over the table. Alternating colors of blue, green, and gold reflected eerily from the dark mirrors of his brooding eyes. "Sorry to pull you all out of bed," he explained as he walked forward. His blond hair and beard sparkled in the translucent waves of light, making it seem as though he passed through the hazy bands of a rainbow. He stopped to the right of the holo. "I've decided to make a major change in our plans. I'm discarding the old Plan A."

Rachel jerked, sucking in a disbelieving breath, and a soft round of disconcerted whispers sounded. Harper

413

and Janowitz exchanged uncomfortable looks.

"But, Jeremiel. . . ." Avel lifted both brows incredulously. "I don't understand. We're completely organized for the original plan. Are you sure it's advisable to make changes at this late hour?"

"Imperative. I've recently obtained some information which demands we refashion our strategy."

"What information?"

He shot a quick glance at Rachel and she tensed. The *Mea*? Seconds passed like centuries before he responded.

"Apparently, the Magistrates have dispatched more battle cruisers for Tikkun than we'd previously thought."

Janowitz paled, jaw slackening. "More than just the *Jataka*? How many more?"

"At least four."

"But we're still a week ahead of them, isn't that right? Can't we put our refugees down and—"

"We can't be sure where those cruisers are. I've checked the long-range navigation signals and found nothing. Still, we must assume they'll be here before we're ready for them. Which means we have to neutralize the intraship threat immediately, put down our refugees, and pray to God we can get the hell out of here before those cruisers cage us."

A dreadful silence descended. Rachel heard the careless scrape of Janowitz's wazer pen across the smooth tabletop, the uneasy rustle of Jeremiel's uniform. Then it broke when Harper breathed, "Blessed God, how are we going to do that?"

Jeremiel bowed his head. When he looked up, he focused solely on Rachel, but his eyes seemed to look through her, into some great future darkness they'd share. The hollow booming of her heart filled her ears. *I trust you,* his eyes said. *For God's sake, don't let me down.*

Silent horrors congealed in her mind, horrors she'd been trying to ignore. They blossomed into a creeping terror that left her weak. Aktariel was the Deceiver. *What if he'd lied to her? What if those ships* weren't *coming at all?* Had Aktariel misled her so that she would force Jeremiel's hand, leading him down this particular path? And where did this path finally terminate? Surely Aktariel knew, or had a damned good idea. Bracing her hands against her chair seat, she straightened up.

"All right, Jeremiel," she murmured. "What do you

want us to do and when do we start?"

He lifted a hand to a green forested area on the North Amman continent; it glowed as darkly as molten jade. "These impenetrable forests are our new target area. Janowitz, get your pilots familiarized with this location. They'll be flying through the deepest darkest wilderness any of them have ever seen. Avel, in half an hour, I want your ten best security teams assembled in the rec room outside of Engineering."

Leaning forward, Jeremiel input a numerical sequence into the table com and the holo of Tikkun switched to a huge square, delineating in blue the herringbone structure of the *Hoyer*'s halls. "This is level seven. I've organized an exact timetable for removal of target groups. Leaders will be taken early and separately. We'll follow with groups of ten thereafter, with a one-to-one ratio of guards, heading them down empty corridors to different landing bays."

Jeremiel perched on the edge of the table and met each of their gazes in turn. "Give your teams clear orders that if their charges display any overt hostility they're to shoot to kill without hesitation. We can't risk anyone escaping to tell their comrades what's happening. If everything goes as planned, the entire operation should be over in about an hour. Then we can start worrying about the refugees."

Jeremiel smoothed his hand over the black petrolon tabletop. "Chris, I'll meet you in landing bay twenty-twelve in fifteen minutes. Avel, I'll meet you in the rec room in twenty-five. The less time we all have to worry about this, the better." He inhaled a deep breath. "One final thing. If worst comes to worst, if I'm dead or missing, and you sight cruisers converging on you from different directions. . . . There are some desperate measures I want you to take."

Rachel's mouth went dry as she listened to him softly explain his final solution to their problems. In the deep recesses of her mind, she could almost hear the pitiful cries of thousands dying.

When Jeremiel had finished, he said simply. "Please get started."

Janowitz and Harper feverishly pushed back from the table and headed for the exit. Rachel stood, gazing questioningly at Jeremiel. He waited until the door closed behind Avel and Chris.

"Rachel, I have a special assignment for you. But first, let's discuss the content of any *dreams* you might have head recently."

"What do you want to know?"

"How's Aktariel? Any word from him on when those cruisers might show up on our horizon?"

She braced her palms against the table, blinking ominously at the reflection of the blue herringbone patterns. "You sound like you believe he really exists."

"Irrelevant. The information he provides in your dreams may make the difference between Gamant survival and destruction."

She nodded. "I haven't heard from him. I don't know why."

He put his hands on his hips and nodded. "Well, then I guess we're on our own. Unfortunately."

"What do you want me to do?"

"I've assigned you a critical and difficult task. I want you to take Cole Tahn from his cabin down to room twenty-oh-nine—and keep him there no matter what. Kill him if you have to. I want you to get started immediately and don't discuss your actions with anyone."

"And what are you going to do?"

He breathed out a worried breath. "I'm going down to Tikkun to do a reconnaissance of Magisterial operations. I'll be taking Halloway with me. She can—"

"No!" she blurted. "No, you . . . *you have to take Tahn.*"

He tilted his head inquisitively. "Is that recommendation based on military strategy, or divine revelation?"

She shrugged noncommittally. "I don't know for certain. There are some things Aktariel told me that I haven't told you, I just couldn't bring myself to—"

"Why not?"

"Because I'm terrified he's using both of us for his own ends. Name of God! He's the Deceiver!"

Jeremiel stroked his beard thoughtfully, but his blue eyes gleamed with an odd light. "So long as his goals correspond with ours, what difference does it make?"

Her mouth quivered. *It makes a difference, Jeremiel. He's playing his own deep game. I can* feel *the patterns of it deep inside me*—in strands and conjunctions. *I just*

416

can't figure out the weave.

Rachel leaned forward over the table and studied the splotches of green and gold light that splashed the black surface. Jeremiel walked closer, staring at her ominously.

"Let me decide what's true and false, Rachel. I need every scrap of information if I'm to—"

"All right," she blurted agonizingly. "I should have told you long ago, but I've been so frightened that Aktariel was using me as a tool to deceive you. I—I don't know why you have to take Tahn, but. . . ."

* * *

Sarah Norton nervously paced her cabin, waiting for her usual morning escort to the class she was teaching on Magisterial weaponry. Her nerves hummed with hatred and hope. Last night, she'd watched Millhyser introduce the com virus that would disable the *Hoyer*. She'd inserted it into a teaching file on singularity physics that tied, in a roundabout, tenuous way, into the auxiliary com in the maintenance department. From that point forward, every time a program was accessed, the virus gave a delete command. No one would know, not even the great Jeremiel Baruch, until too late. Depending upon how rapidly the green Gamant crew accessed programs, the problem might not become obvious for hours. The thought sent a thrill through her. Then she could wash her hands of these filthy Gamant ignoramuses forever. Her fingers itched for the comforting weight of a rifle. Tahn had laid their plans with painstaking attention to detail. Even if six of the arms in their sevenfold attack format failed, they could still take this ship back. Goddamned Gamants, they deserved what they were about to get. *Annihilation.*

She smiled grimly. Her gaze drifted admiringly over the colorful abstract holos composed of lavender and green splatters on her walls. Soon, she'd have her old life back. She'd be traveling the stars, fighting to protect distant planets from pirates, bringing supplies to developing worlds, running hard and fast when they had to rescue populations from unsuspected natural disasters. Her soul ached with pleasant memories.

"Not long," she promised in a hushed voice. "A few more hours and we'll blow every filthy Gamant out the hatches just like Baruch did our crewmates."

Her door com buzzed right on time, the familiar

Gamant voice of her daily escort, Uriah, coming through: "Lieutenant Norton? Time for class. Are you ready?"

She clenched her fists and pounded the exit patch. Uriah stood with his rifle pointed at her middle. Black hair hung in dirty strands around his temples, accentuating the flush in his cheeks. She frowned. He looked like he was struggling to keep his face from reflecting emotions that tormented his gut.

He licked his lips nervously. "Let's go, ma'am. You know the way."

She stared at him for an instant and then began walking, heading for the seventh level classroom she'd grown so used to sitting in for eighteen hours a day. His steps sounded unnaturally quiet behind her. Was it just her own strained nerves or were his footfalls as calculated and soft as an assassin's?

By the time she'd reached the final turn, sweat drenched her sides.

"Halt," Uriah said with such hushed intensity it made her whirl on her toes to stare at him.

"Why?"

"We're going in the other direction." He pointed down the opposite corridor with his rifle barrel and took a step backward, clearing a new path for her.

She looked him over thoroughly, searching for any hint of his orders. Had they been found out? Was this some Gamant countermove they hadn't anticipated. Another of Baruch's insane tactics? *No, no, don't panic. There've been no leaks.* But her mind riveted on Neil Dannon's tortured face the last time she'd been forced to keep him company. He'd looked like a man on the verge of murder—or treason. Hesitantly, she started walking. "Where are we going?"

"You'll find that out soon enough, ma'am."

They made two more turns, striding quickly down empty hallways, then he ushered her into a transport tube.

Norton stepped out of the tube into the midst of chaos. Gamants in rags raced to and from down the hall, panting, feet thudding dully against the white tile floor. Men and women shouted orders back and forth. Like quick hard thrusts of a sword in her belly, she caught their gist. *They'd just initiated some plan of their own.*

"Straight ahead," Uriah ordered coolly.

She pushed around the horde in the corridor, but her steps halted when Uriah stiffly commanded, "Take the next left."

"Into the landing bay?"

"Yes, ma'am. You'll need to hurry. We haven't much time."

She stared aghast, feeling her knees start to knock gently together. "Where are you taking me?"

"Your pilot will inform you." He gestured sharply for her to pass through the door. The longer she stalled, the harder his black eyes grew until she felt that gaze like hot flames against bare skin.

"My pilot?"

"Move."

She stumbled backward through the doorway and came face to face with Lieutenants Macey, Ronan, Kleemer. . . . Her gaze darted quickly over the rest, logging each as her fears swelled suffocatingly. They had their hands bound behind their backs with EM restraints. In the center of the bay, a shuttle waited, gangplank down.

From all around, a circle of armed Gamants closed in, rifles kicked up to full force, hums shredding the heavy air.

Tears blurred her vision as the guards herded them toward the ship.

* * *

Rachel sprinted down the hall, her black braid tapping against her back. The empty corridor seemed forebodingly quiet. Only the dry-leaf rustle of her crisp purple and gray uniform disturbed the somber urgency. Coming to an abrupt halt in front of Tahn's door, she fought for a moment to control her breathing, then struck the com patch. "Captain? It's Rachel Eloel."

"Come in, Rachel."

The door slipped open and she stepped inside, regripping her rifle in clammy palms. He took in the action without any apparent alarm, but a soft curiosity lit the depths of his blue-violet eyes. Dressed in a fresh uniform, his shoulders seemed even broader, muscles more clearly defined, bulging through the fabric. Brown wisps fringed his forehead. He evaluated her combative stance and the sergeant's stripes on her arms, then spoke with soft deliberateness:

"Are we orbiting Tikkun?"

"Yes, Captain. Commander Baruch would like you to come to the bridge. Please hurry."

He stood quietly. "I suppose he wants me to talk to Lichtner? I don't blame him, but I'm not going to like it any better than he would."

In a graceful motion, he strode past her into the corridor. She exited his cabin, giving him a sideways glance. She could almost feel the tension in his bunched muscles. It wrapped around her like an opaque black serpent.

He walked slightly ahead of her in silence, but she noted how carefully his gaze surveyed the corridor.

When they reached the tube, he obligingly hit the patch and casually remarked, "Is it just you and me today? Where's Janowitz?"

"Chris is on another assignment."

"Tormenting my crew, no doubt."

"No doubt."

His eyes gleamed with some hidden suspicion. "Well, if Baruch has dropped my guard to one, I must have ceased being the ship's most desperate character—which is a credit to your talent. Who's taken my place? Halloway?"

"I wouldn't know."

"Uh-huh."

She reached out to pound the patch with a fist. Where the hell was the tube? He watched her closely, then his face slackened in some understanding.

"Rachel, just between us, am I walking into something worse than I think?"

"You'll have to ask Jeremiel."

"When accuracy counts, I'll take your story any day."

"I'm not at liberty to say, sorry."

His gaze sharpened, becoming keen and alert, studying every uneasy movement she made. She strained to keep still, but found it nearly impossible. Anxiously, he tilted his head back and shoved his hands in his pockets.

"If this is a swan song I'm about to pull off, I'd like to know it beforehand. At this point in time, it can't possibly hurt Baruch for me to know such minor details of his plans."

"A swan song?"

"A *last* song."

"He's not going to kill you. I mean, I don't think so."

Tahn lifted a brow. "Well, that's vaguely comforting. So what's this really all about? Is it just Lichtner we're dealing with? Or is there someone else I need to prepare for?"

"If we're going to have a pleasant chat about each other's strategy, why don't you tell me if you've already initiated your attack to take this ship back?"

His face fell into blank inscrutable lines, but he pointed at her rifle. "I'm not in much of a position to do that, am I?"

"I've studied your personnel file. I'd never be so bold as to underestimate you."

He chuckled disdainfully. "Did the file say I was a magician?"

She fixed him with hard midnight eyes. *"Yes."*

Blessedly, the tube arrived and they strode inside, taking opposite sides of the compartment. He leaned a shoulder against the wall.

"Is that what this is about? Baruch wants to grill me? He's not planning on resorting to the probes, is he? I thought he had moral objections to them? Or did he decide they weren't quite so distasteful in my case?"

She kept quiet, concentrating on the flashing level numbers as though they had some deep significance. Could he tell how frightened she was, how her whole soul quaked in anticipation of the next few hours?

"Rachel," he commanded softly, "look at me."

She shifted her gaze and met piercing blue-violet eyes filled with a dread so tangible she seemed to feel it in her own chest, heavy, pressing the air from her lungs.

"Just tell me one thing," he said quietly, "does he have the probes set up?"

"He's not probing you, Captain. Don't worry about that."

Almost imperceptibly, she saw him exhale in relief.

* * *

Chris Janowitz strode briskly to Lieutenant Millhyser's cabin. Quietly, he examined the long empty hallway. The blue wall chronometer read 09:00 hours. He nodded to himself and rang the door com, calling, "Lieutenant. I'm here to escort you to your classes."

He waited. After several seconds he rang again. "Lieutenant Millhyser? This is Janowitz. Please acknowledge or I'll have to force entry into your cabin."

His throat went tight. He gripped his universal access patch and hastily fixed it to Millhyser's door. It snicked open, revealing a barren cabin. He ran inside, quickly checking every possible hiding place. Then he charged from the room, racing down the hall toward the next corridor where Samual Luce was supposed to be grabbing Paul Urquel.

He found Luce in the hall, his throat slit. Blood pooled like a shiny crimson lake around his head.

"Oh, God. They've done it."

Chris ran in the opposite direction, trying to get off level seven before Tahn's crew cornered him.

CHAPTER 45

Jeremiel rubbed the sleeves of his purple uniform between his fingers, grimacing slightly, feeling soiled by it. In the shiny white panels on the walls, he could dimly make out his reflection—he looked like a dark-haired demon. He'd shaved his beard, leaving only his mustache, and had colored his hair a dark brown. Avel Harper stood close beside him, black face taut with worry, eyes fixed on the flashing numbers of the tube.

"How are the shuttles moving, Avel?"

"Better than I would have thought. The pilots accepted the changes in the plans with no problems. And your shuttle is waiting. I had it reprogrammed and assigned Uriah to act as copilot. I hope that—"

"Negative. Reassign him to the *Hoyer*. You'll need him here. I'll handle it."

He felt more than saw Harper tense. "Jeremiel, I know you have to find out what's happening on Tikkun, but how can you copilot a ship into the heart of Magisterial territory and guard a prisoner, too?"

"Leave that to me."

The door snicked back and they stepped out onto the bridge. Carey Halloway whirled when they entered. She squinted at him, then, as recognition dawned, she stiffened. Standing alone in front of the forward monitor, she looked uncommonly beautiful, hair pulled back over her ears so that it fell in soft waves to her shoulders. A twinge of longing and regret tormented Jeremiel. The hours they'd spent together had been filled with warmth and talk and shared laughter. He'd miss them. . . .

She'd been watching dozens of shuttles descending toward Tikkun. "Where's the rest of my bridge crew?" she demanded. "What have you done with them?"

"They're safe." He glanced at the screen and her face paled.

"Those . . . those shuttles are filled with your refugees, correct?"

"Not exactly."

He shifted his eyes to the planet, tracing the familiar lines of the continent of Amman which turned like a huge uneven diamond below them.

"Avel," he ordered. "Take the communications console."

"Aye, Jeremiel." He quickly descended to the second level and slid into the chair. Hitting a few buttons on the main com, he spoke softly to Kirtain in Engineering, arranging to have the controls released to the bridge. Turning back around, Harper announced, "We're ready when you are."

He nodded and stepped down to the second level, walking quietly toward Halloway. "Carey," he said, "Rachel will be here in a few minutes. I want you to go with her."

"Where to?"

"A safe place."

"Why?"

"It's necessary."

"Am I about to vanish into the same null singularity my bridge crew has?"

"No."

He concentrated on Tikkun, struggling to find some bastion against the tide of foreboding sweeping over him. Oh, how he'd love to be coming home to peace, to warm sunny days in fragrant meadows, to a safe place where he could allow himself to feel his hurts without fear it would

423

weaken everyone around him. Why was it he never had time for grief anymore? He needed time. Raw wounds seemed to be collecting on his soul, festering . . . killing him.

He gazed at the lights of Derow; they shone a pale amber beneath the coming wash of dawn. He hadn't realized when he left Tikkun and began the Underground movement that the price he'd pay for protecting home and hearth was eternal banishment from both. Were there no sheltering walls left in the galaxy for Gamants? No quiet places where a man could go and lick his wounds? "Let it go."

He didn't even realize he'd spoken the words until Halloway responded, "You'd better, if you're going to survive."

"You care if I survive?"

"Yes. Unfortunately." She barely whispered the last word.

Jeremiel leaned closer so no one could overhear, and said, "Drop the vulnerable act. I like you better as the hard soldier you are than——"

"What you do or don't like is irrelevant." She put a cool hand on his arm and gripped it brutally. Her face had gone hard, calculating. "In an hour, I can drop the act. Until then, *you need me to maintain it.*"

He frowned, catching the implication that her act shielded him in some way. She held his arm so tightly it hurt. He gave her a withering look. "Let's be honest. Tahn has us pitted against each other, hasn't he? I'm sure he has. Not that I mind. It's a good solid move on his part. You're the only member of his crew I might turn my back on. But, sorry, I can't give you the chance to carry out your mission."

"And you think I would?"

He hesitated, giving her a sidelong look. "Perhaps we need to clarify the topic of this discussion. Are you trying to tell me you've decided to accept my offer and switch allegiances?"

For a short interval they just stared at each other. Then the door to the bridge opened and he heard the sound of booted feet. Neither of them looked. He knew who the entrants were, and she seemed to sense it for she turned, her back to the tube, as though to keep the expression on her face hidden, or, perhaps, because she didn't want to see her captain's.

"Well?" he pressed very softly. "Whose side are you on? Mine or Tahn's? I'll take you any day. And I'll treat you better than he does."

"You'll give me the galaxy on a *silver platter,* right?"

The words cut like shards of glass. He shook his head. "Sorry. That's beyond my abilities, but I'll give you what I can. I think a desperate life with the Underground would suit you."

She started to walk away, but stopped when she caught Tahn's powerful gaze. As though hating the message in his eyes, Carey's face tensed. She turned first one way then the other, as though vacillating—then she hurried back. She'd readopted her vulnerable act. Softly, she said, "Jeremiel, tell me where you're going?"

He pursed his lips disapprovingly. *So Tahn wants you to play it? Or expects you to? I don't get it, Carey. You and I both know it's an act. So if you know it doesn't work on me . . . who are you fooling?* He shrugged warily, silently asking her what she was up to. "To Tikkun."

"No. . . . *Don't!*" she half-shouted. *Clearly for Tahn's benefit.* "You're too valuable to risk! Without you on this ship, your people will fall apart! And Lichtner may be a slimy sonofabitch, but he's not a fool. What if he suspects who you are? If he captures you, you'll doom your people to—"

Angry and confused, he reached out and grabbed her hand, jerking her closer to him. "*Let's talk,* quietly, honestly."

She whispered, "It's too risky."

"Tell me what you're doing. If you're on my side . . . *let me help you.*"

He met and held those hard emerald eyes. Desperation lurked just beneath her controlled facade. Carey searched his face, then shook her head. "You don't—"

"Listen to me! I'll put your friends off safely on any planet you name. Tell me what you think is best for them and I'll do everything in my power to protect them. Just . . . just fight for the right side."

Straightforwardly, she said, "The thing that's best for them is to win their ship back so the Magistrates will forget their former sins. But . . . I don't want you hurt."

He ignored the last. "What makes you think they'll forget? Have you accessed the recent reports on Garold

425

Silbersay?"

She looked up suddenly. "They're open? I thought they'd be—"

"They're open. Simple personnel files. Though why I don't know, unless the information is meant as a lesson for every other high ranking human officer in the Service."

"What lesson?"

"Slothen ordered all of Silbersay's memories over the age of twelve erased."

She gasped softly. "You're a liar!"

"Am I? Check it out for yourself—and don't forget the *Annum*."

She wet her lips anxiously. Waging a battle, he fervently hoped, with the most unbreakable vows in her life: loyalties to her ship, crew, and captain. He glanced back at Tahn who pinned him with a fierce gaze. His bitter expression said he knew from Carey's face that Jeremiel was trying to subvert her, and, if possible, despised him even more for it.

In response to Carey's silence, Jeremiel shoved her away, then in a hard voice instructed: "Go with Rachel, Halloway. And Rachel? Give her full access to all com files relating to personnel and neurophysiological experiments. You know the files I mean?"

Rachel nodded. "Yes. I understand."

"No!" Carey dropped her voice to a bare murmur. *"Dannon told Tahn you'd put all the Magisterial crew down first. Tahn's made alternate plans! If you leave this ship, by the time you get back, you'll have* lost *it."*

He gazed steadily at her. Dread and mistrust beat a staccato in his chest. But what if she was telling the truth? "Go with Rachel."

"Jeremiel, you don't understand, you've—"

"Carey, please . . ."

Suddenly, she was in his arms, her forehead pressed against his cheek. Her arms went around his waist, pulling him close. He could feel tears warm against his throat. He caressed her hair one last time. "It won't work," he whispered. "You know that. Why are you—"

"This game is more complicated than you think. Tell your people to guard the level seven-twelve security access tunnel."

"Why?"

"Because I said so."

"Why should I believe you?"

Over the top of her head, he saw Tahn clench his fists, turning away angrily. Ruse? Probably.

Carey pressed her lips to his ear. "I'm not on your side—but I do love you."

Then she pushed away and turned, steps echoing in brisk military cadence across the bridge. He noted the quick look she shared with Tahn before entering the transport tube. After that look, Tahn seemed relieved, his confidence restored.

Jeremiel sucked in a deep breath and let it out slowly. "Harper, contact Major Lichtner. Inform him Captain Tahn is arriving in exactly thirty minutes to inspect his operations in Block 10. He'll be accompanied by a single security officer."

Harper struck the appropriate keys and the com aura glowed around his ebony hair, instantaneously relaying his thoughts.

Tahn defiantly propped his hands on his hips, taking in Jeremiel's brown hair and mustache. "What's Block 10?"

"A quaint experimental center I need to see. And you need to see it, too—*apparently*. Come on, we'll discuss it more in the shuttle."

Almost as an afterthought, Jeremiel pulled his pistol and gestured toward the tube. "You should have talked to me, Tahn. We could have made this a lot easier. *Move*, Captain."

CHAPTER 46

Neil Dannon sat slumped against a weapons terminal. Grim amusement tormented him. So that's why Jeremiel had left Tahn free to roam the *Hoyer*. He'd been counting on Tahn using Dannon's knowledge. *Oh, yes, good, Jeremiel. Good!* Green and red lights flared above him, indicating the status of various units. Millhyser stood a short distance away, encircled by ten Magisterial officers. The hushed violence in their voices only increased his amusement.

He listened to them halfheartedly, wondering what Jeremiel would be doing right now? Trying to jettison refugees and Magisterial soldiers as fast as he could so he could escape conflict with the *Jataka*? Probably. And Rudy was nearby. He knew it because he felt Kopal's presence in the very marrow of his bones.

"Dannon?" Millhyser called roughly.

He refused to look up. He studied his hands, curiously lifting them to the bluish light. *Remember, Rudy? Remember when I saved your life with these?* He smiled. They'd been crawling on their bellies through the steaming jungles of Gerona. A platoon of government soldiers had cornered them. Rudy had fought like an Orillian tiger, but. . . .

"Dannon!"

He slowly lowered his hands to his lap. "What do you want?"

The ugly blonde strode up to loom over him. Her mouth puckered disdainfully. She'd confiscated his weapons, leaving him defenseless again. "Get up, Dannon. We've got to figure out what to do with you."

"What do you mean *do* with me?"

"Baruch's move caught us off guard. Our numbers are critically depleted. We need every hand. That means I can't spare anyone to guard you." She folded her arms, glaring. "Be of some use. Think up a safe location where we can stash you until the fighting is over."

He laughed bitterly. "Just give me a vacuum suit, Lieutenant. I'll take care of myself."

"As an officer in the Magisterial fleet, I'm obliged to protect you—not throw you to the dogs. Try to think for a change, Dannon. Where—"

"Shut your mouth! I'll do better alone than with you, Lieutenant. I give your people six hours against Baruch's forces—poorly trained or not." He lifted a hand and waved it dismissively. "Get away from me! *I don't need you!*"

Millhyser gave him a cold smile. Over her shoulder, she called, "Faniels? Bring Dannon a vacuum suit. We're going to leave him on his own. He doesn't *need* us."

Faniels trotted over and threw it at Neil. Then, like a school of fish at a thrown rock, the Magisterial soldiers vanished into the nooks and crannies of the ship.

Neil toyed with the suit, fastening and unfastening the pockets. Finally, he stood up and started to walk away.

A pistol whined shrilly, the purple arc panning erratically through the niche. A console exploded in a charcoal flash of shrapnel. Dannon hit the floor on his belly, scrambling for cover. When he got halfway across the niche, he dove behind a stack of crates—and came face-to-face with a dark barrel. He lifted his gaze without moving a muscle. A tall old man with a mop of gray hair stood grinning. "I got him!" he called.

From around the crates a short pudgy elder wearing spectacles low on his nose emerged, panting, running on unsteady legs. "Well, what are we waiting for? Let's get out of here!"

"Who are you?" Neil demanded. But he already knew they were Gamants from their accents.

The tall man said, "I'm Funk. He's Calas."

Dannon's brow furrowed. "Yosef Calas? Zadok's brother?"

Calas looked forlorn, mouth pursed as though against some regrettable duty. "Get up Mister Dannon," he said gently. "We must be going."

Neil searched the surroundings for Millhyser. Where the hell had she gone to so quickly? "But wait, I don't—"

"Why do you want to take him somewhere?" Funk demanded. "I say we put the grease on the rat-fuck sonofabitch right now!"

Calas squinted disbelievingly and shoved Funk hard, kicking him in the ankles until he got in the proper place behind Neil.

"All right! All right!" Funk yielded. "Quit it!"

Neil glanced from one to the other. Good God, they were nothing but old men with delusions of grandeur. But both had pistols. He'd have to wait for the right opportunity to take them.

Funk whispered, maliciously, "Don't get any ideas, brain boy. I've never had a conscience and I'm too old to grow one now. I'll kill you pretty quick if you so much as lift your hand too fast. Get up!"

Neil slowly got to his feet, standing stiffly, waiting for instructions. "Where are you taking me?"

Calas hobbled forward as though in pain. "Oh, we'll figure that out as we go along."

Funk prodded Neil in the shoulders and sides with his pistol barrel, forcing him to follow Calas.

* * *

Baruch led Tahn through a maze of rushing people on level twenty, so many that his anxiety level soared to dangerous levels. He wanted to run, to break away and find out what the hell was happening! Baruch stopped briefly at the landing bay door to speak to Janowitz.

Tahn studied their changing facial expressions, the glances Janowitz shot in his direction. Something in their still postures, their low interchange of words, gripped Tahn like the fists of doom. Finally, Baruch walked back toward him, gesturing to the door with his pistol.

"You know how to pilot shuttles, don't you, Tahn?"

"I'm a little rusty, but I'll manage."

"Good. Move."

Tahn headed into the bay and toward the shuttle *Eugnostos*. Baruch eased around him, going to open the side door. Cole stepped inside and gazed around the cramped white interior. Composed of two compartments, the crew area was clean. Benches lined the walls. Tahn strode forward into the command cabin.

"I assume you want me to take the pilot's seat, is that right?"

"Good guess."

Tahn stepped around the floor storage cabinet and went to the appropriate chair. Leaning back, he glanced sideways at Baruch. The Underground leader's pistol aimed unambiguously at his head. *Not a pretty sight.* The purple and gray uniform Baruch had adopted grated on his nerves like sandpaper on bare fingertips. He ached to get his hands around Baruch's throat. Obviously, fate wasn't going to grant him the favor for a while. Morosely, the reached forward to the control console. . . .

"Just a minute, Tahn," Baruch ordered sternly. Hitting the EM restraints, he snugged back in the copilot's seat, brown hair and mustache shimmering in the bright command cabin.

"I thought you were in a hurry to get to Tikkun?"

"Not that much of a hurry. We need to have a brief discussion about the special alterations I've made in the operation of this shuttle."

"I didn't think you'd leave me control of the weapons, Baruch, not even with the incentive of your pistol pointed at my ear."

Baruch leaned forward to tap four screens in the tri-level com display. "Not only that, Captain. Take note that all other major controls have also been shifted to the copilot's console, including life systems and emergency operations. You can't initiate any functions for ejection, internal atmosphere or heat control, vertical or horizontal stabilization, or flight modulation beyond steady-state flying, basic navigation and landing—among other things which I'm sure you can see. And I have override veto on those."

Tahn checked each com screen in detail, nothing specifically what other functions had been removed from his control. He heaved a disgruntled sigh and nodded. "Pretty thorough."

"Damned thorough."

With exaggerated politeness, Tahn inquired, "Would you like me to initiate takeoff now?"

"I would. And remember," Baruch said, conspicuously gripping his pistol tighter. "I can kill you and still have no trouble flying this ship alone."

"I can see that from the control reprogramming, Baruch. No need to be brazen."

"I just wanted to make sure we understood each other." Baruch reached forward, without taking his eyes from Tahn, to strike the patch that opened the landing bay doors.

Tahn watched the white panels pull back and gazed anxiously out at the heavens. Their orbit had taken them around to the morning side of Tikkun. The atmosphere glittered like a tawny aura of sunlit dust around the planet. Hundreds of miles below, the continent of Amman rotated. Major geological features stood out starkly against the background of vast deserts and forests. A central band of volcanoes stained the land mass like a lumpy charcoal blanket carelessly tossed over an interlocking weave of green and brown farms. With interest, Tahn noted that Baruch's refugee shuttles were descending toward one of the densest, most inaccessible forest regions. A curious choice on his part. And yet another thing Dannon had assessed incorrectly.

He initiated takeoff and they gently eased out of the

bay into space. Behind them, he saw the *Hoyer* hanging silently, her hull gleaming silver, edges tinged with the palest of golds, and his heart ached. At this very moment, Millhyser's computer virus would be ensnarling every fundamental program except life and singularity maintenance systems, but it would be another hour before his crew initiated their attack. Would he be back in time to orchestrate it? Probably not. It didn't matter. With just five key players, the strategy could be implemented. He'd taken great care to assure that if Baruch caught on and killed ninety-nine percent of his people, he could still take his ship back. And Baruch's green crew would sure as hell fare worse without their commander than Tahn's seasoned soldiers would without him.

He nosed the shuttle downward toward the far deserts outside the capital city of Derow. As they turned, he noticed the shuttle wings gleaming. In the sunlight, they burned with a fringe of opalescent fire. He glanced sideways at Baruch. The man sat calmly, one boot propped unprofessionally against the forward bulkhead camera. Not that they'd need it, but it looked bad.

Tahn irritably demanded, "What specific coordinates did Lichtner transmit?"

"Eleven-seventeen-nine by ten-five-two. That sounded particularly hostile. Are you upset about something?"

He pursed his lips incredulously. "Get your goddamned boot off the camera."

"What for?"

"It would improve my mood."

Baruch leaned back in his seat to prop his other boot blasphemously alongside the first. He rested his pistol on his knee. The camera almost seemed to groan beneath the treatment.

Tahn ground his teeth. "Will you tell me something?"

"I might. What?"

"How does the Underground survive when its people abuse essential equipment?"

"We don't abuse our own."

"Ah, then you've accepted the fact that this shuttle will never be yours?"

Baruch frowned contemplatively and removed his boots, stretching his long legs across the floor. "Clever point."

"I thought you'd appreciate that one. Now, let's discuss Block 10. Obviously it's in the middle of the Yaguthian Desert. What is it? And what do you expect to find there?"

"I'm not sure. The data available on the project are fragmented at best. I haven't been able to—"

"Fragmented?" Truth or a good lie? It could be a dattran error, but if not the implications bespoke a major undertaking of questionable ethics. He frowned out the side portal. "You think the government's initiated an incoherency cover-up?"

"Looks like it."

He shifted positions uncomfortably. "Well, that explains why they'd put Lichtner in charge. The project must be so iffy Slothen's afraid to get someone in there who might have a shred of morality."

Baruch eyed him curiously. "I didn't know the government had any employees with a shred of morality."

"Didn't you? I'm relieved. That means you don't know Carey nearly as well as it appeared on the bridge."

Baruch made no comment. He merely exhaled a deep breath, as though thinking long and hard.

"That's an interesting look, Baruch," Tahn taunted. "You're not in love with my second in command, are you?"

Baruch casually lifted his pistol, clicking off the safety. "Shall I help you out with your suicidal tendencies?"

Tahn's gut crawled. That cool threat hadn't been idle. He blinked and looked back at the com console, studying the navigational readings. Obviously Carey had affected Baruch's emotional foundations. But how much?

They sat in silence, each occasionally glancing speculatively at the other. When they could see the spiny ridges of Yaguth shining maroon in the slanting rays of sunrise, Tahn leaned forward to peer out the portal. A transparent veil of smoky pink lay over the desert. Drifting clouds glowed like shredded rose petals. Below, a photon shield formed a mustard colored bubble beside a towering cliff.

Baruch gave Tahn a sidelong look. "Set her down easy, Captain."

"Affirmative."

He made a gentle, sweeping turn, circling the complex, noting the number of ships and men stationed outside the walls. It looked like a goddamned prisoner-of-war

433

camp. The words stung. An involuntary shiver went up his back. Images of Old Earth reared in his memories. The cathedral of Notre Dame and the shining bars of his light cage seeped through his recently regained shell of protection. Baruch, he noticed, had started to breathe shallowly, hand threateningly caressing the pistol in his lap.

"This the first time you've been home in years, isn't it?" Tahn asked.

"It is."

"How does it feel?"

Baruch turned slowly, a dull taciturn glitter in his eyes. "Bad, Captain. Very bad. Land in front of the main gate."

"I was planning on it."

Tahn set the shuttle down softly and watched twenty guards trot up outside. A shower of dust sprang up, darkening the skies like a bloody smear. He hit the EM restraints and started to rise.

Baruch shoved him back in his chair. Somehow the brown hair and neatly trimmed mustache made him seem even more sinister. "When we're in the complex, Tahn, remember, I can have my pistol out in the blink of an eye—and you'll be the first thing I target." A haunted smile touched his lips. "I've wanted to kill you for a long time. Try not to give me an excuse."

"Do you need an excuse?"

"Not much of one."

"I didn't think so. Trust me. I'm not near as suicidal as you think."

He eased out of his chair, hands over his head, and slowly walked toward the side door. Baruch holstered his pistol and followed.

CHAPTER 47

Rachel cast a wary look over her shoulder at Halloway, then leaned against the table in the small conference room on level twenty and watched the wall monitor. Tikkun whirled in a staggering array of colors. Shuttles still came and went, shining silver in the sunlight. They'd completed the evacuation of all Magisterial personnel they could find, but ten had disappeared into the bowels of the cruiser. Harper had search teams out. They'd turned up nothing. Rachel studied the descending spray of shuttles. Filled with Gamant refugees now, they streaked toward the Sacla Seven Islands. Her gaze caressed the magnificent oceans and jade green forests. Her heart ached for the comforts of fragrant grass and cool rock, for rain-scented winds and damp earth. Would she forever be condemned to white odorless halls?

Aktariel? Where are you? What are you doing?

She waited, but not even a breath of his presence touched the room. Feeling impotent and frightened, she looked around absently. Built to hold no more than a dozen, the room felt cramped and stuffy. A drink dispenser adorned the wall opposite the monitor. The oval table in the center took up almost every inch of space, leaving barely enough room for two people to walk abreast around the circumference. A com unit sat at each end of the table, cursors blinking rhythmically. She ran a hand inside her purple collar and tugged at the artificial fabric. If something didn't happen soon, she'd explode from the building tension.

Carey Halloway sat immobile at the far end of the table, eyes glued to the com screen, reading the files Jeremiel had named. She'd been very quiet, but as she read, her breathing grew progressively more labored, hissing irregularly through her nostrils.

Sliding off the table, Rachel wandered to the drink

435

dispenser and keyed in for a cup of taza. It came out steaming, its earthy fragrance bathing Rachel's face. She set it on the table and turned to Halloway. "Can I order you something to drink?"

"Strong coffee." The words were sharp-edged, brittle.

Rachel keyed in and pulled it out, then walked across the room, setting it on the table. The dark liquid still boiled, bubbles frothing in the center of the cup. Halloway leaned back in her chair and pushed auburn hair behind her ear. Her purple uniform had grown dark sweat stains beneath the arms in the past hour.

"Thank you."

Rachel nodded as she slowly walked around the table sipping her taza. "Those files are interesting, aren't they?"

"No," Halloway said as she shook her head. "They're terrifying. I would have never believed this could happen in our age. Never."

Rachel scrutinized Halloway; she had a haunted look in her eyes—as though she'd just witnessed the death of everything she loved and her soul hovered in a numb vacuum of terror. Rachel dropped her gaze. *You're probably projecting your own feelings onto her. Stop it. You can't afford to feel sympathy for this woman.*

Taking a breath, Rachel asked, "Do you understand the entries regarding brain chemicals and the interpreter?"

"Not completely."

"What do they mean by the 'interpreter'?"

"Oh, there's a mechanism in human brains which formulates data and constructs visions of what's real and what isn't. The Gamant notion of 'soul' comes close."

"What about the misfiring circuitry part?"

"I don't know. I think they're suggesting that either Gamant brain structure or an excess of certain neurotransmitters triggers a misfiring of nerve circuits which results in the 'interpreter' getting inadequate information and, consequently, making incorrect conclusions regarding reality."

"What does that mean?"

"That you're irrationally violent—dangerously and irreparably flawed."

"Hopeless barbarians? Well. . . ." She stared into her cup bitterly, watching the light flash in silver waves through the dark liquid. Memories of Horeb's bloody civil war, Adom's pained and forgiving eyes, wafted through her mind. "I wouldn't argue about that. That's why they want to sterilize our women?"

Halloway massaged her forehead. "Yes, it's like burning out plague villages. It's a final solution that gets rid of the pestilence forever—and all the bleeding heart citizens don't have to endure any of the unpleasant ravages of war. It's clean."

Rachel laughed caustically. She had the strangling desire to hurt something, anything, to relieve the unbearable sensations of silent violation. "Right. Clean. Because sterilization is more politically popular than full-scale war? You—"

"No. Because it's more economical." Halloway braced her elbows on the table and steepled her fingers before her lips. Rachel watched her shaking hands with intrigue. "Scorch attacks are expensive. Both in terms of military costs and political liabilities. Union planets have been screaming for the Magistrates' blue blood for months, blaming them for leaving quadrant seven open to raiders."

Rachel walked forward and leaned against the table beside Halloway, closing her hands tightly around her taza cup to fight the rising tide of futility that stalked her. "So, it is genocide we're talking about."

"It seems so."

"But not massive murder. This is more insidious, don't you think? They're going to do it slowly, by mutilating our women. How ingenious."

Halloway aimlessly shoved her cup, once, then twice; it scritched across the table. "Maybe."

"Maybe *what?*" Rachel demanded fiercely. Was this woman blind? The truth stared them in the face!

Halloway gazed up at her through hard green eyes. "Maybe massive murder has been excluded. We can't be sure."

Rachel couldn't breathe. The words burned through her like a baptism by fire. Her gaze settled blindly on the com screen. The amber letters gleamed forebodingly. But, slowly, it seeped through Rachel's emotional haze that something had changed. Halloway had pulled up the Silbersay file, which Rachel had looked at only hours before—but now the words appeared scrambled, lines staggered irregularly, irrelevant symbols interspersed throughout the report. Before her shocked eyes, the words jumped again, shuffling—then the screen fluttered. In a flash, it went blank.

The cup of taza in Rachel's still hands sent a wave of steam curling around her face. She set the cup on the table and lurched to her feet, fixing Halloway with a deadly glare. *"What happened to that file?"*

Halloway leaned back in her chair. "It's begun."

"What the hell are you talking about?"

When Halloway didn't answer, Rachel pulled her pistol and pointed it at the lieutenant's head. "Answer me! Is this part of Tahn's plan to take his ship back? Damn you, Halloway! You know what the government is doing to my people! How can you help them?"

The only response she received was a hollow stare.

"Tell me! I ought to kill you right now. Jeremiel should have killed you days ago!"

"Jeremiel. . . ." Halloway murmured. Her pale face tightened. She leaned forward over the table and dropped her head in her hands, gripping handfuls of hair tightly. "Yes," she repeated softly. "He should have."

Rachel grabbed her by the arm and jerked her out of her chair. "Come on. We're going to the bridge where we can monitor what's happening on the ship."

Halloway studied Rachel's hand, made a slight shift as if to attack—Rachel's mind reeled with the knowledge that she'd gotten too close. But Halloway stopped, struggle plain on her face. Rachel felt the woman's hard muscles go slack and trembling in her palm—as though Halloway had managed the feat through sheer force of will.

"Well," Halloway said. She laughed softly—an agonized sound filled with self-reproach, disbelief. She took a deep breath and held it before saying, "We won't be able to monitor the ship. Things are too far along for that now. All intership com links will be down. But maybe we can raise the planet. Long-range communications will be one of the last systems to go. I'd . . . I'd like to talk to Cole."

Rachel gave her the barest of nods and gestured with her pistol. "Come on. I'll let you try."

* * *

Avel Harper threw Janowitz a rifle. Chris caught it deftly and checked the charge. They stood in the bright wardroom outside of Engineering where Jeremiel had ordered all the weapons stored. Now the racks shone nearly empty. Silver brackets gleamed beneath the overhead panels. They'd armed nearly every civilian heading for the planet's surface.

Harper stuffed a belt with extra charges, then strapped it around his waist. "Jeremiel said to take a small strike force? You're sure? That doesn't make any sense. If the brunt of their attack will come through that access tunnel, we should have it heavily guarded."

Chris tilted his head. He jammed a new charge into his rifle, then ejected it, testing the reliability of the mechanism. "I don't generally question his orders. I figure he knows what he's doing."

"How many people are you taking?"

"Ten. That's a one-to-one ratio."

"Assuming they only have ten soldiers. We never did know for certain if we'd found all the hideouts in the ship."

Harper heaved a confused sigh. "Jeremiel didn't specifically say how many you should take?"

"No."

"Then why don't you take twenty?"

Janowitz braced the butt of his rifle on his knee and looked up guardedly. "'Cause I don't consider that a 'small' strike force."

Harper waved a hand anxiously. "Chris, we can't afford to lose you or any of the—"

"Avel," he said, wiping his sweaty forehead on his sleeve. "I don't like this any better than you do, but in another hour we'll have put down damn near every nonessential body. We'll only have a hundred people left aboard. Jeremiel said his sources were unreliable. He wanted the tunnel guarded, but he didn't want to risk more people than absolutely necessary."

Harper threw up his hands. "*I'm not sure ten people is enough!*"

"Well, to tell you the truth, neither am I. But keep in mind that the Magisterial forces only have the weapons they've managed to take off our dead in the past hour. We ought to be able to hold them no matter what they try."

"I'd feel better if you took twenty, Chris."

Janowitz shook his head uncertainly. "I don't think it's a good idea."

Harper wrapped his arms over his burning stomach. "I tell you what. Let's compromise. You take ten people and guard the main entryway to the level seven-twelve tube. I'll bring five more and guard the adjacent halls. That way my group won't be in immediate danger. What do you say to that?"

Chris gazed around the broad empty room, landing on shelves of extra charges, food rations, and silver storage compartments. He indecisively fumbled with the scope on his rifle. Lifting it to his shoulder, he sighted on the opposite side of the room, then slowly lowered it to rest on his knee again. "I guess that'll be all right," he said simply. "But I thought you were assigned to guard Sybil and Mikael?"

Harper wet his dry lips. "I am. I put them both in Mikael's cabin under four guards. I told them I'd meet them there in an hour. If I'm detained, they'll still be safe."

Janowitz's blond brows drew together. He filled his cheeks with air and blew out a breath. "Well," he said reluctantly. "Let's get going then. I'll meet you at the level seven-twelve transport tube in fifteen minutes?"

"Yes, fifteen is fine." Harper nodded and reached out taking Chris' hand in a hard grip.

CHAPTER 48

Tahn stepped out of the shuttle and his boots sank into the soft red sand. The shadows of morning crept into the hollows of the rocky cliffs that surrounded Block 10, pooling like ink in the crevices. Scattered puffs of cloud blew steadily southward, reddening to flame in the first rays of sunrise. The tang of Tikkun sage carried on the warm wind. Baruch walked up beside him.

"Curtain time," Tahn murmured as seven guards in purple uniforms trotted around the side of the shuttle, rifles humming.

"Captain Tahn?" the skinny bald man in the middle greeted. "I'm Jaron Manstein."

Tahn extended a hand, shaking. "Good evening, Sergeant." Manstein shifted his hand to Baruch, who shook firmly, and Tahn had to think fast. "This is Lieutenant Barcus."

"Pleased to meet you," Baruch said in a surprisingly calm voice.

Manstein bowed slightly. "And you, Lieutenant. If you'll both follow me, Major Lichtner is waiting in his office to give you a tour of the compound."

"Thank you, Manstein. Lead on," Tahn said.

As they walked around the shuttle, the immensity of the compound struck him. It hadn't seemed this large from the air—a distortion net to disguise its size? The photon shield stretched endlessly into the lingering blue of dawn—an amber womb comprising perhaps five or six hundred acres.

Tahn's eyes narrowed as they strode through the front gate and into the installation. In the huge square complex, windowless gray buildings rose on all sides around a central parade ground. Raucous laughter came from somewhere ahead, *drunken* laughter, he thought. And another sound, delicate, like a child's muffled cries, wound through the din. He glanced at Baruch. The Underground leader carried himself in strict military fashion, but he'd noticed the laughter, too—his eyes riveted on the location, face wearing a thin veil of hatred.

Manstein turned slightly. "How was your trip in, Captain?"

"Oh, rather uneventful. You know how boring the light vault is. The crew spent the entire time grumbling about how badly they needed vacations. I think they're ready to slit their wrists."

"Well, at least you have Baruch's capture to buoy their spirits. Here, we have nothing." He waved a hand gruffly to the compound. "Every day it's the same thing, shunting filthy Gamants to one experiment here and shunting them to another there. We can barely breathe around them, they stink so badly."

Tahn kept silent.

Manstein turned right, leading them down a narrow alleyway to a gate formed of the thickest black petrolon. He lifted his palm and placed it over a gray patch. Nothing happened; he murmured a subvocal curse. "Say, Barcus," he called, "could you give me hand with this."

Baruch hesitated, eyes glimmering suddenly, as though he suspected a trap, but as all the other guards turned their gazes on him, he answered, "Sure," and strode forward, putting his palm next to Manstein's.

The gate slipped open and they passed through into a small inner courtyard filled with hanging pots of flowers and tan stone benches. All around, buildings rose five and six stories high. A single lustreglobe cast a bluish hue over the shiny brown tiles beneath their feet. Music drifted down from somewhere above, the melancholy strains of a violin twining between buildings. Manstein led them toward a shadowed doorway on the far side of the courtyard. Hitting the door com, the sergeant called, "Corporal Uman? This is Manstein. Please tell Major Lichtner we're here."

A moment later the door opened and Manstein made a sweeping gesture with his arm. Tahn strode by him, Baruch on his heels, into a magnificent room, so magnificent that Tahn's steps faltered. Spreading at least a hundred feet square and twenty high, a chandelier of the finest Arpeggian crystal hung from the ceiling, each faceted piece glistening in a rainbow of colors. Upon the marble staircase to his right, they cast a kaleidoscopic light. An enormous crimson and jade rug covered tiny porcelain tiles decorated with the most delicate of spiderweb designs. Along every wall, priceless pieces of furniture from around the galaxy sat: high-backed Carinan chairs, carved "cherubim" tables from Pegasus III, Cassiopian emerald clocks.

Tahn took it all in quietly, but revulsion stirred within him.

"Captain," a familiar voice called, sickeningly sweet in its tone. "Welcome to Block 10."

Tahn turned to see Lichtner coming gracefully down the staircase. The man's purple uniform garishly boasted dozens of medals, undoubtedly every medal he'd ever won—or, more likely, bought.

Tahn inclined his head. "Major. You're looking well."

Lichtner came across the floor swaying slightly, his

smile gloating. When he got close enough, Tahn could smell the strong scent of wine on his breath. Lichtner extended a manicured hand. "And you're looking poorly, Captain. Those bags under your eyes speak of hard days and harder nights."

Tahn smiled, obligingly shaking that soft white hand, wanting to slap that smug smile off Lichtner's face. "The nights we won't discuss—as to the days, we've been riding herd on these fanatical Gamants for over a year, Major. It begins to weigh on the *best* of men after a time."

Lichtner laughed, a low laugh that made Tahn tense every muscle in his body. "Well, shall we have a glass of wine before I show you around, Captain?"

"I'd prefer a smooth whiskey, Major, if you have it."

"Of course. And for your security officer?"

"Oh," Tahn said apologetically. He turned and gave Baruch a formal smile. "Forgive me. Major Lichtner, this is Lieutenant Barcus."

Baruch stepped forward, bowing and extending a hand. "Major," he said so reverently that Tahn gave him a look of grudging admiration. "It's a pleasure to meet you. I'll also take a whiskey, thank you."

Lichtner smiled plastically, but his gaze surreptitiously examined Baruch's facial features, going carefully over his brown hair and mustache, noting the pistol on his hip. In a quick glance, Lichtner checked Tahn's barren hip. Tahn straightened, hope lighting a fire in his belly. Could someone have tipped Lichtner off? *Bogomil?*

"Very well," Lichtner said, "please follow me."

They walked in single file across the plush rug to the ornately carved liquor cabinet sitting beside a table and eight chairs. Briefly, Tahn's gaze touched Baruch's: the Underground leader's blue eyes filled with warning. Tahn shifted to watch Lichtner take a fine crystal decanter from the shelf and fill two glasses, handing them over with infinite grace.

"So," Tahn began, sipping his whiskey. "Tell us about Block 10. As I understand it, this is a neurophysiological research center, is that correct?"

"For the most part," Lichtner said. His square face seemed to glow, highlighting his brown eyes. "Please, sit down." He gestured to the table with the high-backed chairs. "We've at least twenty minutes before we need to

443

start heading across the compound. We've brought in a new group of study subjects today and are getting rid of an old group. I'm sure you'll appreciate the efficiency of both operations."

"It sounds interesting." Tahn smiled pleasantly, watching Lichtner place the bottle of wine and the whiskey decanter on opposite sides of the table. Drawing lines? A damned good idea. "I think both Barcus and I would appreciate a few minutes of conversation first."

"Manstein," Lichtner called, waving a hand as though shooing away flies. "Please take your men and wait outside. We'll be along shortly."

"Yes, sir." Manstein and all the other guards filed out, shutting the door softly behind them.

With just three of them, Tahn felt even more uncomfortable. Lichtner and Baruch were armed. All he had was his highly agitated body.

They took seats, Baruch dropping to the chair on his right, Lichtner across the table. He didn't miss the way Baruch subtly shifted, turning sideways so Tahn could see his hand resting on the butt of his holstered pistol. Baruch smiled professionally at Tahn. He smiled back, then shifted his gaze to Lichtner. Under normal circumstances, he'd have been obnoxious to the major, but he strongly suspected that wasn't the proper attitude at this moment.

"Well, Lichtner, what sorts of experiments are you performing here?" He sipped his whiskey, lifting his brows. Excellent.

Lichtner leaned back in his chair and took a long drink of his wine, nearly emptying the glass. He refilled it from the bottle before answering. "Oh, a variety. Most of them are concerned with the limbic system and temporal lobes, whatever those are. You know how it is, Captain, these neurobiologists go about their experiments and we administrators handle all the important things."

Tahn nodded obligingly. "Of course. Scientists—and politicians, I might add—rarely perceive the whole picture. I understand."

"And the Magistrates have been quite demanding. Every day it seems we get another order to step up our operations."

"The Magistrates are *always* demanding, Major."

"Yes, but too often it's over trivial things."

"I've noticed that myself in the past."

Lichtner lifted his chin curiously. "Well, we're certainly getting along better this evening, Tahn, than at our last meeting."

Tahn nodded amiably, but a violent fire blazed inside him. He longed to reach across the table and feel Lichtner's trachea beneath his fingers. "Silmar was a bit hectic."

"Hectic?" Lichtner responded indignantly. "I should have filed charges against you. I seriously considered it."

"Well, I appreciate the fact that you didn't. I was—"

"It would have been a little silly. I didn't have any witnesses, after all." Lichtner gave Tahn a glazed look of loathing.

"Yes, well, at any rate, I appreciate your forbearance. I was strung pretty tight that day. If I offended you, I humbly apologize."

Lichtner laughed in a low cruel way, swirling his red wine roughly. "You were extremely unprofessional, Captain. Pleroma was a Gamant slut. Just because you disagreed with my methods was no reason—"

"As I said, I'm sorry. My conduct was *admittedly* reprehensible." Tahn looked askance at Baruch; he sat unmoving, but his nostrils flared with shallow breaths. Their gazes met for an instant and Tahn flinched. Goddamn, what would Baruch do if Lichtner discussed the details of Silmar? Dannon's words about Baruch's emotional flaws fluttered through his mind. One rash act could get them all killed.

Lichtner seemed to give no notice to the hint to shut up. He ran a hand through his light brown hair and his thin lips set into a hard line. "Yes, *admittedly.* I should have filed charges. By all rights you should have been court-martialed and imprisoned for striking a superior officer."

He caught Baruch's curious glance, but kept his attention riveted on Lichtner who lifted his wine glass and drained it dry, then refilled it.

Tahn leaned across the table. "Look Lichtner, I'd rather not discuss this. What's past is past. I'd like to—"

"You've never been a true professional, Captain," Lichtner said with smooth arrogance. "If you were, you'd have understood my methods that day on Silmar. Gamants are too primitive to respect sophisticated means of information gathering. You have to treat them like the wild animals they are. Besides," Lichtner murmured with suave brutality, "Syene Pleroma was most ardent—a true delight—though her screams were a little disconcerting at first. You'd have benefited from playing along with me. I had her four times before I gave her over to my men and I'd have certainly allowed you—"

"Damn it!" Tahn said, rising halfway out of his chair. Beside him, he felt Baruch move, shifting so that if the need arose he could pull his pistol with one smooth movement and fire. Swiftly and certainly, Tahn finished, "I don't want to talk about it, Lichtner!"

The major's eyes narrowed to slits. "You're weak, Tahn. Your *ridiculous* morals make you feeble."

Tahn lifted his whiskey glass, bolting the contents with one quick throw of the hand. For a breathless, timeless moment, he forgot Baruch sat beside him. He leaned over the table, glaring into Lichtner' face. "Do you know what would happen if I filed a complete report of your activities that day, Lichtner? You violated every regulation in the government Ethics Directive. Hmm? How would you like that? Shall I file a report? I've at least five officers who'll stand as witnesses."

Incensed, Lichtner dramatically drummed his fingers on the table. "Threats won't improve our relationship, Captain. Perhaps it would be better if we both forgot Silmar?

Tahn leaned back, breathing hard, rage building to a crescendo in his chest. "Perhaps."

Lichtner turned to gaze at one of the emerald clocks. "At any rate, we should be going. I've some special operations I want to show you. We take care of all our dirty work early in the morning, before our scientists come on duty." He shoved his chair back and stood up, straightening his uniform.

Tahn poured himself another glass of whiskey and bolted it, then rose. He noticed Baruch hadn't so much as touched his glass.

"Yes, let's go," Tahn said. "I want to find out what Block 10 is *really* all about."

Lichtner briskly led the way toward the door, back so straight he looked like he'd swallowed a broomstick. Tahn followed. Baruch quietly brought up the rear. Tahn's spine prickled eerily. Baruch moved with the throttled silence of a skilled hit man.

They exited through the door into a crowd of eight guards. The courtyard seemed even brighter after two whiskeys, the flowers obscenely scenting the air with a rich sweetness. They strode headlong through the far gate and out into the compound.

Quietly, Baruch murmured, "Tahn, some day I'd like to discuss what you did on Silmar. It seems I may owe you something and I'd like to—"

"Forget it. I didn't do it for you, Baruch."

Heading across the parade ground, Tahn heard, once again, the guttural laughter of a half dozen men, the choking whimpers of a girl interspersed with sharp muffled cries of pain. His skin crawled as they neared the source of those sounds.

They rounded a corner and Tahn stopped dead in his tracks. The soft opalescent rays of dawn streamed down over the photon shield, scattering patches of brilliant gold down the alley. Lichtner and his men strode by heedlessly, as though the scene didn't exist. Five men stood in a circle in the alley, naked. They had a tiny girl, no more than twelve, captive between them—her breasts had barely begun to bud, yet white stains of semen traced rivulets down the insides of her thighs. They shoved her from one man to the next, laughing, tormenting, eyes bright with cruel desire.

"What the *hell's* going on here?" Tahn demanded in a low savage voice. He clenched his hands into shaking fists.

One of the men gave him an imperious look, a slow smile creeping over his face. "We're conducting experiments on Gamant fertilization," he announced, laughing. "Want to help? Come on, we'll give you a chance, too." He brutally shoved the child into Tahn's arms.

Cole caught her. Her young skin felt soft and clammy beneath his fingers. Stringy brown hair draped down over the girl's narrow chest. She seemed as frail and transparent as a blade of grass. She looked up at him pleadingly and he couldn't move—his muscles had gone rigid. She had the face of a Renaissance angel, sad, eyes wide and afflicted.

From behind, he heard Baruch's irrationally calm voice say, "Captain, we need to see what Major Lichtner considers important. *Captain . . . let's go.*"

447

Seconds later, Baruch gripped him by the arm and pulled him away. Stunned, Tahn released the girl and allowed himself to be guided quickly across the parade ground. The raucous laughter began again and his very soul withered to dust. Ahead, he caught sight of Lichtner's back.

"I can't believe . . ." he began.

"Can't you?" Baruch whispered. "The Magistrates did a similar thing on Jumes before you were ordered to scorch it."

Tahn stopped, roughly shaking off Baruch's hand. He glared in rage. "Don't give me that goddamned bullshit! I know—"

"Do you? Did you review the clandestine files? Maybe we'll *both* go review them when we get back to the *Hoyer*. That way the facts can stand for themselves."

Tahn's breathing came in shallow gasps. Could it be true? He *hadn't* checked the secret documents. Had the Magistrates established such programs on Jumes? Is that why the populace had revolted? And he'd. . . . His whole body cried out for him to leave this place, but he strode hastily forward, following in Lichtner's path. Behind, he could hear Baruch's resolutely quiet steps.

They had to sprint to catch up, rounding a corner which led out away from the compound. The photon shield cast a curiously filtered light, like the golden shadow of a veiled full moon. In the distance, Tahn could see a line of people standing before a ditch: naked, pitifully starved, hands bound behind their backs. Old women, young women, and little girls. A series of crisply uniformed soldiers stood on the opposite side of the ditch, rifles aimed.

Tahn shoved past Lichtner's guards, running to grab the major's arm and ruthlessly swing him around. "What is this?" he demanded with hushed fury.

Lichtner glared at his restraining hand, then smiled maliciously. "A routine elimination of useless subjects, Captain. The science team culls them out and we ensure they're properly disposed of."

"Disposed of?"

"Certainly. They're of no use. Come, come, Captain. They're just Gamants. You, of all people, know they're subhuman beasts. Indeed, our experiments here prove it. Just wait until you read the reports on—"

The shrill sound of rifles discharging jarred Tahn, he whirled, heart pounding. Violet beams slashed relentlessly through the old women, bearing down toward the children. Some whimpered, most held their chins high, defiantly staring death in the face.

"We've ordered our men to limit both the number and length of their shots to two, one-tenth second bursts for each victim," Lichtner explained proudly. "And, yes, I know very well the Magistrates order five shots, but we don't need to waste our energy resources on Gamants."

Tahn jerked with each renewed blast, feeling the shots as if they slashed his own body. The high energy shots literally burst the atoms of the victims' flesh. A fine mist of blood filled the air. *And from somewhere deep in his mind voices called, strained voices, tears in them, fear.* Jumbled images of Paris flashed, the Arc de Triumphe, the Pont Neuf. . . . From that part of his mind that had gone insane in self-defense, he felt tendrils rising up, thin wispy fingers grasping at him. *No! No, leave me alone! For God's sake, leave me alone!*

The soldiers kept firing into the women and children until the sandy soil ran red with blood. Like the wails from ancient banshees, Lichtner started screaming, "*Stop it! Stop! That's too many shots! I said two! TWO! DAMN YOU ALL—STOP IT!*"

The firing ceased and Lichtner stamped around, fuming, waving his arms violently, cursing his men. Even before the last moan faded, men with mechanical equipment approached from behind, bulldozing the dead into the ditch.

Tahn reeled on his feet. Another flash—the old pagan temple before the cathedral of Notre Dame, sunken. The dead eyes of hundreds stared out at him where he lay huddled on his side in his cage.

"No . . ." he murmured through gritted teeth, struggling to keep his mind blank—*blank! Keep it blank! Yes . . . yes, that's it . . . blank . . . blank . . .* He started to feel blessedly numb, like a sleepwalker running silently through a nightmare that seemed to have no beginning or end.

He inhaled unsteadily and his gaze landed on the bloodied corpse of a two- or three-year-old girl; she kicked one last time, body shuddering as a dozer shoved her into the ditch.

And . . . from somewhere far away and long ago the sound of insidious alien laughter wafted—creeping from a dark door he thought he'd managed to rebolt. On the other side of the ditch, the ruby-eyed demon appeared; it smiled and lifted a hand, beckoning him across. When he didn't move, the beast laughed, a hideous laugh that echoed thunderously. "*Welcome to Moriah, Tahn.*"

"Captain," he heard Baruch say softly from beside him, too softly for anyone else to hear. "We'd like to see the rest of the compound. Tell Lichtner."

Tahn shook his head. "No. No, I can't. I don't—"

"Yes, you do. We have to know the full story here. Do it!"

Tahn swallowed convulsively and gave Baruch a desperate glance. The demon faded into nothingness. Cole clenched his jaw so tightly his head shook. Where had it gone? What the hell was Moriah?

"Tahn," Baruch whispered insistently. "Tell Lichtner."

Cole shook his head. How could Baruch take this so calmly? Had he lost his mind? These were his people, for God's sake, dying for nothing. Nothing! Then it occurred to Cole that perhaps Baruch could take it because he'd seen it so often, because he'd had to learn to steel himself against this stunning feeling of violation and despair. For an eternity, he stared into those hard blue eyes.

"Lichtner," Tahn said coolly, "we don't have all night. We'd like to see the scientific facilities."

Lichtner's lip curled. "Very well, Captain, but they're nowhere near as entertaining." Pivoting on his heel, Lichtner signaled his men to follow and they marched off toward a far building. Tahn and Baruch followed.

Outside, a crowd of perhaps fifty stood. Men and boys, they held hats and coats in their hands. Magisterial officers in clean, crisply pressed uniforms shouted at them: "You filthy Gamant swine, move!" "Stop!" "Don't look me in the eye or I'll kill you right now!" "Go on, get out of here!" "Run! Run! Run! To the registration booths over there! Hurry it up!"

Lichtner turned, briefly explaining, "These are new subjects. We just shipped them in today from Derow." Haughtily, Lichtner and his guards strode away, leaving Tahn and Baruch alone.

The crowd ran obediently, passing by Tahn. One little

boy staggered toward the end, sobbing, tears streaking his dirty face. Dressed in brown rags, he lifted a weak hand. "Where's my daddy? Do you know where my daddy is? Please, let me stay with my dad? Where is he?"

Tahn started to kneel, to talk to the child, but Baruch shoved him out of the way and knelt himself. In a bare whisper, Baruch said something in Gamant. The boy's mouth dropped open slightly and a small flame grew in his eyes. He reached out and took Baruch's hand, kissing it, wiping his tears on the big callused palm, murmuring soft sobbing words. Then he quickly turned and forced his trembling legs to run. He caught up with the group before they entered the booths.

As they followed Lichtner, Tahn whispered, "What did you tell the boy?"

"I told him to stay strong, not to lose heart, that the Underground was on the way to free him."

"You lied to him?"

Baruch gazed at him hard. "Maybe. Doesn't matter. Every extra breath he gets into his lungs helps defeat you and yours, Captain."

The words seared Tahn's soul. Baruch marched forward, leaving him to follow into the facility; it smelled dank with the odors of petrolon and mildew. Stark white walls extended fifty feet high, enclosing a building that must have covered ten acres. Crates littered the floor, stacked fifteen feet high in places. They maneuvered around them, winding down narrow walkways.

"Captain," Lichtner cast over his shoulder. "We are about to enter a surgical wing. Research here centers around disrupting the reward-generating system of the brain. I don't really understand it. You'll have to talk to one of our physicians when they come on duty in two hours. If you like, I'll arrange a special tour for you."

"Yes, do that. I want to talk to somebody who knows something."

Lichtner's thin mouth pursed tightly in anger. Guards flowed around them, heading for a door ahead. They opened it and Tahn nearly choked; scents of stale sweat and urine flooded over him like a foul tidal wave.

Lichtner led the way inside, briskly outdistancing everyone as if anxious to have this over and done with. They walked down a long white corridor and out into a large room.

When Tahn entered the room, his steps faltered, heart pounding so violently he thought it would burst through his ribs. People crouched in light cages down the length of both walls, huddling against the bright golden bars, staring at him through haunted eyes. He took a step backward.

"Major?" Baruch asked unemotionally. "Do you know what types of surgical operations are being performed?"

"Oh," Lichtner waved a hand irritably, "it seems to me that I remember one of our biologists saying that when lesions are made in particular parts of the temporal lobes, it affects the reward system. That's all I know."

"What sorts of conclusions are these experiments leading to?"

As Lichtner walked on, he cast over his shoulder, "Apparently Gamants have peculiar arousal systems that cause them to be aggressive. You know, Lieutenant, that irrational fear of peace they have? They're always fighting. If they can't slit our throats, they'll slit their own just to release their aggressions."

"That's a Gamant for you," Baruch stated calmly.

They rounded a corner into a new section of cages and Tahn caught his breath. Involuntarily a shudder took his body. A woman with long blonde hair lay on her side in one cage, wavy tresses spreading like a rippling blanket over her face and naked torso. A trickle of blood flowed out of her cage, spreading across the floor, soaking the stones. . . .

"*Cole? Oh, Cole . . . forgive me. . . .*"

Rifle fire. Mortar blasts. The sound of weeds rustling, rustling in the cold winds. The sky changed to a sickly mustard color—and Cole's soul became a long soundless cry.

He whirled. The broken cathedral stood like a huge gaping mouth in the distance. "For God's sake, Williston," he whispered. "They're coming fast. Get out of here. Go!"

Williston grabbed him roughly by the arms as he tried to run. "Tahn? Are you all right?"

Hard blue eyes looked into his. "Daryl! Get the hell out of here! I gave you a direct order. What do you think you're doing? Go! Go!"

He struggled against iron arms, fear swelling to smother him. The shrill whine of discharging cannons split the day and Tahn spun. Grabbing Williston, he hurled him to the ground, trying to cover his friend with his own body. "Stay down, Daryl. Down!"

Jagged screams. Dirt raining over on them. Williston shoved out from beneath him, glaring into his face, eyes wide with disbelief. Another explosion.

Tahn screamed and slammed a fist into Daryl's shoulder, then crawled madly for the trenches. The vile odors of ionized air and blood strangled him. A moment later, Williston gripped his arm tightly, pulling him sideways. They struggled wildly against each other, rolling across the floor. For a split second, Tahn felt cold petrolon against his fingers. He reached down and grasped the pistol from Daryl's belt holster and leveled it at the oncoming wave of Pegasan invaders. Williston slapped it out of his hand, knocking it across the ground.

"Daryl, goddamn it, can't you see what's happening? They're going to kill us, man. Run!"

"Tahn, listen to me." Daryl's voice had gone so gentle, so quiet, it did not seem his at all. The hard hands on his arms loosened. "You're not on Earth. You're on Tikkun. The year is 5414. You listening to me? *The year is 5414.*"

Tahn shook his head, hearing the words, but barely understanding them. Shadows seemed to loom behind Daryl, moving, whispering, one voice—insidiously gloating—stabbed at him like a bright shining sword.

"Tahn," Daryl said softly. "It's all right. You're all right. You understand me? You're not on Earth."

Cole stopped writhing and lay panting, gazing up into sharp blue eyes filled now with something he didn't understand—some touch of reluctant camaraderie. And in a sudden, shocking moment, he realized whose arms pinned him to the floor. "Baruch. . . ." he whispered, shaking his head. "What . . . what happened?"

"Baruch?" Lichtner's voice penetrated his haze.

An instant later, rifle fire slashed the ward, and Tahn saw Baruch running, fighting to get away, but Manstein's shot took him in the shoulder, hurling him to the floor. The Underground leader writhed, trying to drag himself to the door. A wide trail of blood stained the stone floor. Four guards surrounded him, pistols aimed at his head and chest. Weakly, Tahn pushed up on his elbows. Two guards lay dead, blown in half.

"Take him to the mind-probe room," Lichtner ordered his guards.

"No!" Baruch shouted. *"Tahn! Tell them no!"*

But the guards dragged him from the room. Lichtner strolled lazily to stand over Tahn. An exultant smile lit his square face. "Well, you may not have been able to capture Baruch, Captain, but I have. I suspected his identity earlier."

Tahn felt dizzy, weak with trembling, but he gingerly got to his feet. "No mind probes," he ordered with as much harshness as he could muster. He stabbed a finger into Lichtner's chest. "You got that, Major? *No probes!"*

Lichtner stiffened, glancing down at his chest as though Tahn's touch had soiled him. "All right. No probes. Now get back to your ship, Tahn. *I'm* in charge in Block 10."

Lichtner left the room. Tahn wiped sweat from his brow and propped hands on his hips, lungs heaving as his thoughts whirled. Why hadn't Baruch killed him when he had the chance? If he'd pulled his weapon in the initial stages, he could have killed every Magisterial soldier in the room and gotten clean away. Why hadn't he?

Shaking, Tahn headed for the door, forcing his eyes to stay riveted to the floor, but a stray image of blonde waves twisted his stomach. He groped for the wall, steadying himself as he vomited.

Forcing his weak knees to move, he ran for his shuttle.

CHAPTER 49

Sybil and Mikael lay underneath his bed, holding each other's hand tightly, watching the lights of his cabin flicker on and off irregularly. They'd been playing checkers to try and forget the scary things going on around them. The drink dispenser didn't work anymore—or when it did it shot out nasty smelling things, so they'd stopped using it.

Mikael looked over at Sybil. Her dark eyes glittered like shiny brown rocks underwater. She didn't look scared, but he was. His heart clip-clopped like a running horse in his chest.

"Don't worry, Mikael," Sybil said confidently, patting his hand. "Avel's coming. He wouldn't leave us by ourselves."

Mikael jerked a nod, but he wasn't sure he believed it. He didn't want to tell Sybil that maybe Avel couldn't come, that maybe Avel was dead like everybody in his family except his Uncle Yosef. "Sure. I know that."

"He probably just got held up somewhere. It happens." She brushed brown curls out of her eyes and gazed at him seriously. "When I was on Horeb, Avel put me in this cave to keep me safe. It had a bunch of books and food and lots of candles and water. I cried for a while because it scared me to be alone in there and I didn't think he was coming back. But finally, when it was safe, Avel came to get me again. He'll come get us, too."

They both jumped when a bunch of loud screeches blared through his door com—like bursts of rifle fire in the corridor outside. Mikael grabbed Sybil's arm and dragged her farther under his bed, until they both pressed against the back wall, breathing hard.

Sybil reached forward and pulled his blanket down so that it touched the floor, forming a gray curtain in front of them. Nobody would be able to see them if they came into the cabin. Mikael felt better. He gazed around their dark hiding place. Only the foot of his bed let light through—that scary on and off light. He smiled at Sybil.

"Thanks, Sybil. I'd have never thought of that."

She grabbed his hand again, holding it tight. He could see her cheeks moving while she ground her teeth. Her forehead had wrinkles in it, like she was thinking hard.

"Sybil?" he asked timidly. "When do you think Captain Erinyes is going to come get us?"

"I don't know." She shook her head. "I guess sometime before the ship gets attacked."

"Do we need to take anything with us?"

"I don't think so. But that dream never came back, so I'm not sure."

Mikael bit his lower lip. He felt so worried his fingers had gone cold and numb. He and Sybil had put on their best clothes because they knew they'd be going somewhere pretty soon. He studied the tiny silver threads shimmering in Sybil's red robe, then looked at his own black robe, embroidered on the sleeves and hem with light blue swirls. He guessed they looked all right.

Sybil patted his hand again. "Are you cold, Mikael?"

"Just a little."

"Yeah, I bet. I think maybe whatever's going wrong with the ship made our thermostat weird, too." Sybil pulled the sleeve of her robe down to cover both their hands, then breathed on his fingers.

A chill went up his back; it felt good. He slid closer to her and put his free arm over her shoulders. "Sybil? Thanks for being my friend. I feel lots better with you close to me."

She smiled brightly and he felt as good as he used to when the first flowers of springtime came out to dot the mountains of Kayan. He leaned his head against her shoulder and stroked her other arm.

In a brilliant flare of purple, their locked door burst inward, petrolon fragments smashing the walls like a thousand thrown rocks. Sybil screamed and dove to cover Mikael. He lay still, whimpering, feeling her warm body pressing down on him.

"Mikael Calas?" a strange voice called.

A sob of fear caught in his throat, choking him. He tried to swallow it, but it didn't quite work. "Who is it?"

"My name's Sergeant Jason West, son. Come on out from there."

Mikael twisted his head to look up at Sybil and saw her dark eyes darting with thought. Finally, Sybil nodded and slid off him. They both crawled out from under the bed. A tall man with light-brown hair and a skinny nose stood in the blasted doorway, a rifle in his hands.

Mikael stood up and helped Sybil. "What do you want, sir?"

West smiled in a kindly way. "I'm going to take you to a safe place. Captain Tahn's orders. He didn't want to take any chances you might get hurt in the fight for the ship."

Mikael's eyes filled with tears. He didn't know whether he should trust this soldier or not. He looked pleadingly at Sybil.

Her dark eyes narrowed. "Mister West," she said, "we want to stay with our people."

"I'm truly sorry, little lady, but I can't let you do that. It would be very dangerous."

Sybil licked her lips and swallowed hard. She looked back at Mikael. "I guess we'd better go with him," she said, then lowered her voice to a faint whisper. "It's probably part of the plan anyway."

Mikael rubbed a fist in his tear-filled eyes. "Okay."

He took a step forward, then ran across his cabin, grabbing the stamps the captain had given him. He tucked them in his pocket, before running back to grab Sybil's hand.

* * *

Bogomil strode briskly out of the transport tube and onto the bridge of the *Jataka*. He'd showered and gotten a full eight hours of sleep. He felt almost human again. The braid on his purple uniform shimmered like chains of gold. Around the bridge, a blue alert flashed. On the forward screen, the entire spectrum wavered, ripples of purple and yellow glimmering around the edges.

"Lieutenant Dharon," he called as he stepped over to stand beside his command chair. "How long until we exit vault?"

She leaned forward to check the chronometer on her console. Her salt and pepper hair hung in damp strands around her square face. "About twenty seconds, sir."

"Good. If everything has gone correctly, we should all be exiting within minutes of each other."

"Aye, sir."

Bogomil dropped into his chair and drummed his fingers on his leg. *Relax. You still have hours to complete battle strategy.* They'd enter the Lysomian system from five different directions, hurtling toward Tikkun where they'd form up into the Star at the last minute. He had a good three hours before he had to worry about bringing his weapons to full power.

"*Scipio* on screen, sir." Winnow announced. She sat stiffly at her com console, on edge, dark hair fluffing around her shoulders. "Abruzzi is sending an 'all's well' message."

Bogomil looked up, seeing the light appear on the high-range magnification screen. "Fine. Right on time." Two other lights streaked in around the edges.

"Which ships are those, Dharon?"

"*Aratus* and . . . *Leimon*."

Bogomil ground his teeth, frowning at the screen, waiting. His bridge crew, he noticed, did the same. Their eyes were frozen on the shimmering tubes of light that cut across the black background of space.

Winnow looked at him over her shoulder. "I have all three captains on line, sir. Shall I wait longer for *Klewe*?"

He shifted uncomfortably, rubbing his chin. He hesitated for several more minutes before muttering under his breath, "Blast you, Joel."

Dharon spun around in her chair to give him a disgruntled look. "Where the hell's Erinyes, Brent? If that sonofabitch—"

"Easy," he said. "Leave it to me. If this is some political ploy, I'll wring his neck myself."

"Fine. You take Joel baby. I'll take Uncle Nafred."

He gave her a look of mock severity. "That's enough. We don't know for certain—"

"Sir?" Winnow interrupted. "Captain Abruzzi is requesting visual."

"Put him on. No. Put them all on—simultaneously."

"Aye, aye, sir."

As the faces formed on the monitors around him, Bogomil sat up nervously.

* * *

Avel Harper gripped his rifle and peered around the corner. He watched Janowitz through the annoying flashing of the overhead panels. The erratic lights washed out the scene, making it seem a slow-motion run of an ancient black and white film. Chris had stationed six people along the walls outside of access tunnel twelve on level seven. Four more guarded the immediately adjacent halls, rifles held in tight fists. Sweat drenched every face. Avel turned to check the positioning of his own people. They each stood guard over an intersecting corridor.

He braced a shoulder against the wall and sucked in a deep breath. Was this all a ruse? They'd seen no sign at all of Magisterial forces and they'd been waiting over an hour. An eternity.

Avel massaged the back of his neck, wondering where Jeremiel was and what he'd discovered on Tikkun. Per instructions, Harper had already laid plans for evacuating those same refugees if Jeremiel found anything unpleasant on the surface. *If we can escape before those cruisers get here.*

458

He saw Janowitz stand up and trot back toward him. His blond hair shone silver in the fluctuating lights.

"Avel, listen," Chris said, mouth pinched. "I think this is a diversion for something else. Maybe you'd better take your people and go guard something more critical."

"Where? We've got most of our people stationed in Engineering and Life Systems."

Chris shook his head. "I don't know, but I think this is a waste of all our energies. Maybe you should go take care of Mikael and Sybil after all."

Harper put hands on his hips and expelled a long exhale. "All right. I have to check on operations on level twenty before I can go pick up Mikael and Sybil. I'll be there if you need me. If nothing happens in the next half hour, maybe you ought to call off this vigil completely."

"No," Chris shook his head. "I think I'll leave a small contingency force just in case."

"Do whatever you think is best. But let's try to stick to the original plans. I'll meet you in wardroom twenty-fourteen at 0:1200."

Chris nodded. "If I'm able, I'll be there." He gave Avel a wry smile and backed away, trotting to crouch again outside the access tunnel.

Harper waved harshly to his people, gathering them up and heading purposefully down the hall.

Chris Janowitz shifted positions to ease the strain in his cramped legs. He glanced around at the people beside him. A good crew, one and all—if only half-trained. He smiled faintly to himself. When they'd been on Horeb, each of these men had spent their days going about monastic duties—striving diligently to keep their souls pure for God. Images of their angelic, calm faces in the caves of the Desert Fathers flitted through his mind, overlaid with the faces that currently studied him through granite hard eyes.

Chris leaned his head back against the wall, staring at the floor. If they didn't get out of here soon, the flashing lights would drive them all madder than hatters. He sucked in a deep breath, vaguely perceiving the slight, very slight trace of sweetness in the air.

"Marcus?" he called to the brown-haired boy at the end of the hall. "What time you got?" The wall chronometers had long ago ceased to make sense.

"09:00 hours, Chris. Don't tell me you're itching to get out of here?"

A round of laughter echoed through the hall. Chris smiled. "Me? Hell, no. You?"

"I figured the lot of us would spend the night here."

Boos and hisses seeped like twined serpents through the hall. Chris laughed. He suddenly felt desperately tired. He smoothed his hand over his rifle. The gray petrolon felt cool and comforting beneath his callused fingers.

"Well since you're so tough, Marcus, maybe we'll just let you spend the night here by yourself. Eh, boys? How does that. . . ."

Chris' lungs burned, blossoming into a fiery pain. "Oh, no. . . ." He tried to lurch to his feet, but he found himself unable to control his limbs. He fell sideways, croaking, *"Get . . . out! Go! Hurry!"*

Two men made it to their hands and knees. They crawled by him, collapsing in heaps a few feet before they reached the next intersecting corridor. Chris blinked blurry eyes. Gasps and choking sounds filled his ears, but he felt too tired to listen, too tired to move.

He felt his body go completely limp, lungs expelling a final hoarse breath. For a time, he lay facedown, a tiny thread of panic keeping his attention. Vaguely, as though in a dream, he felt someone lift the rifle from his hand and heard a husky female voice jubiliantly say, "Thank God for Halloway. *Now we've got weapons.*"

* * *

Sick with dread, Carey Halloway stepped onto the empty bridge. Her body had gone so numb she seemed to be walking on air. Lights flickered here, too, casting an eerie silver glow over the blank coms of eight duty stations. On the three-sixty overhead monitors, bits of data flashed, distorted, capricious nonsense.

Eloel gently prodded her in the back with her pistol. "Go to your com."

Carey nodded tiredly and stepped down to the second level, dropping heavily into her chair. She braced her elbows on her console and steepled her fingers before her mouth, staring hollowly at the rotating image of Tikkun that graced the forward monitor. She felt like a thin bit of interstellar dust caught in a line of cannon fire.

"Where would I find a vacuum suit, Lieutenant?"

Rachel inquired.

"In the storage compartment to your left."

Eloel marched to it quickly and unfastened the lock. The door slid back to reveal suits and a variety of emergency supplies.

"Pull out two," Carey said matter-of-factly.

Rachel glanced at her curiously. "You think I want you alive when this is all over?"

"Might be a good idea—since I'm on your side . . . now."

"You must think I'm a trusting sort."

"I don't care whether you are or not, but it would make things easier. You can always shoot me if it looks like I lied."

Eloel gazed reflectively at her, then nodded and pulled out two suits and helmets. "I will, Lieutenant." She stepped into her suit and fastened it all the way up before striding across the room and tossing Carey a suit and helmet. "But just in case you're telling the truth. . . ." Rachel hesitantly extended a hand. Distinctly non-Gamant—clearly an effort to bridge old hurts. "Glad to have you fighting on the right side, Lieutenant."

Carey took her hand, shaking hard, and noticed the tiny letters AKT branded into Eloel's forehead just at the hairline. Curious. She wondered what they meant. "For the moment, it feels good. Now, let's get this show on the road. We haven't much time."

Eloel nodded and walked toward the command chair. She dropped gracefully into it and glanced at Tikkun. The planet whirled placidly. "Can you do something about these crazy lights. Turn them off or something? It would be easier to concentrate."

As Carey put on her suit, she said, "No, sorry."

Rachel grimaced and focused on the forward monitor. They'd passed to the night side of the planet. The lights of cities sparkled like strewn jewels, emeralds and diamonds, rubies and amber. Carey looked down with a tense longing. Where was Cole? Jeremiel?

"Rachel," she said, "I'm going to try to get Tahn."

"Go ahead, but be very careful what you say. I'd rather not. . . ." Eloel jerked abruptly and Carey's gaze shot to the monitor. The spark of silver caught her eye, too. It appeared and disappeared. A short time later, the spark became a prolonged glimmer, sliding through space toward them.

Eloel sat forward. "Is it them?"

"Let's see."

Carey took a few seconds to input the sequence, then she braced herself for other voices, unknown people whom she'd have to bluff—and called, "Captain Tahn? This is Halloway? Do you read?"

A static distorted voice responded, "Carey? What the hell are you. . . . Are you on . . . bridge?"

"Aye, Captain."

"What's happening there?"

"Unknown. I haven't had access to the crew. But . . . Cole, there are some things we need to discuss. I've just reviewed the clandestine files about the Tikkun projects."

A garbled sentence came through, then Cole's voice rose above it, *"Trying to tell me something . . . Carey?"*

She opened her mouth to respond, but no words would form. She fought the inner welling of traitorous guilt.

Cole came on again, voice calm. "Switching sides, Lieutenant?"

Her heart thudded. She propped a fist on the table, feeling so barrenly empty she could barely stand it. She loved Cole Tahn. Going against him was like a cold blade ripping her soul in half. *"Aye, Captain."*

Silence.

A roll of static filled with half words.

Finally, she heard him say, "Good. The thought of fighting . . . you turned my stomach. Get hold of Eloel. Tell . . . we need arms. But it's got to be just you and me, Carey. I don't want . . . implicate the crew."

"Understood," she whispered. Relief brought tears to her eyes. "Rachel and I will meet you in the bay. Halloway out."

She whirled around in her chair to find Eloel staring at her through glittering eyes. Carey's brows drew together. Eloel looked as though she stood over a corpse, blood on her hands, and didn't recognize the dead face that gazed back at her.

Rachel murmured darkly, "That's why he wanted Jeremiel to take Tahn."

"Who?"

"And why he wanted you to stay here." Rachel shook her head and lurched unsteadily to her feet. Her long

462

black hair glistened like a shroud around her shoulders. "Hurry. Let's go."

Carey ran past Rachel, hitting the transport tube patch. The door shrieked at them, but stayed closed. Carey pounded her fist into it again and again. "Damn it. Come on! It'll take us an hour if we have to use the duct system."

Rachel holstered her pistol and slammed her palm into the patch with Carey. Finally it snicked open and they rushed inside.

CHAPTER 50

Dannon followed as Yosef Calas led the way down a long flickering corridor on level twenty. His purple uniform stuck to his back and chest, bathed in sweat. It had taken them forever to find transport tubes that worked, and then they'd had trouble getting them to stop at the right floors. The com virus Tahn had introduced had been running through the ship like wildfire across a bone-dry prairie. And Funk and Calas refused to let Neil touch any of the controls. The fools. If he could have gotten into the manual override system, he'd have saved them half the time. As they neared an intersecting corridor, Neil slowed his steps.

"Move!" Funk said and jabbed his pistol barrel into Neil's back. The old coot had been acting like a tomcat who'd just caught a mouse and wanted to swat it around for a while before it sank its teeth in. All in all, Neil had been attempting to take it in quiet good grace—but that seemed to stimulate Funk like catnip. The old man ungently prodded his back again.

Dannon shouted angrily, "I'm not going to have any kidneys left if you keep that up, old man!"

"Good!" Ari blustered. "I hope you've passed your last pint!"

Neil grimaced. Yosef turned to gaze curiously at them,

463

then sighed and walked back. "Ari, stop that. You've tortured him enough."

Funk blinked owlishly. "Compared to *what?* Slow poison is too good for this worthless—"

"Then poison him," Calas suggested. "But quit jabbing him in his vital parts!"

"Vital? I haven't even aimed there yet. I was saving that for later."

"Try to be professional, will you?"

Neil nodded heartily. Black hair dangled in wet strands in his eyes. He shook them back. "You tell him, Gramps."

Calas scowled, then indignantly pulled his head up. "Never mind, Ari. Torture him." He waved a hand and waddled forward again.

Neil grunted at the sharp pains, trying to twist away from the afflicting barrel. He'd been holding off, waiting for a better opportunity, but if Funk didn't stop this soon, he'd make his move and one of these old codgers would end up dead.

Ari snickered. "Sure. Professional. Like Torquemada. Like Pleros of Antares III. You bet. I can do that."

Dannon let out a disgruntled yowl. "For God's sake, Funk! Just kill me outright. I can't stand much more of this!"

"No need to rush," Ari responded with maddening suaveness.

Yosef trudged onward and Neil obediently followed, hands held high.

"So, Yosef?" Ari called, sounding far more professional. "What do you think we ought to do with this waste product who betrayed all of Gamant civilization and tried to get Jeremiel killed?"

Dannon's guts tightened. His traitorous mind drew up the expression on Jeremiel's face a few days ago—the abiding remnants of love in those stony blue eyes pierced Neil's soul. *Where are you, old friend? Are you all right?*

Funk continued, "I say we bury him alive."

Yosef grimaced condescendingly. "You romantic. There's not a shred of dirt aboard this entire ship."

"Who needs dirt? There are a thousand things we could use." An eerie smile lit Ari's face. "You remember that dinner they fed us last week? The texture alone ought to do it."

"Don't be ridiculous. We need his body to prove we got him. That stuff would eat through Io-titanium in ten seconds flat."

Dannon glanced back and forth between them, brow furrowed, feeling dismayed and grudgingly amused. He shook his head and let out an exasperated breath. "You know, it's hard to take you two seriously."

Funk laughed demonically, "Good," and prodded Neil in the kidney again.

They rounded a corner into a new corridor and Yosef's steps floundered. The dark hall carried traces of a strange cloying odor. Panic reared in Neil's breast. Yosef started to go forward again, but he gripped the old man's sleeve and jerked him back.

"Let go of him, Dannon!" Funk shouted. His pistol hummed loudly as he kicked the charge up to full.

"Wait, Ari!" Yosef shook off Neil's restraining hand and glowered. "What is it?"

"I just saved your life, Calas. Back up."

Neil slowly eased out of the hallway. His captors followed, glancing worriedly over their shoulders. A nervous twitch plagued Dannon's left cheek, but his eyes gleamed, studying the wavering overhead light panels, the shade of the walls.

"Did you smell it?" Neil asked.

"That sweet scent?" Calas answered.

"Yes. Some sort of petrolon gas. I'm not sure which variety."

"Gas?" Funk gasped, eyes widening like a startled owl. "Like nerve gas?"

Neil shook his head. "This is much more sophisticated. It acts on brain chemicals, bonding to neurotransmitters, changing their composition."

Funk inhaled a deep breath, then thought better of it and expelled it in a coughing fit. "Is that bad?"

"It'll turn your brain to mush, Funk." He gave Ari a critical sideways glance. "Though you may not have anything to worry about—and anyway, it dissipates fast, becoming harmless in ordinary atmospheres after about sixty seconds. Let's wait here a while."

Calas shot a worried look at Funk—but they waited, shifting from foot to foot.

Finally, Neil nodded. "I think that's more than long enough."

Ari said, "Fine. You go first, expert."

Dannon heaved a taut breath and stepped out, cautiously proceeding down the hall, stopping frequently to sniff the air or examine the lights, looking for the characteristic color distortion caused when octopetrolon gas lingered in lethal concentrations in the air. They plodded with slow care for several minutes until they neared the entrance to Engineering on level twenty. Dannon turned a corner, then stepped back hurriedly, bumping into Yosef.

"What's wrong?" Calas demanded.

Neil leaned heavily against the wall and wiped a sleeve across his watering mouth. "I don't know who you were hoping to take me to, Calas—but I think you've lost your chance."

Yosef glared questioningly, then strode forward, around the corner. The old man made a small sorrow-laden sound. Neil sucked in a deep halting breath. Five men lay in contorted heaps in that hall, eyes wide and dead. All Gamants.

Calas stumbled into Funk's supporting arms and lifted a hand to rub his throat. "Ari," he croaked. "Harper. . . ."

"What?" Funk's withered face lined with terror. He released Calas and strode around the corner himself. A few seconds later, he whispered, "But he . . . he was supposed to be taking care of Mikael and Sybil."

Calas started to shiver. "Not the children. Oh, Ari, not the children! Surely the Magisterial soldiers aboard have human souls?"

"Yosef," Ari murmured hoarsely. "We have to hurry. I think this means we've lost Engineering. We have to—"

"Good guess, old man," Dannon said, though he knew that wasn't the case. If Tahn's people had recaptured Engineering, they'd have already corrected the com virus and flooded every deck but their own with toxic gas—that or decompressed the ship again.

Neil straightened up as Funk pointed his pistol; it shook in the wrinkled fist. "Yosef, we have to get rid of Dannon and go find Sybil and Mikael. They're probably—"

"Yes," Yosef murmured in agony. "Let's hurry."

Ari stepped forward, extending a hand to get Dannon moving in the right direction. Neil whirled with the

466

supreme grace of a ballet dancer, gripping Funk's arm and twisting it until the old man cried out in pain. Dannon grasped the pistol and stepped back, leveling it at Calas' chest. Drop your gun, old man!"

Calas did as instructed, gently placing his pistol on the floor. Neil reached down and picked it up and tucked it in the waistband of his trousers.

Calas rushed to Funk's aid, shoving up his sleeve to look at his hurt arm. Ari made a choked back sound of agony. The wounded look in Calas' faded eyes made Neil wince.

"I didn't break it," Dannon assured, backing farther down the corridor. "Get out of here, you two old fools. Tahn's people don't have any soft spots for Gamants. Go find some place safe to hide."

Calas' mouth puckered as he gently stroked Funk's arm. He looked up at Neil angrily. "Where is that, Mister Dannon? I don't believe any safe place exists for Gamants anymore—not in this galaxy."

Neil regripped his pistol. From out of the depths of his memories Jeremiel's deep voice spun like a silken web of sound, *"Without us, Neil, there'll be no sanctuaries for Gamants. No place where any of our people will be able to sleep two nights in a row. I know you hate this. I don't like it either. But it's either the Underground, or oblivion."*

Neil shuddered. He could still clearly feel the weight of Jeremiel's strong hand on his shoulder, squeezing warmly.

Calas watched him through sharp eyes as though he suspected something of what Neil must be feeling. He left Funk's side to hobble forward. His wizened face slackened into kinder lines. He looked up, unafraid of the pistol Neil leveled at his bald head.

"Mister Dannon, it's never too late. Our side still needs trained soldiers. Come back to us?" He extended a withered old hand. *"Come back. . . ."*

Neil clamped his jaw, fighting the urge to grasp those elderly fingers. "You think Jeremiel will forgive my sins, Calas? Don't be a fool. He wants me dead."

"I don't think he does. I think he hates you only because he still loves you so much and he has to punish himself for those feelings; it's tearing him apart."

An old and brutal ache stirred in Neil's breast. "Get out of here, Calas. Go find a niche in one of the bays.

They're nonessential. Tahn's people won't check them until they have leisure time. Which shouldn't be for a few hours."

He turned and ran lightly down the corridor, heading for the bridge where he knew emergency supplies existed. But he couldn't get Calas' words out of his mind—they lingered like a festering stab wound in his heart.

Yosef watched Dannon disappear down the hall and looked anxiously at Ari. "Where can we go, Ari?"

"Engineering."

"But I thought you said—"

"I did, but that look on Dannon's face made me rethink." Ari waved his good arm disgustedly. "If Tahn's balloon brains were in Engineering, every Gamant aboard would be dead. Come on. Those have to be our people in there."

Holding his injured arm, Ari trudged down the hall, stepping wide around the dead bodies that littered the floor. Yosef swallowed to keep his stomach down, and followed in Ari's footsteps.

CHAPTER 51

The 20th of Tishri.

Morning sunlight burned along the edges of the highest cliffs like a flaming curtain of woven cornsilk. Pavel's eyes drifted over the magnificence. The towering stone wall that sheltered Block 10 rose at least a thousand feet straight up from the valley floor. Today, they had the photon shield turned low, extending only twenty feet beyond the walls. High above, ser hawks soared on thermals, wings spread in a gesture of such freedom that Pavel felt his captivity like a hangman's noose against his throat.

Around him, grunts and gasps slashed the air. Men and women worked tirelessly to complete the new wing of the hospital. The Magistrates had sophisticated equipment which could accomplish the task far more quickly and efficiently, yet they forced the prisoners to build and build until they thought they'd drop from the ravages of heat and thirst. Beside him, Jasper labored to lift another shovelful of dirt into the back of a truck. His thin arms trembled with the effort.

Pavel wiped his sweaty forehead on his forearm, glancing fearfully at the black ships that dotted the azure sky. Guards had come and herded the boys away that morning—just to talk to them the guards said, just to give them a little lecture about anatomy. And every hour that passed, a chill bubble of fear swelled larger in Pavel's chest until now he felt desperate to run and find Yael.

"Grandpa, I'm worried about Yael. Maybe they'd let me just go look—"

"Don't be foolish. You saw what happened to young Pona. They mowed him down without a second thought for asking for an extra ration of bread. Stay put. Yael will be all right. And there's nothing you can do just now anyway."

"But, Grandpa, what if they find out—"

"There's nothing you can do." Jasper hefted another shovel-load of dirt, wobbling on his weak knees. "Besides, they told us all to be prepared for a special show at seven-thirty. If you're missing, there's no telling what they'll do."

Pavel nodded obediently, but continued to worry. None of them had seen any of the women, and they'd been marched all over camp several times. Had they moved them? Ships came and went all the time. They could have. His mind had been wound so tightly around Yael, he'd barely thought of Aunt Sekan. It made him ashamed of himself. And his father, dear Epagael, how was his father? Dead? Yes . . . almost certainly. Tears welled uncontrollably in his eyes. He stopped working, leaning on the handle of his shovel.

"Grandpa, are you all right?"

"Don't worry about me. You're the one they beat half to death. How are you?"

Pavel gazed forlornly into those wise old eyes. A sheen of sweat glazed Jasper's bald head, puddling in the wrinkles of his long face.

"I'll make it." He inhaled deeply of the searing air, steadying himself.

"Did you tell the doctors who bandaged your ribs that Lichtner and his boys did it?"

Pavel put all of his weight into his shovel, adding to the growing mound in the truck, delaying answering. Grandpa would chastise him, tell him he should have stood up for himself, but he couldn't help what he'd done. He was more afraid than he'd ever been in his life. "I told them I fell down the stairs outside the amphitheater."

"You. . . !" Grandpa began, then silently recanted. "Well, maybe that was for the best. But they might have been able to put a stop to such brutality if you'd told them the truth."

"Maybe. But I believe Lichtner's threats. I don't want any more trouble."

Jasper tried to lift another shovelful but lost his balance and stumbled into the hot metal tailgate. The blue truck was a monstrous thing, holding maybe ten tons of dirt, and they'd barely dented the gaping maw.

"Grandpa, why don't you sneak around the side of the truck into the shadows. I'll keep watch on the ships to make sure they don't catch on. Rest for a while. I'll keep shoveling. Maybe they won't notice you're gone until you feel better."

"Why are there so many ships today? Are we such threatening men?"

Jasper braced a hand on the tailgate to support himself while he made his way to the shadows. He gripped Pavel's shoulder lovingly as he passed by, but Pavel barely noticed; his eyes were glued to the ships. They didn't move and he heard no scathing voice boom over the speakers.

"I think you're safe, Jasper. Sit down. Rest your legs."

"You're a good boy, Pavel. You know that?"

"I thought you didn't like me, Grandpa."

"Don't be foolish. I've just been trying to teach you to be a fighter. I only spent time on you because I love you. But you'd never listen to me. You thought I was just a crazy old man."

"I was young—in more ways than one."

He threw his weight behind his shovel, working enough for two men. He didn't know how long he'd be able to keep it up, but maybe long enough for Jasper to catch his breath. They'd no right, *no right,* to force a three-hundred-year-old man to work like a field animal.

"Pavel?"

"What?"

"What do you think this show is today?"

The sweat on his body suddenly chilled. He shivered, shoveling harder. "I don't know. I'm worried about it."

"You've heard the rumors?"

Harshly, he answered, "I don't believe them! What would Jeremiel be doing here? Eh? Why would he come to the pit of darkness without his fleet at his back? *It's impossible.*"

Jasper wheezed softly. "I hope to God you're right." Then, as though gathering his strength, he paused. "Pavel? What did those doctors tell you? You've been talking about it in your sleep. Tossing and turning like it's driving you mad."

He paled. "Have I?"

"Yes, but I don't understand most of the things you say. And I want to know what's going on. Tell me."

He'd been hoping Grandpa wouldn't ask, hoping no one would. Not that most of them would understand, but Lichtner had been clear—*tell no one.* He vied with himself for a minute, then two, finally deciding Jasper had a right to know. Besides, Pavel could trust him and he desperately needed to talk about it.

"You can't tell anyone, Grandpa. I know they're all asking, but if Lichtner were to—"

"I won't tell!"

"All right," he sighed. "The Magistrates are toying with the notion that Gamants possess their own brand of mental illness."

"Bah! What? They think we're all crazy?"

"Crazy and dangerous. They're using the rebellions of the past and the Gamant Leader's journey through the *Mea* to God as examples of our bizarre delusional behavior."

"The *Mea*'s not bizarre."

"To them it is. They consider it to be a symbol of our particular brand of lunacy."

"It's a source of comfort, not insanity. Gamant children are raised knowing that if things really get bad, they can go talk to God to get it worked out."

"And Magisterial citizens are raised believing comfort

471

comes from Slothen's economic system."

"That's because they're stupid. Do you feel comfortable? Eh?" Jasper waved an arm irritably.

"Not at this particular moment, but I used to. I never needed to take a trip to ask Epagael for advice. The government lulled us into believing we were safe, valued citizens of the regime."

"So what do these hoity-toity doctors think the problem is with our brains?"

Pavel gazed around at the men working nearby. Starved and exhausted beyond comprehension, none seemed to be paying them the slightest attention. Some still bore the blackening bruises of the fight last night in the cafeteria. One desperately hungry old man had snatched a piece of bread from his neighbor's plate and tried to run away with it. A gang had gathered to chase him down, beating him until they could take it away and divide it amongst themselves. Now, beneath the hot sun, sweat flooded down their dusty bodies, leaving trails of mud. Their tortured faces reminded him of the painted hollow-eyed masks worn by theater actors. Fill the shovel and lift, that's all they knew on this terrible day.

Pavel exhaled tiredly and answered Jasper's query. "They think there's an imbalance of some sort that makes us feel vulnerable even when there's no threat. They see our—"

"No threat! *Where the hell have they been?* They've blasted a half dozen of our planets in the past year! The idiots. Of course we feel vulnerable! And what does feeling vulnerable have to do with the *Mea*?"

"They say our trips to Epagael are our brains' way of coping with it—by creating comforting delusions."

"And what do they think causes the vulnerability?"

"A genetic malfunction. An excess of endorphins or too many receptors—"

"Like the fishes?"

"That's dolphins." Pavel shook his head, wanting to laugh for the first time in a week. But he couldn't quite remember the sound. "It's a lot different. These are chemicals involved in the brain's reward system—"

"Malfunction, hooey!" Jasper grunted and Pavel saw him extend his long legs across the sand, knees still shaking beneath his thin white robe. "They're worried, that's what. Old Zadok went to talk to Epagael during the last Revolt and we wiped out a few hundred thousand Magisterial soldiers. I bet they wish they could get their filthy blue hands on a *Mea* so they could go through, too!"

Pavel chuckled despite himself. "They'd get lost in the void before they ever reached the gate to the first heaven. Even—"

"And if they reached it, the angel Sedriel would make them name the five gillion secret names of God and they'd get thrown back into the void."

For a moment, they both smiled, amused by the thought of one of the Magistrates going through Epagael's seven heavens. The men around them looked up in astonishment that anyone here—in this horrifying place—could laugh. Pavel glanced worriedly at the ships. They still hadn't moved. Hot wind whimpered through the weave of huge natural stones scattering the ground, sucking moisture from his exhausted body. He licked the sweat from his upper lip.

"So, we have too much of the fish chemical. So what?"

"Well, if your limbic system and temporal lobes—"

Jasper leaned around the tire to give him a scorching look. His grimy white sleeves ruffled in the searing wind. Indignantly, he demanded, "Talk Gamant."

"Sorry. . . . When the world around you no longer makes you feel safe, your interpreter works overtime trying to figure out why not. But since there's a chemical imbalance, the interpreter doesn't get the facts right, so—"

"So our brains figure wrong, is that it?"

"That's it. The interpreter makes up a story to fit the only facts it has which are partial facts. The scary thing is that they think after prolonged craziness, these delusions take on a life of their own, forming a whole new set of crazy memories to support the delusions. They become part of our psychohistory and forever influence the way we think."

"So the entire history of our People's struggle is delusional?"

Pavel heaved another shovel load into the truck and wiped his drenched nose on his sleeve. "That's about it."

"They're stupid!" Jasper charged. "They know nothing about Gamant history! If they did. . . ."

They both stopped. The ships had started to move.

From around the perimeter of the camp, guards closed their net, pushing prisoners toward the central parade ground. Laborers from throughout this far section of the camp formed up into rows of five abreast, walking forward blindly.

"Get up, Grandpa. *Hurry!*"

Jasper shoved to his feet, leaning against the truck on shaking legs. He grabbed his shovel and squinted at the black ships. They slowly closed ranks, forming interlocking chevrons.

"Come on," Pavel said, going to Jasper and gripping his arm in support. "We'd better go, too."

Jasper nodded obligingly. They blended in with the rank and file, shuffling toward the parade ground. As they neared, he made out a naked prisoner, hands bound behind his back, surrounded by guards with white wands in their fists. The victim's shoulder wore a thick bandage, but blood had seeped through, draining in rivulets down his chest to soak his muscular thighs in lurid patterns. He seemed half-mad, writhing against the iron hands of the guards who held him. Brown hair straggled about his ears, matted to his cheeks by clotted blood.

Pavel craned his neck to see over the heads of those in front of him. As they got closer, he stumbled, gripping Jasper's sleeve for support. "Blessed Epagael," he whispered. "It is *him*. His hair is different, but his face. . . . Oh, God."

The guards herded them into an irregular circle around the spectacle. When they'd calmed, stunned by the name that passed like lightning through the crowd, Major Lichtner strolled out to stand before them. Two guards with white wands in their hands took places on either side of him. He smiled savagely and beat his baton on his leg. Around him, two dozen guards formed parallel lines. Imperiously Lichtner called, "Quiet down! Shut your mouths!"

A thunderous hush fell over the gathering. Pavel looked around him. How could they be so quiet? How could they look so calm, so placidly interested, when the victim who stood at the head of the line was the last hope of nearly every man, woman, and child in the camp? It sent a hot flash of rage through him. Yet . . . yet, he hadn't the courage to do differently. Pavel wanted to run away, quickly and to the ends of the world, but his feet wouldn't move.

Lichtner strode around haughtily, slapping his baton on his purple pants. In the morning light, his medals gleamed like molten gold. He shouted, "To all you swine who thought your pathetic Underground would rescue you, I give you your leader!"

One of the guards lifted his white wand and a glacial blue thread of light shot out, striking Jeremiel in the side. Baruch writhed like a man caught in a fire storm of flame, fighting the hands that held him. A huge blister of blood rose on Jeremiel's side and burst, running like water down his leg. Breathlessly, he looked out over the swelling gathering. In a deep, booming voice, Baruch shouted, "You can fight them! *Fight!*"

The crowd backed away a few paces, withering in upon itself. Pavel glanced at Jasper. The old man's face had gone hard, eyes moist. "He's right. We're spineless, Pavel. A bunch of filthy stinking cowards. Look how we outnumber them!"

Pavel looked around at the terrified faces and bowed his head in shame. "They have guns, Grandpa. We have nothing."

"We have the strength of our hands!"

"It's not enough. They'll just kill us all."

Lichtner's cruel laugh carried like the stench of carrion over the crowd. He strode up and bashed Jeremiel across the face with his baton. "You urge these stinking vermin to revolt?" He chuckled disdainfully. "There are no greater cowards in the galaxy than Gamants! Where is your fleet, great leader? Why aren't they here to save you?"

No response. Then, in a choking voice, Baruch said to the crowd, "Don't . . . don't let them do this to you. You can win . . . stand up—"

"I'll tell you why!" Lichtner shouted gleefully. "We destroyed half his fleet in the Abulafian system and the other half ran like leprous dogs for the far reaches of the galaxy! Eh, Baruch? Isn't that right?"

Pavel's heart shriveled to dust. Could it be true? Was there no help on the way? *No. . . .*

Lichtner gestured shortly to his guards.

The tall one with curly red hair switched on his wand and the blue flame danced over Baruch's chest. So many huge blisters rose and burst in quick succession that his

475

skin seemed to boil. Pavel found himself straining to hear any word—but Baruch stayed deathly silent. Silver tears traced glistening lines down his cheeks.

Lichtner's rage swelled. He stamped around as though he'd explode. "Send him down the line!" he ordered.

The two guards who'd held Jeremiel shoved him forward. The first guards turned on their wands, striking Baruch in the back. He stumbled forward, almost falling as he weaved down the line. The blue threads of light seared and blackened his neck and chest. Puffs of steam and smoke encircled his tormented face.

As the sun rose higher in the sky it threw a harsh funereal light into their eyes. Pavel lifted a hand, shielding his face—his mind. He silently thanked God for his infinite wisdom in creating a world where sunlight blinded. *Baruch atta adonai. . . .*

As Baruch neared Pavel and Jasper, they almost gagged at the strong acrid scent of burning flesh and fear-sweat. For an instant, Jeremiel's blue eyes touched Pavel's and Pavel gripped the white fabric over his heart in horror. That silent agony struck him with the impact of Judgment Day.

The guards at the end of the line grabbed Baruch's wounded shoulders and whirled him around, forcing him to stagger back down the line toward Lichtner. The blue threads danced like animate demons, blackening his thighs and calves, searing the toes from his right foot. By the time Baruch reached the other end, he'd bent double, dragging that foot behind him, struggling with his last ounce of strength to make it.

Lichtner's treble laughter sounded so sweet and high that Pavel felt sickness rise. Jeremiel straightened, trembling all over. Blackened flesh crisscrossed his muscular body like the pus-filled bloated flesh of a plague victim. "You can . . . *fight!*" Baruch whispered wretchedly. "*You . . . can!*"

"Hold him!" Lichtner shouted.

Hesitantly, two guards approached, turning their heads at the odor as they gripped Baruch's arms tightly. Pavel stared aghast as Lichtner himself jerked a wand from the hand of one of his guards. No one breathed. Jeremiel looked at him through hate-filled eyes, then he lifted his contorted face toward the heavens. In a deep voice that quaked, Baruch began: *"Yisgadal ve'yiskadash. . . ."*

Pavel caught his breath. On the day he stood before God and listened to his own judgment read out, it would be no more terrible than this. Almost without being consciously aware, his lips picked up the rhythm of the mourner's kedis. As one, the crowd joined Baruch. Softly at first, but the crescendo of their voices soon rose to a thunderous wave that must have shaken the very foundations of heaven itself.

". . . sh'mey rabbo. Be'ol'mo deevro chiroosey. U'vyowmey—"

"Stop it! Stop it!" Lichtner cried. He waved wildly to his guards. "Make them shut up! Shut them up!"

". . . Ye'hey sh'mey rabbo me'vorach le'olam. . . ."

"Quiet!" Lichtner screamed insanely. "Shut up, all of you! Shut up or I'll kill him! You hear me? I'll kill your filthy hero!"

". . . Le'ylo min kol birchoso ve'sheeroso. . . ." The rumble ascended, borne by the hot wind, crashing over the camp like the unspeakable roar of the river of fire that flowed before the throne of God.

"That's enough! I warned you! I warned you!" Lichtner aimed his wand and the deadly blue thread shot out and into Jeremiel's right eye. A small, wretched cry escaped Baruch's lips. He staggered and the guards let him drop to his knees. He fell forward, forehead braced against the ground. Brown hair draped like a damp veil around his face.

A wave of hatred and shock overcame the crowd. Voices cried out in terror and indignation. Around him, Pavel saw men moving. One by one, they all turned away. They all showed the soldiers the wall of their white backs. Pavel bravely joined the wave, trembling in his boots as he turned. A brief burst of joy passed amongst them, weaving them once again into men—not dogs kicked so often they feared to lift their heads. "Here," the man next to Pavel said softly, "take my hand. We'll show them. We'll show them." Hands locked everywhere. Each man graced the comrade next to him with a lifted chin and a gaze strong in united defiance.

Then the guards moved in, thrashing with their truncheons, beating people about the heads and backs until tortured screams laced the wind. Pavel saw the man next to him fall and huddled in anticipation.

"You stupid idiots!" the guard who slammed Pavel's ribs shouted. "Look! *Look* before we blind you all for good!"

The guard passed, striking others, treating them like animals for refusing to stand witness to their own deaths. *And everyone knew that's what it was; they all felt it.* Jeremiel—on his knees—was each and every one of them. They lived his every heartbeat, his every breath. It came to Pavel like a truth whispered by an angel in his ear. Each lash Jeremiel had withstood, he could withstand. Each cry Jeremiel had suppressed, *so could he!*

Pavel dared to look up. Jeremiel lay sprawled facedown in the dirt. Flies had started to gather. They swarmed hungrily over his wounded body. He lay so still he seemed dead—but his hands . . . his hands dug into the soil. He clawed his way forward—toward Lichtner, who shouted, then shrieked madly for his guards. Dozens of black ships swooped down from the cerulean sky, skimming the red cliffs.

As though in a nightmare, Pavel heard Jasper scream, felt the hard old hands that shoved him out of the way. Purple arcs of light wove an eerie luminescent web of death around them. The crowd ran toward the center, huddling against each other, weeping, shaking fists weary with futility.

Pavel stood quietly, staring up. A tiny dagger of flame had crept into his heart like a thief in the night. A wild blaze had been kindled in his soul.

CHAPTER 52

Tahn circled the *Hoyer* three times, watching landing bay doors open and close at random. The cruiser glided effortlessly, beautiful, wings gleaming a pale gold in the glare of Tikkun's sun—even though internally she bore deep wounds.

"It's all right," he promised lovingly. "I'll have you

mended in no time."

He searched until he found a bay door that seemed stuck in the open position.

He hit his com switch. "Carey? Bay nineteen-six."

"Give . . . ten minutes to get there, Cole."

"Affirmative. Tahn out."

He set his controls on auto and climbed out of his chair, opening the emergency locker behind the pilot's station. He pulled out a vacuum suit and stepped into it, trying to take his time fastening it all the way up. The soft white fabric glistened like veils of pearlescent silk beneath the harsh lustreglobes. He set his helmet on the floor by the copilot's chair, then reseated himself.

He brought the *Eugnostos* back around, keeping perfect pace with the *Hoyer* so that he seemed to hover in front of the bay. Inside, he could see shuttles shackled to the floor like rows of ebony spear points. Where was Halloway? Hadn't ten minutes passed yet?

Since that terrible moment in Block 10, his world had seemed timeless—a thrumming eternity of ache and hatred. His nerves appeared to be leading a life of their own; they pulsed so vibrantly he had trouble staying in his seat.

"Calm down," he softly urged himself. "Get control. You're going to need it to pull this off."

From the corner of his eye, he caught a flash of white in the bay and turned. Two vacuum-suited forms clung to wall braces at the far end. He swung the shuttle around in a narrow arc, gliding into the bay. Applying constant upward thrust, he kept the ship stationary while Carey, he presumed, sailed forward in ghostly slow motion and clamped down the shackles on the *Eugnostos.*

Cole picked up his helmet and secured it in place, then sprinted to the zero-g compartment and sealed himself in—keeping the central command cabin pressurized and ready.

When he opened the side door, he gripped the outer handholds and pulled himself along the hull of the ship. Carey waited at the far end. As he closed on her position, she lifted an arm and wrapped it around his shoulder, pulling him close and patting his back.

Her first question worried him. "Where's Jeremiel?"

"Captured. We have to hurry."

She pulled back. He could see her desperate eyes

through the visor. "We need a secure place to talk," he said. "Have you made arrangements?"

"Yes." Her voice sounded a little scratchy through the speakers. "We've set up in conference room nineteen-ten."

He playfully bumped helmets with her. Having her on his side had always made him feel better—and never more than now when he still couldn't bring himself to say the word "treason" aloud. "Let's go. We've got damned little time."

They made their way across the bay to Rachel, who gripped a rifle in one arm, while holding the door brace with the other.

"Captain," she greeted. She shifted her head, as though looking past him toward the shuttle, waiting. "Where's Jeremiel?"

Tahn lifted a glove and placed it on her shoulder. "On Tikkun. I'll explain everything inside."

She briskly gestured with her rifle for him to lead the way into the foyer. He obliged. Once the door had snicked closed behind them, he hit the appropriate patches to repressurize the compartment.

Nothing happened.

"Goddamn it," he cursed, slamming his fist into the console.

He tried again . . . and again. Finally, he ripped the cover off the console and accessed the manual override system. The compartment filled with air. They all removed their helmets.

They strode out into the barrenly empty, strobe-lit hall. Carey trotted out in front. He and Rachel brought up the rear. Eloel looked frightened and uncertain, still holding her rifle pointed in the general vicinity of his stomach. She'd braided her long hair so that it hung in a black silken cord over her shoulder. Her heart-shaped face gleamed with a sheen of sweat.

"Captain," she demanded as they turned the corner. "Tell me now. What happened?"

"Lichtner captured him. You and I . . ." he threw her a faint smile, "are going to go get him back."

Rachel jerked to look at him. "I'm willing, but I question your judgment. Why me? Why not Halloway?"

"I need her on the *Hoyer*. Besides, would you trust two Magisterial soldiers to bring him back alive?"

Rachel's lips pressed into a tight line. "No."

"I didn't think so."

Carey entered the conference room and stood aside as he and Rachel entered. A deep hush fell as the door closed. The overhead panels here were dark. Only an oil lamp lit the center of the table, casting their shadows like long-dead ghouls across the walls.

Cole propped his helmet on the table and dropped into the chair at the head. Halloway and Eloel took seats on either side of him. He braced his elbows on the black tabletop and laced his fingers. Carey gazed at him through cool green eyes, but her nostrils flared with rapid breaths.

"Lieutenant," he said gently. "Let's discuss you and me first."

She brushed damp auburn hair behind her ears and fixed him with a warm wry look that made him smile in return. "You're setting us up to be the fall guys if this doesn't work out, right?"

"Yes."

"And our story?"

Cole lowered his gaze to his fingers. He'd unconsciously clenched them into a tight white-knuckled weave. "*My* story. I'll take full responsibility for the Baruch debacle, claiming I ordered the security stand-down from level one to three. That'll clear the crew. As for you, Lieutenant, being seduced into . . . treason . . . by your captain is a secondary offense. They'll only throw half the book at you."

"Don't be ridiculous," Carey said blithely. "They'll never take me alive to stand trial."

He threw her a broad daring smile. "Good, then we're in agreement."

"What's next?"

"From this moment forward, Carey, everything you do, everything you say, has to appear to be mutinous. I suggest you begin by finding and isolating our crew. Preferably unhurt and in the brig. Then you should put Gamant trainees into all key positions. *Lastly,* kill the com virus. In a worst case scenario, you can use a com foul-up as an excuse to gain time and leverage with Brent."

He turned to Rachel. She watched him intently, black eyes pools of suspicion. "I believe you have the authority,

481

Miss Eloel, to order your crew to obey Halloway's commands?"

She looked as grim as if Death had just appeared out of an explosion of fire and brimstone and demanded her soul. She held his gaze but said nothing.

Cole heaved an anxious breath. "Look, Rachel, I'd just as soon you trusted me because I'm a hell of a nice guy, but since it's obvious that you don't, what collateral can I give you to insure your taking the necessary risk?"

She fumbled awkwardly with the rifle lying across her lap. "A nice guy?" She laughed softly, as though in self-mockery. *A just man—decent to a fault.* "I . . . I believe you. But my crew won't—not until they see your people in the brig and the ship clearly in their hands."

He nodded. "I understand that. What if you and Carey both talk to them together. Assign your best security people to help Carey find and capture our crew. That should provide some instant gratification and build confidence. Next, I suggest you handpick your most competent trainees to fill Bridge and Engineering positions. Get them in place immediately." He lightly pounded a fist on the table. "I've no idea how much time we have before Bogomil roars over the horizon. We've got to be prepared—"

"Bogomil," Rachel said, "and those four other cruisers."

Tahn spun to glare at her. "*What* four other cruisers?"

"I don't know, but they're planning on surrounding us in a Laced Star maneuver."

The breath went out of his lungs as a hot flood of adrenaline scorched his body. "How do you . . . ? No, never mind, that's irrelevant. God Above. What plans had Baruch made to counter that maneuver?"

She gave him a clear-eyed deadly stare. "He'd planned on setting the *Hoyer* down on the planet."

Cole's heartbeat grew deafeningly loud in his ears. "Insane."

"He considered it the only way to avoid having everyone aboard captured and hauled off to the nearest neurophysiology center. That included the remnants of your crew, incidentally. He figured some of them would guess what might happen to them if the Magistrates picked them up. He wanted to give them the same chance he was giving his own people."

Cole shook his head disbelievingly. "He didn't plan on trying to fight first? I can't imagine——"

"He said the green Gamant crew would never be able to hold their own against five Magisterial crews. He figured they'd have a better chance of surviving on the planet's surface."

He breathed out a long exhale and ran a hand through his hair. "He's right. But, Lord, I would have never guessed he'd do something so. . . . Well, he must have planned on making that last-ditch move when he first sighted the cruisers converging. That would give the *Hoyer*'s people enough time to land and head for the hills."

"Yes," Rachel said softly. "He did. That was the main reason he wanted to go down with you and check out Magisterial operations on Tikkun. So we'd know what to expect when we got to the planet."

A glacial hand tightened around Cole's heart. After seeing Block 10, Baruch must have felt desperate to the point of madness. They'd boxed him tighter than he'd ever been boxed and he *hadn't* opted to blow up the ship—he'd opted to try and save his people's lives.

His eyes darted over the lamplit room, then landed on Halloway. Her stern gaze had never left him. She studied him pensively, waiting for him to give her another option. "Carey, if I'm not here—if you have to make a desperate play—do it. Set the *Hoyer* down on the planet near the largest population center you can find and run for the center of the city. They'll play hell for months trying to find you. But *only* as a swan song. Until that time, play along with Brent. Do whatever he says—make him believe that the *Hoyer* is still a Magisterial ship. Understand? *Do whatever he says.* At least, anything short of letting him board you. That would end our little show pretty damned quick."

She ground her teeth softly. Her pearl-smooth cheeks vibrated. "Set the *Hoyer* down?"

"Yes."

C-J class cruisers were built for space travel, not gravity wells. He could see the hurt on her face. He'd just told her to murder their ship, to condemn it to being stripped and sliced into scrap. His gaze caressed the stark white walls lovingly, in silent apology, before he forced it back to Carey.

"Aye, Captain. But if I wait—if I play with Brent—won't it be too late?"

He sucked in a deep breath. "Might be. But I don't think Brent will fire on you if he knows you're heading for the surface."

"You mean because he'll assume, and correctly, that he'll be able to capture nearly everyone who flees the downed vessel."

"Yes."

Carey's gaze softened. "All right. Well, one last question."

He rubbed a fist over his mouth. "What?"

"If none of this works—if something totally unexpected happens—what's our story about Baruch's capture on Tikkun?"

She'd said the words calmly, but her mouth trembled. Cole leaned back in his chair. "Hmm. Good point. They'll wonder why, if I could organize the resistance, I didn't stay with my crew. . . . Let's go with this: Everything happened just the way it did—except I gave the stand-down order and later, while we were trying to retake the ship—I blundered. Baruch captured me and forced me to the planet as his hostage."

Carey laughed bitterly, shaking her head. "It doesn't make any sense. Why would he? And no one who knows you will believe you could make such a blunder."

"Fortunately, by then we'll be dealing with the Magistrates. And I'll have had more time to think about it." He got lithely to his feet. The fluttering lamplight threw his shadow in an amorphous black wave across the back wall. "Any other questions?"

Carey shook her head.

Rachel shoved out of her chair. "When are we leaving for Tikkun?"

"As quickly as we can. Get to your people and set them up with Carey, then meet me in the landing bay. I need to reprogram the shuttle so I can handle her if it comes to a fight on Tikkun."

Carey looked up at him. "Cole, when you're in the bay, if you can access the ship-wide link. . . ."

"Yes." He closed his eyes against the thought. His stomach churned sickeningly. "Sorry I didn't think of that. If I can, I'll . . . I'll talk to our people and order them to assemble outside of Engineering. You, Rachel, will kindly advise your people not to disrupt my trap by killing anyone who appears there."

"Understood."

"Is that it? Good. Let's move."

Halloway stepped around the table and embraced him in a hug so hard it drove the air from his lungs. He noticed for the first time the delicate fragrance that clung to her hair. He nuzzled his cheek against the top of her head, hugging her back.

"Don't take any unnecessary risks," he murmured. "I plan on both of us living long and boring lives in hiding. Understand?"

"Got it. I hear there are some great holes in the wall on Vensyl."

He grimaced distastefully. "Vensyl's a dive and you know it. I was thinking more of the caves on Acre. Those nomadic goatherders make some damned fine stouts."

She laughed, burying her face against her shoulder. "We'll argue about it later."

"Affirmative."

She released him and stepped back. In strict military fashion, she spun and sprinted for the door. Tahn turned and gave Rachel a confident smile. "See you in half an hour?"

"Less if I can arrange it." In a hesitant gesture, she lifted her rifle and handed it to him. "Welcome to the side of the angels, Captain."

He reached out, taking it and cradling it in his arms. A euphoria of pride and inexplicable contentment filled him briefly, before the image of the little girl kicking beside the ditch smothered every other emotion. "Yes," he said, checking the rifle's charge. "I believe it is."

* * *

Neil Dannon sat in the command chair on the bridge, laughing hysterically. Tears rolled down his cheeks. His body shuddered so hard that the pistols tucked into his belt jammed against his ribs. He carelessly pulled them out and dropped them to the floor beside the command chair. Tahn's voice echoed through the ship, broken, fragmented, but his message rang out loud and clear. *They'd won!* Baruch had been captured by Lichtner on Tikkun and Tahn himself had Engineering.

When that powerful, jubilant voice ceased, Neil lifted his gaze to the serene image of his home world on the monitor. An ache like a poor sword thrust accosted him. He sat forward to brace his elbows on his knees. He was safe. Safe.

Dropping his face in his hands, he laughed again. Loudly and raucously. The deep-throated sound grew drier, more husky, as the seconds swept by, changing to sobs before he could stop himself.

He ought to be down there on Tikkun.

Killing Lichtner.

Getting Jeremiel out.

He ought to.

CHAPTER 53

Carey Halloway stood in the hall outside of Engineering, a rifle in her arms, pistol on her hip. Alone. She listened to Cole's voice booming all over the ship. He sounded so confident, so utterly in control. *Everybody probably does—once they've given themselves up for dead.* And she figured he had. She had. Still, his voice soothed her fears. He sounded so much the old Cole of a year ago, before the government began its mad assault on Gamant civilians and he'd been carried away in the cyclone. Just his triumphant tone sent her spirits soaring—like it must have those of every other member of his crew.

She shifted to brace a shoulder against the wall. Rachel's people had been willing, but wary. Without the voice of Yosef Calas on her side, she doubted they would have ever accepted her as their commanding officer.

Down the hall, she saw Carlene Millhyser and Jason West emerge, rifles clutched in tight fists, herding Mikael Calas and another child in front of them. Mikael had tears tracing his cheeks. The little girl looked dangerously upset, like none of them had better turn their backs on her or she'd rip their throats out. How could such a young girl look so fierce, Carey wondered? But then this child was Gamant, she'd probably seen more horror in her short life than Carey had.

Millhyser and West spotted her and broad smiles lit their faces. Carlene trotted forward, lifting an arm to embrace Halloway. She hugged her back, patting her meaty shoulders.

"Glad to see you made it, Carlene. Damn good work." She released her and reached out for West. "Jason? You look all right. No direct hits anyway."

He laughed and hugged her tightly. "I'm all right, Lieutenant."

Millhyser chuckled in joy and relief. "We had a time of it on level seven, I'll tell you that. If you hadn't set up that ambush outside of the security tunnel, I doubt we'd have ever gotten weapons."

She smiled. "I may have set it up, but *you* carried it off. I'm proud of you. So's the captain. Come on inside. Tahn dug a bottle of Sartrian brandy out of some hole and is waiting to open it until everybody arrives."

West did a little dance of sheer happiness in the hall, then put his hands at the children's backs while Millhyser hit the patch to open the double doors that led into Engineering. When they snicked back, Carey led the way inside. West, Millhyser, and the children followed unwittingly—falling straight into the arms of six Gamant guards.

"Uncle Yosef!" Mikael cried, running headlong across the room.

Halloway quickly pounded a fist into the patch. The doors closed before anyone coming up the hall could hear the screams of disbelief and rage.

* * *

Erinyes roughly rubbed his earlobe, grimacing at Ornias. The ambassador leaned seductively over Saren Lil's shoulder pretending to watch her go about her com duties. She kept casting imploring looks at Erinyes, obviously begging him to save her.

He'd been holding off, hoping Tetrax would figure it out for himself. "Ambassador," Erinyes said with silky threat. "I'm sure the lieutenant could carry out her responsibilities more effectively if you weren't fogging up her monitor."

Ornias straightened and gave him a slit-eyed appraisal.

"Since nothing's coming in over com, I hardly see that it matters."

Erinyes thrust a hand at the wavering splash of colors on the forward monitor. "We are just about to exit vault. Why don't you sit your fat . . . your *self* down."

Ornias smiled that plastic smile that made Erinyes want to slit his throat. Dressed in a long azure robe embroidered with golden threads, Tetrax looked—and acted—like royalty in exile; it irritated Erinyes. A government employee should dress like one, for God's sake.

"Captain, have you made arrangements to retrieve Calas from the *Hoyer*?"

"Of course." Then, with exaggerated politeness, he continued, "Don't worry about *anything.*"

Ornias opened his mouth to say something undoubtedly vituperative, but Lulen's sharp voice stopped him.

"Captain," she said, "we're out of vault. Ships on screen."

Erinyes heaved a sigh of relief. "Put in a tran to the *Hoyer*. Notify them of our mission. At the same time, send that Clandestine One message from the Magistrates to all the other Magisterial vessels out there."

Ornias caressed his braided beard, lime green eyes gleaming. "And what, pray tell, will you do if Tahn refuses to turn the boy over?"

"Then we'll know for certain he's not in control of the *Hoyer* and we'll fall into the Laced Star maneuver. Eventually, Ambassador, we'll get the child."

Ornias lifted a brow. "We want him *alive,* Erinyes. He won't do us any good dead."

Erinyes glowered. "I'm quite familiar with the necessities of treating political hostages delicately."

* * *

Brent Bogomil grimaced, watching the tube of light streak directly at the *Hoyer*. "Dharon? What ship is that?"

She paused, brown eyes glued to her console. "The *Klewe*, Captain. I don't know what the hell he thinks he's—"

Bogomil lurched out of his chair. "Get him on com! He'll undermine our entire maneuver! *Nobody* is supposed to make contact until we've safely established the Star and surrounded the *Hoyer!*"

"Sir?" Winnow called. "Clandestine One message

coming over com. Do you want it on screen or—"

"Give it to me in the aura." He dropped back into his chair as the golden halo snapped on around his head. He listened to Slothen's terse alien voice giving new orders and sank back into his seat. "Blast it. This is ridiculous—"

"Brent!" Dharon shouted, rising halfway out of her chair. "Ships on screen!"

"What?" He pounded a fist into his chair arm unit to kill the aura. Six, then seven, tubes of light streaked across the blackness of space, heading straight for Tikkun. "Who is that, Dharon?"

"I don't know, but from the readings, those are AO class vessels." She whirled around to pin him with a gaze wild with fear.

Hoarsely, he whispered, "The *Underground?* Get Abruzzi and the others on com! Tell them to fan out around the *Hoyer*. We've got to go in now!"

CHAPTER 54

Rachel eased down into the copilot's seat, hitting the EM restraints. Beside her, Tahn did the same. He looked cool, handsome in his soiled uniform. His brown hair clung in tiny curls to his temples. Those piercing blue-violet eyes had taken on a preoccupied, calculating look.

"I take it your crew had no problems aligning with Halloway?" he asked.

"They're worried, but they'll obey her orders." She frowned at the brittle sound of her voice. *Where was Sybil? Uriah said they'd found Harper dead.* Since that moment, the hard surface beneath her feet had melted to quicksand. Her knees had gone wobbly with the fear that her world might have already ended and she just didn't know it yet.

Tahn gave her a sideways glance. "What's wrong?"

She shook her head, not quite willing to discuss family

489

with this newfound ally. "Nothing. I'm all right. Just on edge."

"Uh-huh. Sounded like more than that. You have a daughter aboard, don't you?"

She met his gaze; beneath the hard glitter, a friendly sympathy shone. Reluctantly, she nodded. "Yes. I don't know where she is."

He keyed something into his com console and the ship began to lift like a feather borne on spring breezes. Rachel braced herself as the shuttle eased out through the open bay doors and into space. Below, the continent of Amman whirled, covered by a patchy opalescent layer of golden clouds. The dark red wrinkles of a mountain range showed through in places.

Tahn nosed the shuttle down and Rachel unconsciously braced her feet against the floor, straining against the motion—which was no motion at all, but it *looked* like it. He watched her for a second, amusement in his eyes.

"Won't help," he said. "We're going down regardless."

"I feared as much."

He smiled and leaned back in his chair. "We've got about twenty minutes. Let's discuss your daughter. What's her name?"

"Sybil. But I don't need—"

"I think you do. When we're on the planet I don't want you distracted. You're going to have to be sharper than I suspect you've ever been—"

"Indeed?" Rachel said. "And what do you know about me?"

He lifted a shoulder. "You're right, I'm an idiot. Forgive my pretentiousness. Where was Sybil supposed to be?"

"Avel Harper was assigned to take care of her and Mikael Calas. Harper's dead. I don't know where the children—"

"In Mikael's cabin on level nineteen?"

She frowned at him. How did he know that? "Yes."

He keyed in a new sequence of coordinates on his console and the ship tilted sideways. "Then I suspect Sybil is quite all right. One of my crew's first moves was to capture Mikael and take him some place safe. If Sybil was with him, my people will have taken her, too. Which means she's probably already in Gamant hands again."

Rachel exhaled a relieved breath—wanting to believe, not quite able to. "Thank you for telling me."

"You're welcome. Feel better?"

"A little."

"Good. Now I'm going to make you feel bad again. Let's discuss Tikkun. There are things happening there that might . . . shock you."

Rachel tilted her head back to rest on the soft blue chair back. Her long black braid fell over her shoulder. Memories of Horeb fluttered: the holocaust of Old Believers in the square. The terrors of the civil war. Murdering Adom. "I doubt it," she said. "But go ahead."

He swiveled his chair around to face her. Through the window behind him, she could see the triangular wings of the shuttle gleaming with an eerie wavering fire. "Lichtner has begun his own Magisterially-approved reign of terror against the Gamants on Tikkun. You've read the neuro files. But I think you should know—"

"I didn't understand very much of what they said."

He laced his fingers in his lap and tightened them anxiously. "The philosophy behind it doesn't matter. What does are the methods the Magistrates have approved for conducting the experiments. They're brutal and inhuman at best. Be prepared for the worst you can imagine."

She lifted her head inquiringly. *Jeremiel?* "The worst I can imagine, Captain, is that he's used those methods on Baruch."

Tahn's face darkened. He swung back around to his control console, pretending to check readouts. "I ordered him not to use mind probes, but he doesn't have to take my orders. I don't know what else he might have done. However, you mustn't let whatever you see affect you. You have to act like one of my finest security officers, *Sergeant Eloel*. Leave anything else to me."

"I will."

The shuttle began to level out and Tahn fell silent, concentrating on angling down over a broad red and tan banded desert. Rachel watched the landscape flash by below. Rain misted the air, creating a clinging gray haze. In the distance, a mustard-colored bubble rose from the sands, shiny, shimmering like a festered wound.

"Block 10," Tahn said simply.

Rachel girded herself for battle. The shuttle swung around the camp twice and her gaze lingered on the high cliffs. The rain turned the red crevices into dark bloody chasms.

"Note how many ships are outside," Tahn said. "If we have to make a run for it, chances are we're dead. Understand? We don't want to have to fight anybody. We just want Baruch back."

"Understood."

Tahn threw her a gravely serious look. "How many charges have you got for that rifle of yours? It would appear unseemly for me to carry one. I'll have to make do with my pistols." One hung on each of his hips, just like Rachel's own.

Professionally, she tapped each belt compartment around her waist. "I have five."

"That should do."

"Should? With these I could clear out the entire camp. What kind of trouble are you expecting? How many people are incarcerated here?"

"Unknown. I'd guess a thousand."

"And Magisterial forces?"

"Two hundred, perhaps."

Tahn set the shuttle down in front of the compound. Rachel tensed, watching twenty to twenty-five guards surround the ship. Tahn's face hardened as he studied their rifles and hostile glares.

"This isn't right," he muttered. "Something's wrong. Be on your toes." He got out of his chair and headed for the side door. Rachel checked her weapons one final time, then followed.

* * *

Dannon stood up as the cruiser dove out of the sunlit heavens on the other side of Tikkun, coming fast, shields up. Heart in his throat, he walked forward, down to the second level to stand before the forward screen. The dark bridge was frighteningly silent. The air seemed to have gotten colder, bearing on its breath the faint scent of death.

Neil watched the ship's approach and felt his throat tighten. In his memories, the two impregnable fortresses of his life crumbled to dust again—Jeremiel's friendship . . . and the sanctuary of Gamant culture. All the wails he'd ever heard from dying people, all the pleas and cries

492

of fleeing children swelled like the voice of God in his ears.

He felt light-headed. So much so, that he didn't even hear the bridge door slip open and eight booted feet race inside.

"Dannon?" Halloway demanded. "What the hell are you doing here? Get out!"

He stumbled in fear, breathing hard, to see seven men and women lunge to take consoles, checking readings, eyes wide with apprehension.

"Halloway, where's Tahn?"

She trotted to the command chair and stopped, looking curiously at him as she bent to retrieve the two pistols lying like crossed sabers on the floor. She dropped quickly into the chair, tucking the pistols beside her right hip. "If you're not going to leave, Dannon, *sit down!*"

His gaze swiftly drifted over the scene, officers fumbling at consoles, whispering fearfully to each other, asking subvocally for God's mercy. *Gamants.* His heart stopped. A wrenching feeling like being disemboweled overcame him. He sank to the floor.

* * *

Carey shouted, "Uriah? See if you can get that ship on com."

The dark-haired young man licked his lips, almost petrified with panic. His shaking hand input the correct sequence. No com aura flared around his head. She'd only just killed the com virus and it would take another hour before the ship had corrected itself, pulling out backup files, recorrelating programs, reengaging hardware.

A visual image swam into focus on the forward screen. The weasel-thin face and coppery hair set her stomach to aching.

"Goddamn it, Erinyes!" she shouted. "What the hell are you doing flying in at me out of attack mode? I'd have shot the hell out of you if I'd had any weapons!"

In a testy voice, he responded, "Greetings, Lieutenant. What do you mean, if you'd had any weapons?"

"We've had a major com malfunction. We're basically adrift in space, Captain. Partial com, no weapons, no—"

"Ah, that's why we haven't been able to reach you. You've had everyone across four sectors of space on the verge of hysteria, I'm afraid."

493

"Not our fault—"

"Let me speak to Tahn, Lieutenant," Erinyes ordered brusquely.

She lifted a brow. "The captain is on the planet's surface. May I help you?"

"I suppose you'll have to." He heaved a disgruntled sigh, obviously disturbed he had to deal with her instead of Cole. "The *Klewe* is on a special Clandestine One mission authorized by Slothen himself. I believe you have in your possession a boy, the new leader of Gamant civilization, Mikael Calas?"

"Affirmative." The hair at the back of her neck crawled.

"You are to immediately turn him over to me. The Magistrates want him." He flicked a hand at someone on his bridge, then turned back to Halloway. "We are transmitting the orders to you at this moment. I hope, given your curious circumstances, that you receive them."

Carey's green eyes narrowed. Around the bridge, she saw the Gamant crew cast questioning looks at each other. Against the far wall where Dannon had slumped, a soft laugh sounded—half hysterical; he shook his head, as though appreciative of Erinyes' move.

Carey got out of her seat to go look over Uriah's shoulder. The message had come through brokenly, but was still understandable.

Greetings Capt. Tahn. You . . . ordered to turn over . . . Calas to Capt. Erinyes without . . . delay. Report . . . Bogomil. Notify immediately . . . Baruch's status.

Magistrate Slothen.

Carey swallowed nervously. Cole had said to do whatever they ordered, not to arouse suspicion under any circumstances. Would her Gamant crew let her turn the boy over? She folded her arms and gave Erinyes a cool stare. "What for, Captain?"

Erinyes' diabolical face went crimson. "I don't believe that's your concern, Lieutenant. Your orders are simply to turn Calas over to me."

She had no alternative. If she hesitated for very long,

Erinyes would know something wasn't right. She nodded tersely. "Please give us a few minutes, Captain. We'll need to get him ready."

A low rumble started across her bridge, disapproving Gamant voices rising. Carey lunged for the com switch, cutting the connection. Better Erinyes think her a rude bitch, than hear the outrage of her crew. Angry eyes turned suspiciously toward her, jaws clenched.

Dannon's low laugh made her blood run cold. "Carey, Carey," he said in an intimate tone. "What *are* you going to do now?"

She propped her hands on her hips. "Uriah? Get Yosef Calas and the boy up here."

* * *

Mikael clutched Sybil's hand tightly as they rode up the transport tube. His Uncle Yosef and Ari stood on the other side of the tube with bad looks on their faces. It made Mikael scared.

Sybil leaned close to him, whispering in his ear. "This is it, I think."

"Yeah. I guess so."

The door opened so fast it made Mikael jump. Uncle Yosef put a hand at his back and guided him out onto the bridge. Mikael's eyes widened. He'd never been on a bridge. All the brightly colored screens fascinated him. He blinked wide-eyed at them.

"Lieutenant," Uncle Yosef said softly. "What's this all about?"

Lieutenant Halloway spun around in the command chair. Auburn hair hung in wet strands around her face. "We've been ordered by the Magistrates to turn over Mikael, Mister Calas. We've little choice, sir. Am I going to have trouble from you or your people if I comply?"

Mikael looked up anxiously. His uncle's spectacles had slipped down on his nose. Ari's face looked mean, eyes riveted on Sybil. She gave Ari a confident nod—as though they were silently talking. Mikael tugged his uncle's gray sleeve.

"Uncle Yosef?" he whispered.

Yosef looked down at him through watery old eyes. "What is it, Mikael?"

"We need to go. It's okay. Me and Sybil. We have to."

Yosef knelt down, knees crackling like a campfire. He stroked Mikael's black curls gently. "Why do you say that, Nephew? We don't know what they want with you."

"But I do, sir. Magistrate Slothen? He wants to talk to me about what he should do with Gamants. And I have to go tell him. Grandfather told me what I have to say." He gave his uncle a brave smile. "Don't worry about us. We'll come back. I don't know when for sure. But some day."

Sybil slid up behind Mikael and patted his back. "Tell him about the books on Horeb."

Mikael frowned, looking at her over his shoulder. He whispered, "I can't yet. Grandpa said so."

Sybil's eyes widened. "Oh, okay. We'd better go, then. You know . . . before . . . *before.*"

Mikael nodded gravely. Before the ship got attacked and they couldn't get away. He turned to Lieutenant Halloway. "Ma'am, could you tell Captain Erinyes that we want to go now—fast."

She lifted her chin slowly, a frown making lines in her forehead. "How did you know who—"

"Sybil has dreams, sometimes."

Sybil nodded hastily. "Yes, ma'am, I do."

Halloway just stared at them, then gazed at Uncle Yosef. "I've received orders only for Mikael. I don't think it would be wise for me to include Sybil."

Mikael's heart raced. He bit his lower lip, looking at his best friend. She looked as frightened as he felt. He reached up and pulled hard on his uncle's sleeve. "Uncle Yosef? I can't go without Sybil. She *has* to come. *She has to!*"

"Shh. It's all right, Mikael," Uncle Yosef said. He stroked Mikael's back and that made the boy feel a little better. "Why does she have to go? I don't think it would be a good idea either without asking her mother first."

"Can't you call her mother?"

"Negative." Halloway said. "Rachel and Cole are on the surface. Sending a tran would endanger their mission there."

Tears pressed against Mikael's lids. He could tell from these grown-ups' faces that they weren't going to let Sybil go with him. His jaw trembled, but he gathered his courage to shout, "I *won't* go without Sybil! You can't make me!"

The grown-ups all looked down at the floor or up at the ceiling and Mikael started to cry. Sybil reached over and squeezed his hand good and hard, then she stepped out in front of him so people couldn't see his face.

She brushed brown curls out of her eyes. "Ari?" she said. "You know I have dreams."

Ari nodded. "I know."

"I have to go," Sybil pleaded. "My mom won't mind. You just tell her I had a *funny* dream about it. She'll understand. But I *have* to go. That Captain Erinyes is a mean man."

Halloway's brows drew together, like she knew it, too. Mikael lifted a finger and tucked it in his mouth, sucking softly, trying to cover the sound of his cries.

"Yosef," Ari said, "what if we go with them both? With us there as guardians, I bet Rachel would give her permission."

Sybil smiled up at him and ran over to hug him around the leg. "Sure, that sounds great. Doesn't it, Mikael?"

He nodded hurriedly. Uncle Yosef didn't look like he was so sure about it. Mikael started to hiccup. It always happened when he got really scared, but it made him mad. He figured there had to be better times for it than right now. He tried to swallow them as soon as they came up.

Finally, Uncle Yosef breathed out through his nose and frowned at Halloway. "Will Captain Erinyes accept us going with Mikael and Sybil as guardians?"

"I think I can arrange that, sir. You'll take responsibility for Sybil?"

Yosef and Ari both nodded at the same time. "Yes."

Halloway lightly pounded a fist on her chair arm. "All right. Please get down to Transportation. I'll inform Erinyes that he has four guests coming." She waved a hand to Samual Lovejoy. "Sergeant, could you escort them?"

"Aye, Lieutenant."

The man jumped out of his chair and ran toward them. Mikael walked back into the tube and huddled close beside Sybil. Her arm felt cool against his. She looked at him through smiling brown eyes.

"It's okay," she whispered. "We did it."

He inhaled a shaky breath and smiled back. "I know, but I'm still scared."

Mikael looked up at Yosef and Ari. They were talking quietly to each other about what would happen when they were all on board that big enemy ship. It made Mikael's stomach hurt. He dropped a hand to rub it.

The tube opened and they stepped out into Transportation. When they got to the landing bay, Mikael saw a black triangular ship sitting on the white tiles. Six guards with guns trotted down the gangplank and surrounded them, forcing them into the ship. Mikael went to sit on one of the long benches in the long cigar-shaped room behind the command cabin. He felt the ship lift and twisted his hands nervously until Sybil scooted over beside him and put her arm around his shoulders. Ari and Uncle Yosef sat down on the opposite side of the ship and four guards sat at the ends of the benches, giving them mean looks.

"It's okay," Sybil whispered confidently. "We're going to be okay. Don't worry."

Mikael sniffed his runny nose. "Sybil? What if Magistrate Slothen won't let us go back to Horeb? What if we never get the books?"

She blew out a breath and lifted a shoulder. "I guess we'll have to figure out some way to win the war without them. But you know what? I don't think God would let Slothen keep us from winning the war. God can do anything."

"Yeah." But Mikael thought about all the terrible stories his grandfather had told him about the last Gamant Revolt. Lots of good people had gotten killed in the fighting before Zadok came back from heaven. If God could do anything, why had he let that happen?

The ship made a soft bumping sound and all the guards got up and pointed their rifles. In a little while, the pilot and copilot came out from the front of the ship and the side door to the shuttle slipped open. A new landing bay gleamed outside. Mikael gripped Sybil's hand tightly and stood up.

"Calas?" the pilot ordered, "take the kids and go first. Funk, you bring up the rear."

Mikael heard Ari whisper something about purple-coated asses. Sybil dragged him forward to stand behind Uncle Yosef, then they walked down the gangplank.

A bunch of people marched across the bay toward them. One of the men had a braided beard and wore a red robe embroidered with gold threads. He looked like a Gamant, but . . . . Mikael leapt sideways when Sybil let out a shriek. She threw down his hand and raced forward, clawing and screaming at the man.

"It's him!" Sybil raged. *"Ornias! Ornias!"*

"Get this brat off of me!" the man shouted and two guards gripped Sybil and wrestled her away.

Mikael watched in mute horror. Sybil fought and shrieked, biting at the guards until they shoved her down on the floor. She curled onto her side and cried.

Anger burned through Mikael. He *hated* these people! He ran forward and sat down beside Sybil. He patted her brown hair. "It's okay, Sybil," he said quietly. "It's okay. I'm right here. Don't be afraid."

The ugly man in the captain's uniform glowered at Mikael, then turned to one of the lieutenants and barked, "Monti, get on the com and tell Lulen to fly us out of here and initiate light vault before Bogomil begins his attack run. We can't afford to be in the vicinity when the heavens burst wide."

"Aye, sir," Monti said and strode away.

Mikael reached down and hugged Sybil. Her shaking shoulders scared him worse than the coming attack. He hugged her tighter. "I love you, Sybil," he whispered into her ear. "It's okay. Don't cry."

In a choking voice, she whispered back. "I love you, too, Mikael."

CHAPTER 55

Tahn and Rachel stepped down to the wet sand and Rachel's black boots sank two inches. Misty rain poured out of the heavens, drenching the cliffs, turning the pale desert plants into jade green walls of brush.

Twenty soldiers came trotting up, rifles humming on full power, all pointed unambiguously at their middles. Tahn lifted a brow. "Sergeant Manstein," he demanded of the thin bald man in front. "What's all the hardware?"

Manstein made an apologetic bow. "Forgive me, Captain. Major Lichtner saw your approach and requests information on the nature of your visit."

Tahn looked surprised and outraged. "I beg your pardon? Is this a Magisterial installation or not? I don't *need* his permission, mister!"

Manstein swallowed convulsively. "The nature of your visit, Captain?"

Tahn's gritted teeth set his jaw at an awkward angle. "You tell that slimy sonofa. . . ." He took a deep breath, steadying himself. "Inform your commanding officer that he promised me a tour with somebody who *knew* something, and I damned well plan on having it!"

"Certainly, Captain. Please wait here a moment." Manstein took off his belt com and walked a short distance away. His low voice grated on Rachel's nerves.

Tahn stamped around cursing expertly, glaring at each and every guard; they responded by stiffening their necks and refusing to meet his angry gaze. When Tahn walked near her, he threw her a fleeting look of worry and then went back to cursing.

Rachel watched the scene with silent intrigue. The rifle in her hands grew clammy with her sweat. Finally, Manstein walked back.

He bowed deferentially again. "Forgive me, Captain. Major Lichtner says it slipped his mind. He'll set up a tour immediately. Please follow me inside."

"I'll bet it *slipped.*" Tahn growled and walked briskly toward the gate. Rachel followed professionally, throwing the guards nasty looks.

When they entered the compound, she gazed around at the tall gray buildings and the immensity of the camp. It seemed to stretch forever. The photon shield glimmered like a wall of ulcerated gold twenty feet over the fence top. Above it, the red cliffs leaned precariously forward. Rachel hid a shiver. Everything about this place made her feel in danger.

Manstein strode up to Tahn's side. "Captain, the major requests that you meet him in his apartment."

Tahn gave the man an evil look. "Then let's go. I've got a ship to run, Sergeant. I haven't got all damned day like Lichtner has."

Rachel strode briskly along at Tahn's side. They walked down a narrow alleyway to a black gate. Manstein placed his palm against the gray patch on the left side and the door instantly opened, revealing a small square surrounded by six-story buildings. They entered a beautiful courtyard. Rachel took in the flowers with her eyes, wanting to bend down and touch the old-style brown tiles that formed a lattice beneath her feet. Stone benches sat beneath sheltered arbors. It felt so peaceful she longed to sit down for a while and study the splash of colors. How long had it been since she'd seen such manicured beauty? Aeons.

They approached a shadowed doorway and Manstein stepped forward, hitting the door com. "Uman? We're here."

The door slid back and Tahn marched by everyone. Rachel followed him into the apartment to stand beneath the most magnificent crystal chandelier she'd ever seen. Its diamond-shaped pieces cast the light of a thousand rainbows over the red and green rug at her feet. Her gaze lingered on the clocks. She'd never seen anything similar before, but they looked like emerald—long thinly sliced panels of the rare gem adorned the time-pieces.

From her right, a brusque, high voice—almost shrill —called, "Tahn, I'd forgotten your impudence in wanting a 'scientific' tour. Forgive me."

A tall man with light brown hair and a drooping mustache stood regally poised on the staircase. His square face and sharply pointed nose accentuated his paper thin lips. He wore dozens of medals across the chest of his purple uniform.

"Listen, Lichtner," Tahn said with repressed violence. "I've only asked for common courtesy—the ordinary things due from one commander to another. Now if you have objections, let's get on the com to Palaia and get this worked out." He pointed a finger sternly. "Because I won't stand for any more insolent treatment from you or your people!"

"Insolent?" Lichtner scoffed, laughing. "I capture Baruch and rescue your ship and you call—"

"My ship? What the hell are you talking about? The *Hoyer* was never in danger!"

Lichtner looked spitefully confused. "But I thought— that is, Bogomil suggested—"

"Brent didn't know what the hell was going on aboard my ship! We've had a major com malfunction for the past

501

week. Our communications have been erratic at best."

"Then how did Baruch——"

Tahn threw up his arms angrily. "*I* made a mistake and he took me hostage, forcing me down here with him."

Lichtner blinked in surprise, then a gloating smile twisted his mouth. "Indeed? Do you blunder as often as it appears, Captain? The Magistrates should find that intriguing."

"I suspect they'll find it about as intriguing as the ethics charges I've decided to file against you, Major."

Lichtner lifted his blunt chin, fuming, but worried enough that his eyes darted nervously over Tahn's face. "I hardly think this the time for accusations, Captain. My scientific staff is still running trying to prepare for your visit. May I pour you a whiskey while we wait?"

Tahn glared. *"No."*

Lichtner came down the staircase with the poor grace of a bad mime artist. He swaggered by Tahn, heading to an elaborately carved liquor cabinet across the room.

Tahn followed. Rachel matched his long strides and could smell the pleasant musky odor of him, could see the perspiration beading on his forehead. Ethics charges? For what? Rachel's steps floundered when she saw the *Mea* lying in a coil on the table. Lichtner must have confiscated it from Jeremiel.

Tahn slumped into a chair and Rachel cautiously took the seat beside him. The *Mea* seemed to sense her presence. The blue glow dimmed to a dusty slate color. *Aktariel? Can you hear me now? What's happening? Talk to me!* She forced herself to look away to Lichtner. The major reached up and grabbed a beautifully faceted whiskey bottle and stopped—as though seeing her for the first time. His barely parted lips half-hid the glint of wolfish canines. He brazenly looked her up and down.

"Who is your security officer, Tahn?"

"Sergeant Eloel."

Rachel inclined her head. "Pleased to meet you, Major."

Lichtner sloshed a glass of whiskey for himself and brusquely set it on the table, then came around the chairs and made a blundering bow. "Miss Eloel, how refreshing it is to have someone of your beauty on our dirty little planet. May I offer you a drink?"

"No. Thank you."

502

He lifted his eyes, unsettled. "Not even a glass of sweet dessert wine or—"

"No."

Tahn gripped Lichtner's sleeve and gruffly pulled him away. "She's a temperance advocate, Major. Leave her alone!"

Lichtner scowled and took a seat opposite Rachel; he smiled deprecatingly as he swallowed his whiskey in one quick bolt, then poured himself another.

Tahn glowered at the action and got irritably out of his chair to pace. "Major, the camp seems uncommonly quiet today. Why is that? I saw no one out and about."

Lichtner waved a hand dismissively. "Oh, we're culling boys on the other side of the camp. It will take another hour or so. Until that time, all of the participants in our programs are ordered to stay inside their barracks. They get so distraught over routine elimination procedures."

Rachel glanced at Tahn. He straightened to his full height, tall, commanding. His blue-violet eyes looked ravaged. Her gaze slid back to Lichtner. He, too, had stiffened, as though he and Tahn shared an understanding of what that meant: elimination. Her heart raced. Murder? It must be. But . . . boys? Children?

Tahn snapped, "Your scientific team, I presume, is involved in the culling process and that's why they're unavailable?"

"Correct."

"Fine. Sergeant Eloel and I would like to see some other part of the camp while we're waiting for them, if you don't mind."

"Shall I interrupt my own schedule to accommodate you, Tahn?"

Tahn smiled challengingly. "Kind of you to offer, Major. Thank you. One of the first things I'd like to see is what you've done with *my* prisoner. Baruch."

Lichtner's face pinched nervously, like a thief caught in the act. He shoved his chair back with a loud squeal. "I hardly think you're qualified—"

"If we're going to argue custodianship, Lichtner, perhaps we should circumvent nasty bickering and tran the Magistrates. They *authorized* my custody of him."

"But, after all, Captain, you lost him when you became his hostage."

"According to manual 1141, legal prisoner transfers occur only when the authorized officer—me, in this case—requests assistance and relinquishes the prisoner after dutifully filing the 1141 paperwork. *I don't recall doing either.*"

Lichtner smiled insidiously. "He rather treated you like a brother, Tahn. You didn't seem to be his hostage, you looked like his . . . accomplice."

Tahn clenched his fists. "I suggest you don't repeat that, Major."

Lichtner's lips puckered offensively. "Well . . . . Come with me. We'll find something to *occupy* you, Tahn."

"Baruch."

Lichtner downed his glass of whiskey and walked haughtily across the room. His dozen security officers followed like pet lap dogs. Tahn fell in line. Rachel quickly grabbed the *Mea* and shoved it in her pants pocket before trotting to catch up. The sacred gate felt curiously cold—like the flesh of a corpse frozen in a glacier. Lichtner stopped by the door to pick up a ruby-handled pistol from a table and tuck it into his belt holster, then he exited into the courtyard.

Rachel leaned close to Tahn as they approached the door. "Too easy. Why did he give in?"

Tahn shook his head. "Don't know. Unless he's already received orders concerning Baruch from somebody I don't know about."

"Orders?"

"Later."

As they strode through the flower garden, out the gate, and onto the parade ground, Rachel's thumb played with the safety of her rifle. She surreptitiously noted the positions of Lichtner's security people—arranged strategically in an elongated diamond around them. They proceeded quietly and quickly by a series of gray windowless buildings and headed out across an empty expanse of red dirt.

The open area seemed mostly to be coarse gravel heaped carelessly in mounds. The rain had nearly stopped. An amorphous cloud of mist still clung to the tops of buildings, splashing Rachel's face with an occasional drop. In the distance the vague rumble of thunder rolled over the desert.

To her right, Rachel saw movement. She jumped,

staring openmouthed as she swung the barrel of her rifle around. Small explosions tormented the ground, shooting wisps of dirt high into the damp air. She shook her head, baffled. Lichtner's guards laughed, nudging each other as they pointed at her.

Tahn came up beside Rachel. She could feel the warmth of his arm against her shoulder. "Come on," he said. "You don't need to see this."

"But what is it?" she asked, loudly enough that Lichtner overheard.

The major stepped forward, smiling proudly. "My Gamants are buried here," he boasted. "Those from last spring. I suspect we've accumulated twelve or thirteen thousand in this camp alone."

Rachel couldn't breathe. The explosions. Gases released by the buried decaying bodies of . . . of thousands. The rifle in her arms became a flimsy lifeboat. *How could she stand here so calmly?* Somewhere in the past months she must have lost her mind. She who had screamed in rage and terror at the murder of a few hundred on Horeb *stood here calmly?* What had happened to her? Her soul ached as though aflame. Why? *Why didn't her hands rise like talons to rip out her eyes to prevent her from witnessing this?* How could she keep them clenched so still, so tight, around her rifle and not lift it to blot out this obscenity? She turned to glare in fiery hatred at Lichtner.

"Major?" Tahn commanded sharply. "We'd like to see Baruch."

Lichtner's proud smile dimmed. He shifted to throw out his chest. "Very well, Captain, but let me warn you, he tried to escape this morning. We had to take defensive action."

Rachel's eyes glazed. *If you've hurt Jeremiel . . . .*

Lichtner plowed across the field with Tahn in hot pursuit.

Rachel followed, but with each step she took her heart pounded more painfully. She could feel the heels of her boots grinding into the emaciated faces of people she almost recognized—relatives long-lost in the fickle mists of time. In a desperate motion, she reached down and clasped a handful of sand and put it in her pocket—hoping she could carry one victim away from this unholy ground.

They strode toward a new building, partially completed. It loomed like a tall gray monster over a broad plaza. Outside, a line of children stood. Boys. Crying. She saw Tahn's shoulder muscles bulge as though in self-defense against the mournful sounds. A short distance away, a group of perhaps sixty men labored on the building, filling trucks with dirt, lifting pipes, hammering ruthlessly. Surrounding them, twenty armed guards milled.

As Lichtner passed, the lead guard, a tough looking criminal of a man, sidled up to him. "Eh, Major? You want me to save the fun part for you? You have time today?"

Lichtner sniffed, and glanced at Tahn. A slow smile crept over his face. "Yes. Save it, Blobel." Then he strode by, leading the way up a short series of steps and into a broad white room.

A long desk sat in the front. A male nurse manned the com console behind it. Doctors moved purposefully up and down the halls, bowing their heads to Lichtner.

They passed two doors and stopped at the third. Lichtner stood aside. Tahn swept by him, into the room. Rachel heard his outraged whispers before she, too, entered.

Lying in the bed beneath a white sheet, Jeremiel had a bandage wrapped around the right side of his head, covering one eye. Was he asleep—or dead? The visible flesh of his face bore deep burns, salved with a yellow gluelike substance. Frantically, Rachel's gaze searched the area of his chest. Did it move?

Tahn walked forward and threw off the sheet. Rachel's stomach rose into her throat. She took a half-step forward. Hideous oozing wounds covered his muscular body, each plastered with the yellow glue. Rachel heard Tahn's labored breathing, saw him tighten his hands into fists. As though in slow motion, he turned and lunged at Lichtner.

"Guards!" the major shrieked, shuffling away.

Two soldiers caught Tahn's arms and held him back. "What the hell did you do, Lichtner?" he demanded. "This is no defensive action. *What did you do?*"

Shuddering with anger, Lichtner shouted, "How dare you question my word! My guards will testify that's how Baruch received his wounds. And I immediately ordered my staff to care for him! I know what a valuable cargo he is!"

Voices rose in bitter cries of rage and recriminations, but Rachel ceased to hear. She walked forward, insuring her body hid her actions, and gently rested a hand on Jeremiel's exposed arm. He felt so hot. So very hot. *What have they done to you? I'll kill him, Jeremiel. I promise.*

She closed her grip on his wrist, squeezing tenderly. For the briefest of moments, she saw his eye flutter open. In that instant, their gazes touched and she read his alarm, his dark dread that she stood next to him. His lips trembled as though he fought to speak. Then, silently, he mouthed, "Don't try. Get out. Now."

She squeezed his wrist again and backed away. Behind her, Tahn yelled in rage, "Get a gurney, goddamn you! You'll transport him to my shuttle immediately, or by God, Lichtner, I'll—"

"Don't threaten me!"

Tahn stood red-faced, so angry the tendons in his neck stood out. He shook off the restraining hands of the guards. His eyes glowed like living starbursts. "Lichtner," he said in a low voice that burned. "I guarantee you an inquiry. And I'll certainly be bringing up the Silmar affair to back my charges. *You understand me?*"

Lichtner's chin jutted out. "Then there'll be mutual charges, Captain. I'm not going to let you get off. They'll court-martial you—"

"Get a gurney!" Tahn took a threatening step forward, daring the guards to halt him. He glared into Lichtner's face. "I want Baruch in my shuttle in fifteen minutes. I've got better medical facilities aboard the *Hoyer* than you'll ever dream of down here. Move!"

"Don't order me around Tahn. You don't have *any* authority. . . ."

The words died in Lichtner's mouth as Rachel calmly lifted her rifle and aimed it at his white face. She switched off the safety with a loud click. "I believe my captain requested you to release this prisoner to him, Major. I suggest you do it."

Lichtner's mouth dropped open in outrage, but he wisely waved to one of his men. "Do it, Sokal. I wash my hands of this entire affair!" Turning, he raced out of the room. His guards followed.

When Rachel and Tahn stood alone, she noticed how badly his hands quaked. He came up beside her, eyes wild with renewed fear. "God forbid, I'm beginning to like Gamant brassiness, *Lieutenant* Eloel. Now, we've got to hurry. I don't know how long he'll stay backed down. He may be tranning the Magistrates right now."

"Tell me what to do."

He took a faltering breath. "I'll search the bedside table for belongings. When they get Baruch on that gurney, you slip one of your pistols under the sheet. I doubt he's got the strength to—"

"I do," a weak voice whispered.

Rachel spun. Jeremiel's one eye opened drowsily. A smile flitted across Tahn's face. "I figured you did."

A clattering sounded in the hall and two men dressed in white gowns pushed an antigrav gurney in. They glanced at Tahn's flaming granite face and seemed to visibly wince as they hurried to the bed. Undoubtedly everyone within five miles had heard his enraged commands. Rachel stood stiffly, watching them prepare to slide Jeremiel off the bed onto the carrier; he groaned, squeezing his eyes closed against the pain. In the foray of lifting and hurried instructions, Tahn brashly searched the bedside table. Finding nothing, he backed away, a fierce look on his face as he eyed the hospital staff. "Both of you," he ordered gruffly, "come outside with me." He belligerently shoved one of the interns into the hall.

Rachel quickly tucked a pistol beneath the sheet, putting it in Jeremiel's hand. She felt his feeble fingers go tight around the grips. With Tahn's loud angry voice as cover, she whispered, "Hang on. We're going to get you out of here."

". . . Tahn?"

"On our side."

"Hoyer?"

"Ours. Halloway is commanding."

His eye flickered open, questioning. At her confirming nod, a smile touched his lips. He seemed to sink back into the soft white sheet, breathing easier.

Tahn stalked imperiously back into the room, two grim interns behind him. He stabbed a hand out, "Take him. And make it quick!"

"Yes, sir," the dark-haired man piped shrilly. He took the handlebars by Jeremiel's head and carefully pushed the gurney out of the room, the other intern walking at his side.

Rachel and Tahn fell in behind them, eyes roving the white corridors for anyone who might try to stop them. The interns pushed out through the front doors and Tahn held one open for Rachel. She stepped outside.

Rain had started to fall again, drops misty, glistening like wavering sheets of silver across the compound. The interns took off at a trot, pushing the floating gurney between them for the front gate. Rachel started to step out behind Tahn, who had broken into a run, but her feet went leaden, melting into the white petrolon steps like poured metal.

Lichtner emerged from the midst of a group of guards. He stamped around, cursing, shouting at the laborers who looked on in horror from near the trucks. "You filthy Gamants! You think you can hide the sex of your children? Did you think we'd never check! Well, now you've asked for it! You *asked* for it! You stupid fools." He jerked one of his ruby-handled pistols from its holster and pointed it at the little boys lined up against the hospital wall.

One child, almond-eyed with short brown hair, lifted his hands to the nearby Gamant adults, crying, "Daddy, Daddy, Daddy!"

Rachel saw a black-haired man with a black beard start forward, but the group around him tackled him, knocking him to the ground. He screamed, raging, kicking, trying to get to his child. "Yael! Yael!" he shrieked madly.

Lichtner laughed and shot the first child in line. A little blond boy crumpled to the wet ground like a frail twig. Blood spattered the white wall at his back. Rachel didn't move a muscle, but something deep inside her seemed to snap. Her eyes grew crystal clear. The world shimmered. *How can this place exist in a universe with a shred of goodness? Oh, Aktariel. . . .*

Lichtner targeted the next child.

"Major!" Rachel shouted. She took a step down the staircase. "Not the children! No more!"

He gave her a disdainful glare. "You've been around Tahn too long, Sergeant. You've picked up his sentimentalism. We mustn't permit ourselves to be robbed of the legitimate uses of terror just because a few stupid, bourgeois mollycoddlers exist in our own ranks!"

He whirled to glare at Tahn, who had stopped, nostrils quivering in rage. The gurney and interns still rushed headlong toward the shuttle. Rachel saw them exit the front gate and enter the shuttle. Lichtner lifted his pistol again and aimed at the next child—the little almond-eyed one, so skinny he seemed nearly transparent in his white gown. A gust of wind pressed the fabric to his narrow chest, revealing thin bars of ribs. The boy reached out to Lichtner, crying incomprehensible words. The black-bearded man in the Gamant ranks, shrieked, "No! No! For the sake of God, she's just a baby! Leave her alone!"

She? Rachel's heart jammed against her ribs. Girls. They were all girls. Lichtner's words congealed into a horrifying truth. Suddenly, every child's face became Sybil's. Every pitiful cry sounded like one she'd heard and comforted a thousand times.

Lichtner hesitated, smiling at Rachel. "Any poltroon who can't bear suffering had better get out of the service! Eh, Sergeant? Perhaps your captain should join a sewing circle?" The twenty guards around him laughed deprecatingly.

Lichtner lifted his pistol again, sighting on the child.

The entire world died around Rachel. The brutal laughter of the guards no longer accosted her ears. She could see Tahn's mouth moving in desperate shouts—but she couldn't hear him. He started to run back. Only when he fell into a crouch and his hand dropped for his pistol did she awaken again to the terror.

Her thumb pushed up the safety with cold efficiency. Lichtner stood so close, she barely had to aim. She felt the slight vibration of the rifle when she pulled the trigger. The shot caught Lichtner in the lower back, ripping him in half, flinging his bloody upper torso into the circle of his guards. They stood stunned, cruel smiles still lingering, frozen on their faces. Rachel numbly panned the group, killing a dozen in the first sweep of her rifle, then a half-dozen more as she brought the barrel back around.

Tahn's pistol whined shrilly and she could hear him now. "Rachel, get down! *Get down!*"

She dove for the red soil as pandemonium broke loose. She hit the wet soil, crawling. A shot flashed in front of her, spraying dirt and stinging gravel into her face. She rolled, scrambling madly for cover. The whine of discharging rifles and screams rose to a deafening roar.

"Get their guns!" she heard someone yell and saw the black-bearded man running with his girl on his hip, a rifle in one arm. "We can fight them!" he screamed. *"We can fight them!"*

Everywhere, Gamants burst up like a flock of frightened birds, flying into the guards in wave after wave, taking their weapons, racing like starved wolves through the compound, killing, killing, killing.

"Rachel!" Tahn yelled.

He was running headlong back for her, pistol spitting blares of purple. She got to her feet and ran to meet him. He grabbed her arm in the hard careless grip of a stranger. "Hurry! This way!"

Dragging her behind a tall gray building, he released her and they ran, darting down a long alley, passing bin after bin of dead children. Rachel's soul twisted in unendurable agony. *Aktariel . . . I can understand now why you. . . .*

Over his shoulder, Tahn shouted, "In about two minutes this place is going to explode with insane Gamants with guns—and you and I are going to be among their first targets!"

The purple uniform clinging in drenched folds to her body suddenly became her greatest enemy. She picked up her feet and ran madly. They rounded a corner, heading for the front gate, and collided head-on with a group of four Magisterial soldiers. The enemy stumbled in surprise. Tahn didn't even break stride. He killed them quickly, cleanly, with single bursts from his pistol. Grabbing Rachel's sleeve, he swung her around the carnage and headed her down a new alley. "Go. Go! Run hard!"

Her feet pounded on the muddy ground. Ahead, she glimpsed the front gate. She raced for it, leaping a jumbled mess of empty crates piled in the alley.

"Rachel, stop!"

She had to grab the drainage chamber on the corner of the building to slow herself down. Tahn ran up behind her, eyes wide and hard, easing up to peer around the corner. "Damn it."

"What is it?"

"There are fifty guards in front of the gate. They've

erected barricades."

"How are we going to get out? What about Jeremiel?" Panic gripped her like an iron fist.

"He's either in the shuttle or he's not. We haven't time to. . . ."

From nowhere, everywhere, a mayhem of insane screams erupted, feet pounding, rifles and pistols splitting the cool rain-drenched wind. Like a rumbling tidal wave, it came, rushing thunderously toward the gate. Tahn slammed an arm across her chest, forcing Rachel back against the wall, out of sight. A foul-smelling wave of men, women, and children threw themselves at the barricade.

And a violet lightning storm of death slashed the rainy world.

Through the narrow slit between buildings, Rachel saw hundreds stagger to fall face-first into the dirt. How long? How long did she stand there, Tahn's hard arm pressing into her breasts, listening to his rapid breathing? A minute? Two? Finally, the shrieks of death turned into a rushing symphony of disbelieving triumph.

She started to edge forward, but a dull thudding of erratic steps sounded and three Gamants in blood-soaked white gowns tumbled into the alley with them. Tahn started to shove Rachel to the ground, but stopped in mid-push. The men were dead, bodies slashed fatally. Blood shot in spurts from their mangled wounds.

Tahn took a step forward and then turned to stare wild-eyed at Rachel. "Get out of your clothes!" he ordered.

In a flash of flying arms and legs, she'd undressed. She stood naked, her olive skin shiny with sweat. He barely looked at her as he stripped one of the victims and threw a blood-soaked white robe her way. She slipped it over her head, studying the red splatters. Blood shed for all of them. . . . She lowered her fingers to touch the moist spots. In front of her, Tahn undressed. For a brief instant she allowed her gaze to linger on the hard swell of muscles covering his tall body. A few fading bruises blotched his upper arms and chest. Jeremiel's attack in the landing bay? She wanted to reach out and soothe those hurts in penance for all the Gamant hurts he'd ever suffered.

512

He straightened up and caught the look on her face. "What's the matter?"

"Nothing. I'm just glad you're on our side."

He gave her a brief smile and threw her uniform at her. "Tuck it up under your gown." He grabbed her hand and pulled her around the corner into an undulating sea of Gamant bodies.

"Don't let go of me!" he shouted.

They struggled to stay upright in the shoving, crying swarm that surged up and over the dead bodies of Magisterial soldiers, bursting like a raging river through the barricades.

Beyond the gate, Rachel saw their shuttle gleaming a tarnished silver beneath the cloudy skies. Rain beaded on the hull like glistening tears. Gamants washed around it heedlessly, more interested in running as far and fast as they could from Block 10 than in investigating government property. They sprinted out across the desert like bloody beasts set free from ancient cages.

Tahn dragged her toward the shuttle's side doors. He hit the patch and she hustled through the open door. Once inside, he locked it. Rachel saw Jeremiel and inhaled a deep grateful breath. The interns had secured his gurney to a bench with EM restraints before fleeing the shuttle. He lay deathly still, but she saw the rise and fall of his broad chest. He'd managed to lift his pistol. It still lay clenched in his hand and propped across his stomach. His eye fluttered open.

In a barely audible voice, he asked, ". . . All right?"

"Yes," she answered as she went to his bedside. "We liberated the camp. Lichtner's dead."

His eye fell closed and almost instantly, he went limp, head rolling to the side in sleep—or unconsciousness. She gripped his wrist, checking his pulse, then shook her head, realizing he'd forced himself to stay awake to wait for them. And she strongly suspected that had he needed to, had they not come back, he'd have gotten out of that bed somehow and crawled every inch of the way to find them.

"Come on," Tahn said curtly. "They're rallying out there." He sprinted into the command cabin.

Rachel tenderly stroked Jeremiel's pistol hand before following.

CHAPTER 56

Rudy Kopal paced the bridge of the *Zilpah*, glaring at the image of the *Hoyer* hanging lifelessly before him. The cruiser, *Klewe*, had just flown in, dispatched a shuttle and received cargo or a *prisoner* and hastily retreated, running for the vault like a bat out of the pit of darkness. Four other cruisers sat in a semicircular formation around the *Hoyer*. Protecting her?

"Merle? Any intraship communications?"

"None." She shoved black hair over her shoulder. "All we know, Rudy, is that they're not firing on the *Hoyer*. Surely if Jeremiel were in control. . . ." She let the sentence dangle like a sword over his head. He swallowed the pain that rose.

"You think that ship was picking him up?"

"Unknown. But we'll be in range of those cruisers in exactly four minutes. Who do I target first, Rudy?"

He felt hatred well up inside him, hatred and desperate fear. Where was Jeremiel? How far had the Magistrates' programs gone on Tikkun? How many Gamants were still alive down there? Rudy folded his arms and hugged himself tightly. On the adjacent monitors, he saw his own ships forming up behind him, facing off against Tahn's. He rushed back to his command chair. "Merle, try to contact our bases on the planet. We'll need ground support when we—"

"*Rudy?*" Merle shouted.

He whirled. On the righthand monitor, seven ships dropped out of vault behind them, hurtling forward insanely. He dove for his arm console, checking the readings. "*That lead ship is one of ours. Merle, target—*"

Before he could finish the command, a dagger of violet shot out, slamming the lead ship. It burst open like a dropped egg, fragments spinning hideously, fires blazing through every portion and instantly freezing. Clouds of vapor congealed around the tumbling wreckage.

"We're picking up a cross-message, Rudy."

"Put it on audio."

His breathing went shallow as Penzer Gorgon's distinct baritone rang out, reporting the kill of the Underground vessel *Vinnitsa*, and requesting instructions for his role in the Tikkun maneuver. Rudy eased down into his command chair. Shoshi Luna had been in command. Her steel gray eyes seemed to stare out of the wreckage at him. Shoshi had been with Qaf around Abulafia. What did that mean about the rest of the fleet? A cold tingle traced its way up his spine.

"Sixty seconds to range, Rudy. What are we doing?"

He glared at the *Hoyer*, hanging so placidly in space. "We'll hit Tahn. Tell Cray, Jesse, Petras, and Diro to choose and target the other four. Have Mica and Lansford run a flanking maneuver. They'll need to try to cover our tails from Gorgon's fleet."

* * *

Carey's heart went cold in her chest as the first shot blasted the *Hoyer*'s shields, sending blinding waves of purple across the screens. Alert sirens blared, blue lights flashing over the bridge. "Uriah!" she screamed, "Get them on com! Who the hell is that?"

From the far corner of the ship where Dannon sat on the floor, knees drawn against his chest, a low laugh rumbled, growing louder. Black hair hung in a drenched mop around his pale handsome face.

"Dannon, damn you! Shut your mouth. Do you know who that is?"

He threw his head back, laughing so hysterically he could barely speak. "Uriah . . . send to the *Zilpah*. Rudy . . . Rudy Kopal in command."

"Belay that order!" Carey shouted as Uriah started to key in the sequence. Her face slackened. She lowered herself into her chair. *The Underground? And she had no weapons!*

"Carey, darling," Dannon cooed. "If I were you, I'd get on com rather quickly. You really must send something that sounds distinctly like Jeremiel."

She gripped her chair arms hard. "I don't need your advice, Dannon! What if Bogomil intercepts a message like that?"

He laughed again, shaking his head. "Bogomil isn't currently firing at you. I'd worry about him later. At this

515

particular moment, Kopal needs to hear something subtle and reassuring, like, *Rudy, what the hell are you doing? You're supposed to be on my side!* That, Lieutenant, will certainly get his attention."

The second shot seemed to spin out of nowhere, everywhere in its proximity. Repeated cannon shots. They slammed the *Hoyer* brutally. The ship lunged sideways, throwing half her bridge crew on the floor. Carey clung desperately to the command chair. Sirens blared in her ears, broken, erratic. The three-sixty monitors flashed partial damage-control data. Shields four and five gone. Level seventeen breached.

Her face slackened. The entire starboard of the cruiser lay open to attack. Just one more direct hit and. . . .

"Uriah!" she shouted, as people scrambled back into their seats. "Get on com! Go ahead. Send that message to Kopal!"

It began as a whisper in her mind, then seemed to grow in strength to echo from everywhere on the bridge—a deep startlingly beautiful voice. "Please countermand that order, Lieutenant."

"What?" She rose out of her chair, gaze flashing over every part of the bridge. "Who said that?" She saw Uriah's hand hovering shakily over his console, unsure what to do. As he started to lower it to comply with her order, she raged, "Wait!"

A shadow crept across the back of the room, like a gigantic writhing serpent of the deepest black. In a brilliant flash of light, a man of the purest gold appeared. Dressed in a dark green velvet cloak, he cocked his head, looking at her through the saddest eyes she'd ever seen. Magnetic, those eyes drew Carey powerfully.

"Lieutenant," he greeted in a calm voice. "Thank you."

He stepped down to the second level, walking gracefully and purposefully over to Neil Dannon. Dannon looked up at him in shock, mouth slightly ajar. Carey could only watch, too stunned to speak.

"Who . . . who are you?" Dannon asked.

The man of light's amber eyes seemed to flare more brightly. "Your people need you, Captain Dannon. Will you help them?"

"What?"

"You must get into the navigation chair. Lieutenant

Halloway's weapons will be back on line in a few seconds and she needs an *expert* weapons officer—or everybody aboard this vessel will die." The alien being smiled sorrowfully at Dannon. "You don't really want that to happen, do you?"

Dannon didn't seem to be breathing. He started to shake his head, then stopped. "I . . . I don't think I can."

"Try. The road back is not nearly as hard as you imagine. Let me help you. Give me your hand." The being extended glowing fingers. They cast a saffron glow over Dannon's frozen features.

"Who *are* you?"

"I offer you salvation, Captain. Will you take responsibility for your sins?" the alien said soothingly. "Do you know that Jeremiel has wished a thousand times in the past few months that he had you at his side? He's prayed for the clock to be reversed so he could talk to you—as you asked him to do so many times." He stretched his hand farther, hovering only a few inches from Dannon's. "Come, help *him*. Help your people."

"Are you . . . are you an angel?"

Carey found herself hanging breathlessly on his answer. From the first time she'd read the ancient remnants of the *Pseudepigrapha,* she'd harbored a secret belief that "angels" existed—as a reclusive alien species. The glowing being turned slightly to throw her a curious smile, as though he'd read her thoughts. Then he lowered his gaze, looking back to Dannon.

"Yes, Captain. I'm an angel. Now, please, we haven't much time. You were always particularly brilliant with weapons strategy. Remember the maneuver you pulled in the Opus system?"

Dannon blinked. Tears glistened in his eyes. Finally, he nodded. "You mean we've got to pivot—"

"Yes. Exactly, Captain. You see, the message you want to send to Rudy will only make him hurt for a split second before he decides it's a ruse of Tahn's. In that instant, I'm afraid Captain Bogomil will pick up your transmission and you'll be struck devastatingly from both sides at once."

Carey gripped her chair, digging her nails into the gray petrolon. "Blessed God."

Dannon lifted a quaking hand a few inches. The angel

reached out and took it, helping Dannon to his feet and smiling in quiet pride. "Please, take your chair, Captain."

Olam Lars instantly yielded the nav console, running to strap into the auxiliary weapons center on the far wall. Dannon sprinted across the room, sitting down. Carey's eyes widened as the *Hoyer*'s systems seemed to come back on line in a massive flood. The three-sixty monitors flared insistently with complete information. The audio com babbled, picking up several signals at once. Uriah nervously slapped controls to silence it. The thrum of a ship on full power eddied across the bridge.

And on the forward monitor, the Underground fleet started their next run, four lining out, two swinging around. A chill premonition of doom made Carey shiver; she braced herself.

The angel's eyes caressed her face for an instant before he walked over to her command chair. She fought the urge to back away from him. His cloak swayed with his movements. Hesitantly, so as not to frighten her, he reached out a hand and gently touched her shoulder.

"Lieutenant," he said softly, for her ears alone. "Be kind to Jeremiel. He's been hurt enough."

She gazed into those gentle amber eyes and heard herself murmur, "Yes. I will."

A gush of warm wind swept the bridge. A huge dark maw spun out, blotting the sight of the transport tube. He backed away into it, vanishing in a swirl of green cloak. It spun closed behind him.

"Carey?" Dannon called with controlled urgency. His eyes were focused on the forward monitor. "Are you ready?"

"I am. Just tell me what the hell we're doing."

* * *

CHAPTER 57

The acceleration pressed Rachel back into her chair like a rough hand. She watched Tahn check and recheck the monitors. He took the ship straight up, then swung around and headed back for Block 10. Rachel panicked. "What are you doing?"

"Cleanup duty."

They soared over brush and stony plateaus. In the distance, Rachel could see Gamants racing in three distinct groups of a few hundred each across the sands. At the gate of Block 10 twenty or thirty Magisterial officers stood. Several more soldiers ran for the ships lined up outside the walls.

"Damn it," Tahn cursed.

He roughly nosed the *Eugnostos* down and Rachel watched the determination on his face when he programmed the weapons. He struck the "fire" button and brilliant purple arcs lanced out from the shuttle, panning the soldiers in front of the gate and slashing through the pilots who fought desperately to get into their ships. Rifle bursts splashed their shields like lavender paint. Diligently, expertly, Tahn swung back around and battered each vessel. The ships ruptured, throwing dirt, men, machinery, and chunks of Block 10's walls into the rain-drenched skies of Tikkun.

As the *Eugnostos* swooped up and started to head away, Rachel reached over and gripped Tahn's forearm hard. He gave her a deadly look.

"What's the matter?"

Rachel's heart thundered. "Hit the camp."

He shook his head lightly. "But what if there's still some survivors in there. They might—"

"Anybody who's left in there will consider death a gift from God compared to what awaits them when the Magistrates retake Block 10."

Tahn's blue-violet eyes softened—as though he, too, could visualize the horror of the probe deaths these victims would be forced to endure.

"Understood," he said.

They hurtled down again. When the cannons let loose, the camp's photon shield flared like molten gold—warping and fluctuating into an obscene wound before it vanished. Tahn methodically hit the gray buildings inside, sending fragments tumbling like huge bits of shrapnel into the air. When he pounded Lichtner's personal quarters, he took special care to leave nothing standing but a jagged mass of rubble.

"Yes," she hissed. "Yes."

They shot up and away. Below them, the continent of Amman shone half in sun, half lost in dark clouds. Across the eastern portion, dark tangles of trees fringed the borders of an aquarmarine ocean. Rachel gazed contemplatively at it, remembering the magnificent cerulean expanse that spread outside of Dor—longing for it.

She shifted her gaze back to the Yaguthian Desert. Sunset crept over the westernmost edges, darkening the cliffs with patchwork shadows. A few flecks of gold sparkled in strangely regular patterns, equidistant, formed into rough squares. Fighting against the acceleration, she leaned forward, to get more of the portal's view.

"Captain?" she asked. "Do you know what those patterns of lights are?"

"I'd suspect more camps like Block 10."

"More. . . ." She sat in stunned immobility. More of them? But, of course, undoubtedly nine other Blocks existed before number ten. How many after? Lichtner boasted of killing at least twelve thousand. If each camp had a similar record . . . . She bowed her head in silent prayer to a God she no longer believed possessed any compassion.

Tahn reached over and started to punch one of the com patches, but his hand halted in mid-motion. He stopped so suddenly that Rachel's breath caught. She spun to look at him. His eyes were glued to the long front portal, chin squared so bluntly that it seemed he fought a tearing inner pain. Rachel saw the arteries in his throat throbbing rapidly.

"What's wrong?" she demanded.

"Cruisers, lining out. We might have to . . ."

In a move so violent it made her cling to her chair, the shuttle veered sharply right, angling down like an out of control missile. The ground rose up in a swirling sickening rush of green and brown.

"Where are we going?" she shouted.

"Someplace safe!"

They dove toward the night side of the planet, toward a dark forest. For a few minutes, Rachel concentrated on the horizon. Stars twinkled dully through a layer of fog. Tahn skimmed the tops of the trees, cursing softly, slamming a fist repeatedly into his leg. He turned the ship in a tight circle, nosing down toward a small irregularly shaped meadow, covered almost completely by a canopy of trees. They landed amidst a spray of dry multicolored leaves. The ship made a dull thud when it struck too suddenly.

Tahn immediately shut off his EM restraints. His hands darted over the patches and Rachel saw the front portal change. The vision of trees swaying through the fog vanished. A new image crystallized in holographic detail. Ships, rushing headlong at each other. She jerked as a violet web of actinic brilliance lashed the scene. Three or four cruisers flared in silent agony, then went out. Several more wavered under fire, shields faltering. Then both sides veered away, swinging around. One ship shot across into the opposing side, forming up with them. Every ship moved—but one. A cold pit expanded in Rachel's stomach.

"Is that the *Hoyer*?" she asked.

His gaze was riveted on the scene. "Yes. She's taken at least six hits."

"What does that mean? Is she. . . ."

"No. Not yet." He shook his head. "But Carey's caught in the middle." Anguish tinged his strong voice. He input several commands into his control com, waiting a few seconds for readouts. Then he slowly sank back in his chair.

"Those are Underground cruisers on the left."

Her heart fluttered with hope. "And on the right?"

"Magisterial."

"So, the Magistrates have more ships."

"Might not matter. The Underground has better positioning. I'd wager they're evenly matched."

Sybil? "Can we do something?"

"I . . . I don't think so." He caressed his forehead. "Trying to reach Carey could kill her. She's obviously played her hand well. Did you notice that none of the Magisterial vessels fired on her? Just the Underground. I suspect that's Kopal up there and if he hears my voice, the *Hoyer* is certainly dead."

In a flash, Tahn climbed out of his chair. He hurried into the rear compartment. Rachel swung her chair around, watching him go to Jeremiel's bedside. "Baruch?" He took a hand-corder and ran it over the length of Jeremiel's body, checking vital signs. "Too weak," she heard Tahn murmur. "And we don't have any drugs to bring him out."

From the corner of her eye, Rachel caught movement on the holo. She looked back. The cruisers had begun another run. *"Tahn?"*

He careened back into the command cabin, eyes on the holo, breathing fast and light. He pressed a fist to his mouth as he watched.

Cruisers reconfigured, fanning out, facing off. They both took a deep breath and held it. Then something strange happened. Just as the Magisterial ships approached the *Hoyer's* position, and the Underground came into firing range, the *Hoyer* pivoted like a supremely skilled ballerina, coming full around to fire into the onslaught of Magisterial vessels. The lead government ship flared and vanished. Another died swiftly, brilliantly. The others braked violently, swerving in erratic patterns, suddenly realizing they'd fallen into a trap. The Underground cruisers seemed momentarily confused. *They held their fire!* Swooping down around the *Hoyer,* four ships fell into formation with her, combining firepower. The remaining ships came to near halts, five against four, pouring ergs into each other.

"What the hell are they doing!" Tahn demanded, teeth gritted. "Get out of there! *Get out!*"

Rachel leaned forward breathlessly. "What's happening? It looks like a standoff."

"Gridlock," he whispered miserably and shook his head. "The Underground waited too long to start firing. The Magisterial ships got too close, now none of them can pull away—without dying. They've got to fight it out."

An incapacitating rush of fear and sorrow brought tears to Rachel's eyes. *Sybil. My baby.* She folded her arms tightly over her aching breast.

Tahn glanced at the com, then back to the *Hoyer*. He chewed his fist in indecision, then lunged for the patch. He quickly input a long sequence—scrambled? Secret?

In a voice as confident as God's Himself, he said, *"Carey? One-eighty. Dive. DIVE!"*

* * *

Carey stood nervelessly on the bridge, smoke choking her lungs, making her eyes stream with tears. All of her crew except Dannon lay strewn across the deck, probably dead. Dannon sat at his console like a tall, haze-enveloped statue.

Carey coughed, on the verge of retching. Smoke roiled so thickly she couldn't see the forward screen. She stumbled back, falling into the command chair.

"Neil?" she choked. "Status?"

"Forward shields. . . ." he coughed violently. "Holding!"

A brief thread of hope wound through her—then she heard the crackle of fire. Spinning in her chair, she saw a mass of flames spreading like a marmalade wall toward her, so hot it ran in a wave over the fireproof carpet, swallowing everything.

Oh, blessed God, we're dead. Dead! She'd been holding off, hoping some of the people on the floor still lived. "Neil!" She gasped a hoarse breath. "Helmet! I'm going to depressurize."

With lightning speed, he reached down to the floor and gripped his helmet, fastening it on his head. Carey did the same and instantly decompressed the bridge. The swift sucking sound would have been deafening if not for the protection of their helmets.

Carey gasped deep breaths of the sterile, life-support air, watching the smoke disappear in a wash. *Now those people are gone.* Through bleary eyes, she saw Dannon fall forward over his console, coughing so hard he couldn't straighten up. When he could, he shouted, "Carey! Shield two failing. Shall I divert power from weapons?"

She stared blindly at the screen. Purple arcs obscured their vision of other vessels. Suicide—either way. Without both forward shields, the *Hoyer* would be devoured.

523

Without full power to the weapons, they'd be pushed back, back until their shields died anyway.

She started laughing, a rich slightly insane laugh. "Do you prefer it quick or slow, Dannon?"

He gave her a wild stare, then, as her meaning dawned, a smile crept over his face. "I've never liked things to drag out."

She laughed harder, until she felt physically ill. He laughed with her, shaking his head. When the laughter began to change, to become husky with tears, she forced herself to stop.

"Dannon? You're a hell of a fine officer," she called. "Thanks."

His smile faded, dark eyes wet and wide. "You, too, Lieutenant. Sorry we couldn't have served together under different circumstances." In a forlorn voice, he quipped, "So much for angels."

"Indeed. Indeed!"

"By the way, what was that tête-à-tête he had with you when nobody could hear?"

She swallowed, taking a breath. It couldn't possibly hurt to tell anybody now. "He told me to be kind to Jeremiel. That he'd been hurt enough."

Dannon held her gaze for a second, then bowed his head, turning his face away so she couldn't see his expression. He fumbled purposelessly with the petrolon frame of his console. "I knew there was something between you two."

"Something much too brief," she said through a long exhalation.

"Well," he said barrenly. "I'm sorry God wasn't on our side. Maybe if he had been you could have . . .."

As though in a dream, Cole's voice boomed all over the ship, deep, commanding: *"Carey? One-eighty. Dive. DIVE!"*

She sat unmoving. He wanted her to back out of the maneuver, to swing behind the cruiser on their flank, using it as cover while they escaped. The other Underground vessels would have to provide covering fire to keep themselves alive. They were all dead anyway, but. . . . Her captain had given her an order.

"Dannon?" She sat up straight. "One-eighty. We'll—"

"Negative!"

"What?" she demanded. "Do it!"

524

He laughed softly, as though truly amused by himself. "Negative. I know those people out there. Together we still have a slim chance of winning. Not much, I'll grant you, but some."

"But they hate you!"

"Well, that doesn't really matter, does it? I still love them."

"Neil, we can break free if we—"

"I've never felt more free than right now, Lieutenant." He gave her an insolent smile and swung back around to his console.

Carey started to rise, to challenge him for the com, but a strong gentle voice penetrated her emotional haze. Almost as though she lay in his arms again, she could feel the tender movements of Jeremiel's hands over her bare back, see the serious look in his blue eyes. . . . *It means being free to fight for a cause you know is right, to fight with all your heart without ever expecting.* . . .

She'd never disobeyed Cole. "Belay that last order, Dannon. I think I understand."

"Do you?" he asked. He gave her a flamboyant look, dark brows arching villainously.

"Yes."

"Good. Then maybe you'll understand this, too. I don't need you here. It only takes one to handle this focused maneuver. Get out. Access one of the pods. Shove as many people in it as you can and go."

Her heart began a painful staccato against her ribs. "Negative. I'm staying."

"Get out, damn it! I'm telling you I don't need you or anybody to carry this off! If you can get down to Transportation, you might be able to save everybody who's still alive. I seriously doubt Jeremiel had time to teach the Gamants aboard about desperate emergency mechanisms like pods."

"Neil, I'm not going to leave you to—"

"Blast you, Carey! There's not a chance in hell that those cruisers will divert firepower to kill a jettisoned pod. *You might make it!* Go. I can hold the ship by myself. At least, as long as she *can* be held."

He gazed at her through warm confident eyes. Through his helmet visor, she could see black hair hanging in drenched wisps over his pale face. Carey got out of her chair and walked to stand behind him, gazing at the forward screen. Waves of purple lanced shield two; it fluctuated wildly. It would be gone soon—and they'd be dead.

"Negative," she said. "If I stay, that increases both our chances for survival. But I appreciate the offer."

She lowered a friendly hand to his shoulder and he caught her completely by surprise. She was stunned by how quickly he pivoted, knocking her to the floor, his powerful body pinning her arms. She saw his hand flash over her helmet and felt, with a shock, the air vanish. She writhed against him, slashing out with her hands, trying to . . . to. . . .

* * *

Cole slammed a fist into the wall. "Damn it, Carey. What are you doing? Dive!"

"She can't," Rachel murmured. She watched the screen through moist eyes. "When she switched sides, she meant it."

He propped a fist against the portal. He felt as if he teetered on the edge of a precipice, about to lose everything that had ever meant anything to him. His ship, his best friend, his crew. "But the chances of them surviving are next to nothing."

"She knows that. Everyone aboard will understand . . . except the . . . the children."

Cole leaned his head against the wall. He looked down into Rachel's dazed, hurt expression and he felt if he stayed in the shuttle another minute, he'd start screaming. More than that, he couldn't bear to see the *Hoyer*'s death happen before his very eyes. He glanced one final time at the cruisers locked in a death duel and headed for the side door of the shuttle.

Stepping down to the wet leaf-strewn carpet of the forest, he sank back against the hull of the ship. He felt so empty, so barren inside himself he wondered what the future could possibly hold. A neuro center if they caught him. But he wasn't going to let them capture him. And then, there were things he could do if they did, to keep himself out of the centers. He shook his head. He and Rachel would make a run for it, all right, but just where they'd go he hadn't the slightest idea. *Well, you'd damn well better think about it.*

"Soon," he promised himself. He gazed at the dark forest around him. Mist twined through the autumn-dusted branches. The damp night air brushed his face with coolness.

Footsteps sounded inside the ship. He saw Rachel step down and sit on the gangplank—a strategic location—she could see him, Baruch, and the holo in the command cabin.

"Cole," she said hollowly. "I just wanted to thank you. Gamant civilization can never—"

"Stop it, Rachel." He thrust an arm out at the heavens. "If I'd been up there instead of down here, *I guarantee you* your daughter and my. . . ." He stopped seeing pain glaze her eyes. Guilt swelled in his gut. "I would have gotten the hell out of there, that's all."

"I know you would have. You don't owe the Underground anything. I think Halloway believes she does." In a voice violent in its softness, she said, "God's to blame for all this. He enjoys our suffering." She reached into her pocket and pulled out a dull gray ball on a long golden chain.

"What is that?" he said.

"A token from the pit of darkness. Actually, it belongs to Jeremiel. . . ." She stopped and laughed softly, bitterly, as though chastising herself. "I wish I'd never laid eyes on it."

She held it out to him and he took it. A faint blue light lit the center, as though some entity inside were probing him. Rachel sucked in a startled breath. Cole felt oddly hollow, cold. The light vanished almost as soon as it had appeared.

Tahn studied the stiffness of Rachel's posture, the square set of her jaw, then he shifted his gaze to the fog twining in the tops of the trees. "Well—I'm astounded that after seeing what's been happening on Tikkun you can still believe in a God. If He is up there, He certainly isn't a friend of ours. Though, who knows, maybe He's on the Magistrates' side." He glowered uncertainly at the *Mea*.

Rachel nodded, twisting her hands. "Would you end the suffering, if you could?"

"Hell, yes."

"No matter what it took?"

He shrugged, but he noticed how intently she watched him, as though hanging on his next words. He reconsidered the offhand remark he had been going to make. "It

527

would depend on what ending it entailed."

"If you could end it all—at once—in a moment." She threw up her arms in a gesture of absolute and total annihilation. "Would you?"

"You mean would I destroy the entire universe to end it? Well, that's one I'd have to think about for awhile."

"I think about it all the time." An eerie calm had possessed her—as though the probable death of her daughter had snuffed all the light in her life.

He frowned. "Do you think the universe should die to kill suffering?"

She tucked her fingers beneath her arms to protect them from the damp chill of the mist. Rocking back and forth slowly, she answered, "I don't know."

"Block 10 makes you wonder though, doesn't it? How could a beneficent God allow such a place to exist?"

"Block 10 is proof enough that God isn't beneficent." Her olive skin turned a dull clay color. She wet her lips anxiously and looked up at him. "Do you regret helping us?"

With the toe of his boot, he turned over a clutter of dead leaves, watching their red and green edges shimmer in the light cast by the shuttle. "No, Rachel, I don't regret a single moment of it."

She started to say something, but she jerked around suddenly, looking at the holo. "Come on," she whispered. Getting to her feet, she ran for the command cabin.

He shoved the *Mea* in his pocket and leaped into the shuttle behind her—fearing what he'd see—knowing the duel had gone on too long. Somebody's shields must have failed, or their systems overloaded. A brilliant flash lit the cabin. He shielded his eyes, stopping in the entryway. Two Underground ships exploded, leaving Carey completely open. He watched in horror as the *Hoyer* dove, but not for the planet. It hurtled straight forward into the line of Magisterial vessels. In a moment of disbelief and desperation, the government vessels shifted their fire to the *Hoyer*. The remaining three Underground vessels shot out and away, accelerating for vault, vanishing into the blackness of space.

Cole forced a swallow down his dry throat. Kopal knew a sacrifice move when he saw it—Carey'd just saved the lives of a few thousand Gamant soldiers.

Tahn watched with tears in his eyes as the *Hoyer* exploded, the splash of light so enormous and violent, he knew instantly what Carey had done. Curiously, he studied the mini supernova that spread over the dark skies of Tikkun. Light rolled out in blinding waves, consuming every remaining Magisterial vessel in its wake. Carey had pushed the engines, nursed them until she knew one or more of the singularities was on the verge of evaporation. Then she'd made her move.

"Get down!" he ordered. Grabbing a stunned Rachel, he pushed her to the floor, covering her body with his own. The shock wave struck the planet like a roaring fist. The ground shuddered, tossing the shuttle back and forth before it ceased.

A terrible silence engulfed them. Neither of them breathed. "It's all right," he assured. "It's over."

"Yes," she whispered. "All over."

He felt her tears running warmly against his face. He slipped his arms beneath her shoulders and embraced her tightly.

"Cole?" she shouted. "What's that?"

He spun, staring at the holo which still gleamed with a bright silver wash. Two tiny streaks burned through the planet's atmosphere. He got to his feet, extending a hand to help Rachel up as he watched the specks of white soar downward.

"Fragments of the ship?" she asked.

He shook his head, frowning. "Not from the *Hoyer*. Discounting the ferocity of the explosion, the timing's wrong. To be entering the atmosphere now, those had to have been cast away minutes ago." He leaned forward, accessing the navigation console. He traced the paths of the specks, noting their straight line flights. "They dropped somewhere in the south. Near the Hentopan Sea."

He heard Rachel's sharp intake of breath. "Shuttles?"

"No," he said certainly. "Mass readings are too small." Then his eyes widened. *"But they could sure as hell be pods!"*

She clutched her throat. "Hurry. Let's hurry."

"Damned right. We've got to find them before somebody else does."

He climbed into the pilot's chair and began powering up as Rachel hit her EM restraints.

CHAPTER 58

Carey lifted a crate of food rations and carried it out of the pod, setting it on the sandy shore. Twenty people worked around her, lifting, carrying crates and boxes into the nearby caves that bordered the sea like an intricate honeycomb. A dense jade forest spread on the other side of the caves. Just after their landing, Millhyser and two other Magisterial soldiers had made a break for it, vanishing into the tangled vegetation. Carey hadn't assigned a search party. She couldn't spare anyone—and she hadn't the heart to kill those people.

She wiped a hand over her sweating brow. The dusty radiance of sunset glimmered on the beach, setting each grain to sparkling like a diamond. In the distance, Tikkun's sun hung like a crimson ball over the azure water.

She inhaled deeply of the warm salt-scented air. She'd awakened in the pod, hurtling toward the planet, but she'd seen the demise of the *Hoyer*. Her heart still ached—for her ship and the friends she couldn't save—and for a man she'd despised for too long. Surely, it had been *that* Neil Dannon that Jeremiel Baruch had called his best friend.

A numbness swelled in her chest. She shook herself, not daring to think about Jeremiel or Cole yet. She lifted her gaze to the pearlescent skies of dusk, searching for ships. Already the military installations would have mobilized, having seen the pods on their scanners. They'd have watched the battle, noted the *Hoyer*'s treason, and jumped into their ships before it was even over to come looking for the traitors. Before that happened, she wanted to scavenge everything she could and hide it away in the thousands of caves and crevices of this area. She and what remained of the Gamant crew would undoubtedly need the supplies in the coming months while they scrambled for cover.

"Pray to Epagael, we can avoid capture." She anxiously fingered the pistol on her hip.

"Lieutenant?" Sandy Joad called. A young man, short and skinny, he had a calm sallow face. His pinkish hair dangled to the collar of his brown jumpsuit. She'd only met him in the shuttle, but already she'd grown to like his competent quiet ways. He'd taken over organizing the salvage parties, leaving the more critical duties for Carey.

"What is it, Sandy?"

"Ma'am, what should we do with the injured? We've got about six that are sure to die if we don't get them tended pretty quick."

Smoke inhalation and burns had taken the most serious tolls. "There are two antigrav gurneys in each pod. Find somebody to break out the med supplies in the emergency lockers, then put the injured in the largest, most sheltered cave you can find."

"On my way." He sprinted toward the far pod, sitting like an octagonal ball at the edge of the trees.

Carey stretched her aching back muscles and picked up her rations crate again, hauling it across the damp beach to the foot of the caves where the others were stacked. She saw Joad rushing the first victim, an old Gamant woman with straggly gray hair, into a cave tucked into the forest about a hundred feet from her.

Using her dirty purple sleeve, Carey wiped her face and started back to the pod for another load.

Joad's voice stopped her. "Lieutenant!"

She spun and saw him running toward her. "What's wrong?"

"We got company, ma'am." He pointed to the sky, glowing carnelian now in the fires of sunset.

She shaded her eyes, looking up. "I don't see anything."

"It's there. I saw a glint of silver."

Carey pulled her pistol and gripped it in a sweaty hand, gaze darting madly across every tatter of cloud that drifted westward. Nothing. Yet, her spine tingled.

"Sandy, get the people into the caves. Go! Move it!" She slapped him on the shoulder and they ran across the sands, waving arms, yelling, "Take cover. Get in the caves! *Run!*"

Everywhere, people dropped crates and picked up their feet, fading into the honeycomb of tan rock like

531

ghosts in some misty netherworlds. Carey and Sandy ran into a tiny niche no more than six feet high and five around. She slid back against the wall, peering out cautiously. Remnants of sunlight flashed in gold and silver from the deepening blue of the sea.

"If it's the government, Sandy," Carey said huskily, "I'll try to provide covering fire. Take as many people as you can and head for the forest. You'll have to have solid rock between you and them or their ships will find you. You understand that?"

He nodded once. "I do."

Carey heard the splash of sand as a ship landed. She eased forward, peering out. Silhouetted against the lavender skies, a shuttle sat. A tall man stood in the dark shadow at its side, pistol drawn.

He took a step forward, out of the obscuring shadow, and Carey felt as though her heart would burst. She darted out of the cave. A few steps later, Cole saw her and broke into a run.

"Carey?"

He caught her up and swung her around, his arms crushing her ribs. She laughed with sheer jubilation.

"I thought you were dead," he said softly.

"I wasn't so sure about you either."

He held her at arm's length, gaze caressing her face. "But if that wasn't you that pulled that brilliant maneuver—"

"Neil Dannon."

He seemed stunned. He tilted his head in thought, then nodded his acceptance. "Well, I suspect Baruch will be interested to hear that."

Carey's heart fluttered. "Jeremiel's all right? Where is he? Why isn't he. . . ." She tried to break free from his grasp to run to the shuttle, but he held her wrists in a viselike grip.

"Carey. He's not all right."

She felt the ground beneath her boots tremble. For a moment, she couldn't speak. "What's wrong? Tell me quickly, Cole."

He wrapped an arm around her shoulders and headed her in the direction of the shuttle. The sun had set, but its hidden rays burned through the drifting clouds like flame.

"He'll be all right," he said gently. "Lichtner apparently took out all his pent up frustrations with Gamants on Baruch. He's got third-degree burns over about seventy percent of his body."

A cry of anger and futility caught in her throat. She put a hand to her mouth and then forced it down. "Is he conscious?"

"Barely. The entire flight down, he's been delirious. We have painkillers in the shuttle, but very little else."

She nodded. "I understand. We brought. . . . Dannon had the Gamant refugees pack every shred of med supplies he could find into our pods."

"Maybe he had a premonition about his ex-best friend."

As they neared the shuttle's side doors, she stopped, bracing her suddenly weak knees. "No," she said softly. "Just *his best friend.*"

Rachel emerged from the shuttle, running, face taut. "Halloway? My daughter? Is she. . . ."

Carey shook her head, then realized the implications and quickly amended, "She's at Palaia with Mikael."

Rachel's steps faltered. "What?"

"Just before the battle began, we were ordered to turn Mikael over and Sybil demanded to go with him. I sent Funk and Calas along as guardians. I think they're probably all right."

Rachel's face darkened, but she nodded.

Carey strode past her, climbing into the shuttle. The bright white lights seemed an abomination after the subtle pastel shades of the planet. Jeremiel lay on the far side, covered by a white sheet. Carey clenched her jaw. Her gaze lingered on the burns on his pale cheeks, the bandage around his right eye.

"Damn you, Jeremiel," she murmured, walking forward. "I tell you I love you and you almost get yourself killed."

A faint smile curled his mouth. "Didn't mean to," he said weakly. His unbandaged eye opened drowsily. It glistened with fevered brilliance. His lungs filled as though he fought to find the breath to speak. "What happened?"

"It's a long story. A Neil Dannon story. How strong are you? Do you want to hear it now or—"

"Now."

She nodded. "We were being hit hard by the Underground. I. . . ."

He looked at her with dire hope. "Kopal?"

"Yes, but he's gone. He left when he had the first opening."

"Good."

"We'd sustained six hits. I thought for sure we were dead. Neil took over the nav console and just before Kopal reached firing range in his second run, Dannon pivoted the *Hoyer* and fired into the oncoming Magisterial wave. We—"

"Opus move. Neil . . . best weapons strategist I ever knew."

"Yes. Me, too. We gridlocked." Jeremiel's face slackened with fear and she reached down to tenderly stroke his wounded cheek. His one eye struggled to stay focused on her face. "That's when Neil attacked me and dragged me down to a bay to shove me into a pod. After he jettisoned us, he flew into the Magisterial formation, firing, and the three remaining Underground ships beat hell for the vault."

"Singularities . . . evaporating?"

"Yes. Dannon saved nearly everyone aboard and three of Kopal's vessels."

He closed his one eye and his mouth tightened with restrained emotion—as though remembering and hurting for the friend he'd loved, not the man who'd betrayed him. When he spoke, his voice whispered with pain. "He . . . knew what he was doing. You all right?"

"Oh, yes."

"Glad you were there . . . with Neil. Would have never worked . . . if Tahn had been. They'd have killed each other."

"I suspect so. Not only that, but I doubt Cole would have known what to do when the. . . ." She hesitated, lifting her brows and venting a long sigh. Behind her, she heard someone enter the shuttle to stand silently and turned to see Rachel silhouetted in the entry.

"Go on," Jeremiel urged.

Carey lifted a shoulder. "Well, I know it sounds like I'm mad, but an angel appeared on the bridge just before the *Hoyer*'s systems came back on line. It was him, the angel, who convinced Dannon to take the nav com."

Jeremiel stared fearfully at her. "What did he look like?"

"Beautiful. Like a golden glowing god."

The shuttle went silent. The proverbial pin could have been dropped with thunderous effect. Neither Jeremiel nor Rachel so much as moved a muscle—as though they both walked a silver thread over the abyss.

Jeremiel's eye flashed darkly over the shuttle's ceiling panels. "Must have been. Mustn't it, Rachel?"

"Yes. I—I think so."

Carey frowned, looking from one to the other. "Been. . . ?"

She straightened when she saw Cole come up behind Rachel.

"How is he?" Tahn asked.

"Awake."

"Fine," Jeremiel insisted.

Tahn lifted his brows and shook his head. "He's as stubborn as a Giclasian. Anybody else would have died with dignity by now."

"After I see you in an Underground uniform."

Tahn scowled and walked forward. "Where the hell did you get the energy to be so goddamned brassy? I thought that shot I gave you knocked you out?"

"Not yet."

"Well, here, then," Cole said, drawing a curious necklace from his pocket. He placed it on Jeremiel's stomach, next to his hand. "I understand this is yours."

In a shaky gesture, Jeremiel touched the gray globe. After a moment, he snaked his hand closer, wrapping his fingers around it. To Carey's eyes, the gray quality seemed to deepen, as foreboding as roiling storm clouds on the horizon. Slowly, Jeremiel lifted his gaze to Rachel. Her eyes flared like full black moons—as if the globe in Baruch's hand answered all the cataclysmic questions that wedded her soul to the Darkness.

"Forsaken?" Jeremiel whispered. "Both of us?"

A swallow went down Rachel's throat. "Only by God."

Baruch exhaled quietly. "Seen our friend?"

"No. I—I haven't," Rachel stammered. She'd started to shake. She backed away and Carey heard her feet retreat across the sand.

"What's wrong with her?" Carey demanded.

Jeremiel breathed out a sigh and seemed to drift off,

eye opening and closing lazily. His voice was heavy with sleep. *"Mashiah . . . Antimashiah. . . . She no longer knows what's good or what's evil. . . . Nor do I."* His head lolled to the side and his eye closed.

"Carey," Cole said ominously. "We've got to find shelter. This beach is the last place on Tikkun we need to be."

She laid a hand on Jeremiel's fevered brow, touching him tenderly one last time. "There are some interesting rock formations about ten miles from here. We saw them on the way down. They're in the depths of the forest. I was thinking—"

"And I'm sure you're right. Let's go."

CHAPTER 59

Mikael stood uneasily in the front room of Magistrate Slothen's office on Palaia Station. The blue man behind the desk scowled at him and Mikael shuffled away to press against Sybil's shoulder. Around them, Ambassador Ornias, Captain Erinyes, and Ari and Yosef stood.

Mikael brushed Sybil's brown hair out of the way and cupped a hand to her ear, whispering, "This is the right place, isn't it?"

Sybil nodded certainly, then cupped a hand to his ear. "Sure. Didn't you see those funny yellow skies and pointed buildings? This is it, all right."

"Okay. Sybil, did you have *funny* dreams on the cruiser on the way here?"

She shook her head and gazed at him questioningly. Mikael shrugged it off and focused again on the ugly blue creature behind the desk. Mikael had slept for most of the journey. He'd had very strange dreams. Metatron kept coming to him, telling him things, asking him questions, and showing him funny pictures from the future: *Mikael could still feel the cool wind that tousled his hair when he stood between the Horns of the Calf on*

Palaia. He could still hear the screams from men and women dying on the plains below and see the ships that soared overhead and slashed the hills with violet fire. The clouds burned. . . .

For three mornings, he'd awakened with a terrible headache. And—he felt different, older, as though Metatron had done things to his brain to make him think like a fifteen-year-old or something. Even more frightening, Mikael remembered Metatron telling him that he'd created little gates in Mikael's head, gates that Mikael could open or close at will. Metatron had shown him how to do it—to shut off certain parts of his brain. He'd been experimenting in his dreams most of the way here.

Shifting from one foot to the other, Mikael tried to think of exactly what he had to say to Slothen. His grandfather had told him what God wanted, but he had to say it just right. He was thinking about it when the blue man stood up and said, "Magistrate Slothen will see you now."

"Well, it's about time," Captain Erinyes said nastily. He led the way down a long lavender hall.

Mikael trembled, looking from Sybil to his Uncle Yosef.

"Let me take your hand, Mikael?" Yosef said, looking down at him through loving eyes. He extended wrinkled fingers.

Mikael took them, holding them tightly. As they started off, he motioned for Sybil to come take his other hand. She ran forward to do it. Her palm felt warm against his. Ari followed behind, cursing quietly to himself about blue sonsabitches.

Two guards in purple uniforms stood by a big door. Captain Erinyes and Ambassador Ornias swept by them like the wind, but Mikael stopped, blinking up.

"Hello," he said shyly. "How are you?" He'd watched his grandfather for most of his life. His grandfather talked nice to everybody. It was important.

The tall dark-haired guard glared sternly for a little bit, then his face melted like ice in the sun and he smiled. "I'm fine. How are you, son?"

Mikael smiled back. "All right, sir. Thank you."

Uncle Yosef smiled at the guard and tugged Mikael's hand. They walked into a big office. Beautiful pictures hung on the walls, stars and things. He looked at them with interest, then he turned to stare at the blue man behind the white desk.

"Leader Calas," the man said, "welcome to Palaia Station. I'm Magistrate Slothen."

Mikael's heart thumped. Bravely, he let go of Yosef's and Sybil's fingers and stepped forward. He formed his hands into the sacred Gamant triangle and bowed. "I'm pleased to meet you, sir. Thank you for letting me come." He extended a hand toward his family. "This is my Uncle Yosef and his friend Ari Funk and this is my best friend Sybil."

"Good day," Magistrate Slothen said stiffly and smiled.

It scared Mikael a little, because he had long pointed teeth under bright red lips that reminded Mikael of blood. "Sir? We need to talk about what to do with Gamants."

Slothen's blue wormy hair crawled. Mikael grimaced. "Gamants are very uncooperative. I'm not sure we can negotiate anymore. But, please sit down. We'll at least talk. What did you have in mind?"

Mikael watched people sit down, everybody except Sybil and Ambassador Ornias. Sybil glared at the ambassador like she wanted to hit him again. The tall man came forward and knelt beside Mikael, smiling sideways at Magistrate Slothen. Mikael squinted.

"Listen, Calas," Ornias whispered. "Let me help you. I know these people. They're—"

"He's a pig!" Sybil accused, glowering at the ambassador. "He killed my dad, and he tried to kill me and my mom!"

Mikael lifted his chin and said. "Get away from us. We don't need your help."

"But, really, Mikael," Ornias pressed quietly. "You don't know Giclasians, they have strange ways."

"You're a pig!" Mikael echoed Sybil. "I don't like you. Get away from me!"

Ornias' eyes narrowed. He got to his feet and looked down harshly at Sybil, then turned in a whirl of black robes and went back to sit beside Captain Erinyes.

Mikael kept standing, mostly because he felt too nervous to sit. Sybil stood in front of her chair, like she was waiting for him to tell her it was okay. He nodded and she nodded back, then slid onto the seat.

Mikael walked timidly over to stand before Slothen. His eyes just reached above the top of the desk. He curled his fingers over it to pull himself up a little higher. He braced his chin on the desktop. "Sir? Captain Tahn told me you didn't really hate Gamants. Is that right, sir?"

Slothen leaned back in his chair and rubbed a finger over his ruby red lips. Behind him, ships dove through the yellow skies, swooping over the tall buildings. "Hatred is not a Giclasian emotion."

Mikael smiled uncertainly. "I guess that means no, then. I'm glad, because, Gamants don't really mean to be bad. It's just that sometimes they think they have to because they're afraid you want to hurt them." He licked his lips and watched the frown form on that blue monster face.

"What do you suggest we do to stop the violence, Leader Calas?"

Mikael slid his chin around to glance at Sybil. She nodded to him, telling him to go ahead and say what his grandfather had told him God wanted. "Well," he said thoughtfully, "I think, sir, that we need to move Gamants to one planet."

"Move them? You're *asking* for forced relocation?"

Uncle Yosef sat forward, eyes glistening fearfully. He whispered softly to Ari, who shook his head.

Mikael chewed his lower lip and decided he'd just go on and not tell Slothen he didn't understand what "relocation" meant. "Yes, sir, move them. To one planet."

Slothen twined his fingers together and made a twisted face. "What planet did you have in mind?"

"Horeb, sir. Could you do that?"

"Mikael?" Uncle Yosef said sharply. Sweat had broken out across his bald head, gleaming in the bright sunlight streaming through the windows. "I don't think that's such a good idea."

Mikael blinked. "But Grandfather said we had to. Epagael wants us there, Uncle Yosef."

Yosef's face tightened. "Do you realize, Mikael, that after the scorch attack, Horeb will be a terrible place. We won't be able to grow food or hunt animals to support ourselves. We'll have to rely totally on the government for food and clothes and everything else."

Mikael's gaze darted around. His grandfather hadn't

told him that. He'd just said that Epagael wanted all Gamants to go to Horeb because it was very far from Palaia Station and safer. And Metatron had said the books that would help them win the war were there.

"We'll manage," Mikael assured his uncle.

Slothen inclined his head. "Will you order your people to comply with my relocation program?"

"Does that mean you want me to tell them it's okay for them to move to Horeb?"

Slothen smiled that sharp-toothed smile again. "Yes. That's what I mean."

"Yes, sir. I'll tell them."

Slothen nodded and leaned forward, getting closer; Mikael stiffened his muscles, trying not to be afraid.

"I suspect it will take a few years to complete the relocation, but we'll begin immediately. I assume you want to be one of the first immigrants?"

Mikael shrugged, wondering what that meant. "I want to be one of the first people to go there, yes, sir. That way—"

From behind him, he heard Sybil's footsteps. She ran up and cupped a hand to his ear, whispering, "Do you want to tell him about the Cave of Treasures?"

Mikael thought about it. Metatron hadn't told him he could and he worried about keeping secrets good enough. Sometimes he forgot and told people, then his friends got mad at him.

He shook his head. Sybil patted his shoulder and backed away, clasping her hands behind her back and looking at Magistrate Slothen meanly. Sometimes she did that, just to let people know she wasn't stupid or anything.

"Is that all, Leader Calas?" Slothen asked, glancing at Sybil.

Mikael looked at Sybil, too. She nodded confidently and Mikael smiled. "Yes, sir. We'd like to go to Horeb now, if that's all right."

"I promise to take you there as soon as you've instructed all the Gamant planets to comply with my relocation program."

"All right, sir."

Slothen stood up and put four hands on his white desk. Mikael took a step backward and bumped into Sybil; she squeezed his arm to make him feel better. Slothen

540

squinted at them. "Then good-bye. I'll talk to you again soon."

"Good-bye, sir."

Mikael took Sybil's hand and together they ran down the hall, their hearts bursting with happiness. *Now they could go study the books in the Cave of Treasures and lead the war!*

When they reached the end of the hall and Mikael saw Uncle Yosef's worried face, he ran back, giggling, to throw himself in Yosef's thin arms.

"We get to go back to Horeb, Uncle Yosef!"

He watched as his Uncle Yosef bowed his head sadly; tears filled his faded eyes. He pulled Mikael close and stroked his back lovingly.

Slothen swiveled his chair around to gaze out the window. Fighters shot through the lemon skies, practicing wedge maneuvers, swooping down over the city like glimmering diamonds. He shook his head.

To have the leader's permission to herd Gamants into a pen was too much to have expected. Oh, how very easy it would be to control them once he'd confined them to that godforsaken gravity well. Yet . . . Gamants were unpredictable. He'd certainly see to it that both the little boy and the girl were thoroughly probed while at Palaia. Perhaps through skillful neural manipulation, he could assure that the residents of Horeb would have a leader who mouthed Magisterial propaganda.

He twined his fingers nervously and frowned at the fighters as they soared up through the flaxen clouds.

CHAPTER 60

You must become Light in the Spirit of Silence. I have struck off the chains. I have broken down the door of the Pitiless. . . . I came because of the pride of the archigenitor and his angels, who say, 'We are gods!'

Trample underfoot their Sepulchers! Let their yoke be broken!

The Sophia of Yesu
Manuscript in the Sahidic Dialect of Old Earth, 4th century, Common Era.
Fragment found in Boskion caves, Pitbon, 5212.

* * *

Rachel stood on a rocky plateau in a grove of trees on the far side of the Hentopan Sea. She propped a boot on a granite boulder. Fish and moss scented the cool breezes that caressed her face, swirling her loose hair over her eyes in long black strands. Behind her, she could hear the sounds of men and women laboring in the forest. In the past two weeks, they'd discovered and moved into a series of underground caves that seemed to stretch for uncounted miles around and beneath the ocean. They'd cannibalized and set up the shuttle's scanning system. But even with it serving as a warning beacon, they still found themselves scrambling every day to stay out of sight of the numerous Magisterial ships that invaded their skies. Efforts to find them had intensified since the government found the abandoned shuttle and pods they'd hidden in the forest on the other side of the sea, miles distant. Tahn warned that as soon as the Magistrates had the luxury of dispatching a cruiser to aid the search, they'd play hell hiding from the vessel's sophisticated sensing equipment.

Tahn and Jeremiel spent every day searching the heavens for Rudy Kopal or any remnant of the Underground fleet—and Rachel wandered the caves, worrying over whether Sybil really was alive and if she'd ever see her again.

Rachel lifted her eyes to the clear azure heavens, praying that the Underground found them before the Magisterial cruisers arrived. "So much suffering, Epagael. Why?"

Memories of the *Mea* glowing a dull gray beneath Jeremiel's fingers haunted her. What reason could God have for denying him access to heaven? Unless it was to punish her? Or all Gamants?

Below, the surf pounded against the rocky parapet, throwing foam into the crystal sunlight where it shimmered as bright and beautiful as stardust.

The soft footfalls that approached from her side didn't surprise her—she'd heard them a thousand times in her dreams. She stood silently, watching a gull wheel through the cloudless sky. She caught a glimpse of blond curls and his frost-colored robe. His gold-stitched collar ruffled in the breeze.

Lifting her face to the warm sunshine, she asked, "We needed Cole Tahn on our side, was that it?"

"Mostly."

Aktariel's voice sounded so gentle. Rachel braced a hand against the limb of the tree over her head. He didn't even question her usage of *our,* but she'd known he wouldn't. When she'd made her decision, she'd felt the very waves of air retreat from around her—like throwing a huge stone into a tiny wilderness pond.

Had he not felt it, too, he wouldn't have come.

"Why Tahn?" she asked.

"He knows stochastic mechanics and singularity engineering."

"Which relate directly to the Treasures of Light?"

He looked at Rachel through wide brown eyes, as though baring his soul. Blond curls danced around his face in the warm sea-scented winds. "Yes."

"What makes you think Tahn will help us? You hurt him a great deal, you know. You killed his ship and friends. You made him an outcast among his own kind."

He propped his hands on his hips. "No being is formed without the Serpent entering his or her soul, Rachel. We've all been sown in the soil of fire and water now."

Aktariel reached into his pocket and drew out a *Mea.* He studied it contemplatively, then handed it to her. "Sybil has been crying all night wanting you."

Rachel's throat ached. She glanced in terror at the Sacred Gate that had haunted her people for millennia. "When can I go see her?"

"As soon as you take this from my hand."

"Do I have to. I hate *Meas.*"

"Let me teach you their secrets. I think you'll change your mind. And it's the only way you'll be able to see Sybil again in the near future."

Rachel steeled herself and reached out. He draped the golden chain across her open fingers. The *Mea* flared brilliantly, brighter than it had even in his own hand, casting a cerulean halo around them.

"I'll help you in the beginning," he murmured. "Then I'll set you free."

She saw the half-frightened glimmer in his dark eyes, as though he feared that once she had the chance she'd vanish forever. Would the *Mea* give her such forbidden freedom?

"On Horeb," she said, "in the ice cave, you admitted you'd stolen all the *Meas*. What did you do with them?"

Wind whipped his robe into snapping folds around his arms and legs. "The ancient legends tell you."

"That you gave them to the Magistrates."

"Yes."

"And did you?"

He tipped his smooth, tanned face to the fragrant breeze, inhaling deeply of the scents. "Not all the *Meas* —but enough. They exist in charged synchronous orbits inside Palaia Station."

Astonished, she leaned back against the cool trunk of the tree. "Why would you give them to the government?"

"Because, my dear Rachel," he murmured as he gazed out over the glimmering azure sea. "Soon, very soon, God will send out his Great Light, and in Darkness the judgment will take place. Only a being whose blood is Light will survive." He turned to stare piercingly at her. "Do you understand?"

"No."

He extended his hand and his frost-colored sleeve danced before her eyes like windblown shreds of cloud. Tenderly, he caressed the letters branded into her forehead.

"You will."